INVISIBLE MAN

Ralph Waldo Ellison was born in Oklahoma in 1914. At the age of nineteen he won a scholarship to study music at the Booker T. Washington Tuskegee Institute. In 1936 he went to New York and there met Langston Hughes and Richard Wright. He started contributing to the Federal Writers' Project, set up as part of Roosevelt's New Deal, and soon his short stories and articles began to appear in magazines and journals. In 1943 he joined the United States Merchant Marines, returning to New York after the war. Awarded a Rosenwald fellowship, he was able to concentrate on his writing and, seven years after starting it, *Invisible Man* (1952) was published. Immediately recognized as a classic in its own time, it won the National Book Award and established Ellison as one of the major figures of twentieth-century fiction. Ellison was highly regarded by both the literary and academic worlds. He was Fellow of the American Academy in Rome from 1955 to 1957 and on his return held several visiting professorships. He received the United States Medal of Freedom in 1969, became Chevalier de l'ordre des Arts et Lettres in 1970, and received the National Medal of Arts in 1985. He died in 1994.

Jp King is an artist, designer and writer. He runs Paper Pusher printworks, a small Risograph publishing and printing operation. His work explores contemporary mythology, masculinity, garbage and collective activity, and his obsession with paper manifests itself in collage, installation, murals and multiples. He lives in Toronto. jpking.ca

D1158953

RALPH ELLISON

Invisible Man

PENGUIN BOOKS

PENGUIN ESSENTIALS

Published by the Penguin Group
Penguin Books Ltd, 80 Strand, London WC2R ORL, England
Penguin Group (USA) Inc., 375 Hudson Street, New York, New York 10014, USA
Penguin Group (Canada), 90 Eglinton Avenue East, Suite 700, Toronto, Ontario, Canada M4P 2Y3
(a division of Pearson Penguin Canada Inc.)
Penguin Ireland, 25 St Stephen's Green, Dublin 2, Ireland (a division of Penguin Books Ltd)
Penguin Group (Australia), 707 Collins Street, Melbourne, Victoria 3008, Australia
(a division of Pearson Australia Group Pty Ltd)
Penguin Books India Pvt Ltd, 11 Community Centre, Panchsheel Park, New Delhi – 110 017, India
Penguin Group (NZ), 67 Apollo Drive, Rosedale, Auckland 0632, New Zealand
(a division of Pearson New Zealand Ltd)
Penguin Books (South Africa) (Pty) Ltd, Block D, Rosebank Office Park,
181 Jan Smuts Avenue, Parktown North, Gauteng 2193, South Africa

Penguin Books Ltd, Registered Offices: 80 Strand, London WC2R ORL, England

www.penguin.com

First published in the USA by Random House Inc., 1952
Published in Great Britain by Gollancz 1953
Published in Penguin Books 1965
This Penguin Essentials edition published 2014

003

Printed in Great Britain by Clays Ltd, St Ives plc

ISBN: 978-0-241-97056-0

www.greenpenguin.co.uk

To Ida

Author's   Introduction

What, if anything, is there that a novelist can say about his work that wouldn't be better left to the critics? They at least have the advantage of dealing with the words on the page, while for him the task of accounting for the process involved in putting them there is similar to that of commanding a smoky genie to make an orderly retreat—not simply back into the traditional bottle, but into the ribbon and keys of a by now defunct typewriter. And in this particular instance all the more so, because from the moment of its unexpected inception this has been a most self-willed and self-generating piece of fiction. For at a time when I was struggling with a quite different narrative it announced itself in what were to become the opening words of its pro-logue, moved in, and proceeded to challenge my imagination for some seven years. What is more, despite its peacetime scen-ery it erupted out of what had been conceived as a war novel.

It all began during the summer of 1945, in a barn in Waitsfield, Vermont, where I was on sick leave from service in the merchant marine, and with the war's end it continued to preoccupy me in various parts of New York City, including its crowded subways: In a converted 141st Street stable, in a one-room ground-floor apartment on St. Nicholas Avenue and, most unexpectedly, in a suite otherwise occupied by jewelers located on the eighth floor of Number 608 Fifth Avenue. It was there, thanks to the generosity of Beatrice and Francis Steegmuller, then spending a year abroad, I discovered that writing could be just as difficult in a fellow writer's elegant office as in a crowded Harlem apartment. There were, however, important differences, some of which worked wonders for my shaky self-confidence and served, perhaps, as a catalyst for the wild mixture of elements that went into the evolving fiction.

The proprietors of the suite, Sam and Augusta Mann, saw to it that I worked undisturbed, took time off for lunch (often at their own expense) and were most encouraging of my efforts. Thanks to them I found myself keeping a businessman's respectable hours, and the suite's constant flow of beautiful objects and its occupants' expert evaluations of pearls and diamonds, platinum and gold gave me a sense of living far above my means. Thus actually and symbolically the eighth floor was the highest elevation upon which the novel unfolded, but it was a long, far cry from our below-street-level apartment and might well have proved disorienting had I not been consciously concerned with a fictional character who was bent upon finding his way in areas of society whose manners, motives and rituals were baffling.

Interestingly enough, it was only the elevator operators who questioned my presence in such an affluent building, but this, after all, was during a period when the doormen of buildings located in middle- and upper-class neighborhoods routinely directed such as myself to their service elevators. I hasten to add, however, that nothing of the kind ever happened at 608, for once the elevator men became accustomed to my presence they were quite friendly. And that was true even of the well-read immigrant among them who found the idea of my being a writer quite amusing.

By contrast, certain of my St. Nicholas Avenue neighbors considered me of questionable character. This, ostensibly, was because Fanny, my wife, came and went with the regularity of one who held a conventional job while I was often at home and could be seen at odd hours walking our Scottish terriers. But basically it was because I fitted none of the roles, legal or illegal, with which my neighbors were familiar. I was neither a thug, numbers-runner, nor pusher, postal worker, doctor, dentist, lawyer, tailor, undertaker, barber, bartender nor preacher. And, while my speech revealed a degree of higher education, it was also clear that I was not of the group of professionals who lived or worked in the neighborhood. My indefinite status was therefore a subject of speculation and a source of unease, especially among those whose attitudes and modes of conduct were at odds with the dictates of law and order. This made for a nodding relationship in which my neighbors kept their distance and I kept mine. But I remained suspect, and one snowy afternoon as I walked down a shady street into the winter sunshine a wino lady let me know exactly how I rated on her checklist of sundry types and characters.

Leaning blearily against the façade of a corner bar as I approached, and directing her remarks at me through her woozy companions, she said, "Now that nigger *there* must be some kinda sweetback, 'cause while his wife has her some kinda little 'slave,' all I ever see *him* do is walk them damn dogs and shoot some damn pictures!"

Frankly, I was startled by such a low rating, for by "sweetback" she meant a man who lived off the earnings of a woman, a type usually identified by his leisure, his flashy clothes, flamboyant personal style and the ruthless business enterprise of an out-and-out pimp—all qualities of which I was so conspicuously lacking that she had to laugh at her own provocative sally. However the ploy was intended to elicit a response, whether angry or conciliatory she was too drunk or reckless to care as long as it threw some light into the shadows of my existence. Therefore I was less annoyed than amused, and since I was returning home with fifty legally earned dollars from a photographic assignment I could well afford to smile while remaining silently concealed in my mystery.

Even so, the wino lady had come fairly close to one of the economic arrangements which made my writing a possibility, and that too is part of the story behind this novel. My wife did indeed provide the more dependable contributions to our income while mine came catch-as-catch-can. During the time the novel was in progress she worked as a secretary for several organizations and was to crown her working career as the executive director of the American Medical Center for Burma, a group that supported the work of Dr. Gordon S. Seagrave, the famous "Burma Surgeon." As for myself, I reviewed a few books, sold a few articles and short stories, did free-lance photography (including book-jacket portraits of Francis Steegmuller and Mary McCarthy), built audio amplifiers and installed high-fidelity sound systems. There were also a few savings from my work on ships, a Rosenwald grant and its renewal, a small publisher's advance and, for a while, a monthly stipend from our friend and patron of the arts, the late Mrs. J. Caesar Guggenheimer.

Naturally our neighbors knew nothing of this, and neither did our landlord, who considered writing to be such a questionable occupation for a healthy young man that during our absence he was not above entering our apartment and prowling through my papers. Still, such annoyances were to be endured as a part of the desperate gamble involved in my becoming a novelist. Fortunately my wife had faith in my talent, a fine sense of humor and a capacity for neighborly charity. Nor was I unappreciative of the hilarious inversion of what is usually a racially restricted social mobility that took me on daily journeys from a Negro neighborhood, wherein strangers questioned my moral character on nothing more substantial than our common color and my vague deviation from accepted norms, to find sanctuary in a predominantly white environment wherein that same color and vagueness of role rendered me anonymous, and hence beyond public concern. In retrospect it was as though writing about invisibility had rendered me either transparent or opaque and set me bouncing back and forth between the benighted provincialism of a small village and the benign disinterestedness of a great metropolis. Which, given the difficulty of gaining an authorial knowledge of this diverse society, was not a bad discipline for an American writer.

But the Fifth Avenue interval aside, most of the novel still managed to get itself written in Harlem, where it drew much of its substance from the voices, idioms, folklore, traditions and political concerns of those whose racial and cultural origins I share. So much then for the economics, geography and sociology of the struggle sustained in writing the novel, and back to the circumstances in which it began.

The narrative that was upstaged by the voice which spoke so knowingly of invisibility (pertinent here because it turned out to have been a blundering step toward the present novel), focused upon the experiences of a captured American pilot who found himself in a Nazi prisoner-of-war camp in which he was the officer of highest rank and thus by a convention of war the designated spokesman for his fellow prisoners. Predictably, the dramatic conflict arose from the fact that he was the only Negro among the Americans, and the resulting racial tension was exploited by the German camp commander for his own amusement. Having to choose between his passionate rejection of both native and foreign racisms while upholding those democratic values which he held in common with his white countrymen, my pilot was forced to find support for his morale in his sense of individual dignity and in his newly awakened awareness of human loneliness. For him that war-born vision of virile fraternity of which Malraux wrote so eloquently was not forthcoming, and much to his surprise he found his only justification for attempting to deal with his countrymen as comrades-in-arms lay precisely in those old betrayed promises proclaimed in such national slogans and turns-of-phrase as those the hero of Hemingway's *A Farewell to Arms* had found so obscene during the chaotic retreat from Caporetto. But while Hemingway's hero managed to put the war behind him and opt for love, for my pilot there was neither escape nor a loved one waiting. Therefore he had either to affirm the transcendent ideals of democracy and his own dignity by aiding those who despised him, or accept his situation as hopelessly devoid of meaning; a choice tantamount to rejecting his own humanity. The crowning irony of all this lay in the fact that neither of his adversaries was aware of his inner struggle.

Undramatized, all this might sound a bit extreme, yet historically most of this nation's conflicts of arms have been— at least for Afro-Americans—wars-within-wars. Such was true of the Civil War, the last of the Indian Wars, of the Spanish American War, and of World Wars I and II. And in order for the Negro to fulfill his duty as a citizen it was often necessary that he fight for his self-affirmed right to fight. Accordingly, my pilot was prepared to make the ultimate wartime sacrifice that most governments demand of their able-bodied citizens, but his was one that regarded his life as of lesser value than the lives of whites making the same sacrifice. This reality made for an existential torture, which was given a further twist of the screw by his awareness that once the peace was signed, the German camp commander could immigrate to the United States and immediately take advantage of freedoms that were denied the most heroic of Negro servicemen. Thus democratic ideals and military valor alike were rendered absurd by the prevailing mystique of race and color.

I myself had chosen the merchant marine as a more democratic mode of service (as had a former colleague, a poet, who was lost off Murmansk on his first trip to sea), and as a seaman ashore in Europe I had been encountering numerous Negro soldiers who gave me vivid accounts of the less-than-democratic conditions under which they fought and labored. But having had a father who fought on San Juan Hill, in the Philippines and in China, I knew that such complaints grew out of what was by then an archetypical American dilemma: How could you treat a Negro as equal in war and then deny him equality during times of peace? I also knew something of the trials of Negro airmen, who after being trained in segregated units and undergoing the abuse of white officers and civilians alike were prevented from flying combat missions.

Indeed, I had published a short story which dealt with such a situation, and it was in that attempt to convert experience into fiction that I discovered that its implicit drama was far more complex than I had assumed. For while I had conceived of it in terms of a black-white, majority-minority conflict, with white officers refusing to recognize the humanity of a Negro who saw mastering the highly technical skills of a pilot as a dignified way of serving his country while improving his economic status, I came to realize that my pilot was also experiencing difficulty in seeing *himself*. And this had to do with his ambivalence before his own group's divisions of class and diversities of culture; an ambivalence which was brought into focus after he crash-landed on a southern plantation and found himself being aided by a Negro tenant farmer whose outlook and folkways were a painful reminder of his own tenuous military status and their common origin in slavery. A man of two worlds, my pilot felt himself to be misperceived in both and thus was at ease in neither. In brief, the story depicted his conscious struggle for self-definition and for an invulnerable support for his individual dignity. I by no means was aware of his relationship to the invisible man, but clearly he possessed some of the symptoms.

During the same period I had published yet another story in which a young Afro-American seaman, ashore in Swansea, South Wales, was forced to grapple with the troublesome "American" aspects of his identity after white Americans had blacked his eye during a wartime blackout on the Swansea street called Straight (no, his name was *not* Saul nor did he become a Paul!). But here the pressure toward self-scrutiny came from a group of Welshmen who rescued him and surprised him by greeting him as a "Black Yank" and inviting him to a private club, and then sang the American National Anthem in his honor. Both stories were published in 1944, but now in 1945 on a Vermont farm, the theme of a young Negro's quest for identity was reasserting itself in a far more bewildering form.

For while I had structured my short stories out of familiar experiences and possessed concrete images of my characters and their backgrounds, now I was confronted by nothing more substantial than a taunting, disembodied voice. And while I was in the process of plotting a novel based on the war then in progress, the conflict which that voice was imposing upon my attention was one that had been ongoing since the Civil War. Given the experiences of the past, I had felt on safe historical grounds even though the literary problem of conveying the complex human emotions and philosophical decisions faced by a unique individual remained. It was, I thought, an intriguing idea for an American novel but a difficult task for a fledgling novelist. Therefore I was most annoyed to have my efforts interrupted by an ironic, down-home voice that struck me as being as irreverent as a honky-tonk trumpet blasting through a performance, say, of Britten's *War Requiem*.

And all the more so because the voice seemed well aware that a piece of science fiction was the last thing I aspired to write. In fact, it seemed to tease me with allusions to that pseudoscientific sociological concept which held that most Afro-American difficulties sprang from our "high visibility"; a phrase as double-dealing and insidious as its more recent oxymoronic cousins, "benign neglect" and "reverse discrimination," both of which translate "Keep those Negroes running—but in their same old place." My friends had made wry jokes out of the term for many years, suggesting that while the darker brother was clearly "checked and balanced"—and kept far more checked than balanced—on the basis of his darkness he glowed, nevertheless, within the American conscience with such intensity that most whites feigned moral blindness toward his predicament; and these included the waves of late arrivals who refused to recognize the vast extent to which they too benefited from his second-class status while placing all of the blame on white southerners.

Thus despite the bland assertions of sociologists, "high visibility" actually rendered one *un*-visible—whether at high noon in Macy's window or illuminated by flaming torches and flashbulbs while undergoing the ritual sacrifice that was dedicated to the ideal of white supremacy. After such knowledge, and given the persistence of racial violence and the unavailability of legal protection, I asked myself, what else *was* there to sustain our will to persevere but laughter? And could it be that there was a subtle triumph hidden in such laughter that I had missed, but one which still was more affirmative than raw anger? A secret, hard-earned wisdom that might, perhaps, offer a more effective strategy through which a floundering Afro-American novelist could convey his vision?

It was a startling idea, yet the voice was so persuasive with echoes of blues-toned laughter that I found myself being nudged toward a frame of mind in which, suddenly, current events, memories and artifacts began combining to form a vague but intriguing new perspective.

Shortly before the spokesman for invisibility intruded, I had seen, in a nearby Vermont village, a poster announcing the performance of a "Tom Show," that forgotten term for blackface minstrel versions of Mrs. Stowe's *Uncle Tom's Cabin.* I had thought such entertainment a thing of the past, but there in a quiet northern village it was alive and kicking, with Eliza, frantically slipping and sliding on the ice, still trying—and that during World War II!—to escape the slavering hounds. . . . *Oh, I went to the hills/ To hide my face/ The hills cried out. No hiding place/ There's no hiding place/ Up here!*

No, because what is commonly assumed to be past history is actually as much a part of the living present as William Faulkner insisted. Furtive, implacable and tricky, it inspirits both the observer and the scene observed, artifacts, manners and atmosphere and it speaks even when no one wills to listen.

And so, as I listen, things once obscure began falling into place. Odd things, unexpected things. Such as the poster that reminded me of the tenacity which a nation's moral evasions can take on when given the trappings of racial stereotypes, and the ease with which its deepest experience of tragedy could be converted into blackface farce. Even information picked up about the backgrounds of friends and acquaintances fell into the slowly emerging pattern of implication. The wife of the racially mixed couple who were our hosts was the granddaughter of a Vermonter who had been a general in the Civil War, adding a new dimension to the poster's presence. Details of old photographs and rhymes and riddles and children's games, church services and college ceremonies, practical jokes and political activities observed during my prewar days in Harlem— all fell into place. I had reported the riot of 1943 for the *New York Post* and had agitated earlier for the release of Angelo Herndon and the Scottsboro Boys, had marched behind Adam Clayton Powell, Jr., in his effort to desegregate the stores along 125th Street, and had been part of a throng which blocked off Fifth Avenue in protest of the role being played by Germany and Italy in the Spanish Civil War. Everything and anything appeared as grist for my fictional mill. Some speaking up clearly, saying, "Use me right here," while others were disturbingly mysterious.

Like my sudden recall of an incident from my college days when, opening a vat of Plasticine donated to an invalid sculptor friend by some northern studio, I found enfolded within the oily mass a frieze of figures modeled after those depicted on Saint-Gaudens's monument to Colonel Robert Gould Shaw and his 54th Massachusetts Negro Regiment, a memorial which stands on the Boston Common. I had no idea as to why it should surface, but perhaps it was to remind me that since I was writing fiction and seeking vaguely for images of black and white fraternity I would do well to recall that Henry James's brother Wilky had fought as an officer with those Negro soldiers, and that Colonel Shaw's body had been thrown into a ditch with those of his men. Perhaps it was also to remind me that war could, with art, be transformed into something deeper and more meaningful than its surface violence . . .

At any rate, it now appeared that the voice of invisibility issued from deep within our complex American underground. So how crazy-logical that I should finally locate its owner living—and oh, so garrulously—in an abandoned cellar. Of course, the process was far more disjointed than I make it sound, but such was the inner-outer, subjective-objective process of the developing fiction, its pied rind and surreal heart . . .

Even so, I was still inclined to close my ears and get on with my interrupted novel, but like many writers atoss in what Conrad described as the "destructive element," I had floundered into a state of hyperreceptivity; a desperate condition in which a fiction writer finds it difficult to ignore even the most nebulous idea-emotion that might arise in the process of creation. For he soon learns that such amorphous projections might well be unexpected gifts from his daydreaming muse that might, when properly perceived, provide exactly the materials needed to keep afloat in the turbulent tides of composition. On the other hand, they might wreck him, drown him in the quicksands of indecision. I was already having enough difficulty trying to avoid writing what might turn out to be nothing more than another novel of racial protest instead of the dramatic study in comparative humanity which I felt any worthwhile novel should be, and the voice appeared to be leading me precisely in that direction. But then as I listened to its taunting laughter and speculated as to what kind of individual would speak in such accents, I decided that it would be one who had been forged in the underground of American experience and yet managed to emerge less angry than ironic. That he would be a blues-toned laugher-at-wounds who included himself in his indictment of the human condition. I liked the idea, and as I tried to visualize the speaker I came to relate him to those ongoing conflicts, tragic and comic, that had claimed my group's energies since the abandonment of the Reconstruction.

And after coaxing him into revealing a bit more about himself, I concluded that he was without question a "character," and that in the dual meaning of the term. And I saw that he was young, powerless (reflecting the difficulties of Negro leaders of the period) and ambitious for a role of leadership; a role at which he was doomed to fail. Having nothing to lose, and by way of providing myself the widest field for success or failure, I associated him, ever so distantly, with the narrator of Dostoevsky's *Notes from Underground,* and with that *I* began to structure the movement of my plot, while *he* began to merge with my more specialized concerns with fictional form and with certain problems arising out of the pluralistic literary tradition from which I spring.

Among these was the question of why most protagonists of Afro-American fiction (not to mention the black characters in fiction written by whites) were without intellectual depth. Too often they were figures caught up in the most intense forms of social struggle, subject to the most extreme forms of the human predicament but yet seldom able to articulate the issues which tortured them. Not that many worthy individuals aren't in fact inarticulate, but that there were, and are, enough exceptions in real life to provide the perceptive novelist with models. And even if they did not exist it would be necessary, both in the interest of fictional expressiveness and as examples of human possibility, to invent them. Henry James had taught us much with his hyperconscious, "Super subtle fry," characters who embodied in their own cultured, upper-class way the American virtues of conscience and consciousness. Such ideal creatures were unlikely to turn up in the world I inhabited, but one never knew because so much in this society is unnoticed and unrecorded. On the other hand, I felt that one of the ever-present challenges facing the American novelist was that of endowing his inarticulate characters, scenes and social processes with eloquence. For it is by such attempts that he fulfills his social responsibility as an American artist.

Here it would seem that the interests of art and democracy converge, the development of conscious, articulate citizens being an established goal of this democratic society, and the creation of conscious, articulate characters being indispensable to the creation of resonant compositional centers through which an organic consistency can be achieved in the fashioning of fictional forms. By way of imposing meaning upon our disparate American experience the novelist seeks to create forms in which acts, scenes and characters speak for more than their immediate selves, and in this enterprise the very nature of language is on his side. For by a trick of fate (and our racial problems notwithstanding) the human imagination is integrative—and the same is true of the centrifugal force that inspirits the democratic process. And while fiction is but a form of symbolic action, a mere game of "as if," therein lies its true function and its potential for effecting change. For at its most serious, just as is true of politics at its best, it is a thrust toward a human ideal. And it approaches that ideal by a subtle process of negating the world of things as given in favor of a complex of man-made positives.

So if the ideal of achieving a true political equality eludes us in reality—as it continues to do—there is still available that fictional *vision* of an ideal democracy in which the actual combines with the ideal and gives us representations of a state of things in which the highly placed and the lowly, the black and the white, the northerner and the southerner, the native-born and the immigrant are combined to tell us of transcendent truths and possibilities such as those discovered when Mark Twain set Huck and Jim afloat on the raft.

Which suggested to me that a novel could be fashioned as a raft of hope, perception and entertainment that might help keep us afloat as we tried to negotiate the snags and whirlpools that mark our nation's vacillating course toward and away from the democratic ideal. There are, of course, other goals for fiction. Yet I recalled that during the early, more optimistic days of this republic it was assumed that each individual citizen could become (and should prepare to become) President. For democracy was considered not only a collectivity of individuals, as was defined by W. H. Auden, but a collectivity of politically astute citizens who, by virtue of our vaunted system of universal education and our freedom of opportunity, would be prepared to govern. As things turned out it was an unlikely possibility—but not entirely, as is attested by the recent examples of the peanut farmer and the motion-picture actor.

And even for Afro-Americans there was the brief hope that had been encouraged by the presence of black congressmen in Washington during the Reconstruction. Nor could I see any reason for allowing our more chastened view of political possibility (not too long before I began this novel A. Phillip Randolph had to threaten our beloved F.D.R. with a march on Washington before our war industries were opened to Negroes) to impose undue restrictions upon my novelist's freedom to manipulate imaginatively those possibilities that existed both in Afro-American personality and in the restricted structure of American society. My task was to transcend those restrictions. And as an example, Mark Twain had demonstrated that the novel *could* serve as a comic antidote to the ailments of politics, and since in 1945, as well as now, Afro-Americans were usually defeated in their bouts with circumstance, there was no reason why they, like Brer Rabbit and his more literary cousins, the great heroes of tragedy and comedy, shouldn't be allowed to snatch the victory of conscious perception from the forces that overwhelmed them. Therefore I would have to create a narrator who could think as well as act, and I saw a capacity for conscious self-assertion as basic to his blundering quest for freedom.

So my task was one of revealing the human universals hidden within the plight of one who was both black and American, and not only as a means of conveying my personal vision of possibility, but as a way of dealing with the sheer rhetorical challenge involved in communicating across our barriers of race and religion, class, color and region—barriers which consist of the many strategies of division that were designed, and still function, to prevent what would otherwise have been a more or less natural recognition of the reality of black and white fraternity. And to defeat this national tendency to deny the common humanity shared by my character and those who might happen to read of his experience, I would have to provide him with something of a worldview, give him a consciousness in which serious philosophical questions could be raised, provide him with a range of diction that could play upon the richness of our readily shared vernacular speech and construct a plot that would bring him in contact with a variety of American types as they operated on various levels of society. Most of all, I would have to approach racial stereotypes as a given fact of the social process and proceed, while gambling with the reader's capacity for fictional truth, to reveal the human complexity which stereotypes are intended to conceal.

It would be misleading, however, to leave the impression that all of the process of writing was so solemn. For in fact there was a great deal of fun along the way. I knew that I was composing a work of fiction, a work of literary art and one that would allow me to take advantage of the novel's capacity for telling the truth while actually telling a "lie," which is the Afro-American folk term for an improvised story. Having worked in barbershops where that form of oral art flourished, I knew that I could draw upon the rich culture of the folk tale as well as that of the novel, and that being uncertain of my skill I would have to improvise upon my materials in the manner of a jazz musician putting a musical theme through a wild star-burst of metamorphosis. By the time I realized that the words of the Prologue contained the germ of the ending as well as that of the beginning, I was free to enjoy the surprises of incident and character as they popped into view.

And there were surprises. Five years before the book was completed, Frank Taylor, who had given me my first book contract, showed a section to Cyril Connolly, the editor of the English magazine *Horizon*, and it was published in an issue devoted to art in America. This marked the initial publication of the first chapter, which appeared in America shortly afterward in the 1948 volume of the now-defunct *Magazine of the Year*—a circumstance which accounts for the 1947 and 1948 copyright dates that have caused confusion for scholars. The actual publication date of the complete volume was 1952.

These surprises were both encouraging and intimidating because after savoring that bit of success I became afraid that this single section, which contained the "battle royal" scene, might well be the novel's only incident of interest. But I persisted and finally arrived at the moment when it became meaningful to work with my editor, Albert Erskine. The rest, as the saying goes, is history. My highest hope for the novel was that it would sell enough copies to prevent my publishers from losing on their investment and my editor from having wasted his time. But, as I said in the beginning, this has always been a most willful, most self-generating novel, and the proof of that statement is witnessed by the fact that here, thirty astounding years later, it has me writing about it again.

Ralph Ellison
November 10, 1981

Invisible Man

Prologue

I am an invisible man. No, I am not a spook like those who haunted Edgar Allan Poe; nor am I one of your Hollywood-movie ectoplasms. I am a man of substance, of flesh and bone, fiber and liquids—and I might even be said to possess a mind. I am invisible, understand, simply because people refuse to see me. Like the bodiless heads you see sometimes in circus sideshows, it is as though I have been surrounded by mirrors of hard, distorting glass. When they approach me they see only my surroundings, themselves, or figments of their imagination—indeed, everything and anything except me.

Nor is my invisibility exactly a matter of a biochemical accident to my epidermis. That invisibility to which I refer occurs because of a peculiar disposition of the eyes of those with whom I come in contact. A matter of the construction of their *inner* eyes, those eyes with which they look through their physical eyes upon reality. I am not complaining, nor am I protesting either. It is sometimes advantageous to be unseen, although it is most often rather wearing on the nerves. Then

3

too, you're constantly being bumped against by those of poor vision. Or again, you often doubt if you really exist. You wonder whether you aren't simply a phantom in other people's minds. Say, a figure in a nightmare which the sleeper tries with all his strength to destroy. It's when you feel like this that, out of resentment, you begin to bump people back. And, let me confess, you feel that way most of the time. You ache with the need to convince yourself that you do exist in the real world, that you're a part of all the sound and anguish, and you strike out with your fists, you curse and you swear to make them recognize you. And, alas, it's seldom successful.

One night I accidentally bumped into a man, and perhaps because of the near darkness he saw me and called me an insulting name. I sprang at him, seized his coat lapels and demanded that he apologize. He was a tall blond man, and as my face came close to his he looked insolently out of his blue eyes and cursed me, his breath hot in my face as he struggled. I pulled his chin down sharp upon the crown of my head, butting him as I had seen the West Indians do, and I felt his flesh tear and the blood gush out, and I yelled, "Apologize! Apologize!" But he continued to curse and struggle, and I butted him again and again until he went down heavily, on his knees, profusely bleeding. I kicked him repeatedly, in a frenzy because he still uttered insults though his lips were frothy with blood. Oh yes, I kicked him! And in my outrage I got out my knife and prepared to slit his throat, right there beneath the lamplight in the deserted street, holding him in the collar with one hand, and opening the knife with my teeth—when it occurred to me that the man had not *seen* me, actually; that he, as far as he knew, was in the midst of a walking nightmare! And I stopped the blade, slicing the air as I pushed him away, letting him fall back to the street. I stared at him hard as the lights of a car stabbed through the darkness. He lay there, moaning on the asphalt; a man almost killed by a phantom. It unnerved me. I was both disgusted and ashamed. I was like a drunken man myself, wavering about on weakened legs. Then I was amused: Something in this man's thick head had sprung out and beaten him within an inch of his life. I began to laugh at this crazy discovery. Would he have awakened at the point of death? Would Death himself have freed him for wakeful living? But I didn't linger. I ran away into the dark, laughing so hard I feared I might rupture myself. The next day I saw his picture in the *Daily News*, beneath a caption stating that he had been "mugged." Poor fool, poor blind fool, I thought with sincere compassion, mugged by an invisible man!

Most of the time (although I do not choose as I once did to deny the violence of my days by ignoring it) I am not so overtly violent. I remember that I am invisible and walk softly so as not to awaken the sleeping ones. Sometimes it is best not to awaken them; there are few things in the world as dangerous as sleepwalkers. I learned in time though that it is possible to carry on a fight against them without their realizing it. For instance, I have been carrying on a fight with Monopolated Light & Power for some time now. I use their service and pay them nothing at all, and they don't know it. Oh, they suspect that power is being drained off, but they don't know where. All they know is that according to the master meter back there in their power station a hell of a lot of free current is disappearing somewhere into the jungle of Harlem. The joke, of course, is that I don't live in Harlem but in a border area. Several years ago (before I discovered the advantages of being invisible) I went through the routine process of buying service and paying their outrageous rates. But no more. I gave up all that, along with my apartment, and my old way of life: That way based upon the fallacious assumption that I, like other men, was visible. Now, aware of my invisibility, I live rent-free in a building rented strictly to whites, in a section of the basement that was shut off and forgotten during the nineteenth century, which I discovered when I was trying to escape in the night from Ras the Destroyer. But that's getting too far ahead of the story, almost to the end, although the end is in the beginning and lies far ahead.

The point now is that I found a home—or a hole in the ground, as you will. Now don't jump to the conclusion that because I call my home a "hole" it is damp and cold like a grave; there are cold holes and warm holes. Mine is a warm hole. And remember, a bear retires to his hole for the winter and lives until spring; then he comes strolling out like the Easter chick breaking from its shell. I say all this to assure you that it is incorrect to assume that, because I'm invisible and live in a hole, I am dead. I am neither dead nor in a state of suspended animation. Call me Jack-the-Bear, for I am in a state of hibernation.

My hole is warm and full of light. Yes, *full* of light. I doubt if there is a brighter spot in all New York than this hole of mine, and I do not exclude Broadway. Or the Empire State Building on a photographer's dream night. But that is taking advantage of you. Those two spots are among the darkest of our whole civilization—pardon me, our whole *culture* (an important distinction, I've heard)—which might sound like a hoax, or a contradiction, but that (by contradiction, I mean) is how the world moves: Not like an arrow, but a boomerang. (Beware of those who speak of the *spiral* of history; they are preparing a boomerang. Keep a steel helmet handy.) I know; I have been boomeranged across my head so much that I now can see the darkness of lightness. And I love light. Perhaps you'll think it strange that an invisible man should need light, desire light, love light. But maybe it is exactly because I *am* invisible. Light confirms my reality, gives birth to my form. A beautiful girl once told me of a recurring nightmare in which she lay in the center of a large dark room and felt her face expand until it filled the whole room, becoming a formless mass while her eyes ran in bilious jelly up the chimney. And so it is with me. Without light I am not only invisible, but formless as well; and to be unaware of one's form is to live a death. I myself, after existing some twenty years, did not become alive until I discovered my invisibility.

That is why I fight my battle with Monopolated Light & Power. The deeper reason, I mean: It allows me to feel my vital aliveness. I also fight them for taking so much of my money before I learned to protect myself. In my hole in the basement there are exactly 1,369 lights. I've wired the entire ceiling, every inch of it. And not with fluorescent bulbs, but with the older, more-expensive-to-operate kind, the filament type. An act of sabotage, you know. I've already begun to wire the wall. A junk man I know, a man of vision, has supplied me with wire and sockets. Nothing, storm or flood, must get in the way of our need for light and ever more and brighter light. The truth is the light and light is the truth. When I finish all four walls, then I'll start on the floor. Just how that will go, I don't know. Yet when you have lived invisible as long as I have you develop a certain ingenuity. I'll solve the problem. And maybe I'll invent a gadget to place my coffee pot on the fire while I lie in bed, and even invent a gadget to warm my bed—like the fellow I saw in one of the picture magazines who made himself a gadget to warm his shoes! Though invisible, I am in the great American tradition of tinkers. That makes me kin to Ford, Edison and Franklin. Call me, since I have a theory and a concept, a "thinker-tinker." Yes, I'll warm my shoes; they need it, they're usually full of holes. I'll do that and more.

Now I have one radio-phonograph; I plan to have five.

There is a certain acoustical deadness in my hole, and when I have music I want to *feel* its vibration, not only with my ear but with my whole body. I'd like to hear five recordings of Louis Armstrong playing and singing "What Did I Do to Be so Black and Blue"—all at the same time. Sometimes now I listen to Louis while I have my favorite dessert of vanilla ice cream and sloe gin. I pour the red liquid over the white mound, watching it glisten and the vapor rising as Louis bends that military instrument into a beam of lyrical sound. Perhaps I like Louis Armstrong because he's made poetry out of being invisible. I think it must be because he's unaware that he *is* invisible. And my own grasp of invisibility aids me to understand his music. Once when I asked for a cigarette, some jokers gave me a reefer, which I lighted when I got home and sat listening to my phonograph. It was a strange evening. Invisibility, let me explain, gives one a slightly different sense of time, you're never quite on the beat. Sometimes you're ahead and sometimes behind. Instead of the swift and imperceptible flowing of time, you are aware of its nodes, those points where time stands still or from which it leaps ahead. And you slip into the breaks and look around. That's what you hear vaguely in Louis' music.

Once I saw a prizefighter boxing a yokel. The fighter was swift and amazingly scientific. His body was one violent flow of rapid rhythmic action. He hit the yokel a hundred times while the yokel held up his arms in stunned surprise. But suddenly the yokel, rolling about in the gale of boxing gloves, struck one blow and knocked science, speed and footwork as cold as a well-digger's posterior. The smart money hit the canvas. The long shot got the nod. The yokel had simply stepped inside of his opponent's sense of time. So under the spell of the reefer I discovered a new analytical way of listening to music. The unheard sounds came through, and each melodic line existed of itself, stood out clearly from all the rest, said its piece, and waited patiently for the other voices to speak. That night I found myself hearing not only in time, but in space as well. I not only entered the music but descended, like Dante, into its depths. And *beneath the swiftness of the hot tempo there was a slower tempo and a cave and I entered it and looked around and heard an old woman singing a spiritual as full of Welt-schmerz as flamenco, and beneath that lay a still lower level on which I saw a beautiful girl the color of ivory pleading in a voice like my mother's as she stood before a group of slaveowners who bid for her naked body, and below that I found a lower level and a more rapid tempo and I heard someone shout:*

"Brothers and sisters, my text this morning is the 'Blackness of Blackness.'"

And a congregation of voices answered: "That blackness is most black, brother, most black . . ."

"In the beginning . . ."

"At the very start," they cried.

". . . there was blackness . . ."

"Preach it . . ."

". . . and the sun . . ."

"The sun, Lawd . . ."

". . . was bloody red . . ."

"Red . . ."

"Now black is . . ." the preacher shouted.

"Bloody . . ."

"I said black is . . ."

"Preach it, brother . . ."

". . . an' black ain't . . ."

"Red, Lawd, red: He said it's red!"

"Amen, brother . . ."

"Black will git you . . ."

"Yes, it will . . ."

"Yes, it will . . ."

"*. . . an' black won't . . .*"

"*Naw, it won't!*"

"*It do . . .*"

"*It do, Lawd . . .*"

"*. . . an' it don't.*"

"*Halleluiah . . .*"

"*. . . It'll put you, glory, glory, Oh my Lawd, in the* WHALE'S BELLY."

"*Preach it, dear brother . . .*"

"*. . . an' make you tempt . . .*"

"*Good God a-mighty!*"

"*Old Aunt Nelly!*"

"*Black will make you . . .*"

"*Black . . .*"

"*. . . or black will un-make you.*"

"*Ain't it the truth, Lawd?*"

And at that point a voice of trombone timbre screamed at me, "Git out of here, you fool! Is you ready to commit treason?"

And I tore myself away, hearing the old singer of spirituals moaning, "Go curse your God, boy, and die."

I stopped and questioned her, asked her what was wrong.

"I dearly loved my master, son," she said.

"You should have hated him," I said.

"He gave me several sons," she said, "and because I loved my sons I learned to love their father though I hated him too."

"I too have become acquainted with ambivalence," I said. "That's why I'm here."

"What's that?"

"Nothing, a word that doesn't explain it. Why do you moan?"

"I moan this way 'cause he's dead," she said.

"Then tell me, who is that laughing upstairs?"

"Them's my sons. They glad."

"Yes, I can understand that too," I said.

"I laughs too, but I moans too. He promised to set us free but he never could bring hisself to do it. Still I loved him . . ."

"Loved him? You mean . . . ?"

"Oh yes, but I loved something else even more."

"What more?"

"Freedom."

"Freedom," I said. "Maybe freedom lies in hating."

"Naw, son, it's in loving. I loved him and give him the poison and he withered away like a frost-bit apple. Them boys woulda tore him to pieces with they homemade knives."

"A mistake was made somewhere," I said, "I'm confused."
And I wished to say other things, but the laughter upstairs became too loud and moan-like for me and I tried to break out of it, but I couldn't. Just as I was leaving I felt an urgent desire to ask her what freedom was and went back. She sat with her head in her hands, moaning softly; her leather-brown face was filled with sadness.

"Old woman, what is this freedom you love so well?" I asked around a corner of my mind.

She looked surprised, then thoughtful, then baffled. "I done forgot, son. It's all mixed up. First I think it's one thing, then I think it's another. It gits my head to spinning. I guess now it ain't nothing but knowing how to say what I got up in my head. But it's a hard job, son. Too much is done happen to me in too short a time. Hit's like I have a fever. Ever' time I starts to walk my head gits to swirling and I falls down. Or if it ain't that, it's the boys; they gits to laughing and wants to kill up the white folks. They's bitter, that's what they is . . ."

"But what about freedom?"

"Leave me 'lone, boy; my head aches!"

I left her, feeling dizzy myself. I didn't get far.

Suddenly one of the sons, a big fellow six feet tall, appeared out of nowhere and struck me with his fist.

"What's the matter, man?" I cried.

"You made Ma cry!"

"But how?" I said, dodging a blow.

"Askin' her them questions, that's how. Git outa here and stay, and next time you got questions like that, ask yourself!"

He held me in a grip like cold stone, his fingers fastening upon my windpipe until I thought I would suffocate before he finally allowed me to go. I stumbled about dazed, the music beating hysterically in my ears. It was dark. My head cleared and I wandered down a dark narrow passage, thinking I heard his footsteps hurrying behind me. I was sore, and into my being had come a profound craving for tranquillity, for peace and quiet, a state I felt I could never achieve. For one thing, the trumpet was blaring and the rhythm was too hectic. A tom-tom beating like heart-thuds began drowning out the trumpet, filling my ears. I longed for water and I heard it rushing through the cold mains my fingers touched as I felt my way, but I couldn't stop to search because of the footsteps behind me.

"Hey, Ras," I called. "Is it you, Destroyer? Rinehart?"

No answer, only the rhythmic footsteps behind me. Once I tried crossing the road, but a speeding machine struck me, scraping the skin from my leg as it roared past.

Then somehow I came out of it, ascending hastily from this underworld of sound to hear Louis Armstrong innocently asking,

> *What did I do*
> *To be so black*
> *And blue?*

At first I was afraid; this familiar music had demanded action, the kind of which I was incapable, and yet had I lingered there beneath the surface I might have attempted to act. Nevertheless, I know now that few really listen to this music.

I sat on the chair's edge in a soaking sweat, as though each of my 1,369 bulbs had every one become a klieg light in an individual setting for a third degree with Ras and Rinehart in charge. It was exhausting—as though I had held my breath continuously for an hour under the terrifying serenity that comes from days of intense hunger. And yet, it was a strangely satisfying experience for an invisible man to hear the silence of sound. I had discovered unrecognized compulsions of my being—even though I could not answer "yes" to their promptings. I haven't smoked a reefer since, however; not because they're illegal, but because to *see* around corners is enough (that is not unusual when you are invisible). But to hear around them is too much; it inhibits action. And despite Brother Jack and all that sad, lost period of the Brotherhood, I believe in nothing if not in action.

Please, a definition: A hibernation is a covert preparation for a more overt action.

Besides, the drug destroys one's sense of time completely. If that happened, I might forget to dodge some bright morning and some cluck would run me down with an orange and yellow street car, or a bilious bus! Or I might forget to leave my hole when the moment for action presents itself.

Meanwhile I enjoy my life with the compliments of Monopolated Light & Power. Since you never recognize me even when in closest contact with me, and since, no doubt, you'll hardly believe that I exist, it won't matter if you know that I tapped a power line leading into the building and ran it into my hole in the ground. Before that I lived in the darkness into which I was chased, but now I see. I've illuminated the blackness of my invisibility—and vice versa. And so I play the invisible music of my isolation. The last statement doesn't seem just right, does it? But it is; you hear this music simply because music is heard and seldom seen, except by musicians. Could this compulsion to put invisibility down in black and white be thus an urge to make music of invisibility? But I am an orator, a rabble rouser—Am? I *was*, and perhaps shall be again. Who knows? All sickness is not unto death, neither is invisibility.

I can hear you say, "What a horrible, irresponsible bastard!" And you're right. I leap to agree with you. I am one of the most irresponsible beings that ever lived. Irresponsibility is part of my invisibility; any way you face it, it is a denial. But to whom can I be responsible, and why should I be, when you refuse to see me? And wait until I reveal how truly irresponsible I am. Responsibility rests upon recognition, and recognition is a form of agreement. Take the man whom I almost killed: Who was responsible for that near murder—I? I don't think so, and I refuse it. I won't buy it. You can't give it to me. *He* bumped *me*, *he* insulted *me*. Shouldn't he, for his own personal safety, have recognized my hysteria, my "danger potential"? He, let us say, was lost in a dream world. But didn't *he* control that dream world—which, alas, is only too real!— and didn't *he* rule me out of it? And if he had yelled for a policeman, wouldn't *I* have been taken for the offending one? Yes, yes, yes! Let me agree with you, I was the irresponsible one; for I should have used my knife to protect the higher interests of society. Some day that kind of foolishness will cause us tragic trouble. All dreamers and sleepwalkers must pay the price, and even the invisible victim is responsible for the fate of all. But I shirked that responsibility; I became too snarled in the incompatible notions that buzzed within my brain. I was a coward . . .

But what did *I* do to be so blue? Bear with me.

Chapter one

It goes a long way back, some twenty years. All my life I had been looking for something, and everywhere I turned someone tried to tell me what it was. I accepted their answers too, though they were often in contradiction and even self-contradictory. I was naïve. I was looking for myself and asking everyone except myself questions which I, and only I, could answer. It took me a long time and much painful boomeranging of my expectations to achieve a realization everyone else appears to have been born with: That I am nobody but myself. But first I had to discover that I am an invisible man!

And yet I am no freak of nature, nor of history. I was in the cards, other things having been equal (or unequal) eighty-five years ago. I am not ashamed of my grandparents for having been slaves. I am only ashamed of myself for having at one time been ashamed. About eighty-five years ago they were told that they were free, united with others of our country in everything pertaining to the common good, and, in everything social, separate like the fingers of the hand. And they believed it. They exulted in it. They stayed in their place, worked hard, and brought up my father to do the same. But my grandfather is the one. He was an odd old guy, my grandfather, and I am told I take after him. It was he who caused the trouble. On his deathbed he called my father to him and said, "Son, after I'm gone I want you to keep up the good fight. I never told you, but our life is a war and I have been a traitor all my born days, a spy in the enemy's country ever since I give up my gun back in the Reconstruction. Live with your head in the lion's mouth. I want you to overcome 'em with yeses, undermine 'em with grins, agree 'em to death and destruction, let 'em swoller you till they vomit or bust wide open." They thought the old man had gone out of his mind. He had been the meekest of men. The younger children were rushed from the room, the shades drawn and the flame of the lamp turned so low that it sputtered on the wick like the old man's breathing. "Learn it to the younguns," he whispered fiercely; then he died.

But my folks were more alarmed over his last words than over his dying. It was as though he had not died at all, his words caused so much anxiety. I was warned emphatically to forget what he had said and, indeed, this is the first time it has been mentioned outside the family circle. It had a tremendous effect upon me, however. I could never be sure of what he meant. Grandfather had been a quiet old man who never made any trouble, yet on his deathbed he had called himself a traitor and a spy, and he had spoken of his meekness as a dangerous activity. It became a constant puzzle which lay unanswered in the back of my mind. And whenever things went well for me I remembered my grandfather and felt guilty and uncomfortable. It was as though I was carrying out his advice in spite of myself. And to make it worse, everyone loved me for it. I was praised by the most lily-white men of the town. I was consid-

ered an example of desirable conduct—just as my grandfather
had been. And what puzzled me was that the old man had
defined it as *treachery*. When I was praised for my conduct I
felt a guilt that in some way I was doing something that was
really against the wishes of the white folks, that if they had
understood they would have desired me to act just the opposite, that I should have been sulky and mean, and that that
really would have been what they wanted, even though they
were fooled and thought they wanted me to act as I did. It
made me afraid that some day they would look upon me as a
traitor and I would be lost. Still I was more afraid to act any
other way because they didn't like that at all. The old man's
words were like a curse. On my graduation day I delivered an
oration in which I showed that humility was the secret, indeed,
the very essence of progress. (Not that I believed this—how
could I, remembering my grandfather?—I only believed that it
worked.) It was a great success. Everyone praised me and I was
invited to give the speech at a gathering of the town's leading
white citizens. It was a triumph for our whole community.

It was in the main ballroom of the leading hotel. When
I got there I discovered that it was on the occasion of a smoker,
and I was told that since I was to be there anyway I might as
well take part in the battle royal to be fought by some of my
schoolmates as part of the entertainment. The battle royal came
first.

All of the town's big shots were there in their tuxedoes,
wolfing down the buffet foods, drinking beer and whiskey and
smoking black cigars. It was a large room with a high ceiling.
Chairs were arranged in neat rows around three sides of a
portable boxing ring. The fourth side was clear, revealing a
gleaming space of polished floor. I had some misgivings over
the battle royal, by the way. Not from a distaste for fighting,
but because I didn't care too much for the other fellows who

were to take part. They were tough guys who seemed to have no grandfather's curse worrying their minds. No one could mistake their toughness. And besides, I suspected that fighting a battle royal might detract from the dignity of my speech. In those pre-invisible days I visualized myself as a potential Booker T. Washington. But the other fellows didn't care too much for me either, and there were nine of them. I felt superior to them in my way, and I didn't like the manner in which we were all crowded together into the servants' elevator. Nor did they like my being there. In fact, as the warmly lighted floors flashed past the elevator we had words over the fact that I, by taking part in the fight, had knocked one of their friends out of a night's work.

We were led out of the elevator through a rococo hall into an anteroom and told to get into our fighting togs. Each of us was issued a pair of boxing gloves and ushered out into the big mirrored hall, which we entered looking cautiously about us and whispering, lest we might accidentally be heard above the noise of the room. It was foggy with cigar smoke. And already the whiskey was taking effect. I was shocked to see some of the most important men of the town quite tipsy. They were all there—bankers, lawyers, judges, doctors, fire chiefs, teachers, merchants. Even one of the more fashionable pastors. Something we could not see was going on up front. A clarinet was vibrating sensuously and the men were standing up and moving eagerly forward. We were a small tight group, clustered together, our bare upper bodies touching and shining with anticipatory sweat; while up front the big shots were becoming increasingly excited over something we still could not see. Suddenly I heard the school superintendent, who had told me to come, yell, "Bring up the shines, gentlemen! Bring up the little shines!"

We were rushed up to the front of the ballroom, where

it smelled even more strongly of tobacco and whiskey. Then we were pushed into place. I almost wet my pants. A sea of faces, some hostile, some amused, ringed around us, and in the center, facing us, stood a magnificent blonde—stark naked. There was dead silence. I felt a blast of cold air chill me. I tried to back away, but they were behind me and around me. Some of the boys stood with lowered heads, trembling. I felt a wave of irrational guilt and fear. My teeth chattered, my skin turned to goose flesh, my knees knocked. Yet I was strongly attracted and looked in spite of myself. Had the price of looking been blindness, I would have looked. The hair was yellow like that of a circus kewpie doll, the face heavily powdered and rouged, as though to form an abstract mask, the eyes hollow and smeared a cool blue, the color of a baboon's butt. I felt a desire to spit upon her as my eyes brushed slowly over her body. Her breasts were firm and round as the domes of East Indian temples, and I stood so close as to see the fine skin texture and beads of pearly perspiration glistening like dew around the pink and erected buds of her nipples. I wanted at one and the same time to run from the room, to sink through the floor, or go to her and cover her from my eyes and the eyes of the others with my body; to feel the soft thighs, to caress her and destroy her, to love her and murder her, to hide from her, and yet to stroke where below the small American flag tattooed upon her belly her thighs formed a capital V. I had a notion that of all in the room she saw only me with her impersonal eyes.

And then she began to dance, a slow sensuous movement; the smoke of a hundred cigars clinging to her like the thinnest of veils. She seemed like a fair bird-girl girdled in veils calling to me from the angry surface of some gray and threatening sea. I was transported. Then I became aware of the clarinet playing and the big shots yelling at us. Some threatened us if we looked and others if we did not. On my right I saw one boy faint. And now a man grabbed a silver pitcher from a table and stepped close as he dashed ice water upon him and stood him up and forced two of us to support him as his head hung and moans issued from his thick bluish lips. Another boy began to plead to go home. He was the largest of the group, wearing dark red fighting trunks much too small to conceal the erection which projected from him as though in answer to the insinuating low-registered moaning of the clarinet. He tried to hide himself with his boxing gloves.

And all the while the blonde continued dancing, smiling faintly at the big shots who watched her with fascination, and faintly smiling at our fear. I noticed a certain merchant who followed her hungrily, his lips loose and drooling. He was a large man who wore diamond studs in a shirtfront which swelled with the ample paunch underneath, and each time the blonde swayed her undulating hips he ran his hand through the thin hair of his bald head and, with his arms upheld, his posture clumsy like that of an intoxicated panda, wound his belly in a slow and obscene grind. This creature was completely hypnotized. The music had quickened. As the dancer flung herself about with a detached expression on her face, the men began reaching out to touch her. I could see their beefy fingers sink into the soft flesh. Some of the others tried to stop them and she began to move around the floor in graceful circles, as they gave chase, slipping and sliding over the polished floor. It was mad. Chairs went crashing, drinks were spilt, as they ran laughing and howling after her. They caught her just as she reached a door, raised her from the floor, and tossed her as college boys are tossed at a hazing, and above her red, fixed-smiling lips I saw the terror and disgust in her eyes, almost like my own terror and that which I saw in some of the other boys. As I watched, they tossed her twice and her soft breasts seemed to flatten against the air and her legs flung wildly as she spun. Some of the more sober ones helped her to escape. And I started off the floor, heading for the anteroom with the rest of the boys.

Some were still crying and in hysteria. But as we tried to leave we were stopped and ordered to get into the ring. There was nothing to do but what we were told. All ten of us climbed under the ropes and allowed ourselves to be blindfolded with broad bands of white cloth. One of the men seemed to feel a bit sympathetic and tried to cheer us up as we stood with our backs against the ropes. Some of us tried to grin. "See that boy over there?" one of the men said. "I want you to run across at the bell and give it to him right in the belly. If you don't get him, I'm going to get you. I don't like his looks." Each of us was told the same. The blindfolds were put on. Yet even then I had been going over my speech. In my mind each word was as bright as flame. I felt the cloth pressed into place, and frowned so that it would be loosened when I relaxed.

But now I felt a sudden fit of blind terror. I was unused to darkness. It was though I had suddenly found myself in a dark room filled with poisonous cottonmouths. I could hear the bleary voices yelling insistently for the battle royal to begin.

"Get going in there!"

"Let me at that big nigger!"

I strained to pick up the school superintendent's voice, as though to squeeze some security out of that slightly more familiar sound.

"Let me at those black sonsabitches!" someone yelled.

"No, Jackson, no!" another voice yelled. "Here, somebody, help me hold Jack."

"I want to get at that ginger-colored nigger. Tear him limb from limb," the first voice yelled.

I stood against the ropes trembling. For in those days I

was what they called ginger-colored, and he sounded as though he might crunch me between his teeth like a crisp ginger cookie.

Quite a struggle was going on. Chairs were being kicked about and I could hear voices grunting as with a terrific effort. I wanted to see, to see more desperately than ever before. But the blindfold was tight as a thick skin-puckering scab and when I raised my gloved hands to push the layers of white aside a voice yelled, "Oh, no you don't, black bastard! Leave that alone!"

"Ring the bell before Jackson kills him a coon!" someone boomed in the sudden silence. And I heard the bell clang and the sound of the feet scuffing forward.

A glove smacked against my head. I pivoted, striking out stiffly as someone went past, and felt the jar ripple along the length of my arm to my shoulder. Then it seemed as though all nine of the boys had turned upon me at once. Blows pounded me from all sides while I struck out as best I could. So many blows landed upon me that I wondered if I were not the only blindfolded fighter in the ring, or if the man called Jackson hadn't succeeded in getting me after all.

Blindfolded, I could no longer control my motions. I had no dignity. I stumbled about like a baby or a drunken man. The smoke had become thicker and with each new blow it seemed to sear and further restrict my lungs. My saliva became like hot bitter glue. A glove connected with my head, filling my mouth with warm blood. It was everywhere. I could not tell if the moisture I felt upon my body was sweat or blood. A blow landed hard against the nape of my neck. I felt myself going over, my head hitting the floor. Streaks of blue light filled the black world behind the blindfold. I lay prone, pretending that I was knocked out, but felt myself seized by hands and yanked to my feet. "Get going, black boy! Mix it up!" My arms were like lead, my head smarting from blows. I managed to feel my way to the ropes and held on, trying to catch my breath. A glove landed in my mid-section and I went over again, feeling as though the smoke had become a knife jabbed into my guts. Pushed this way and that by the legs milling around me, I finally pulled erect and discovered that I could see the black, sweat-washed forms weaving in the smoky-blue atmosphere like drunken dancers weaving to the rapid drum-like thuds of blows.

Everyone fought hysterically. It was complete anarchy. Everybody fought everybody else. No group fought together for long. Two, three, four, fought one, then turned to fight each other, were themselves attacked. Blows landed below the belt and in the kidney, with the gloves open as well as closed, and with my eye partly opened now there was not so much terror. I moved carefully, avoiding blows, although not too many to attract attention, fighting from group to group. The boys groped about like blind, cautious crabs crouching to protect their mid-sections, their heads pulled in short against their shoulders, their arms stretched nervously before them, with their fists testing the smoke-filled air like the knobbed feelers of hypersensitive snails. In one corner I glimpsed a boy violently punching the air and heard him scream in pain as he smashed his hand against a ring post. For a second I saw him bent over holding his hand, then going down as a blow caught his unprotected head. I played one group against the other, slipping in and throwing a punch then stepping out of range while pushing the others into the melee to take the blows blindly aimed at me. The smoke was agonizing and there were no rounds, no bells at three-minute intervals to relieve our exhaustion. The room spun round me, a swirl of lights, smoke, sweating bodies surrounded by tense white faces. I bled from both nose and mouth, the blood spattering upon my chest.

The men kept yelling, "Slug him, black boy! Knock his guts out!"

"Uppercut him! Kill him! Kill that big boy!"

Taking a fake fall, I saw a boy going down heavily beside me as though we were felled by a single blow, saw a sneaker-clad foot shoot into his groin as the two who had knocked him down stumbled upon him. I rolled out of range, feeling a twinge of nausea.

The harder we fought the more threatening the men became. And yet, I had begun to worry about my speech again. How would it go? Would they recognize my ability? What would they give me?

I was fighting automatically when suddenly I noticed that one after another of the boys was leaving the ring. I was surprised, filled with panic, as though I had been left alone with an unknown danger. Then I understood. The boys had arranged it among themselves. It was the custom for the two men left in the ring to slug it out for the winner's prize. I discovered this too late. When the bell sounded two men in tuxedoes leaped into the ring and removed the blindfold. I found myself facing Tatlock, the biggest of the gang. I felt sick at my stomach. Hardly had the bell stopped ringing in my ears than it clanged again and I saw him moving swiftly toward me. Thinking of nothing else to do I hit him smash on the nose. He kept coming, bringing the rank sharp violence of stale sweat. His face was a black blank of a face, only his eyes alive—with hate of me and aglow with a feverish terror from what had happened to us all. I became anxious. I wanted to deliver my speech and he came at me as though he meant to beat it out of me. I smashed him again and again, taking his blows as they came. Then on a sudden impulse I struck him lightly and as we clinched, I whispered, "Fake like I knocked you out, you can have the prize."

"I'll break your behind," he whispered hoarsely.

"For *them?*"

"For *me,* sonofabitch!"

They were yelling for us to break it up and Tatlock spun me half around with a blow, and as a joggled camera sweeps in a reeling scene, I saw the howling red faces crouching tense beneath the cloud of blue-gray smoke. For a moment the world wavered, unraveled, flowed, then my head cleared and Tatlock bounced before me. That fluttering shadow before my eyes was his jabbing left hand. Then falling forward, my head against his damp shoulder, I whispered,

"I'll make it five dollars more."

"Go to hell!"

But his muscles relaxed a trifle beneath my pressure and I breathed, "Seven?"

"Give it to your ma," he said, ripping me beneath the heart.

And while I still held him I butted him and moved away. I felt myself bombarded with punches. I fought back with hopeless desperation. I wanted to deliver my speech more than anything else in the world, because I felt that only these men could judge truly my ability, and now this stupid clown was ruining my chances. I began fighting carefully now, moving in to punch him and out again with my greater speed. A lucky blow to his chin and I had him going too—until I heard a loud voice yell, "I got my money on the big boy."

Hearing this, I almost dropped my guard. I was confused: Should I try to win against the voice out there? Would not this go against my speech, and was not this a moment for humility, for nonresistance? A blow to my head as I danced about sent my right eye popping like a jack-in-the-box and settled my dilemma. The room went red as I fell. It was a dream fall, my body languid and fastidious as to where to land, until the floor became impatient and smashed up to meet me. A moment later I came to. An hypnotic voice said FIVE emphatically. And I lay there, hazily watching a dark red spot of my own blood shaping itself into a butterfly, glistening and soaking into the soiled gray world of the canvas.

When the voice drawled TEN I was lifted up and dragged to a chair. I sat dazed. My eye pained and swelled with each throb of my pounding heart and I wondered if now I would be allowed to speak. I was wringing wet, my mouth still bleeding. We were grouped along the wall now. The other boys ignored me as they congratulated Tatlock and speculated as to how much they would be paid. One boy whimpered over his smashed hand. Looking up front, I saw attendants in white jackets rolling the portable ring away and placing a small square rug in the vacant space surrounded by chairs. Perhaps, I thought, I will stand on the rug to deliver my speech.

Then the M.C. called to us, "Come on up here boys and get your money."

We ran forward to where the men laughed and talked in their chairs, waiting. Everyone seemed friendly now.

"There it is on the rug," the man said. I saw the rug covered with coins of all dimensions and a few crumpled bills. But what excited me, scattered here and there, were the gold pieces.

"Boys, it's all yours," the man said. "You get all you grab."

"That's right, Sambo," a blond man said, winking at me confidentially.

I trembled with excitement, forgetting my pain. I would get the gold and the bills, I thought. I would use both hands. I would throw my body against the boys nearest me to block them from the gold.

"Get down around the rug now," the man commanded, "and don't anyone touch it until I give the signal."

"This ought to be good," I heard.

As told, we got around the square rug on our knees. Slowly the man raised his freckled hand as we followed it upward with our eyes.

I heard, "These niggers look like they're about to pray!"

Then, "Ready," the man said. "Go!"

I lunged for a yellow coin lying on the blue design of the carpet, touching it and sending a surprised shriek to join those rising around me. I tried frantically to remove my hand but could not let go. A hot, violent force tore through my body, shaking me like a wet rat. The rug was electrified. The hair bristled up on my head as I shook myself free. My muscles jumped, my nerves jangled, writhed. But I saw that this was not stopping the other boys. Laughing in fear and embarrassment, some were holding back and scooping up the coins knocked off by the painful contortions of the others. The men roared above us as we struggled.

"Pick it up, goddamnit, pick it up!" someone called like a bass-voiced parrot. "Go on, get it!"

I crawled rapidly around the floor, picking up the coins, trying to avoid the coppers and to get greenbacks and the gold. Ignoring the shock by laughing, as I brushed the coins off quickly, I discovered that I could contain the electricity—a contradiction, but it works. Then the men began to push us onto the rug. Laughing embarrassedly, we struggled out of their hands and kept after the coins. We were all wet and slippery and hard to hold. Suddenly I saw a boy lifted into the air, glistening with sweat like a circus seal, and dropped, his wet back landing flush upon the charged rug, heard him yell and saw him literally dance upon his back, his elbows beating a frenzied tattoo upon the floor, his muscles twitching like the flesh of a horse stung by many flies. When he finally rolled off, his face was gray and no one stopped him when he ran from the floor amid booming laughter.

"Get the money," the M.C. called. "That's good hard American cash!"

And we snatched and grabbed, snatched and grabbed. I was careful not to come too close to the rug now, and when I felt the hot whiskey breath descend upon me like a cloud of foul air I reached out and grabbed the leg of a chair. It was occupied and I held on desperately.

"Leggo, nigger! Leggo!"

The huge face wavered down to mine as he tried to push me free. But my body was slippery and he was too drunk. It was Mr. Colcord, who owned a chain of movie houses and "entertainment palaces." Each time he grabbed me I slipped out of his hands. It became a real struggle. I feared the rug more than I did the drunk, so I held on, surprising myself for a moment by trying to topple *him* upon the rug. It was such an enormous idea that I found myself actually carrying it out. I tried not to be obvious, yet when I grabbed his leg, trying to tumble him out of the chair, he raised up roaring with laughter, and, looking at me with soberness dead in the eye, kicked me viciously in the chest. The chair leg flew out of my hand and I felt myself going and rolled. It was as though I had rolled through a bed of hot coals. It seemed a whole century would pass before I would roll free, a century in which I was seared through the deepest levels of my body to the fearful breath within me and the breath seared and heated to the point of explosion. It'll all be over in a flash, I thought as I rolled clear. It'll all be over in a flash.

But not yet, the men on the other side were waiting, red faces swollen as though from apoplexy as they bent forward in their chairs. Seeing their fingers coming toward me I rolled away as a fumbled football rolls off the receiver's fingertips, back into the coals. That time I luckily sent the rug sliding out of place and heard the coins ringing against the floor and the boys scuffling to pick them up and the M.C. calling, "All right, boys, that's all. Go get dressed and get your money."

I was limp as a dish rag. My back felt as though it had been beaten with wires.

When we had dressed the M.C. came in and gave us each five dollars, except Tatlock, who got ten for being last in the ring. Then he told us to leave. I was not to get a chance to deliver my speech, I thought. I was going out into the dim alley in despair when I was stopped and told to go back. I returned to the ballroom, where the men were pushing back their chairs and gathering in groups to talk.

The M.C. knocked on a table for quiet. "Gentlemen," he said, "we almost forgot an important part of the program. A most serious part, gentlemen. This boy was brought here to deliver a speech which he made at his graduation yesterday . . ."

"Bravo!"

"I'm told that he is the smartest boy we've got out there in Greenwood. I'm told that he knows more big words than a pocket-sized dictionary."

Much applause and laughter.

"So now, gentlemen, I want you to give him your attention."

There was still laughter as I faced them, my mouth dry, my eye throbbing. I began slowly, but evidently my throat was tense, because they began shouting, "Louder! Louder!"

"We of the younger generation extol the wisdom of that great leader and educator," I shouted, "who first spoke these flaming words of wisdom: 'A ship lost at sea for many days suddenly sighted a friendly vessel. From the mast of the unfortunate vessel was seen a signal: "Water, water; we die of thirst!" The answer from the friendly vessel came back: "Cast down your bucket where you are." The captain of the distressed vessel, at last heeding the injunction, cast down his bucket, and it came up full of fresh sparkling water from the mouth of the Amazon River.' And like him I say, and in his words, 'To those of my race who depend upon bettering their condition in a foreign land, or who underestimate the importance of cultivating friendly relations with the southern white man, who is his next-door neighbor, I would say: "Cast down your bucket where you are"—cast it down in making friends in every manly way of the people of all races by whom we are surrounded . . .' "

I spoke automatically and with such fervor that I did not realize that the men were still talking and laughing until my dry mouth, filling up with blood from the cut, almost strangled me. I coughed, wanting to stop and go to one of the tall brass, sand-filled spittoons to relieve myself, but a few of the men, especially the superintendent, were listening and I was afraid. So I gulped it down, blood, saliva and all, and continued. (What powers of endurance I had during those days! What enthusiasm! What a belief in the rightness of things!) I spoke even louder in spite of the pain. But still they talked and still they laughed, as though deaf with cotton in dirty ears. So I spoke with greater emotional emphasis. I closed my ears and swallowed blood until I was nauseated. The speech seemed a hundred times as long as before, but I could not leave out a single word. All had to be said, each memorized nuance considered, rendered. Nor was that all. Whenever I uttered a word of three or more syllables a group of voices would yell for me to repeat it. I used the phrase "social responsibility" and they yelled:

"What's that word you say, boy?"

"Social responsibility," I said.

"What?"

"Social . . ."

"Louder."

". . . responsibility."

"More!"

"Respon—"

"Repeat!"

"—sibility."

The room filled with the uproar of laughter until, no doubt distracted by having to gulp down my blood, I made a mistake and yelled a phrase I had often seen denounced in newspaper editorials, heard debated in private.

"Social . . ."

"What?" they yelled.

". . . equality—"

The laughter hung smokelike in the sudden stillness. I opened my eyes, puzzled. Sounds of displeasure filled the room. The M.C. rushed forward. They shouted hostile phrases at me. But I did not understand.

A small dry mustached man in the front row blared out, "Say that slowly, son!"

"What, sir?"

"What you just said!"

"Social responsibility, sir," I said.

"You weren't being smart, were you, boy?" he said, not unkindly.

"No, sir!"

"You sure that about 'equality' was a mistake?"

"Oh, yes, sir," I said. "I was swallowing blood."

"Well, you had better speak more slowly so we can understand. We mean to do right by you, but you've got to know your place at all times. All right, now, go on with your speech."

I was afraid. I wanted to leave but I wanted also to speak and I was afraid they'd snatch me down.

"Thank you, sir," I said, beginning where I had left off, and having them ignore me as before.

Yet when I finished there was a thunderous applause. I

was surprised to see the superintendent come forth with a package wrapped in white tissue paper, and, gesturing for quiet, address the men.

"Gentlemen, you see that I did not overpraise this boy. He makes a good speech and some day he'll lead his people in the proper paths. And I don't have to tell you that that is important in these days and times. This is a good, smart boy, and so to encourage him in the right direction, in the name of the Board of Education I wish to present him a prize in the form of this . . ."

He paused, removing the tissue paper and revealing a gleaming calfskin brief case.

". . . in the form of this first-class article from Shad Whitmore's shop."

"Boy," he said, addressing me, "take this prize and keep it well. Consider it a badge of office. Prize it. Keep developing as you are and some day it will be filled with important papers that will help shape the destiny of your people."

I was so moved that I could hardly express my thanks. A rope of bloody saliva forming a shape like an undiscovered continent drooled upon the leather and I wiped it quickly away. I felt an importance that I had never dreamed.

"Open it and see what's inside," I was told.

My fingers a-tremble, I complied, smelling the fresh leather and finding an official-looking document inside. It was a scholarship to the state college for Negroes. My eyes filled with tears and I ran awkwardly off the floor.

I was overjoyed; I did not even mind when I discovered that the gold pieces I had scrambled for were brass pocket tokens advertising a certain make of automobile.

When I reached home everyone was excited. Next day the neighbors came to congratulate me. I even felt safe from grandfather, whose deathbed curse usually spoiled my triumphs. I stood beneath his photograph with my brief case in hand and smiled triumphantly into his stolid black peasant's face. It was a face that fascinated me. The eyes seemed to follow everywhere I went.

That night I dreamed I was at a circus with him and that he refused to laugh at the clowns no matter what they did. Then later he told me to open my brief case and read what was inside and I did, finding an official envelope stamped with the state seal; and inside the envelope I found another and another, endlessly, and I thought I would fall of weariness. "Them's years," he said. "Now open that one." And I did and in it I found an engraved document containing a short message in letters of gold. "Read it," my grandfather said. "Out loud!"

"To Whom It May Concern," I intoned. "Keep This Nigger-Boy Running."

I awoke with the old man's laughter ringing in my ears.

(It was a dream I was to remember and dream again for many years after. But at that time I had no insight into its meaning. First I had to attend college.)

Chapter two

It was a beautiful college. The buildings were old and covered with vines and the roads gracefully winding, lined with hedges and wild roses that dazzled the eyes in the summer sun. Honeysuckle and purple wisteria hung heavy from the trees and white magnolias mixed with their scents in the bee-humming air. I've recalled it often, here in my hole: How the grass turned green in the springtime and how the mocking birds fluttered their tails and sang, how the moon shone down on the buildings, how the bell in the chapel tower rang out the precious short-lived hours; how the girls in bright summer dresses promenaded the grassy lawn. Many times, here at night, I've closed my eyes and walked along the forbidden road that winds past the girls' dormitories, past the hall with the clock in the tower, its windows warmly aglow, on down past the small white Home Economics practice cottage, whiter still in the moonlight, and on down the road with its sloping and turning, paralleling the black powerhouse with its engines droning earth-shaking rhythms in the dark, its windows red from the glow of the furnace, on to where the road became a bridge over a dry riverbed, tangled with brush and clinging vines; the bridge of rustic logs, made for trysting, but virginal and untested by lovers; on up the road, past the buildings, with the southern verandas half-a-city-block long, to the sudden forking, barren of buildings, birds, or grass, where the road turned off to the insane asylum.

I always come this far and open my eyes. The spell breaks and I try to re-see the rabbits, so tame through having never been hunted, that played in the hedges and along the road. And I see the purple and silver of thistle growing between the broken glass and sunheated stones, the ants moving nervously in single file, and I turn and retrace my steps and come back to the winding road past the hospital, where at night in certain wards the gay student nurses dispensed a far more precious thing than pills to lucky boys in the know; and I come to a stop at the chapel. And then it is suddenly winter, with the moon high above and the chimes in the steeple ringing and a sonorous choir of trombones rendering a Christmas carol; and over all is a quietness and an ache as though all the world were loneliness. And I stand and listen beneath the high-hung moon, hearing "A Mighty Fortress Is Our God," majestically mellow on four trombones, and then the organ. The sound floats over all, clear like the night, liquid, serene, and lonely. And I stand as for an answer and see in my mind's eye the cabins surrounded by empty fields beyond red clay roads, and beyond a certain road a river, sluggish and covered with algae more yellow than green in its stagnant stillness; past more empty fields, to the sun-shrunk shacks at the railroad crossing where the disabled veterans visited the whores, hobbling down the tracks on crutches and canes; sometimes pushing the legless, thighless one in a red wheelchair. And sometimes I listen to hear if music reaches that far, but recall only the drunken laughter of sad, sad whores. And I stand in the circle where three roads converge near the statue, where we drilled four-abreast down the smooth asphalt and pivoted and entered the chapel on Sundays, our uniforms pressed, shoes shined, minds laced up, eyes blind like those of robots to visitors and officials on the low, whitewashed reviewing stand.

It's so long ago and far away that here in my invisibility I wonder if it happened at all. Then in my mind's eye I see the bronze statue of the college Founder, the cold Father symbol, his hands outstretched in the breathtaking gesture of lifting a veil that flutters in hard, metallic folds above the face of a kneeling slave; and I am standing puzzled, unable to decide whether the veil is really being lifted, or lowered more firmly in place; whether I am witnessing a revelation or a more efficient blinding. And as I gaze, there is a rustle of wings and I see a flock of starlings flighting before me and, when I look again, the bronze face, whose empty eyes look upon a world I have never seen, runs with liquid chalk—creating another ambiguity to puzzle my groping mind: Why is a bird-soiled statue more commanding than one that is clean?

Oh, long green stretch of campus, Oh, quiet songs at dusk, Oh, moon that kissed the steeple and flooded the perfumed nights, Oh, bugle that called in the morning, Oh, drum that marched us militarily at noon—what was real, what solid, what more than a pleasant, time-killing dream? For how could it have been real if now I am invisible? If real, why is it that I can recall in all that island of greenness no fountain but one that was broken, corroded and dry? And why does no rain fall through my recollections, sound through my memories, soak through the hard dry crust of the still so recent past? Why do I recall, instead of the odor of seed bursting in springtime, only the yellow contents of the cistern spread over the lawn's dead grass? Why? And how? How and why?

The grass did grow and the green leaves appeared on the

trees and filled the avenues with shadow and shade as sure as
the millionaires descended from the North on Founders' Day
each spring. And how they arrived! Came smiling, inspecting,
encouraging, conversing in whispers, speechmaking into the
wide-open ears of our black and yellow faces—and each leaving
a sizeable check as he departed. I'm convinced it was the prod-
uct of a subtle magic, the alchemy of moonlight; the school a
flower-studded wasteland, the rocks sunken, the dry winds hidden, the lost crickets chirping to yellow butterflies.

And oh, oh, oh, those multimillionaires!

THEY were all such a part of that other life that's dead that I
can't remember them all. (Time was as I was, but neither that
time nor that "I" are anymore.) But this one I remember:
near the end of my junior year I drove for him during the
week he was on the campus. A face pink like St. Nicholas',
topped with a shock of silk white hair. An easy, informal manner, even with me. A Bostonian, smoker of cigars, teller of
polite Negro stories, shrewd banker, skilled scientist, director,
philanthropist, forty years a bearer of the white man's burden,
and for sixty a symbol of the Great Traditions.

We were driving, the powerful motor purring and filling
me with pride and anxiety. The car smelled of mints and cigar
smoke. Students looked up and smiled in recognition as we
rolled slowly past. I had just come from dinner and in bending
forward to suppress a belch, I accidentally pressed the button
on the wheel and the belch became a loud and shattering blast
of the horn. Folks on the road turned and stared.

"I'm awfully sorry, sir," I said, worried lest he report me
to Dr. Bledsoe, the president, who would refuse to allow me
to drive again.

"Perfectly all right. Perfectly."

"Where shall I drive you, sir?"

"Let me see . . ."

Through the rear-view mirror I could see him studying a wafer-thin watch, replacing it in the pocket of his checked waistcoat. His shirt was soft silk, set off with a blue-and-white polka-dotted bow tie. His manner was aristocratic, his movements dapper and suave.

"It's early to go in for the next session," he said. "Suppose you just drive. Anywhere you like."

"Have you seen all the campus, sir?"

"Yes, I think so. I was one of the original founders, you know."

"Gee! I didn't know that, sir. Then I'll have to try some of the roads."

Of course I knew he was a founder, but I knew also that it was advantageous to flatter rich white folks. Perhaps he'd give me a large tip, or a suit, or a scholarship next year.

"Anywhere else you like. The campus is part of my life and I know my life rather well."

"Yes, sir."

He was still smiling.

In a moment the green campus with its vine-covered buildings was behind us. The car bounded over the road. How was the campus part of his life, I wondered. And how did one learn his life "rather well"?

"Young man, you're part of a wonderful institution. It is a great dream become reality . . ."

"Yes, sir," I said.

"I feel as lucky to be connected with it as you no doubt do yourself. I came here years ago, when all your beautiful campus was barren ground. There were no trees, no flowers, no fertile farmland. That was years ago before you were born . . ."

I listened with fascination, my eyes glued to the white

line dividing the highway as my thoughts attempted to sweep back to the times of which he spoke.

"Even your parents were young. Slavery was just recently past. Your people did not know in what direction to turn and, I must confess, many of mine didn't know in what direction they should turn either. But your great Founder did. He was my friend and I believed in his vision. So much so, that sometimes I don't know whether it was his vision or mine . . ."

He chuckled softly, wrinkles forming at the corners of his eyes.

"But of course it was his; I only assisted. I came down with him to see the barren land and did what I could to render assistance. And it has been my pleasant fate to return each spring and observe the changes that the years have wrought. That has been more pleasant and satisfying to me than my own work. It has been a pleasant fate, indeed."

His voice was mellow and loaded with more meaning than I could fathom. As I drove, faded and yellowed pictures of the school's early days displayed in the library flashed across the screen of my mind, coming fitfully and fragmentarily to life—photographs of men and women in wagons drawn by mule teams and oxen, dressed in black, dusty clothing, people who seemed almost without individuality, a black mob that seemed to be waiting, looking with blank faces, and among them the inevitable collection of white men and women in smiles, clear of features, striking, elegant and confident. Until now, and although I could recognize the Founder and Dr. Bledsoe among them, the figures in the photographs had never seemed actually to have been alive, but were more like signs or symbols one found on the last pages of the dictionary . . . But now I felt that I was sharing in a great work and, with the car leaping leisurely beneath the pressure of my foot, I identified myself with the rich man reminiscing on the rear seat . . .

"A pleasant fate," he repeated, "and I hope yours will be as pleasant."

"Yes, sir. Thank you, sir," I said, pleased that he wished something pleasant for me.

But at the same time I was puzzled: How could anyone's fate be *pleasant*? I had always thought of it as something painful. No one I knew spoke of it as pleasant—not even Woodridge, who made us read Greek plays.

We were beyond the farthest extension of the school-owned lands now and I suddenly decided to turn off the highway, down a road that seemed unfamiliar. There were no trees and the air was brilliant. Far down the road the sun glared cruelly against a tin sign nailed to a barn. A lone figure bending over a hoe on the hillside raised up wearily and waved, more a shadow against the skyline than a man.

"How far have we come?" I heard over my shoulder.

"Just about a mile, sir."

"I don't remember this section," he said.

I didn't answer. I was thinking of the first person who'd mentioned anything like fate in my presence, my grandfather. There had been nothing pleasant about it and I had tried to forget it. Now, riding here in the powerful car with this white man who was so pleased with what he called his fate, I felt a sense of dread. My grandfather would have called this treachery and I could not understand in just what way it was. Suddenly I grew guilty at the realization that the white man might have thought so too. What would he have thought? Did he know that Negroes like my grandfather had been freed during those days just before the college had been founded?

As we came to a side road I saw a team of oxen hitched to a broken-down wagon, the ragged driver dozing on the seat beneath the shade of a clump of trees.

"Did you see that, sir?" I asked over my shoulder.

"What was it?"

"The ox team, sir."

"Oh! No, I can't see it for the trees," he said looking back. "It's good timber."

"I'm sorry, sir. Shall I turn back?"

"No, it isn't much," he said. "Go on."

I drove on, remembering the lean, hungry face of the sleeping man. He was the kind of white man I feared. The brown fields swept out to the horizon. A flock of birds dipped down, circled, swung up and out as though linked by invisible strings. Waves of heat danced above the engine hood. The tires sang over the highway. Finally I overcame my timidity and asked him:

"Sir, why did you become interested in the school?"

"I think," he said, thoughtfully, raising his voice, "it was because I felt even as a young man that your people were somehow closely connected with my destiny. Do you understand?"

"Not so clearly, sir," I said, ashamed to admit it.

"You have studied Emerson, haven't you?"

"Emerson, sir?"

"Ralph Waldo Emerson."

I was embarrassed because I hadn't. "Not yet, sir. We haven't come to him yet."

"No?" he said with a note of surprise. "Well, never mind. I am a New Englander, like Emerson. You must learn about him, for he was important to your people. He had a hand in your destiny. Yes, perhaps that is what I mean. I had a feeling that your people were somehow connected with my destiny. That what happened to you was connected with what would happen to me . . ."

I slowed the car, trying to understand. Through the glass

I saw him gazing at the long ash of his cigar, holding it delicately in his slender, manicured fingers.

"Yes, you are my fate, young man. Only you can tell me what it really is. Do you understand?"

"I *think* I do, sir."

"I mean that upon you depends the outcome of the years I have spent in helping your school. That has been my real life's work, not my banking or my researches, but my first-hand organizing of human life."

I saw him now, leaning toward the front seat, speaking with an intensity which had not been there before. It was hard not to turn my eyes from the highway and face him.

"There is another reason, a reason more important, more passionate and yes, even more sacred than all the others," he said, no longer seeming to see me, but speaking to himself alone. "Yes, even more sacred than all the others. A girl, my daughter. She was a being more rare, more beautiful, purer, more perfect and more delicate than the wildest dream of a poet. I could never believe her to be my own flesh and blood. Her beauty was a well-spring of purest water-of-life, and to look upon her was to drink and drink and drink again . . . She was rare, a perfect creation, a work of purest art. A delicate flower that bloomed in the liquid light of the moon. A nature not of this world, a personality like that of some biblical maiden, gracious and queenly. I found it difficult to believe her my own . . ."

Suddenly he fumbled in his vest pocket and thrust something over the back of the seat, surprising me.

"Here, young man, you owe much of your good fortune in attending such a school to her."

I looked upon the tinted miniature framed in engraved platinum. I almost dropped it. A young woman of delicate, dreamy features looked up at me. She was very beautiful, I thought at the time, so beautiful that I did not know whether I should express admiration to the extent I felt it or merely act polite. And yet I seemed to remember her, or someone like her, in the past. I know now that it was the flowing costume of soft, flimsy material that made for the effect; today, dressed in one of the smart, well-tailored, angular, sterile, streamlined, engine-turned, air-conditioned modern outfits you see in the women's magazines, she would appear as ordinary as an expensive piece of machine-tooled jewelry and just as lifeless. Then, however, I shared something of his enthusiasm.

"She was too pure for life," he said sadly; "too pure and too good and too beautiful. We were sailing together, touring the world, just she and I, when she became ill in Italy. I thought little of it at the time and we continued across the Alps. When we reached Munich she was already fading away. While we were attending an embassy party she collapsed. The best medical science in the world could not save her. It was a lonely return, a bitter voyage. I have never recovered. I have never forgiven myself. Everything I've done since her passing has been a monument to her memory."

He became silent, looking with his blue eyes far beyond the field stretching away in the sun. I returned the miniature, wondering what in the world had made him open his heart to me. That was something I never did; it was dangerous. First, it was dangerous if you felt like that about anything, because then you'd never get it or something or someone would take it away from you; then it was dangerous because nobody would understand you and they'd only laugh and think you were crazy.

"So you see, young man, you are involved in my life quite intimately, even though you've never seen me before. You are bound to a great dream and to a beautiful monument. If you become a good farmer, a chef, a preacher, doctor, singer, mechanic—whatever you become, and even if you fail, you are my fate. And you must write me and tell me the outcome."

I was relieved to see him smiling through the mirror. My feelings were mixed. Was he kidding me? Was he talking to me like someone in a book just to see how I would take it? Or could it be, I was almost afraid to think, that this rich man was just the tiniest bit crazy? How could I tell him *his* fate? He raised his head and our eyes met for an instant in the glass, then I lowered mine to the blazing white line that divided the highway.

The trees along the road were thick and tall. We took a curve. Flocks of quail sailed up and over a field, brown, brown, sailing down, blending.

"Will you promise to tell me my fate?" I heard.

"Sir?"

"Will you?"

"Right *now*, sir?" I asked with embarrassment.

"It is up to you. Now, if you like."

I was silent. His voice was serious, demanding. I could think of no reply. The motor purred. An insect crushed itself against the windshield, leaving a yellow, mucous smear.

"I don't know now, sir. This is only my junior year . . ."

"But you'll tell me when you know?"

"I'll try, sir."

"Good."

When I took a quick glance into the mirror he was smiling again. I wanted to ask him if being rich and famous and helping to direct the school to become what it was, wasn't enough; but I was afraid.

"What do you think of my idea, young man?" he said.

"I don't know, sir. I only think that you have what you're looking for. Because if I fail or leave school, it doesn't seem to me it would be your fault. Because you helped make the school what it is."

"And you think that enough?"

"Yes, sir. That's what the president tells us. You have yours, and you got it yourself, and we have to lift ourselves up the same way."

"But that's only part of it, young man. I have wealth and a reputation and prestige—all that is true. But your great Founder had more than that, he had tens of thousands of lives dependent upon his ideas and upon his actions. What he did affected your whole race. In a way, he had the power of a king, or in a sense, of a god. That, I've come to believe, is more important than my own work, because more depends upon you. *You* are important because if you fail *I* have failed by one individual, one defective cog; it didn't matter so much before, but now I'm growing old and it has become very important . . ."

But you don't even know my name, I thought, wondering what it was all about.

". . . I suppose it is difficult for you to understand how this concerns me. But as you develop you must remember that I am dependent upon you to learn my fate. Through you and your fellow students I become, let us say, three hundred teachers, seven hundred trained mechanics, eight hundred skilled farmers, and so on. That way I can observe in terms of living personalities to what extent my money, my time and my hopes have been fruitfully invested. I also construct a living memorial to my daughter. Understand? I can see the fruits produced by the land that your great Founder has transformed from barren clay to fertile soil."

His voice ceased and I saw the strands of pale blue smoke drifting across the mirror and heard the electric lighter snap back on its cable into place behind the back of the seat.

"I think I understand you better, now, sir," I said.

"Very good, my boy."

"Shall I continue in this direction, sir?"

45

"By all means," he said, looking out at the country-side. "I've never seen this section before. It's new territory for me."

Half-consciously I followed the white line as I drove, thinking about what he had said. Then as we took a hill we were swept by a wave of scorching air and it was as though we were approaching a desert. It almost took my breath away and I leaned over and switched on the fan, hearing its sudden whirr.

"Thank you," he said as a slight breeze filled the car.

We were passing a collection of shacks and log cabins now, bleached white and warped by the weather. Sun-tortured shingles lay on the roofs like decks of water-soaked cards spread out to dry. The houses consisted of two square rooms joined together by a common floor and roof with a porch in between. As we passed we could look through to the fields beyond. I stopped the car at his excited command in front of a house set off from the rest.

"Is that a *log* cabin?"

It was an old cabin with its chinks filled with chalk-white clay, with bright new shingles patching its roof. Suddenly I was sorry that I had blundered down this road. I recognized the place as soon as I saw the group of children in stiff new overalls who played near a rickety fence.

"Yes, sir. It is a log cabin," I said.

It was the cabin of Jim Trueblood, a sharecropper who had brought disgrace upon the black community. Several months before he had caused quite a bit of outrage up at the school, and now his name was never mentioned above a whis-per. Even before that he had seldom come near the campus but had been well liked as a hard worker who took good care of his family's needs, and as one who told the old stories with a sense of humor and a magic that made them come alive. He was also a good tenor singer, and sometimes when special white guests visited the school he was brought up along with the members of a country quartet to sing what the officials called "their primitive spirituals" when we assembled in the chapel on Sunday evenings. We were embarrassed by the earthy harmonies they sang, but since the visitors were awed we dared not laugh at the crude, high, plaintively animal sounds Jim Trueblood made as he led the quartet. That had all passed now with his disgrace, and what on the part of the school officials had been an attitude of contempt blunted by tolerance, had now become a contempt sharpened by hate. I didn't understand in those pre-invisible days that their hate, and mine too, was charged with fear. How all of us at the college hated the black-belt people, the "peasants," during those days! We were trying to lift them up and they, like Trueblood, did everything it seemed to pull us down.

"It appears quite old," Mr. Norton said, looking across the bare, hard stretch of yard where two women dressed in new blue-and-white checked ginghams were washing clothes in an iron pot. The pot was soot-black and the feeble flames that licked its sides showed pale pink and bordered with black, like flames in mourning. Both women moved with the weary, full-fronted motions of far-gone pregnancy.

"It is, sir," I said. "That one and the other two like it were built during slavery times."

"You don't say! I would never have believed that they were so enduring. Since slavery times!"

"That's true, sir. And the white family that owned the land when it was a big plantation still lives in town."

"Yes," he said, "I know that many of the old families still survive. And individuals too, the human stock goes on, even though it degenerates. But these cabins!" He seemed surprised and confounded.

"Do you suppose those women know anything about the age and history of the place? The older one looks as though she might."

"I doubt it, sir. They—they don't seem very bright."

"Bright?" he said, removing his cigar. "You mean that they wouldn't talk with me?" he asked suspiciously.

"Yes, sir. That's it."

"Why not?"

I didn't want to explain. It made me feel ashamed, but he sensed that I knew something and pressed me.

"It's not very nice, sir. But I don't think those women would talk to us."

"We can explain that we're from the school. Surely they'll talk then. You may tell them who I am."

"Yes, sir," I said, "but they hate us up at the school. They never come there . . ."

"What!"

"No, sir."

"And those children along the fence down there?"

"They don't either, sir."

"But why?"

"I don't really know, sir. Quite a few folks out this way don't, though. I guess they're too ignorant. They're not interested."

"But I can't believe it."

The children had stopped playing and now looked silently at the car, their arms behind their backs and their new oversized overalls pulled tight over their little pot bellies as though they too were pregnant.

"What about their men folk?"

I hesitated. Why did he find this so strange?

"He hates us, sir," I said.

"You say *he*; aren't both the women married?"

I caught my breath. I'd made a mistake. "The old one is, sir," I said reluctantly.

"What happened to the young woman's husband?"

"She doesn't have any— That is . . . I—"

"What is it, young man? Do you know these people?"

"Only a little, sir. There was some talk about them up on the campus a while back."

"What talk?"

"Well, the young woman is the old woman's daughter . . ."

"And?"

"Well, sir, they say . . . you see . . . I mean they say the daughter doesn't have a husband."

"Oh, I see. But that shouldn't be so strange. I understand that your people— Never mind! Is that all?"

"Well, sir . . ."

"Yes, what else?"

"They say that her father did it."

"What!"

"Yes, sir . . . that he gave her the baby."

I heard the sharp intake of breath, like a toy-balloon suddenly deflated. His face reddened. I was confused, feeling shame for the two women and fear that I had talked too much and offended his sensibilities.

"And did anyone from the school investigate this matter?" he asked at last.

"Yes, sir," I said.

"What was discovered?"

"That it was true—they say."

"But how does he explain his doing such a—a—such a monstrous thing?"

He sat back in the seat, his hands grasping his knees, his knuckles bloodless. I looked away, down the heat-dazzling concrete of the highway. I wished we were back on the other side of the white line, heading back to the quiet green stretch of the campus.

"It is said that the man took both his wife and his daughter?"

"Yes, sir."

"And that he is the father of *both* their children?"

"Yes, sir."

"No, no, no!"

He sounded as though he were in great pain. I looked at him anxiously. What had happened? What had I said?

"Not that! No . . ." he said, with something like horror.

I saw the sun blaze upon the new blue overalls as the man appeared around the cabin. His shoes were tan and new and he moved easily over the hot earth. He was a small man and he covered the yard with a familiarity that would have allowed him to walk in the blackest darkness with the same certainty. He came and said something to the woman as he fanned himself with a blue bandanna handkerchief. But they appeared to regard him sullenly, barely speaking, and hardly looking in his direction.

"Would that be the man?" Mr. Norton asked.

"Yes, sir. I think so."

"Get out!" he cried. "I must talk with him."

I was unable to move. I felt surprise and a dread and resentment of what he might say to Trueblood and his women, the questions he might ask. Why couldn't he leave them alone!

"Hurry!"

I climbed from the car and opened the rear door. He clambered out and almost ran across the road to the yard, as though compelled by some pressing urgency which I could not understand. Then suddenly I saw the two women turn and run frantically behind the house, their movements heavy and flat-footed. I hurried behind him, seeing him stop when he reached the man and the children. They became silent, their faces clouding over, their features becoming soft and negative, their eyes bland and deceptive. They were crouching behind their eyes waiting for him to speak—just as I recognized that I was trembling behind my own. Up close I saw what I had not seen from the car: The man had a scar on his right cheek, as though he had been hit in the face with a sledge. The wound was raw and moist and from time to time he lifted his handkerchief to fan away the gnats.

"I, I—" Mr. Norton stammered, "I must talk with you!"

"All right, suh," Jim Trueblood said without surprise and waited.

"Is it true . . . I mean did you?"

"Suh?" Trueblood asked, as I looked away.

"You have survived," he blurted. "But is it true . . . ?"

"*Sub?*" the farmer said, his brow wrinkling with bewilderment.

"I'm sorry, sir," I said, "but I don't think he understands you."

He ignored me, staring into Trueblood's face as though reading a message there which I could not perceive.

"You did and are unharmed!" he shouted, his blue eyes blazing into the black face with something like envy and indignation. Trueblood looked helplessly at me. I looked away. I understood no more than he.

"You have looked upon chaos and are not destroyed!"

"No suh! I feels all right."

"You do? You feel no inner turmoil, no need to cast out the offending eye?"

"*Sub?*"

"Answer me!"

"I'm all right, suh," Trueblood said uneasily. "My eyes is all right too. And when I feels po'ly in my gut I takes a little soda and it goes away."

"No, no, no! Let us go where there is shade," he said,

looking about excitedly and going swiftly to where the porch cast a swath of shade. We followed him. The farmer placed his hand on my shoulder, but I shook it off, knowing that I could explain nothing. We sat on the porch in a semi-circle in camp chairs, me between the sharecropper and the millionaire. The earth around the porch was hard and white from where wash water had long been thrown.

"How are you faring now?" Mr. Norton asked. "Perhaps I could help."

"We ain't doing so bad, suh. 'Fore they heard 'bout what happen to us out here I couldn't git no help from nobody. Now lotta folks is curious and goes outta they way to help. Even the biggity school folks up on the hill, only there was a catch to it! They offered to send us clean outta the county, pay our way and everything and give me a hundred dollars to git settled with. But we likes it here so I told 'em No. Then they sent a fellow out here, a big fellow too, and he said if I didn't leave they was going to turn the white folks loose on me. It made me mad and it made me scared. Them folks up there to the school is in strong with the white folks and that scared me. But I thought when they first come out here that they was different from when I went up there a long time ago looking for some book learning and some points on how to handle my crops. That was when I had my own place. I thought they was trying to he'p me, on accounta I got two women due to birth 'bout the same time.

"But I got mad when I found they was tryin' to git rid of us 'cause they said we was a disgrace. Yessuh, I got real mad. So I went down to see Mr. Buchanan, the boss man, and I tole him 'bout it and he give me a note to the sheriff and tole me to take it to him. I did that, jus' like he tole me. I went to the jailhouse and give Sheriff Barbour the note and he ask me to tell him what happen, and I tole him and he called in some more men and they made me tell it again. They wanted to hear about the gal lots of times and they gimme somethin' to eat and drink and some tobacco. Surprised me, 'cause I was scared and spectin' somethin' different. Why, I guess there ain't a colored man in the county who ever got to take so much of the white folkses' time as I did. So finally they tell me not to worry, that they was going to send word up to the school that I was to stay right where I am. Them big nigguhs didn't bother me, neither. It just goes to show yuh that no matter how biggity a nigguh gits, the white folks can always cut him down. The white folks took up for me. And the white folks took to coming out here to see us and talk with us. Some of 'em was big white folks, too, from the big school way cross the State. Asked me lots 'bout what I thought 'bout things, and 'bout my folks and the kids, and wrote it all down in a book. But best of all, suh, I got more work now than I ever did have before . . ."

He talked willingly now, with a kind of satisfaction and no trace of hesitancy or shame. The old man listened with a puzzled expression as he held an unlit cigar in his delicate fingers.

"Things is pretty good now," the farmer said. "Ever time I think of how cold it was and what a hard time we was having I gits the shakes."

I saw him bite into a plug of chewing tobacco. Something tinkled against the porch and I picked it up, gazing at it from time to time. It was a hard red apple stamped out of tin.

"You see, suh, it was cold and us didn't have much fire. Nothin' but wood, no coal. I tried to git help but wouldn't nobody help us and I couldn't find no work or nothin'. It was so cold all of us had to sleep together; me, the ole lady and the gal. That's how it started, suh."

He cleared his throat, his eyes gleaming and his voice

taking on a deep, incantatory quality, as though he had told the story many, many times. Flies and fine white gnats swarmed about his wound.

"That's the way it was," he said. "Me on one side and the ole lady on the other and the gal in the middle. It was dark, plum black. Black as the middle of a bucket of tar. The kids was sleeping all together in they bed over in the corner. I must have been the last one to go to sleep, 'cause I was think-ing 'bout how to git some grub for the next day and 'bout the gal and the young boy what was startin' to hang 'round her. I didn't like him and he kept comin' through my thoughts and I made up my mind to warn him away from the gal. It was black dark and I heard one of the kids whimper in his sleep and the last few sticks of kindlin' crackin' and settlin' in the stove and the smell of the fat meat seemed to git cold and still in the air just like meat grease when it gits set in a cold plate of molasses. And I was thinkin' 'bout the gal and this boy and feelin' her arms besides me and hearing the ole lady snorin' with a kinda moanin' and a-groanin' on the other side. I was worryin' 'bout my family, how they was goin' to eat and all, and I thought 'bout when the gal was little like the younguns sleepin' over in the corner and how I was her favorite over the ole lady. There we was, breathin' together in the dark. Only I could see 'em in my mind, knowin' 'em like I do. In my mind I looked at all of 'em, one by one. The gal looks just like the ole lady did when she was young and I first met her, only better lookin'. You know, we gittin' to be a better-lookin' race of people . . .

"Anyway, I could hear 'em breathin' and though I hadn't been it made me sleepy. Then I heard the gal say, 'Daddy,' soft and low in her sleep and I looked, tryin' to see if she was still awake. But all I can do is smell her and feel her breath on my hand when I go to touch her. She said it so soft I couldn't be sure I had heard anything, so I just laid there listenin'. Seems like I heard a whippoorwill callin', and I thought to myself, Go on away from here, we'll whip ole Will when we find him. Then I heard the clock up there at the school strikin' four times, lonesome like.

"Then I got to thinkin' 'bout way back when I left the farm and went to live in Mobile and 'bout a gal I had me then. I was young then—like this young fellow here. Us lived in a two-story house 'longside the river, and at night in the summertime we used to lay in bed and talk, and after she'd gone off to sleep I'd be awake lookin' out at the lights comin' up from the water and listenin' to the sounds of the boats movin' along. They used to have musicianers on them boats, and sometimes I used to wake her up to hear the music when they come up the river. I'd be layin' there and it would be quiet and I could hear it comin' from way, way off. Like when you quail huntin' and it's getting dark and you can hear the boss bird whistlin' tryin' to get the covey together again, and he's coming toward you slow and whistlin' soft, 'cause he knows you somewhere around with your gun. Still he got to round them up, so he keeps on comin'. Them boss quails is like a good man, what he got to do he *do*.

"Well, that's the way the boats used to sound. Comin' close to you from far away. First one would be comin' to you when you almost sleep and it sounded like somebody hittin' at you slow with a big shiny pick. You see the pick-point comin' straight at you, comin' slow too, and you can't dodge; only when it goes to hit you it ain't no pick a'tall but somebody far away breakin' little bottles of all kindsa colored glass. It's still comin' at you though. Still comin'. Then you hear it close up, like when you up in the second-story window and look down on a wagonful of watermelons, and you see one of them young juicy melons split wide open a-layin' all spread out and cool

and sweet on top of all the striped green ones like it's waitin'
just for you, so you can see how red and ripe and juicy it is
and all the shiny black seeds it's got and all. And you could
hear the sidewheels splashin' like they don't want to wake nobody up; and us, me and the gal, would lay there feelin' like
we was rich folks and them boys on the boats would be playin'
sweet as good peach brandy wine. Then the boats would be
past and the lights would be gone from the window and the
music would be goin' too. Kinda like when you watch a gal in
a red dress and a wide straw hat goin' past you down a lane
with the trees on both sides, and she's plump and juicy and
kinda switchin' her tail 'cause she knows you watchin' and you
know she know, and you just stands there and watches 'til you
can't see nothin' but the top of her red hat and then that goes
and you know she done dropped behind a hill—I seen me a
gal like that once. All I could hear then would be that Mobile
gal—name of Margaret—she be breathin' beside me, and maybe
'bout that time she'd say, 'Daddy, you still 'wake?' and then
I'd grunt, "Uhhuh" and drop on off—Gent'mens," Jim Trueblood said, "I likes to recall them Mobile days.

"Well, it was like that when I heard Matty Lou say,
'Daddy,' and I knowed she musta been dreamin' 'bout somebody from the way she said it and I gits mad wonderin' if it's
that boy. I listen to her mumblin' for a while tryin' to hear if
she calls his name, but she don't, and I remember that they
say if you put the hand of a person who's talkin' in his sleep
in warm water he'll say it all, but the water is too cold and I
wouldn't have done it anyway. But I'm realizin' that she's a
woman now, when I feels her turn and squirm against me and
throw her arm across my neck, up where the cover didn't reach
and I was cold. She said somethin' I couldn't understand, like
a woman says when she wants to tease and please a man. I
knowed then she was grown and I wondered how many times

it'd done happened and was it that doggone boy. I moved her arm and it was soft, but it didn't wake her, so I called her, but that didn't wake her neither. Then I turned my back and tried to move away, though there wasn't much room and I could still feel her touchin' me, movin' close to me. Then I musta dropped into the dream. I have to tell you 'bout that dream.''

I looked at Mr. Norton and stood up, thinking that now was a good time to leave; but he was listening to Trueblood so intensely he didn't see me, and I sat down again, cursing the farmer silently. To hell with his dream!

"I don't quite remember it all, but I remember that I was lookin' for some fat meat. I went to the white folks downtown and they said go see Mr. Broadnax, that he'd give it to me. Well, he lives up on a hill and I was climbin' up there to see him. Seems like that was the highest hill in the world. The more I climbed the farther away Mr. Broadnax's house seems to git. But finally I do reach there. And I'm so tired and restless to git to the man, I goes through the front door! I knows it's wrong, but I can't help it. I goes in and I'm standin' in a big room full of lighted candles and shiny furniture and pictures on the walls, and soft stuff on the floor. But I don't see a livin' soul. So I calls his name, but still don't nobody come and don't nobody answer. So I sees a door and goes through that door and I'm in a big white bedroom, like I seen one time when I was a little ole boy and went to the big house with my Ma. Everything in the room was white and I'm standin' there knowin' I got no business in there, but there anyhow. It's a woman's room too. I tries git out, but I don't find the door; and all around me I can smell woman, can smell it gittin' stronger all the time. Then I looks over in a corner and sees one of them tall grandfather clocks and I hears it strikin' and the glass door is openin' and a white lady is steppin' out of it. She got on a nightgown of soft white silky stuff and nothin' else, and she looks straight at me. I don't know what to do. I wants to run, but the only door I see is the one in the clock she's standin' in—and anyway, I can't move and this here clock is keepin' up a heapa racket. It's gittin' faster and faster all the time. I tries to say somethin', but I caint. Then she starts to screamin' and I thinks I done gone deef, 'cause though I can see her mouth working, I don't *hear* nothin'. Yit I can still hear the clock and I tries to tell her I'm just lookin' for Mr. Broadnax but she don't hear me. Instead she runs up and grabs me around the neck and holds tight, tryin' to keep me out of the clock. I don't know what to do then, sho 'nough. I tries to talk to her, and I tries to git away. But she's holdin' me and I'm scared to touch her 'cause she's white. Then I gits so scared that I throws her on the bed and tries to break her holt. That woman just seemed to sink outta sight, that there bed was so soft. It's sinkin' down so far I think it's going to smother both of us. Then swoosh! all of a sudden a flock of little white geese flies out of the bed like they say you see when you go to dig for buried money. Lawd! they hadn't no more'n disappeared than I heard a door open and Mr. Broadnax's voice said, 'They just nigguhs, leave 'em do it.'"

How can he tell this to white men, I thought, when he knows they'll say that all Negroes do such things? I looked at the floor, a red mist of anguish before my eyes.

"And I caint stop—although I got a feelin' somethin' is wrong. I git aloose from the woman now and I'm runnin' for the clock. At first I couldn't git the door open, it had some kinda crinkly stuff like steel wool on the facing. But I gits it open and gits inside and it's hot and dark in there. I goes up a dark tunnel, up near where the machinery is making all that noise and heat. It's like the power plant they got up to the school. It's burnin' hot as iffen the house was caught on fire, and I starts to runnin', tryin' to git out. I runs and runs till I should be tired but ain't tired but feelin' more rested as I runs, and runnin' so good it's like flyin' and I'm flyin' and sailin' and floatin' right up over the town. Only I'm still in the *tunnel*. Then way up ahead I sees a bright light like a jack-o-lantern over a graveyard. It gits brighter and brighter and I know I got to catch up with it or else. Then all at once I was right up with it and it burst like a great big electric light in my eyes and scalded me all over. Only it wasn't a scald, but like I was drownin' in a lake where the water was hot on the top and had cold numbin' currents down under it. Then all at once I'm through it and I'm relieved to be out and in the cool daylight agin.

"I wakes up intendin' to tell the ole lady 'bout my crazy dream. Morning done come, and it's gettin' almost light. And there I am, lookin' straight in Matty Lou's face and she's beatin' me and scratchin' and tremblin' and shakin' and cryin' all at the same time like she's havin' a fit. I'm too surprised to move. She's cryin', 'Daddy, Daddy, oh Daddy,' just like that. And all at once I remember the ole lady. She's right beside us snorin' and I can't move 'cause I figgers if I moved it would be a sin. And I figgers too, that if I don't move it maybe ain't no sin, 'cause it happened when I was asleep—although maybe some-times a man can look at a little ole pigtail gal and see him a whore—you'all know that? Anyway, I realizes that if I don't move the ole lady will see me. I don't want that to happen. That would be *worse* than sin. I'm whisperin' to Matty Lou, tryin' to keep her quiet and I'm figurin' how to git myself out of the fix I'm in without sinnin'. I almost chokes her.

"But once a man gits hisself in a tight spot like that there ain't much he can do. It ain't up to him no longer. There I was, tryin' to git away with all my might, yet having to move *without* movin'. I flew in but I had to walk out. I had to move without movin'. I done thought 'bout it since a heap, and when you think right hard you see that that's the way things is always been with me. That's just about been my life. There was only one way I can figger that I could git out: that was with a knife. But I didn't have no knife, and if you'all ever seen them geld them young boar pigs in the fall, you know I knowed that that was too much to pay to keep from sinnin'. Everything was happenin' inside of me like a fight was goin' on. Then just the very thought of the fix I'm in puts the iron back in me.

"Then if that ain' bad enough, Matty Lou can't hold out no longer and gits to movin' herself. First she was tryin' to push me away and I'm tryin' to hold her down to keep from sinnin'. Then I'm pullin' away and shushin' her to be quiet so's not to wake her Ma, when she grabs holt to me and holds tight. She didn't want me to go then—and to tell the honest-to-God truth I found out that I didn't want to go neither. I guess I felt then, at that time—and although I been sorry since—just 'bout like that fellow did down in Birmingham. That one what locked hisself in his house and shot at them police until they set fire to the house and burned him up. I was lost. The more wringlin' and twistin' we done tryin' to git away, the more we wanted to stay. So like that fellow, I stayed, I had to fight it on out to the end. He mighta died, but I suspects now that he got a heapa satisfaction before he went. I *know* there ain't nothin' like what I went through, I caint tell how it was. It's like when a real drinkin' man gits drunk, or like when a real sanctified religious woman gits so worked up she jumps outta her clothes, or when a real gamblin' man keeps on gamblin' when he's losin'. You got holt to it and you caint let go even though you want to."

"Mr. Norton, sir," I said in a choked voice, "it's time we were getting back to the campus. You'll miss your appointments . . ."

He didn't even look at me. *"Please,"* he said, waving his hand in annoyance.

Trueblood seemed to smile at me behind his eyes as he looked from the white man to me and continued.

"I couldn't even let go when I heard Kate scream. It was a scream to make your blood run cold. It sounds like a woman who was watchin' a team of wild horses run down her baby chile and she caint move. Kate's hair is standin' up like she done seen a ghost, her gown is hanging open and the veins in her neck is 'bout to bust. And her eyes! Lawd, them eyes. I'm lookin' up at her from where I'm layin' on the pallet with Matty Lou, and I'm too weak to move. She screams and starts to pickin' up the first thing that comes to her hand and throwin' it. Some of them misses me and some of them hits me. Little things and big things. Somethin' cold and strong-stinkin' hits me and wets me and bangs against my head. Somethin' hits the wall—boom-a-loom-a-loom!—like a cannon ball, and I tries to cover up my head. Kate's talkin' the unknown tongue, like a wild woman.

" 'Wait a minit, Kate,' I says. 'Stop it!'

"Then I hears her stop a second and I hears her runnin' across the floor, and I twists and looks and Lawd, she done got my double-barrel shotgun!

"And while she's foamin' at the mouth and cockin' the gun, she gits her speech.

" 'Git up! Git up!' she says.

" 'HEY! NAW! KATE!' I says.

" 'Goddam yo' soul to hell! Git up offa my chile!'

" 'But woman, Kate, lissen . . .'

" 'Don't talk, MOVE!'

" 'Down that thing, Kate!'

" 'No down, UP!'

" 'That there's buckshot, woman, BUCKshot!'

" 'Yes, it is!'

" 'Down it, I say!'

" 'I'm gon blast your soul to hell!'

" 'You gon hit Matty Lou!'

" 'Not Matty Lou—YOU!'

" 'It spreads, Kate. Matty Lou!'

"She moves around, aimin' at me.

" 'I done warn you, Jim . . .'

" 'Kate, it was a dream. Lissen to me . . .'

" 'You the one who lissen—UP FROM THERE!'

"She jerks the gun and I shuts my eyes. But insteada thunder and lightin' bustin' me, I hears Matty Lou scream in my ear,

" 'Mamma! Oooooo, MAMA!'

"I rolls almost over then and Kate hesitates. She looks at the gun, and she looks at us, and she shivers a minit like she got the fever. Then all at once she drops the gun, and ZIP! quick as a cat, she turns and grabs somethin' off the stove. It catches me like somebody diggin' into my side with a sharp spade. I caint breathe. She's throwin' and talkin' all at the same time.

"And when I looks up, Maan, Maaan! she's got a iron in her hand!

"I hollers, 'No blood, Kate. Don't spill no blood!'

" 'You low-down dog,' she says, 'it's better to spill than to foul!'

" 'Naw, Kate. Things ain't what they 'pear! Don't make no blood-sin on accounta no dream-sin!'

" 'Shut up, nigguh. You done *fouled*!'

"But I sees there ain't no use reasonin' with her then. I makes up my mind that I'm goin' to take whatever she gimme. It seems to me that all I can do is take my punishment. I tell myself, Maybe if you suffer for it, it will be best. Maybe you owe it to Kate to let her beat you. You ain't guilty, but she thinks you is. You don't want her to beat you, but she thinks she got to beat you. You want to git up, but you too weak to move.

"I was too. I was frozen to where I was like a youngun what done stuck his lip to a pump handle in the wintertime. I was just like a jaybird that the yellow jackets done stung 'til he's paralyzed—but still alive in his eyes and he's watchin' 'em sting his body to death.

"It made me seem to go way back a distance in my head, behind my eyes, like I was standin' behind a windbreak durin' a storm. I looks out and sees Kate runnin' toward me draggin' something behind her. I tries to see what it is 'cause I'm curious 'bout it and sees her gown catch on the stove and her hand comin' in sight with somethin' in it. I thinks to myself, It's a handle. What she got the handle to? Then I sees her right up on me, big. She's swingin' her arms like a man swingin' a ten-pound sledge and I sees the knuckles of her hand is bruised and bleedin', and I sees it catch in her gown and I sees her gown go up so I can see her thighs and I sees how rusty and gray the cold done made her skin, and I sees her bend and straightenin' up and I hears her grunt and I sees her swing and I smells her sweat and I knows by the shape of the shinin' wood what she's got to put on me. Lawd, yes! I sees it catch on a quilt this time and raise that quilt up and drop it on the floor. Then I sees that ax come free! It's shinin', shinin' from the sharpenin' I'd give it a few days before, and man, way back in myself, behind that windbreak, I says,

" 'NAAW! KATE—Lawd, Kate, NAW!!!' "

Suddenly his voice was so strident that I looked up startled. Trueblood seemed to look straight through Mr. Norton, his eyes glassy. The children paused guiltily at their play, looking toward their father.

"I might as well been pleadin' with a switch engine," he
went on. "I sees it comin' down. I sees the light catchin' on
it, I sees Kate's face all mean and I tightens my shoulders and
stiffens my neck and I waits—ten million back-breakin' years,
it seems to me like I waits. I waits so long I remembers all the
wrong things I ever done; I waits so long I opens my eyes and
closes 'em and opens my eyes agin, and I sees it fallin'. It's
fallin' fast as flops from a six-foot ox, and while I'm waitin' I
feels somethin' wind up inside of me and turn to water. I sees
it, Lawd, yes! I sees it and seein' it I twists my head aside.
Couldn't help it; Kate has a good aim, but for that. I moves.
Though I meant to keep still, I moves! Anybody but Jesus
Christ hisself woulda moved. I feel like the whole side of my
face is smashed clear off. It hits me like hot lead so hot that
insteada burnin' me it numbs me. I'm layin' there on the floor,
but inside me I'm runnin' round in circles like a dog with his
back broke, and back into that numbness with my tail tucked
between my legs. I feels like I don't have no skin on my
face no more, only the naked bone. But this is the part I
don't understand: more'n the pain and numbness I feels relief.
Yes, and to git some more of that relief I seems to run out
from behind the windbreak again and up to where Kate's
standin' with the ax, and I opens my eyes and waits. That's
the truth. I wants some more and I waits. I sees her swing it,
lookin' down on me, and I sees it in the air and I holds my
breath, then all of a sudden I sees it stop like somebody done
reached down through the roof and caught it, and I sees her
face have a spasm and I sees the ax fall, back of her this time,
and hit the floor, and Kate spews out some puke and I close
my eyes and waits. I can hear her moanin' and stumblin' out
of the door and fallin' off the porch into the yard. Then I
hears her pukin' like all her guts is coming up by the roots.
Then I looks down and seen blood runnin' all over Matty

64

Lou. It's my blood, my face is bleedin'. That gits me to movin'
I gits up and stumbles out to find Kate, and there she is
under the cottonwood tree out there, on her knees, and she's
moanin'.

" 'What have I done, Lawd! What have I done!'

"She's droolin' green stuff and gits to pukin' agin, and
when I goes to touch her it gits worse. I stands there holdin'
my face and tryin' to keep the blood from flowin' and wonders
what on earth is gonna happen. I looks up at the mornin' sun
and expects somehow for it to thunder. But it's already bright
and clear and the sun comin' up and the birds is chirpin' and
I gits more afraid then than if a bolt of lightnin' had struck
me. I yells, 'Have mercy, Lawd! Lawd, have mercy!' and waits.
And there's nothin' but the clear bright mornin' sun.

"But don' nothin' happen and I knows then that somethin' worse than anything I ever heard 'bout is in store for me.
I musta stood there stark stone still for half an hour. I was
still standin' there when Kate got off her knees and went back
into the house. The blood was runnin' all over my clothes
and the flies was after me, and I went back inside to try and
stop it.

"When I see Matty Lou stretched out there I think she's
dead. Ain't no color in her face and she ain't hardly breathin'.
She gray in the face. I tries to help her but I can't do no good
and Kate won't speak to me nor look at me even; and I thinks
maybe she plans to try to kill me agin, but she don't. I'm in
such a daze I just sits there the whole time while she bundles
up the younguns and takes 'em down the road to Will Nich-
ols'. I can see but I caint do nothin'.

"And I'm still settin' there when she comes back with
some women to see 'bout Matty Lou. Won't nobody speak to
me, though they looks at me like I'm some new kinda cotton-
pickin' machine. I feels bad. I tells them how it happened in

a dream, but they scorns me. I gits plum out of the house then. I goes to see the preacher and even he don't believe me. He tells me to git out of his house, that I'm the most wicked man he's ever seen and that I better go confess my sin and make my peace with God. I leaves tryin' to pray, but I caint. I thinks and thinks, until I thinks my brain go'n bust, 'bout how I'm guilty and how I ain't guilty. I don't eat nothin' and I don't drink nothin' and caint sleep at night. Finally, one night, way early in the mornin', I looks up and sees the stars and I starts singin'. I don't mean to, I didn't think 'bout it, just start singin'. I don't know what it was, some kinda church song, I guess. All I know is I *ends up* singin' the blues. I sings me some blues that night ain't never been sang before, and while I'm singin' them blues I makes up my mind that I ain't nobody but myself and ain't nothin' I can do but let whatever is gonna happen, happen. I made up my mind that I was goin' back home and face Kate; yeah, and face Matty Lou too.

"When I gits here everybody thinks I done run off. There's a heap of women here with Kate and I runs 'em out. And when I runs 'em out I sends the younguns out to play and locks the door and tells Kate and Matty Lou 'bout the dream and how I'm sorry, but that what done happen is done happen.

" 'How come you don't go on 'way and leave us?' is the first words Kate says to me. 'Ain't you done enough to me and this chile?'

" 'I caint leave you,' I says. 'I'm a man and man don't leave his family.'

"She says, 'Naw you ain't no man. No man'd do what you did.'

" 'I'm still a man,' I says.

" 'But what you gon do after it happens?' says Kate.

" 'After *what* happens?' I says.

" 'When yo black 'bomination is birthed to bawl yo wicked sin befo the eyes of God!' (She musta learned them words from the preacher.)

" 'Birth?' I says. '*Who* birth?'

" 'Both of us. Me birth and Matty Lou birth. Both of us birth, you dirty lowdown wicked dog!'

"That liketa killed me. I can understand then why Matty Lou won't look at me and won't speak a word to nobody.

" 'If you stay I'm goin' over an' git Aunt Cloe for both of us,' Kate says. She says, 'I don't aim to birth no sin for folks to look at all the rest of my life, and I don't aim for Matty Lou to neither.'

"You see, Aunt Cloe is a midwife, and even weak as I am from this news I knows I don't want her foolin' with my womenfolks. That woulda been pilin' sin up on toppa sin. So I told Kate, naw, that if Aunt Cloe come near this house I'd kill her, old as she is. I'da done it too. That settles it. I walks out of the house and leaves 'em here to cry it out between 'em. I wanted to go off by myself agin, but it don't do no good tryin' to run off from somethin' like that. It follows you wherever you go. Besides, to git right down to the facts, there wasn't nowhere I could go. I didn't have a cryin' dime!

"Things got to happenin' right off. The nigguhs up at the school come down to chase me off and that made me mad. I went to see the white folks then and they gave me help. That's what I don't understand. I done the worse thing a man could ever do in his family and instead of chasin' me out of the country, they gimme more help than they ever give any other colored man, no matter how good a nigguh he was. Except that my wife an' daughter won't speak to me, I'm better off than I ever been before. And even if Kate won't speak to me she took the new clothes I brought her from up in town and now she's gettin' some eyeglasses made what she been needin' for so long. But what I don't understand is how I done the worse thing a man can do in his own family and 'stead of things gittin' bad, they got better. The nigguhs up at the school don't like me, but the white folks treats me fine.''

HE WAS some farmer. As I listened I had been so torn between humiliation and fascination that to lessen my sense of shame I had kept my attention riveted upon his intense face. That way I did not have to look at Mr. Norton. But now as the voice ended I sat looking down at Mr. Norton's feet. Out in the yard a woman's hoarse contralto intoned a hymn. Children's voices were raised in playful chatter. I sat bent over, smelling the sharp dry odor of wood burning in the hot sunlight. I stared at the two pairs of shoe before me. Mr. Norton's were white, trimmed with black. They were custom made and there beside the cheap tan brogues of the farmer they had the elegantly slender well-bred appearance of fine gloves. Finally someone cleared his throat and I looked up to see Mr. Norton staring silently into Jim Trueblood's eyes. I was startled. His face had drained of color. With his bright eyes burning into Trueblood's black face, he looked ghostly. Trueblood looked at me questioningly.

"Lissen to the younguns," he said in embarrassment. "Playin' 'London Bridge's Fallin' Down.' "

Something was going on which I didn't get. I had to get Mr. Norton away.

"Are you all right, sir?" I asked.

He looked at me with unseeing eyes. "All right?" he said.

"Yes, sir. I mean that I think it's time for the afternoon session," I hurried on.

He stared at me blankly.

I went to him. "Are you sure you're all right, sir?"

"Maybe it's the heat," Trueblood said. "You got to be born down here to stand this kind of heat."

"Perhaps," Mr. Norton said, "it is the heat. We'd better go."

He stood shakily, still staring intently at Trueblood. Then I saw him removing a red Moroccan-leather wallet from his coat pocket. The platinum-framed miniature came with it, but he did not look at it this time.

"Here," he said, extending a banknote. "Please take this and buy the children some toys for me."

Trueblood's mouth fell agape, his eyes widened and filled with moisture as he took the bill between trembling fingers. It was a hundred-dollar bill.

"I'm ready, young man," Mr. Norton said, his voice a whisper.

I went before him to the car and opened the door. He stumbled a bit climbing in and I gave him my arm. His face was still chalk white.

"Drive me away from here," he said in a sudden frenzy. "Away!"

"Yes, sir."

I saw Jim Trueblood wave as I threw the car into gear. "You bastard," I said under my breath. "You no-good bastard! *You* get a hundred-dollar bill!"

When I had turned the car and started back I saw him still standing in the same place.

Suddenly Mr. Norton touched me on the shoulder. "I must have a stimulant, young man. A little whiskey."

"Yes, sir. Are you all right, sir?"

"A little faint, but a stimulant . . ."

His voice trailed off. Something cold formed within my chest. If anything happened to him Dr. Bledsoe would blame me. I stepped on the gas, wondering where I could get him some whiskey. Not in the town, that would take too long. There was only one place, the Golden Day.

"I'll have you some in a few minutes, sir," I said.

"As soon as you can," he said.

Chapter three

I saw them as we approached the short stretch that lay between the railroad tracks and the Golden Day. At first I failed to recognize them. They straggled down the highway in a loose body, blocking the way from the white line to the frazzled weeds that bordered the sun-heated concrete slab. I cursed them silently. They were blocking the road and Mr. Norton was gasping for breath. Ahead of the radiator's gleaming curve they looked like a chain gang on its way to make a road. But a chain gang marches single file and I saw no guards on horseback. As I drew nearer I recognized the loose gray shirts and pants worn by the veterans. Damn! They were heading for the Golden Day.

"A little stimulant," I heard behind me.

"In a few minutes, sir."

Up ahead I saw the one who thought he was a drum major strutting in front, giving orders as he moved energetically in long, hip-swinging strides, a cane held above his head, rising and falling as though in time to music. I slowed the car as I saw him turn to face the men, his cane held at chest level as he shortened the pace. The men continued to ignore him, walking along in a mass, some talking in groups and others talking and gesticulating to themselves.

Suddenly, the drum major saw the car and shook his cane-baton at me. I blew the horn, seeing the men move over to the side as I nosed the car slowly forward. He held his ground, his legs braced, hands on hips, and to keep from hitting him I slammed on the brakes.

The drum major rushed past the men toward the car, and I heard the cane bang down upon the hood as he rushed toward me.

"Who the hell you think you are, running down the army? Give the countersign. Who's in command of this outfit? You trucking bastards was always too big for your britches. Countersign me!"

"This is General Pershing's car, sir," I said, remembering hearing that he responded to the name of his wartime Commander-in-Chief. Suddenly the wild look changed in his eyes and he stepped back and saluted with stiff precision. Then looking suspiciously into the back seat, he barked,

"Where's the General?"

"There," I said, turning and seeing Mr. Norton raising himself, weak and white-faced, from the seat.

"What is it? Why have we stopped?"

"The sergeant stopped us, sir . . ."

"Sergeant? What sergeant?" He sat up.

"Is that you, General?" the vet said, saluting. "I didn't know you were inspecting the front lines today. I'm very sorry, sir."

"What . . . ?" Mr. Norton said.

"The General's in a hurry," I said quickly.

"Sure is," the vet said. "He's got a lot to see. Discipline is bad. Artillery's shot to hell." Then he called to the men walking up the road, "Get the hell out of the General's road. General Pershing's coming through. Make way for General Pershing!"

He stepped aside and I shot the car across the line to avoid the men and stayed there on the wrong side as I headed for the Golden Day.

"Who was that man?" Mr. Norton gasped from the back seat.

"A former soldier, sir. A vet. They're all vets, a little shellshocked."

"But where is the attendant?"

"I don't see one, sir. They're harmless though."

"Nevertheless, they should have an attendant."

I had to get him there and away before they arrived. This was their day to visit the girls, and the Golden Day would be pretty rowdy. I wondered where the rest of them were. There should have been about fifty. Well, I would rush in and get the whiskey and leave. What was wrong with Mr. Norton anyway, why should he get *that* upset over Trueblood? I had felt ashamed and several times I had wanted to laugh, but it had made him sick. Maybe he needed a doctor. Hell, he didn't ask for any doctor. Damn that bastard Trueblood.

I would run in, get a pint, and run out again, I thought. Then he wouldn't see the Golden Day. I seldom went there myself except with some of the fellows when word got out that a new bunch of girls had arrived from New Orleans. The school had tried to make the Golden Day respectable, but the local white folks had a hand in it somehow and they got nowhere. The best the school could do was to make it hot for any student caught going there.

He lay like a man asleep as I left the car and ran into the Golden Day. I wanted to ask him for money but decided to use my own. At the door I paused; the place was already full, jammed with vets in loose gray shirts and trousers and women in short, tight-fitting, stiffly starched gingham aprons. The stale beer smell struck like a club through the noise of voices and the juke box. Just as I got inside the door a stolid-faced man gripped me by the arm and looked stonily into my eyes.

"It will occur at 5:30," he said, looking straight through me.

"What?"

"The great all-embracing, absolute Armistice, the end of the world!" he said.

Before I could answer, a small plump woman smiled into my face and pulled him away.

"It's your turn, Doc," she said. "Don't let it happen till after me and you done been upstairs. How come I always have to come get you?"

"No, it is true," he said. "They wirelessed me from Paris this morning."

"Then, baby, me an' you better hurry. There's lots of money I got to make in here before that thing happens. You hold it back a while, will you?"

She winked at me as she pulled him through the crowd toward the stairs. I elbowed my way nervously toward the bar.

Many of the men had been doctors, lawyers, teachers, Civil Service workers; there were several cooks, a preacher, a politician, and an artist. One very nutty one had been a psychiatrist. Whenever I saw them I felt uncomfortable. They were supposed to be members of the professions toward which at various times I vaguely aspired myself, and even though they never seemed to see me I could never believe that they were really patients. Sometimes it appeared as though they played some vast and complicated game with me and the rest of the school folk, a game whose goal was laughter and whose rules and subtleties I could never grasp.

Two men stood directly in front of me, one speaking with intense earnestness. ". . . and Johnson hit Jeffries at an angle of 45 degrees from his lower left lateral incisor, producing an instantaneous blocking of his entire thalamic rine, frosting it over like the freezing unit of a refrigerator, thus shattering his autonomous nervous system and rocking the big brick-laying creampuff with extreme hyperspasmic muscular tremors which dropped him dead on the extreme tip of his coccyx, which, in turn, produced a sharp traumatic reaction in his sphincter nerve and muscle, and then, my dear colleague, they swept him up, sprinkled him with quicklime and rolled him away in a barrow. Naturally, there was no other therapy possible."

"Excuse me," I said, pushing past.

Big Halley was behind the bar, his dark skin showing through his sweat-wet shirt.

"Whatcha saying, school-boy?"

"I want a double whiskey, Halley. Put it in something deep so I can get it out of here without spilling it. It's for somebody outside."

His mouth shot out, "Hell, naw!"

"Why?" I asked, surprised at the anger in his thyroid eyes.

"You still up at the school, ain't you?"

"Sure."

"Well, those bastards is trying to close me up again, that's why. You can drink till you blue in the face in here, but I wouldn't sell you enough to spit through your teeth to take outside."

"But I've got a sick man out in the car."

"What car? You never had no car."

"The white man's car. I'm driving for him."

"Ain't you in school?"

"He's *from* the school."

"Well, who's sick?"

"He is."

"He too good to come in? Tell him we don't Jimcrow nobody."

"But he's sick."

"He can die!"

"He's important, Halley, a trustee. He's rich and sick and if anything happens to him, they'll have me packed and on my way home."

"Can't help it, school-boy. Bring him inside and he can buy enough to swim in. He can drink outta my own private bottle."

He sliced the white heads off a couple of beers with an ivory paddle and passed them up the bar. I felt sick inside. Mr. Norton wouldn't want to come in here. He was too sick. And besides I didn't want him to see the patients and the girls. Things were getting wilder as I made my way out. Supercargo, the white-uniformed attendant who usually kept the men quiet, was nowhere to be seen. I didn't like it, for when he was upstairs they had absolutely no inhibitions. I made my way out to the car. What could I tell Mr. Norton? He was lying very still when I opened the door.

"Mr. Norton, sir. They refuse to sell me whiskey to bring out."

He lay very still.

"Mr. Norton."

He lay like a figure of chalk. I shook him gently, feeling dread within me. He barely breathed. I shook him violently, seeing his head wobble grotesquely. His lips parted, bluish, revealing a row of long, slender, amazingly animal-like teeth.

"SIR!"

In a panic I ran back into the Golden Day, bursting through the noise as through an invisible wall.

"Halley! Help me, he's dying!"

I tried to get through but no one seemed to have heard me. I was blocked on both sides. They were jammed together.

"Halley!"

Two patients turned and looked at me in the face, their eyes two inches from my nose.

"What is wrong with this gentleman, Sylvester?" the tall one said.

"A man's dying outside!" I said.

"Someone is always dying," the other one said.

"Yes, and it's good to die beneath God's great tent of sky."

"He's got to have some whiskey!"

"Oh, that's different," one of them said and they began pushing a path to the bar. "A last bright drink to keep the anguish down. Step aside, please!"

"School-boy, you back already?" Halley said.

"Give me some whiskey. He's dying!"

"I done told you, school-boy, you better bring him in here. He can die, but I still got to pay my bills."

"Please, they'll put me in jail."

"You going to college, figure it out," he said.

"You'd better bring the gentleman inside," the one called Sylvester said. "Come, let us assist you."

We fought our way out of the crowd. He was just as I left him.

"Look, Sylvester, it's Thomas Jefferson!"

"I was just about to say, I've long wanted to discourse with him."

I looked at them speechlessly; they were both crazy. Or were they joking?

"Give me a hand," I said.

"Gladly."

I shook him. "Mr. Norton!"

"We'd better hurry if he's to enjoy his drink," one of them said thoughtfully.

We picked him up. He swung between us like a sack of old clothes.

"Hurry!"

As we carried him toward the Golden Day one of the men stopped suddenly and Mr. Norton's head hung down, his white hair dragging in the dust.

"Gentlemen, this man is my grandfather!"

"But he's *white*, his name's Norton."

"I should know my own grandfather! He's Thomas Jefferson and I'm his grandson—on the 'field-nigger' side," the tall man said.

"Sylvester, I do believe that you're right. I certainly do," he said, staring at Mr. Norton. "Look at those features. Exactly like yours—from the identical mold. Are you sure he didn't spit you upon the earth, fully clothed?"

"No, no, that was my father," the man said earnestly.

And he began to curse his father violently as we moved for the door. Halley was there waiting. Somehow he'd gotten the crowd to quieten down and a space was cleared in the center of the room. The men came close to look at Mr. Norton.

"Somebody bring a chair."

"Yeah, let Mister Eddy sit down."

"That ain't no Mister Eddy, man, that's John D. Rockefeller," someone said.

"Here's a chair for the Messiah."

"Stand back y'all," Halley ordered. "Give him some room."

Burnside, who had been a doctor, rushed forward and felt for Mr. Norton's pulse.

"It's solid! This man has a *solid* pulse! Instead of beating, it *vibrates*. That's very unusual. Very."

Someone pulled him away. Halley reappeared with a bottle and a glass. "Here, some of y'all tilt his head back."

And before I could move, a short, pock-marked man appeared and took Mr. Norton's head between his hands, tilting it at arm's length and then, pinching the chin gently like a barber about to apply a razor, gave a sharp, swift movement.

"Pow!"

Mr. Norton's head jerked like a jabbed punching bag. Five pale red lines bloomed on the white cheek, glowing like fire beneath translucent stone. I could not believe my eyes. I wanted to run. A woman tittered. I saw several men rush for the door.

"Cut it out, you damn fool!"

"A case of hysteria," the pock-marked man said quietly.

"Git the hell out of the way," Halley said. "Somebody git that stool-pigeon attendant from upstairs. Git him down here, quick!"

"A mere mild case of hysteria," the pock-marked man said as they pushed him away.

"Hurry with the drink, Halley!"

"Heah, school-boy, you hold the glass. This here's brandy I been saving for myself."

Someone whispered tonelessly into my ear, "You see, I told you that it would occur at 5:30. Already the Creator has come." It was the stolid-faced man.

I saw Halley tilt the bottle and the oily amber of brandy sloshing into the glass. Then tilting Mr. Norton's head back, I put the glass to his lips and poured. A fine brown stream ran from the corner of his mouth, down his delicate chin. The room was suddenly quiet. I felt a slight movement against my hand, like a child's breast when it whimpers at the end of a spell of crying. The fine-veined eyelids flickered. He coughed. I saw a slow red flush creep, then spurt, up his neck, spreading over his face.

"Hold it under his nose, school-boy. Let 'im smell it."

I waved the glass beneath Mr. Norton's nose. He opened his pale blue eyes. They seemed watery now in the red flush that bathed his face. He tried to sit up, his right hand fluttering to his chin. His eyes widened, moved quickly from face to face. Then coming to mine, the moist eyes focused with recognition.

"You were unconscious, sir," I said.

"Where am I, young man?" he asked wearily.

"This is the Golden Day, sir."

"What?"

"The Golden Day. It's a kind of sporting-and-gambling house," I added reluctantly.

"Now give him another drinka brandy," Halley said.

I poured a drink and handed it to him. He sniffed it, closed his eyes as in puzzlement, then drank; his cheeks filled out like small bellows; he was rinsing his mouth.

"Thank you," he said, a little stronger now. "What is this place?"

"The Golden Day," said several patients in unison.

He looked slowly around him, up to the balcony, with its scrolled and carved wood. A large flag hung lank above the floor. He frowned.

"What was this building used for in the past?" he said.

"It was a church, then a bank, then it was a restaurant and a fancy gambling house, and now *we* got it," Halley explained. "I think somebody said it used to be a jailhouse too."

"They let us come here once a week to raise a little hell," someone said.

"I couldn't buy a drink to take out, sir, so I had to bring you inside," I explained in dread.

He looked about him. I followed his eyes and was amazed to see the varied expressions on the patients' faces as they silently returned his gaze. Some were hostile, some cringing, some horrified; some, who when among themselves were most violent, now appeared as submissive as children. And some seemed strangely amused.

"Are all of you patients?" Mr. Norton asked.

"Me, I just runs the joint," Halley said. "These here other fellows . . ."

"We're patients sent here as therapy," a short, fat, very intelligent-looking man said. "But," he smiled, "they send along an attendant, a kind of censor, to see that the therapy fails."

"You're nuts. I'm a dynamo of energy. I come to charge my batteries," one of the vets insisted.

"I'm a student of history, sir," another interrupted with dramatic gestures. "The world moves in a circle like a roulette wheel. In the beginning, black is on top, in the middle epochs, white holds the odds, but soon Ethiopia shall stretch forth her noble wings! Then place your money on the black!" His voice throbbed with emotion. "Until then, the sun holds no heat, there's ice in the heart of the earth. Two years from now and I'll be old enough to give my mulatto mother a bath, the half-white bitch!" he added, beginning to leap up and down in an explosion of glassy-eyed fury.

Mr. Norton blinked his eyes and straightened up.

"I'm a physician, may I take your pulse?" Burnside said, seizing Mr. Norton's wrist.

"Don't pay him no mind, mister. He ain't been no doctor in ten years. They caught him trying to change some blood into money."

"I did too!" the man screamed. "I discovered it and John D. Rockefeller stole the formula from me."

"Mr. Rockefeller did you say?" Mr. Norton said. "I'm sure you must be mistaken."

"WHAT'S GOING ON DOWN THERE?" a voice shouted from the balcony. Everyone turned. I saw a huge black giant of a man, dressed only in white shorts, swaying on the stairs. It was Supercargo, the attendant. I hardly recognized him without his hard-starched white uniform. Usually he walked around threatening the men with a strait jacket which he always carried over his arm, and usually they were quiet and submissive in his presence. But now they seemed not to recognize him and began shouting curses.

"How you gon keep order in the place if you gon git drunk?" Halley shouted. "Charlene! Charlene!"

"Yeah?" a woman's voice, startling in its carrying power, answered sulkily from a room off the balcony.

"I want you to git that stool-pigeoning, joy-killing, nut-crushing bum back in there with you and sober him up. Then git him in his white suit and down here to keep order. We got white folks in the house."

A woman appeared on the balcony, drawing a woolly pink robe about her. "Now you lissen here, Halley," she drawled, "I'm a woman. If you want him dressed, you can do it yourself. I don't put on but one man's clothes and he's in N'Orleans."

"Never mind all that. Git that stool pigeon sober!"

"I want order down there," Supercargo boomed, "and if there's white folks down there, I wan's *double* order."

Suddenly there was an angry roar from the men back near the bar and I saw them rush the stairs.

"Get him!"

"Let's give him some order!"

"Out of my way."

Five men charged the stairs. I saw the giant bend and clutch the posts at the top of the stairs with both hands, bracing himself, his body gleaming bare in his white shorts. The little man who had slapped Mr. Norton was in front, and, as he sprang up the long flight, I saw the attendant set himself and kick, catching the little man just as he reached the top, hard in the chest, sending him backwards in a curving dive into the midst of the men behind him. Supercargo got set to swing his leg again. It was a narrow stair and only one man could get up at a time. As fast as they rushed up, the giant kicked them back. He swung his leg, kicking them down like a fungo-hitter batting out flies. Watching him, I forgot Mr. Norton. The Golden Day was in an uproar. Half-dressed women appeared from the rooms off the balcony. Men hooted and yelled as at a football game.

"I WANT ORDER!" the giant shouted as he sent a man flying down the flight of stairs.

"THEY THROWING BOTTLES OF LIQUOR!" a woman screamed. "REAL LIQUOR!"

"That's a order he don't want," someone said.

A shower of bottles and glasses splashing whiskey crashed against the balcony. I saw Supercargo snap suddenly erect and grab his forehead, his face bathed in whiskey. "Eeeee!" he cried, "Eeeee!" Then I saw him wave, rigid from his ankles upward. For a moment the men on the stairs were motionless, watching him. Then they sprang forward.

Supercargo grabbed wildly at the balustrade as they snatched his feet from beneath him and started down. His head bounced against the steps making a sound like a series of gunshots as they ran dragging him by his ankles, like volunteer firemen running with a hose. The crowd surged forward. Halley yelled near my ear. I saw the man being dragged toward the center of the room.

"Give the bastard some order!"

"Here I'm forty-five and he's been acting like he's my old man!"

"So you like to kick, huh?" a tall man said, aiming a shoe at the attendant's head. The flesh above his right eye jumped out as though it had been inflated.

Then I heard Mr. Norton beside me shouting, "No, no! Not when he's down!"

"Lissen at the white folks," someone said.

"He's the white folks' man!"

Men were jumping upon Supercargo with both feet now and I felt such an excitement that I wanted to join them. Even the girls were yelling, "Give it to him good!" "He never pays me!" "Kill him!"

"Please, y'all, not in here! Not in my place!"

"You can't speak your mind when he's on duty!"

"Hell, no!"

Somehow I got pushed away from Mr. Norton and found myself beside the man called Sylvester.

"Watch this, school-boy," he said. "See there, where his ribs are bleeding?"

I nodded my head.

"Now don't move your eyes."

I watched the spot as though compelled, just beneath the lower rib and above the hip-bone, as Sylvester measured carefully with his toe and kicked as though he were punting a football. Supercargo let out a groan like an injured horse.

"Try it, school-boy, it feels so good. It gives you relief," Sylvester said. "Sometimes I get so afraid of him I feel that he's inside my head. There!" he said, giving Supercargo another kick.

As I watched, a man sprang on Supercargo's chest with both feet and he lost consciousness. They began throwing cold beer on him, reviving him, only to kick him unconscious again. Soon he was drenched in blood and beer.

"The bastard's out cold."

"Throw him out."

"Naw, wait a minute. Give me a hand somebody."

They threw him upon the bar, stretching him out with his arms folded across his chest like a corpse.

"Now, let's have a drink!"

Halley was slow in getting behind the bar and they cursed him.

"Get back there and serve us, you big sack of fat!"

"Gimme a rye!"

"Up here, funk-buster!"

"Shake them sloppy hips!"

"Okay, okay, take it easy," Halley said, rushing to pour them drinks. "Just put y'all's money where your mouth is."

With Supercargo lying helpless upon the bar, the men whirled about like maniacs. The excitement seemed to have tilted some of the more delicately balanced ones too far. Some made hostile speeches at the top of their voices against the hospital, the state and the universe. The one who called himself a composer was banging away the one wild piece he seemed to know on the out-of-tune piano, striking the keyboard with fists and elbows and filling in other effects in a bass voice that moaned like a bear in agony. One of the most educated ones touched my arm. He was a former chemist who was never seen without his shining Phi Beta Kappa key.

"The men have lost control," he said through the uproar. "I think you'd better leave."

"I'm trying to," I said, "as soon as I can get over to Mr. Norton."

Mr. Norton was gone from where I had left him. I rushed here and there through the noisy men, calling his name.

When I found him he was under the stairs. Somehow he had been pushed there by the scuffling, reeling men and he lay sprawled in the chair like an aged doll. In the dim light his features were sharp and white and his closed eyes well-defined lines in a well-tooled face. I shouted his name above the roar of the men, and got no answer. He was out again. I shook him, gently, then roughly, but still no flicker of his wrinkled lids. Then some of the milling men pushed me up against him and suddenly a mass of whiteness was looming two inches from my eyes; it was only his face but I felt a shudder of nameless horror. I had never been so close to a white person before. In a panic I struggled to get away. With his eyes closed he seemed more threatening than with them open. He was like a formless white death, suddenly appeared before me, a death which had been there all the time and which had now revealed itself in the madness of the Golden Day.

"Stop screaming!" a voice commanded, and I felt myself pulled away. It was the short fat man.

I clamped my mouth shut, aware for the first time that the shrill sound was coming from my own throat. I saw the man's face relax as he gave me a wry smile.

"That's better," he shouted into my ear. "He's only a man. Remember that. He's only a man!"

I wanted to tell him that Mr. Norton was much more than that, that he was a rich white man and in my charge; but the very idea that I was responsible for him was too much for me to put into words.

"Let us take him to the balcony," the man said, pushing me toward Mr. Norton's feet. I moved automatically, grasping the thin ankles as he raised the white man by the armpits and backed from beneath the stairs. Mr. Norton's head lolled upon his chest as though he were drunk or dead.

The vet started up the steps still smiling, climbing backwards a step at a time. I had begun to worry about him, whether he was drunk like the rest, when I saw three of the girls who had been leaning over the balustrade watching the brawl come down to help us carry Mr. Norton up.

"Looks like pops couldn't take it," one of them shouted.

"He's high as a Georgia pine."

"Yeah, I tell you this stuff Halley got out here is too strong for white folks to drink."

"Not drunk, ill!" the fat man said. "Go find a bed that's not being used so he can stretch out awhile."

"Sho, daddy. Is there any other little favors I can do for you?"

"That'll be enough," he said.

One of the girls ran up ahead. "Mine's just been changed. Bring him down here," she said.

In a few minutes Mr. Norton was lying upon a three-quarter bed, faintly breathing. I watched the fat man bend over him very professionally and feel for his pulse.

"You a doctor?" a girl asked.

"Not now, I'm a patient. But I have a certain knowledge."

Another one, I thought, pushing him quickly aside. "He'll be all right. Let him come to so I can get him out of here."

"You needn't worry, I'm not like those down there, young fellow," he said. "I really was a doctor. I won't hurt him. He's had a mild shock of some kind."

We watched him bend over Mr. Norton again, feeling his pulse, pulling back his eyelid.

"It's a mild shock," he repeated.

"This here Golden Day is enough to shock anybody," a girl said, smoothing her apron over the smooth sensuous roll of her stomach.

Another brushed Mr. Norton's white hair away from his forehead and stroked it, smiling vacantly. "He's kinda cute," she said. "Just like a little white baby."

"What kinda ole baby?" the small skinny girl asked.

"That's the kind, an *ole* baby."

"You just like white men, Edna. That's all," the skinny one said.

Edna shook her head and smiled as though amused at herself. "I sho do. I just love 'em. Now this one, old as he is, he could put his shoes under my bed any night."

"Shucks, me I'd kill an old man like that."

"Kill him nothing," Edna said. "Girl, don't you know that all these rich ole white men got monkey glands and billy goat balls? These old bastards don't never git enough. They want to have the whole world."

The doctor looked at me and smiled. "See, now you're learning all about endocrinology," he said. "I was wrong when I told you that he was only a man; it seems now that he's either part goat or part ape. Maybe he's both."

"It's the truth," Edna said. "I used to have me one in Chicago—"

"Now you ain't never been to no Chicago, gal," the other one interrupted.

"How you know I ain't? Two years ago . . . Shucks, you don't know nothing. That ole white man right there might have him a coupla jackass balls!"

The fat man raised up with a quick grin. "As a scientist and a physician I'm forced to discount that," he said. "That is one operation that has yet to be performed." Then he managed to get the girls out of the room.

"If he should come around and hear that conversation," the vet said, "it would be enough to send him off again. Besides, their scientific curiosity might lead them to investigate whether he really does have a monkey gland. And that, I'm afraid, would be a bit obscene."

"I've got to get him back to the school," I said.

"All right," he said, "I'll do what I can to help you. Go see if you can find some ice. And don't worry."

I went out on the balcony, seeing the tops of their heads. They were still milling around, the juke box baying, the piano thumping, and over at the end of the room, drenched with beer, Supercargo lay like a spent horse upon the bar.

Starting down, I noticed a large piece of ice glinting in the remains of an abandoned drink and seized its coldness in my hot hand and hurried back to the room.

The vet sat staring at Mr. Norton, who now breathed with a slightly irregular sound.

"You were quick," the man said, as he stood and reached for the ice. "Swift with the speed of anxiety," he added, as if to himself. "Hand me that clean towel—there, from beside the basin."

I handed him one, seeing him fold the ice inside it and apply it to Mr. Norton's face.

"Is he all right?" I said.

"He will be in a few minutes. What happened to him?"

"I took him for a drive," I said.

"Did you have an accident or something?"

"No," I said. "He just talked to a farmer and the heat knocked him out . . . Then we got caught in the mob downstairs."

"How old is he?"

"I don't know, but he's one of the trustees . . ."

"One of the very first, no doubt," he said, dabbing at the blue-veined eyes. "A trustee of consciousness."

"What was that?" I asked.

"Nothing . . . There now, he's coming out of it."

I had an impulse to run out of the room. I feared what Mr. Norton would say to me, the expression that might come into his eyes. And yet, I was afraid to leave. My eyes could not leave the face with its flickering lids. The head moved from side to side in the pale glow of the light bulb, as though denying some insistent voice which I could not hear. Then the lids opened, revealing pale pools of blue vagueness that finally solidified into points that froze upon the vet, who looked down unsmilingly.

Men like us did not look at a man like Mr. Norton in that manner, and I stepped hurriedly forward.

"He's a real doctor, sir," I said.

"I'll explain," the vet said. "Get a glass of water."

I hesitated. He looked at me firmly. "Get the water," he said, turning to help Mr. Norton to sit up.

Outside I asked Edna for a glass of water and she led me down the hall to a small kitchen, drawing it for me from a green old-fashioned cooler.

"I got some good liquor, baby, if you want to give him a drink," she said.

"This will do," I said. My hands trembled so that the water spilled. When I returned, Mr. Norton was sitting up unaided, carrying on a conversation with the vet.

"Here's some water, sir," I said, extending the glass.

He took it. "Thank you," he said.

"Not too much," the vet cautioned.

"Your diagnosis is exactly that of my specialist," Mr. Norton said, "and I went to several fine physicians before one could diagnose it. How did you know?"

"I too was a specialist," the vet said.

"But how? Only a few men in the whole country possess the knowledge—"

"Then one of them is an inmate of a semi-madhouse," the vet said. "But there's nothing mysterious about it. I escaped for awhile—I went to France with the Army Medical Corps and remained there after the Armistice to study and practice."

"Oh yes, and how long were you in France?" Mr. Norton asked.

"Long enough," he said. "Long enough to forget some fundamentals which I should never have forgotten."

"What fundamentals?" Mr. Norton said. "What do you mean?"

The vet smiled and cocked his head. "Things about life. Such things as most peasants and folk peoples almost always know through experience, though seldom through conscious thought . . ."

"Pardon me, sir," I said to Mr. Norton, "but now that you feel better, shouldn't we go?"

"Not just yet," he said. Then to the doctor, "I'm very interested. What happened to you?" A drop of water caught in one of his eyebrows glittered like a chip of active diamond. I went over and sat on a chair. Damn this vet to hell!

"Are you sure you would like to hear?" the vet asked.

"Why, of course."

"Then perhaps the young fellow should go downstairs and wait . . ."

The sound of shouting and destruction welled up from below as I opened the door.

"No, perhaps you should stay," the fat man said. "Perhaps had I overheard some of what I'm about to tell you when I was a student up there on the hill, I wouldn't be the casualty that I am."

"Sit down, young man," Mr. Norton ordered. "So you were a student at the college," he said to the vet.

I sat down again, worrying about Dr. Bledsoe as the fat man told Mr. Norton of his attending college, then becoming a physician and going to France during the World War.

"Were you a successful physician?" Mr. Norton said.

"Fairly so. I performed a few brain surgeries that won me some small attention."

"Then why did you return?"

"Nostalgia," the vet said.

"Then what on earth are you doing here in this . . . ?" Mr. Norton said, "With your ability . . ."

"Ulcers," the fat man said.

"That's terribly unfortunate, but why should ulcers stop your career?"

"Not really, but I learned along with the ulcers that my work could bring me no dignity," the vet said.

"Now you sound bitter," Mr. Norton said, just as the door flew open.

A brown-skinned woman with red hair looked in. "How's white-folks making out?" she said, staggering inside. "White-folks, baby, you done come to. You want a drink?"

"Not now, Hester," the vet said. "He's still a little weak."

"He sho looks it. That's how come he needs a drink. Put some iron in his blood."

"Now, now, Hester."

"Okay, okay . . . But what y'all doing looking like you at a funeral? Don't you know this is the Golden Day?" She staggered toward me, belching elegantly and reeling. "Just look at y'all. Here school-boy looks like he's scared to death. And white-folks here is acting like y'all two strange poodles. Be happy y'all! I'm going down and get Halley to send you up some drinks." She patted Mr. Norton's cheek as she went past and I saw him turn a glowing red. "Be happy, white-folks."

"Ah, hah!" the vet laughed, "you're blushing, which means that you're better. Don't be embarrassed. Hester is a great humanitarian, a therapist of generous nature and great skill, and the possessor of a healing touch. Her catharsis is absolutely tremendous—ha, ha!"

"You do look better, sir," I said, anxious to get out of the place. I could understand the vet's words but not what they conveyed, and Mr. Norton looked as uncomfortable as I felt.

The one thing which I did know was that the vet was acting toward the white man with a freedom which could only bring on trouble. I wanted to tell Mr. Norton that the man was crazy and yet I received a fearful satisfaction from hearing him talk as he had to a white man. With the girl it was different. A woman usually got away with things a man never could.

I was wet with anxiety, but the vet talked on, ignoring the interruption.

"Rest, rest," he said, fixing Mr. Norton with his eyes. "The clocks are all set back and the forces of destruction are rampant down below. They might suddenly realize that you are what you are, and then your life wouldn't be worth a piece of bankrupt stock. You would be canceled, perforated, voided, become the recognized magnet attracting loose screws. Then what would you do? Such men are beyond money, and with Supercargo down, out like a felled ox, they know nothing of value. To some, you are the great white father, to others the lyncher of souls, but for all, you are confusion come even into the Golden Day."

"What are you talking about?" I said, thinking: *Lyncher?* He was getting wilder than the men downstairs. I didn't dare look at Mr. Norton, who made a sound of protest.

The vet frowned. "It is an issue which I can confront only by evading it. An utterly stupid proposition, and these hands so lovingly trained to master a scalpel yearn to caress a trigger. I returned to save life and I was refused," he said. "Ten men in masks drove me out from the city at midnight and beat me with whips for saving a human life. And I was forced to the utmost degradation because I possessed skilled hands and the belief that my knowledge could bring me dignity—not wealth, only dignity—and other men health!"

Then suddenly he fixed me with his eyes. "And now, do you understand?"

"What?" I said.

"What you've heard!"

"I don't know."

"Why?"

I said, "I really think it's time we left."

"You see," he said turning to Mr. Norton, "he has eyes and ears and a good distended African nose, but he fails to understand the simple facts of life. *Understand.* Understand? It's worse than that. He registers with his senses but short-circuits his brain. Nothing has meaning. He takes it in but he doesn't digest it. Already he is—well, bless my soul! Behold! a walking zombie! Already he's learned to repress not only his emotions but his humanity. He's invisible, a walking personification of the Negative, the most perfect achievement of your dreams, sir! The mechanical man!"

Mr. Norton looked amazed.

"Tell me," the vet said, suddenly calm. "Why have you been interested in the school, Mr. Norton?"

"Out of a sense of my destined role," Mr. Norton said shakily. "I felt, and I still feel, that your people are in some important manner tied to my destiny."

"What do you mean, destiny?" the vet said.

"Why, the success of my work, of course."

"I see. And would you recognize it if you saw it?"

"Why, of course I would," Mr. Norton said indignantly. "I've watched it grow each year I've returned to the campus."

"Campus? Why the campus?"

"It is there that my destiny is being made."

The vet exploded with laughter. "The campus, what a destiny!" He stood and walked around the narrow room, laughing. Then he stopped as suddenly as he had begun.

"You will hardly recognize it, but it is very fitting that you came to the Golden Day with the young fellow," he said.

"I came out of illness—or rather, he brought me," Mr. Norton said.

"Of course, but you came, and it was fitting."

"What do you mean?" Mr. Norton said with irritation.

"A little child shall lead them," the vet said with a smile. "But seriously, because you both fail to understand what is happening to you. You cannot see or hear or smell the truth of what you see—and you, looking for destiny! It's classic! And the boy, this automaton, he was made of the very mud of the region and he sees far less than you. Poor stumblers, neither of you can see the other. To you he is a mark on the score-card of your achievement, a thing and not a man; a child, or even less—a black amorphous thing. And you, for all your power, are not a man to him, but a God, a force—"

Mr. Norton stood abruptly. "Let us go, young man," he said angrily.

"No, listen. He believes in you as he believes in the beat of his heart. He believes in that great false wisdom taught slaves and pragmatists alike, that white is right. I can tell you *his* destiny. He'll do your bidding, and for that his blindness is his chief asset. He's your man, friend. Your man and your destiny. Now the two of you descend the stairs into chaos and get the hell out of here. I'm sick of both of you pitiful obscenities! Get out before I do you both the favor of bashing in your heads!"

I saw his motion toward the big white pitcher on the washstand and stepped between him and Mr. Norton, guiding Mr. Norton swiftly through the doorway. Looking back, I saw him leaning against the wall making a sound that was a blending of laughter and tears.

"Hurry, the man is as insane as the rest," Mr. Norton said.

"Yes, sir," I said, noticing a new note in his voice.

The balcony was now as noisy as the floor below. The girls and drunken vets were stumbling about with drinks in their hands. Just as we went past an open door Edna saw us and grabbed my arm.

"Where you taking white-folks?" she demanded.

"Back to school," I said, shaking her off.

"You don't want to go up there, white-folks, baby," she said. I tried to push past her. "I ain't lying," she said. "I'm the best little home-maker in the business."

"Okay, but please let us alone," I pleaded. "You'll get me into trouble."

We were going down the stairs into the milling men now and she started to scream, "Pay me then! If he's too good for me, let him pay!"

And before I could stop her she had pushed Mr. Norton, and both of us were stumbling swiftly down the stairs. I landed against a man who looked up with the anonymous familiarity of a drunk and shoved me hard away. I saw Mr. Norton spin past as I sank farther into the crowd. Somewhere I could hear the girl screaming and Halley's voice yelling, "Hey! Hey! Hey, now!" Then I was aware of fresh air and saw that I was near the door and pushed my way free and stood panting and preparing to plunge back for Mr. Norton—when I heard Halley calling, "Make way y'all!" and saw him piloting Mr. Norton to the door.

"Whew!" he said, releasing the white man and shaking his huge head.

"Thanks, Halley—" I said and got no further.

I saw Mr. Norton, his face pale again, his white suit rumpled, topple and fall, his head scraping against the screen of the door.

"Hey!"

I opened the door and raised him up.

"Goddamit, out agin," Halley said. "How come you bring this white man here, school-boy?"

"Is he dead?"

"DEAD!" he said, stepping back indignantly. "He *caint* die!"

"What'll I do, Halley?"

"Not in my place, he caint die," he said, kneeling.

Mr. Norton looked up. "No one is dead or dying," he said acidly. "Remove your hands!"

Halley fell away, surprised. "I sho am glad. You sho you all right? I thought sho you was dead this time."

"For God's sake, be quiet!" I exploded nervously. "You should be glad that he's all right."

Mr. Norton was visibly angry now, a raw place showing on his forehead, and I hurried ahead of him to the car. He climbed in unaided, and I got under the wheel, smelling the heated odor of mints and cigar smoke. He was silent as I drove away.

Chapter four

The wheel felt like an alien thing in my hands as I followed the white line of the highway. Heat rays from the late afternoon sun arose from the gray concrete, shimmering like the weary tones of a distant bugle blown upon still midnight air. In the mirror I could see Mr. Norton staring out vacantly upon the empty fields, his mouth stern, his white forehead livid where it had scraped the screen. And seeing him I felt the fear balled coldly within me unfold. What would happen now? What would the school officials say? In my mind I visualized Dr. Bledsoe's face when he saw Mr. Norton. I thought of the glee certain folks at home would feel if I were expelled. Tatlock's grinning face danced through my mind. What would the white folks think who'd sent me to college? Was Mr. Norton angry at *me*? In the Golden Day he had seemed more curious than anything else— until the vet had started talking wild. Damn Trueblood. It was his fault. If we hadn't sat in the sun so long Mr. Norton would not have needed whiskey and I wouldn't have gone to the Golden Day. And why would the vets act that way with a white man in the house?

I headed the car through the red-brick campus gateposts with a sense of cold apprehension. Now even the rows of neat dormitories seemed to threaten me, the rolling lawns appearing as hostile as the gray highway with its white dividing line. As of its own compulsion, the car slowed as we passed the chapel with its low, sweeping eaves. The sun shone coolly through the avenue of trees, dappling the curving drive. Students strolled through the shade, down a hill of tender grass toward the brick-red stretch of tennis courts. Far beyond, players in whites showed sharp against the red of the courts surrounded by grass, a gay vista washed by the sun. In the brief interval I heard a cheer arise. My predicament struck me like a stab. I had a sense of losing control of the car and slammed on the brakes in the middle of the road, then apologized and drove on. Here within this quiet greenness I possessed the only identity I had ever known, and I was losing it. In this brief moment of passage I became aware of the connection between these lawns and buildings and my hopes and dreams. I wanted to stop the car and talk with Mr. Norton, to beg his pardon for what he had seen; to plead and show him tears, unashamed tears like those of a child before his parent; to denounce all we'd seen and heard; to assure him that far from being like any of the people we had seen, I *hated* them, that I believed in the principles of the Founder with all my heart and soul, and that I believed in his own goodness and kindness in extending the hand of his benevolence to helping us poor, ignorant people out of the mire and darkness. I would do his bidding and teach others to rise up as he wished them to, teach them to be thrifty, decent, upright citizens, contributing to the welfare of all, shunning all but the straight and narrow path that he and the Founder had stretched before us. If only he were not angry with me! If only he would give me another chance!

Tears filled my eyes, and the walks and buildings flowed

and froze for a moment in mist, glittering as in winter when rain froze on the grass and foliage and turned the campus into a world of whiteness, weighting and bending both trees and bushes with fruit of crystal. Then in the twinkling of my eyes, it was gone, and the here and now of heat and greenness returned. If only I could make Mr. Norton understand what the school meant to me.

"Shall I stop at your rooms, sir?" I said. "Or shall I take you to the administration building? Dr. Bledsoe might be worried."

"To my rooms, then bring Dr. Bledsoe to me," he answered tersely.

"Yes, sir."

In the mirror I saw him dabbing gingerly at his forehead with a crinkled handkerchief. "You'd better send the school physician to me also," he said.

I stopped the car in front of a small building with white pillars like those of an old plantation manor house, got out and opened the door.

"Mr. Norton, please, sir . . . I'm sorry . . . I—"

He looked at me sternly, his eyes narrowed, saying nothing.

"I didn't know . . . please . . ."

"Send Dr. Bledsoe to me," he said, turning away and swinging up the graveled path to the building.

I got back into the car and drove slowly to the administration building. A girl waved gaily as I passed, a bunch of violets in her hand. Two teachers in dark suits talked decorously beside a broken fountain.

The building was quiet. Going upstairs I visualized Dr. Bledsoe, with his broad globular face that seemed to take its form from the fat pressing from the inside, which, as air pressing against the membrane of a balloon, gave it shape and buoyancy. "Old Bucket-head," some of the fellows called him. I never had. He had been kind to me from the first, perhaps because of the letters which the school superintendent had sent to him when I arrived. But more than that, he was the example of everything I hoped to be: Influential with wealthy men all over the country; consulted in matters concerning the race; a leader of his people; the possessor of not one, but *two* Cadillacs, a good salary and a soft, good-looking and creamy-complexioned wife. What was more, while black and bald and everything white folks poked fun at, he had achieved power and authority; had, while black and wrinkle-headed, made himself of more importance in the world than most Southern white men. They could laugh at him but they couldn't ignore him . . .

"He's been looking all over for you," the girl at the desk said.

When I walked in he looked up from the telephone and said, "Never mind, he's here now," and hung up. "Where's Mr. Norton?" he demanded excitedly. "Is he all right?"

"Yes, sir. I left him at his rooms and came to drive you down. He wishes to see you."

"Is anything wrong?" he said, getting up hurriedly and coming around the desk.

I hesitated.

"Well, is there!"

The panicky beating of my heart seemed to blur my vision.

"Not now, sir."

"*Now?* What do you mean?"

"Well, sir, he had some kind of fainting spell."

"Aw, my God! I knew something was wrong. Why didn't you get in touch with me?" He grabbed his black homburg, starting for the door. "Come on!"

I followed him, trying to explain. "He's all over it now, sir, and we were too far away for me to phone . . ."

"Why did you take him so far?" he said, moving with great bustling energy.

"But I drove him where he wanted to go, sir."

"Where was that?"

"Back of the slave-quarter section," I said with dread.

"The quarters! Boy, are you a fool? Didn't you know better than to take a trustee out there?"

"He asked me to, sir."

We were going down the walk now, through the spring air, and he stopped to look at me with exasperation, as though I'd suddenly told him black was white.

"Damn what *he* wants," he said, climbing in the front seat beside me. "Haven't you the sense God gave a dog? We take these white folks where we want them to go, we show them what we want them to see. Don't you know that? I thought you had some sense."

Reaching Rabb Hall, I stopped the car, weak with bewilderment.

"Don't sit there," he said. "Come with me!"

Just inside the building I got another shock. As we approached a mirror Dr. Bledsoe stopped and composed his angry face like a sculptor, making it a bland mask, leaving only the sparkle of his eyes to betray the emotion that I had seen only a moment before. He looked steadily at himself for a moment; then we moved quietly down the silent hall and up the stairs.

A co-ed sat at a graceful table stacked with magazines. Before a great window stood a large aquarium containing colored stones and a small replica of a feudal castle surrounded by goldfish that seemed to remain motionless despite the fluttering of their lacy fins, a momentary motionful suspension of time.

"Is Mr. Norton in his room?" he said to the girl.

"Yessir, Dr. Bledsoe, sir," she said. "He said to tell you to come in when you got here."

Pausing at the door I heard him clear his throat, then rap softly upon the panel with his fist.

"Mr. Norton?" he said, his lips already a smile. And at the answer I followed him inside.

It was a large light room. Mr. Norton sat in a huge wing chair with his jacket off. A change of clothing lay on the cool bedspread. Above a spacious fireplace an oil portrait of the Founder looked down at me remotely, benign, sad, and in that hot instant, profoundly disillusioned. Then a veil seemed to fall.

"I've been worried about you, sir," Dr. Bledsoe said. "We expected you at the afternoon session . . ."

Now it's beginning, I thought. Now—

And suddenly he rushed forward. "Mr. Norton, your head!" he cried, a strange grandmotherly concern in his voice. "What happened, sir?"

"It's nothing." Mr. Norton's face was immobile. "A mere scratch."

Dr. Bledsoe whirled around, his face outraged. "Get the doctor over here," he said. "Why didn't you tell me that Mr. Norton had been injured?"

"I've already taken care of that, sir," I said softly, seeing him whirl back.

"Mr. Norton, *Mister Norton!* I'm so sorry," he crooned. "I thought I had sent you a boy who was careful, a sensible young man! Why we've never had an accident before. Never, not in seventy-five years. I assure you, sir, that he shall be disciplined, severely disciplined!"

"But there was no automobile accident," Mr. Norton said kindly, "nor was the boy responsible. You may send him away, we won't need him now."

My eyes suddenly filled. I felt a wave of gratitude at his words.

"Don't be kind, sir," Dr. Bledsoe said. "You can't be soft with these people. We mustn't pamper them. An accident to a guest of this college while he is in the charge of a student is without question the student's fault. That's one of our strictest rules!" Then to me: "Return to your dormitory and remain there until further notice!"

"But it was out of my control, sir," I said, "just as Mr. Norton said . . ."

"I'll explain, young man," Mr. Norton said with a half-smile. "Everything will be explained."

"Thank you, sir," I said, seeing Dr. Bledsoe looking at me with no change of expression.

"On second thought," he said, "I want you to be in chapel this evening, understand me, sir?"

"Yes, sir."

I opened the door with a cold hand, bumping into the girl who had been at the table when we went inside.

"I'm sorry," she said. "Look like you have old Bucket-head kind of mad."

I said nothing as she walked beside me expectantly. A red sun cast its light upon the campus as I started for my dormitory.

"Will you take a message to my boy friend for me?" she said.

"Who is he?" I said, trying hard to conceal my tension and fear.

"Jack Maston," she said.

"Okay, he's in the room next to mine."

"That's swell," she said with a big smile. "The dean put me on duty so I missed him this afternoon. Just tell him that I said the grass is green . . ."

"What?"

"The grass is green. It's our secret code, he'll understand."

"The grass is green," I said.

"That's it. Thank you, lover," she said.

I felt like cursing as I watched her hurrying back into the building, hearing her flat-heeled shoes crunching the graveled walk. Here she was playing with some silly secret code at the very minute my fate for the rest of my life was being decided. The grass was green and they'd meet and she'd be sent home pregnant, but even so, in less disgrace than I . . . If only I knew what they were saying about me . . . Suddenly I had an idea and ran after her, into the building and up the stairs.

In the hall, fine dust played in a shaft of sunlight, stirred by her hurried passing. But she had disappeared. I had thought to ask her to listen at the door and tell me what was said. I gave it up; if she were discovered, I'd have that on my conscience too. Besides, I was ashamed for anyone to know of my predicament, it was too stupid to be believed. Down the long length of the wide hall I heard someone unseen skipping down the stairs singing. A girl's sweet, hopeful voice. I left quietly and hurried to my dorm.

I lay in my room with my eyes closed, trying to think. The tension gripped my insides. Then I heard someone coming up the hall and stiffened. Had they sent for me already? Nearby a door opened and closed, leaving me as tense as ever. To whom could I turn for help? I could think of no one. No one to whom I could even explain what had happened at the Golden Day. Everything was upset inside me. And Dr. Bledsoe's attitude toward Mr. Norton was the most confusing of all. I dared not repeat what he'd said, for fear that it would lessen my chances of remaining in school. It just wasn't true, I had misunderstood. He *couldn't* have said what I thought he had said. Hadn't I seen him approach white visitors too often with his hat in hand, bowing humbly and respectfully? Hadn't he refused to eat in the dining hall with white guests of the school, entering only after they had finished and then refusing to sit down, but remaining standing, his hat in his hand, while he addressed them eloquently, then leaving with a humble bow? Hadn't he, *hadn't* he? I had seen him too often as I peeped through the door between the dining room and the kitchen, I myself. And wasn't his favorite spiritual "Live-a-Humble"? And in the chapel on Sunday evenings upon the platform, hadn't he always taught us to live content in our place in a thousand unambiguous words? He had and I had believed him. I had believed without question his illustrations of the good which came of following the Founder's path. It was my affirmation of life and they couldn't send me away for something I didn't do. They simply couldn't. But that vet! He was so crazy that he corrupted sane men. He had tried to turn the world inside out, goddamn him! He had made Mr. Norton angry. He had no right to talk to a white man as he had, not with me to take the punishment . . .

Someone shook me and I recoiled, my legs moist and trembling. It was my roommate.

"What the hell, roomy," he said. "Let's go to chow."

I looked at his confident mug; *he* was going to be a farmer.

"I don't have an appetite," I said with a sigh.

"Okay now," he said, "you can try to kid me but don't say I didn't wake you."

"No," I said.

"Who're you expecting, a broad-butt gal with ball-bearing hips?"

"No," I said.

"You'd better stop that, roomy," he grinned. "It'll ruin your health, make you a moron. You ought to take you a gal and show her how the moon rises over all that green grass on the Founder's grave, man ..."

"Go to hell," I said.

He left laughing, opening the door to the sound of many footsteps from the hall: supper time. The sound of departing voices. Something of my life seemed to retreat with them into a gray distance, moiling. Then a knock sounded at the door and I sprang up, my heart tense.

A small student wearing a freshman's cap stuck his head in the door, shouting, "Dr. Bledsoe said he wants to see you down at Rabb Hall." And then he was gone before I could question him, his footsteps thundering down the hall as he raced to dinner before the last bell sounded.

AT MR. NORTON's door I stopped with my hand on the knob, mumbling a prayer.

"Come in, young man," he said to my knock. He was dressed in fresh linen, the light falling upon his white hair as upon silk floss. A small piece of gauze was plastered to his forehead. He was alone.

"I'm sorry, sir," I apologized, "but I was told that Dr. Bledsoe wanted to see me here ..."

"That's correct," he said, "but Dr. Bledsoe had to leave. You'll find him in his office after chapel."

"Thank you, sir," I said and turned to go. He cleared his throat behind me. "Young man ..."

I turned hopefully.

"Young man, I have explained to Dr. Bledsoe that you were not at fault. I believe he understands."

I was so relieved that at first I could only look at him, a small silken-haired, white-suited St. Nicholas, seen through misty eyes.

"I certainly do thank you, sir," I managed finally.

He studied me silently, his eyes slightly narrowed.

"Will you need me this evening, sir?" I asked.

"No, I won't be needing the machine. Business is taking me away sooner than I expected. I leave late tonight."

"I could drive you to the station, sir," I said hopefully.

"Thank you, but Dr. Bledsoe has already arranged it."

"Oh," I said with disappointment. I had hoped that by serving him the rest of the week I could win back his esteem. Now I would not have the opportunity.

"Well, I hope you have a pleasant trip, sir," I said.

"Thank you," he said, suddenly smiling.

"And maybe next time you come I'll be able to answer some of the questions you asked me this afternoon."

"Questions?" His eyes narrowed.

"Yes, sir, about . . . about your fate," I said.

"Ah, yes, yes," he said.

"And I intend to read Emerson, too . . ."

"Very good. Self-reliance is a most worthy virtue. I shall look forward with the greatest of interest to learning your contribution to my fate." He motioned me toward the door. "And don't forget to see Dr. Bledsoe."

I left somewhat reassured, but not completely. I still had to face Dr. Bledsoe. And I had to attend chapel.

Chapter five

At the sound of vespers I moved across the campus with groups of students, walking slowly, their voices soft in the mellow dusk. I remember the yellowed globes of frosted glass making lacy silhouettes on the gravel and the walk of the leaves and branches above us as we moved slow through the dusk so restless with scents of lilac, honeysuckle and verbena, and the feel of spring greenness; and I recall the sudden arpeggios of laughter lilting across the tender, springtime grass—gay-welling, far-floating, fluent, spontaneous, a bell-like feminine fluting, then suppressed; as though snuffed swiftly and irrevocably beneath the quiet solemnity of the vespered air now vibrant with somber chapel bells. Dong! Dong! Dong! Above the decorous walking around me, sounds of footsteps leaving the verandas of far-flung buildings and moving toward the walks and over the walks to the asphalt drives lined with whitewashed stones, those cryptic messages for men and women, boys and girls heading quietly toward where the visitors waited, and we moving not in the mood of worship but of judgment; as though even here in the filtering

dusk, here beneath the deep indigo sky, here, alive with loop-
ing swifts and darting moths, here in the hereness of the night
not yet lighted by the moon that looms blood-red behind the
chapel like a fallen sun, its radiance shedding not upon the
here-dusk of twittering bats, nor on the there-night of cricket
and whippoorwill, but focused short-rayed upon our place of
convergence; and we drifting forward with rigid motions, limbs
stiff and voices now silent, as though on exhibit even in the
dark, and the moon a white man's bloodshot eye.

And I move more rigid than all the others with a sense
of judgment; the vibrations of the chapel bells stirring the
depths of my turmoil, moving toward its nexus with a sense
of doom. And I remember the chapel with its sweeping eaves,
long and low as though risen bloody from the earth like the
rising moon; vine-covered and earth-colored as though more
earth-sprung than man-sprung. And my mind rushing for relief
away from the spring dusk and flower scents, away from the
time-scene of the crucifixion to the time-mood of the birth;
from spring-dusk and vespers to the high, clear, lucid moon of
winter and snow glinting upon the dwarfed pines where instead of the bells, the organ and the trombone choir speak
carols to the distances drifted with snow, making of the night
air a sea of crystal water lapping the slumbering land to the
farthest reaches of sound, for endless miles, bringing the new
dispensation even to the Golden Day, even unto the house of
madness. But in the hereness of dusk I am moving toward the
doomlike bells through the flowered air, beneath the rising
moon.

Into the doors and into the soft lights I go, silently, past
the rows of puritanical benches straight and torturous, finding
that to which I am assigned and bending my body to its agony.
There at the head of the platform with its pulpit and rail of
polished brass are the banked and pyramided heads of the stu-

dent choir, faces composed and stolid above uniforms of black and white; and above them, stretching to the ceiling, the organ pipes looming, a gothic hierarchy of dull gilded gold.

Around me the students move with faces frozen in solemn masks, and I seem to hear already the voices mechanically raised in the songs the visitors loved. (Loved? Demanded. Sung? An ultimatum accepted and ritualized, an allegiance recited for the peace it imparted, and for that perhaps loved. Loved as the defeated come to love the symbols of their conquerors. A gesture of acceptance, of terms laid down and reluctantly approved.) And here, sitting rigid, I remember the evenings spent before the sweeping platform in awe and in pleasure, and in the pleasure of awe; remember the short formal sermons intoned from the pulpit there, rendered in smooth articulate tones, with calm assurance purged of that wild emotion of the crude preachers most of us knew in our home towns and of whom we were deeply ashamed, these logical appeals which reached us more like the thrust of a firm and formal design requiring nothing more than the lucidity of uncluttered periods, the lulling movement of multisyllabic words to thrill and console us. And I remember, too, the talks of visiting speakers, all eager to inform us of how fortunate we were to be a part of the "vast" and formal ritual. How fortunate to belong to this family sheltered from those lost in ignorance and darkness.

Here upon this stage the black rite of Horatio Alger was performed to God's own acting script, with millionaires come down to portray themselves; not merely acting out the myth of their goodness, and wealth and success and power and benevolence and authority in cardboard masks, but themselves, these virtues concretely! Not the wafer and the wine, but the flesh and the blood, vibrant and alive, and vibrant even when stooped, ancient and withered. (And who, in face of this, would not believe? Could even doubt?)

And I remember too, how we confronted those others, those who had set me here in this Eden, whom we knew though we didn't know, who were unfamiliar in their familiarity, who trailed their words to us through blood and violence and ridicule and condescension with drawling smiles, and who exhorted and threatened, intimidated with innocent words as they described to us the limitations of our lives and the vast boldness of our aspirations, the staggering folly of our impatience to rise even higher; who, as they talked, aroused furtive visions within me of blood-froth sparkling their chins like their familiar tobacco juice, and upon their lips the curdled milk of a million black slave mammies' withered dugs, a treacherous and fluid knowledge of our being, imbibed at our source and now regurgitated foul upon us. This was our world, they said as they described it to us, this our horizon and its earth, its seasons and its climate, its spring and its summer, and its fall and harvest some unknown millennium ahead; and these its floods and cyclones and they themselves our thunder and lightning; and this we must accept and love and accept even if we did not love. We must accept—even when those were absent, and the men who made the railroads and ships and towers of stone, were before our eyes, in the flesh, their voices different, unweighted with recognizable danger and their delight in our songs more sincere seeming, their regard for our welfare marked by an almost benign and impersonal indifference. But the words of the others were stronger than the strength of philanthropic dollars, deeper than shafts sunk in the earth for oil and gold, more awe-inspiring than the miracles fabricated in scientific laboratories. For their most innocent words were acts of violence to which we of the campus were hypersensitive though we endured them not.

And there on the platform I too had stridden and debated, a student leader directing my voice at the highest beams and farthest rafters, ringing them, the accents staccato upon the ridgepole and echoing back with a tinkling, like words hurled to the trees of a wilderness, or into a well of slate-gray water; more sound than sense, a play upon the resonances of buildings, an assault upon the temples of the ear:

Ha! to the gray-haired matron in the final row. Ha! Miss Susie, Miss Susie Gresham, back there looking at that co-ed smiling at that he-ed—listen to me, the bungling bugler of words, imitating the trumpet and the trombone's timbre, playing thematic variations like a baritone born. Hey! old connoisseur of voice sounds, of voices without messages, of newsless winds, listen to the vowel sounds and the crackling dentals, to the low harsh gutturals of empty anguish, now riding the curve of a preacher's rhythm I heard long ago in a Baptist church, stripped now of its imagery: No suns having hemorrhages, no moons weeping tears, no earthworms refusing the sacred flesh and dancing in the earth on Easter morn. Ha! singing achievement, Ha! booming success, intoning, Ha! acceptance, Ha! a river of word-sounds filled with drowned passions, floating, Ha! with wrecks of unachievable ambitions and stillborn revolts, sweeping their ears, Ha! ranged stiff before me, necks stretched forward with listening ears, Ha! a-spraying the ceiling and a-drumming the dark-stained after rafter, that seasoned crossarm of torturous timber mellowed in the kiln of a thousand voices; playing Ha! as upon a xylophone; words marching like the student band, up the campus and down again, blaring triumphant sounds empty of triumphs. Hey, Miss Susie! the sound of words that were no words, counterfeit notes singing achievements yet unachieved, riding upon the wings of my voice out to you, old matron, who knew the voice sounds of the Founder and knew the accents and echo of his promise; your gray old head cocked with the young around you, your eyes closed, face ecstatic, as I toss the word sounds in my breath, my bellows, my fountain,

*like bright-colored balls in a water spout—bear me, old matron,
justify now this sound with your dear old nod of affirmation, your
closed-eye smile and bow of recognition, who'll never be fooled with
the mere content of words, not my words, not these pinfeathered
flighters that stroke your lids till they flutter with ecstasy with but
the mere echoed noise of the promise. And after the singing and
outward marching, you seize my hand and sing out quavering,
"Boy, some day you'll make the Founder proud!" Ha! Susie
Gresham, Mother Gresham, guardian of the hot young women
on the puritan benches who couldn't see your Jordan's water for
their private steam; you, relic of slavery whom the campus loved
but did not understand, aged, of slavery, yet bearer of something
warm and vital and all-enduring, of which in that island of
shame we were not ashamed—it was to you on the final row I
directed my rush of sound, and it was you of whom I thought
with shame and regret as I waited for the ceremony to begin.*

The honored guests moved silently upon the platform,
herded toward their high, carved chairs by Dr. Bledsoe with
the decorum of a portly head waiter. Like some of the guests,
he wore striped trousers and a swallow-tail coat with black-
braided lapels topped by a rich ascot tie. It was his regular
dress for such occasions, yet for all its elegance, he managed
to make himself look humble. Somehow, his trousers inevitably
bagged at the knees and the coat slouched in the shoulders. I
watched him smiling at first one and then another of the guests,
of whom all but one were white; and as I saw him placing his
hand upon their arms, touching their backs, whispering to a
tall angular-faced trustee who in turn touched his arm familiarly, I felt a shudder. I too had touched a white man today
and I felt that it had been disastrous, and I realized then that
he was the only one of us whom I knew—except perhaps a
barber or a nursemaid—who could touch a white man with

impunity. And I remembered too that whenever white guests came upon the platform he placed his hand upon them as though exercising a powerful magic. I watched his teeth flash as he took a white hand; then, with all seated, he went to his place at the end of the row of chairs.

Several terraces of students' faces above them, the organist, his eyes glinting at the console, was waiting with his head turned over his shoulder, and I saw Dr. Bledsoe, his eyes roaming over the audience, suddenly nod without turning his head. It was as though he had given a downbeat with an invisible baton. The organist turned and hunched his shoulders. A high cascade of sound bubbled from the organ, spreading, thick and clinging, over the chapel, slowly surging. The organist twisted and turned on his bench, with his feet flying beneath him as though dancing to rhythms totally unrelated to the decorous thunder of his organ.

And Dr. Bledsoe sat with a benign smile of inward concentration. Yet his eyes were darting swiftly, first over the rows of students, then over the section reserved for teachers, his swift glance carrying a threat for all. For he demanded that everyone attend these sessions. It was here that policy was announced in broadest rhetoric. I seemed to feel his eyes resting upon my face as he swept the section in which I sat. I looked at the guests on the platform; they sat with that alert relaxation with which they always met our upturned eyes. I wondered to which of them I might go to intercede for me with Dr. Bledsoe, but within myself I knew that there was no one.

In spite of the array of important men beside him, and despite the posture of humility and meekness which made him seem smaller than the others (although he was physically larger), Dr. Bledsoe made his presence felt by us with a far greater impact. I remembered the legend of how he had come to the college, a barefoot boy who in his fervor for education had trudged with his bundle of ragged clothing across two states. And how he was given a job feeding slop to the hogs but had made himself the best slop dispenser in the history of the school; and how the Founder had been impressed and made him his office boy. Each of us knew of his rise over years of hard work to the presidency, and each of us at some time wished that he had walked to the school or pushed a wheelbarrow or performed some other act of determination and sacrifice to attest his eagerness for knowledge. I remembered the admiration and fear he inspired in everyone on the campus; the pictures in the Negro press captioned "EDUCATOR," in type that exploded like a rifle shot, his face looking out at you with utmost confidence. To us he was more than just a president of a college. He was a leader, a "statesman" who carried our problems to those above us, even unto the White House; and in days past he had conducted the President himself about the campus. He was our leader and our magic, who kept the endowment high, the funds for scholarships plentiful and publicity moving through the channels of the press. He was our coal-black daddy of whom we were afraid.

As the organ voices died, I saw a thin brown girl arise noiselessly with the rigid control of a modern dancer, high in the upper rows of the choir, and begin to sing a cappella. She began softly, as though singing to herself of emotions of utmost privacy, a sound not addressed to the gathering, but which they overheard almost against her will. Gradually she increased its volume, until at times the voice seemed to become a disembodied force that sought to enter her, to violate her, shaking her, rocking her rhythmically, as though it had become the source of her being, rather than the fluid web of her own creation.

I saw the guests on the platform turn to look behind

them, to see the thin brown girl in white choir robe standing high against the organ pipes, herself become before our eyes a pipe of contained, controlled and sublimated anguish, a thin plain face transformed by music. I could not understand the words, but only the mood, sorrowful, vague and ethereal, of the singing. It throbbed with nostalgia, regret and repentance, and I sat with a lump in my throat as she sank slowly down; not a sitting but a controlled collapsing, as though she were balancing, sustaining the simmering bubble of her final tone by some delicate rhythm of her heart's blood, or by some mystic concentration of her being, focused upon the sound through the contained liquid of her large uplifted eyes.

There was no applause, only the appreciation of a profound silence. The white guests exchanged smiles of approval. I sat thinking of the dread possibility of having to leave all this, of being expelled; imagining the return home and the rebukes of my parents. I looked out at the scene now from far back in my despair, seeing the platform and its actors as through a reversed telescope; small doll-like figures moving through some meaningless ritual. Someone up there, above the alternating moss-dry and grease-slick heads of the students rowed before me, was making announcements from a lectern on which a dim light shone. Another figure rose and led a prayer. Someone spoke. Then around me everyone was singing *Lead me, lead me to a rock that is higher than I*. And as though the sound contained some force more impervious than the image of the scene of which it was the living connective tissue, I was pulled back to its immediacy.

One of the guests had risen to speak. A man of striking ugliness; fat, with a bullet-head set on a short neck, with a nose much too wide for its face, upon which he wore black-lensed glasses. He had been seated next to Dr. Bledsoe, but so concerned had I been with the president that I hadn't really seen him. My eyes had focused only upon the white men and Dr. Bledsoe. So that now as he arose and crossed slowly to the center of the platform, I had the notion that part of Dr. Bledsoe had arisen and moved forward, leaving his other part smiling in the chair.

He stood before us relaxed, his white collar gleaming like a band between his black face and his dark garments, dividing his head from his body; his short arms crossed before his barrel, like a black little Buddha's. For a moment he stood with his large head lifted, as though thinking; then he began speaking, his voice round and vibrant as he told of his pleasure in being allowed to visit the school once more after many years. Having been preaching in a northern city, he had seen it last in the final days of the Founder, when Dr. Bledsoe was the "second in command." "Those were wonderful days," he droned. "Significant days. Days filled with great portent."

As he talked he made a cage of his hands by touching his fingertips, then with his small feet pressing together, he began a slow, rhythmic rocking; tilting forward on his toes until it seemed he would fall, then back on his heels, the lights catching his black-lensed glasses until it seemed that his head floated free of his body and was held close to it only by the white band of his collar. And as he tilted he talked until a rhythm was established.

Then he was renewing the dream in our hearts:

". . . this barren land after Emancipation," he intoned, "this land of darkness and sorrow, of ignorance and degradation, where the hand of brother had been turned against brother, father against son, and son against father; where master had turned against slave and slave against master; where all was strife and darkness, an aching land. And into this land came a humble prophet, lowly like the humble carpenter of Nazareth, a slave and a son of slaves, knowing only his mother.

A slave born, but marked from the beginning by a high intelligence and princely personality; born in the lowest part of this barren, war-scarred land, yet somehow shedding light upon it where'er he passed through. I'm sure you have heard of his precarious infancy, his precious life almost destroyed by an insane cousin who splashed the babe with lye and shriveled his seed and how, a mere babe, he lay nine days in a deathlike coma and then suddenly and miraculously recovered. You might say that it was as though he had risen from the dead or been reborn.

"Oh, my young friends," he cried, beaming, "my young friends, it is indeed a beautiful story. I'm sure you've heard it many times: Recall how he came upon his initial learning through shrewd questioning of his little masters, the elder masters never suspecting; and how he learned his alphabet and taught himself to read and solve the secret of words, going instinctively to the Holy Bible with its great wisdom for his first knowledge. And you know how he escaped and made his way across mountain and valley to that place of learning and how he persisted and worked noontimes, nights and mornings for the privilege of studying, or, as the old folk would say, of 'rubbing his head against the college wall.' You know of his brilliant career, how already he was a moving orator; then his penniless graduation and his return after years to this country.

"And then his great struggle beginning. Picture it, my young friends: The clouds of darkness all over the land, black folk and white folk full of fear and hate, wanting to go forward, but each fearful of the other. A whole region is caught in a terrible tension. Everyone is perplexed with the question of what must be done to dissolve this fear and hatred that crouched over the land like a demon waiting to spring, and you know how he came and showed them the way. Oh, yes, my friends. I'm sure you've heard it time and time again; of this godly man's labors, his great humility and his undimming vision, the fruits of which you enjoy today; concrete, made flesh; his dream, conceived in the starkness and darkness of slavery, fulfilled now even in the air you breathe, in the sweet harmonies of your blended voices, in the knowledge which each of you—daughters and granddaughters, sons and grandsons, of slaves—all of you partaking of it in bright and well-equipped classrooms. You must see this slave, this black Aristotle, moving slowly, with sweet patience, with a patience not of mere man, but of God-inspired faith—see him moving slowly as he surmounts each and every opposition. Rendering unto Caesar that which was Caesar's, yes; but steadfastly seeking for you that bright horizon which you now enjoy . . .

"All this," he said, spreading his fingers palm down before him, "has been told and retold throughout the land, inspiring a humble but fast-rising people. You have heard it and it—this true story of rich implication, this living parable of proven glory and humble nobility—and it, as I say, has made you free. Even you who have come to this shrine only this semester know it. You have heard his name from your parents, for it was he who led them to the path, guiding them like a great captain; like that great pilot of ancient times who led his people safe and unharmed across the bottom of the blood-red sea. And your parents followed this remarkable man across the black sea of prejudice, safely out of the land of ignorance, through the storms of fear and anger, shouting, LET MY PEOPLE GO! when it was necessary, whispering it during those times when whispering was wisest. And he was heard."

I listened, my back pressing against the hard bench, with a numbness, my emotions woven into his words as upon a loom.

"And remember how," he said, "when he entered a certain state at cotton-picking time, his enemies had plotted to take his life. And recall how during his journey he was stopped by the strange figure of a man whose pitted features revealed no inkling of whether he was black or white . . . Some say he was a Greek. Some a Mongolian. Others a mulatto—and others still, a simple white man of God. Whoever, and whatsoever, and we must not rule out the possibility of an emissary direct from above—oh, yes!—and remember how he appeared suddenly, startling both Founder and horse as he gave warning, telling the Founder to leave the horse and buggy there in the road and proceed immediately to a certain cabin, then slipped silently away, so silently, my young friends, that the Founder doubted his very existence. And you know how the great man continued through the dusk, determined though puzzled as he approached the town. He was lost, lost in reverie until the crack of the first rifle sounded, then the almost fatal volley that creased his skull—oh my!—and left him stunned and apparently lifeless.

"I have heard him tell with his own lips how consciousness returned while they were still upon him examining their foul deed, and how he lay biting his heart lest they hear it and wipe out their failure with a *coup-de-grace*, as the French would say. Ha! And I'm sure you've each of you lived with him through his escape," he said, seeming to look directly into my watered eyes. "You awakened when he awakened, rejoiced when he rejoiced at their leaving without further harm; arising when he arose; seeing with his eyes the prints of their milling footsteps and the cartridges dropped in the dust about the imprint of his fallen body; yes, and the cold, dust-encrusted, but not quite fatal blood. And you hurried with him full of doubt to the cabin designated by the stranger, where he met that seemingly demented black man . . . You remember that old one, laughed at by the children in the town's square, old, comic-faced, crafty, *cotton*-headed. And yet it was he who bound up your wounds with the wounds of the Founder. He, the old slave, showing a surprising knowledge of such matters—*germology* and *scabology*—ha! ha!—he called it, and what a youthful skill of the hands! For he shaved our skull, and cleansed our wound and bound it neat with bandages stolen from the home of an unsuspecting leader of the mob, ha! And you recall how you plunged with the Founder, the Leader, deep into the black art of escape, guided at first, indeed, initiated, by the seemingly demented one who had learned his craft in slavery. You left with the Founder in the black of the night, and I know it. You hurried silently along the river bottom, stung by mosquitoes, hooted by owls, zoomed by bats, buzzed by snakes that rattled among the rocks, mud and fever, darkness and sighing. You hid all the following day in the cabin where thirteen slept in three small rooms, standing until darkness in the fireplace chimney, back in all the soot and ashes—ha! ha!—guarded by the granny who dozed at the hearth seemingly without a fire. You stood in the blackness and when they came with their baying hounds they thought her demented. But she knew, she knew! She knew the fire! She knew the fire! She knew the fire that burned without consuming! My God, yes!"

"My God, yes!" a woman's voice responded, adding to the structure of his vision within me.

"And you left him on the morning, hidden in a wagonload of cotton, in the very center of the fleece, where you breathed the hot air through the barrel of the emergency shotgun; the cartridges, which thank God it was unnecessary to use, held fanwise and ready between the spread fingers of your hand. And you went into this town with him and were hidden by the friendly aristocrat one night, and on the next by the white blacksmith who held no hatred—surprising contradictions of the underground. Escaping, yes! helped by those who knew you and those who didn't know. Because for some it was enough to see him; others helped without even that, black and white. But mostly it was our own who aided, because you were their own and we have always helped our own. And so, my young friends, my sisters and brothers, you went with him, in and out of cabins, by night and early morning, through swamps and hills. On and on, passed from black hand to black hand and some white hands, and all the hands molding the Founder's freedom and our own freedom like voices shaping a deep-felt song. And you, each of you, were with him. Ah, how well you know it, for it was you who escaped to freedom. Ah, yes, and you know the story."

I saw him resting now, and beaming out across the chapel, his huge head turning to all its corners like a beacon, his voice still echoing as I fought back my emotion. For the first time the evocation of the Founder saddened me, and the campus seemed to rush past me, fast retreating, like the fading of a dream at the sundering of slumber. Beside me, the student's eyes swam with a distorting cataract of tears, his features rigid as though he struggled within himself. The fat man was playing upon the whole audience without the least show of exertion. He seemed completely composed, hidden behind his black-lensed glasses, only his mobile features gesturing his vocal drama. I nudged the boy beside me.

"Who is he?" I whispered.

He gave me a look of annoyance, almost of outrage. "Reverend Homer A. Barbee, Chicago," he said.

Now the speaker rested his arm upon the lectern and turned toward Dr. Bledsoe:

"You've heard the bright beginning of the beautiful story, my friends. But there is the mournful ending, and perhaps in many ways the richer side. The setting of this glorious son of the morning."

He turned to Dr. Bledsoe, "It was a fateful day, Dr. Bledsoe, sir, if I may recall it to you, for we were there. Oh yes, my young friends," he said, turning to face us again with a sad proud smile. "I knew him well and loved him, and I was there.

"We had toured through several states to which he was carrying the message. The people had come to hear the prophet, the multitude had responded. The old-fashioned people; women in aprons and Mother Hubbards of calico and gingham, men in their overalls and patched alpacas; a sea of upturned and puzzled faces looking out from beneath old battered straw hats and limp sunbonnets. They who had come by oxen and mule team and by walking long distances. It was the month of September and unseasonably cold. He had spoken peace and confidence into their troubled souls, had set a star before them and we were passing on to other scenes, still carrying the message.

"Ah, those days of ceaseless travel, those youthful days, those springtime days; fertile, blossomy, sun-filled days of promise. Ah, yes, those indescribably glorious days, in which the Founder was building the dream not only here in this then barren valley, but hither and yonder throughout the land, instilling the dream in the hearts of the people. Erecting the scaffolding of a nation. Broadcasting his message that fell like seed on fallow ground, sacrificing himself, fighting and forgiving his enemies of both complexions—oh yes, he had them, of both complexions. But going forward filled with the importance of his message, filled with his dedicated mission; and in his zeal, perhaps in his mortal pride, ignoring the advice of his physician. I see in my mind's eye the fatal atmosphere of that jam-packed auditorium: The Founder holds the audience within the gentle palm of his eloquence, rocking it, soothing it, instructing it; and there below, the rapt faces blushed by the glow of the big pot-bellied stove now turned cherry-red with its glowing; yes, the spellbound rows caught in the imperious truth of his message. And I hear now, again, the great humming hush as his voice reached the end of a mighty period, and one of the listeners, a snowy-headed man, leaps to his feet crying out, 'Tell us what is to be done, sir! For God's sake, tell us! Tell us in the name of the son they snatched from me last week!' And all through the room the voices arising, imploring, 'Tell us, tell us!' And the Founder is suddenly mute with tears.''

Old Barbee's voice rang out, as suddenly he made charged and incomplete movements about the platform, acting out his words. And I watched with a sick fascination, knowing part of the story, yet a part of me fighting against its sad inevitable conclusion.

"And the Founder pauses, then steps forward with his eyes spilling his great emotion. With his arm upraised, he begins to answer and totters. Then all is commotion. We rush forward and lead him away.

"The audience leaps to its feet in consternation. All is terror and turmoil, a moan and a sighing. Until, like a clap of thunder, I hear Dr. Bledsoe's voice ring out whip-like with authority, a song of hope. And as we stretch the Founder upon a bench to rest, I hear Dr. Bledsoe stomping out the time with mighty strokes upon the hollow platform, commanding not in words but in the great gut-tones of his magnificent basso—oh, but wasn't he a singer? Isn't he a singer still today?—and they stand, they calm, and with him they sing out against the tottering of their giant. Sing out their long black songs of blood and bones:

"Meaning HOPE!

"Of hardship and pain:

"Meaning FAITH!

"Of humbleness and absurdity:

"Meaning ENDURANCE!

"Of ceaseless struggle in darkness, meaning:

"TRIUMPH . . .

"Ha!" Barbee cried, slapping his hands, "Ha! Singing verse after verse, until the leader revived!" (Slap, slap of his hands.)

"Addressed them"—

(Slap!) "My God, my God!

"Assured them"—(Slap!)

"That"—(Slap!)

"He was only tired of his ceaseless efforts." (Slap!) "Yes, and dismisses them, sending each on his way rejoicing, giving each a parting handshake of fellowship . . ."

I watched Barbee pace in a semi-circle, his lips compressed, his face working with emotion, his palms meeting but making no sound.

"Ah, those days in which he tilled his mighty fields, those days in which he watched the crops take hold and grow, those youthful, summery, sun-bright days . . ."

Barbee's voice sighed off in nostalgia. The chapel hardly breathed as he sighed deeply. Then I watched him produce a snowy handkerchief, remove his dark glasses and wipe his eyes, and through the increasing distance of my isolation, I watched the men in the seats of honor slowly shake their spellbound heads. Then Barbee's voice began again, disembodied now, and it was as though he had never paused, as though his words, reverberating within us, had continued their rhythmic flow though their source was for a moment stilled:

"Oh, yes, my young friends, oh, yes," he continued with a great sadness. "Man's hope can paint a purple picture, can transform a soaring vulture into a noble eagle or a moaning dove. Oh, yes! But I *knew*," he shouted, startling me. "In spite of that *great, anguished hope within me, I knew—knew* that the great spirit was declining, was approaching its lonely winter; the great sun going down. For sometimes it is given one to know these things ... And I staggered under the awful burden of that knowledge and I cursed myself because I bore it. But such was the Founder's enthusiasm—oh, yes!—that as we sped from country town to country town through the glorious Indian summer, I soon forgot. And then ... And then ... and ... then ..."

I listened to his voice fall to a whisper; his hands were outspread as though he were leading an orchestra into a profound and final diminuendo. Then his voice rose again, crisply, almost matter-of-factly, accelerated:

"I remember the start of the train, how it seemed to groan as it started up the steep grade into the mountain. It was cold. Frost formed its icy patterns upon the window's edges. And the whistle of the train was long-drawn and lonely, a sigh issuing from the depths of the mountain.

"In the car up ahead, in the Pullman assigned him by the very president of the line, the Leader lay tossing. He had been struck with a sudden and mysterious sickness. And I knew in spite of the anguish within me that the sun goeth down, for the heavens themselves conveyed that knowledge. The rush of the train, the clicking of wheels upon the steel. I remember how I looked out of the frosted pane and saw the looming great North Star and lost it, as though the sky had shut its eye. The train was curving the mountain, the engine loping like a great black hound, parallel with the last careening cars, panting forth its pale white vapor as it hurled us ever higher. And shortly the sky was black, without a moon ..."

As his "mooo-o-on" echoed over the chapel, he drew his chin against his chest until his white collar disappeared, leaving him a figure of balanced unbroken blackness, and I could hear the rasp of air as he inhaled.

"It was as though the very constellations knew our impending sorrow," he bugled, his head raised to the ceiling, his voice full-throated. "For against that great—wide—sweep of sable there came the burst of a single jewel-like star, and I saw it shimmer, and break, and streak down the cheek of that coal-black sky like a reluctant and solitary tear . . ."

He shook his head with great emotion, his lips pursed as he moaned, "Mmmmmmmmmm," turning toward Dr. Bledsoe as though he did not quite see him. "At that fateful moment . . . Mmmmmm, I sat with your great president . . . Mmmmmmmmmm! He was deep in meditation as we awaited word from the men of science, and he said to me of that dying star,

" 'Barbee, friend, did you see?'

"And I answered, 'Yes, Doctor, I saw.'

"And at our throats already we felt the cold hands of sorrow. And I said to Dr. Bledsoe, 'Let us pray.' And as we knelt there on the swaying floor our words were less prayers than sounds of mute and terrible sorrow. And it was then, as we pulled to our feet, staggering with the motion of that speeding train, that we saw the physician moving toward us. And we looked with bated breath into the blank and expressionless features of the man of science, asking with our total beings: Do you bring us hope or disaster? And it was then and there he informed us that the Leader was nearing his destination . . .

"It was said, the cruel blow had fallen and we were left numb, but the Founder was still for the moment with us and still in command. And, of all in the traveling party, he sent for him who sits there before you, and for me as a man of God. But he wanted mainly his friend of midnight consultations, his comrade of many battles, who over the weary years had remained steadfast in defeat as in victory.

"Even now I can see it, the dark passage lit with dim

lights and Dr. Bledsoe swaying as he went before me. At the door stood the porter and the conductor, a black man and a white man of the South, both crying. Both weeping. And he looked up as we entered, his great eyes resigned but still aflame with nobility and courage against the white of his pillow; and he looked at his friend and smiled. Smiled warmly at his old campaigner, his loyal champion, his adjunct, that marvelous singer of the old songs who had rallied his spirit during times of distress and discouragement, who with his singing of the old familiar melodies soothed the doubts and fears of the multitude; he who had rallied the ignorant, the fearful and suspicious, those still wrapped in the rags of slavery; him, there, your leader, who calmed the children of the storm. And as the Founder looked up at his companion, he smiled. And reaching out his hand to his friend and companion as I now stretch out my hand to you, he said, 'Come closer. Come closer.' And he moved closer, until he stood beside the berth, and the light slanting across his shoulder as he knelt beside him. And the hand reached out and gently touched him and he said, 'Now, you must take on the burden. Lead them the rest of the way.' And oh, the cry of that train and the pain too big for tears!

"When the train reached the summit of the mountain, he was no longer with us. And as the train dropped down the grade he had departed.

"It had become a veritable train of sorrow. Dr. Bledsoe there, sat weary in mind and heavy of heart. What should he do? The leader was dead and he thrown suddenly at the head of the troops like a cavalryman catapulted into the saddle of his general felled in a charge of battle—vaulted onto the back of his fiery and half-broken charger. Ah! And that great, black, noble beast, wall-eyed with the din of battle and twitching already with its sense of loss. What command should he give?

Should he return with his burden, home, to where already the hot wires were flashing, speaking, rattling the mournful message? Should he turn and bear the fallen soldier down the cold and alien mountain to this valley home? Return with the dear eyes dulled, the firm hand still, the magnificent voice silent, the Leader cold? Return to the warm valley, to the green grounds he could no longer light with his mortal vision? Should he follow his Leader's vision though he had now himself departed?

"Ah, of course you know the story: How he bore the body into the strange city, and the speech he made as his Leader lay in state, and how when the sad news spread, a day of mourning was declared for the whole municipality. Oh, and how rich and poor, black and white, weak and powerful, young and old, all came to pay their homage—many realizing the Leader's worth and their loss only now with his passing. And how, with his mission done, Dr. Bledsoe returned, keeping his sorrowful vigil with his friend in a humble baggage car; and how the people came to pay their respects at the stations . . . A slow train. A sorrowful train. And all along the line, in mountain and valley, wherever the rails found their fateful course, the people were one in their common mourning, and like the cold steel rails, were spiked down to their sorrow. Oh, what a sad departure!

"And what an even sadder arrival. See with me, my young friends, hear with me: The weeping and wailing of those who shared his labors. Their sweet Leader returned to them, rock-cold in the iron immobility of death. He who had left them quick, in the prime of his manhood, author of their own fire and illumination, returned to them cold, already a bronzed statue. Oh, the *despair*, my young friends. The black despair of black people! I see them now; wandering about these grounds, where each brick, each bird, each blade of grass was a reminder of some precious memory; and each memory a hammer stroke driving home the blunt spikes of their sorrow. Oh, yes, some now are here gray-haired among you, still dedicated to his vision, still laboring in the vineyard. But then with the black-draped coffin lying in state among them—inescapably reminding them—they felt the dark night of slavery settling once more upon them. They smelt that old obscene stink of darkness, that old slavery smell, worse than the rank halitosis of hoary death. Their sweet light enclosed in a black-draped coffin, their majestic sun snatched behind a cloud.

"Oh, and the sad sound of weeping bugles! I can hear them now, stationed at the four corners of the campus, sounding taps for the fallen general; announcing and reannouncing the sad tidings, telling and retelling the sad revelation one to the other across the still numbness of the air, as though they could not believe it, could neither comprehend nor accept it; bugles weeping like a family of tender women lamenting their loved one. And the people came to sing the old songs and to express their unspeakable sorrow. Black, black, black! Black people in blacker mourning, the funeral crape hung upon their naked hearts; singing unashamedly their black folk's songs of sorrow, moving painfully, overflowing the curving walks, weeping and wailing beneath the drooping trees and their low murmuring voices like the moans of winds in a wilderness. And finally they gathered on the hill slope and as far as the tear-wet eyes could see, they stood with their heads bowed, singing.

"Then silence. The lonesome hole banked with poignant flowers. The dozen white-gloved hands waiting taut upon the silken ropes. That awful silence. The final words are spoken. A single wild rose tossed farewell, bursts slowly, its petals drifting snowlike upon the reluctantly lowered coffin. Then down into the earth; back to the ancient dust; back to the cold black clay . . . mother . . . of us all."

As Barbee paused the silence was so complete that I could hear the power engines far across the campus throbbing the night like an excited pulse. Somewhere in the audience an old woman's voice began a plaintive wail; the birth of a sad, unformulated song that died stillborn in a sob.

Barbee stood with his head thrown back, his arms rigid at his sides, his fists clenched as though fighting desperately for control. Dr. Bledsoe sat with his face in his hands. Near me someone blew his nose. Barbee took a tottering step forward.

"Oh, yes. Oh, yes," he said. "Oh, yes. That too is part of the glorious story. But think of it not as a death, but as a birth. A great seed had been planted. A seed which has continued to put forth its fruit in its season as surely as if the great creator had been resurrected. For in a sense he was, if not in the flesh, in the spirit. And in a sense in the flesh too. For has not your present leader become his living agent, his physical presence? Look about you if you doubt it. My young friends, my dear young friends! How can I tell you what manner of man this is who leads you? How can I convey to you how well he has kept his pledge to the Founder, how conscientious has been his stewardship?

"First, you must see the school as it was. Already a great institution, to be sure; but then the buildings were eight, now they are twenty; then the faculty was fifty, now it is two hundred; then the student body was a few hundred, where now I'm told you are three thousand. And now where you have roads of asphalt for the passage of rubber tires, then the roads were of crushed stone for the passage of oxen, and mule teams, and horse-drawn wagons. I have not the words to tell you how my heart swelled to return to this great institution after so great a while to move among its wealth of green things, its fruitful farmland and fragrant campus. Ah! and the marvelous plant supplying power to an area larger than many towns—all operated by *black hands*. Thus, my young friends, does the light of the Founder still burn. Your leader has kept his promise a thousandfold. I commend him in his own right, for he is the co-architect of a great and noble experiment. He is a worthy successor to his great friend and it is no accident that his great and intelligent leadership has made him our leading statesman. His is a form of greatness worthy of your imitation. I say to you, pattern yourselves upon him. Aspire, each of you, to some day follow in his footsteps. Great deeds are yet to be performed. For we are a young, though a fast-rising, people. Legends are still to be created. Be not afraid to undertake the burdens of your leader, and the work of the Founder will be one of ever unfolding glory, the history of the race a saga of mounting triumphs."

Barbee stood with his arms outstretched now, beaming over the audience, his Buddha-like body still as an onyx boulder. There was sniffling throughout the chapel. Voices murmured with admiration and I felt more lost than ever. For a few minutes old Barbee had made me see the vision and now I knew that leaving the campus would be like the parting of flesh. I watched him lower his arms now and start back to his chair, moving slowly with his head cocked as though listening to distant music. I had lowered my head to wipe my eyes when I heard the shocked gasp arise.

Looking up, I saw two of the white trustees moving swiftly across the platform to where Barbee floundered upon Dr. Bledsoe's legs. The old man slid forward upon his hands and knees as the two white men took his arms; and now as he stood I saw one of them reach for something on the floor and place it in his hands. It was when he raised his head that I saw it. For a swift instant, between the gesture and the opaque glitter of his glasses, I saw the blinking of sightless eyes. Homer A. Barbee was blind.

Uttering apologies, Dr. Bledsoe helped him to his chair. Then as the old man rested back with a smile, Dr. Bledsoe walked to the edge of the platform and lifted his arms. I closed my eyes as I heard the deep moaning sound that issued from him, and the rising crescendo of the student body joining in. This time it was music sincerely felt, not rendered for the guests, but for themselves; a song of hope and exaltation. I wanted to rush from the building, but didn't dare. I sat stiff and erect, supported by the hard bench, relying upon it as upon a form of hope.

I could not look at Dr. Bledsoe now, because old Barbee had made me both feel my guilt and accept it. For although I had not intended it, any act that endangered the continuity of the dream was an act of treason.

I did not listen to the next speaker, a tall white man who kept dabbing at his eyes with a handkerchief and repeating his phrases in an emotional and inarticulate manner. Then the orchestra played excerpts from Dvořák's *New World Symphony* and I kept hearing "Swing Low, Sweet Chariot" resounding through its dominant theme—my mother's and grandfather's favorite spiritual. It was more than I could stand, and before the next speaker could begin I hurried past the disapproving eyes of teachers and matrons, out into the night.

A mockingbird trilled a note from where it perched upon the hand of the moonlit Founder, flipping its moon-mad tail above the head of the eternally kneeling slave. I went up the shadowy drive, heard it trill behind me. The street lamps glowed brilliant in the moonlit dream of the campus, each light serene in its cage of shadows.

I might well have waited until the end of the services, for I hadn't gone far when I heard the dim, bright notes of the orchestra striking up a march, followed by a burst of voices as the students filed out into the night. With a feeling of dread I headed for the administration building, and upon reaching it, stood in the darkened doorway. My mind fluttered like the moths that veiled the street lamp which cast shadows upon the bank of grass below me. I would now have my real interview with Dr. Bledsoe, and I recalled Barbee's address with resentment. With such words fresh in his mind, I was sure Dr. Bledsoe would be far less sympathetic to my plea. I stood in the darkened doorway trying to probe my future if I were expelled. Where would I go, what would I do? How could I ever return home?

Chapter six

Down the sloping lawn below me the male students moved toward their dormitories, seeming far away from me now, remote, and each shadowy form vastly superior to me, who had by some shortcoming cast myself into the darkness away from all that was worthwhile and inspiring. I listened to one group harmonize quietly as they passed. The smell of fresh bread being prepared in the bakery drifted to me. The good white bread of breakfast; the rolls dripping with yellow butter that I had slipped into my pocket so often to be munched later in my room with wild blackberry jam from home.

Lights began to appear in the girls' dormitories, like the bursting of luminous seeds flung broadside by an invisible hand. Several cars rolled by. I saw a group of old women who lived in the town approaching. One used a cane which from time to time she tapped hollowly upon the walk like a blind man. Snatches of their conversation fluttered to me as they discussed Barbee's talk with enthusiasm, recalled the times of the Founder, their quavering voices weaving and embroidering his story.

Then down the long avenue of trees I saw the familiar Cadillac approaching and started inside the building, suddenly filled with panic. I hadn't gone two steps before I turned and hurried out into the night again. I couldn't stand to face Dr. Bledsoe immediately. I was fairly shivering as I fell in behind a group of boys going up the drive. They were arguing some point heatedly, but I was too agitated to listen and simply followed in their shadows, noticing the dull gleam of their polished shoe-leather in the rays of the street lamps. I kept trying to formulate what I would say to Dr. Bledsoe, and the boys must have turned into their building, for suddenly finding myself outside the gates of the campus and heading down the highway, I turned and ran back to the building.

When I went in he was wiping his neck with a blue-bordered handkerchief. The shaded lamp catching the lenses of his glasses left half of his broad face in the shadow as his clenched fists stretched full forth in the light before him. I stood, hesitating in the door, aware suddenly of the old heavy furnishings, the relics from the times of the Founder, the framed portrait photographs and relief plaques of presidents and industrialists, men of power—fixed like trophies or heraldic emblems upon the walls.

"Come in," he said from the half-shadow; then I saw him move and his head coming forward, his eyes burning.

He began mildly, as if quietly joking, throwing me off balance.

"Boy," he said, "I understand that you not only carried Mr. Norton out to the Quarters but that you wound up at that sinkhole, that Golden Day."

It was a statement, not a question. I said nothing and he looked at me with the same mild gaze. Had Barbee helped Mr. Norton soften him?

"No," he said, "it wasn't enough to take him to the

Quarters, you had to make the complete tour, to give him the full treatment. Was that it?"

"No, sir . . . I mean that he was ill, sir," I said. "He had to have some whiskey . . ."

"And that was the only place you knew to go," he said. "So you went there because you were taking care of him . . ."

"Yes, sir . . ."

"And not only that," he said in a voice that both mocked and marveled, "you took him out and sat him down on the gallery, veranda—piazza—whatever they call it now'days—and introduced him to the quality!"

"Quality?" I frowned. "Oh—but he insisted that I stop, sir. There was nothing I could do . . ."

"Of course," he said. "Of course."

"He was interested in the cabins, sir. He was surprised that there were any left."

"So naturally you stopped," he said, bowing his head again.

"Yes, sir."

"Yes, and I suppose the cabin opened up and told him its life history and all the choice gossip?"

I started to explain.

"Boy!" he exploded. "Are you serious? Why were you out on the road in the first place? Weren't you behind the wheel?"

"Yes, sir . . ."

"Then haven't we bowed and scraped and begged and lied enough decent homes and drives for you to show him? Did you think that white man had to come a thousand miles— all the way from New York and Boston and Philadelphia just for you to show him a slum? Don't just stand there, say something!"

"But I was only driving him, sir. I only stopped there after he ordered me to . . ."

"Ordered you?" he said. "He *ordered* you. Dammit, white folk are always giving orders, it's a habit with them. Why didn't you make an excuse? Couldn't you say they had sickness—smallpox—or picked another cabin? Why that Trueblood shack? My God, boy! You're black and living in the South—did you forget how to lie?"

"Lie, sir? Lie to him, lie to a trustee, sir? Me?"

He shook his head with a kind of anguish. "And me thinking I'd picked a boy with brain," he said. "Didn't you know you were endangering the school?"

"But I was only trying to please him . . ."

"*Please* him? And here you are a junior in college! Why, the dumbest black bastard in the cotton patch knows that the only way to please a white man is to tell him a lie! What kind of education are you getting around here? Who really told you to take him out there?" he said.

"He did, sir. No one else."

"Don't lie to me!"

"That's the truth, sir."

"I warn you now, who suggested it?"

"I swear, sir. No one told me."

"Nigger, this isn't the time to lie. I'm no white man. Tell me the truth!"

It was as though he'd struck me. I stared across the desk thinking, He called me *that* . . .

"Answer me, boy!"

That, I thought, noticing the throbbing of a vein that rose between his eyes, thinking, *He called me that.*

"I wouldn't lie, sir," I said.

"Then who was that patient you were talking with?"

"I never saw him before, sir."

"What was he saying?"

"I can't recall it all," I muttered. "The man was raving."

"Speak up. What did he say?"

"He thinks that he lived in France and that he's a great doctor . . ."

"Continue."

"He said that I believed that white was right," I said.

"What?" Suddenly his face twitched and cracked like the surface of dark water. "And you do, don't you?" Dr. Bledsoe said, suppressing a nasty laugh. "Well, don't you?"

I did not answer, thinking, *You, you . . .*

"Who was he, did you ever see him before?"

"No, sir, I hadn't."

"Was he northern or southern?"

"I don't know, sir."

He struck his desk. "College for Negroes! Boy, what do you know other than how to ruin an institution in half an hour that it took over half a hundred years to build? Did he *talk* northern or southern?"

"He talked like a white man," I said, "except that his voice sounded southern, like one of ours . . ."

"I'll have to investigate him," he said. "A Negro like that should be under lock and key."

Across the campus a clock struck the quarter hour and something inside me seemed to muffle its sound. I turned to him desperately. "Dr. Bledsoe, I'm awfully sorry. I had no intention of going there but things just got out of hand. Mr. Norton understands how it happened . . ."

"Listen to me, boy," he said loudly. "Norton is one man and I'm another, and while he might think he's satisfied, *I* know that he isn't! Your poor judgment has caused this school incalculable damage. Instead of uplifting the race, you've torn it down."

He looked at me as though I had committed the worst crime imaginable. "Don't you know we can't tolerate such a thing? I gave you an opportunity to serve one of our best white friends, a man who could make your fortune. But in return you dragged the entire race into the slime!"

Suddenly he reached for something beneath a pile of papers, an old leg shackle from slavery which he proudly called a "symbol of our progress."

"You've got to be disciplined, boy," he said. "There's no if's and and's about it."

"But you gave Mr. Norton your word . . ."

"Don't stand there and tell me what I already know. Regardless of what I said, as the leader of this institution I can't possibly let this pass. Boy, I'm getting rid of you!"

It must have happened when the metal struck the desk, for suddenly I was leaning toward him, shouting with outrage.

"I'll tell him," I said. "I'll go to Mr. Norton and tell him. You've lied to both of us . . ."

"What!" he said. "You have the nerve to threaten me . . . in my own office?"

"I'll tell him," I screamed. "I'll tell everybody. I'll fight you. I swear it, I'll fight!"

"Well," he said, sitting back, "well, I'll be damn!"

For a moment he looked me up and down and I saw his head go back into the shadow, hearing a high, thin sound like a cry of rage; then his face came forward and I saw his laughter. For an instant I stared; then I wheeled and started for the door, hearing him sputter, "Wait, wait," behind me.

I turned. He gasped for breath, propping his huge head up with his hands as tears streamed down his face.

"Come on, come," he said, removing his glasses and wiping his eyes. "Come on, son," his voice amused and conciliatory. It was as though I were being put through a fraternity initiation and found myself going back. He looked at me, still laughing with agony. My eyes burned.

"Boy, you *are* a fool," he said. "Your white folk didn't

teach you anything and your mother-wit has left you cold. What has happened to you young Negroes? I thought you had caught on to how things are done down here. But you don't even know the difference between the way things are and the way they're supposed to be. My God," he gasped, "what is the race coming to? Why, boy, you can tell anyone you like—sit down there . . . Sit down, sir, I say!"

Reluctantly I sat, torn between anger and fascination, hating myself for obeying.

"Tell anyone you like," he said. "I don't care. I wouldn't raise my little finger to stop you. Because I don't owe anyone a thing, son. Who, Negroes? Negroes don't control this school or much of anything else—haven't you learned even that? No, sir, they don't control this school, nor white folk either. True they *support* it, but *I* control it. I's big and black and I say 'Yes, suh' as loudly as any burrhead when it's convenient, but I'm still the king down here. I don't care how much it appears otherwise. Power doesn't have to show off. Power is confident, self-assuring, self-starting and self-stopping, self-warming and self-justifying. When you have it, you know it. Let the Negroes snicker and the crackers laugh! Those are the facts, son. The only ones I even pretend to please are *big* white folk, and even those I control more than they control me. This is a power set-up, son, and I'm at the controls. You think about that. When you buck against me, you're bucking against power, rich white folk's power, the nation's power—which means government power!"

He paused to let it sink in and I waited, feeling a numb, violent outrage.

"And I'll tell you something your sociology teachers are afraid to tell you," he said. "If there weren't men like me running schools like this, there'd be no South. Nor North, either. No, and there'd be no country—not as it is today. You think about that, son." He laughed. "With all your speech-making and studying I thought you understood something. But you . . . All right, go ahead. See Norton. You'll find that *he* wants you disciplined; he might not know it, but he does. Because he knows that I know what is best for his interests. You're a black educated fool, son. These white folk have news-papers, magazines, radios, spokesmen to get their ideas across. If they want to tell the world a lie, they can tell it so well that it becomes the truth; and if I tell them that you're lying, they'll tell the world even if you prove you're telling the truth. Be-cause it's the kind of lie they want to hear . . ."

I heard the high thin laugh again. "You're nobody, son. You don't exist—can't you see that? The white folk tell every-body what to think—except men like me. I tell *them*; that's my life, telling white folk how to think about the things I know about. Shocks you, doesn't it? Well, that's the way it is. It's a nasty deal and I don't always like it myself. But you listen to me: I didn't make it, and I know that I can't change it. But I've made my place in it and I'll have every Negro in the country hanging on tree limbs by morning if it means staying where I am."

He was looking me in the eye now, his voice charged and sincere, as though uttering a confession, a fantastic reve-lation which I could neither believe nor deny. Cold drops of sweat moved at a glacier's pace down my spine . . .

"I mean it, son," he said. "I had to be strong and pur-poseful to get where I am. I had to wait and plan and lick around . . . Yes, I had to act the nigger!" he said, adding an-other fiery, "Yes!"

"I don't even insist that it was worth it, but now I'm here and I mean to stay—after you win the game, you take the prize and you keep it, protect it; there's nothing else to do." He shrugged. "A man gets old winning his place, son.

So you go ahead, go tell your story; match your truth against my truth, because what I've said is truth, the broader truth. Test it, try it out . . . When I started out I was a young fellow . . ."

But I no longer listened, nor saw more than the play of light upon the metallic disks of his glasses, which now seemed to float within the disgusting sea of his words. Truth, truth, what was truth? Nobody I knew, not even my own mother, would believe me if I tried to tell them. Nor would I tomorrow, I thought, nor would I . . . I gazed helplessly at the grain of the desk, then past his head to the case of loving cups behind his chair. Above the case a portrait of the Founder looked non-committally down.

"Hee, hee!" Bledsoe laughed. "Your arms are too short to box with me, son. And I haven't had to really clip a young Negro in years. No," he said getting up, "they haven't been so cocky as they used to."

This time I could barely move, my stomach was knotted and my kidneys ached. My legs were rubbery. For three years I had thought of myself as a man and here with a few words he'd made me as helpless as an infant. I pulled myself up . . .

"Wait, hold on a second," he said, looking at me like a man about to flip a coin. "I like your spirit, son. You're a fighter, and I like that; you just lack judgment, though lack of judgment can ruin you. That's why I have to penalize you, son. I know how you feel, too. You don't want to go home to be humiliated, I understand that, because you have some vague notions about dignity. In spite of me, such notions seep in along with the gimcrack teachers and northern-trained idealists. Yes, and you have some white folk backing you and you don't want to face them because nothing is worse for a black man than to be humiliated by white folk. I know all about that too; ole doc's been 'buked and scorned and all of that. I don't just *sing* about it in chapel, I *know* about it. But you'll get over it; it's foolish and expensive and a lot of dead weight. You let the white folk worry about pride and dignity—you learn where you are and get yourself power, influence, contacts with powerful and influential people—then stay in the dark and use it!"

How long will I stand here and let him laugh at me, I thought, holding on to the back of the chair, how long?

"You're a nervy little fighter, son," he said, "and the race needs good, smart, disillusioned fighters. Therefore I'm going to give you a hand—maybe you'll feel that I'm giving you my left hand after I'm struck you with my right—if you think I'm the kind of man who'd lead with his right, which I'm most certainly not. But that's all right too, take it or leave it. I want you to go to New York for the summer and save your pride—and your money. You go there and earn your next year's fees, understand?"

I nodded, unable to speak, whirling about furiously within myself, trying to deal with him, to fit what he was saying to what he had said . . .

"I'll give you letters to some of the school's friends to see that you get work," he said. "But this time, use your judgment, keep your eyes open, get in the swing of things! Then, if you make good, perhaps . . . well, perhaps . . . It's up to you."

His voice stopped as he stood, tall and black and disk-eyed, huge.

"That's all, young man," he said, his tone abrupt, official. "You have two days in which to close your affairs."

"Two days?"

"Two days!" he said.

I went down the steps and up the walk in the dark, making it out of the building just before it bent me double beneath the wisteria that hung from the trees on ropelike vines.

Almost a total disembowelment and when it paused I looked up through the trees arched high and cool above me to see a whirling, double-imaged moon. My eyes were out of focus. I started toward my room, covering one eye with my hand to avoid crashing into trees and lampposts projected into my path. I went on, tasting bile and thankful that it was night with no one to witness my condition. My stomach felt raw. From somewhere across the quiet of the campus the sound of an old guitar-blues plucked from an out-of-tune piano drifted toward me like a lazy, shimmering wave, like the echoed whistle of a lonely train, and my head went over again, against a tree this time, and I could hear it splattering the flowering vines.

When I could move, my head started to whirl in a circle. The day's events flowed past. Trueblood, Mr. Norton, Dr. Bledsoe and the Golden Day swept around my mind in a mad surreal whirl. I stood in the path holding my eye and trying to push back the day, but each time I floundered upon Dr. Bledsoe's decision. It still echoed in my mind and it was real and it was final. Whatever my responsibility was for what had occurred, I knew that I would pay for it, knew that I would be expelled, and the very idea stabbed my insides again. I stood there on the moonlit walk, trying to think ahead to its effects, imagining the satisfaction of those who envied my success, the shame and disappointment of my parents. I would never live down my disgrace. My white friends would be disgusted and I recalled the fear that hung over all those who had no protection from powerful whites.

How had I come to this? I had kept unswervingly to the path placed before me, had tried to be exactly what I was expected to be, had done exactly what I was expected to do—yet, instead of winning the expected reward, here I was stumbling along, holding on desperately to one of my eyes in order to keep from bursting out my brain against some familiar object swerved into my path by my distorted vision. And now to drive me wild I felt suddenly that my grandfather was hovering over me, grinning triumphantly out of the dark. I simply could not endure it. For, despite my anguish and anger, I knew of no other way of living, nor other forms of success available to such as me. I was so completely a part of that existence that in the end I had to make my peace. It was either that or admit that my grandfather had made sense. Which was impossible, for though I still believed myself innocent, I saw that the only alternative to permanently facing the world of Trueblood and the Golden Day was to accept the responsibility for what had happened. Somehow, I convinced myself, I had violated the code and thus would have to submit to punishment. Dr. Bledsoe is right, I told myself, he's right; the school and what it stands for have to be protected. There was no other way, and no matter how much I suffered I would pay my debt as quickly as possible and return to building my career . . .

Back in my room I counted my savings, some fifty dollars, and decided to get to New York as quickly as possible. If Dr. Bledsoe didn't change his mind about helping me get a job, it would be enough to pay my room and board at Men's House, about which I had learned from fellows who lived there during their summer vacations. I would leave in the morning.

So while my roommate grinned and mumbled unaware in his sleep I packed my bags.

NEXT morning I was up before the bugle sounded and already on a bench in Dr. Bledsoe's outer office when he appeared. The jacket of his blue serge suit was open, revealing a heavy gold chain linked between his vest pockets as he moved toward me with a noiseless tread. He passed without seeming to see me. Then as he reached his office door he said, "I haven't changed my mind about you, boy. And I don't intend to!"

"Oh, I didn't come for that, sir," I said, seeing him turn quickly, looking down upon me, his eyes quizzical.

"Very well, as long as you understand that. Come in and state your business. I have work to do."

I waited before the desk, watching him place his homburg on an old brass hall-tree. Then he sat before me, making a cage of his fingers and nodding for me to begin.

My eyes burned and my voice sounded unreal. "I'd like to leave this morning, sir," I said.

His eyes retreated. "Why this morning?" he said. "I gave you until tomorrow. Why the hurry?"

"It isn't hurry, sir. But since I have to leave I'd like to get going. Staying until tomorrow won't change matters . . ."

"No, it won't," he said. "That's good sense and you have my permission. And what else?"

"That's all, sir, except that I want to say that I'm sorry for what I did and that I hold no hard feelings. What I did was unintentional, but I'm in agreement with my punishment."

He touched his fingertips together, the thick fingers meeting delicately, his face without expression. "That's the proper attitude," he said. "In other words, you don't intend to become bitter, is that it?"

"Yes, sir."

"Yes, I can see that you're beginning to learn. That's good. Two things our people must do is accept responsibility for their acts and avoid becoming bitter." His voice rose with the conviction of his chapel speeches. "Son, if you don't become bitter, nothing can stop you from success. Remember that."

"I shall, sir," I said. Then my throat thickened and I hoped he would bring up the matter of a job himself.

Instead, he looked at me impatiently and said, "Well? I have work to do. My permission is granted."

"Well, sir, I'd like to ask a favor of you . . ."

"Favor," he said shrewdly. "Now that's another matter. What kind of favor?"

"It isn't much, sir. You suggested that you would put me in touch with some of the trustees who would give me a job. I'm willing to do anything."

"Oh, yes," he said, "yes, of course."

He seemed to think for a moment, his eyes studying the objects on his desk. Then touching the shackle gently with his index finger, he said, "Very well. When do you intend to leave?"

"By the first bus, if possible, sir."

"Are you packed?"

"Yes, sir."

"Very well. Go get your bags and return here in thirty minutes. My secretary will give you some letters addressed to several friends of the school. One of them will do something for you."

"Thanks, sir. Thank you very much," I said as he stood.

"That's all right," he said. "The school tries to look out for its own. Only one thing more. These letters will be sealed; don't open them if you want help. White folk are strict about such things. The letters will introduce you and request them to help you with a job. I'll do my best for you and it isn't necessary for you to open them, understand?"

"Oh, I wouldn't think of opening them, sir," I said.

"Very well, the young lady will have them for you when you return. What about your parents, have you informed them?"

"No, sir, it might make them feel too bad if I told them I was expelled, so I plan to write them after I get there and get a job . . ."

"I see. Perhaps that is best."

"Well, good-bye, sir," I said, extending my hand.

"Good-bye," he said. His hand was large and strangely limp.

He pressed a buzzer as I turned to leave. His secretary brushed past me as I went through the door.

The letters were waiting when I returned, seven of them, addressed to men with impressive names. I looked for Mr. Norton's but his was not among them. Placing them carefully in my inside pocket, I grabbed my bags and hurried for the bus.

Chapter seven

The station was empty, but the ticket window was open and a porter in a gray uniform was pushing a broom. I bought my ticket and climbed into the bus. There were only two passengers seated at the rear of the red and nickel interior, and I suddenly felt that I was dreaming. It was the vet, who gave me a smile of recognition; an attendant sat beside him.

"Welcome, young man," he called. "Imagine, Mr. Crenshaw," he said to the attendant, "we have a traveling companion!"

"Morning," I said reluctantly. I looked around for a seat away from them, but although the bus was almost empty, only the rear was reserved for us and there was nothing to do but move back with them. I didn't like it; the vet was too much a part of an experience which I was already trying to blot out of my consciousness. His way of talking to Mr. Norton had been a foreshadowing of my misfortune—just as I had sensed that it would be. Now having accepted my punishment, I wanted to remember nothing connected with Trueblood or the Golden Day.

Crenshaw, a much smaller man than Supercargo, said nothing. He was not the type usually sent out to accompany violent cases and I was glad until I remembered that the only violent thing about the vet was his tongue. His mouth had already gotten me into trouble and now I hoped he wouldn't turn it upon the white driver—*that* was apt to get us killed. What was he doing on the bus anyway? God, how had Dr. Bledsoe worked that fast? I stared at the fat man.

"How did your friend Mr. Norton make out?" he asked.

"He's okay," I said.

"No more fainting spells?"

"No."

"Did he bawl you out for what happened?"

"He didn't blame me," I said.

"Good. I think I shocked him more than anything else he saw at the Golden Day. I hoped I hadn't caused you trouble. School isn't out so soon, is it?"

"Not quite," I said lightly. "I'm leaving early in order to take a job."

"Wonderful! At home?"

"No, I thought I might make more money in New York."

"New York!" he said. "That's not a place, it's a dream. When I was your age it was Chicago. Now all the little black boys run away to New York. Out of the fire into the melting pot. I can see you after you've lived in Harlem for three months. Your speech will change, you'll talk a lot about 'college,' you'll attend lectures at the Men's House . . . you might even meet a few white folks. And listen," he said, leaning close to whisper, "you might even dance with a white girl!"

"I'm going to New York to work," I said, looking around me. "I won't have time for that."

"You will though," he teased. "Deep down you're thinking about the freedom you've heard about up North, and you'll try it once, just to see if what you've heard is true."

"There's other kinds of freedom beside some ole white trash women," Crenshaw said. "He might want to see him some shows and eat in some of them big restaurants."

The vet grinned. "Why, of course, but remember, Crenshaw, he's only going to be there a few months. Most of the time he'll be working, and so much of his freedom will have to be symbolic. And what will be his or any man's most easily accessible symbol of freedom? Why, a woman, of course. In twenty minutes he can inflate that symbol with all the freedom which he'll be too busy working to enjoy the rest of the time. He'll see."

I tried to change the subject. "Where are you going?" I asked.

"To Washington, D.C.," he said.

"Then you're cured?"

"Cured? There is no cure—"

"He's being transferred," said Crenshaw.

"Yes, I'm headed for St. Elizabeth's," the vet said. "The ways of authority are indeed mysterious. For a year I've tried to get transferred, then this morning I'm suddenly told to pack. I can't but wonder if our little conversation with your friend Mr. Norton had something to do with it."

"How could he have anything to do with it?" I said, remembering Dr. Bledsoe's threat.

"How could he have anything to do with your being on this bus?" he said.

He winked. His eyes twinkled. "All right, forget what I've said. But for God's sake, learn to look beneath the surface," he said. "Come out of the fog, young man. And remember you don't have to be a complete fool in order to succeed. Play the game, but don't believe in it—that much you owe yourself. Even if it lands you in a strait jacket or a padded cell. Play the game, but play it your own way—part of the time at least. Play the game, but raise the ante, my boy. Learn how it operates, learn how *you* operate—I wish I had time to tell you only a fragment. We're an ass-backward people, though. You might even beat the game. It's really a very crude affair. Really pre-Renaissance—and that game has been analyzed, put down in books. But down here they've forgotten to take care of the books and that's your opportunity. You're hidden right out in the open—that is, you would be if you only realized it. They wouldn't see you because they don't expect you to know anything, since they believe they've taken care of that . . ."

"Man, who's this *they* you talking so much about?" said Crenshaw.

The vet looked annoyed. "They?" he said. "They? Why, the same *they* we always mean, the white folks, authority, the gods, fate, circumstances—the force that pulls your strings until you refuse to be pulled any more. The big man who's never there, where you think he is."

Crenshaw grimaced. "You talk too damn much, man," he said. "You talk and you don't say nothing."

"Oh, I have a lot to say, Crenshaw. I put into words things which most men feel, if only slightly. Sure, I'm a compulsive talker of a kind, but I'm really more clown than fool. But, Crenshaw," he said, rolling a wand of the newspaper which lay across his knees, "you don't realize what's happening. Our young friend is going North for the first time! It *is* for the first time, isn't it?"

"You're right," I said.

"Of course. Were you ever North before, Crenshaw?"

"I been all over the country," Crenshaw said. "I know how they do wherever they do it. And I know how to act too. Besides, you ain't going North, not the real North. You going to Washington. It's just another southern town."

"Yes, I know," the vet said, "but think of what this means for the young fellow. He's going free, in the broad daylight and alone. I can remember when young fellows like him had first to commit a crime, or be accused of one, before they tried such a thing. Instead of leaving in the light of morning, they went in the dark of night. And no bus was fast enough—isn't that so, Crenshaw?"

Crenshaw stopped unwrapping a candy bar and looked at him sharply, his eyes narrowed. "How the hell I know?" he said.

"I'm sorry, Crenshaw," the vet said. "I thought that as a man of experience . . ."

"Well, I ain't had that experience. I went North of my own free will."

"But haven't you *beard* of such cases?"

"Hearing ain't 'speriencing," Crenshaw said.

"No, it isn't. But since there's always an element of crime in freedom—"

"I ain't committed no crime!"

"I didn't mean that you had," the vet said. "I apologize. Forget it."

Crenshaw took an angry bite from his candy bar, mumbling, "I wish you'd hurry up and git depressive, maybe then you won't talk so damn much."

"Yes, doctor," the vet said mockingly. "I'll be depressive soon enough, but while you eat your candy just allow me to chew the rag; there's a kind of substance in it."

"Aw, quit trying to show off your education," Crenshaw said. "You riding back here in the Jim Crow just like me. Besides, you're a nut."

The vet winked at me, continuing his flow of words as the bus got under way. We were going at last and I took a last longing look as the bus shot around the highway which circled the school. I turned and watched it recede from the rear window; the sun caught its treetops, bathed its low-set buildings and ordered grounds. Then it was gone. In less than five minutes the spot of earth which I identified with the best of all possible worlds was gone, lost within the wild uncultivated countryside. A flash of movement drew my eye to the side of the highway now, and I saw a moccasin wiggle swiftly along the gray concrete, vanishing into a length of iron pipe that lay beside the road. I watched the flashing past of cotton fields and cabins, feeling that I was moving into the unknown.

The vet and Crenshaw prepared to change busses at the next stop, and upon leaving, the vet placed his hand upon my shoulder and looked at me with kindness, and, as always, he smiled.

"Now is the time for offering fatherly advice," he said, "but I'll have to spare you that—since I guess I'm nobody's father except my own. Perhaps that's the advice to give you: Be your own father, young man. And remember, the world is possibility if only you'll discover it. Last of all, leave the Mr. Nortons alone, and if you don't know what I mean, think about it. Farewell."

I watched him following Crenshaw through the group of passengers waiting to get on, a short, comical figure turning to wave, then disappearing through the door of the red brick terminal. I sat back with a sigh of relief, yet once the passengers were aboard and the bus under way again, I felt sad and utterly alone.

NOT UNTIL we were sailing through the Jersey countryside did my spirits begin to rise. Then my old confidence and optimism revived, and I tried to plan my time in the North. I would work hard and serve my employer so well that he would shower Dr. Bledsoe with favorable reports. And I would save my money and return in the fall full of New York culture. I'd be indisputably the leading campus figure. Perhaps I would attend Town Meeting, which I had heard over the radio. I'd learn the platform tricks of the leading speakers. And I would make the best of my contacts. When I met the big men to whom my letters were addressed I would put on my best manner. I would speak softly, in my most polished tones, smile agreeably and be most polite; and I would remember that if he ("he" meant any of the important gentlemen) should begin a topic of conversation (I would never begin a subject of my own) which I found unfamiliar, I would smile and agree. My shoes would be polished, my suit pressed, my hair dressed (not too much grease) and parted on the right side; my nails would be clean and my armpits well deodorized—you had to watch the last item. You couldn't allow them to think *all* of us smelled bad. The very thought of my contacts gave me a feeling of sophistication, of worldliness, which, as I fingered the seven important letters in my pocket, made me feel light and expansive.

I dreamed with my eyes gazing blankly upon the landscape until I looked up to see a Red Cap frowning down. "Buddy, are you getting off here?" he said. "If so, you better get started."

"Oh, sure," I said, beginning to move. "Sure, but how do you get to Harlem?"

"That's easy," he said. "You just keep heading north."

And while I got down my bags and my prize brief case, still as shiny as the night of the battle royal, he instructed me how to take the subway, then I struggled through the crowd.

Moving into the subway I was pushed along by the milling salt-and-pepper mob, seized in the back by a burly, blue-uniformed attendant about the size of Supercargo, and crammed, bags and all, into a train that was so crowded that everyone seemed to stand with his head back and his eyes bulging, like chickens frozen at the sound of danger. Then the door banged behind me and I was crushed against a huge woman in black who shook her head and smiled while I stared with horror at a large mole that arose out of the oily whiteness of her skin like a black mountain sweeping out of a rainwet plain. And all the while I could feel the rubbery softness of her flesh against the length of my body. I could neither turn sideways nor back away, nor set down my bags. I was trapped, so close that simply by nodding my head, I might have brushed her lips with mine. I wanted desperately to raise my hands to show her that it was against my will. I kept expecting her to scream, until finally the car lurched and I was able to free my left arm. I closed my eyes, holding desperately to my lapel. The car roared and swayed, pressing me hard against her, but when I took a furtive glance around no one was paying me the slightest attention. And even she seemed lost in her own thoughts. The train seemed to plunge downhill now, only to lunge to a stop that shot me out upon a platform feeling like something regurgitated from the belly of a frantic whale. Wrestling with my bags, I swept along with the crowd, up the stairs into the hot street. I didn't care where I was, I would walk the rest of the way.

For a moment I stood before a shop window staring at my own reflection in the glass, trying to recover from the ride against the woman. I was limp, my clothing wet. "But you're up North now," I told myself, "up North." Yes, but suppose she had screamed . . . The next time I used the subway I'd always be sure to enter with my hands grasping my lapels and I'd keep them there until I left the train. Why, my God, they must have riots on those things all the time. Why hadn't I read about them?

I had never seen so many black people against a background of brick buildings, neon signs, plate glass and roaring traffic—not even on trips I had made with the debating team to New Orleans, Dallas or Birmingham. They were everywhere. So many, and moving along with so much tension and noise that I wasn't sure whether they were about to celebrate a holiday or join in a street fight. There were even black girls behind the counters of the Five and Ten as I passed. Then at the street intersection I had the shock of seeing a black policeman directing traffic—and there were white drivers in the traffic who obeyed his signals as though it was the most natural thing in the world. Sure I had heard of it, but this was *real.* My courage returned. This really was Harlem, and now all the stories which I had heard of the city-within-a-city leaped alive in my mind. The vet had been right: For me this was not a city of realities, but of dreams; perhaps because I had always thought of my life as being confined to the South. And now as I struggled through the lines of people a new world of possibility suggested itself to me faintly, like a small voice that was barely audible in the roar of city sounds. I moved wide-eyed, trying to take the bombardment of impressions. Then I stopped still.

It was ahead of me, angry and shrill, and upon hearing it I had a sensation of shock and fear such as I had felt as a child when surprised by my father's voice. An emptiness widened in my stomach. Before me a gathering of people were almost blocking the walk, while above them a short squat man shouted angrily from a ladder to which were attached a collection of small American flags.

"We gine chase 'em out," the man cried. "Out!"

"Tell 'em about it, Ras, mahn," a voice called.

And I saw the squat man shake his fist angrily over the uplifted faces, yelling something in a staccato West Indian accent, at which the crowd yelled threateningly. It was as though a riot would break any minute, against whom I didn't know. I was puzzled, both by the effect of his voice upon me and by the obvious anger of the crowd. I had never seen so many black men angry in public before, and yet others passed the gathering by without even a glance. And as I came alongside, I saw two white policemen talking quietly with one another, their backs turned as they laughed at some joke. Even when the shirt-sleeved crowd cried out in angry affirmation of some remark of the speaker, they paid no attention. I was stunned. I stood gaping at the policemen, my bags settling upon the middle of the walk, until one of them happened to see me and nudged the other, who chewed lazily upon a wad of gum.

"What can we do for you, bud?" he said.

"I was just wondering . . ." I said before I caught myself.

"Yeah?"

"I was just wondering how to get to Men's House, sir," I said.

"Is that all?"

"Yes, sir," I stammered.

"You sure?"

"Yes, sir."

"He's a stranger," the other said. "Just coming to town, bud?"

"Yes, sir," I said, "I just got off the subway."

"You did, huh? Well, you want to be careful."

"Oh, I will, sir."

"That's the idea. Keep it clean," he said, and directed me to Men's House.

I thanked them and hurried on. The speaker had become more violent than before and his remarks were about the government. The clash between the calm of the rest of the street and the passion of the voice gave the scene a strange out-of-joint quality, and I was careful not to look back lest I see a riot flare.

I reached Men's House in a sweat, registered, and went immediately to my room. I would have to take Harlem a little at a time.

Chapter eight

It was a clean little room with a dark orange bedspread. The chair and dresser were maple and there was a Gideon Bible lying upon a small table. I dropped my bags and sat on the bed. From the street below came the sound of traffic, the larger sound of the subway, the smaller, more varied sounds of voices. Alone in the room, I could hardly believe that I was so far away from home, yet there was nothing familiar in my surroundings. Except the Bible; I picked it up and sat back on the bed, allowing its blood-red-edged pages to ripple beneath my thumb. I remembered how Dr. Bledsoe could quote from the Book during his speeches to the student body on Sunday nights. I turned to the book of Genesis, but could not read. I thought of home and the attempts my father had made to institute family prayer, the gathering around the stove at mealtime and kneeling with heads bowed over the seats of our chairs, his voice quavering and full of church-house rhetoric and verbal humility. But this made me homesick and I put the Bible aside. This was New York. I had to get a job and earn money.

I took off my coat and hat and took my packet of letters and lay back upon the bed, drawing a feeling of importance from reading the important names. What was inside, and how could I open them undetected? They were tightly sealed. I had read that letters were sometimes steamed open, but I had no steam. I gave it up, I really didn't need to know their contents and it would not be honorable or safe to tamper with Dr. Bledsoe. I knew already that they concerned me and were addressed to some of the most important men in the whole country. That was enough. I caught myself wishing for someone to show the letters to, someone who could give me a proper reflection of my importance. Finally, I went to the mirror and gave myself an admiring smile as I spread the letters upon the dresser like a hand of high trump cards.

Then I began to map my campaign for the next day. First, I would have a shower, then get breakfast. All this very early. I'd have to move fast. With important men like that you had to be on time. If you made an appointment with one of them, you couldn't bring them any slow c.p. (colored people's) time. Yes, and I would have to get a watch. I would do everything to schedule. I recalled the heavy gold chain that hung between Dr. Bledsoe's vest pockets and the air with which he snapped his watch open to consult the time, his lips pursed, chin pulled in so that it multiplied, his forehead wrinkled. Then he'd clear his throat and give a deeply intoned order, as though each syllable were pregnant with nuances of profoundly important meaning. I recalled my expulsion, feeling quick anger and attempting to suppress it immediately; but now I was not quite successful, my resentment stuck out at the edges, making me uncomfortable. Maybe it was best, I thought hastily. Maybe if it hadn't happened I would never have received an opportunity to meet such important men face to face. In my mind's eye I continued to see him gazing into his watch, but now he was joined by another figure; a younger figure, myself; become shrewd, suave and dressed not in somber garments (like his old-fashioned ones) but in a dapper suit of rich material, cut fashionably, like those of the men you saw in magazine ads, the junior executive types in *Esquire*. I imagined myself making a speech and caught in striking poses by flashing cameras, snapped at the end of some period of dazzling eloquence. A younger version of the doctor, less crude, indeed polished. I would hardly ever speak above a whisper and I would always be—yes, there was no other word, I would be *charming*. Like Ronald Colman. What a voice! Of course you couldn't speak that way in the South, the white folks wouldn't like it, and the Negroes would say that you were "putting on." But here in the North I would slough off my southern ways of speech. Indeed, I would have one way of speaking in the North and another in the South. Give them what they wanted down South, that was the way. If Dr. Bledsoe could do it, so could I. Before going to bed that night I wiped off my brief case with a clean towel and placed the letters carefully inside.

The next morning I took an early subway into the Wall Street district, selecting an address that carried me almost to the end of the island. It was dark with the tallness of the buildings and the narrow streets. Armored cars with alert guards went past as I looked for the number. The streets were full of hurrying people who walked as though they had been wound up and were directed by some unseen control. Many of the men carried dispatch cases and brief cases and I gripped mine with a sense of importance. And here and there I saw Negroes who hurried along with leather pouches strapped to their wrists. They reminded me fleetingly of prisoners carrying their leg irons as they escaped from a chain gang. Yet they seemed aware of some self-importance, and I wished to stop one and ask him why he was chained to his pouch. Maybe they got paid well for this, maybe they were chained to money. Perhaps the man with rundown heels ahead of me was chained to a million dollars!

I looked to see if there were policemen or detectives with drawn guns following, but there was no one. Or if so, they were hidden in the hurrying crowd. I wanted to follow one of the men to see where he was going. Why did they trust him with all that money? And what would happen if he should disappear with it? But of course no one would be that foolish. This was Wall Street. Perhaps it was guarded, as I had been told post offices were guarded, by men who looked down at you through peepholes in the ceiling and walls, watching you constantly, silently waiting for a wrong move. Perhaps even now an eye had picked me up and watched my every movement. Maybe the face of that clock set in the gray building across the street hid a pair of searching eyes. I hurried to my address and was challenged by the sheer height of the white stone with its sculptured bronze façade. Men and women hurried inside, and after staring for a moment I followed, taking the elevator and being pushed to the back of the car. It rose like a rocket, creating a sensation in my crotch as though an important part of myself had been left below in the lobby.

At the last stop I left the car and went down a stretch of marble hallway until I found the door marked with the trustee's name. But starting to enter I lost my nerve and backed away. I looked down the hall. It was empty. White folks were funny; Mr. Bates might not wish to see a Negro the first thing in the morning. I turned and walked down the hall and looked out of the window. I would wait awhile.

Below me lay South Ferry, and a ship and two barges were passing out into the river, and far out and to the right I could make out the Statue of Liberty, her torch almost lost in the fog. Back along the shore, gulls soared through the mist above the docks, and down, so far below that it made me dizzy, crowds were moving. I looked back to a ferry passing the Statue of Liberty now, its backwash a curving line upon the bay and three gulls swooping down behind it.

Behind me the elevator was letting off passengers, and I heard the cheery voices of women going chattering down the hall. Soon I would have to go in. My uncertainty grew. My appearance worried me. Mr. Bates might not like my suit, or the cut of my hair, and my chance of a job would be lost. I looked at his name typed neatly across the envelope and wondered how he earned his money. He was a millionaire, I knew. Maybe he had always been; maybe he was born a millionaire. Never before had I been so curious about money as now that I believed I was surrounded by it. Perhaps I would get a job here and after a few years would be sent up and down the streets with millions strapped to my arms, a trusted messenger. Then I'd be sent South again to head the college—just as the mayor's cook had been made principal of the school after she'd become too lame to stand before her stove. Only I wouldn't stay North that long; they'd need me before that . . . But now for the interview.

Entering the office I found myself face to face with a young woman who looked up from her desk as I glanced swiftly over the large light room, over the comfortable chairs, the ceiling-high bookcases with gold and leather bindings, past a series of portraits and back again, to meet her questioning eyes. She was alone and I thought, Well, at least I'm not too early . . .

"Good morning," she said, betraying none of the antagonism I had expected.

"Good morning," I said, advancing. How should I begin?

"Yes?"

"Is this Mr. Bates' office?" I said.

"Why, yes, it is," she said. "Have you an appointment?"

"No, ma'am," I said, and quickly hated myself for saying "ma'am" to so young a white woman, and in the North too. I removed the letter from my brief case, but before I could explain, she said,

"May I see it, please?"

I hesitated. I did not wish to surrender the letter except to Mr. Bates, but there was a command in the extended hand, and I obeyed. I surrendered it, expecting her to open it, but instead, after looking at the envelope she rose and disappeared behind a paneled door without a word.

Back across the expanse of carpet to the door which I had entered I noticed several chairs but was undecided to go there. I stood, my hat in my hand, looking around me. One wall caught my eyes. It was hung with three portraits of dignified old gentlemen in winged collars who looked down from their frames with an assurance and arrogance that I had never seen in any except white men and a few bad, razor-scarred Negroes. Not even Dr. Bledsoe, who had but to look around him without speaking to set the teachers to trembling, had such assurance. So these were the kind of men who stood behind him. How did they fit in with the southern white folks, with the men who gave me my scholarship? I was still staring, caught in the spell of power and mystery, when the secretary returned.

She looked at me oddly and smiled. "I'm very sorry," she said, "but Mr. Bates is just too busy to see you this morning and asks that you leave your name and address. You'll hear from him by mail."

I stood silent with disappointment. "Write it here," she said, giving me a card.

"I'm sorry," she said again as I scribbled my address and prepared to leave.

"I can be reached here at any time," I said.

"Very good," she said. "You should hear very soon."

She seemed very kind and interested, and I left in good spirits. My fears were groundless, there was nothing to it. This was New York.

I succeeded in reaching several trustees' secretaries during the days that followed, and all were friendly and encouraging. Some looked at me strangely, but I dismissed it since it didn't appear to be antagonism. Perhaps they're surprised to see someone like me with introductions to such important men, I thought. Well, there were unseen lines that ran from North to South, and Mr. Norton had called me his destiny . . . I swung my brief case with confidence.

With things going so well I distributed my letters in the mornings, and saw the city during the afternoons. Walking about the streets, sitting on subways beside whites, eating with them in the same cafeterias (although I avoided their tables) gave me the eerie, out-of-focus sensation of a dream. My clothes felt ill-fitting; and for all my letters to men of power, I was unsure of how I should act. For the first time, as I swung along the streets, I thought consciously of how I had conducted myself at home. I hadn't worried too much about whites as people. Some were friendly and some were not, and you tried not to offend either. But here they all seemed impersonal; and yet when most impersonal they startled me by being polite, by begging my pardon after brushing against me in a crowd. Still I felt that even when they were polite they hardly saw me, that they would have begged the pardon of Jack the Bear, never glancing his way if the bear happened to be walking along minding his business. It was confusing. I did not know if it was desirable or undesirable . . .

But my main concern was seeing the trustees and after more than a week of seeing the city and being vaguely encouraged by secretaries, I became impatient. I had distributed all but the letter to a Mr. Emerson, who I knew from the papers was away from the city. Several times I started down to see what had happened but changed my mind. I did not wish to seem too impatient. But time was becoming short. Unless I found work soon I would never earn enough to enter school by fall. I had already written home that I was working for a member of the trustee board, and the only letter I had received so far was one telling me how wonderful they thought it was and warning me against the ways of the *wicked* city. Now I couldn't write them for money without revealing that I had been lying about the job.

Finally I tried to reach the important men by telephone, only to receive polite refusals by their secretaries. But fortunately I still had the letter to Mr. Emerson. I decided to use it, but instead of handing it over to a secretary, I wrote a letter explaining that I had a message from Dr. Bledsoe and requesting an appointment. Maybe I've been wrong about the secretaries, I thought; maybe they destroyed the letters. I should have been more careful.

I thought of Mr. Norton. If only the last letter had been addressed to him. If only he lived in New York so that I could make a personal appeal! Somehow I felt closer to Mr. Norton, and felt that if he should see me, he would remember that it was I whom he connected so closely to his fate. Now it seemed ages ago and in a different season and a distant land. Actually, it was less than a month. I became energetic and wrote him a letter, expressing my belief that my future would be immeasurably different if only I could work for him; that he would be benefited as well as I. I was especially careful to allow some indication of my ability to come through the appeal. I spent several hours on the typing, destroying copy after copy until I had completed one that was immaculate, carefully phrased and most respectful. I hurried down and posted it before the final mail collection, suddenly seized with the dizzy conviction that it would bring results. I remained about the building for three days awaiting an answer. But the letter brought no reply. Nor, any more than a prayer unanswered by God, was it returned.

My doubts grew. Perhaps all was not well. I remained in my room all the next day. I grew conscious that I was afraid; more afraid here in my room than I had ever been in the South. And all the more, because here there was nothing concrete to lay it to. All the secretaries had been encouraging. In the evening I went out to a movie, a picture of frontier life with heroic Indian fighting and struggles against flood, storm and forest fire, with the out-numbered settlers winning each engagement; an epic of wagon trains rolling ever westward. I forgot myself (although there was no one like me taking part in the adventures) and left the dark room in a lighter mood. But that night I dreamed of my grandfather and awoke depressed. I walked out of the building with a queer feeling that I was playing a part in some scheme which I did not understand. Somehow I felt that Bledsoe and Norton were behind it, and all day I was inhibited in both speech and conduct, for fear that I might say or do something scandalous. But this was all fantastic, I told myself. I was being too impatient. I could wait for the trustees to make a move. Perhaps I was being subjected to a test of some kind. They hadn't told me the rules, I knew, but the feeling persisted. Perhaps my exile would end suddenly and I would be given a scholarship to return to the campus. But when? How long?

Something had to happen soon. I would have to find a job to tide me over. My money was almost gone and anything might happen. I had been so confident that I had failed to put aside the price of train fare home. I was miserable and I dared not talk to anyone about my problems; not even the officials at Men's House, for since they had learned that I was to be assigned to an important job, they treated me with a certain deference; therefore I was careful to hide my growing doubts. After all, I thought, I might have to ask for credit and I'll have to appear a good risk. No, the thing to do was to keep faith. I'd start out once more in the morning. Something was certain to happen tomorrow. And it did. I received a letter from Mr. Emerson.

Chapter   nine

It was a clear, bright day when I went out, and the sun burned warm upon my eyes. Only a few flecks of snowy cloud hung high in the morning-blue sky, and already a woman was hanging wash on a roof. I felt better walking along. A feeling of confidence grew. Far down the island the skyscrapers rose tall and mysterious in the thin, pastel haze. A milk truck went past. I thought of the school. What were they doing now on the campus? Had the moon sunk low and the sun climbed clear? Had the breakfast bugle blown? Did the bellow of the big seed bull awaken the girls in the dorms this morning as on most spring mornings when I was there—sounding clear and full above bells and bugles and early workaday sounds? I hurried along, encouraged by the memories, and suddenly I was seized with a certainty that today was the day. Something would happen. I patted my brief case, thinking of the letter inside. The last had been first—a good sign.

Close to the curb ahead I saw a man pushing a cart piled high with rolls of blue paper and heard him singing in a clear ringing voice. It was a blues, and I walked along behind him remembering the times that I had heard such singing at home. It seemed that here some memories slipped around my life at the campus and went far back to things I had long ago shut out of my mind. There was no escaping such reminders.

> *"She's got feet like a monkey*
> *Legs like a frog—Lawd, Lawd!*
> *But when she starts to loving me*
> *I holler Whoooo, God-dog!*
> *Cause I loves my baabay,*
> *Better than I do myself . . ."*

And as I drew alongside I was startled to hear him call to me:

"Looka-year, buddy . . ."

"Yes," I said, pausing to look into his reddish eyes.

"Tell me just one thing this very fine morning—Hey! Wait a minute, daddy-o, I'm going your way!"

"What is it?" I said.

"What I want to know is," he said, "is you got the *dog?*"

"Dog? What dog?"

"Sho," he said, stopping his cart and resting it on its support. "That's it. *Who—*" he halted to crouch with one foot on the curb like a country preacher about to pound his Bible— "*got . . . the . . . dog,*" his head snapping with each word like an angry rooster's.

I laughed nervously and stepped back. He watched me out of shrewd eyes. "Oh goddog, daddy-o," he said with a sudden bluster, "who got the damn dog? Now I know you from down home, how come you trying to act like you never heard that before! Hell, ain't nobody out here this morning but us colored— Why you trying to deny me?"

Suddenly I was embarrassed and angry. "Deny you? What do you mean?"

"Just answer the question. Is you got him, or ain't you?"

"*A dog?*"

"Yeah, *the* dog."

I was exasperated. "No, not this morning," I said and saw a grin spread over his face.

"Wait a minute, daddy. Now don't go get mad. Damn, man! I thought sho *you* had him," he said, pretending to disbelieve me. I started away and he pushed the cart beside me. And suddenly I felt uncomfortable. Somehow he was like one of the vets from the Golden Day . . .

"Well, maybe it's the other way round," he said. "Maybe he got holt to you."

"Maybe," I said.

"If he is, you lucky it's just a dog—'cause, man, I tell you I believe it's a bear that's got holt to me . . ."

"A bear?"

"Hell, yes! *The* bear. Caint you see these patches where he's been clawing at my behind?"

Pulling the seat of his Charlie Chaplin pants to the side, he broke into deep laughter.

"Man, this Harlem ain't nothing but a bear's den. But I tell you one thing," he said with swiftly sobering face, "it's the best place in the world for you and me, and if times don't get better soon I'm going to grab that bear and turn him every way but loose!"

"Don't let him get you down," I said.

"No, daddy-o, I'm going to start with one my own size!"

I tried to think of some saying about bears to reply, but remembered only Jack the Rabbit, Jack the Bear . . . who were both long forgotten and now brought a wave of homesickness.

I wanted to leave him, and yet I found a certain comfort in walking along beside him, as though we'd walked this way before through other mornings, in other places . . .

"What is all that you have there?" I said, pointing to the rolls of blue paper stacked in the cart.

"Blueprints, man. Here I got 'bout a hundred pounds of blueprints and I couldn't build nothing!"

"What are they blueprints for?" I said.

"Damn if I know—everything. Cities, towns, country clubs. Some just buildings and houses. I got damn near enough to build me a house if I could live in a paper house like they do in Japan. I guess somebody done changed their plans," he added with a laugh. "I asked the man why they getting rid of all this stuff and he said they get in the way so every once in a while they have to throw 'em out to make place for the new plans. Plenty of these ain't never been used, you know."

"You have quite a lot," I said.

"Yeah, this ain't all neither. I got a coupla loads. There's a day's work right here in this stuff. Folks is always making plans and changing 'em."

"Yes, that's right," I said, thinking of my letters, "but that's a mistake. You have to stick to the plan."

He looked at me, suddenly grave. "You kinda young, daddy-o," he said.

I did not answer. We came to a corner at the top of a hill.

"Well, daddy-o, it's been good talking with a youngster from the old country but I got to leave you now. This here's one of them good ole downhill streets. I can coast a while and won't be worn out at the end of the day. Damn if I'm-a let 'em run *me* into my grave. I be seeing you again sometime— And you know something?"

"What's that?"

"I thought you was trying to deny me at first, but now I be pretty glad to see you . . ."

"I hope so," I said. "And you take it easy."

"Oh, I'll do that. All it takes to get along in this here man's town is a little shit, grit and mother-wit. And man, I was bawn with all three. In fact, I'maseventhsonofaseventhson-bawnwithacauloverbotheyesandraisedonblackcatboneshighjohn theconquerorandgreasygreens—" he spieled with twinkling eyes, his lips working rapidly. "You dig me, daddy?"

"You're going too fast," I said, beginning to laugh.

"Okay, I'm slowing down. I'll verse you but I won't curse you— My name is Peter Wheatstraw, I'm the Devil's only son-in-law, so roll 'em! You a southern boy, ain't you?" he said, his head to one side like a bear's.

"Yes," I said.

"Well, git with it! My name's Blue and I'm coming at you with a pitchfork. Fe Fi Fo Fum. Who wants to shoot the Devil one, Lord God Stingeroy!"

He had me grinning despite myself. I liked his words though I didn't know the answer. I'd known the stuff from child-hood, but had forgotten it; had learned it back of school . . .

"You digging me, daddy?" he laughed. "Haw, but look me up sometimes, I'm a piano player and a rounder, a whiskey drinker and a pavement pounder. I'll teach you some good bad habits. You'll need 'em. Good luck," he said.

"So long," I said and watched him going. I watched him push around the corner to the top of the hill, leaning sharp against the cart handle, and heard his voice arise, muffled now, as he started down.

She's got feet like a monkeeee
Legs

Legs, Legs like a maaad
Bulldog . . .

What does it mean, I thought. I'd heard it all my life but suddenly the strangeness of it came through to me. Was it about a woman or about some strange sphinxlike animal? Certainly his woman, *no* woman, fitted that description. And why describe anyone in such contradictory words? Was it a sphinx? Did old Chaplin-pants, old dusty-butt, love her or hate her; or was he merely singing? What kind of woman could love a dirty fellow like that, anyway? And how could even *he* love her if she were as repulsive as the song described? I moved ahead. Perhaps everyone loved someone; I didn't know, I couldn't give much thought to love; in order to travel far you had to be detached, and I had the long road back to the campus before me. I strode along, hearing the cartman's song become a lonesome, broad-toned whistle now that flowered at the end of each phrase into a tremulous, blue-toned chord. And in its flutter and swoop I heard the sound of a railroad train highballing it, lonely across the lonely night. He was the Devil's son-in-law, all right, and he was a man who could whistle a three-toned chord . . . God damn, I thought, they're a hell of a people! And I didn't know whether it was pride or disgust that suddenly flashed over me.

At the corner I turned into a drugstore and took a seat at the counter. Several men were bent over plates of food. Glass globes of coffee simmered above blue flames. I could feel the odor of frying bacon reach deep into my stomach as I watched the counterman open the doors of the grill and turn the lean strips over and bang the doors shut again. Above, facing the counter, a blonde, sunburned college girl smiled down, inviting all and sundry to drink a coke. The counterman came over.

"I've got something good for you," he said, placing a glass of water before me. "How about the special?"

"What's the special?"

"Pork chops, grits, one egg, hot biscuits and coffee!" He leaned over the counter with a look that seemed to say, There, that ought to excite you, boy. Could everyone see that I was southern?

"I'll have orange juice, toast and coffee," I said coldly.

He shook his head. "You fooled me," he said, slamming two pieces of bread into the toaster. "I would have sworn you were a pork chop man. Is that juice large or small?"

"Make it large," I said.

I looked silently at the back of his head as he sliced an orange, thinking, I should order the special and get up and walk out. Who does he think he is?

A seed floated in the thick layer of pulp that formed at the top of the glass. I fished it out with a spoon and then downed the acid drink, proud to have resisted the pork chop and grits. It was an act of discipline, a sign of the change that was coming over me and which would return me to college a more experienced man. I would be basically the same, I thought, stirring my coffee, yet so subtly changed as to intrigue those who had never been North. It always helped at the college to be a little different, especially if you wished to play a leading role. It made the folks talk about you, try to figure you out. I had to be careful though, not to speak too much like a northern Negro; they wouldn't like that. The thing to do, I thought with a smile, was to give them hints that whatever you did or said was weighted with broad and mysterious meanings that lay just beneath the surface. They'd love that. And the vaguer you told things, the better. You had to keep them guessing—just as they guessed about Dr. Bledsoe: Did Dr. Bledsoe stop at an expensive white hotel when he visited

New York? Did he go on parties with the trustees? And how did he act?

"Man, I bet he has him a fine time. They tell me when Ole Doc gets to New York he don't stop for the red lights. Say he drinks his good red whiskey and smokes his good black cigars and forgets all about you ole know-nothing-Negroes down here on the campus. Say when he gets up North he makes everybody call him Mister Doctor Bledsoe."

I smiled as the conversation came back to my mind. I felt good. Perhaps it was all to the best that I had been sent away. I had learned more. Heretofore all the campus gossip had seemed merely malicious and disrespectful; now I could see the advantage for Dr. Bledsoe. Whether we liked him or not, he was never out of our minds. That was a secret of leadership. Strange I should think of it now, for although I'd never given it any thought before, I seemed to have known it all along. Only here the distance from the campus seemed to make it clear and hard, and I thought it without fear. Here it came to hand just as easily as the coin which I now placed on the counter for my breakfast. It was fifteen cents and as I felt for a nickel I took out another dime, thinking, Is it an insult when one of us tips one of them?

I looked for the counterman, seeing him serving a plate of pork chops and grits to a man with a pale blond mustache, and stared; then I slapped the dime on the counter and left, annoyed that the dime did not ring as loud as a fifty-cent piece.

WHEN I reached the door of Mr. Emerson's office it occurred to me that perhaps I should have waited until the business of the day was under way, but I disregarded the idea and went ahead. My being early would be, I hoped, an indication of both how badly I wanted work, and how promptly I would perform any assignment given me. Besides, wasn't there a saying that the first person of the day to enter a business would get a bargain? Or was that said only of Jewish business? I removed the letter from my brief case. Was Emerson a Christian or a Jewish name?

Beyond the door it was like a museum. I had entered a large reception room decorated with cool tropical colors. One wall was almost covered by a huge colored map, from which narrow red silk ribbons stretched tautly from each division of the map to a series of ebony pedestals, upon which sat glass specimen jars containing natural products of the various countries. It was an importing firm. I looked around the room, amazed. There were paintings, bronzes, tapestries, all beautifully arranged. I was dazzled and so taken aback that I almost dropped my brief case when I heard a voice say, "And what would your business be?"

I saw the figure out of a collar ad: ruddy face with blond hair faultlessly in place, a tropical weave suit draped handsomely from his broad shoulders, his eyes gray and nervous behind clear-framed glasses.

I explained my appointment. "Oh, yes," he said. "May I see the letter, please?"

I handed it over, noticing the gold links in the soft white cuffs as he extended his hand. Glancing at the envelope he looked back at me with a strange interest in his eyes and said, "Have a seat, please. I'll be with you in a moment."

I watched him leave noiselessly, moving with a long hip-swinging stride that caused me to frown. I went over and took a teakwood chair with cushions of emerald-green silk, sitting stiffly with my brief case across my knees. He must have been sitting there when I came in, for on a table that held a beautiful dwarf tree I saw smoke rising from a cigarette in a jade ash tray. An open book, something called *Totem and Taboo*, lay beside it. I looked across to a lighted case of Chinese design which held delicate-looking statues of horses and birds, small vases and bowls, each set upon a carved wooden base. The room was quiet as a tomb—until suddenly there was a savage beating of wings and I looked toward the window to see an eruption of color, as though a gale had whipped up a bundle of brightly colored rags. It was an aviary of tropical birds set near one of the broad windows, through which, as the clapping of wings settled down, I could see two ships plying far out upon the greenish bay below. A large bird began a song, drawing my eyes to the throbbing of its bright blue, red and yellow throat. It was startling and I watched the surge and flutter of the birds as their colors flared for an instant like an unfurled oriental fan. I wanted to go and stand near the cage for a better view, but decided against it. It might seem unbusinesslike. I observed the room from the chair.

These folks are the Kings of the Earth! I thought, hearing the bird make an ugly noise. There was nothing like this at the college museum—or anywhere else that I had ever been. I recalled only a few cracked relics from slavery times: an iron pot, an ancient bell, a set of ankle-irons and links of chain, a primitive loom, a spinning wheel, a gourd for drinking, an ugly ebony African god that seemed to sneer (presented to the school by some traveling millionaire), a leather whip with copper brads, a branding iron with the double letter MM . . . Though I had seen them very seldom, they were vivid in my mind. They had not been pleasant and whenever I had visited the room I avoided the glass case in which they rested, preferring instead to look at photographs of the early days after the Civil War, the times close to those blind Barbee had described. And I had not looked even at these too often.

I tried to relax; the chair was beautiful but hard. Where had the man gone? Had he shown any antagonism when he saw me? I was annoyed that I had failed to see him first. One had to watch such details. Suddenly there came a harsh cry from the cage, and once more I saw a mad flashing as though the birds had burst into spontaneous flame, fluttering and beating their wings maliciously against the bamboo bars, only to settle down just as suddenly when the door opened and the blond man stood beckoning, his hand upon the knob. I went over, tense inside me. Had I been accepted or rejected?

There was a question in his eyes. "Come in, please," he said.

"Thank you," I said, waiting to follow him.

"Please," he said with a slight smile.

I moved ahead of him, sounding the tone of his words for a sign.

"I want to ask you a few questions," he said, waving my letter at two chairs.

"Yes, sir?" I said.

"Tell me, what is it that you're trying to accomplish?" he said.

"I want a job, sir, so that I can earn enough money to return to college in the fall."

"To your old school?"

"Yes, sir."

"I see." For a moment he studied me silently. "When do you expect to graduate?"

"Next year, sir. I've completed my junior classes . . ."

"Oh, you have? That's very good. And how old are you?"

"Almost twenty, sir."

"A junior at nineteen? You *are* a good student."

"Thank you, sir," I said, beginning to enjoy the interview.

"Were you an athlete?" he asked.

"No, sir . . ."

"You have the build," he said, looking me up and down. "You'd probably make an excellent runner, a sprinter."

"I've never tried, sir."

"And I suppose it's silly even to ask what you think of your Alma Mater?" he said.

"I think it's one of the best in the world," I said, hearing my voice surge with deep feeling.

"I know, I know," he said, with a swift displeasure that surprised me.

I became alert again as he mumbled something incomprehensible about "nostalgia for Harvard yard."

"But what if you were offered an opportunity to finish your work at some other college?" he said, his eyes widening behind his glasses. His smile had returned.

"*Another* college?" I asked, my mind beginning to whirl.

"Why, yes, say some school in New England . . ."

I looked at him speechlessly. Did he mean Harvard? Was this good or bad? Where was it leading? "I don't know, sir," I said cautiously. "I've never thought about it. I've only a year more, and, well, I know everyone at my old school and they know me . . ."

I came to a confused halt, seeing him look at me with a sigh of resignation. What was on his mind? Perhaps I had been too frank about returning to the college, maybe he was against our having a higher education . . . But hell, he's only a secretary . . . Or *is* he?

"I understand," he said calmly. "It was presumptuous of me to even suggest another school. I guess one's college is really a kind of mother and father . . . a sacred matter."

"Yes, sir. That's it," I said in hurried agreement.

His eyes narrowed. "But now I must ask you an embarrassing question. Do you mind?"

"Why, no, sir," I said nervously.

"I don't like to ask this, but it's quite necessary . . ." He leaned forward with a pained frown. "Tell me, did you *read* the letter which you brought to Mr. Emerson? This," he said, taking the letter from the table.

"Why, no, sir! It wasn't addressed to me, so naturally I wouldn't think of opening it . . ."

"Of course not, I know you wouldn't," he said, fluttering his hand and sitting erect. "I'm sorry and you must dismiss it, like one of those annoying personal questions you find so often nowadays on supposedly impersonal forms."

I didn't believe him. "But was it opened, sir? Someone might have gone into my things . . ."

"Oh, no, nothing like that. Please forget the question . . . And tell me, please, what are your plans after graduation?"

"I'm not sure, sir, I'd like to be asked to remain at the college as a teacher, or as a member of the administrative staff. And . . . Well . . ."

"Yes? And what else?"

"Well—er, I guess I'd really like to become Dr. Bledsoe's assistant . . ."

"Oh, I see," he said, sitting back and forming his mouth into a thin-lipped circle. "You're very ambitious."

"I guess I am, sir. But I'm willing to work hard."

"Ambition is a wonderful force," he said, "but sometimes it can be blinding . . . On the other hand, it can make you successful—like my father . . ." A new edge came into his voice and he frowned and looked down at his hands, which were trembling. "The only trouble with ambition is that it sometimes blinds one to realities . . . Tell me, how many of these letters do you have?"

"I had about seven, sir," I replied, confused by his new turn. "They're—"

"Seven!" He was suddenly angry.

"Yes, sir, that was all he gave me . . ."

"And how many of these gentlemen have you succeeded in seeing, may I ask?"

A sinking feeling came over me. "I haven't seen any of them personally, sir."

"And this is your last letter?"

"Yes, sir, it is, but I expect to hear from the others . . . They said—"

"Of course you will, and from all seven. They're all loyal Americans."

There was unmistakable irony in his voice now, and I didn't know what to say.

"Seven," he repeated mysteriously. "Oh, don't let me upset you," he said with an elegant gesture of self-disgust. "I had a difficult session with my analyst last evening and the slightest thing is apt to set me off. Like an alarm clock without control— Say!" he said, slapping his palms against his thighs. "What on earth does that mean?" Suddenly he was in a state. One side of his face had begun to twitch and swell.

I watched him light a cigarette, thinking, What on earth is this all about?

"Some things are just too unjust for words," he said, expelling a plume of smoke, "and too ambiguous for either speech or ideas. By the way, have you ever been to the Club Calamus?"

"I don't think I've ever heard of it, sir," I said.

"You haven't? It's very well known. Many of my Harlem friends go there. It's a rendezvous for writers, artists and all kinds of celebrities. There's nothing like it in the city, and by some strange twist it has a truly continental flavor."

"I've never been to a night club, sir. I'll have to go there to see what it's like after I've started earning some money," I said, hoping to bring the conversation back to the problem of jobs.

He looked at me with a jerk of his head, his face beginning to twitch again.

"I suppose I've been evading the issue again—as always. Look," he burst out impulsively. "Do you believe that two people, two strangers who have never seen one another before can speak with utter frankness and sincerity?"

"Sir?"

"Oh, damn! What I mean is, do you believe it possible for us, the two of us, to throw off the mask of custom and manners that insulate man from man, and converse in naked honesty and frankness?"

"I don't know what you mean exactly, sir," I said.

"Are you sure?"

"I . . ."

"Of course, of course. If I could only speak plainly! I'm confusing you. Such frankness just isn't possible because all our motives are impure. Forget what I just said. I'll try to put it this way—and remember this, please . . ."

My head spun. He was addressing me, leaning forward confidentially, as though he'd known me for years, and I remembered something my grandfather had said long ago: *Don't let no white man tell you his business, 'cause after he tells you he's liable to git shame he tole it to you and then he'll hate you. Fact is, he was hating you all the time . . .*

". . . I want to try to reveal a part of reality that is most important to you—but I warn you, it's going to hurt. No, let me finish," he said, touching my knee lightly and quickly removing his hand as I shifted my position.

"What I want to do is done very seldom, and, to be honest, it wouldn't happen now if I hadn't sustained a series of impossible frustrations. You see—well, I'm a thwarted . . . Oh, damn, there I go again, thinking only of myself . . . We're both frustrated, understand? Both of us, and I want to help you . . ."

"You mean you'll let me see Mr. Emerson?"

He frowned. "Please don't seem so happy about it, and don't leap to conclusions. I want to help, but there is a tyranny involved . . ."

"A *tyranny?*" My lungs tightened.

"Yes. That's a way of putting it. Because to help you I must disillusion you . . ."

"Oh, I don't think I mind, sir. Once I see Mr. Emerson, it'll be up to me. All I want to do is speak to him."

"*Speak* to him," he said, getting quickly to his feet and mashing his cigarette into the tray with shaking fingers. "No one speaks to him. *He* does the speaking—" Suddenly he broke off. "On second thought, perhaps you'd better leave me your address and I'll mail you Mr. Emerson's reply in the morning. He's really a very busy man."

His whole manner had changed.

"But you said . . ." I stood up, completely confused. Was he having fun with me? "Couldn't you let me talk to him for just five minutes?" I pleaded. "I'm sure I can convince him that I'm worthy of a job. And if there's someone who has tampered with my letter, I'll prove my identity . . . Dr. Bledsoe would—"

"Identity! My God! Who has any identity anymore anyway? It isn't so perfectly simple. Look," he said with an anguished gesture. "Will you trust me?"

"Why, yes, sir, I trust you."

He leaned forward. "Look," he said, his face working violently, "I was trying to tell you that I know many things about you—not you personally, but fellows like you. Not much, either, but still more than the average. With us it's still Jim and Huck Finn. A number of my friends are jazz musicians, and I've been around. I know the conditions under which you live— Why go back, fellow? There is so much you could do here where there is more freedom. You won't find what you're looking for when you return anyway; because so much is involved that you can't possibly know. Please don't misunderstand me; I don't say all this to impress you. Or to give myself some kind of sadistic catharsis. Truly, I don't. But I do know this world you're trying to contact—all its virtues and all its unspeakables— Ha, yes, unspeakables. I'm afraid my father considers *me* one of the unspeakables . . . I'm Huckleberry, you see . . ."

He laughed drily as I tried to make sense of his ramblings. *Huckleberry?* Why did he keep talking about that kid's story? I was puzzled and annoyed that he could talk to me this way because he stood between me and a job, the campus . . .

"But I only want a job, sir," I said. "I only want to make enough money to return to my studies."

"Of course, but surely you suspect there is more to it than that. Aren't you curious about what lies behind the face of things?"

"Yes, sir, but I'm mainly interested in a job."

"Of course," he said, "but life isn't that simple . . ."

"But I'm not bothered about all the other things, whatever they are, sir. They're not for me to interfere with and I'll be satisfied to go back to college and remain there as long as they'll allow me to."

"But I want to help you do what is best," he said. "What's *best*, mind you. Do you wish to do what's best for yourself?"

"Why, yes, sir. I suppose I do . . ."

"Then forget about returning to the college. Go somewhere else . . ."

"You mean leave?"

"Yes, forget it . . ."

"But you said that you would help me!"

"I did and I am—"

"But what about seeing Mr. Emerson?"

"Oh, God! Don't you see that it's best that you do *not* see him?"

Suddenly I could not breathe. Then I was standing, gripping my brief case. "What have you got against me?" I blurted. "What did I ever do to you? You never intended to let me see him. Even though I presented my letter of introduction. Why? Why? I'd never endanger *your* job—"

"No, no, no! Of course not," he cried, getting to his feet. "You've misunderstood me. You mustn't do that! God, there's too much misunderstanding. Please don't think I'm trying to prevent you from seeing my—from seeing Mr. Emerson out of prejudice . . ."

"Yes, sir, I do," I said angrily. "I was sent here by a friend of his. You read the letter, but still you refuse to let me see him, and now you're trying to get me to leave college. What kind of man are you, anyway? What have you got against me? You, a northern white man!"

He looked pained. "I've done it badly," he said, "but you must believe that I am trying to advise you what is best for you." He snatched off his glasses.

"But *I* know what's best for me," I said. "Or at least Dr. Bledsoe does, and if I can't see Mr. Emerson today, just tell me when I can and I'll be here . . ."

He bit his lips and shut his eyes, shaking his head from side to side as though fighting back a scream. "I'm sorry, really sorry that I started all of this," he said, suddenly calm. "It was foolish of me to try to advise you, but please, you mustn't believe that I'm against you . . . or your race. I'm your friend.

Some of the finest people I know are Neg—Well, you see, Mr. Emerson is my father."

"Your father!"

"My father, yes, though I would have preferred it otherwise. But he is, and I could arrange for you to see him. But to be utterly frank, I'm incapable of such cynicism. It would do you no good."

"But I'd like to take my chances, Mr. Emerson, sir. . . . This is very important to me. My whole career depends upon it."

"But you *have* no chance," he said.

"But Dr. Bledsoe sent me here," I said, growing more excited. "I *must* have a chance . . ."

"Dr. Bledsoe," he said with distaste. "He's like my . . . he ought to be horsewhipped! Here," he said, sweeping up the letter and thrusting it crackling toward me. I took it, looking into his eyes that burned back at me.

"Go on, read it," he cried excitedly. "Go on!"

"But I wasn't asking for this," I said.

"Read it!"

My dear Mr. Emerson:

The bearer of this letter is a former student of ours (I say *former* because he shall never, under any circumstances, be enrolled as a student here again) who has been expelled for a most serious defection from our strictest rules of deportment.

Due, however, to circumstances the nature of which I shall explain to you in person on the occasion of the next meeting of the board, it is to the best interests of the college that this young man have no knowledge of the finality of his expulsion. For it is indeed his hope to return here to his classes in the fall. However, it is to the best interests of the great work which we are dedicated to perform, that he continue undisturbed in these vain hopes while remaining as far as possible from our midst.

This case represents, my dear Mr. Emerson, one of the rare, delicate instances in which one for whom we held great expectations has gone grievously astray, and who in his fall threatens to upset certain delicate relationships between certain interested individuals and the school. Thus, while the bearer is no longer a member of our scholastic family, it is highly important that his severance with the college be executed as painlessly as possible. I beg of you, sir, to help him continue in the direction of that promise which, like the horizon, recedes ever brightly and distantly beyond the hopeful traveler.

Respectfully, I am your
humble servant,

A. Hebert Bledsoe

I raised my head. Twenty-five years seemed to have lapsed between his handing me the letter and my grasping its message. I could not believe it, tried to read it again. I could not believe it, yet I had a feeling that it all had happened before. I rubbed my eyes, and they felt sandy as though all the fluids had suddenly dried.

"I'm sorry," he said. "I'm terribly sorry."

"What did I do? I always tried to do the right thing . . ."

"*That* you must tell me," he said. "To what does he refer?"

"I don't know, I don't know . . ."

"But you must have done *something*."

"I took a man for a drive, showed him into the Golden Day to help him when he became ill . . . I don't know . . ."

I told him falteringly of the visit to Trueblood's and the

trip to the Golden Day and of my expulsion, watching his mobile face reflecting his reaction to each detail.

"It's little enough," he said when I had finished. "I don't understand the man. He is very complicated."

"I only wanted to return and help," I said.

"You'll never return. You can't return now," he said. "Don't you see? I'm terribly sorry and yet I'm glad that I gave in to the impulse to speak to you. Forget it; though that's advice which I've been unable to accept myself, it's still good advice. There is no point in blinding yourself to the truth. Don't blind yourself . . ."

I got up, dazed, and started toward the door. He came behind me into the reception room where the birds flamed in the cage, their squawks like screams in a nightmare.

He stammered guiltily, "Please, I must ask you never to mention this conversation to anyone."

"No," I said.

"I wouldn't mind, but my father would consider my revelation the most extreme treason . . . You're free of him now. I'm still his prisoner. You have been freed, don't you understand? I've still my battle." He seemed near tears.

"I won't," I said. "No one would believe me. I can't myself. There must be some mistake. There must be . . ."

I opened the door.

"Look, fellow," he said. "This evening I'm having a party at the Calamus. Would you like to join my guests? It might help you—"

"No, thank you, sir. I'll be all right."

"Perhaps you'd like to be my valet?"

I looked at him. "No, thank you, sir," I said.

"Please," he said. "I really want to help. Look, I happen to know of a possible job at Liberty Paints. My father has sent several fellows there . . . You should try—"

I shut the door.

The elevator dropped me like a shot and I went out and walked along the street. The sun was very bright now and the people along the walk seemed far away. I stopped before a gray wall where high above me the headstones of a church graveyard arose like the tops of buildings. Across the street in the shade of an awning a shoeshine boy was dancing for pennies. I went on to the corner and got on a bus and went automatically to the rear. In the seat in front of me a dark man in a panama hat kept whistling a tune between his teeth. My mind flew in circles, to Bledsoe, Emerson and back again. There was no sense to be made of it. It was a joke. Hell, it couldn't be a joke. Yes, it is a joke ... Suddenly the bus jerked to a stop and I heard myself humming the same tune that the man ahead was whistling, and the words came back:

> O well they picked poor Robin clean
> O well they picked poor Robin clean
> Well they tied poor Robin to a stump
> Lawd, they picked all the feathers round
>   from Robin's rump
> Well they picked poor Robin clean.

Then I was on my feet, hurrying to the door, hearing the thin, tissue-paper-against-the-teeth-of-a-comb whistle following me outside at the next stop. I stood trembling at the curb, watching and half expecting to see the man leap from the door to follow me, whistling the old forgotten jingle about a bare-rumped robin. My mind seized upon the tune. I took the subway and it still droned through my mind after I had reached my room at Men's House and lay across the bed. What was the who-what-when-why-where of poor old Robin? What had he done and who had tied him and why had they plucked him and why had we sung of his fate? It was for a laugh, for a laugh, all the kids had laughed and laughed, and the droll tuba player of the old Elk's band had rendered it solo on his helical horn; with comical flourishes and doleful phrasing, *"Boo boo boo booooo,* Poor Robin clean"—a mock funeral dirge . . . But who was Robin and for what had he been hurt and humiliated?

Suddenly I lay shaking with anger. It was no good. I thought of young Emerson. What if he'd lied out of some ulterior motive of his own? Everyone seemed to have some plan for me, and beneath that some more secret plan. What was young Emerson's plan—and why should it have included me? Who was I anyway? I tossed fitfully. Perhaps it was a test of my good will and faith—But that's a lie, I thought. It's a lie and you know it's a lie. I had seen the letter and it had practically ordered me killed. By slow degrees . . .

"My dear Mr. Emerson," I said aloud. "The Robin bearing this letter is a former student. Please hope him to death, and keep him running. Your most humble and obedient servant, A. H. Bledsoe . . ."

Sure, that's the way it was, I thought, a short, concise verbal *coup de grace*, straight to the nape of the neck. And Emerson would write in reply? Sure: "Dear Bled, have met Robin and shaved tail. Signed, Emerson."

I sat on the bed and laughed. They'd sent me to the rookery, all right. I laughed and felt numb and weak, knowing that soon the pain would come and that no matter what happened to me I'd never be the same. I felt numb and I was laughing. When I stopped, gasping for breath, I decided that I would go back and kill Bledsoe. Yes, I thought, I owe it to the race and to myself. I'll kill him.

And the boldness of the idea and the anger behind it made me move with decision. I had to have a job and I took what I hoped was the quickest means. I called the plant young Emerson had mentioned, and it worked. I was told to report the following morning. It happened so quickly and with such ease that for a moment I felt turned around. Had they planned it this way? But no, they wouldn't catch me again. This time *I* had made the move.

I could hardly get to sleep for dreaming of revenge.

Chapter ten

The plant was in Long Island, and I crossed a bridge in the fog to get there and came down in a stream of workers. Ahead of me a huge electric sign announced its message through the drifting strands of fog:

KEEP AMERICA PURE

WITH

LIBERTY PAINTS

Flags were fluttering in the breeze from each of a maze of buildings below the sign, and for a moment it was like watching some vast patriotic ceremony from a distance. But no shots were fired and no bugles sounded. I hurried ahead with the others through the fog.

I was worried, since I had used Emerson's name without his permission, but when I found my way to the personnel office it worked like magic. I was interviewed by a little droopy-eyed man named Mr. MacDuffy and sent to work for a Mr. Kimbro. An office boy came along to direct me.

"If Kimbro needs him," MacDuffy told the boy, "come

back and have his name entered on the shipping department's payroll."

"It's tremendous," I said as we left the building. "It looks like a small city."

"It's big all right," he said. "We're one of the biggest outfits in the business. Make a lot of paint for the government."

We entered one of the buildings now and started down a pure white hall.

"You better leave your things in the locker room," he said, opening a door through which I saw a room with low wooden benches and rows of green lockers. There were keys in several of the locks, and he selected one for me. "Put your stuff in there and take the key," he said. Dressing, I felt nervous. He sprawled with one foot on a bench, watching me closely as he chewed on a match stem. Did he suspect that Emerson hadn't sent me?

"They have a new racket around here," he said, twirling the match between his finger and thumb. There was a note of insinuation in his voice, and I looked up from tying my shoe, breathing with conscious evenness.

"What kind of racket?" I said.

"Oh, you know. The wise guys firing the regular guys and putting on you colored college boys. Pretty smart," he said. "That way they don't have to pay union wages."

"How did you know I went to college?" I said.

"Oh, there're about six of you guys out here already. Some up in the testing lab. Everybody knows about that."

"But I had no idea that was why I was hired," I said.

"Forget it, Mac," he said. "It's not your fault. You new guys don't know the score. Just like the union says, it's the wise guys in the office. They're the ones who make scabs out of you—Hey! we better hurry."

We entered a long, shed-like room in which I saw a series

of overhead doors along one side and a row of small offices on the other. I followed the boy down an aisle between endless cans, buckets and drums labeled with the company's trademark, a screaming eagle. The paint was stacked in neatly pyramided lots along the concrete floor. Then, starting into one of the offices, the boy stopped short and grinned.

"Listen to that!"

Someone inside the office was swearing violently over a telephone.

"Who's that?" I asked.

He grinned. "Your boss, the terrible Mr. Kimbro. We call him 'Colonel,' but don't let him catch you."

I didn't like it. The voice was raving about some failure of the laboratory and I felt a swift uneasiness. I didn't like the idea of starting to work for a man who was in such a nasty mood. Perhaps he was angry at one of the men from the school, and that wouldn't make him feel too friendly toward me.

"Let's go in," the boy said. "I've got to get back."

As we entered, the man slammed down the phone and picked up some papers.

"Mr. MacDuffy wants to know if you can use this new man," the boy said.

"You damn right I can use him and . . ." the voice trailed off, the eyes above the stiff military mustache going hard.

"Well, can you use him?" the boy said. "I got to go make out his card."

"Okay," the man said finally. "I can use him. I gotta. What's his name?"

The boy read my name off a card.

"All right," he said, "you go right to work. And you," he said to the boy, "get the hell out of here before I give you a chance to earn some of the money wasted on you every payday!"

"Aw, gwan, you slave driver," the boy said, dashing from the room.

Reddening, Kimbro turned to me, "Come along, let's get going."

I followed him into the long room where the lots of paint were stacked along the floor beneath numbered markers that hung from the ceiling. Toward the rear I could see two men unloading heavy buckets from a truck, stacking them neatly on a low loading platform.

"Now get this straight," Kimbro said gruffly. "This is a busy department and I don't have time to repeat things. You have to follow instructions and you're going to be doing things you don't understand, so get your orders the first time and get them right! I won't have time to stop and explain everything. You have to catch on by doing exactly what I tell you. You got that?"

I nodded, noting that his voice became louder when the men across the floor stopped to listen.

"All right," he said, picking up several tools. "Now come over here."

"He's Kimbro," one of the men said.

I watched him kneel and open one of the buckets, stirring a milky brown substance. A nauseating stench arose. I wanted to step away. But he stirred it vigorously until it became glossy white, holding the spatula like a delicate instrument and studying the paint as it laced off the blade, back into the bucket. Kimbro frowned.

"Damn those laboratory blubberheads to hell! There's got to be dope put in every single sonofabitching bucket. And that's what you're going to do, *and* it's got to be put in so it can be trucked out of here before 11:30." He handed me a white enamel graduate and what looked like a battery hydrometer.

"The idea is to open each bucket and put in ten drops

of this stuff," he said. "Then you stir it 'til it disappears. After
it's mixed you take this brush and paint out a sample on one
of these." He produced a number of small rectangular boards
and a small brush from his jacket pocket. "You understand?"

"Yes, sir." But when I looked into the white graduate I
hesitated; the liquid inside was dead black. Was he trying to
kid me?

"What's wrong?"

"I don't know, sir . . . I mean. Well, I don't want to start
by asking a lot of stupid questions, but do you know what's
in this graduate?"

His eyes snapped. "You damn right I know," he said.
"You just do what you're told!"

"I just wanted to make sure, sir," I said.

"Look," he said, drawing in his breath with an exagger-
ated show of patience. "Take the dropper and fill it full . . .
Go on, do it!"

I filled it.

"Now measure ten drops into the paint . . . There, that's
it, not too goddam fast. Now. You want no more than ten,
and no less."

Slowly, I measured the glistening black drops, seeing them
settle upon the surface and become blacker still, spreading suddenly out to the edges.

"That's it. That's all you have to do," he said. "Never
mind how it looks. That's my worry. You just do what you're
told and don't try to think about it. When you've done five or
six buckets, come back and see if the samples are dry . . . And
hurry, we've got to get this batch back off to Washington by
11:30 . . ."

I worked fast but carefully. With a man like this Kimbro
the least thing done incorrectly would cause trouble. So I wasn't
supposed to think! To hell with him. Just a flunkey, a northern

redneck, a Yankee cracker! I mixed the paint thoroughly, then brushed it smoothly on one of the pieces of board, careful that the brush strokes were uniform.

Struggling to remove an especially difficult cover, I wondered if the same Liberty paint was used on the campus, or if this "Optic White" was something made exclusively for the government. Perhaps it was of a better quality, a special mix. And in my mind I could see the brightly trimmed and freshly decorated campus buildings as they appeared on spring mornings—after the fall painting and the light winter snows, with a cloud riding over and a darting bird above—framed by the trees and encircling vines. The buildings had always seemed more impressive because they were the only buildings to receive regular paintings; usually, the nearby houses and cabins were left untouched to become the dull grained gray of weathered wood. And I remembered how the splinters in some of the boards were raised from the grain by the wind, the sun and the rain until the clapboards shone with a satiny, silvery, silver-fish sheen: Like Trueblood's cabin, or the Golden Day . . . The Golden Day had once been painted white; now its paint was flaking away with the years, the scratch of a finger being enough to send it showering down. Damn that Golden Day! But it was strange how life connected up; because I had carried Mr. Norton to the old rundown building with rotting paint, I was here. If, I thought, one could slow down his heartbeats and memory to the tempo of the black drops falling so slowly into the bucket yet reacting so swiftly, it would seem like a sequence in a feverish dream . . . I was so deep in reverie that I failed to hear Kimbro approach.

"How's it coming?" he said, standing with hands on hips.

"All right, sir."

"Let's see," he said, selecting a sample and running his thumb across the board. "That's it, as white as George Washington's Sunday-go-to-meetin' wig and as sound as the all-mighty dollar! That's paint!" he said proudly. "That's paint that'll cover just about anything!"

He looked as though I had expressed a doubt and I hurried to say, "It's certainly white all right."

"White! It's the purest white that can be found. Nobody makes a paint any whiter. This batch right here is heading for a national monument!"

"I see," I said, quite impressed.

He looked at his watch. "Just keep it up," he said. "If I don't hurry I'll be late for that production conference! Say, you're nearly out of dope; you'd better go in the tank room and refill it . . . And don't waste any time! I've got to go."

He shot away without telling me where the tank room was. It was easy to find, but I wasn't prepared for so many tanks. There were seven; each with a puzzling code stenciled on it. It's just like Kimbro not to tell me, I thought. You can't trust any of them. Well, it doesn't matter, I'll pick the tank from the contents of the drip cans hanging from the spigots.

But while the first five tanks contained clear liquids that smelled like turpentine, the last two both contained something black like the dope, but with different codes. So I had to make a choice. Selecting the tank with the drip can that smelled most like the dope, I filled the graduate, congratulating myself for not having to waste time until Kimbro returned.

The work went faster now, the mixing easier. The pigment and heavy oils came free of the bottom much quicker, and when Kimbro returned I was going at top speed. "How many have you finished?" he asked.

"About seventy-five, I think, sir. I lost count."

"That's pretty good, but not fast enough. They've been putting pressure on me to get the stuff out. Here, I'll give you a hand."

They must have given him hell, I thought, as he got grunting to his knees and began removing covers from the buckets. But he had hardly started when he was called away.

When he left I took a look at the last bunch of samples and got a shock: Instead of the smooth, hard surface of the first, they were covered with a sticky goo through which I could see the grain of the wood. What on earth had happened? The paint was not as white and glossy as before; it had a gray tinge. I stirred it vigorously, then grabbed a rag, wiping each of the boards clean, then made a new sample of each bucket. I grew panicky lest Kimbro return before I finished. Working feverishly, I made it, but since the paint required a few minutes to dry I picked up two finished buckets and started lugging them over to the loading platform. I dropped them with a thump as the voice rang out behind me. It was Kimbro.

"What the hell!" he yelled, smearing his finger over one of the samples. "This stuff's still wet!"

I didn't know what to say. He snatched up several of the later samples, smearing them, and letting out a groan. "Of all the things to happen to me. First they take away all my good men and then they send me you. What'd you do to it?"

"Nothing, sir. I followed your directions," I said defensively.

I watched him peer into the graduate, lifting the dropper and sniffing it, his face glowing with exasperation.

"Who the hell gave you this?"

"No one . . ."

"Then where'd you get it?"

"From the tank room."

Suddenly he dashed for the tank room, sloshing the liquid as he ran. I thought, Oh, hell, and before I could follow, he burst out of the door in a frenzy.

"You took the wrong tank," he shouted. "What the hell,

you trying to sabotage the company? That stuff wouldn't work in a million years. It's remover, *concentrated* remover! Don't you know the difference?"

"No, sir, I don't. It looked the same to me. I didn't know what I was using and you didn't tell me. I was trying to save time and took what I thought was right."

"But why this one?"

"Because it smelled the same—" I began.

"Smelled!" he roared. "Goddamit, don't you know you can't smell shit around all those fumes? Come on to my office!"

I was torn between protesting and pleading for fairness. It was not all my fault and I didn't want the blame, but I did wish to finish out the day. Throbbing with anger I followed, listening as he called personnel.

"Hello? Mac? Mac, this is Kimbro. It's about this fellow you sent me this morning. I'm sending him in to pick up his pay . . . What did he do? He doesn't satisfy me, that's what. I don't like his work . . . So the old man has to have a report, so what? Make him one. Tell him goddamit this fellow ruined a batch of government stuff—Hey! No, don't tell him that . . . Listen, Mac, you got anyone else out there? . . . Okay, forget it."

He crashed down the phone and swung toward me. "I swear I don't know why they hire you fellows. You just don't belong in a paint plant. Come on."

Bewildered, I followed him into the tank room, yearning to quit and tell him to go to hell. But I needed the money, and even though this was the North I wasn't ready to fight unless I had to. Here I'd be one against how many?

I watched him empty the graduate back into the tank and noted carefully when he went to another marked SKA-3-69-T-Y and refilled it. Next time I would know.

"Now, for God's sake," he said, handing me the graduate, "be careful and try to do the job right. And if you don't know what to do, ask somebody. I'll be in my office."

I returned to the buckets, my emotions whirling. Kimbro had forgotten to say what was to be done with the spoiled paint. Seeing it there I was suddenly seized by an angry impulse, and, filling the dropper with fresh dope, I stirred ten drops into each bucket and pressed home the covers. Let the government worry about that, I thought, and started to work on the unopened buckets. I stirred until my arm ached and painted the samples as smoothly as I could, becoming more skillful as I went along.

When Kimbro came down the floor and watched I glanced up silently and continued stirring.

"How is it?" he said, frowning.

"I don't know," I said, picking up a sample and hesitating.

"Well?"

"It's nothing . . . a speck of dirt," I said, standing and holding out the sample, a tightness growing within me.

Holding it close to his face, he ran his fingers over the surface and squinted at the texture. "That's more like it," he said. "That's the way it oughta be."

I watched with a sense of unbelief as he rubbed his thumb over the sample, handed it back and left without a further word.

I looked at the painted slab. It appeared the same: a gray tinge glowed through the whiteness, and Kimbro had failed to detect it. I stared for about a minute, wondering if I were seeing things, inspected another and another. All were the same, a brilliant white diffused with gray. I closed my eyes for a moment and looked again and still no change. Well, I thought, as long as he's satisfied . . .

But I had a feeling that something had gone wrong,

something far more important than the paint; that either I had played a trick on Kimbro or he, like the trustees and Bledsoe, was playing one on me . . .

When the truck backed up to the platform I was pressing the cover on the last bucket—and there stood Kimbro above me.

"Let's see your samples," he said.

I reached, trying to select the whitest, as the blue-shirted truckmen climbed through the loading door.

"How about it, Kimbro," one of them said, "can we get started?"

"Just a minute, now," he said, studying the sample, "just a minute . . ."

I watched him nervously, waiting for him to throw a fit over the gray tinge and hating myself for feeling nervous and afraid. What would I say? But now he was turning to the truckmen.

"All right, boys, get the hell out of here."

"And you," he said to me, "go see MacDuffy; you're through."

I stood there, staring at the back of his head, at the pink neck beneath the cloth cap and the iron-gray hair. So he'd let me stay only to finish the mixing. I turned away, there was nothing that I could do. I cursed him all the way to the personnel office. Should I write the owners about what had happened? Perhaps they didn't know that Kimbro was having so much to do with the quality of the paint. Perhaps that is how things are done here, I thought, perhaps the real quality of the paint is *always* determined by the man who ships it rather than by those who mix it. To hell with the whole thing . . . I'll find another job.

But I wasn't fired. MacDuffy sent me to the basement of Building No. 2 on a new assignment.

"When you get down there just tell Brockway that Mr.

Sparland insists that he have an assistant. You do whatever he tells you."

"What is that name again, sir?" I said.

"Lucius *Brockway*," he said. "He's in charge."

It was a deep basement. Three levels underground I pushed upon a heavy metal door marked "Danger" and descended into a noisy, dimly lit room. There was something familiar about the fumes that filled the air and I had just thought *pine*, when a high-pitched Negro voice rang out above the machine sounds.

"Who you looking for down here?"

"I'm looking for the man in charge," I called, straining to locate the voice.

"You talkin' to him. What you want?"

The man who moved out of the shadow and looked at me sullenly was small, wiry and very natty in his dirty overalls. And as I approached him I saw his drawn face and the cottony white hair showing beneath his tight, striped engineer's cap. His manner puzzled me. I couldn't tell whether he felt guilty about something himself, or thought I had committed some crime. I came closer, staring. He was barely five feet tall, his overalls looking now as though he had been dipped in pitch.

"All right," he said. "I'm a busy man. What you want?"

"I'm looking for Lucius," I said.

He frowned. "That's me—and don't come calling me by my first name. To you and all like you I'm *Mister* Brockway . . ."

"You . . . ?" I began.

"Yeah, me! Who sent you down here anyway?"

"The personnel office," I said. "I was told to tell you that Mr. Sparland said for you to be given an assistant!"

"Assistant!" he said. "I don't need no damn assistant!

Old Man Sparland must think I'm getting old as him. Here I been running things by myself all these years and now they keep trying to send me some assistant. You get on back up there and tell 'em that when I want an assistant I'll ask for one!"

I was so disgusted to find such a man in charge that I turned without a word and started back up the stairs. First Kimbro, I thought, and now this old . . .

"Hey! wait a minute!"

I turned, seeing him beckon.

"Come on back here a minute," he called, his voice cutting sharply through the roar of the furnaces.

I went back, seeing him remove a white cloth from his hip pocket and wipe the glass face of a pressure gauge, then bend close to squint at the position of the needle.

"Here," he said, straightening and handing me the cloth, "you can stay 'til I can get in touch with the Old Man. These here have to be kept clean so's I can see how much pressure I'm getting."

I took the cloth without a word and began rubbing the glasses. He watched me critically.

"What's your name?" he said.

I told him, shouting it in the roar of the furnaces.

"Wait a minute," he called, going over and turning a valve in an intricate network of pipes. I heard the noise rise to a higher, almost hysterical pitch, somehow making it possible to hear without yelling, our voices moving blurrily underneath.

Returning, he looked at me sharply, his withered face an animated black walnut with shrewd, reddish eyes.

"This here's the first time they ever sent me anybody like you," he said as though puzzled. "That's how come I called you back. Usually they sends down some young white fellow who thinks he's going to watch me a few days and ask me a heap of questions and then take over. Some folks is too damn simple to even talk about," he said, grimacing and waving his hand in a violent gesture of dismissal. "You an engineer?" he said, looking quickly at me.

"An *engineer?*"

"Yeah, that's what I asked you," he said challengingly.

"Why, no, sir, I'm no engineer."

"You sho?"

"Of course I'm sure. Why shouldn't I be?"

He seemed to relax. "That's all right then. I have to watch them personnel fellows. One of them thinks he's going to git me out of here, when he ought to know by now he's wasting his time. Lucius Brockway not only intends to protect hisself, he *knows how* to do it! Everybody knows I been here ever since there's been a here—even helped dig the first foundation. The Old Man hired me, nobody else; and, by God, it'll take the Old Man to fire me!"

I rubbed away at the gauges, wondering what had brought on this outburst, and was somewhat relieved that he seemed to hold nothing against me personally.

"Where you go to school?" he said.

I told him.

"Is that so? What you learning down there?"

"Just general subjects, a regular college course," I said.

"Mechanics?"

"Oh no, nothing like that, just a liberal arts course. No trades."

"Is that so?" he said doubtfully. Then suddenly, "How much pressure I got on that gauge right there?"

"Which?"

"You see it?" he pointed. "That one right there!"

I looked, calling off, "Forty-three and two-tenths pounds."

"Uh huh, uh huh, that's right." He squinted at the gauge and back at me. "Where you learn to read a gauge so good?"

"In my high-school physics class. It's like reading a clock."

"They teach you that in *high* school?"

"That's right."

"Well, that's going to be one of your jobs. These here gauges have to be checked every fifteen minutes. You ought to be able to do that."

"I think I can," I said.

"Some kin, some caint. By the way, who hired you?"

"Mr. MacDuffy," I said, wondering why all the questions.

"Yeah, then where you been all morning?"

"I was working over in Building No.1."

"That there's a heap of building. Where'bouts?"

"For Mr. Kimbro."

"I see, I see. I knowed they oughtn't to be hiring anybody this late in the day. What Kimbro have you doing?"

"Putting dope in some paint that went bad," I said wearily, annoyed with all the questions.

His lips shot out belligerently. "What paint went bad?"

"I think it was some for the government . . ."

He cocked his head "I wonder how come nobody said nothing to me about it," he said thoughtfully. "Was it in buckets or them little biddy cans?"

"Buckets."

"Oh, that ain't so bad, them little ones is a heap of work." He gave me a high dry laugh. "How you hear about this job?" he snapped suddenly, as though trying to catch me off guard.

"Look," I said slowly, "a man I know told me about the job; MacDuffy hired me; I worked this morning for Mr. Kimbro; and I was sent to you by Mr. MacDuffy."

His face tightened. "You friends to one of those colored fellows?"

"Who?"

"Up in the lab?"

"No," I said. "Anything else you want to know?"

He gave me a long, suspicious look and spat upon a hot pipe, causing it to steam furiously. I watched him remove a heavy engineer's watch from his breast pocket and squint at the dial importantly, then turn to check it with an electric clock that glowed from the wall. "You keep on wiping them gauges," he said. "I got to look at my soup. And look here." He pointed to one of the gauges. "I wants you to keep a 'specially sharp eye on this here sonofabitch. The last couple of days he's 'veloped a habit of building up too fast. Causes me a heap of trouble. You see him gitting past 75, you yell, and yell loud!"

He went back into the shadows and I saw a shaft of brightness mark the opening of a door.

Running the rag over a gauge I wondered how an apparently uneducated old man could gain such a responsible job. He certainly didn't sound like an engineer; yet he alone was on duty. And you could never be sure, for at home an old man employed as a janitor at the Water Works was the only one who knew the location of all of the water mains. He had been employed at the beginning, before any records were kept, and actually functioned as an engineer though he drew a janitor's pay. Perhaps this old Brockway was protecting himself from something. After all, there was antagonism to our being employed. Maybe he was dissimulating, like some of the teachers at the college, who, to avoid trouble when driving through the small surrounding towns, wore chauffeur caps and pretended that their cars belonged to white men. But why was he pretending with me? And what was his job?

I looked around me. It was not just an engine room; I knew, for I had been in several, the last at college. It was something more. For one thing, the furnaces were made differently and the flames that flared through the cracks of the fire chambers were too intense and too blue. And there were the odors. No, he was *making* something down here, something that had to do with paint, and probably something too filthy and dangerous for white men to be willing to do even for money. It was not paint because I had been told that the paint was made on the floors above, where, passing through, I had seen men in splattered aprons working over large vats filled with whirling pigment. One thing was certain: I had to be careful with this crazy Brockway; he didn't like my being here . . . And there he was, entering the room now from the stairs.

"How's it going?" he asked.

"All right," I said. "Only it seems to have gotten louder."

"Oh, it gets pretty loud down here, all right; this here's the uproar department and I'm in charge . . . Did she go over the mark?"

"No, it's holding steady," I said.

"That's good. I been having plenty trouble with it lately. Haveta bust it down and give it a good going over soon as I can get the tank clear."

Perhaps he *is* the engineer, I thought, watching him inspect the gauges and go to another part of the room to adjust a series of valves. Then he went and said a few words into a wall phone and called me, pointing to the valves.

"I'm fixing to shoot it to 'em upstairs," he said gravely. "When I give you the signal I want you to turn 'em wide open. 'N when I give you the second signal I want you to close 'em up again. Start with this here red one and work right straight across . . ."

I took my position and waited, as he took a stand near the gauge.

"Let her go," he called. I opened the valves, hearing the sound of liquids rushing through the huge pipes. At the sound of a buzzer I looked up . . .

"Start closing," he yelled. "What you looking at? Close them valves!"

"What's wrong with you?" he asked when the last valve was closed.

"I expected you to call."

"I said I'd *signal* you. Caint you tell the difference between a signal and a call? Hell, I buzzed you. You don't want to do that no more. When I buzz you I want you to do something and do it quick!"

"You're the boss," I said sarcastically.

"You mighty right, I'm the boss, and don't forgit it. Now come on back here, we got work to do."

We came to a strange-looking machine consisting of a huge set of gears connecting a series of drum-like rollers. Brockway took a shovel and scooped up a load of brown crystals from a pile on the floor, pitching them skillfully into a receptacle on top of the machine.

"Grab a scoop and let's git going," he ordered briskly. "You ever done this before?" he asked as I scooped into the pile.

"It's been a long time," I said. "What is this material?"

He stopped shoveling and gave me a long, black stare, then returned to the pile, his scoop ringing on the floor. You'll have to remember not to ask this suspicious old bastard any questions, I thought, scooping into the brown pile.

Soon I was perspiring freely. My hands were sore and I began to tire. Brockway watched me out of the corner of his eye, snickering noiselessly.

"You don't want to overwork yourself, young feller," he said blandly.

"I'll get used to it," I said, scooping up a heavy load.

"Oh, sho, sho," he said. "Sho. But you better take a rest when you git tired."

I didn't stop. I piled on the material until he said, "That there's the scoop we been trying to find. That's what we want. You better stand back a little, 'cause I'm fixing to start her up."

I backed away, watching him go over and push a switch. Shuddering into motion, the machine gave a sudden scream like a circular saw, and sent a tattoo of sharp crystals against my face. I moved clumsily away, seeing Brockway grin like a dried prune. Then with the dying hum of the furiously whirling drums, I heard the grains sifting lazily in the sudden still-ness, sliding sand-like down the chute into the pot underneath.

I watched him go over and open a valve. A sharp new smell of oil arose.

"Now she's all set to cook down; all we got to do is put the fire to her," he said, pressing a button on something that looked like the burner of an oil furnace. There was an angry hum, followed by a slight explosion that caused something to rattle, and I could hear a low roaring begin.

"Know what that's going to be when it's cooked?"

"No, sir," I said.

"Well that's going to be the guts, what they call the *vee*-hicle of the paint. Least it will be by time I git through putting other stuff with it."

"But I thought the paint was made upstairs . . ."

"Naw, they just mixes in the color, make it look pretty. Right down here is where the real paint is made. Without what I do they couldn't do nothing, they be making bricks without straw. An' not only do I make up the base, I fixes the varnishes and lots of the oils too . . ."

"So that's it," I said. "I was wondering what you did down here."

"A whole lots of folks wonders about that without gitting anywhere. But as I was saying, caint a single doggone drop of paint move out of the factory lessen it comes through Lucius Brockway's hands."

"How long have you been doing this?"

"Long enough to know what I'm doing," he said. "And I learned it without all that education that them what's been sent down here is suppose to have. I learned it by doing it. Them personnel fellows don't want to face the facts, but Liberty Paints wouldn't be worth a plugged nickel if they didn't have me here to see that it got a good strong base. Old Man Sparland know it though. I caint stop laughing over the time when I was down with a touch of pneumonia and they put one of them so-called engineers to pooting around down here. Why, they started to having so much paint go bad they didn't know what to do. Paint was bleeding and wrinkling, wouldn't cover or nothing—you know, a man could make hisself all kinds of money if he found out what makes paint bleed. Anyway, everything was going bad. Then word got to me that they done put that fellow in my place and when I got well I wouldn't come back. Here I been with 'em so long and loyal and everything. Shucks, I just sent 'em word that Lucius Brockway was retiring!

"Next thing you know here come the Old Man. He so old hisself his chauffeur has to help him up them steep stairs at my place. Come in a-puffing and a-blowing, says, 'Lucius, what's this I hear 'bout you retiring?'

" 'Well, sir, Mr. Sparland, sir,' I says, 'I been pretty sick, as you well know, and I'm gitting kinder along in my years, as you well know, and I hear that this here Italian fellow you got in my place is doing so good I thought I'd might as well take it easy round the house.'

"Why, you'd a-thought I'd done cursed him or something. 'What kind of talk is that from you, Lucius Brockway,' he said, 'taking it easy round the house when we need you out to the plant? Don't you know the quickest way to die is to retire? Why, that fellow out at the plant don't know a thing about those furnaces. I'm so worried about what he's going to do, that he's liable to blow up the plant or something that I took out some extra insurance. He can't do your job,' he said. 'He don't have the touch. We haven't put out a first-class batch of paint since you been gone.' Now that was the Old Man hisself!" Lucius Brockway said.

"So what happened?" I said.

"What you mean, what happened?" he said, looking as though it were the most unreasonable question in the world. "Shucks, a few days later the Old Man had me back down here in full control. That engineer got so mad when he found out he had to take orders from me he quit the next day."

He spat on the floor and laughed. "Heh, heh, heh, he was a fool, that's what. A fool! He wanted to boss *me* and I know more about this basement than anybody, boilers and everything. I helped lay the pipes and everything, and what I mean is I knows the location of each and every pipe and switch and cable and wire and everything else—both in the floors and in the walls *and* out in the yard. Yes, sir! And what's more, I got it in my head so good I can trace it out on paper down to the last nut and bolt; and ain't never been to nobody's engineering school neither, ain't even passed by one, as far as I know. Now what you think about that?"

"I think it's remarkable," I said, thinking, I don't like this old man.

"Oh, I wouldn't call it that," he said. "It's just that I been round here so long. I been studying this machinery for over twenty-five years. Sho, and that fellow thinking 'cause he been to some school and learned how to read a blueprint and how to fire a boiler he knows more 'bout this plant than Lucius Brockway. That fool couldn't make no engineer 'cause he can't see what's staring him straight in the face . . . Say, you forgittin' to watch them gauges."

I hurried over, finding all the needles steady.

"They're okay," I called.

"All right, but I'm warning you to keep an eye on 'em. You caint forgit down here, 'cause if you do, you liable to blow up something. They got all this machinery, but that ain't everything; *we the machines inside the machine.*

"You know the best selling paint we got, the one that *made* this here business?" he asked as I helped him fill a vat with a smelly substance.

"No, I don't."

"Our white, Optic White."

"Why the white rather than the others?"

" 'Cause we started stressing it from the first. We make the best white paint in the world, I don't give a damn what nobody says. Our white is so white you can paint a chunka coal and you'd have to crack it open with a sledge hammer to prove it wasn't white clear through!"

His eyes glinted with humorless conviction and I had to drop my head to hide my grin.

"You notice that sign on top of the building?"

"Oh, you can't miss that," I said.

"You read the slogan?"

"I don't remember, I was in such a hurry."

"Well, you might not believe it, but I helped the Old Man make up that slogan. 'If It's Optic White, It's the Right White,' " he quoted with an upraised finger, like a preacher quoting holy writ. "I got me a three-hundred-dollar bonus for helping to think that up. These newfangled advertising folks is been tryin' to work up something about the other colors, talking about rainbows or something, but hell, *they* caint get no-where."

" 'If It's Optic White, It's the Right White,' " I repeated and suddenly had to repress a laugh as a childhood jingle rang through my mind:

" 'If you're white, you're right,' " I said.

"That's it," he said. "And that's another reason why the Old Man ain't goin' to let nobody come down here messing with me. *He* knows what a lot of them new fellers don't; *he* knows that the reason our paint is so good is because of the way Lucius Brockway puts the pressure on them oils and resins before they even leaves the tanks." He laughed maliciously. "They thinks 'cause everything down here is done by machinery, that's all there is to it. They crazy! Ain't a continental thing that happens down here that ain't as iffen I done put my black hands into it! Them machines just do the cooking, these here hands right here do the sweeting. Yes, sir! Lucius Brockway hit it square on the head! I dips my finger in and sweets it! Come on, let's eat . . ."

"But what about the gauges?" I said, seeing him go over and take a thermos bottle from a shelf near one of the furnaces.

"Oh, we'll be here close enough to keep an eye on 'em. Don't you worry 'bout that."

"But I left my lunch in the locker room over at Building No. 1."

"Go on and git it and come back here and eat. Down here we have to always be on the job. A man don't need no more'n fifteen minutes to eat no-how; then I say let him git on back on the job."

Upon opening the door I thought I had made a mistake. Men dressed in splattered painters' caps and overalls sat about on benches, listening to a thin tubercular-looking man who was addressing them in a nasal voice. Everyone looked at me and I was starting out when the thin man called, "There's plenty of seats for late comers. Come in, brother . . ."

Brother? Even after my weeks in the North this was surprising. "I was looking for the locker room," I spluttered.

"You're in it, brother. Weren't you told about the meeting?"

"Meeting? Why, no, sir, I wasn't."

The chairman frowned. "You see, the bosses are not co-operating," he said to the others. "Brother, who's your foreman?"

"Mr. Brockway, sir," I said.

Suddenly the men began scraping their feet and cursing. I looked about me. What was wrong? Were they objecting to my referring to Brockway as *Mister*?

"Quiet, brothers," the chairman said, leaning across his table, his hand cupped to his ear. "Now what was that, brother; who is your foreman?"

"Lucius Brockway, sir," I said, dropping the *Mister*.

But this seemed only to make them more hostile. "Get him the hell out of here," they shouted. I turned. A group on the far side of the room kicked over a bench, yelling, "Throw him out! Throw him out!"

I inched backwards, hearing the little man bang on the table for order. "Men, brothers! Give the brother a chance . . ."

"He looks like a dirty fink to me. A first-class enameled fink!"

The hoarsely voiced word grated my ears like "nigger" in an angry southern mouth . . .

"Brothers, *please!*" The chairman was waving his hands

as I reached out behind me for the door and touched an arm, feeling it snatch violently away. I dropped my hand.

"Who sent this fink into the meeting, brother chairman? Ask him that!" a man demanded.

"No, wait," the chairman said. "Don't ride that word too hard . . ."

"Ask him, brother chairman!" another man said.

"Okay, but don't label a man a fink until you know for sure." The chairman turned to me. "How'd you happen in here, brother?"

The men quieted, listening.

"I left my lunch in my locker," I said, my mouth dry.

"You weren't *sent* into the meeting?"

"No, sir, I didn't know about any meeting."

"The hell he says. None of these finks ever knows!"

"Throw the lousy bastard out!"

"Now, wait," I said.

They became louder, threatening.

"Respect the chair!" the chairman shouted. "We're a democratic union here, following democratic—"

"Never mind, git rid of the fink!"

". . . procedures. It's our task to make friends with all the workers. And I mean *all*. That's how we build the union strong. Now let's hear what the brother's got to say. No more of that beefing and interrupting!"

I broke into a cold sweat, my eyes seeming to have become extremely sharp, causing each face to stand out vivid in its hostility.

I heard, "When were you hired, friend?"

"This morning," I said.

"See, brothers, he's a new man. We don't want to make the mistake of judging the worker by his foreman. Some of you also work for sonsabitches, remember?"

Suddenly the men began to laugh and curse. "Here's one right here," one of them yelled.

"Mine wants to marry the boss's daughter—a frigging eight-day wonder!"

This sudden change made me puzzled and angry, as though they were making me the butt of a joke.

"Order, brothers! Perhaps the brother would like to join the union. How about it, brother?"

"Sir . . . ?" I didn't know what to say. I knew very little about unions—but most of these men seemed hostile . . . And before I could answer a fat man with shaggy gray hair leaped to his feet, shouting angrily.

"I'm against it! Brothers, this fellow could be a fink, even if he was hired right this minute! Not that I aim to be unfair to anybody, either. Maybe he ain't a fink," he cried passionately, "but brothers, I want to remind you that nobody knows it; and it seems to me that anybody that would work under that sonofabitching, double-crossing Brockway for more than fifteen minutes is just as apt as not to be *naturally* fink-minded! Please, brothers!" he cried, waving his arms for quiet. "As some of you brothers have learned, to the sorrow of your wives and babies, a fink don't have to know about trade unionism to be a fink! Finkism? Hell, I've made a study of finkism! Finkism is *born* into some guys. It's born into some guys, just like a good eye for color is born into other guys. That's right, that's the honest, scientific truth! A fink don't even have to have heard of a union before," he cried in a frenzy of words. "All you have to do is bring him around the neighborhood of a union and next thing you know, why, zip! he's finking his finking ass off!"

He was drowned out by shouts of approval. Men turned violently to look at me. I felt choked. I wanted to drop my head but faced them as though facing them was itself a denial of his statements. Another voice ripped out of the shouts of approval, spilling with great urgency from the lips of a little fellow with glasses who spoke with the index finger of one hand upraised and the thumb of the other crooked in the suspender of his overalls:

"I want to put this brother's remarks in the form of a motion: I move that we determine through a thorough investigation whether the new worker is a fink or no; and if he is a fink, let us discover who he's finking for! And this, brother members, would give the worker time, if he *ain't* a fink, to become acquainted with the work of the union and its aims. After all, brothers, we don't want to forget that workers like him aren't so highly developed as some of us who've been in the labor movement for a long time. So *I* says, let's give him time to see what we've done to improve the condition of the workers, and then, if he *ain't* a fink, we can decide in a democratic way whether we want to accept this brother into the union. Brother union members, I thank you!" He sat down with a bump.

The room roared. Biting anger grew inside me. So I was not so highly developed as they! What did he mean? Were they all Ph.D.'s? I couldn't move; too much was happening to me. It was as though by entering the room I had automatically applied for membership—even though I had no idea that a union existed, and had come up simply to get a cold pork chop sandwich. I stood trembling, afraid that they would ask me to join but angry that so many rejected me on sight. And worst of all, I knew they were forcing me to accept things on their own terms, and I was unable to leave.

"All right, brothers. We'll take a vote," the chairman shouted. "All in favor of the motion, signify by saying 'Aye' . . ."

The ayes drowned him out.

"The ayes carried it," the chairman announced as several

men turned to stare at me. At last I could move. I started out, forgetting why I had come.

"Come in, brother," the chairman called. "You can get your lunch now. Let him through, you brothers around the door!"

My face stung as though it had been slapped. They had made their decision without giving me a chance to speak for myself. I felt that every man present looked upon me with hostility; and though I had lived with hostility all my life, now for the first time it seemed to reach me, as though I had expected more of these men than of others—even though I had not known of their existence. Here in this room my defenses were negated, stripped away, checked at the door as the weapons, the knives and razors and owlhead pistols of the country boys were checked on Saturday night at the Golden Day. I kept my eyes lowered, mumbling "Pardon me, pardon me," all the way to the drab green locker, where I removed the sandwich, for which I no longer had an appetite, and stood fumbling with the bag, dreading to face the men on my way out. Then still hating myself for the apologies made coming over, I brushed past silently as I went back.

When I reached the door the chairman called, "Just a minute, brother, we want you to understand that this is nothing against you personally. What you see here is the results of certain conditions here at the plant. We want you to know that we are only trying to protect ourselves. Some day we hope to have you as a member in good standing."

From here and there came a half-hearted applause that quickly died. I swallowed and stared unseeing, the words spurting to me from a red, misty distance.

"Okay, brothers," the voice said, "let him pass."

. . .

I STUMBLED through the bright sunlight of the yard, past the office workers chatting on the grass, back to Building No. 2, to the basement. I stood on the stairs, feeling as though my bowels had been flooded with acid. Why hadn't I simply left, I thought with anguish. And since I had remained, why hadn't I *said* something, defended myself? Suddenly I snatched the wrapper off a sandwich and tore it violently with my teeth, hardly tasting the dry lumps that squeezed past my constricted throat when I swallowed. Dropping the remainder back into the bag, I held onto the handrail, my legs shaking as though I had just escaped a great danger. Finally, it went away and I pushed open the metal door.

"What kept you so long?" Brockway snapped from where he sat on a wheelbarrow. He had been drinking from a white mug now cupped in his grimy hands.

I looked at him abstractedly, seeing how the light caught on his wrinkled forehead, his snowy hair.

"I said, what kept you so long!"

What had he to do with it, I thought, looking at him through a kind of mist, knowing that I disliked him and that I was very tired.

"I say . . ." he began, and I heard my voice come quiet from my tensed throat as I noticed by the clock that I had been gone only twenty minutes.

"I ran into a union meeting—"

"Union!" I heard his white cup shatter against the floor as he uncrossed his legs, rising. "I knowed you belonged to that bunch of troublemaking foreigners! I knowed it! Git out!" he screamed. "Git out of my basement!"

He started toward me as in a dream, trembling like the needle of one of the gauges as he pointed toward the stairs, his voice shrieking. I stared; something seemed to have gone wrong, my reflexes were jammed.

"But what's the matter?" I stammered, my voice low and my mind understanding and yet failing exactly to understand. "What's wrong?"

"You heard me. Git out!"

"But I don't understand . . ."

"Shut up and git!"

"But, Mr. Brockway," I cried, fighting to hold something that was giving way.

"You two-bit, trouble-making union louse!"

"Look, man," I cried, urgently now, "I don't belong to any union."

"If you don't git outta here, you low-down skunk," he said, looking wildly about the floor, "I'm liable to kill you. The Lord being my witness, I'LL KILL YOU!"

It was incredible, things were speeding up. "You'll do what?" I stammered.

"I'LL KILL YOU, THAT'S WHAT!"

He had said it again and something fell away from me, and I seemed to be telling myself in a rush: *You were trained to accept the foolishness of such old men as this, even when you thought them clowns and fools; you were trained to pretend that you respected them and acknowledged in them the same quality of authority and power in your world as the whites before whom they bowed and scraped and feared and loved and imitated, and you were even trained to accept it when, angered or spiteful, or drunk with power, they came at you with a stick or strap or cane and you made no effort to strike back, but only to escape unmarked.* But this was too much . . . he was not grandfather or uncle or father, nor preacher or teacher. Something uncoiled in my stomach and I was moving toward him, shouting, more at a black blur that irritated my eyes than at a clearly defined human face, "YOU'LL KILL WHO?"

"*YOU*, THAT'S WHO!"

"Listen here, you old fool, don't talk about killing me! Give me a chance to explain. I don't belong to anything—Go on, pick it up! Go on!" I yelled, seeing his eyes fasten upon a twisted iron bar. "You're old enough to be my grandfather, but if you touch that bar, I swear I'll make you eat it!"

"I done tole you, GIT OUTTA MY BASEMENT! *You impudent son'bitch*," he screamed.

I moved forward, seeing him stoop and reach aside for the bar; and I was throwing myself forward, feeling him go over with a grunt, hard against the floor, rolling beneath the force of my lunge. It was as though I had landed upon a wiry rat. He scrambled beneath me, making angry sounds and striking my face as he tried to use the bar. I twisted it from his grasp, feeling a sharp pain stab through my shoulder. He's using a knife, flashed through my mind and I slashed out with my elbow, sharp against his face, feeling it land solid and seeing his head fly backwards and up and back again as I struck again, hearing something fly free and skitter across the floor, thinking, It's gone, the knife is gone . . . and struck again as he tried to choke me, jabbing at his bobbing head, feeling the bar come free and bringing it down at his head, missing, the metal clinking against the floor, and bringing it up for a second try and him yelling, "No, no! You the best, you the best!"

"I'm going to beat your brains out!" I said, my throat dry, "stabbing me . . ."

"No," he panted. "I got enough. Ain't you heard me say I got enough?"

"So when you can't win you want to stop! Damn you, if you've cut me bad, I'll tear your head off!"

Watching him warily, I got to my feet. I dropped the bar, as a flash of heat swept over me: His face was caved in.

"What's wrong with you, old man?" I yelled nervously. "Don't you know better than to attack a man a third your age?"

He blanched at being called old, and I repeated it, adding insults I'd heard my grandfather use. "Why, you old-fashioned, slavery-time, mammy-made, handkerchief-headed bastard, you should know better! What made you think you could threaten *my* life? You meant nothing to me, I came down here because I was sent. I didn't know anything about you or the union either. Why'd you start riding me the minute I came in? Are you people crazy? Does this paint go to your head? Are you drinking it?"

He glared, panting tiredly. Great tucks showed in his overalls where the folds were stuck together by the goo with which he was covered, and I thought, Tar Baby, and wanted to blot him out of my sight. But now my anger was flowing fast from action to words.

"I go to get my lunch and they ask me who I work for and when I tell them, they call me a fink. *A fink!* You people must be out of your minds. No sooner do I get back down here than *you* start yelling that you're going to kill me! What's going on? What have you got against me? What did I do?"

He glowered at me silently, then pointed to the floor.

"Reach and draw back a nub," I warned.

"Caint a man even git his teeth?" he mumbled, his voice strange.

"TEETH?"

With a shamed frown, he opened his mouth. I saw a blue flash of shrunken gums. The thing that had skittered across the floor was not a knife, but a plate of false teeth. For a fraction of a second I was desperate, feeling some of my justification for wanting to kill him slipping away. My fingers leaped to my shoulder, finding wet cloth but no blood. The old fool had *bitten* me. A wild flash of laughter struggled to rise from beneath my anger. He had bitten me! I looked on the floor, seeing the smashed mug and the teeth glinting dully across the room.

"Get them," I said, growing ashamed. Without his teeth, some of the hatefulness seemed to have gone out of him. But I stayed close as he got his teeth and went over to the tap and held them beneath a stream of water. A tooth fell away beneath the pressure of his thumb, and I heard him grumbling as he placed the plate in his mouth. Then, wiggling his chin, he became himself again.

"You was really trying to kill me," he said. He seemed unable to believe it.

"You started the killing. I don't go around fighting," I said. "Why didn't you let me explain? Is it against the law to belong to the union?"

"That damn union," he cried, almost in tears. "That *damn* union! They after my job! I know they after my job! For one of us to join one of them damn unions is like we was to bite the hand of the man who teached us to bathe in a bathtub! I hates it, and I mean to keep on doing all I can to chase it outta the plant. They after my job, the chickenshit bastards!"

Spittle formed at the corners of his mouth; he seemed to boil with hatred.

"But what have I to do with that?" I said, feeling suddenly the older.

" 'Cause them young colored fellers up in the lab is trying to join that outfit, that's what! Here the white man done give 'em jobs," he wheezed as though pleading a case. "He done give 'em *good* jobs too, and they so ungrateful they goes and joins up with that backbiting union! I never seen such a no-good ungrateful bunch. All they doing is making things bad for the rest of us!"

"Well, I'm sorry," I said, "I didn't know about all that. I came here to take a temporary job and I certainly didn't intend to get mixed up in any quarrels. But as for us, I'm ready to forget our disagreement—if you are ..." I held out my hand, causing my shoulder to pain.

He gave me a gruff look. "You ought to have more self-respect than to fight an old man," he said. "I got grown boys older than you."

"I thought you were trying to kill me," I said, my hand still extended. "I thought you had stabbed me."

"Well, I don't like a lot of bickering and confusion my-self," he said, avoiding my eyes. And it was as though the closing of his sticky hand over mine was a signal. I heard a shrill hissing from the boilers behind me and turned, hearing Brockway yell, "I tole you to watch them gauges. Git over to the big valves, quick!"

I dashed for where a series of valve wheels projected from the wall near the crusher, seeing Brockway scrambling away in the other direction, thinking, Where's he going? as I reached the valves, and hearing him yell, "Turn it! Turn it!"

"Which?" I yelled, reaching.

"The white one, fool, the white one!"

I jumped, catching it and pulling down with all my weight, feeling it give. But this only increased the noise and I seemed to hear Brockway laugh as I looked around to see him scrambling for the stairs, his hands clasping the back of his head, and his neck pulled in close, like a small boy who has thrown a brick into the air.

"Hey you! Hey you!" I yelled. "Hey!" But it was too late. All my movements seemed too slow, ran together. I felt the wheel resisting and tried vainly to reverse it and tried to let go, and it sticking to my palms and my fingers stiff and sticky, and I turned, running now, seeing the needle on one of the gauges swinging madly, like a beacon gone out of control, and trying to think clearly, my eyes darting here and there through the room of tanks and machines and up the stairs so far away and hearing the clear new note arising while I seemed to run swiftly up an incline and shot forward with sudden acceleration into a wet blast of black emptiness that was somehow a bath of whiteness.

It was a fall into space that seemed not a fall but a suspension. Then a great weight landed upon me and I seemed to sprawl in an interval of clarity beneath a pile of broken machinery, my head pressed back against a huge wheel, my body splattered with a stinking goo. Somewhere an engine ground in furious futility, grating loudly until a pain shot around the curve of my head and bounced me off into blackness for a distance, only to strike another pain that lobbed me back. And in that clear instant of consciousness I opened my eyes to a blinding flash.

Holding on grimly, I could hear the sound of someone wading, sloshing, nearby, and an old man's garrulous voice saying, "I tole 'em these here young Nineteen-Hundred boys ain't no good for the job. They ain't got the nerves. Naw, sir, they just ain't got the nerves."

I tried to speak, to answer, but something heavy moved again, and I was understanding something fully and trying again to answer but seemed to sink to the center of a lake of heavy water and pause, transfixed and numb with the sense that I had lost irrevocably an important victory.

Chapter eleven

I was sitting in a cold, white rigid chair and a man was looking at me out of a bright third eye that glowed from the center of his forehead. He reached out, touching my skull gingerly, and said something encouraging, as though I were a child. His fingers went away.

"Take this," he said. "It's good for you." I swallowed. Suddenly my skin itched, all over. I had on new overalls, strange white ones. The taste ran bitter through my mouth. My fingers trembled.

A thin voice with a mirror on the end of it said, "How is he?"

"I don't think it's anything serious. Merely stunned."

"Should he be sent home now?"

"No, just to be certain we'll keep him here a few days. Want to keep him under observation. Then he may leave."

Now I was lying on a cot, the bright eye still burning into mine, although the man was gone. It was quiet and I was numb. I closed my eyes only to be awakened.

"What is your name?" a voice said.

"My head . . ." I said.

"Yes, but your name. Address?"

"My head—that burning eye . . ." I said.

"Eye?"

"Inside," I said.

"Shoot him up for an X-ray," another voice said.

"My head . . ."

"Careful!"

Somewhere a machine began to hum and I distrusted the man and woman above me.

They were holding me firm and it was fiery and above it all I kept hearing the opening motif of Beethoven's *Fifth*—three short and one long buzz, repeated again and again in varying volume, and I was struggling and breaking through, rising up, to find myself lying on my back with two pink-faced men laughing down.

"Be quiet now," one of them said firmly. "You'll be all right." I raised my eyes, seeing two indefinite young women in white, looking down at me. A third, a desert of heat waves away, sat at a panel arrayed with coils and dials. Where was I? From far below me a barber-chair thumping began and I felt myself rise on the tip of the sound from the floor. A face was now level with mine, looking closely and saying something without meaning. A whirring began that snapped and cracked with static, and suddenly I seemed to be crushed between the floor and ceiling. Two forces tore savagely at my stomach and back. A flash of cold-edged heat enclosed me. I was pounded between crushing electrical pressures; pumped between live electrodes like an accordion between a player's hands. My lungs were compressed like a bellows and each time my breath returned I yelled, punctuating the rhythmical action of the nodes.

"Hush, goddamit," one of the faces ordered. "We're trying to get you started again. Now shut up!"

The voice throbbed with icy authority and I quieted and tried to contain the pain. I discovered now that my head was encircled by a piece of cold metal like the iron cap worn by the occupant of an electric chair. I tried unsuccessfully to struggle, to cry out. But the people were so remote, the pain so immediate. A face moved in and out of the circle of lights, peering for a moment, then disappeared. A freckled, red-haired woman with gold nose-glasses appeared; then a man with a circular mirror attached to his forehead—a doctor. Yes, he was a doctor and the women were nurses; it was coming clear. I was in a hospital. They would care for me. It was all geared toward the easing of pain. I felt thankful.

I tried to remember how I'd gotten here, but nothing came. My mind was blank, as though I had just begun to live. When the next face appeared I saw the eyes behind the thick glasses blinking as though noticing me for the first time.

"You're all right, boy. You're okay. You just be patient," said the voice, hollow with profound detachment.

I seemed to go away; the lights receded like a tail-light racing down a dark country road. I couldn't follow. A sharp pain stabbed my shoulder. I twisted about on my back, fighting something I couldn't see. Then after a while my vision cleared.

Now a man sitting with his back to me, manipulating dials on a panel. I wanted to call him, but the *Fifth Symphony* rhythm racked me, and he seemed too serene and too far away. Bright metal bars were between us and when I strained my neck around I discovered that I was not lying *on* an operating table but *in* a kind of glass and nickel box, the lid of which was propped open. Why was I here?

"Doctor! Doctor!" I called.

No answer. Perhaps he hadn't heard, I thought, calling again and feeling the stabbing pulses of the machine again and feeling myself going under and fighting against it and coming up to hear voices carrying on a conversation behind my head.

The static sounds became a quiet drone. Strains of music, a Sunday air, drifted from a distance. With closed eyes, barely breathing, I warded off the pain. The voices droned harmoniously. Was it a radio I heard—a phonograph? The *vox humana* of a hidden organ? If so, what organ and where? I felt warm. Green hedges, dazzling with red wild roses appeared behind my eyes, stretching with a gentle curving to an infinity empty of objects, a limpid blue space. Scenes of a shaded lawn in summer drifted past; I saw a uniformed military band arrayed decorously in concert, each musician with well-oiled hair, heard a sweet-voiced trumpet rendering "The Holy City" as from an echoing distance, buoyed by a choir of muted horns; and above, the mocking obligato of a mocking bird. I felt giddy. The air seemed to grow thick with fine white gnats, filling my eyes, boiling so thickly that the dark trumpeter breathed them in and expelled them through the bell of his golden horn, a live white cloud mixing with the tones upon the torpid air.

I came back. The voices still droned above me and I disliked them. Why didn't they go away? Smug ones. Oh, doctor, I thought drowsily, did you ever wade in a brook before breakfast? Ever chew on sugar cane? You know, doc, the same fall day I first saw the hounds chasing black men in stripes and chains my grandmother sat with me and sang with twinkling eyes:

> *"Godamighty made a monkey*
> *Godamighty made a whale*
> *And Godamighty made a 'gator*
> *With hickeys all over his tail . . ."*

Or you, nurse, did you know that when you strolled in pink organdy and picture hat between the rows of cape jasmine, cooing to your beau in a drawl as thick as sorghum, we little black boys hidden snug in the bushes called out so loud that you daren't hear:

> *"Did you ever see Miss Margaret boil water?*
> *Man, she hisses a wonderful stream,*
> *Seventeen miles and a quarter,*
> *Man, and you can't see her pot for the steam ..."*

But now the music became a distinct wail of female pain. I opened my eyes. Glass and metal floated above me.

"How are you feeling, boy?" a voice said.

A pair of eyes peered down through lenses as thick as the bottom of a Coca-Cola bottle, eyes protruding, luminous and veined, like an old biology specimen preserved in alcohol.

"I don't have enough room," I said angrily.

"Oh, that's a necessary part of the treatment."

"But I need more room," I insisted. "I'm cramped."

"Don't worry about it, boy. You'll get used to it after a while. How is your stomach and head?"

"Stomach?"

"Yes, and your head?"

"I don't know," I said, realizing that I could feel nothing beyond the pressure around my head and on the tender surface of my body. Yet my senses seemed to focus sharply.

"I don't feel it," I cried, alarmed.

"Aha! You see! My little gadget will solve everything!" he exploded.

"I don't know," another voice said. "I think I still prefer surgery. And in this case especially, with this, uh ... background, I'm not so sure that I don't believe in the effectiveness of simple prayer."

"Nonsense, from now on do your praying to my little machine. I'll deliver the cure."

"I don't know, but I believe it a mistake to assume that solutions—cures, that is—that apply in, uh . . . primitive instances, are, uh . . . equally effective when more advanced conditions are in question. Suppose it were a New Englander with a Harvard background?"

"Now you're arguing politics," the first voice said banteringly.

"Oh, no, but it *is* a problem."

I listened with growing uneasiness to the conversation fuzzing away to a whisper. Their simplest words seemed to refer to something else, as did many of the notions that unfurled through my head. I wasn't sure whether they were talking about me or someone else. Some of it sounded like a discussion of history . . .

"The machine will produce the results of a prefrontal lobotomy without the negative effects of the knife," the voice said. "You see, instead of severing the prefrontal lobe, a single lobe, that is, we apply pressure in the proper degrees to the major centers of nerve control—our concept is Gestalt—and the result is as complete a change of personality as you'll find in your famous fairy-tale cases of criminals transformed into amiable fellows after all that bloody business of a brain operation. And what's more," the voice went on triumphantly, "the patient is both physically and neurally whole."

"But what of his psychology?"

"Absolutely of no importance!" the voice said. "The patient will live as he has to live, and with absolute integrity. Who could ask more? He'll experience no major conflict of motives, and what is even better, society will suffer no traumata on his account."

There was a pause. A pen scratched upon paper. Then, "Why not castration, doctor?" a voice asked waggishly, causing me to start, a pain tearing through me.

"There goes your love of blood again," the first voice laughed. "What's that definition of a surgeon, 'A butcher with a bad conscience'?"

They laughed.

"It's not so funny. It would be more scientific to try to define the case. It has been developing some three hundred years—"

"Define? Hell, man, we know all that."

"Then why don't you try more current?"

"You suggest it?"

"I do, why not?"

"But isn't there a danger . . . ?" the voice trailed off.

I heard them move away; a chair scraped. The machine droned, and I knew definitely that they were discussing me and steeled myself for the shocks, but was blasted nevertheless. The pulse came swift and staccato, increasing gradually until I fairly danced between the nodes. My teeth chattered. I closed my eyes and bit my lips to smother my screams. Warm blood filled my mouth. Between my lids I saw a circle of hands and faces, dazzling with light. Some were scribbling upon charts.

"Look, he's dancing," someone called.

"No, really?"

An oily face looked in. "They really do have rhythm, don't they? Get hot, boy! Get hot!" it said with a laugh.

And suddenly my bewilderment suspended and I wanted to be angry, murderously angry. But somehow the pulse of current smashing through my body prevented me. Something had been disconnected. For though I had seldom used my capacities for anger and indignation, I had no doubt that I possessed them; and, like a man who knows that he must fight, whether angry or not, when called a son of a bitch, I tried to *imagine* myself angry—only to discover a deeper sense of remoteness. I was beyond anger. I was only bewildered. And

those above seemed to sense it. There was no avoiding the
shock and I rolled with the agitated tide, out into the blackness.

When I emerged, the lights were still there. I lay beneath
the slab of glass, feeling deflated. All my limbs seemed ampu-
tated. It was very warm. A dim white ceiling stretched far
above me. My eyes were swimming with tears. Why, I didn't
know. It worried me. I wanted to knock on the glass to attract
attention, but I couldn't move. The slightest effort, hardly more
than desire, tired me. I lay experiencing the vague processes of
my body. I seemed to have lost all sense of proportion. Where
did my body end and the crystal and white world begin?
Thoughts evaded me, hiding in the vast stretch of clinical
whiteness to which I seemed connected only by a scale of
receding grays. No sounds beyond the sluggish inner roar of
the blood. I couldn't open my eyes. I seemed to exist in some
other dimension, utterly alone; until after a while a nurse bent
down and forced a warm fluid between my lips. I gagged,
swallowed, feeling the fluid course slowly to my vague middle.
A huge iridescent bubble seemed to enfold me. Gentle hands
moved over me, bringing vague impressions of memory. I was
laved with warm liquids, felt gentle hands move through the
indefinite limits of my flesh. The sterile and weightless texture
of a sheet enfolded me. I felt myself bounce, sail off like a ball
thrown over the roof into mist, striking a hidden wall beyond
a pile of broken machinery and sailing back. How long it took,
I didn't know. But now above the movement of the hands I
heard a friendly voice, uttering familiar words to which I could
assign no meaning. I listened intensely, aware of the form and
movement of sentences and grasping the now subtle rhythmical
differences between progressions of sound that questioned and
those that made a statement. But still their meanings were lost
in the vast whiteness in which I myself was lost.

Other voices emerged. Faces hovered above me like inscrutable fish peering myopically through a glass aquarium wall. I saw them suspended motionless above me, then two floating off, first their heads, then the tips of their finlike fingers, moving dreamily from the top of the case. A thoroughly mysterious coming and going, like the surging of torpid tides. I watched the two make furious movements with their mouths. I didn't understand. They tried again, the meaning still escaping me. I felt uneasy. I saw a scribbled card, held over me. All a jumble of alphabets. They consulted heatedly. Somehow I felt responsible. A terrible sense of loneliness came over me; they seemed to enact a mysterious pantomime. And seeing them from this angle was disturbing. They appeared utterly stupid and I didn't like it. It wasn't right. I could see smut in one doctor's nose; a nurse had two flabby chins. Other faces came up, their mouths working with soundless fury. But we are all human, I thought, wondering what I meant.

A man dressed in black appeared, a long-haired fellow, whose piercing eyes looked down upon me out of an intense and friendly face. The others hovered about him, their eyes anxious as he alternately peered at me and consulted my chart. Then he scribbled something on a large card and thrust it before my eyes:

WHAT IS YOUR NAME?

A tremor shook me; it was as though he had suddenly given a name to, had organized the vagueness that drifted through my head, and I was overcome with swift shame. I realized that I no longer knew my own name. I shut my eyes and shook my head with sorrow. Here was the first warm attempt to communicate with me and I was failing. I tried again, plunging into the blackness of my mind. It was no use;

I found nothing but pain. I saw the card again and he pointed slowly to each word:

WHAT . . . IS . . . YOUR . . . NAME?

I tried desperately, diving below the blackness until I was limp with fatigue. It was as though a vein had been opened and my energy syphoned away; I could only stare back mutely. But with an irritating burst of activity he gestured for another card and wrote:

WHO . . . ARE . . . YOU?

Something inside me turned with a sluggish excitement. This phrasing of the question seemed to set off a series of weak and distant lights where the other had thrown a spark that failed. Who am I? I asked myself. But it was like trying to identify one particular cell that coursed through the torpid veins of my body. Maybe I was just this blackness and bewilderment and pain, but that seemed less like a suitable answer than something I'd read somewhere.

The card was back again:

WHAT IS YOUR MOTHER'S NAME?

Mother, who *was* my mother? Mother, the one who screams when you suffer—but who? This was stupid, you always knew your mother's name. Who was it that screamed? Mother? But the scream came from the machine. A machine my mother? . . . Clearly, I was out of my head.

He shot questions at me: *Where were you born? Try to think of your name.*

I tried, thinking vainly of many names, but none seemed

to fit, and yet it was as though I was somehow a part of all of them, had become submerged within them and lost.

You must remember, the placard read. But it was useless. Each time I found myself back in the clinging white mist and my name just beyond my fingertips. I shook my head and watched him disappear for a moment and return with a companion, a short, scholarly looking man who stared at me with a blank expression. I watched him produce a child's slate and a piece of chalk, writing upon it:

WHO WAS YOUR MOTHER?

I looked at him, feeling a quick dislike and thinking, half in amusement, I don't play the dozens. And how's *your* old lady today?

THINK

I stared, seeing him frown and write a long time. The slate was filled with meaningless names.

I smiled, seeing his eyes blaze with annoyance. Old Friendly Face said something. The new man wrote a question at which I stared in wide-eyed amazement:

WHO WAS BUCKEYE THE RABBIT?

I was filled with turmoil. Why should he think of *that*? He pointed to the question, word by word. I laughed, deep, deep inside me, giddy with the delight of self-discovery and the desire to hide it. Somehow *I* was Buckeye the Rabbit . . . or had been, when as children we danced and sang barefoot in the dusty streets:

Buckeye the Rabbit
Shake it, shake it
Buckeye the Rabbit
Break it, break it . . .

Yes, I could not bring myself to admit it, it was too ridiculous—and somehow too dangerous. It was annoying that he had hit upon an old identity and I shook my head, seeing him purse his lips and eye me sharply.

BOY, WHO WAS BRER RABBIT?

He was your mother's back-door man, I thought. Anyone knew they were one and the same: "Buckeye" when you were very young and hid yourself behind wide innocent eyes; "Brer," when you were older. But why was he playing around with these childish names? Did they think I was a child? Why didn't they leave me alone? I would remember soon enough when they let me out of the machine . . . A palm smacked sharply upon the glass, but I was tired of them. Yet as my eyes focused upon Old Friendly Face he seemed pleased. I couldn't understand it, but there he was, smiling and leaving with the new assistant.

Left alone, I lay fretting over my identity. I suspected that I was really playing a game with myself and that they were taking part. A kind of combat. Actually they knew as well as I, and I for some reason preferred not to face it. It was irritating, and it made me feel sly and alert. I would solve the mystery the next instant. I imagined myself whirling about in my mind like an old man attempting to catch a small boy in some mischief, thinking, Who am I? It was no good. I felt like a clown. Nor was I up to being both criminal and detective—though why criminal I didn't know.

I fell to plotting ways of short-circuiting the machine. Perhaps if I shifted my body about so that the two nodes would come together—No, not only was there no room but it might electrocute me. I shuddered. Whoever else I was, I was no Samson. I had no desire to destroy myself even if it destroyed the machine; I wanted freedom, not destruction. It was exhausting, for no matter what the scheme I conceived, there was one constant flaw—myself. There was no getting around it. I could no more escape than I could think of my identity. Perhaps, I thought, the two things are involved with each other. When I discover who I am, I'll be free.

It was as though my thoughts of escape had alerted them. I looked up to see two agitated physicians and a nurse, and thought, It's too late now, and lay in a veil of sweat watching them manipulate the controls. I was braced for the usual shock, but nothing happened. Instead I saw their hands at the lid, loosening the bolts, and before I could react they had opened the lid and pulled me erect.

"What's happened?" I began, seeing the nurse pause to look at me.

"Well?" she said.

My mouth worked soundlessly.

"Come on, get it out," she said.

"What hospital is this?" I said.

"It's the factory hospital," she said. "Now be quiet."

They were around me now, inspecting my body, and I watched with growing bewilderment, thinking, what is a *factory* hospital?

I felt a tug at my belly and looked down to see one of the physicians pull the cord which was attached to the stomach node, jerking me forward.

"What is this?" I said.

"Get the shears," he said.

"Sure," the other said. "Let's not waste time."

I recoiled inwardly as though the cord were part of me. Then they had it free and the nurse clipped through the belly band and removed the heavy node. I opened my mouth to speak but one of the physicians shook his head. They worked swiftly. The nodes off, the nurse went over me with rubbing alcohol. Then I was told to climb out of the case. I looked from face to face, overcome with indecision. For now that it appeared that I was being freed, I dared not believe it. What if they were transferring me to some even more painful machine? I sat there, refusing to move. Should I struggle against them?

"Take his arm," one of them said.

"I can do it," I said, climbing fearfully out.

I was told to stand while they went over my body with the stethoscope.

"How's the articulation?" the one with the chart said as the other examined my shoulder.

"Perfect," he said.

I could feel a tightness there but no pain.

"I'd say he's surprisingly strong, considering," the other said.

"Shall we call in Drexel? It seems rather unusual for him to be so strong."

"No, just note it on the chart."

"All right, nurse, give him his clothes."

"What are you going to do with me?" I said. She handed me clean underclothing and a pair of white overalls.

"No questions," she said. "Just dress as quickly as possible."

The air outside the machine seemed extremely rare. When I bent over to tie my shoes I thought I would faint, but fought it off. I stood shakily and they looked me up and down.

"Well, boy, it looks as though you're cured," one of them said. "You're a new man. You came through fine. Come with us," he said.

We went slowly out of the room and down a long white corridor into an elevator, then swiftly down three floors to a reception room with rows of chairs. At the front were a number of private offices with frosted glass doors and walls.

"Sit down there," they said. "The director will see you shortly."

I sat, seeing them disappear inside one of the offices for a second and emerge, passing me without a word. I trembled like a leaf. Were they really freeing me? My head spun. I looked at my white overalls. The nurse said that this was the factory hospital . . . Why couldn't I remember what kind of factory it was? And why a *factory* hospital? Yes . . . I did remember some vague factory; perhaps I was being sent back there. Yes, and he'd spoken of the director instead of the head doctor; could they be one and the same? Perhaps I was in the factory already. I listened but could hear no machinery.

ACROSS the room a newspaper lay on a chair, but I was too concerned to get it. Somewhere a fan droned. Then one of the doors with frosted glass was opened and I saw a tall austere-looking man in a white coat, beckoning to me with a chart.

"Come," he said.

I got up and went past him into a large simply furnished office, thinking, *Now, I'll know. Now.*

"Sit down," he said.

I eased myself into the chair beside his desk. He watched me with a calm, scientific gaze.

"What is your name? Oh here, I have it," he said, studying the chart. And it was as though someone inside of me tried to tell him to be silent, but already he had called my name and I heard myself say, "Oh!" as a pain stabbed through my head and I shot to my feet and looked wildly around me and sat down and got up and down again very fast, remembering. I don't know why I did it, but suddenly I saw him looking at me intently, and I stayed down this time.

He began asking questions and I could hear myself replying fluently, though inside I was reeling with swiftly changing emotional images that shrilled and chattered, like a sound-track reversed at high speed.

"Well, my boy," he said, "you're cured. We are going to release you. How does that strike you?"

Suddenly I didn't know. I noticed a company calendar beside a stethoscope and a miniature silver paint brush. Did he mean from the hospital or from the job?. . .

"Sir?" I said.

"I said, how does that strike you?"

"All right, sir," I said in an unreal voice. "I'll be glad to get back to work."

He looked at the chart, frowning. "You'll be released, but I'm afraid that you'll be disappointed about the work," he said.

"What do you mean, sir?"

"You've been through a severe experience," he said. "You aren't ready for the rigors of industry. Now I want you to rest, undertake a period of convalescence. You need to become re-adjusted and get your strength back."

"But, sir—"

"You mustn't try to go too fast. You're glad to be re-leased, are you not?"

"Oh, yes. But how shall I live?"

"Live?" his eyebrows raised and lowered. "Take another job," he said. "Something easier, quieter. Something for which you're better prepared."

"Prepared?" I looked at him, thinking, Is he in on it too? "I'll take anything, sir," I said.

"That isn't the problem, my boy. You just aren't prepared for work under our industrial conditions. Later, perhaps, but not now. And remember, you'll be adequately compensated for your experience."

"Compensated, sir?"

"Oh, yes," he said. "We follow a policy of enlightened humanitarianism; all our employees are automatically insured. You have only to sign a few papers."

"What kind of papers, sir?"

"We require an affidavit releasing the company of responsibility," he said. "Yours was a difficult case, and a number of specialists had to be called in. But, after all, any new occupation has its hazards. They are part of growing up, of becoming adjusted, as it were. One takes a chance and while some are prepared, others are not."

I looked at his lined face. Was he doctor, factory official, or both? I couldn't get it; and now he seemed to move back and forth across my field of vision, although he sat perfectly calm in his chair.

It came out of itself: "Do you know Mr. Norton, sir?" I said.

"Norton?" His brows knitted. "What Norton is this?"

Then it was as though I hadn't asked him; the name sounded strange. I ran my hand over my eyes.

"I'm sorry," I said. "It occurred to me that you might. He was just a man I used to know."

"I see. Well"—he picked up some papers—"so that's the way it is, my boy. A little later perhaps we'll be able to do something. You may take the papers along if you wish. Just mail them to us. Your check will be sent upon their return. Meanwhile, take as much time as you like. You'll find that we are perfectly fair."

I took the folded papers and looked at him for what seemed to be too long a time. He seemed to waver. Then I heard myself say, "Do you know him?" my voice rising.

"Who?"

"Mr. Norton," I said. "Mr. Norton!"

"Oh, why, no."

"No," I said, "no one knows anybody and it was too long a time ago."

He frowned and I laughed. "They picked poor Robin clean," I said. "Do you happen to know Bled?"

He looked at me, his head to one side. "Are these people friends of yours?"

"Friends? Oh, yes," I said, "we're all good friends. Buddies from way back. But I don't suppose we get around in the same circles."

His eyes widened. "No," he said, "I don't suppose we do. However, good friends are valuable to have."

I felt light-headed and started to laugh and he seemed to waver again and I thought of asking him about Emerson, but now he was clearing his throat and indicating that he was finished.

I put the folded papers in my overalls and started out. The door beyond the rows of chairs seemed far away.

"Take care of yourself," he said.

"And you," I said, thinking, It's time, it's past time.

Turning abruptly, I went weakly back to the desk, seeing him looking up at me with his steady scientific gaze. I was overcome with ceremonial feelings but unable to remember the proper formula. So as I deliberately extended my hand I fought down laughter with a cough.

"It's been quite pleasant, our little palaver, sir," I said. I listened to myself and to his answer.

"Yes, indeed," he said.

He shook my hand gravely, without surprise or distaste. I looked down, he was there somewhere behind the lined face and outstretched hand.

"And now our palaver is finished," I said. "Good-bye."

He raised his hand. "Good-bye," he said, his voice non-committal.

Leaving him and going out into the paint-fuming air I had the feeling that I had been talking beyond myself, had used words and expressed attitudes not my own, that I was in the grip of some alien personality lodged deep within me. Like the servant about whom I'd read in psychology class who, during a trance, had recited pages of Greek philosophy which she had overheard one day while she worked. It was as though I were acting out a scene from some crazy movie. Or perhaps I was catching up with myself and had put into words feelings which I had hitherto suppressed. Or was it, I thought, starting up the walk, that I was no longer afraid? I stopped, looking at the buildings down the bright street slanting with sun and shade. I *was* no longer afraid. Not of important men, not of trustees and such; for knowing now that there was nothing which I could expect from them, there was no reason to be afraid. Was that it? I felt light-headed, my ears were ringing. I went on.

Along the walk the buildings rose, uniform and close together. It was day's end now and on top of every building the flags were fluttering and diving down, collapsing. And I felt that I would fall, had fallen, moved now as against a current sweeping swiftly against me. Out of the grounds and up the street I found the bridge by which I'd come, but the stairs leading back to the car that crossed the top were too dizzily steep to climb, swim or fly, and I found a subway instead.

Things whirled too fast around me. My mind went alternately bright and blank in slow rolling waves. We, he, him—

my mind and I—were no longer getting around in the same circles. Nor my body either. Across the aisle a young platinum blonde nibbled at a red Delicious apple as station lights rippled past behind her. The train plunged. I dropped through the roar, giddy and vacuum-minded, sucked under and out into late afternoon Harlem.

Chapter twelve

Whan I came out of the subway, Lenox Avenue seemed to career away from me at a drunken angle, and I focused upon the teetering scene with wild, infant's eyes, my head throbbing. Two huge women with spoiled-cream complexions seemed to struggle with their massive bodies as they came past, their flowered hips trembling like threatening flames. Out across the walk before me they moved, and a bright orange slant of sun seemed to boil up and I saw myself going down, my legs watery beneath me, but my head clear, too clear, recording the crowd swerving around me: legs, feet, eyes, hands, bent knees, scuffed shoes, teethy-eyed excitement; and some moving on unhalting.

And the big dark woman saying, *Boy, is you all right, what's wrong?* in a husky-voiced contralto. And me saying, *I'm all right, just weak,* and trying to stand, and her saying, *Why don't y'all stand back and let the man breathe? Stand back there y'all,* and now echoed by an official tone, *Keep moving, break it up.* And she on one side and a man on the other, helping me to stand and the policeman saying, *Are you all right?* and

me answering, *Yes, I just felt weak, must have fainted but all
right now,* and him ordering the crowd to move on and the
others moving on except the man and woman and him saying,
You sure you okay, daddy, and me nodding yes, and her saying,
Where you live son, somewhere around here? And me telling her
Men's House and her looking at me shaking her head saying,
*Men's House, Men's House, shucks that ain't no place for nobody
in your condition what's weak and needs a woman to keep an eye
on you awhile.* And me saying, *But I'll be all right now,* and
her, *Maybe you will and maybe you won't. I live just up the
street and round the corner, you better come on round and rest
till you feel stronger. I'll phone Men's House and tell 'em where
you at.* And me too tired to resist and already she had one
arm and was instructing the fellow to take the other and we
went, me between them, inwardly rejecting and yet accepting
her bossing, hearing, *You take it easy, I'll take care of you like I
done a heap of others, my name's Mary Rambo, everybody knows
me round this part of Harlem, you heard of me, ain't you?* And
the fellow saying, *Sure, I'm Jenny Jackson's boy, you know I
know you, Miss Mary.* And her saying, *Jenny Jackson, why, I
should say you do know me and I know you, you Ralston, and
your mama got two more children, boy named Flint and gal
named Laura-jean, I should say I know you—me and your mama
and your papa useta—* And me saying, *I'm all right now, really
all right.* And her saying, *And looking like that, you must be
worse off even than you look,* and pulling me now, saying, *Here's
my house right here, hep me git him up the steps and inside, you
needn't worry, son, I ain't never laid eyes on you before and it
ain't my business and I don't care what you think about me but
you weak and caint hardly walk and all and you look what's
more like you hungry, so just come on and let me do something
for you like I hope you'd do something for ole Mary in case she
needed it, it ain't costing you a penny and I don't want to git in*

your business, I just want you to lay down till you rested and then you can go. And the fellow taking it up, saying, *You in good hands, daddy, Miss Mary always helping somebody and you need some help 'cause here you black as me and white as a sheet, as the ofays would say—watch these steps.* And going up some steps and then some more, growing weaker, and the two warm around me on each side of me, and then inside a cool dark room, hearing, *Here, here's the bed, lie him down there, there, there now, that's it, Ralston, now put his legs up—never mind the cover—there, that's it, now go out there in the kitchen and pour him a glass of water, you'll find a bottle in the ice-box.* And him going and her placing another pillow beneath my head, saying, *Now you'll be better and when you git all right you'll know how bad a shape you been in, here, now taka sip of this water,* and me drinking and seeing her worn brown fingers holding the bright glass and a feeling of old, almost forgotten relief coming over me and thinking in echo of her words, *If I don't think I'm sinking, look what a hole I'm in,* and then the soft cool splash of sleep.

I saw her across the room when I awoke, reading a newspaper, her glasses low across the bridge of her nose as she stared at the page intently. Then I realized that though the glasses still slanted down, the eyes were no longer focused on the page, but on my face and lighting with a slow smile.

"How you feel now?" she said.

"Much better."

"I thought you would be. And you be even better after you have a cup of soup I got for you in the kitchen. You slept a good long time."

"Did I?" I said. "What time is it?"

"It's about ten o'clock, and from the way you slept I

suspects all you needed was some rest . . . No, don't git up yet. You got to drink your soup, then you can go," she said, leaving.

She returned with a bowl in a plate. "This here'll fix you up," she said. "You don't get this kind of service up there at Men's House, do you? Now, you just sit there and take your time. I ain't got nothing to do but read the paper. And I like company. You have to make time in the morning?"

"No, I've been sick," I said. "But I have to look for a job."

"I knowed you wasn't well. Why you try to hide it?"

"I didn't want to be trouble to anyone," I said.

"Everybody has to be trouble to *somebody*. And you just come from the hospital too."

I looked up. She sat in the rocking chair bent forward, her arms folded at ease across her aproned lap. Had she searched my pockets?

"How did you know that?" I said.

"There you go getting suspicious," she said sternly. "That's what's wrong with the world today, don't nobody trust nobody. I can smell that hospital smell on you, son. You got enough ether in those clothes to put to sleep a dog!"

"I couldn't remember telling you that I had been in the hospital."

"No, and you didn't have to. I smelled that out. You got people here in the city?"

"No, ma'm," I said. "They're down South. I came up here to work so I could go to school, and I got sick."

"Now ain't that too bad! But you'll make out all right. What you plan to make out of yourself?"

"I don't know now; I came here wanting to be an educator. Now I don't know."

"So what's wrong with being an educator?"

I thought about it while sipping the good hot soup. "Nothing, I suppose, I just think I'd like to do something else."

"Well, whatever it is, I hope it's something that's a credit to the race."

"I hope so," I said.

"Don't hope, make it that way."

I looked at her, thinking of what I'd tried to do and of where it had gotten me, seeing her heavy, composed figure before me.

"It's you young folks what's going to make the changes," she said. "Y'all's the ones. You got to lead and you got to fight and move us all on up a little higher. And I tell you something else, it's the ones from the South that's got to do it, them what knows the fire and ain't forgot how it burns. Up here too many forgits. They finds a place for theyselves and forgits the ones on the bottom. Oh, heap of them *talks* about doing things, but they done really forgot. No, it's you young ones what has to remember and take the lead."

"Yes," I said.

"And you have to take care of yourself, son. Don't let this Harlem git you. I'm in New York, but New York ain't in me, understand what I mean? Don't git corrupted."

"I won't. I'll be too busy."

"All right now, you looks to me like you might make something out of yourself, so you be careful."

I got up to go, watching her raise herself out of her chair and come with me to the door.

"You ever decide you want a room somewhere beside Men's House, try me," she said. "The rent's reasonable."

"I'll remember that," I said.

. . . .

I WAS to remember sooner than I had thought. The moment I entered the bright, buzzing lobby of Men's House I was overcome by a sense of alienation and hostility. My overalls were causing stares and I knew that I could live there no longer, that that phase of my life was past. The lobby was the meeting place for various groups still caught up in the illusions that had just been boomeranged out of my head: college boys working to return to school down South; older advocates of racial progress with utopian schemes for building black business empires; preachers ordained by no authority except their own, without church or congregation, without bread or wine, body or blood; the community "leaders" without followers; old men of sixty or more still caught up in post–Civil War dreams of freedom within segregation; the pathetic ones who possessed nothing beyond their dreams of being gentlemen, who held small jobs or drew small pensions, and all pretending to be engaged in some vast, though obscure, enterprise, who affected the pseudo-courtly manners of certain southern congressmen and bowed and nodded as they passed like senile old roosters in a barnyard; the younger crowd for whom I now felt a contempt such as only a disillusioned dreamer feels for those still unaware that they dream—the business students from southern colleges, for whom business was a vague, abstract game with rules as obsolete as Noah's Ark but who yet were drunk on finance. Yes, and that older group with similar aspirations, the "fundamentalists," the "actors" who sought to achieve the status of brokers through imagination alone, a group of janitors and messengers who spent most of their wages on clothing such as was fashionable among Wall Street brokers, with their Brooks Brothers suits and bowler hats, English umbrellas, black calfskin shoes and yellow gloves; with their orthodox and passionate argument as to what was the correct tie to wear with what shirt, what shade of gray was correct for spats and what would the Prince of Wales wear at a certain seasonal event; should field glasses be slung from the right or from the left shoulder; who never read the financial pages though they purchased the *Wall Street Journal* religiously and carried it beneath the left elbow, pressed firm against the body and grasped in the left hand—always manicured and gloved, fair weather or foul— with an easy precision (Oh, they had style) while the other hand whipped a tightly rolled umbrella back and forth at a calculated angle; with their homburgs and Chesterfields, their polo coats and Tyrolean hats worn strictly as fashion demanded.

I could feel their eyes, saw them all and saw too the time when they would know that my prospects were ended and saw already the contempt they'd feel for me, a college man who had lost his prospects and pride. I could see it all and I knew that even the officials and the older men would despise me as though, somehow, in losing my place in Bledsoe's world I had betrayed them . . . I saw it as they looked at my overalls.

I had started toward the elevator when I heard the voice raised in laughter and turned to see him holding forth to a group in the lobby chairs and saw the rolls of fat behind the wrinkled, high-domed, close-cut head, and I was certain that it was he and stooped without thought and lifted it shining, full and foul, and moved forward two long steps, dumping its great brown, transparent splash upon the head warned too late by someone across the room. And too late for me to see that it was not Bledsoe but a preacher, a prominent Baptist, who shot up wide-eyed with disbelief and outrage, and I shot around and out of the lobby before anyone could think to stop me.

No one followed me and I wandered the streets amazed at my own action. Later it began to rain and I sneaked back near Men's House and persuaded an amused porter to slip my things out to me. I learned that I had been barred from the building for "ninety-nine years and a day."

"You might not can come back, man," the porter said, "but after what you did, I swear, they never will stop talking about you. You really baptized ole Rev!"

So THAT same night I went back to Mary's, where I lived in a small but comfortable room until the ice came.

It was a period of quietness. I paid my way with my compensation money and found living with her pleasant except for her constant talk about leadership and responsibility. And even this was not too bad as long as I could pay my way. It was, however, a small compensation, and when after several months my money ran out and I was looking again for a job, I found her exceedingly irritating to listen to. Still, she never dunned me and was as generous with her servings of food during mealtime as ever. "It's just hard times you going through," she'd say. "Everybody worth his salt has his hard times, and when you git to be somebody you'll see these here very same hard times helped you a heap."

I didn't see it that way. I had lost my sense of direction. I spent my time, when not looking for work, in my room, where I read countless books from the library. Sometimes, when there was still money, or when I had earned a few dollars waiting table, I'd eat out and wander the streets until late at night. Other than Mary I had no friends and desired none. Nor did I think of Mary as a "friend"; she was something more—a force, a stable, familiar force like something out of my past which kept me from whirling off into some unknown which I dared not face. It was a most painful position, for at the same time, Mary reminded me constantly that something was expected of me, some act of leadership, some newsworthy achievement; and I was torn between resenting her for it and loving her for the nebulous hope she kept alive.

I had no doubt that I could do something, but what, and how? I had no contacts and I believed in nothing. And the obsession with my identity which I had developed in the factory hospital returned with a vengeance. Who was I, how had I come to be? Certainly I couldn't help being different from when I left the campus; but now a new, painful, contradictory voice had grown up within me, and between its demands for revengeful action and Mary's silent pressure I throbbed with guilt and puzzlement. I wanted peace and quiet, tranquillity, but was too much aboil inside. Somewhere beneath the load of the emotion-freezing ice which my life had conditioned my brain to produce, a spot of black anger glowed and threw off a hot red light of such intensity that had Lord Kelvin known of its existence, he would have had to revise his measurements. A remote explosion had occurred somewhere, perhaps back at Emerson's or that night in Bledsoe's office, and it had caused the ice cap to melt and shift the slightest bit. But that bit, that fraction, was irrevocable. Coming to New York had perhaps been an unconscious attempt to keep the old freezing unit going, but it hadn't worked; hot water had gotten into its coils. Only a drop, perhaps, but that drop was the first wave of the deluge. One moment I believed, I was dedicated, willing to lie on the blazing coals, do anything to attain a position on the campus—then snap! It was done with, finished, through. Now there was only the problem of forgetting it. If only all the contradictory voices shouting inside my head would calm down and sing a song in unison, whatever it was I wouldn't care as long as they sang without dissonance; yes, and avoided the uncertain extremes of the scale. But there was no relief. I was wild with resentment but too much under "self-control," that frozen virtue, that freezing vice. And the more resentful I became, the more my old urge to make speeches returned. While walking along the streets words would spill from my lips in a mumble over which I had little control. I became afraid of what I might do. All things were indeed awash in my mind. I longed for home.

And while the ice was melting to form a flood in which I threatened to drown I awoke one afternoon to find that my first northern winter had set.

Chapter thirteen

At first I had turned away from the window and tried to read but my mind kept wandering back to my old problems and, unable to endure it any longer, I rushed from the house, extremely agitated but determined to get away from my hot thoughts into the chill air.

At the entrance I bumped against a woman who called me a filthy name, only causing me to increase my speed. In a few minutes I was several blocks away, having moved to the next avenue and downtown. The streets were covered with ice and soot-flecked snow and from above a feeble sun filtered through the haze. I walked with my head down, feeling the biting air. And yet I was hot, burning with an inner fever. I barely raised my eyes until a car, passing with a thudding of skid chains whirled completely around on the ice, then turned cautiously and thudded off again.

I walked slowly on, blinking my eyes in the chill air, my mind a blur with the hot inner argument continuing. The whole of Harlem seemed to fall apart in the swirl of snow. I imagined

I was lost and for a moment there was an eerie quiet. I imagined I heard the fall of snow upon snow. What did it mean? I walked, my eyes focused into the endless succession of barber shops, beauty parlors, confectioneries, luncheonettes, fish houses, and hog maw joints, walking close to the windows, the snowflakes lacing swift between, simultaneously forming a curtain, a veil, and stripping it aside. A flash of red and gold from a window filled with religious articles caught my eye. And behind the film of frost etching the glass I saw two brashly painted plaster images of Mary and Jesus surrounded by dream books, love powders, God-Is-Love signs, money-drawing oil and plastic dice. A black statue of a nude Nubian slave grinned out at me from beneath a turban of gold. I passed on to a window decorated with switches of wiry false hair, ointments guaranteed to produce the miracle of whitening black skin. "You too can be truly beautiful," a sign proclaimed. "Win greater happiness with whiter complexion. Be outstanding in your social set."

I hurried on, suppressing a savage urge to push my fist through the pane. A wind was rising, the snow thinning. Where would I go? To a movie? Could I sleep there? I ignored the windows now and walked along, becoming aware that I was muttering to myself again. Then far down at the corner I saw an old man warming his hands against the sides of an odd-looking wagon, from which a stove pipe reeled off a thin spiral of smoke that drifted the odor of baking yams slowly to me, bringing a stab of swift nostalgia. I stopped as though struck by a shot, deeply inhaling, remembering, my mind surging back, back. At home we'd bake them in the hot coals of the fireplace, had carried them cold to school for lunch; munched them secretly, squeezing the sweet pulp from the soft peel as we hid from the teacher behind the largest book, the *World's Geography*. Yes, and we'd loved them candied, or baked in a cobbler, deep-fat fried in a pocket of dough, or roasted with pork and glazed with the well-browned fat; had chewed them raw—yams and years ago. More yams than years ago, though the time seemed endlessly expanded, stretched thin as the spiraling smoke beyond all recall.

I moved again. "Get yo' hot, baked Car'lina yam," he called. At the corner the old man, wrapped in an army overcoat, his feet covered with gunny sacks, his head in a knitted cap, was puttering with a stack of paper bags. I saw a crude sign on the side of the wagon proclaiming YAMS, as I walked flush into the warmth thrown by the coals that glowed in a grate underneath.

"How much are your yams?" I said, suddenly hungry.

"They ten cents and they sweet," he said, his voice quavering with age. "These ain't none of them binding ones neither. These here is real, sweet, yaller yams. How many?"

"One," I said. "If they're that good, one should be enough."

He gave me a searching glance. There was a tear in the corner of his eye. He chuckled and opened the door of the improvised oven, reaching gingerly with his gloved hand. The yams, some bubbling with syrup, lay on a wire rack above glowing coals that leaped to low blue flame when struck by the draft of air. The flash of warmth set my face aglow as he removed one of the yams and shut the door.

"Here you are, suh," he said, starting to put the yam into a bag.

"Never mind the bag, I'm going to eat it. Here . . ."

"Thanks." He took the dime. "If that ain't a sweet one, I'll give you another one free of charge."

I knew that it was sweet before I broke it; bubbles of brown syrup had burst the skin.

"Go ahead and break it," the old man said. "Break it

and I'll give you some butter since you gon' eat it right here. Lots of folks takes 'em home. They got their own butter at home."

I broke it, seeing the sugary pulp steaming in the cold.

"Hold it over here," he said. He took a crock from a rack on the side of the wagon. "Right here."

I held it, watching him pour a spoonful of melted butter over the yam and the butter seeping in.

"Thanks."

"You welcome. And I'll tell you something."

"What's that?" I said.

"If that ain't the best eating you had in a long time, I give you your money back."

"You don't have to convince me," I said. "I can look at it and see it's good."

"You right, but everything what looks good ain't necessarily good," he said. "But these is."

I took a bite, finding it as sweet and hot as any I'd ever had, and was overcome with such a surge of homesickness that I turned away to keep my control. I walked along, munching the yam, just as suddenly overcome by an intense feeling of freedom—simply because I was eating while walking along the street. It was exhilarating. I no longer had to worry about who saw me or about what was proper. To hell with all that, and as sweet as the yam actually was, it became like nectar with the thought. If only someone who had known me at school or at home would come along and see me now. How shocked they'd be! I'd push them into a side street and smear their faces with the peel. What a group of people we were, I thought. Why, you could cause us the greatest humiliation simply by confronting us with something we liked. Not *all* of us, but so many. Simply by walking up and shaking a set of chitterlings or a well-boiled hog maw at them during the clear light of day! What consternation it would cause! And I saw myself advancing upon Bledsoe, standing bare of his false humility in the crowded lobby of Men's House, and seeing him there and him seeing me and ignoring me and me enraged and suddenly whipping out a foot or two of chitterlings, raw, uncleaned and dripping sticky circles on the floor as I shake them in his face, shouting:

"Bledsoe, you're a shameless chitterling eater! I accuse you of relishing hog bowels! Ha! And not only do you eat them, you sneak and eat them in *private* when you think you're unobserved! You're a sneaking chitterling lover! I accuse you of indulging in a filthy habit, Bledsoe! Lug them out of there, Bledsoe! Lug them out so we can see! I accuse you before the eyes of the world!" And he lugs them out, yards of them, with mustard greens, and racks of pigs' ears, and pork chops and black-eyed peas with dull accusing eyes.

I let out a wild laugh, almost choking over the yam as the scene spun before me. Why, with others present, it would be worse than if I had accused him of raping an old woman of ninety-nine years, weighing ninety pounds . . . blind in one eye and lame in the hip! Bledsoe would disintegrate, disinflate! With a profound sigh he'd drop his head in shame. He'd lose caste. The weekly newspapers would attack him. The captions over his picture: *Prominent Educator Reverts to Field-Niggerism!* His rivals would denounce him as a bad example for the youth. Editorials would demand that he either recant or retire from public life. In the South his white folks would desert him; he would be discussed far and wide, and all of the trustees' money couldn't prop up his sagging prestige. He'd end up an exile washing dishes at the Automat. For down South he'd be unable to get a job on the honey wagon.

This is all very wild and childish, I thought, but to hell

with being ashamed of what you liked. No more of that for me. I am what I am! I wolfed down the yam and ran back to the old man and handed him twenty cents. "Give me two more," I said.

"Sho, all you want, long as I got 'em. I can see you a serious yam eater, young fellow. You eating them right away?"

"As soon as you give them to me," I said.

"You want 'em buttered?"

"Please."

"Sho, that way you can get the most out of 'em. Yes-suh," he said, handing over the yams, "I can see you one of these old-fashioned yam eaters."

"They're my birthmark," I said. "I yam what I am!"

"Then you must be from South Car'lina," he said with a grin.

"South Carolina nothing, where I come from we really go for yams."

"Come back tonight or tomorrow if you can eat some more," he called after me. "My old lady'll be out here with some hot sweet potato fried pies."

Hot fried pies, I thought sadly, moving away. I would probably have indigestion if I ate one—now that I no longer felt ashamed of the things I had always loved, I probably could no longer digest very many of them. What and how much had I lost by trying to do only what was expected of me instead of what I myself had wished to do? What a waste, what a senseless waste! But what of those things which you actually didn't like, not because you were not supposed to like them, not because to dislike them was considered a mark of refinement and education—but because you actually found them distasteful? The very idea annoyed me. How could you know? It involved a problem of choice. I would have to weigh many things carefully before deciding and there would be some things that would cause quite a bit of trouble, simply because I had never formed a personal attitude toward so much. I had accepted the accepted attitudes and it had made life seem simple . . .

But not yams, I had no problem concerning them and I would eat them whenever and wherever I took the notion. Continue on the yam level and life would be sweet—though somewhat yellowish. Yet the freedom to eat yams on the street was far less than I had expected upon coming to the city. An unpleasant taste bloomed in my mouth now as I bit the end of the yam and threw it into the street; it had been frost-bitten.

The wind drove me into a side street where a group of boys had set a packing box afire. The gray smoke hung low and seemed to thicken as I walked with my head down and eyes closed, trying to avoid the fumes. My lungs began to pain; then emerging, wiping my eyes and coughing, I almost stumbled over it: It was piled in a jumble along the walk and over the curb into the street, like a lot of junk waiting to be hauled away. Then I saw the sullen-faced crowd, looking at a building where two white men were totting out a chair in which an old woman sat; who, as I watched, struck at them feebly with her fists. A motherly-looking old woman with her head tied in a handkerchief, wearing a man's shoes and a man's heavy blue sweater. It was startling: The crowd watching silently, the two white men lugging the chair and trying to dodge the blows and the old woman's face streaming with angry tears as she thrashed at them with her fists. I couldn't believe it. Something, a sense of foreboding, filled me, a quick sense of un-cleanliness.

"Leave us alone," she cried, "leave us alone!" as the men pulled their heads out of range and sat her down abruptly at the curb, hurrying back in the building.

What on earth, I thought, looking above me. What on earth? The old woman sobbed, pointing to the stuff piled along the curb. "Just look what they doing to us. Just look," looking straight at me. And I realized that what I'd taken for junk was actually worn household furnishings.

"Just look at what they're doing," she said, her teary eyes upon my face.

I looked away embarrassed, staring into the rapidly growing crowd. Faces were peering sullenly from the windows above. And now as the two men reappeared at the top of the steps carrying a battered chest of drawers, I saw a third man come out and stand behind them, pulling at his ear as he looked out over the crowd.

"Shake it up, you fellows," he said, "shake it up. We don't have all day."

Then the men came down with the chest and I saw the crowd give way sullenly, the men trudging through, grunting and putting the chest at the curb, then returning into the building without a glance to left or right.

"Look at that," a slender man near me said. "We ought to beat the hell out of those paddies!"

I looked silently into his face, taut and ashy in the cold, his eyes trained upon the men going up the steps.

"Sho, we ought to stop 'em," another man said, "but ain't that much nerve in the whole bunch."

"There's plenty nerve," the slender man said. "All they need is someone to set it off. All they need is a leader. You mean *you* don't have the nerve."

"Who me?" the man said. "Who me?"

"Yes, you."

"Just look," the old woman said, "just look," her face still turned toward mine. I turned away, edging closer to the two men.

"Who are those men?" I said, edging closer.

"Marshals or something. I don't give a damn who they is."

"Marshals, hell," another man said. "Those guys doing all the toting ain't nothing but trusties. Soon as they get through they'll lock 'em up again."

"I don't care who they are, they got no business putting these old folks out on the sidewalk."

"You mean they're putting them out of their apartment?" I said. "They can do that up *here?*"

"Man, where *you* from?" he said, swinging toward me. "What does it look they puttin' them out of, a Pullman car? They being evicted!"

I was embarrassed; others were turning to stare. I had never seen an eviction. Someone snickered.

"Where did *he* come from?"

A flash of heat went over me and I turned. "Look, friend," I said, hearing a hot edge coming into my voice. "I asked a civil question. If you don't care to answer, don't, but don't try to make me look ridiculous."

"Ridiculous? Hell, all scobos is ridiculous. Who the hell is you?"

"Never mind, I am who I am. Just don't beat up your gums at me," I said, throwing him a newly acquired phrase.

Just then one of the men came down the steps with an armful of articles, and I saw the old woman reach up, yelling, "Take your hands off my Bible!" And the crowd surged forward.

The white man's hot eyes swept the crowd. "Where, lady?" he said. "I don't see any Bible."

And I saw her snatch the Book from his arms, clutching it fiercely and sending forth a shriek. "They can come in your home and do what they want to you," she said. "Just come stomping and jerk your life up by the roots! But this here's the last straw. They ain't going to bother with my Bible!"

The white man eyed the crowd. "Look, lady," he said, more to the rest of us than to her, "I don't want to do this, I *have* to do it. They sent me up here to do it. If it was left to me, you could stay here till hell freezes over . . ."

"These white folks, Lord. These white folks," she moaned, her eyes turned toward the sky, as an old man pushed past me and went to her.

"Hon, Hon," he said, placing his hand on her shoulder. "It's the agent, not these gentlemen. He's the one. He says it's in the bank, but you know he's the one. We've done business with him for over twenty years."

"Don't tell me," she said. "It's all the white folks, not just one. They all against us. Every stinking low-down one of them."

"She's right!" a hoarse voice said. "She's right! They *all* is!"

Something had been working fiercely inside me, and for a moment I had forgotten the rest of the crowd. Now I recognized a self-consciousness about them, as though they, we, were ashamed to witness the eviction, as though we were all unwilling intruders upon some shameful event; and thus we were careful not to touch or stare too hard at the effects that lined the curb; for we were witnesses of what we did not wish to see, though curious, fascinated, despite our shame, and through it all the old female, mind-plunging crying.

I looked at the old people, feeling my eyes burn, my throat tighten. The old woman's sobbing was having a strange effect upon me—as when a child, seeing the tears of its parents, is moved by both fear and sympathy to cry. I turned away, feeling myself being drawn to the old couple by a warm, dark, rising whirlpool of emotion which I feared. I was wary of what the sight of them crying there on the sidewalk was making me begin to feel. I wanted to leave, but was too ashamed to leave, was rapidly becoming too much a part of it to leave.

I turned aside and looked at the clutter of household objects which the two men continued to pile on the walk. And as the crowd pushed me I looked down to see looking out of an oval frame a portrait of the old couple when young, seeing the sad, stiff dignity of the faces there; feeling strange memories awakening that began an echoing in my head like that of a hysterical voice stuttering in a dark street. Seeing them look back at me as though even then in that nineteenth-century day they had expected little, and this with a grim, unillusioned pride that suddenly seemed to me both a reproach and a warning. My eyes fell upon a pair of crudely carved and polished bones, "knocking bones," used to accompany music at country dances, used in black-face minstrels; the flat ribs of a cow, a steer or sheep, flat bones that gave off a sound, when struck, like heavy castanets (had he been a minstrel?) or the wooden block of a set of drums. Pots and pots of green plants were lined in the dirty snow, certain to die of the cold; ivy, canna, a tomato plant. And in a basket I saw a straightening comb, switches of false hair, a curling iron, a card with silvery letters against a background of dark red velvet, reading "God Bless Our Home"; and scattered across the top of a chiffonier were nuggets of High John the Conqueror, the lucky stone; and as I watched the white men put down a basket in which I saw a whiskey bottle filled with rock candy and camphor, a small Ethiopian flag, a faded tintype of Abraham Lincoln, and the smiling image of a Hollywood star torn from a magazine. And on a pillow several badly cracked pieces of delicate china, a commemorative plate celebrating the St. Louis World's Fair . . . I stood in a kind of daze, looking at an old folded lace fan studded with jet and mother-of-pearl.

The crowd surged as the white men came back, knocking over a drawer that spilled its contents in the snow at my feet. I stooped and starting replacing the articles: a bent Masonic emblem, a set of tarnished cuff links, three brass rings, a dime pierced with a nail hole so as to be worn about the ankle on a string for luck, an ornate greeting card with the message "Grandma, I love you" in childish scrawl; another card with a picture of what looked like a white man in black-face seated in the door of a cabin strumming a banjo beneath a bar of music and the lyric "Going back to my old cabin home"; a useless inhalant, a string of bright glass beads with a tarnished clasp, a rabbit foot, a celluloid baseball scoring card shaped like a catcher's mitt, registering a game won or lost years ago; an old breast pump with rubber bulb yellowed with age, a worn baby shoe and a dusty lock of infant hair tied with a faded and crumpled blue ribbon. I felt nauseated. In my hand I held three lapsed life insurance policies with perforated seals stamped "Void"; a yellowing newspaper portrait of a huge black man with the caption: MARCUS GARVEY DEPORTED.

I turned away, bending and searching the dirty snow for anything missed by my eyes, and my fingers closed upon something resting in a frozen footstep: a fragile paper, coming apart with age, written in black ink grown yellow. I read: FREE PAPERS. *Be it known to all men that my negro, Primus Provo, has been freed by me this sixth day of August, 1859. Signed: John Samuels. Macon.* . . . I folded it quickly, blotting out the single drop of melted snow which glistened on the yellowed page, and dropped it back into the drawer. My hands were trembling, my breath rasping as if I had run a long distance or come upon a coiled snake in a busy street. *It has been longer than that, further removed in time,* I told myself, and yet I knew that it hadn't been. I replaced the drawer in the chest and pushed drunkenly to the curb.

But it wouldn't come up, only a bitter spurt of gall filled my mouth and splattered the old folk's possessions. I turned and stared again at the jumble, no longer looking at what was before my eyes, but inwardly-outwardly, around a corner into the dark, far-away-and-long-ago, not so much of my own memory as of remembered words, of linked verbal echoes, images, heard even when not listening at home. And it was as though I myself was being dispossessed of some painful yet precious thing which I could not bear to lose; something confounding, like a rotted tooth that one would rather suffer indefinitely than endure the short, violent eruption of pain that would mark its removal. And with this sense of dispossession came a pang of vague recognition: this junk, these shabby chairs, these heavy, old-fashioned pressing irons, zinc wash tubs with dented bottoms—all throbbed within me with more meaning than there should have been: *And why did I, standing in the crowd, see like a vision my mother hanging wash on a cold windy day, so cold that the warm clothes froze even before the vapor thinned and hung stiff on the line, and her hands white and raw in the skirt-swirling wind and her gray head bare to the darkened sky— why were they causing me discomfort so far beyond their intrinsic meaning as objects? And why did I see them now, as behind a veil that threatened to lift, stirred by the cold wind in the narrow street?*

A scream, "I'm going in!" spun me around. The old couple were on the steps now, the old man holding her arm, the white men leaning forward above, and the crowd pressing me closer to the steps.

"You can't go in, lady," the man said.

"I want to pray!" she said.

"I can't help it, lady. You'll have to do your praying out here."

"I'm go'n in!"

"Not in here!"

"All we want to do is go in and pray," she said, clutching her Bible. "It ain't right to pray in the street like this."

"I'm sorry," he said.

"Aw, let the woman go in to pray," a voice called from the crowd. "You got all their stuff out here on the walk—what more do you want, blood?"

"Sure, let them old folks pray."

"That's what's wrong with us now, all this damn praying," another voice called.

"You don't go back, see," the white man said. "You were legally evicted."

"But all we want to do is go in an' kneel on the floor," the old man said. "We been living right here for over twenty years. I don't see why you can't let us go just for a few minutes . . ."

"Look, I've told you," the man said. "I've got my orders. You're wasting my time."

"We go'n in!" the woman said.

It happened so suddenly that I could barely keep up with it: I saw the old woman clutching her Bible and rushing up the steps, her husband behind her and the white man stepping in front of them and stretching out his arm. "I'll jug you," he yelled, "by God, I'll jug you!"

"Take your hands off that woman!" someone called from the crowd.

Then at the top of the stairs they were pushing against the man and I saw the old woman fall backwards, and the crowd exploded.

"Get that paddie sonofabitch!"

"He struck her!" a West Indian woman screamed into my ear. "The filthy brute, he struck her!"

"Stand back or I'll shoot," the man called, his eyes wild as he drew a gun and backed into the doorway where the two trusties stood bewildered, their arms full of articles. "I swear I'll shoot! You don't know what you're doing, but I'll shoot!"

They hesitated. "Ain't but six bullets in that thing," a little fellow called. "Then what you going to do?"

"Yeah, you damn sho caint hide."

"I advise you to stay out of this," the marshal called.

"Think you can come up here and hit one of our women, you a fool."

"To hell with all this talk, let's rush that bastard!"

"You better think twice," the white man called.

I saw them start up the steps and felt suddenly as though my head would split. I knew that they were about to attack the man and I was both afraid and angry, repelled and fascinated. I both wanted it and feared the consequences, was outraged and angered at what I saw and yet surged with fear; not for the man or of the consequences of an attack, but of what the sight of violence might release in me. And beneath it all there boiled up all the shock-absorbing phrases that I had learned all my life. I seemed to totter on the edge of a great dark hole.

"No, no," I heard myself yelling. "Black men! Brothers! Black Brothers! That's not the way. We're law-abiding. We're a law-abiding people and a slow-to-anger people."

Forcing my way quickly through the crowd, I stood on the steps facing those in front, talking rapidly without thought but out of my clashing emotions. "We're a law-abiding people and a slow-to-anger people . . ." They stopped, listening. Even the white man was startled.

"Yeah, but we mad now," a voice called out.

"Yes, you're right," I called back. "We're angry, but let us be wise. Let us, I mean let us not . . . Let us learn from that great leader whose wise action was reported in the newspaper the other day . . ."

"What mahn? Who?" a West Indian voice shouted.

"Come on! To hell with this guy, let's get that paddie before they send him some help . . ."

"No, wait," I yelled. "Let's follow a leader, let's organize. *Organize.* We need someone like that wise leader, you read about him, down in Alabama. He was strong enough to choose to do the wise thing in spite of what he felt himself . . ."

"Who, mahn? Who?"

This was it, I thought, they're listening, eager to listen. Nobody laughed. If they laugh, I'll die! I tensed my diaphragm.

"That wise man," I said, "you read about him, who when that fugitive escaped from the mob and ran to his school for protection, that wise man who was strong enough to do the legal thing, the law-abiding thing, to turn him over to the forces of law and order . . ."

"Yeah," a voice rang out, "yeah, so they could lynch his ass."

Oh, God, this wasn't it at all. Poor technique and not at all what I intended.

"He was a wise leader," I yelled. "He was within the law. Now wasn't that the wise thing to do?"

"Yeah, he was wise all right," the man laughed angrily. "Now get out of the way so we can jump this paddie."

The crowd yelled and I laughed in response as though hypnotized.

"But wasn't that the human thing to do? After all, he had to protect himself because—"

"He was a handkerchief-headed rat!" a woman screamed, her voice boiling with contempt.

"Yes, you're right. He was wise and cowardly, but what about us? What are we to do?" I yelled, suddenly thrilled by the response. "Look at him," I cried.

"Yes, just look at him!" an old fellow in a derby called out as though answering a preacher in church.

"And look at that old couple . . ."

"Yeah, what about Sister and Brother Provo?" he said. "It's an ungodly shame!"

"And look at their possessions all strewn there on the sidewalk. Just look at their possessions in the snow. How old are you, sir?" I yelled.

"I'm eighty-seven," the old man said, his voice low and bewildered.

"How's that? Yell so our slow-to-anger brethren can hear you."

"I'm eighty-seven years old!"

"Did you hear him? He's eighty-seven. Eighty-seven and look at all he's accumulated in eighty-seven years, strewn in the snow like chicken guts, and we're a law-abiding, slow-to-anger bunch of folks turning the other cheek every day in the week. What are we going to do? What would you, what would I, what would he have done? *What is to be done?* I propose we do the wise thing, the law-abiding thing. Just look at this junk! Should two old folks live in such junk, cooped up in a filthy room? It's a great danger, a fire hazard! Old cracked dishes and broken-down chairs. Yes, yes, yes! Look at that old woman, somebody's mother, somebody's grandmother, maybe. We call them 'Big Mama' and they spoil us and—*you* know, *you* remember . . . Look at her quilts and broken-down shoes. I know she's somebody's mother because I saw an old breast pump fall into the snow, and she's somebody's grandmother, because I saw a card that read 'Dear Grandma' . . . but we're law-abiding . . . I looked into a basket and I saw some bones, not neck-bones, but rib bones, knocking bones . . . This old couple used to dance . . . I saw— What kind of work do you do, Father?" I called.

"I'm a day laborer . . ."

". . . A day laborer, you heard him, but look at his stuff strewn like chitterlings in the snow . . . Where has all his labor gone? Is he lying?"

"Hell, no, he ain't lying."

"Naw, suh!"

"Then where did his labor go? Look at his old blues records and her pots of plants, they're down-home folks, and everything tossed out like junk whirled eighty-seven years in a cyclone. Eighty-seven years, and *poof!* like a snort in a wind storm. Look at them, they look like my mama and my papa and my grandma and grandpa, and I look like you and you look like me. Look at them but remember that we're a wise, law-abiding group of people. And remember it when you look up there in the doorway at that law standing there with his forty-five. Look at him, standing with his blue steel pistol and his blue serge suit, or one forty-five, you see ten for every one of us, ten guns and ten warm suits and ten fat bellies and ten million laws. *Laws*, that's what we call them down South! Laws! And we're wise, and law-abiding. And look at this old woman with her dog-eared Bible. What's she trying to bring off here? She's let her religion go to her head, but we all know that religion is for the heart, not for the head. 'Blessed are the pure in heart,' it says. Nothing about the poor in head. What's she trying to do? What about the clear of head? And the clear of eye, the ice-water-visioned who see too clear to miss a lie? Look out there at her cabinet with its gaping drawers. Eighty-seven years to fill them, and full of brick and brack, a brica-brac, and she wants to break the law . . . What's happened to them? They're our people, your people and mine, your parents and mine. What's happened to 'em?"

"I'll tell you!" a heavyweight yelled, pushing out of the crowd, his face angry. "Hell, they been dispossessed, you crazy sonofabitch, get out the way!"

"Dispossessed?" I cried, holding up my hand and allowing the word to whistle from my throat. "That's a good word, 'Dispossessed'! 'Dispossessed,' eighty-seven years and dispossessed of what? They ain't *got* nothing, they caint *get* nothing, they never *had* nothing. So who was dispossessed?" I growled. "We're law-abiding. So who's being dispossessed? Can it be us? These old ones are out in the snow, but we're here with them. Look at their stuff, not a pit to hiss in, nor a window to shout the news and us right with them. Look at them, not a shack to pray in or an alley to sing the blues! They're facing a gun and we're facing it with them. They don't want the world, but only Jesus. They only want Jesus, just fifteen minutes of Jesus on the rug-bare floor . . . How about it, Mr. Law? Do we get our fifteen minutes worth of Jesus? You got the world, can we have our Jesus?"

"I got my orders, Mac," the man called, waving the pistol with a sneer. "You're doing all right, tell 'em to keep out of this. This is legal and I'll shoot if I have to . . ."

"But what about the prayer?"

"They don't go back!"

"Are you positive?"

"You could bet your life," he said.

"Look at him," I called to the angry crowd. "With his blue steel pistol and his blue serge suit. You heard him, he's the law. He says he'll shoot us down because we're a law-abiding people. So we've been dispossessed, and what's more, he thinks he's God. Look up there backed against the post with a criminal on either side of him. Can't you feel the cold wind, can't you hear it asking, 'What did you do with your heavy labor? What did you do?' When you look at all you haven't got in eighty-seven years you feel ashamed—"

"Tell 'em about it, brother," an old man interrupted. "It makes you feel you ain't a man."

"Yes, these old folks had a dream book, but the pages

went blank and it failed to give them the number. It was called the Seeing Eye, The Great Constitutional Dream Book, The Secrets of Africa, The Wisdom of Egypt—but the eye was blind, it lost its luster. It's all cataracted like a cross-eyed carpenter and it doesn't saw straight. All we have is the Bible and this Law here rules that out. So where do we go? Where do we go from here, without a pot—"

"We going after that paddie," the heavyweight called, rushing up the steps.

Someone pushed me. "No, wait," I called.

"Get out the way now."

There was a rush against me and I fell, hearing a single explosion, backward into a whirl of milling legs, overshoes, the trampled snow cold on my hands. Another shot sounded above like a bursting bag. Managing to stand, I saw atop the steps the fist with the gun being forced into the air above the crowd's bobbing heads and the next instant they were dragging him down into the snow; punching him left and right, uttering a low tense swelling sound of desperate effort; a grunt that exploded into a thousand softly spat, hate-sizzling curses. I saw a woman striking with the pointed heel of her shoe, her face a blank mask with hollow black eyes as she aimed and struck, aimed and struck, bringing spurts of blood, running along beside the man who was dragged to his feet now as they punched him gauntlet-wise between them. Suddenly I saw a pair of handcuffs arc gleaming into the air and sail across the street. A boy broke out of the crowd, the marshal's snappy hat on his head. The marshal was spun this way and that, then a swift tattoo of blows started him down the street. I was beside myself with excitement. The crowd surged after him, milling like a huge man trying to turn in a cubbyhole—some of them laughing, some cursing, some intently silent.

"The brute stuck that gentle woman, poor thing!" the West Indian woman chanted. "Black men, did you ever see such a brute? Is he a gentleman, I ask you? The brute? Give it back to him, black men. Repay the brute a thousandfold! Give it back to him unto the third and fourth generations. Strike him, our fine black men. Protect your black women! Repay the arrogant creature to the third and fourth generations!"

"We're dispossessed," I sang at the top of my voice, "dispossessed and we want to pray. Let's go in and pray. Let's have a big prayer meeting. But we'll need some chairs to sit in . . . rest upon as we kneel. We'll need some chairs!"

"Here's some chairs down here," a woman called from the walk. "How 'bout taking in some chairs?"

"Sure," I called, "take everything. Take it all, hide that junk! Put it back where it came from. It's blocking the street and the sidewalk, and that's against the law. We're law-abiding, so clear the street of the debris. Put it out of sight! Hide it, hide their shame! Hide *our* shame!"

"Come on, men," I yelled, dashing down the steps and seizing a chair and starting back, no longer struggling against or thinking about the nature of my action. The others followed, picking up pieces of furniture and lugging it back into the building.

"We ought to done this long ago," a man said.

"We damn sho should."

"I feel so good," a woman said. "I feel so *good!*"

"Black men, I'm proud of you," the West Indian woman shrilled. "Proud!"

We rushed into the dark little apartment that smelled of stale cabbage and put the pieces down and returned for more. Men, women and children seized articles and dashed inside shouting, laughing. I looked for the two trusties, but they seemed to have disappeared. Then, coming down into the street, I thought I saw one. He was carrying a chair back inside.

"So you're law-abiding too," I called, only to become

aware that it was someone else. A white man but someone else altogether.

The man laughed at me and continued inside. And when I reached the street there were several of them, men and women, standing about, cheering whenever another piece of furniture was returned. It was like a holiday. I didn't want it to stop.

"Who are those people?" I called from the steps.

"What people?" someone called back.

"Those," I said, pointing.

"You mean those ofays?"

"Yes, what do they want?"

"We're friends of the people," one of the white men called.

"Friends of what people?" I called, prepared to jump down upon him if he answered, *"You* people."

"We're friends of *all* the common people," he shouted. "We came up to help."

"We believe in brotherhood," another called.

"Well, pick up that sofa and come on," I called. I was uneasy about their presence and disappointed when they all joined the crowd and started lugging the evicted articles back inside. Where had I heard of them?

"Why don't we stage a march?" one of the white men called, going past.

"Why don't we march!" I yelled out to the sidewalk before I had time to think.

They took it up immediately.

"Let's march . . ."

"It's a good idea."

"Let's have a demonstration . . ."

"Let's parade!"

I heard the siren and saw the scout cars swing into the block in the same instant. It was the police! I looked into the crowd, trying to focus upon their faces, hearing someone yell, "Here come the cops," and others answering, "Let 'em come!"

Where is all this leading? I thought, seeing a white man run inside the building as the policemen dashed from their cars and came running up.

"What's going on here?" a gold-shield officer called up the steps.

It had become silent. No one answered.

"I said, what's going on here," he repeated. "You," he called, pointing straight at me.

"We've . . . we've been clearing the sidewalk of a lot of junk," I called, tense inside.

"What's that?" he said.

"It's a clean-up campaign," I called, wanting to laugh. "These old folks had all their stuff cluttering up the sidewalk and we cleared the street . . ."

"You mean you're interfering with an eviction," he called, starting through the crowd.

"He ain't doing nothing," a woman called from behind me.

I looked around, the steps behind were filled with those who had been inside.

"We're all together," someone called, as the crowd closed in.

"Clear the streets," the officer ordered.

"That's what we were doing," someone called from back in the crowd.

"Mahoney!" he bellowed to another policeman, "send in a riot call!"

"What riot?" one of the white men called to him. "There's no riot."

"If I say there's a riot, there's a riot," the officer said. "And what are you white people doing up here in Harlem?"

"We're citizens. We go anywhere we like."

"Listen! Here come some more cops!" someone called.

"Let them come!"

"Let the Commissioner come!"

It became too much for me. The whole thing had gotten out of hand. What had I said to bring on all this? I edged to the back of the crowd on the steps and backed into the hallway. Where would I go? I hurried up to the old couple's apartment. But I can't hide here, I thought, heading back for the stairs.

"No. You can't go that way," a voice said.

I whirled. It was a white girl standing in the door.

"What are you doing in here?" I shouted, my fear turning to feverish anger.

"I didn't mean to startle you," she said. "Brother, that was quite a speech you made. I heard just the end of it, but you certainly moved them to action . . ."

"Action," I said, "action—"

"Don't be modest, brother," she said, "I heard you."

"Look, Miss, we'd better get out of here," I said, finally controlling the throbbing in my throat. "There are a lot of policemen downstairs and more coming."

"Oh, yes. You'd better go over the roof," she said. "Otherwise, someone is sure to point you out."

"Over the roof?"

"It's easy. Just go up to the roof of the building and keep crossing until you reach the house at the end of the block. Then open the door and walk down as though you've been visiting. You'd better hurry. The longer you remain unknown to the police, the longer you'll be effective."

Effective? I thought. What did she mean? And what was this "brother" business?

"Thanks," I said, and hurried for the stairs.

"Good-bye," her voice rose fluidly behind me. I turned, glimpsing her white face in the dim light of the darkened doorway.

I took the flight in a bound and cautiously opened the door, and suddenly the sun flared bright on the roof and it was windy cold. Before me the low, snow-caked walls dividing the buildings stretched hurdle-like the long length of the block to the corner, and before me empty clotheslines trembled in the wind. I made my way through the wind-carved snow to the next roof and then to the next, going with swift caution. Planes were rising over an airfield far to the southeast, and I was running now and seeing all the church steeples rising and falling and stacks with smoke leaning sharp against the sky, and below in the street the sound of sirens and shouting. I hurried. Then, climbing over a wall I looked back, seeing a man hurrying after me, slipping, sliding, going over the low dividing walls of the roofs with puffing, bustling effort. I turned and ran, trying to put the rows of chimneys between us, wondering why he didn't yell "Halt!" or shout, or shoot. I ran, dodging behind an elevator housing, then dashing to the next roof, going down, the snow cold to my hands, knees striking, toes gripping, and up and running and looking back, seeing the short figure in black still running after. The corner seemed a mile away. I tried to count the number of roofs that bounced before me yet to be crossed. Getting to seven, I ran, hearing shouts, more sirens, and looking back and him still behind me, running in a short-legged scramble, still behind me as I tried to open the door of a building to go down and finding it stuck and running once more, trying to zig-zag in the snow and feeling the crunch of gravel underneath, and behind me still, as I swung over a partition and went brushing past a huge cote and arousing a flight of frantic white birds, suddenly as large as buzzards as they beat furiously against my eyes, dazzling the sun as they fluttered up and away and around in a furious glide and me running again and looking back and for a split second thinking him gone and once more seeing him bobbing after. Why doesn't he shoot? Why? If only it were like at home where I knew someone in *all* the houses, knew them by sight and by name, by blood and by background, by shame and pride, and by religion.

It was a carpeted hall and I moved down with pounding heart as a dog set up a terrific din within the top apartment. Then I moved quickly, my body like glass inside as I skipped downward off the edges of the stairs. Looking down the stairwell I saw pale light filtering through the door glass, far below. But what had happened to the girl, had she put the man on my trail? What was she doing there? I bounded down, no one challenging me, and I stopped in the vestibule, breathing deeply and listening for his hand upon the door above and brushing my clothing into order. Then I stepped into the street with a nonchalance copied from characters I had seen in the movies. No sound from above, not even the malicious note of the barking dog.

It was a long block and I had come down into a building that faced not the street but the avenue. A squad of mounted policemen lashed themselves around the corner and galloped past, the horseshoes thudding dully through the snow, the men rising high in their saddles, shouting. I picked up speed, careful not to run, heading away. This was awful. What on earth had I said to have brought on all this? How would it end? Someone might be killed. Heads would be pistol-whipped. I stopped at the corner, looking for the pursuing man, the detective, and for a bus. The long white stretch of street was empty, the aroused pigeons still circling overhead. I scanned the roofs, expecting to see him peering down. The sound of shouting continued to rise, then another green and white patrol car was whining around the corner and speeding past me, heading for the block. I cut through a block in which there were close to a dozen funeral parlors, each decked out with neon signs, all set up in old brownstone buildings. Elaborate funeral cars stood along the curb, one a dull black with windows shaped like Gothic arches, through which I saw funeral flowers piled upon a casket. I hurried on.

I could see the girl's face still, below the short flight of stairs. But who was the figure that had crossed the roof behind me? Chased me? Why had he been so silent, and why was there only one? Yes, and why hadn't they sent a patrol car to pick me up? I hurried out of the block of funeral parlors into the bright sun that swept the snow of the avenue, slowing to a leisurely walk now, trying to give the impression of a complete lack of haste. I longed to look stupid, utterly incapable of thought or speech, and tried to shuffle my feet over the walk, but quit with distaste after stealing a glance behind me. Just ahead I saw a car pull up and a man leap out with a physician's bag.

"Hurry, Doctor," a man called from the stoop, "she's already in labor!"

"Good," the doctor called. "That's what we've been waiting for, isn't it?"

"Yeah, but it didn't start when we expected it."

I watched them disappear inside the hall. What a hell of a time to be born, I thought. At the corner I joined several people waiting for the lights to change. I had just about convinced myself that I had escaped successfully when a quiet, penetrating voice beside me said, "That was a masterful bit of persuasion, brother."

Suddenly wound tight as a tensioned spring I turned almost lethargically. A short insignificant-looking bushy-eyebrowed man with a quiet smile on his face stood beside me, looking not at all like a policeman.

"What do you mean?" I asked, my voice lazy, distant.

"Don't be alarmed," he said, "I'm a friend."

"I've got nothing to be alarmed about, and you're no friend of mine."

"Then say that I'm an admirer," he said pleasantly.

"Admirer of what?"

"Of your speech," he said. "I was listening."

"What speech? I made no speech," I said.

He smiled knowingly. "I can see that you have been well trained. Come, it isn't good for you to be seen with me here in the street. Let's go somewhere for a cup of coffee."

Something told me to refuse, but I was intrigued and, underneath it all, was probably flattered. Besides, if I refused to go, it would be taken as an admission of guilt. And he didn't look like a policeman or a detective. I went silently beside him to a cafeteria down near the end of the block, seeing him peer inside through the window before we entered.

"You get the table, brother. Over there near the wall where we can talk in peace. I'll get the coffee."

I watched him going across the floor with a bouncy, rolling step, then found a table and sat watching him. It was warm in the cafeteria. It was late afternoon now and only a few customers were scattered at the tables. I watched the man going familiarly to the food counter and ordering. His movements, as he peered through the brightly lighted shelves of pastry, were those of a lively small animal, a fyce, interested in detecting only the target cut of cake. So he's heard my speech; well, I'll hear what he has to say, I thought, seeing him start toward me with his rapid, rolling, bouncy, heel-and-toey step. It was as though he had taught himself to walk that way and I had a feeling that somehow he was acting a part; that something about him wasn't exactly real—an idea which I dismissed immediately, since there was a quality of unreality over the whole afternoon. He came straight to the table without having to look about for me, as though he had expected me to take that particular table and no other—although many tables were vacant. He was balancing a plate of cake on top of each cup, setting them down deftly and shoving one toward me as he took his chair.

"I thought you might like a piece of cheese cake," he said.

"Cheese cake?" I said. "I've never heard of it."

"It's nice. Sugar?"

"Go ahead," I said.

"No, after you, brother."

I looked at him, then poured three spoonfuls and shoved the shaker toward him. I was tense again.

"Thanks," I said, repressing an impulse to call him down about the "brother" business.

He smiled, cutting into his cheese cake with a fork and shoving far too large a piece into his mouth. His manners are extremely crude, I thought, trying to put him at a disadvantage in my own mind by pointedly taking a small piece of the cheesy stuff and placing it neatly into my mouth.

"You know," he said, taking a gulp of coffee, "I haven't heard such an effective piece of eloquence since the days when I was in—well, in a long time. You aroused them so quickly to action. I don't understand how you managed it. If only some of *our* speakers could have listened! With a few words you had them involved in action! Others would have still been wasting time with empty verbiage. I want to thank you for a most instructive experience!"

I drank my coffee silently. Not only did I distrust him, I didn't know how much I could safely say.

"The cheese cake here is good," he said before I could answer. "It's really very good. By the way, where did you learn to speak?"

"Nowhere," I said, much too quickly.

"Then you're very talented. You are a natural. It's hard to believe."

"I was simply angry," I said, deciding to admit this much in order to see what he would reveal.

"Then your anger was skillfully controlled. It had eloquence. Why was that?"

"Why? I suppose I felt sorry—I don't know. Maybe I just felt like making a speech. There was the crowd waiting, so I said a few words. You might not believe it, but I didn't know what I was going to say . . ."

"Please," he said, with a knowing smile.

"What do you mean?" I said.

"You try to sound cynical, but I see through you. I know, I listened very carefully to what you had to say. You were enormously moved. Your emotions were touched."

"I guess so," I said. "Maybe seeing them reminded me of something."

He leaned forward, watching me intensely now, the smile still on his lips.

"Did it remind you of people you know?"

"I guess it did," I said.

"I think I understand. You were watching a death—"

I dropped my fork. "No one was killed," I said tensely. "What are you trying to do?"

"A *Death on the City Pavements*—that's the title of a detective story or something I read somewhere . . ." He laughed. "I only mean meta-phor-ically speaking. They're living, but dead. Dead-in-living . . . a unity of opposites."

"Oh," I said. What kind of double talk was this?

"The old one, they're agrarian types, you know. Being ground up by industrial conditions. Thrown on the dump heaps and cast aside. You pointed it out very well. 'Eighty-seven years and nothing to show for it,' you said. You were absolutely correct."

"I suppose that seeing them like that made me feel pretty bad," I said.

"Yes, of course. And you made an effective speech. But you mustn't waste your emotions on individuals, they don't count."

"*Who* doesn't count?" I said.

"Those old ones," he said grimly. "It's sad, yes. But they're already dead, defunct. History has passed them by. Unfortunate, but there's nothing to do about them. They're like dead limbs that must be pruned away so that the tree may bear young fruit or the storms of history will blow them down anyway. Better the storm should hit them—"

"But look—"

"No, let me continue. These people are old. Men grow old and types of men grow old. And these are very old. All they have left is their religion. That's all they can think about. So they'll be cast aside. They're dead, you see, because they're incapable of rising to the necessity of the historical situation."

"But I *like* them," I said. "I like them, they reminded me of folks I know down South. It's taken me a long time to feel it, but they're folks just like me, except that I've been to school a few years."

He wagged his round red head. "Oh, no, brother; you're mistaken and you're sentimental. You're not like them. Perhaps you were, but you're not any longer. Otherwise you'd never have made that speech. Perhaps you were, but that's all past, dead. You might not recognize it just now, but that part of you is dead! You have not completely shed that self, that old agrarian self, but it's dead and you will throw it off completely and emerge something new. *History* has been born in your brain."

"Look," I said, "I don't know what you're talking about. I've never lived on a farm and I didn't study agriculture, but I do know why I made that speech."

"Then why?"

"Because I was upset over seeing those old folks put out

in the street, that's why. I don't care what *you* call it, I was angry."

He shrugged. "Let's not argue about it," he said. "I've a notion you could do it again. Perhaps you would be interested in working for us."

"For whom?" I asked, suddenly excited. What was he trying to do?

"With our organization. We need a good speaker for this district. Someone who can articulate the grievances of the people," he said.

"But nobody cares about their grievances," I said. "Suppose they were articulated, who would listen or care?"

"They exist," he said with his knowing smile. "They exist, and when the cry of protest is sounded, there are those who will hear it and act."

There was something mysterious and smug in the way he spoke, as though he had everything figured out—whatever he was talking about. Look at this very most certain white man, I thought. He didn't even realize that I was afraid and yet he speaks so confidently. I got to my feet, "I'm sorry," I said, "I have a job and I'm not interested in anyone's grievances but my own . . ."

"But you were concerned with that old couple," he said with narrowed eyes. "Are they relatives of yours?"

"Sure, we're both black," I said, beginning to laugh.

He smiled, his eyes intense upon my face.

"Seriously, are they your relatives?"

"Sure, we were burned in the same oven," I said.

The effect was electric. "Why do you fellows always talk in terms of race!" he snapped, his eyes blazing.

"What other terms do you know?" I said, puzzled. "You think I would have been around there if they had been white?"

He threw up his hands and laughed. "Let's not argue

that now," he said. "You were very effective in helping them. I can't believe that you're such an individualist as you pretend. You appeared to be a man who knew his duty toward the people and performed it well. Whatever you think about it personally, you were a spokesman for your people and you have a duty to work in their interest."

He was too complicated for me. "Look, my friend, thanks for the coffee and cake. I have no more interest in those old folks than in your job. I wanted to make a speech. I *like* to make speeches. What happened afterwards is a mystery to me. You picked the wrong man. You should have stopped one of those fellows who started yelling at the policeman . . ." I stood up.

"Wait a second," he said, producing a piece of envelope and scribbling something. "You might change your mind. As for those others, I know them already."

I looked at the white paper in his extended hand.

"You are wise to distrust me," he said. "You don't know who I am and you don't trust me. That's as it should be. But I don't give up hope, because some day you will look me up on your own accord and it will be different, for then you'll be ready. Just call this number and ask for Brother Jack. You needn't give me your name, just mention our conversation. Should you decide tonight, give me a ring about eight."

"Okay," I said, taking the paper. "I doubt if I'll ever need it, but who knows?"

"Well, you think about it, brother. Times are grave and you seem very indignant."

"I only wanted to make a speech," I said again.

"But you were indignant. And sometimes the difference between individual and organized indignation is the difference between criminal and political action," he said.

I laughed, "So what? I'm neither a criminal nor a politician, brother. So you picked the wrong man. But thanks again for the coffee and cheese cake—*brother.*"

I left him sitting with a quiet smile on his face. When I had crossed the avenue I looked through the glass, seeing him still there, and it occurred to me that he was the same man who had followed me over the roof. He hadn't been chasing me at all but only going in the same direction. I hadn't understood much of what he had said, only that he had spoken with great confidence. Anyway, I had been the better runner. Perhaps it was a trick of some kind. He gave the impression that he understood much and spoke out of a knowledge far deeper than appeared on the surface of his words. Perhaps it was only the knowledge that he had escaped by the same route as I. But what had *he* to fear? I had made the speech, not he. That girl in the apartment had said that the longer I remained unseen the longer I'd be effective, which didn't make much sense either. But perhaps that was why he had run. He wanted to remain unseen and effective. Effective at what? No doubt he was laughing at me. I must have looked silly hurtling across the roofs, and like a black-face comedian shrinking from a ghost when the white pigeons shot up around me. To hell with him. He needn't be so smug, I knew of some things he didn't know. Let him find someone else. He only wanted to use me for something. Everybody wanted to use you for some purpose. Why should he want *me* as a speaker? Let him make his own speeches. I headed for home, feeling a growing satisfaction that I had dismissed him so completely.

It was turning dark now, and much colder. Colder than I had ever known. What on earth was it, I mused, bending my head to the wind, that made us leave the warm, mild weather of home for all this cold, and never to return, if not something worth hoping for, freezing for, even being evicted for? I felt sad. An old woman passed, bent down with two shopping bags, her eyes upon the slushy walk, and I thought of the old couple at the eviction. How had it ended and where were they now? What an awful emotion. What had he called it—a death on the city pavements? How often did such things occur? And what would he say of Mary? She was far from dead, or of being ground to bits by New York. Hell, she knew very well how to live here, much better than I with my college training—training! *Bledsoing*, that was the term. And I was the one being ground up, not Mary. Thinking of her made me feel better. I couldn't imagine Mary being as helpless as the old woman at the eviction, and by the time I reached the apartment I had begun to lose my depression.

Chapter fourteen

The odor of Mary's cabbage changed my mind. Standing engulfed in the fumes filling the hall, it struck me that I couldn't realistically reject the job. Cabbage was always a depressing reminder of the leaner years of my childhood and I suffered silently whenever she served it, but this was the third time within the week and it dawned on me that Mary must be short of money.

And here I've been congratulating myself for refusing a job, I thought, when I don't even know how much money I owe her. I felt a quick sickness grow within me. How could I face her? I went quietly to my room and lay upon the bed, brooding. There were other roomers, who had jobs, and I knew she received help from relatives; still there was no mistake, Mary loved a variety of food and this concentration upon cabbage was no accident. Why hadn't I noticed? She'd been too kind, never dunning me, and I lay there hearing her, "Don't come bothering me with your little troubles, boy. You'll git something bye and bye"—when I would try to apologize for not paying my rent and board. Perhaps another roomer had moved, or lost his job. What were Mary's problems anyway; who "articulated her grievances," as the red-headed man had put it? She had kept me going for months, yet I had no idea. What kind of man was I becoming? I had taken her so much for granted that I hadn't even thought of my debt when I refused the job. Nor had I considered the embarrassment I might have caused her should the police come to her home to arrest me for making that wild speech. Suddenly I felt an urge to go look at her, perhaps I had really never seen her. I had been acting like a child, not a man.

Taking out the crumpled paper, I looked at the telephone number. He had mentioned an organization. What was it called? I hadn't inquired. What a fool! At least I should have learned what I was turning down, although I distrusted the red-headed man. Had I refused out of fear as well as from resentment? Why didn't he just tell me what it was all about instead of trying to impress me with his knowledge?

Then from down the hall I could hear Mary singing, her voice clear and untroubled, though she sang a troubled song. It was the "Back Water Blues." I lay listening as the sound flowed to and around me, bringing me a calm sense of my indebtedness. When it faded I got up and put on my coat. Perhaps it was not too late. I would find a telephone and call him; then he could tell me exactly what he wanted and I could make a sensible decision.

Mary heard me this time. "Boy, when you come home?" she said, sticking her head out of the kitchen. "I didn't even hear you."

"I came in a short while ago," I said. "You were busy so I didn't bother you."

"Then where you going so soon, ain't you going to eat supper?"

"Yes, Mary," I said, "but I've got to go out now. I forgot to take care of some business."

"Shucks! What kind of business you got on a cold night like this?" she said.

"Oh, I don't know, I might have a surprise for you."

"Won't nothing surprise me," she said. "And you hurry on back here and git something hot in your stomach."

Going through the cold seeking a telephone booth I realized that I had committed myself to bring her some kind of surprise, and as I walked I became mildly enthusiastic. It was, after all, a job that promised to exercise my talent for public speaking, and if the pay was anything at all it would be more than I had now. At least I could pay Mary something of what I owed her. And she might receive some satisfaction that her prediction had proved correct.

I seemed to be haunted by cabbage fumes; the little luncheonette in which I found the telephone was reeking.

Brother Jack didn't sound at all surprised upon receiving my call.

"I'd like some information about—"

"Get here as quickly as you can, we're leaving shortly," he said, giving me a Lenox Avenue address and hanging up before I could finish my request.

I went out into the cold, annoyed both by his lack of surprise and by the short, clipped manner in which he'd spoken, but I started out, taking my own time. It wasn't far, and just as I reached the corner of Lenox a car pulled up and I saw several men inside, Jack among them, smiling.

"Get in," he said. "We can talk where we're going. It's a party; you might like it."

"But I'm not dressed," I said. "I'll call you tomorrow—"

"Dressed?" he chuckled. "You're all right, get in."

I got in beside him and the driver, noticing that there were three men in the back. Then the car moved off.

No one spoke. Brother Jack seemed to sink immediately into deep thought. The others looked out into the night. It was as though we were mere chance passengers in a subway car. I felt uneasy, wondering where we were going, but decided to say nothing. The car shot swiftly over the slush.

Looking out at the passing night I wondered what kind of men they were. Certainly they didn't act as though they were heading for a very sociable evening. I was hungry and I wouldn't get back in time for supper. Well, maybe it would be worth it, both to Mary and to me. At least I wouldn't have to eat that cabbage!

For a moment the car paused for the traffic light, then we were circling swiftly through long stretches of snow-covered landscape lighted here and there by street lamps and the nervously stabbing beams of passing cars: We were flashing through Central Park, now completely transformed by the snow. It was as though we had plunged suddenly into mid-country peace, yet I knew that here, somewhere close by in the night, there was a zoo with its dangerous animals. The lions and tigers in heated cages, the bears asleep, the snakes coiled tightly underground. And there was also the reservoir of dark water, all covered by snow and by night, by snow-fall and by night-fall, buried beneath black and white, gray mist and gray silence. Then past the driver's head I could see a wall of buildings looming beyond the windshield. The car nosed slowly into traffic, dropped swiftly down a hill.

We stopped before an expensive-looking building in a strange part of the city. I could see the word *Chthonian* on the storm awning stretched above the walk as I got out with the others and went swiftly toward a lobby lighted by dim bulbs set behind frosted glass, going past the uniformed doorman

with an uncanny sense of familiarity; feeling now, as we entered a sound-proof elevator and shot away at a mile a minute,
that I had been through it all before. Then we were stopping
with a gentle bounce and I was uncertain whether we had gone
up or down. Brother Jack guided me down the hall to a door
on which I saw a bronze door-knocker in the shape of a large-
eyed owl. Now he hesitated a moment, his head thrust forward
as though listening, then his hand covered the owl from view,
producing instead of the knock which I expected, an icy peal
of clear chimes. Shortly the door swung partly open, revealing
a smartly dressed woman, whose hard, handsome face broke
into smiles.

"Come in, brothers," she said, her exotic perfume filling
the foyer.

I noticed a clip of blazing diamonds on her dress as I
tried to stand aside for the others, but Brother Jack pushed me
ahead.

"Excuse me," I said, but she held her ground, and I was
pressing tensely against her perfumed softness, seeing her smile
as though there were only she and I. Then I was past, disturbed
not so much by the close contact, as by the sense that I had
somehow been through it all before. I couldn't decide if it were
from watching some similar scene in the movies, from books
I'd read, or from some recurrent but deeply buried dream.
Whatsoever, it was like entering a scene which, because of
some devious circumstance, I had hitherto watched only from
a distance. How could they have such an expensive place, I
wondered.

"Put your things in the study," the woman said. "I'll go
see about drinks."

We entered a room lined with books and decorated with
old musical instruments: An Irish harp, a hunter's horn, a clarinet and a wooden flute were suspended by the neck from the

wall on pink and blue ribbons. There were a leather divan and a number of easy chairs.

"Throw your coat on the divan," Brother Jack said.

I slid out of my overcoat and looked around. The dial of the radio built into a section of the natural mahogany bookshelf was lighted, but I couldn't hear any sound; and there was an ample desk on which rested silver and crystal writing things, and, as one of the men came to stand gazing at the bookcase, I was struck by the contrast between the richness of the room and their rather poor clothing.

"Now we'll go into the other room," Brother Jack said, taking me by the arm.

We entered a large room in which one entire wall was hung with Italian-red draperies that fell in rich folds from the ceiling. A number of well-dressed men and women were gathered in groups, some beside a grand piano, the others lounging in the pale beige upholstery of the blond wood chairs. Here and there I saw several attractive young women but carefully avoided giving them more than a glance. I felt extremely uncomfortable, although after brief glances no one paid me any special attention. It was as though they hadn't seen me, as though I were here, and yet not here. The others were moving away to join the various groups now, and Brother Jack took my arm.

"Come, let's get a drink," he said, guiding me toward the end of the room.

The woman who'd let us in was mixing drinks behind a handsome free-form bar which was large enough to have graced a night club.

"How about a drink for us, Emma?" Brother Jack said.

"Well, now, I'll have to think about it," she said, tilting her severely drawn head and smiling.

"Don't think, act," he said. "We're very thirsty men. This young man pushed history ahead twenty years today."

"Oh," she said, her eyes becoming intent. "You must tell me about him."

"Just read the morning papers, Emma. Things have begun to move. Yes, leap ahead." He laughed deeply.

"What would you like, Brother?" she said, her eyes brushing slowly over my face.

"Bourbon," I said, a little too loudly, as I remembered the best the South had to offer. My face was warm, but I returned her glance as steadily as I dared. It was not the harsh uninterested-in-you-as-a-human-being stare that I'd known in the South, the kind that swept over a black man as though he were a horse or an insect; it was something more, a direct, what-type-of-mere-man-have-we-here kind of look that seemed to go beneath my skin ... Somewhere in my leg a muscle twitched violently.

"Emma, the bourbon! *Two* bourbons," Brother Jack said.

"You know," she said, picking up a decanter, "I'm intrigued."

"Naturally. Always," he said. "Intrigued and intriguing. But we're dying of thirst."

"Only of impatience," she said, pouring the drinks. "I mean *you* are. Tell me, where did you find this young hero of the people?"

"I didn't," Brother Jack said. "He simply arose out of a crowd. The people always throw up their leaders, you know ..."

"*Throw* them up," she said. "Nonsense, they chew them up and spit them out. Their leaders are made, not born. Then they're destroyed. You've always said that. Here you are, Brother."

He looked at her steadily. I took the heavy crystal glass

and raised it to my lips, glad for an excuse to turn from her eyes. A haze of cigarette smoke drifted through the room. I heard a series of rich arpeggios sound on the piano behind me and turned to look, hearing the woman Emma say not quite softly enough, "But don't you think he should be a little blacker?"

"Shhh, don't be a damn fool," Brother Jack said sharply. "We're not interested in his looks but in his voice. And I suggest, Emma, that you make it *your* interest too . . ."

Suddenly hot and breathless, I saw a window across the room and went over and stood looking out. We were up very high; street lamps and traffic cut patterns in the night below. So she doesn't think I'm black enough. What does she want, a black-face comedian? Who is she, anyway, Brother Jack's wife, his girl friend? Maybe she wants to see me sweat coal tar, ink, shoe polish, graphite. What was I, a man or a natural resource?

The window was so high that I could barely hear the sound of traffic below . . . This was a bad beginning, but hell, I was being hired by Brother Jack, if he still wanted me, not this Emma woman. I'd like to show her how really black I am, I thought, taking a big drink of the bourbon. It was smooth, cold. I'd have to be careful with the stuff. Anything might happen if I had too much. With these people I'll have to be careful. Always careful. With all people I'll have to be careful . . .

"It's a pleasant view, isn't it?" a voice said, and I whirled to see a tall dark man. "But now would you mind joining us in the library?" he said.

Brother Jack, the men who had come along in the car, and two others whom I hadn't seen before were waiting.

"Come in, Brother," Jack said. "Business before pleasure, is always a good rule, whoever you are. Some day the rule shall be business *with* pleasure, for the joy of labor shall have been restored. Sit down."

I took the chair directly before him, wondering what this speech was all about.

"You know, Brother," he said, "we don't ordinarily interrupt our social gatherings with business, but with you it's necessary."

"I'm very sorry," I said. "I should have called you earlier."

"Sorry? Why, we're only too glad to do so. We've been waiting for you for months. Or for someone who could do what you've done."

"But what . . . ?" I said.

"What are we doing? What is our mission? It's simple; we are working for a better world for all people. It's that simple. Too many have been dispossessed of their heritage, and we have banded together in brotherhood so as to do something about it. What do you think of that?"

"Why, I think it's fine," I said, trying to take in the full meaning of his words. "I think it's excellent. But how?"

"By moving them to action just as you did this morning . . . Brothers, I was there," he said to the others, "and he was magnificent. With a few words he set off an effective demonstration against evictions!"

"I was present too," another said. "It was amazing."

"Tell us something of your background," Brother Jack said, his voice and manner demanding truthful answers. And I explained briefly that I had come up looking for work to pay my way through college and had failed.

"Do you still plan to return?"

"Not now," I said. "I'm all done with that."

"It's just as well," Brother Jack said. "You have little to learn down there. However, college training is not a bad thing—although you'll have to forget most of it. Did you study economics?"

"Some."

"Sociology?"

"Yes."

"Well, let me advise you to forget it. You'll be given books to read along with some material that explains our program in detail. But we're moving too fast. Perhaps you aren't interested in working for the Brotherhood."

"But you haven't told me what I'm supposed to do," I said.

He looked at me fixedly, picking up his glass slowly and taking a long swallow.

"Let's put it this way," he said. "How would you like to be the new Booker T. Washington?"

"What!" I looked into his bland eyes for laughter, seeing his red head turned slightly to the side. "Please, now," I said.

"Oh, yes, I'm serious."

"Then I don't understand you." Was *I* drunk? I looked at him; he *seemed* sober.

"What do you think of the idea? Or better still, what do you think of Booker T. Washington?"

"Why, naturally, I think he was an important figure. At least most people say so."

"But?"

"Well," I was at a loss for words. He was going too fast again. The whole idea was insane and yet the others were looking at me calmly; one of them was lighting up an under-slung pipe. The match sputtered, caught fire.

"What is it?" Brother Jack insisted.

"Well, I guess I don't think he was as great as the Founder."

"Oh? And why not?"

"Well, in the first place, the Founder came before him and did practically everything Booker T. Washington did and a lot more. And more people believed in him. You hear a lot of arguments about Booker T. Washington, but few would argue about the Founder . . ."

"No, but perhaps that is because the Founder lies outside history, while Washington is still a living force. However, the *new* Washington shall work for the poor . . ."

I looked into my crystal glass of bourbon. It was unbelievable, yet strangely exciting and I had the sense of being present at the creation of important events, as though a curtain had been parted and I was being allowed to glimpse how the country operated. And yet none of these men was well known, or at least I'd never seen their faces in the newspapers.

"During these times of indecision when all the old answers are proven false, the people look back to the dead to give them a clue," he went on. "They call first upon one and then upon another of those who have acted in the past."

"If you please, Brother," the man with the pipe interrupted, "I think you should speak more concretely."

"Please don't interrupt," Brother Jack said icily.

"I wish only to point out that a scientific terminology exists," the man said, emphasizing his words with his pipe. "After all, we call ourselves scientists here. Let us speak as scientists."

"In due time," Brother Jack said. "In due time . . . You see, Brother," he said, turning to me, "the trouble is that there is little the dead can do; otherwise they wouldn't be the dead. No! But on the other hand, it would be a great mistake to assume that the dead are absolutely powerless. They are powerless only to give the full answer to the new questions posed for the living by history. But they try! Whenever they hear the imperious cries of the people in a crisis, the dead respond. Right now in this country, with its many national groups, all the old heroes are being called back to life—Jefferson, Jackson, Pulaski, Garibaldi, Booker T. Washington, Sun Yat-sen, Danny O'Connell, Abraham Lincoln and countless others are being asked to step once again upon the stage of history. I can't say too emphatically that we stand at a terminal point in history, at a moment of supreme world crisis. Destruction lies ahead unless things are changed. And things *must* be changed. And changed by the people. Because, Brother, the enemies of man are dispossessing the world! Do you understand?"

"I'm beginning to," I said, greatly impressed.

"There are other terms, other more accurate ways of saying all this, but we haven't time for that right now. We speak now in terms that are easy to understand. As you spoke to the crowd this morning."

"I see," I said, feeling uncomfortable under his stare.

"So it isn't a matter of whether you *wish* to be the new Booker T. Washington, my friend. Booker Washington was resurrected today at a certain eviction in Harlem. He came out from the anonymity of the crowd and spoke to the people. So you see, I don't joke with you. Or play with words either. There is a scientific explanation for this phenomenon—as our learned brother has graciously reminded me—you'll learn it in time, but whatever you call it the reality of the world crisis is a fact. We are all realists here, and materialists. It is a question of who shall determine the direction of events. That is why we've brought you into this room. This morning you answered the people's appeal and we want you to be the true interpreter of the people. You shall be the new Booker T. Washington, but even greater than he."

There was silence. I could hear the wet cracking of the pipe.

"Perhaps we should allow the brother to express himself as to how he feels about all this," the man with the pipe said.

"Well, Brother?" Brother Jack said.

I looked into their waiting faces.

"It's all so new to me that I don't know exactly what I do think," I said. "Do you really think you have the right man?"

"You mustn't let that worry you," Brother Jack said. "You will rise to the task; it is only necessary that you work hard and follow instructions."

They stood up now. I looked at them, fighting a sense of unreality. They stared at me as the fellows had done when I was being initiated into my college fraternity. Only this was real and now was the time for me to decide or to say I thought they were crazy and go back to Mary's. But what is there to lose? I thought. At least they've invited me, one of us, in at the beginning of something big; and besides, if I refused to join them, where would I go—to a job as porter at the railroad station? At least here was a chance to speak.

"When shall I start?" I said.

"Tomorrow, we must waste no time. By the way, where are you living?"

"I rent a room from a woman in Harlem," I said.

"A housewife?"

"She's a widow," I said. "She rents rooms."

"What is her educational background?"

"She's had very little."

"More or less like the old couple that was evicted?"

"Somewhat, but better able to take care of herself. She's tough," I said with a laugh.

"Does she ask a lot of questions? Are you friendly with her?"

"She's been very nice to me," I said. "She allowed me to stay on after I was unable to pay my rent."

He shook his head. "No."

"What is it?" I said.

"It is best that you move," he said. "We'll find you a place further downtown so that you'll be within easy call . . ."

"But I have no money, and she's entirely trustworthy."

"That will be taken care of," he said, waving his hand. "You must realize immediately that much of our work is opposed. Our discipline demands therefore that we talk to no one and that we avoid situations in which information might be given away unwittingly. So you must put aside your past. Do you have a family?"

"Yes."

"Are you in touch with them?"

"Of course. I write home now and then," I said, beginning to resent his method of questioning. His voice had become cold, searching.

"Then it's best that you cease for a while," he said. "Anyway, you'll be too busy. Here." He fished into his vest pocket for something and got suddenly to his feet.

"What is it?" someone asked.

"Nothing, excuse me," he said, rolling to the door and beckoning. In a moment I saw the woman appear.

"Emma, the slip of paper I gave you. Give it to the new brother," he said as she stepped inside and closed the door.

"Oh, so it's you," she said with a meaningful smile.

I watched her reach into the bosom of her taffeta hostess gown and remove a white envelope.

"This is your new identity," Brother Jack said. "Open it."

Inside I found a name written on a slip of paper.

"That is your new name," Brother Jack said. "Start thinking of yourself by that name from this moment. Get it down so that even if you are called in the middle of the night you will respond. Very soon you shall be known by it all over the country. You are to answer to no other, understand?"

"I'll try," I said.

"Don't forget his living quarters," the tall man said.

"No," Brother Jack said with a frown. "Emma, please, some funds."

"How much, Jack?" she said.

He turned to me. "Do you owe much rent?"

"Too much," I said.

"Make it three hundred, Emma," he said.

"Never mind," he said as I showed my surprise at the sum. "This will pay your debts and buy you clothing. Call me in the morning and I'll have selected your living quarters. For a start your salary will be sixty dollars a week."

Sixty a week! There was nothing I could say. The woman had crossed the room to the desk and returned with the money, placing it in my hand.

"You'd better put it away," she said expansively.

"Well, Brothers, I believe that's all," he said. "Emma, how about a drink?"

"Of course, of course," she said, going to a cabinet and removing a decanter and a set of glasses in which she poured about an inch of clear liquid.

"Here you are, Brothers," she said.

Taking his, Brother Jack raised it to his nose, inhaling deeply. "To the Brotherhood of Man . . . to History and to Change," he said, touching my glass.

"To History," we all said.

The stuff burned, causing me to lower my head to hide the tears that popped from my eyes.

"Aaaah!" someone said with deep satisfaction.

"Come along," Emma said. "Let's join the others."

"Now for some pleasure," Brother Jack said. "And remember your new identity."

I wanted to think but they gave me no time. I was swept

into the large room and introduced by my new name. Everyone smiled and seemed eager to meet me, as though they all knew the role I was to play. All grasped me warmly by the hand.

"What is your opinion of the state of women's rights, Brother?" I was asked by a plain woman in a large black velvet tam. But before I could open my mouth, Brother Jack had pushed me along to a group of men, one of whom seemed to know all about the eviction. Nearby, a group around the piano were singing folk songs with more volume than melody. We moved from group to group, Brother Jack very authoritative, the others always respectful. He must be a powerful man, I thought, not a clown at all. But to hell with this Booker T. Washington business. I would do the work but I would be no one except myself—whoever I was. I would pattern my life on that of the Founder. They might think I was acting like Booker T. Washington; let them. But what I thought of myself I would keep to myself. Yes, and I'd have to hide the fact that I had actually been afraid when I made my speech. Suddenly I felt laughter bubbling inside me. I'd have to catch up with this science of history business.

We had come to stand near the piano now, where an intense young man questioned me about various leaders of the Harlem community. I knew them only by name, but pretended that I knew them all.

"Good," he said, "good, we have to work with all these forces during the coming period."

"Yes, you're quite right," I said, giving my glass a tinkling twirl. A short broad man saw me and waved the others to a halt. "Say, Brother," he called. "Hold the music, boys, hold it!"

"Yes, uh . . . Brother," I said.

"You're just who we need. We been looking for you."

"Oh," I said.

"How about a spiritual, Brother? Or one of those real good ole Negro work songs? Like this: *Ah went to Atlanta—nevah been there befo','*" he sang, his arms held out from his body like a penguin's wings, glass in one hand, cigar in the other. *"White man sleep in a feather bed, Niggah sleep on the flo'* . . . Ha! Ha! How about it, Brother?"

"The brother *does not sing!*" Brother Jack roared staccato.

"Nonsense, *all* colored people sing."

"This is an outrageous example of unconscious racial chauvinism!" Jack said.

"Nonsense, I *like* their singing," the broad man said doggedly.

"The brother *does not sing!*" Brother Jack cried, his face turning a deep purple.

The broad man regarded him stubbornly. "Why don't you let *him* say whether he can sing or not . . . ? Come on, Brother, git hot! *Go Down, Moses,*" he bellowed in a ragged baritone, putting down his cigar and snapping his fingers. *"Way down in Egypt's land. Tell dat ole Pharaoh to let ma colored folks sing!* I'm for the rights of the colored brother to sing!" he shouted belligerently.

Brother Jack looked as if he would choke; he raised his hand, signaling. I saw two men shoot from across the room and lead the short man roughly away. Brother Jack followed them as they disappeared beyond the door, leaving an enormous silence.

For a moment I stood there, my eyes riveted upon the door, then I turned, the glass hot in my hand, my face feeling as though it would explode. Why was everyone staring at me as though I were responsible? Why the hell were they staring at me? Suddenly I yelled, "What's the matter with you? Haven't you ever seen a drunk—" when somewhere off the foyer the broad man's voice staggered drunkenly to us, *"St. Louis mammieeeee—with her diamond riiiings . . ."* and was clipped off by a slamming door, leaving a roomful of bewildered faces. And suddenly I was laughing hysterically.

"He hit me in the face," I wheezed. "He hit me in the face with a yard of chitterlings!"—bending double, roaring, the whole room seeming to dance up and down with each rapid eruption of laughter.

"He threw a hog maw," I cried, but no one seemed to understand. My eyes filled, I could barely see. "He's high as a Georgia pine," I laughed, turning to the group nearest me. "He's abso-lutely drunk . . . off music!"

"Yes. Sure," a man said nervously. "Ha, ha . . ."

"Three sheets in the wind," I laughed, getting my breath now, and discovering that the silent tension of the others was ebbing into a ripple of laughter that sounded throughout the room, growing swiftly to a roar, a laugh of all dimensions, intensities and intonations. Everyone was joining in. The room fairly bounced.

"And did you see Brother Jack's face," a man shouted, shaking his head.

"It was murder!"

"Go Down Moses!"

"I tell you it was murder!"

Across the room they were pounding someone on the back to keep him from choking. Handkerchiefs appeared, there was much honking of noses, wiping of eyes. A glass crashed to the floor, a chair was overturned. I fought against the painful laughter, and as I calmed I saw them looking at me with a sort of embarrassed gratitude. It was sobering and yet they seemed bent upon pretending that nothing unusual had happened. They smiled. Several seemed about to come over and pound my back, shake my hand. It was as though I had told them something which they'd wished very much to hear, had rendered them an important service which I couldn't understand. But there it was, working in their faces. My stomach ached. I wanted to leave, to get their eyes off me. Then a thin little woman came over and grasped my hand.

"I'm so sorry that this had to happen," she said in a slow Yankee voice, "really and truly sorry. Some of our brothers aren't so highly developed, you know. Although they mean very well. You must allow me to apologize for him . . ."

"Oh, he was only tipsy," I said, looking into her thin New England face.

"Yes, I know, and revealingly so. *I* would never ask our colored brothers to sing, even though I love to hear them. Because I know that it would be a very backward thing. You are here to fight along with us, not to entertain. I think you understand me, don't you, Brother?"

I gave her a silent smile.

"Of course you do. I must go now, good-bye," she said, extending her little white-gloved hand and leaving.

I was puzzled. Just what did she mean? Was it that she understood that we resented having others think that we were all entertainers and natural singers? But now after the mutual laughter something disturbed me: Shouldn't there be some way for us to be asked to sing? Shouldn't the short man have the right to make a mistake without his motives being considered consciously or unconsciously malicious? After all, *he* was singing, or trying to. What if I asked *him* to sing? I watched the little woman, dressed in black like a missionary, winding her way through the crowd. What on earth was she doing here? What part did she play? Well, whatever she meant, she's nice and I like her.

Just then Emma came up and challenged me to dance

and I led her toward the floor as the piano played, thinking of the vet's prediction and drawing her to me as though I danced with such as her every evening. For having committed myself, I felt that I could never allow myself to show surprise or upset—even when confronted with situations furthest from my experience. Otherwise I might be considered undependable, or unworthy. I felt that somehow they expected me to perform even those tasks for which nothing in my experience—except perhaps my imagination—had prepared me. Still it was nothing new, white folks seemed always to expect you to know those things which they'd done everything they could think of to prevent you from knowing. The thing to do was to be prepared—as my grandfather had been when it was demanded that he quote the entire United States Constitution as a test of his fitness to vote. He had confounded them all by passing the test, although they still refused him the ballot . . . Anyway, these were different.

It was close to five A.M., many dances and many bourbons later, when I reached Mary's. Somehow, I felt surprised that the room was still the same—except that Mary had changed the bed linen. Good old Mary. I felt sadly sobered. And as I undressed I saw my outworn clothes and realized that I'd have to shed them. Certainly it was time. Even my hat would go; its green was sun-faded and brown, like a leaf struck by the winter's snows. I would require a new one for my new name. A black broad-brimmed one; perhaps a homburg . . . humbug? I laughed. Well, I could leave packing for tomorrow—I had very little, which was perhaps all to the good. I would travel light, far and fast. They were fast people, all right. What a vast difference between Mary and those for whom I was leaving her. And why should it be this way, that the very job which might make it possible for me to do some of the things which she expected of me required that I leave her?

What kind of room would Brother Jack select for me and why wasn't I left to select my own? It didn't seem right that in order to become a Harlem leader I should live elsewhere. Yet nothing seemed right and I would have to rely upon their judgment. They seemed expert in such matters.

But how far could I trust them, and in what way were they different from the trustees? Whatever, I was committed; I'd learn in the process of working with them, I thought, remembering the money. The bills were crisp and fresh and I tried to imagine Mary's surprise when I paid her all my back rent and board. She'd think that I was kidding. But money could never repay her generosity. She would never understand my wanting to move so quickly after getting a job. And if I had any kind of success at all, it would seem the height of ingratitude. How would I face her? She had asked for nothing in return. Or hardly anything, except that I make something of myself that she called a "race leader." I shivered in the cold. Telling her that I was moving would be a hard proposition. I didn't like to think of it, but one couldn't be sentimental. As Brother Jack had said, History makes harsh demands of us all. But they were demands that had to be met if men were to be the masters and not the victims of their times. Did I believe that? Perhaps I had already begun to pay. Besides, I might as well admit right now, I thought, that there are many things about people like Mary that I dislike. For one thing, they seldom know where their personalities end and yours begins; they usually think in terms of "we" while I have always tended to think in terms of "me"—and that has caused some friction, even with my own family. Brother Jack and the others talked in terms of "we," but it was a different, bigger "we."

Well, I had a new name and new problems. I had best leave the old behind. Perhaps it would be best not to see Mary at all, just place the money in an envelope and leave it on the kitchen table where she'd be sure to find it. It would be better that way, I thought drowsily; then there'd be no need to stand before her and stumble over emotions and words that were at best all snarled up and undifferentiated ... One thing about the people at the Chthonian, they all seemed able to say just what they felt and meant in hard, clear terms. That too, I'd have to learn ... I stretched out beneath the covers, hearing the springs groan beneath me. The room was cold. I listened to the night sounds of the house. The clock ticked with empty urgency, as though trying to catch up with the time. In the street a siren howled.

Chapter fifteen

Then I was awake
and not awake, sitting bolt upright in bed and trying to peer
through the sick gray light as I sought the meaning of the
brash, nerve-jangling sound. Pushing the blanket aside I clasped
my hands to my ears. Someone was pounding the steam line,
and I stared helplessly for what seemed minutes. My ears
throbbed. My side began itching violently and I tore open my
pajamas to scratch, and suddenly the pain seemed to leap from
my ears to my side and I saw gray marks appearing where the
old skin was flaking away beneath my digging nails. And as I
watched I saw thin lines of blood well up in the scratches,
bringing pain and joining time and place again, and I thought,
The room has lost its heat on my last day at Mary's, and
suddenly I was sick at heart.

The clock, its alarm lost in the larger sound, said seven-
thirty, and I got out of bed. I'd have to hurry. There was
shopping to do before I called Brother Jack for my instructions
and I had to get the money to Mary— Why didn't they stop
that noise? I reached for my shoes, flinching as the knocking

seemed to sound an inch above my head. Why don't they stop, I thought. And why do I feel so let down? The bourbon? My nerves going bad?

Suddenly I was across the room in a bound, pounding the pipe furiously with my shoe heel.

"Stop it, you ignorant fool!"

My head was splitting. Beside myself, I struck pieces of silver from the pipe, exposing the black and rusted iron. He was using a piece of metal now, his blows ringing with a ragged edge.

If only I knew who it was, I thought, looking for something heavy with which to strike back. If only I knew!

Then near the door I saw something which I'd never noticed there before: the cast-iron figure of a very black, red-lipped and wide-mouthed Negro, whose white eyes stared up at me from the floor, his face an enormous grin, his single large black hand held palm up before his chest. It was a bank, a piece of early Americana, the kind of bank which, if a coin is placed in the hand and a lever pressed upon the back, will raise its arm and flip the coin into the grinning mouth. For a second I stopped, feeling hate charging within me, then dashed over and grabbed it, suddenly as enraged by the tolerance or lack of discrimination, or whatever, that allowed Mary to keep such a self-mocking image around, as by the knocking.

In my hand its expression seemed more of a strangulation than a grin. It was choking, filled to the throat with coins.

How the hell did it get here, I wondered, dashing over and striking the pipe a blow with the kinky iron head. "Shut up!" I screamed, which seemed only to enrage the hidden knocker. The din was deafening. Tenants up and down the entire line of apartments joined in. I hammered back with the iron naps, seeing the silver fly, striking like driven sand against my face. The pipe fairly hummed with the blows. Windows were going up. Voices yelled obscenities down the airshaft.

Who started all this, I wondered, who's responsible?

"Why don't you act like responsible people living in the twentieth century?" I yelled, aiming a blow at the pipe. "Get rid of your cottonpatch ways! Act civilized!"

Then came a crash of sound and I felt the iron head crumble and fly apart in my hand. Coins flew over the room like crickets, ringing, rattling against the floor, rolling. I stopped dead.

"Just listen to 'em! Just listen to 'em!" Mary called from the hall. "Enough noise to wake the dead! They know when the heat don't come up that the super's drunk or done walked off the job looking for his woman, or something. Why don't folks act according to what they know?"

She was at my door now, knocking stroke for stroke with the blows landing on the pipe, calling, "Son! Ain't some of that knocking coming from in there?"

I turned from side to side in indecision, looking at the pieces of broken head, the small coins of all denominations that were scattered about.

"You hear me, boy?" she called.

"What is it?" I called, dropping to the floor and reaching frantically for the broken pieces, thinking, If she opens the door, I'm lost . . .

"I said is any of that racket coming from in there?"

"Yes, it is, Mary," I called, "but I'm all right . . . I'm already awake."

I saw the knob move and froze, hearing, "Sounded to me like a heap of it was coming from in there. You got your clothes on?"

"No," I cried. "I'm just dressing. I'll have them on in a minute."

"Come on out to the kitchen," she said. "It's warm out there. And there's some hot water on the stove to wash your face in . . . and some coffee. Lawd, just listen at the racket!"

I stood as though frozen, until she moved away from the door. I'd have to hurry. I kneeled, picking up a piece of the bank, a part of the red-shirted chest, reading the legend, FEED ME in a curve of white iron letters, like the team name on an athlete's shirt. The figure had gone to pieces like a grenade, scattering jagged fragments of painted iron among the coins. I looked at my hand; a small trickle of blood showed. I wiped it away, thinking, I'll have to hide this mess! I can't take her this and the news that I'm moving at the same time. Taking a newspaper from the chair I folded it stiffly and swept the coins and broken metal into a pile. Where would I hide it, I wondered, looking with profound distaste at the iron kinks, the dull red of a piece of grinning lip. Why, I thought with anguish, would Mary have something like this around anyway? Just why? I looked under the bed. It was dustless there, no place to hide anything. She was too good a housekeeper. Besides, what of the coins? Hell! Maybe the thing was left by the former roomer. Anyway, whosoever it was, it had to be hidden. There was the closet, but she'd find it there too. After I was gone a few days she'd clean out my things and there it'd be. The knocking had gone beyond mere protest over heatlessness now, they had fallen into a ragged rumba rhythm:

Knock!
Knock-knock
Knock-knock!

Knock!
Knock-knock
Knock-knock!

vibrating the very floor.

"Just a few minutes more, you bastards," I said aloud, "and I'll be gone! No respect for the individual. Why don't you think about those who might wish to sleep? What if some-one is near a nervous breakdown . . . ?''

But there was still the package. There was nothing to do but get rid of it along the way downtown. Making a tight bundle, I placed it in my overcoat pocket. I'd simply have to give Mary enough money to cover the coins. I'd give her as much as I could spare, half of what I had, if necessary. That should make up for some of it. She should appreciate that. And now I realized with a feeling of dread that I *had* to meet her face to face. There was no way out. Why can't I just tell her that I'm leaving and pay her and go on off? She was a landlady, I was a tenant—No, there was more to it and I wasn't hard enough, scientific enough, even to tell her that I was leaving. I'll tell her I have a job, anything, but it has to be now.

She was sitting at the table drinking coffee when I went in, the kettle hissing away on the stove, sending up jets of steam.

"Gee, but you slow this morning," she said. "Take some of that water in the kettle and go wash your face. Though sleepy as you look, maybe you ought to just use cold water."

"This'll do," I said flatly, feeling the steam drifting upon my face, growing swiftly damp and cold. The clock above the stove was slower than mine.

In the bathroom I put in the plug and poured some of the hot water and cooled it from the spigot. I kept the tear-warm water upon my face a long time, then dried and returned to the kitchen.

"Run it full again," she said when I returned. "How you feel?"

"So-so," I said.

She sat with her elbows upon the enameled table top, her cup held in both hands, one work-worn little finger delicately curved. I went to the sink and turned the spigot, feeling the cold rush of water upon my hand, thinking of what I had to do . . .

"That's enough there, boy," Mary said, startling me. "Wake up!"

"I guess I'm not all here," I said. "My mind was wandering."

"Well, call it back and come get you some coffee. Soon's I've had mine, I'll see what kind of breakfast I can whip together. I guess after last night you can eat this morning. You didn't come back for supper."

"I'm sorry," I said. "Coffee will be enough for me."

"Boy, you better start eating again," she warned, pouring me a full cup of coffee.

I took the cup and sipped it, black. It was bitter. She glanced from me to the sugar bowl and back again but remained silent, then swirled her cup, looking into it.

"Guess I'll have to get some better filters," she mused. "These I got just lets through the grounds along with the coffee, the good with the bad. I don't know though, even with the best of filters you apt to find a ground or two at the bottom of your cup."

I blew upon the steaming liquid, avoiding Mary's eyes. The knocking was becoming unbearable again. I'd have to get away. I looked at the hot metallic surface of the coffee, noticing an oily, opalescent swirl.

"Look, Mary," I said, plunging in, "I want to talk to you about something."

"Now see here, boy," she said gruffly, "I don't want you worrying me about your rent this morning. I'm not worried 'cause when you get it I know you'll pay me. Meanwhile you forget it. Nobody in this house is going to starve. You having any luck lining up a job?"

"No—I mean not exactly," I stammered, seizing the opportunity. "But I've got an appointment to see about one this morning . . ."

Her face brightened. "Oh, that's fine. You'll get something yet. I know it."

"But about my debt," I began again.

"Don't worry about it. How about some hotcakes?" she asked, rising and going to look into the cabinet. "They'll stick with you in this cold weather."

"I won't have time," I said. "But I've got something for you . . ."

"What's that?" she said, her voice coming muffled as she peered inside the cabinet.

"Here," I said hurriedly, reaching into my pocket for the money.

"What?—Let's see if I got some syrup . . ."

"But look," I said eagerly, removing a hundred-dollar bill.

"Must be on a higher shelf," she said, her back still turned.

I sighed as she dragged a step ladder from beside the cabinet and mounted it, holding onto the doors and peering upon an upper shelf. I'd never get it said . . .

"But I'm trying to give you something," I said.

"Why don't you quit bothering me, boy? You trying to give me *what*?" she said looking over her shoulder.

I held up the bill. "This," I said.

She craned her head around. "Boy, what you got there?"

"It's money."

"Money? Good God, boy!" she said, almost losing her balance as she turned completely around. "Where'd you get all that much money? You been playing the numbers?"

"That's it. My number came up," I said thankfully—

thinking, What'll I say if she asks what the number was? I didn't know. I had never played.

"But how come you didn't tell me? I'd have at least put a nickel on it."

"I didn't think it would do anything," I said.

"Well, I declare. And I bet it was your first time too."

"It was."

"See there, I knowed you was a lucky one. Here I been playing for years and the first drop of the bucket you hits for that kinda money. I'm sho glad for you, son. I really am. But I don't want your money. You wait 'til you get a job."

"But I'm not giving you all of it," I said hastily. "This is just on account."

"But that's a *hundred*-dollar bill. I take that an' try to change it and the white folks'll want to know my whole life's history." She snorted. "They want to know where I was born, where I work, and where I been for the last six months, and when I tell 'em they still gonna think I stole it. Ain't you got nothing smaller?"

"That's the smallest. Take it," I pleaded. "I'll have enough left."

She looked at me shrewdly. "You sho?"

"It's the truth," I said.

"Well, I de-clare—Let me get down from up here before I fall and break my neck! Son," she said, coming down off the ladder, "I sho do appreciate it. But I tell you, I'm just going to keep part of it for myself and the rest I'm going to save for you. You get hard up just come to Mary."

"I think I'll be all right now," I said, watching her fold the money carefully, placing it in the leather bag that always hung on the back of her chair.

"I'm really glad, 'cause now I can take care of that bill they been bothering me about. It'll do me so much good to go in there and plop down some money and tell them folks to quit bothering me. Son, I believe your luck done changed. You dream that number?"

I glanced at her eager face. "Yes," I said, "but it was a mixed-up dream."

"What was the figger—Jesus! What's this!" she cried, getting up and pointing at the linoleum near the steam line.

I saw a small drove of roaches trooping frantically down the steam line from the floor above, plummeting to the floor as the vibration of the pipe shook them off.

"Get the broom!" Mary yelled. "Out of the closet there!"

Stepping around the chair I snatched the broom and joined her, splattering the scattering roaches with both broom and feet, hearing the pop and snap as I brought the pressure down upon them vehemently.

"The filthy, stinking things," Mary cried. "Git that one under the table! Yon' he goes, don't let him git away! The nasty rascal!"

I swung the broom, battering and sweeping the squashed insects into piles. Breathing excitedly Mary got the dust pan and handed it to me.

"Some folks just live in filth," she said disgustedly. "Just let a little knocking start and here it comes crawling out. All you have to do is shake things up a bit."

I looked at the damp spots on the linoleum, then shakily replaced the pan and broom and started out of the room.

"Aren't you going to eat no breakfast?" she said. "Soon's I wipe up this mess I'm going to start."

"I don't have time," I said, my hand on the knob. "My appointment is early and I have a few things to do before-hand."

"Then you better stop and have you something hot soon as you can. Don't do to go around in this cold weather without something in your belly. And don't think you gon' start eating out just 'cause you got some money!"

"I don't. I'll take care of it," I said to her back as she washed her hands.

"Well, good luck, son," she called. "You really give me a pleasant surprise this morning—and if *that's* a lie, I hope something big'll bite me!"

She laughed gaily and I went down the hall to my room and closed the door. Pulling on my overcoat I got down my prized brief case from the closet. It was still as new as the night of the battle royal, and sagged now as I placed the smashed bank and coins inside and locked the flap. Then I closed the closet door and left.

The knocking didn't bother me so much now. Mary was singing something sad and serene as I went down the hall, and still singing as I opened the door and stepped into the outside hall. Then I remembered, and there beneath the dim hall light I took the faintly perfumed paper from my wallet and carefully unfolded it. A tremor passed over me; the hall was cold. Then it was gone and I squinted and took a long, hard look at my new Brotherhood name.

The night's snowfall was already being churned to muck by the passing cars, and it was warmer. Joining the pedestrians along the walk, I could feel the brief case swinging against my leg from the weight of the package, and I determined to get rid of the coins and broken iron at the first ash can. I needed nothing like this to remind me of my last morning at Mary's.

I made for a row of crushed garbage cans lined before a row of old private houses, coming alongside and tossing the package casually into one of them and moving on—only to hear a door open behind me and a voice ring out,

"Oh, no you don't, oh, no you don't! Just come right back here and get it!"

Turning, I saw a little woman standing on the stoop with

a green coat covering her head and shoulders, its sleeves hanging limp like extra atrophied arms.

"I mean you," she called. "Come on back an' get your trash. An' don't *ever* put your trash in my can again!"

She was a short yellow woman with a pince-nez on a chain, her hair pinned up in knots.

"We keep our place clean and respectable and we don't want you field niggers coming up from the South and ruining things," she shouted with blazing hate.

People were stopping to look. A super from a building down the block came out and stood in the middle of the walk, pounding his fist against his palm with a dry, smacking sound. I hesitated, embarrassed and annoyed. Was this woman crazy?

"I mean it! Yes, you! I'm talking to you! Just take it right out! Rosalie," she called to someone inside the house, "call the police, Rosalie!"

I can't afford that, I thought, and walked back to the can. "What does it matter, Miss?" I called up to her. "When the collectors come, garbage is garbage. I just didn't want to throw it into the street. I didn't know that some kinds of garbage were better than others."

"Never mind your impertinence," she said. "I'm sick and tired of having you southern Negroes mess up things for the rest of us!"

"All right," I said, "I'll get it out."

I reached into the half-filled can, feeling for the package, as the fumes of rotting swill entered my nostrils. It felt unhealthy to my hand, and the heavy package had sunk far down. Cursing, I pushed back my sleeve with my clean hand and probed until I found it. Then I wiped off my arm with a handkerchief and started away, aware of the people who paused to grin at me.

"It serves you right," the little woman called from the stoop.

And I turned and started upward. "That's enough out of you, you piece of yellow gone-to-waste. Unless you still want to call the police." My voice had taken on a new shrill pitch. "I've done what you wanted me to do; another word and I'll do what I want to do—"

She looked at me with widening eyes. "I believe you would," she said, opening the door. "I believe you would."

"I not only would, I'd love it," I said.

"I can see that you're no gentleman," she called, slamming the door.

At the next row of cans I wiped off my wrist and hands with a piece of newspaper, then wrapped the rest around the package. Next time I'd throw it into the street.

Two blocks further along my anger had ebbed, but I felt strangely lonely. Even the people who stood around me at the intersection seemed isolated, each lost in his own thoughts. And now just as the lights changed I let the package fall into the trampled snow and hurried across, thinking, There, it's done.

I had covered two blocks when someone called behind me, "Say, buddy! Hey, there! You, Mister . . . Wait a second!" and I could hear the hurried crunching of footsteps upon the snow. Then he was beside me, a squat man in worn clothes, the strands of his breath showing white in the cold as he smiled at me, panting.

"You was moving so fast I thought I wasn't going to be able to stop you," he said. "Didn't you lose something back there a piece?"

Oh, hell, a friend in need, I thought, deciding to deny it. "Lose something?" I said. "Why, no."

"You sure?" he said, frowning.

"Yes," I said, seeing his forehead wrinkle with uncertainty, a hot charge of fear leaping to his eyes as he searched my face.

"But I *seen* you— Say, buddy," he said, looking swiftly, back up the street, "what you trying to do?"

"Do? What do you mean?"

"I mean talking 'bout you didn't lose nothing. You working a con game or something?" He backed away, looking hurriedly at the pedestrians back up the street from where he'd come.

"What on earth are you talking about now?" I said. "I tell you I didn't lose anything."

"Man, don't tell me! I *seen* you. What the hell you mean?" he said, furtively removing the package from his pocket. "This here feels like money or a gun or something and I know damn well I seen you drop it."

"Oh, *that*," I said. "That isn't anything—I thought you—"

"That's right, 'Oh.' So you remembers now, don't you? I think I'm doing you a favor and you play me for a fool. You some kind of confidence man or dope peddler or something? You trying to work one of those pigeon drops on me?"

"*Pigeon drop?*" I said. "You're making a mistake—"

"Mistake, hell! Take this damn stuff," he said, thrusting the package in my hands as though it were a bomb with a lighted fuse. "I got a family, man. I try to do you a favor and here you trying to get me into trouble— You running from a detective or somebody?"

"Wait a minute," I said. "You're letting your imagination run away; this is nothing but garbage—"

"Don't try to hand me that simple-minded crap," he wheezed. "I know what kind of garbage it is. You young New York Negroes is a blip! I swear you is! I hope they catch you and put your ass under the jail!"

He shot away as though I had smallpox. I looked at the package. He thinks it's a gun or stolen goods, I thought, watching him go. A few steps farther along I was about to toss it boldly into the street when upon looking back I saw him, joined by another man now, gesturing toward me indignantly. I hurried away. Give him time and the fool'll call a policeman. I dropped the package back into the brief case. I'd wait until I got downtown.

On the subway people around me were reading their morning papers, pressing forward their unpleasant faces. I rode with my eyes shut, trying to make my mind blank to thoughts of Mary. Then turning, I saw the item *Violent Protest Over Harlem Eviction*, just as the man lowered his paper and moved out of the breaking doors. I could hardly wait until I reached 42nd Street, where I found the story carried on the front page of a tabloid, and I read it eagerly. I was referred to only as an unknown "rabble rouser" who had disappeared in the excitement, but that it referred to me was unmistakable. It had lasted for two hours, the crowd refusing to vacate the premises. I entered the clothing store with a new sense of self-importance.

I selected a more expensive suit than I'd intended, and while it was being altered I picked up a hat, shirts, shoes, underwear and socks, then hurried to call Brother Jack, who snapped his orders like a general. I was to go to a number on the upper East Side where I'd find a room, and I was to read over some of the Brotherhood's literature, which had been left there for me, with the idea of my making a speech at a Harlem rally to be held that evening.

The address was that of an undistinguished building in a mixed Spanish-Irish neighborhood, and there were boys throwing snowballs across the street when I rang the super's bell. The door was opened by a small pleasant-faced woman who smiled.

"Good morning, Brother," she said. "The apartment is all ready for you. He said you'd come about this time and I've just this minute come down. My, just look at that snow."

I followed her up the three flights of stairs, wondering what on earth I'd do with a whole apartment.

"This is it," she said, removing a chain of keys from her pocket and opening a door at the front of the hall. I went into a small comfortably furnished room that was bright with the winter sun. "This is the living room," she said proudly, "and over here is your bedroom."

It was much larger than I needed, with a chest of drawers, two upholstered chairs, two closets, a bookshelf and a desk on which was stacked the literature to which he'd referred. A bathroom lay off the bedroom, and there was a small kitchen.

"I hope you like it, Brother," she said, as she left. "If there's anything you need, please ring my bell."

The apartment was clean and neat and I liked it—especially the bathroom with its tub and shower. And as quickly as I could I drew a bath and soaked myself. Then, feeling clean and exhilarated, I went out to puzzle over the Brotherhood books and pamphlets. My brief case with the broken image lay on the table. I would get rid of the package later; right now I had to think about tonight's rally.

Chapter sixteen

At seven-thirty Brother Jack and some of the others picked me up and we shot up to Harlem in a taxi. As before, no one spoke a word. There was only the sound made by a man in the corner who drew noisily on a pipeful of rum-flavored tobacco, causing it to glow on and off, a red disk in the dark. I rode with mounting nervousness; the taxi seemed unnaturally warm. We got out in a side street and went down a narrow alley in the dark to the rear of the huge, barnlike building. Other members had already arrived.

"Ah, here we are," Brother Jack said, leading the way through a dark rear door to a dressing room lighted by naked, low-hanging bulbs—a small room with wooden benches and a row of steel lockers with a network of names scratched on the doors. It had a football-locker smell of ancient sweat, iodine, blood and rubbing alcohol, and I felt a welling up of memories.

"We remain here until the building fills," Brother Jack said. "Then we make our appearances—just at the height of their impatience." He gave me a grin. "Meanwhile, you think about what you'll say. Did you look over the material?"

"All day," I said.

"Good. I suggest, however, that you listen carefully to the rest of us. We'll all precede you so that you can get the pointers for your remarks. You'll be last."

I nodded, seeing him take two of the other men by the arm and retreat to a corner. I was alone, the others were studying their notes, talking. I went across the room to a torn photograph tacked to the faded wall. It was a shot, in fighting stance, of a former prizefight champion, a popular fighter who had lost his sight in the ring. It must have been right here in this arena, I thought. That had been years ago. The photograph was that of a man so dark and battered that he might have been of any nationality. Big and loose-muscled, he looked like a good man. I remembered my father's story of how he had been beaten blind in a crooked fight, of the scandal that had been suppressed, and how the fighter had died in a home for the blind. Who would have thought I'd ever come here? How things were twisted around! I felt strangely sad and went and slouched on a bench. The others talked on, their voices low. I watched them with a sudden resentment. Why did *I* have to come last? What if they bored the audience to death before I came on! I'd probably be shouted down before I could get started . . . But perhaps not, I thought, jabbing my suspicions away. Perhaps I could make an effect through the sheer contrast between my approach and theirs. Maybe that was the strategy . . . Anyway, I had to trust them. I had to.

Still a nervousness clung to me. I felt out of place. From beyond the door I could hear a distant scrape of chairs, a murmur of voices. Little worries whirled up within me: That I might forget my new name; that I might be recognized from the audience. I bent forward, suddenly conscious of my legs in new blue trousers. But how do you know they're your legs? What's your name? I thought, making a sad joke with myself.

It was absurd, but it relieved my nervousness. For it was as though I were looking at my own legs for the first time— independent objects that could of their own volition lead me to safety or danger. I stared at the dusty floor. Then it was as though I stood simultaneously at opposite ends of a tunnel. I seemed to view myself from the distance of the campus while yet sitting there on a bench in the old arena; dressed in a new blue suit; sitting across the room from a group of intense men who talked among themselves in hushed, edgy voices; while yet in the distance I could hear the clatter of chairs, more voices, a cough. I seemed aware of it all from a point deep within me, yet there was a disturbing vagueness about what I saw, a disturbing unformed quality, as when you see yourself in a photo exposed during adolescence; the expression empty, the grin without character, the ears too large, the pimples, "courage bumps," too many and too well-defined. This was a new phase, I realized, a new beginning, and I would have to take that part of myself that looked on with remote eyes and keep it always at the distance of the campus, the hospital machine, the battle royal—all now far behind. Perhaps the part of me that observed listlessly but saw all, missing nothing, was still the malicious, arguing part; the dissenting voice, my grandfather part; the cynical, disbelieving part—the traitor self that always threatened internal discord. Whatever it was, I knew that I'd have to keep it pressed down. I had to. For if I were successful tonight, I'd be on the road to something big. No more flying apart at the seams, no more remembering forgotten pains . . . No, I thought, shifting my body, they're the same legs on which I've come so far from home. And yet they were somehow new. The new suit imparted a newness to me. It was the clothes and the new name and the circumstances. It was a newness too subtle to put into thought, but there it was. I was becoming someone else.

I sensed vaguely and with a flash of panic that the moment I walked out upon the platform and opened my mouth I'd be someone else. Not just a nobody with a manufactured name which might have belonged to anyone, or to no one. But another personality. Few people knew me now, but after tonight ... How was it? Perhaps simply to be known, to be looked upon by so many people, to be the focal point of so many concentrating eyes, perhaps this was enough to make one different; enough to transform one into something else, someone else; just as by becoming an increasingly larger boy one became one day a man; a man with a deep voice—although my voice had been deep since I was twelve. But what if someone from the campus wandered into the audience? Or someone from Mary's—even Mary herself? "No, it wouldn't change it," I heard myself say softly, "that's all past." My name was different; I was under orders. Even if I met Mary on the street, I'd have to pass her by unrecognized. A depressing thought— and I got up abruptly and went out of the dressing room and into the alley.

Without my overcoat it was cold. A feeble light burned above the entrance, sparkling the snow. I crossed the alley to the dark side, stopping near a fence that smelled of carbolic acid, which, as I looked back across the alley, caused me to remember a great abandoned hole that had been the site of a sports arena that had burned before my birth. All that was left, a cliff drop of some forty feet below the heat-buckled walk, was the shell of concrete with weirdly bent and rusted rods that had been its basement. The hole was used for dumping, and after a rain it stank with stagnant water. And now in my mind I stood upon the walk looking out across the hole past a Hooverville shanty of packing cases and bent tin signs, to a railroad yard that lay beyond. Dark depthless water lay without motion in the hole, and past the Hooverville a switch engine idled upon the shining rails, and as a plume of white steam curled slowly from its funnel I saw a man come out of the shanty and start up the path which led to the walk above. Stooped and dark and sprouting rags from his shoes, hat and sleeves, he shuffled slowly toward me, bringing a threatening cloud of carbolic acid. It was a syphilitic who lived alone in the shanty between the hole and the railroad yard, coming up to the street only to beg money for food and disinfectant with which to soak his rags. Then in my mind I saw him stretching out a hand from which the fingers had been eaten away and I ran—back to the dark, and the cold and the present.

I shivered, looking toward the street, where up the alley through the tunneling dark, three mounted policemen loomed beneath the circular, snow-sparkling beam of the street lamp, grasping their horses by their bridles, the heads of both men and animals bent close, as though plotting; the leather of saddles and leggings shining. Three white men and three black horses. Then a car passed and they showed in full relief, their shadows flying like dreams across the sparkle of snow and darkness. And, as I turned to leave, one of the horses violently tossed its head and I saw the gauntleted fist yanked down. Then there was a wild neigh and the horse plunged off in the dark, the crisp, frantic clanking of metal and the stomping of hooves followed me to the door. Perhaps this was something for Brother Jack to know.

But inside they were still in a huddle, and I went back and sat on the bench.

I watched them, feeling very young and inexperienced and yet strangely old, with an oldness that watched and waited quietly within me. Outside, the audience had begun to drone; a distant, churning sound that brought back some of the terror of the eviction. My mind flowed. There was a child standing in rompers outside a chicken-wire fence, looking in upon a huge black-and-white dog, log-chained to an apple tree. It was Master, the bulldog; and I was the child who was afraid to touch him, although, panting with heat, he seemed to grin back at me like a fat good-natured man, the saliva roping silvery from his jowls. And as the voices of the crowd churned and mounted and became an impatient splatter of hand claps, I thought of Master's low hoarse growl. He had barked the same note when angry or when being brought his dinner, when lazily snapping flies, or when tearing an intruder to shreds. I liked, but didn't trust old Master; I wanted to please, but did not trust the crowd. Then I looked at Brother Jack and grinned: That was it; in some ways, he was like a toy bull terrier.

But now the roar and clapping of hands became a song and I saw Brother Jack break off and bounce to the door. "Okay, Brothers," he said, "that's our signal."

We went in a bunch, out of the dressing room and down a dim passage aroar with the distant sound. Then it was brighter and I could see a spotlight blazing the smoky haze. We moved silently, Brother Jack following two very black Negroes and two white men who led the procession, and now the roar of the crowd seemed to rise above us, flaring louder. I noticed the others falling into columns of four, and I was alone in the rear, like the pivot of a drill team. Ahead, a slanting shaft of brightness marked the entrance to one of the levels of the arena, and now as we passed it the crowd let out a roar. Then swiftly we were in the dark again, and climbing, the roar seeming to sink below us and we were moved into a bright blue light and down a ramp; to each side of which, stretching away in a curve, I could see rows of blurred faces—then suddenly I was blinded and felt myself crash into the man ahead of me.

"It always happens the first time," he shouted, stopping to let me get my balance, his voice small in the roar. "It's the spotlight!"

It had picked us up now, and, beaming just ahead, led us into the arena and encircled us full in its beam, the crowd thundering. The song burst forth like a rocket to the marching tempo of clapping hands:

> *John Brown's body lies a-mold'ring*
> *in the grave*
> *John Brown's body lies a-mold'ring*
> *in the grave*
> *John Brown's body lies a-mold'ring*
> *in the grave*
> *—His soul is marching on!*

Imagine that, I thought, they make the old song sound new. At first I was as remote as though I stood in the highest balcony looking on. Then I walked flush into the vibrations of the voices and felt an electric tingling along my spine. We marched toward a flag-draped platform set near the front of the arena, moving through an aisle left between rows of people in folding chairs, then onto the platform past a number of women who stood when we came on. With a nod Brother Jack indicated our chairs and we faced the applause standing.

Below and above us was the audience, row after row of faces, the arena a bowl-shaped aggregation of humanity. Then I saw the policemen and was disturbed. What if they recognized me? They were all along the wall. I touched the arm of the man ahead, seeing him turn, his mouth halting in a verse of the song.

"Why all the police?" I said, leaning forward on the back of his chair.

"Cops? Don't worry. Tonight they're ordered to protect us. This meeting is of great political consequences!" he said, turning away.

Who ordered them to protect us? I thought— But now the song was ending and the building rang with applause, yells, until the chant burst from the rear and spread:

> *No more dispossessing of the dispossessed!*
> *No more dispossessing of the dispossessed!*

The audience seemed to have become one, its breathing and articulation synchronized. I looked at Brother Jack. He stood up front beside a microphone, his feet planted solidly on the dirty canvas-covered platform, looking from side to side; his posture dignified and benign, like a bemused father listening to the performance of his adoring children. I saw his hand go up in a salute, and the audience thundered. And I seemed to move in close, like the lens of a camera, focusing into the scene and feeling the heat and excitement and the pounding of voice and applause against my diaphragm, my eyes flying from face to face, swiftly, fleetingly, searching for someone I could recognize, for someone from the old life, and seeing the faces become vaguer and vaguer the farther they receded from the platform.

The speeches began. First an invocation by a Negro preacher; then a woman spoke of what was happening to the children. Then came speeches on various aspects of the economic and political situation. I listened carefully, trying to snatch a phrase here, a word there, from the arsenal of hard, precise terms. It was becoming a high-keyed evening. Songs flared between speeches, chants exploded as spontaneously as shouts at a southern revival. And I was somehow attuned to it all, could feel it physically. Sitting with my feet on the soiled canvas I felt as though I had wandered into the percussion section of a symphony orchestra. It worked on me so thoroughly that I soon gave up trying to memorize phrases and simply allowed the excitement to carry me along.

Someone pulled on my coat sleeve—my turn had come. I went toward the microphone where Brother Jack himself waited, entering the spot of light that surrounded me like a seamless cage of stainless steel. I halted. The light was so strong that I could no longer see the audience, the bowl of human faces. It was as though a semi-transparent curtain had dropped between us, but through which they could see me—for they were applauding—without themselves being seen. I felt the hard, mechanical isolation of the hospital machine and I didn't like it. I stood, barely hearing Brother Jack's introduction. Then he was through and there was an encouraging burst of applause. And I thought, They remember; some of them were there.

The microphone was strange and unnerving. I approached it incorrectly, my voice sounding raspy and full of air, and after a few words I halted, embarrassed. I was getting off to a bad start, something had to be done. I leaned toward the vague audience closest to the platform and said, "Sorry, folks. Up to now they've kept me so far away from these shiny electric gadgets I haven't learned the technique . . . And to tell you the truth, it looks to me like it might bite! Just look at it, it looks like the steel skull of a man! Do you think he died of dispossession?"

It worked and while they laughed someone came and made an adjustment. "Don't stand too close," he advised.

"How's that?" I said, hearing my voice boom deep and vibrant over the arena. "Is that better?"

There was a ripple of applause.

"You see, all I needed was a chance. You've granted it, now it's up to me!"

The applause grew stronger and from down front a man's

far-carrying voice called out, "We with you, Brother. You pitch 'em we catch 'em!"

That was all I needed, I'd made a contact, and it was as though his voice was that of them all. I was wound up, nervous. I might have been anyone, might have been trying to speak in a foreign language. For I couldn't remember the correct words and phrases from the pamphlets. I had to fall back upon tradition and since it was a political meeting, I selected one of the political techniques that I'd heard so often at home: The old down-to-earth, I'm-sick-and-tired-of-the-way-they've-been-treating-us approach. I couldn't see them so I addressed the microphone and the co-operative voice before me.

"You know, there are those who think we who are gathered here are dumb," I shouted. "Tell me if I'm right."

"That's a strike, Brother," the voice called. "You pitched a strike."

"Yes, they think we're dumb. They call us the 'common people.' But I've been sitting here listening and looking and trying to understand what's so *common* about us. I think they're guilty of a gross mis-statement of fact—we are the uncommon people—"

"Another strike," the voice called in the thunder, and I paused holding up my hand to halt the noise.

"Yes, we're the uncommon people—and I'll tell you why. They call us dumb and they treat us dumb. And what do they do with dumb ones? Think about it, look around! They've got a slogan and a policy, they've got what Brother Jack would call a 'theory and a practice.' It's 'Never give a sucker an even break!' It's dispossess him! Evict him! Use his empty head for a spittoon and his back for a door mat! It's break him! Deprive him of his wages! It's use his protest as a sounding brass to frighten him into silence, it's beat his ideas and his hopes and homely aspirations into a tinkling cymbal! A small, cracked cymbal to tinkle on the Fourth of July! Only muffle it! Don't let it sound too loud! Beat it in stoptime, give the dumb bunnies the soft-shoe dance! The Big Wormy Apple, the Chicago Get Away, the Shoo Fly Don't Bother Me!

"And do you know what makes us so uncommon?" I whispered hoarsely. *"We let them do it!"*

The silence was profound. The smoke boiled in the spotlight.

"Another strike," I heard the voice call sadly. "Ain't no use to protest the decision!" And I thought, Is he with me or against me?

"Dispossession! *Dis*-possession is the word!" I went on. "They've tried to dispossess us of our manhood and womanhood! Of our childhood and adolescence— You heard the sister's statistics on our infant mortality rate. Don't you know you're lucky to be uncommonly born? Why, they even tried to dispossess us of *our dislike of being dispossessed!* And I'll tell you something else—if we don't resist, pretty soon they'll succeed! These are the days of dispossession, the season of homelessness, the time of evictions. We'll be dispossessed of the very brains in our heads! And we're so *un*-common that we can't even see it! Perhaps we're too polite. Perhaps we don't care to look at unpleasantness. They think we're blind—*un*-commonly blind. And I don't wonder. Think about it, they've dispossessed us each of one eye from the day we're born. So now we can only see in straight white lines. We're a nation of one-eyed mice— Did you ever see such a sight in your life? Such an *un*-common sight!"

"An' ain't a farmer's wife in the house," the voice called through the titters of bitter laughter. "It's another strike!"

I leaned forward. "You know, if we aren't careful, they'll slip up on our blind sides and—*plop!* out goes our last good eye and we're blind as bats! Someone's afraid we'll see something. Maybe that's why so many of our fine friends are present tonight—blue steel pistols and blue serge suits and all!—but I believe one eye is enough to lose without resistance and I think that's your belief. So let's get together. Did you ever notice, my dumb one-eyed brothers, how two totally blind men can get together and help one another along? They stumble, they bump into things, but they avoid dangers too; they get along. Let's get together, uncommon people. With both our eyes we may see what makes us so uncommon, we'll see *who* make us so uncommon! Up to now we've been like a couple of one-eyed men walking down opposite sides of the street. Someone starts throwing bricks and we start blaming each other and fighting among ourselves. But we're mistaken! Because there's a third party present. There's a smooth, oily scoundrel running down the *middle* of the wide gray street throwing stones— He's the one! He's doing the damage! He claims he needs the space— he calls it his *freedom.* And he knows he's got us on our blind side and he's been popping away till he's got us silly— *uncommonly* silly! In fact, *his* freedom has got us damn-nigh blind! Hush now, don't call no names!" I called, holding up my palm. "I say to hell with this guy! I say come on, cross over! Let's make an alliance! I'll look out for you, and you look out for me! I'm good at catching and I've got a damn good pitching arm!"

"You don't pitch no balls, Brother! Not a single one!"

"Let's make a miracle," I shouted. "Let's take back our pillaged eyes! Let's reclaim our sight; let's combine and spread our vision. Peep around the corner, there's a storm coming. Look down the avenue, there's only one enemy. Can't you see his face?"

It was a natural pause and there was applause, but as it burst I realized that the flow of words had stopped. What would I do when they started to listen again? I leaned forward, straining to see through the barrier of light. They were mine, out there, and I couldn't afford to lose them. Yet I suddenly felt naked, sensing that the words were returning and that something was about to be said that I shouldn't reveal.

"Look at me!" The words ripped from my solar plexus. "I haven't lived here long. Times are hard, I've known despair. I'm from the South, and since coming here I've know eviction. I'd come to distrust the world . . . But look at me now, something strange is happening. I'm here before you. I must confess . . ."

And suddenly Brother Jack was beside me, pretending to adjust the microphone. "Careful now," he whispered. "Don't end your usefulness before you've begun."

"I'm all right," I said, leaning toward the mike.

"May I confess?" I shouted. "You are my friends. We share a common disinheritance, and it's said that confession is good for the soul. Have I your permission?"

"You batting .500, Brother," the voice called.

There was a stir behind me. I waited until it was quiet and hurried on.

"Silence is consent," I said, "so I'll have it out, I'll confess it!" My shoulders were squared, my chin thrust forward and my eyes focused straight into the light. *"Something strange and miraculous and transforming is taking place in me right now . . . as I stand here before you!"*

I could feel the words forming themselves, slowly falling into place. The light seemed to boil opalescently, like liquid soap shaken gently in a bottle.

"Let me describe it. It is something odd. It's something that I'm sure I'd never experience anywhere else in the world. I feel your eyes upon me. I hear the pulse of your breathing. And now, at this moment, with your black and white eyes upon me, I feel . . . I feel . . ."

I stumbled in a stillness so complete that I could hear the gears of the huge clock mounted somewhere on the balcony gnawing upon time.

"What is it, son, what do you feel?" a shrill voice cried.

My voice fell to a husky whisper, "I feel, I feel suddenly that I have become *more human*. Do you understand? More human. Not that I have become a man, for I was born a man. But that I am more human. I feel strong, I feel able to get things done! I feel that I can see sharp and clear and far down the dim corridor of history and in it I can hear the footsteps of militant fraternity! No, wait, let me confess . . . I feel the urge to affirm my feelings . . . I feel that here, after a long and desperate and uncommonly blind journey, I have come home . . . Home! With your eyes upon me I feel that I've found my true family! My true people! My true country! I am a new citizen of the country of your vision, a native of your fraternal land. I feel that here tonight, in this old arena, the new is being born and the vital old revived. In each of you, in me, in us all.

"SISTERS! BROTHERS!

"WE ARE THE TRUE PATRIOTS! THE CITIZENS OF TOMORROW'S WORLD!

"WE'LL BE DISPOSSESSED NO MORE!"

The applause struck like a clap of thunder. I stood transfixed, unable to see, my body quivering with the roar. I made an indefinite movement. What should I do—wave to them? I faced the shouts, cheers, shrill whistling, my eyes burning from the light. I felt a large tear roll down my face and I wiped it away with embarrassment. Others were starting down. Why didn't someone help me get out of the spot before I spoiled everything? But with the tears came an increase of applause and I lifted my head, surprised, my eyes streaming. The sound seemed to roar up in waves. They had begun to stomp the floor and I was laughing and bowing my head now unashamed. It grew in volume, the sound of splitting wood came from the rear. I grew tired, but still they cheered until, finally, I gave up and started back toward the chairs. Red spots danced before my eyes. Someone took my hand, and leaned toward my ear.

"You did it, goddamnit! You did it!" And I was puzzled by the hot mixture of hate and admiration bursting through his words as I thanked him and removed my hand from his crushing grasp.

"Thanks," I said, "but the others had raised them to the right pitch."

I shuddered; he sounded as though he would like to throttle me. I couldn't see and there was much confusion and suddenly someone spun me around, pulling me off balance, and I felt myself pressed against warm feminine softness, holding on.

"Oh, Brother, Brother!" a woman's voice cried into my ear, "Little Brother!" and I felt the hot moist pressure of her lips upon my cheek.

Blurred figures bumped about me. I stumbled as in a game of blindman's buff. My hands were shaken, my back pounded. My face was sprayed with the saliva of enthusiasm, and I decided that the next time I stood in the spotlight it would be wise to wear dark glasses.

It was a deafening demonstration. We left them cheering, knocking over chairs, stomping the floor. Brother Jack guided me off the platform. "It's time we left," he shouted. "Things have truly begun to move. All that energy must be organized!"

He guided me through the shouting crowd, hands continuing to touch me as I stumbled along. Then we entered the dark passage and when we reached the end the spots faded from my eyes and I began to see again. Brother Jack paused at the door.

"Listen to them," he said. "Just waiting to be told what to do!" And I could still hear the applause booming behind us. Then several of the others broke off their conversation and faced us, as the applause muffled down behind the closing door.

"Well, what do you think?" Brother Jack said enthusiastically. "How's that for a starter?"

There was a tense silence. I looked from face to face, black and white, feeling swift panic. They were grim.

"Well?" Brother Jack said, his voice suddenly hard.

I could hear the creaking of someone's shoes.

"Well?" he repeated.

Then the man with the pipe spoke up, a swift charge of tension building with his words.

"It was a most unsatisfactory beginning," he said quietly, punctuating the "unsatisfactory" with a stab of his pipe. He was looking straight at me and I was puzzled. I looked at the others. Their faces were noncommittal, stolid.

"Unsatisfactory!" Brother Jack exploded. "And what alleged process of thought led to that brilliant pronouncement?"

"This is no time for cheap sarcasm, Brother," the brother with the pipe said.

"Sarcasm? You made the sarcasm. No, it isn't a time for sarcasms nor for imbecilities. Nor for plain damn-fooleries! This is a key moment in the struggle, things have just begun to move—and suddenly you are unhappy. You are afraid of success? What's wrong? Isn't this just what we've been working for?"

"Again, ask yourself. You are the great leader. Look into your crystal ball."

Brother Jack swore.

"Brothers!" someone said.

Brother Jack swore and swung to another brother. "You,"

he said to the husky man. "Have you the courage to tell me what's going on here? Have we become a street-corner gang?"

Silence. Someone shuffled his feet. The man with the pipe was looking now at me.

"Did I do something wrong?" I said.

"The worst you could have done," he said coldly.

Stunned, I looked at him wordlessly.

"Never mind," Brother Jack said, suddenly calm. "Just what is the problem, Brother? Let's have it out right here. Just what is your complaint?"

"Not a complaint, an opinion. If we are still allowed to express our opinions," the brother with the pipe said.

"Your opinion, then," Brother Jack said.

"In my opinion the speech was wild, hysterical, politically irresponsible and dangerous," he snapped. "And worse than that, it was *incorrect!*" He pronounced "incorrect" as though the term described the most heinous crime imaginable, and I stared at him openmouthed, feeling a vague guilt.

"Soooo," Brother Jack said, looking from face to face, "there's been a caucus and decisions have been made. Did you take minutes, Brother Chairman? Have you recorded your wise disputations?"

"There was no caucus and the opinion still holds," the brother with the pipe said.

"No meeting, but just the same there has been a caucus and decisions have been reached even before the event is finished."

"But, Brother," someone tried to intervene.

"A most brilliant operation," Brother Jack went on, smiling now. "A consummate example of skilled theoretical Nijinskys leaping ahead of history. But come down, Brothers, come down or you'll land on your dialectics; the stage of history hasn't built that far. The month after next, perhaps, but not yet. And what do you think, Brother Wrestrum?" he asked, pointing to a big fellow of the shape and size of Supercargo.

"I think the brother's speech was backward and reactionary!" he said.

I wanted to answer but could not. No wonder his voice had sounded so mixed when he congratulated me. I could only stare into the broad face with its hate-burning eyes.

"And you," Brother Jack said.

"I liked the speech," the man said, "I thought it was quite effective."

"And you?" Brother Jack said to the next man.

"I am of the opinion that it was a mistake."

"And just why?"

"Because we must strive to reach the people through their intelligence . . ."

"Exactly," the brother with the pipe said. "It was the antithesis of the scientific approach. Ours is a reasonable point of view. We are champions of a scientific approach to society, and such a speech as we've identified ourselves with tonight destroys everything that has been said before. The audience isn't thinking, it's yelling its head off."

"Sure, it's acting like a mob," the big black brother said.

Brother Jack laughed. "And this mob," he said, "is it a mob *against* us, or is it a mob *for* us—how do our musclebound scientists answer that?"

But before they could answer he continued, "Perhaps you're right, perhaps it is a mob; but if it is, then it seems to be a mob that's simply boiling over to come along with us. And I shouldn't have to tell you theoreticians that science bases its judgments upon *experiment!* You're jumping to conclusions before the experiment has run its course. In fact, what's happening here tonight represents only one step in the experiment. The *initial* step, the release of energy. I can understand that it should make you timid—you're afraid of carrying through to the next step—because it's up to you to organize that energy. Well, it's going to be organized and not by a bunch of timid sideline theoreticians arguing in a vacuum, but by getting out and leading the people!"

He was fighting mad, looking from face to face, his red head bristling, but no one answered his challenge.

"It's disgusting," he said, pointing to me. "Our new brother has succeeded by instinct where for two years your 'science' has failed, and now all you can offer is destructive criticism."

"I beg to differ," the brother with the pipe said. "To point out the dangerous nature of his speech isn't destructive criticism. Far from it. Like the rest of us, the new brother must learn to speak scientifically. He must be trained!"

"So at last it occurs to you," Brother Jack said, pulling down the corners of his mouth. *"Training.* All is not lost. There's hope that our wild but effective speaker may be tamed. The scientists perceive a possibility! Very well, it has been arranged; perhaps not scientifically but arranged nevertheless. For the next few months our new brother is to undergo a period of intense study and indoctrination under the guidance of Brother Hambro. That's right," he said, as I started to speak. "I meant to tell you later."

"But that's a long time," I said. "How am I going to live?"

"Your salary will continue," he said. "Meanwhile, you'll be guilty of no further unscientific speeches to upset our brothers' scientific tranquillity. In fact, you are to stay completely out of Harlem. Perhaps then we'll see if you brothers are as swift at organizing as you are at criticizing. It's your move, Brothers."

"I think Brother Jack is correct," a short, bald man said.

"And I don't think that we, of all people, should be afraid of the people's enthusiasm. What we've got to do is to guide it into channels where it will do the most good."

The rest were silent, the brother with the pipe looking at me unbendingly.

"Come," Brother Jack said. "Let's get out of here. If we keep our eyes on the real goal our chances are better than ever before. And let's remember that science isn't a game of chess, although chess may be played scientifically. The other thing to remember is that if we are to organize the masses we must first organize ourselves. Thanks to our new brother, things have changed; we mustn't fail to make use of our opportunity. From now on it's up to you."

"We shall see," the brother with the pipe said. "And as for the new brother, a few talks with Brother Hambro wouldn't harm anyone."

Hambro, I thought, going out, who the hell is he? I suppose I'm lucky they didn't fire me. So now I've got to go to school again.

Out in the night the group was breaking up and Brother Jack drew me aside. "Don't worry," he said. "You'll find Brother Hambro interesting, and a period of training was inevitable. Your speech tonight was a test which you passed with flying colors, so now you'll be prepared for some real work. Here's the address; see Brother Hambro the first thing in the morning. He's already been notified."

When I reached home, tiredness seemed to explode within me. My nerves remained tense even after I had had a hot shower and crawled into bed. In my disappointment, I wanted only to sleep, but my mind kept wandering back to the rally. It had actually happened. I had been lucky and had said the right things at the right time and they had liked me. Or perhaps I had said the wrong things in the right places—

whatever, they had liked it regardless of the brothers, and from now on my life would be different. It was different already. For now I realized that I meant everything that I had said to the audience, even though I hadn't known that I was going to say those things. I had intended only to make a good appearance, to say enough to keep the Brotherhood interested in me. What had come out was completely uncalculated, as though another self within me had taken over and held forth. And lucky that it had, or I might have been fired.

Even my technique had been different; no one who had known me at college would have recognized the speech. But that was as it should have been, for I *was* someone new—even though I had spoken in a very old-fashioned way. I had been transformed, and now, lying restlessly in bed in the dark, I felt a kind of affection for the blurred audience whose faces I had never clearly seen. They had been with me from the first word. They had wanted me to succeed, and fortunately I had spoken for them and they had recognized my words. I belonged to them. I sat up, grasping my knees in the dark as the thought struck home. Perhaps this was what was meant by being "dedicated and set aside." Very well, if so, I accepted it. My possibilities were suddenly broadened. As a Brotherhood spokesman I would represent not only my own group but one that was much larger. The audience was mixed, their claims broader than race. I would do whatever was necessary to serve them well. If they could take a chance with me, then I'd do the very best that I could. How else could I save myself from disintegration?

I sat there in the dark trying to recall the sequence of the speech. Already it seemed the expression of someone else. Yet I knew that it was mine and mine alone, and if it was recorded by a stenographer, I would have a look at it tomorrow.

Words, phrases, skipped through my mind; I saw the blue haze again. What had I meant by saying that I had become "more human"? Was it a phrase that I had picked up from some preceding speaker, or a slip of the tongue? For a moment I thought of my grandfather and quickly dismissed him. What had an old slave to do with humanity? Perhaps it was something that Woodridge had said in the literature class back at college. I could see him vividly, half-drunk on words and full of contempt and exaltation, pacing before the blackboard chalked with quotations from Joyce and Yeats and Sean O'Casey; thin, nervous, neat, pacing as though he walked a high wire of meaning upon which no one of us would ever dare venture. I could hear him: "Stephen's problem, like ours, was not actually one of creating the uncreated conscience of his race, but of creating the *uncreated features of his face*. Our task is that of making ourselves individuals. The conscience of a race is the gift of its individuals who see, evaluate, record . . . We create the race by creating ourselves and then to our great astonishment we will have created something far more important: We will have created a culture. Why waste time creating a conscience for something that doesn't exist? For, you see, blood and skin do not think!"

But no, it wasn't Woodridge. "More human" . . . Did I mean that I had become less of what I was, less a Negro, or that I was less a being apart; less an exile from down home, the South? . . . But all this is negative. To become less—in order to become more? Perhaps that was it, but in what way *more* human? Even Woodridge hadn't spoken of such things. It was a mystery once more, as at the eviction I had uttered words that had possessed me.

I thought of Bledsoe and Norton and what they had done. By kicking me into the dark they'd made me see the possibility of achieving something greater and more important than I'd ever dreamed. Here was a way that didn't lead through the back door, a way not limited by black and white, but a way which, if one lived long enough and worked hard enough, could lead to the highest possible rewards. Here was a way to have a part in making the big decisions, of seeing through the mystery of how the country, the world, really operated. For the first time, lying there in the dark, I could glimpse the possibility of being more than a member of a race. It was no dream, the possibility existed. I had only to work and learn and survive in order to go to the top. Sure I'd study with Hambro, I'd learn what he had to teach and a lot more. Let tomorrow come. The sooner I was through with this Hambro, the sooner I could get started with my work.

Chapter seventeen

Four months later when Brother Jack called the apartment at midnight to tell me to be prepared to take a ride I became quite excited. Fortunately, I was awake and dressed, and when he drove up a few minutes later I was waiting expectantly at the curb. Maybe, I thought, as I saw him hunched behind the wheel in his topcoat, this is what I've been waiting for.

"How have you been, Brother?" I said, getting in.

"A little tired," he said. "Not enough sleep, too many problems."

Then, as he got the car under way, he became silent, and I decided not to ask any questions. That was one thing I had learned thoroughly. There must be something doing at the Chthonian, I thought, watching him staring at the road as though lost in thought. Maybe the brothers are waiting to put me through my paces. If so, fine; I've been waiting for an examination . . .

But instead of going to the Chthonian I looked out to discover that he had brought me to Harlem and was parking the car.

356

"We'll have a drink," he said, getting out and heading for where the neon-lighted sign of a bull's head announced the El Toro Bar.

I was disappointed. I wanted no drink; I wanted to take the next step that lay between me and an assignment. I followed him inside with a surge of irritation.

The barroom was warm and quiet. The usual rows of bottles with exotic names were lined on the shelves, and in the rear, where four men argued in Spanish over glasses of beer, a juke box, lit up green and red, played "Media Luz." And as we waited for the bartender, I tried to figure the purpose of the trip.

I had seen very little of Brother Jack after beginning my studies with Brother Hambro. My life had been too tightly organized. But I should have known that if anything was going to happen, Brother Hambro would have let me know. Instead, I was to meet him in the morning as usual. That Hambro, I thought, is *be* a fanatic teacher! A tall, friendly man, a lawyer and the Brotherhood's chief theoretician, he had proved to be a hard taskmaster. Between daily discussions with him and a rigid schedule of reading, I had been working harder than I'd ever found necessary at college. Even my nights were organized; every evening found me at some rally or meeting in one of the many districts (though this was my first trip to Harlem since my speech) where I'd sit on the platform with the speakers, making notes to be discussed with him the next day. Every occasion became a study situation, even the parties that sometimes followed the meetings. During these I had to make mental notes on the ideological attitudes revealed in the guests' conversations. But I had soon learned the method in it: Not only had I been learning the many aspects of the Brotherhood's policy and its approach to various social groupings, but the city-wide membership had grown familiar with me. My part in the eviction was kept very much alive, and although I was under orders to make no speeches, I had grown accustomed to being introduced as a kind of hero.

Yet it had been mainly a time for listening and, being a talker, I had grown impatient. Now I knew most of the Brotherhood arguments so well—those I doubted as well as those I believed—that I could repeat them in my sleep, but nothing had been said about my assignment. Thus I had hoped the midnight call meant some kind of action was to begin . . .

Beside me, Brother Jack was still lost in thought. He seemed in no hurry to go elsewhere or to talk, and as the slow-motion bartender mixed our drinks I puzzled vainly as to why he had brought me here. Before me, in the panel where a mirror is usually placed, I could see a scene from a bullfight, the bull charging close to the man and the man swinging the red cape in sculptured folds so close to his body that man and bull seemed to blend in one swirl of calm, pure motion. Pure grace, I thought, looking above the bar to where, larger than life, the pink and white image of a girl smiled down from a summery beer ad on which a calendar said April One. Then, as our drinks were placed before us, Brother Jack came alive, his mood changing as though in the instant he had settled whatever had been bothering him and felt suddenly free.

"Here, come back," he said, nudging me playfully. "She's only a cardboard image of a cold steel civilization."

I laughed, glad to hear him joking. "And that?" I said, pointing to the bullfight scene.

"Sheer barbarism," he said, watching the bartender and lowering his voice to a whisper. "But tell me, how have you found your work with Brother Hambro?"

"Oh, fine," I said. "He's strict, but if I'd had teachers like him in college, I'd know a few things. He's taught me a lot, but whether enough to satisfy the brothers who disliked my arena speech, I don't know. Shall we converse scientifically?"

He laughed, one of his eyes glowing brighter than the other. "Don't worry about the brothers," he said. "You'll do very well. Brother Hambro's reports on you have been excellent."

"Now, that's nice to hear," I said, aware now of another bullfight scene further down the bar in which the matador was being swept skyward on the black bull's horns. "I've worked pretty hard trying to master the ideology."

"Master it," Brother Jack said, "but don't overdo it. Don't let it master you. There is nothing to put the people to sleep like dry ideology. The ideal is to strike a medium between ideology and inspiration. Say what the people want to hear, but say it in such a way that they'll do what we wish." He laughed. "Remember too, that theory always comes after practice. Act first, theorize later; that's also a formula, a devastatingly effective one!"

He looked at me as though he did not see me and I could not tell whether he was laughing *at* me or *with* me. I was sure only that he was laughing.

"Yes," I said, "I'll try to master all that is required."

"You can," he said. "And now you don't have to worry about the brothers' criticism. Just throw some ideology back at them and they'll leave you alone—provided, of course, that you have the right backing and produce the required results. Another drink?"

"Thanks, I've had enough."

"Are you sure?"

"Sure."

"Good. Now to your assignment: Tomorrow you are to become chief spokesman of the Harlem District . . ."

"What!"

"Yes. The committee decided yesterday."

"But I had no idea."

"You'll do all right. Now listen. You are to continue

what you started at the eviction. Keep them stirred up. Get them active. Get as many to join as possible. You'll be given guidance by some of the older members, but for the time being you are to see what you can do. You will have freedom of action—*and* you will be under strict discipline to the committee."

"I see," I said.

"No, you don't quite see," he said, "but you will. You must not underestimate the discipline, Brother. It makes you answerable to the entire organization for what you do. Don't underestimate the discipline. It is very strict, but within its framework you are to have full freedom to do your work. And your work is very important. Understand?" His eyes seemed to crowd my face as I nodded yes. "We'd better go now so that you can get some sleep," he said, draining his glass. "You're a soldier now, your health belongs to the organization."

"I'll be ready," I said.

"I know you will. Until tomorrow then. You'll meet with the executive committee of the Harlem section at nine A.M. You know the location of course?"

"No, Brother, I don't."

"Oh? That's right—then you'd better come up with me for a minute. I have to see someone there and you can take a look at where you'll work. I'll drop you off on the way down," he said.

THE district offices were located in a converted church structure, the main floor of which was occupied by a pawnshop, its window crammed with loot that gleamed dully in the darkened street. We took a stair to the third floor, entering a large room beneath a high Gothic ceiling.

"It's down here," Brother Jack said, making for the end of the large room where I saw a row of smaller ones, only one of which was lighted. And now I saw a man appear in the door and limp forward.

"Evening, Brother Jack," he said.

"Why, Brother Tarp, I expected to find Brother Tobitt."

"I know. He was here but he had to leave," the man said. "He left this envelope for you and said he'd call you later on tonight."

"Good, good," Brother Jack said. "Here, meet a new brother . . ."

"Pleased to meet you," the brother said, smiling. "I heard you speak at the arena. You really told 'em."

"Thanks," I said.

"So you liked it, did you, Brother Tarp?" Brother Jack said.

"The boy's all right with me," the man said.

"Well, you're going to see a lot of him, he's your new spokesman."

"That's fine," the man said. "Looks like we're going to get some changes made."

"Correct," Brother Jack said. "Now let's take a look at his office and we'll be going."

"Sure, Brother," Tarp said, limping before me into one of the dark rooms and snapping on a light. "This here is the one."

I looked into a small office, containing a flat-top desk with a telephone, a typewriter on its table, a bookcase with shelves of books and pamphlets, and a huge map of the world inscribed with ancient nautical signs and a heroic figure of Columbus to one side.

"If there's anything you need, just see Brother Tarp," Brother Jack said. "He's here at all times."

"Thanks, I shall," I said. "I'll get oriented in the morning."

"Yes, and we'd better go so you can get some sleep.

Good night, Brother Tarp. See that everything is ready for him in the morning."

"He won't have to worry about a thing, Brother. Good night."

"It's because we attract men like Brother Tarp there that we shall triumph," he said as we climbed into the car. "He's old physically, but ideologically he's a vigorous young man. He can be depended upon in the most precarious circumstance."

"He sounds like a good man to have around," I said.

"You'll see," he said and lapsed into a silence that lasted until we reached my door.

THE committee was assembled in the hall with the high Gothic ceiling when I arrived, sitting in folding chairs around two small tables pushed together to form a unit.

"Well," Brother Jack said, "you are on time. Very good, we favor precision in our leaders."

"Brother, I shall always try to be on time," I said.

"Here he is, Brothers and Sisters," he said, "your new spokesman. Now to begin. Are we all present?"

"All except Brother Tod Clifton," someone said.

His red head jerked with surprise. "So?"

"He'll be here," a young brother said. "We were working until three this morning."

"Still, he should be on time— Very well," Brother Jack said, taking out a watch, "let us begin. I have only a little time here, but a little time is all that is needed. You all know the events of the recent period, and the role our new brother has played in them. Briefly, you are here to see that it isn't wasted. We must achieve two things: We must plan methods of increasing the effectiveness of our agitation, and we must organize the energy that has already been released. This calls for a rapid increase of membership. The people are fully aroused; if we fail to lead them into action, they will become passive, or they will become cynical. Thus it is necessary that we strike immediately and strike hard!

"For this purpose," he said, nodding toward me, "our brother has been appointed district spokesman. You are to give him your loyal support and regard him as the new instrument of the committee's authority . . ."

I heard the slight applause splatter up—only to halt with the opening of the door, and I looked down past the rows of chairs to where a hatless young man about my own age was coming into the hall. He wore a heavy sweater and slacks, and as the others looked up I heard the quick intake of a woman's pleasurable sigh. Then the young man was moving with an easy Negro stride out of the shadow into the light, and I saw that he was very black and very handsome, and as he advanced mid-distance into the room, that he possessed the chiseled, black-marble features sometimes found on statues in northern museums and alive in southern towns in which the white off-spring of house children and the black offspring of yard chil-dren bear names, features and character traits as identical as the rifling of bullets fired from a common barrel. And now close up, leaning tall and relaxed, his arms outstretched stiffly upon the table, I saw the broad, taut span of his knuckles upon the dark grain of the wood, the muscular, sweatered arms, the curving line of the chest rising to the easy pulsing of his throat, to the square, smooth chin, and saw a small X-shaped patch of adhesive upon the subtly blended, velvet-over-stone, granite-over-bone, Afro-Anglo-Saxon contour of his cheek.

He leaned there, looking at us all with a remote aloofness in which I sensed an unstated questioning beneath a friendly charm. Sensing a possible rival, I watched him warily, won-dering who he was.

"Ah, so, Brother Tod Clifton is late," Brother Jack said. "Our leader of the youth is late. Why is this?"

The young man pointed to his cheek and smiled. "I had to see the doctor," he said.

"What is this?" Brother Jack said, looking at the cross of adhesive on the black skin.

"Just a little encounter with the nationalists. With Ras the Exhorter's boys," Brother Clifton said. And I heard a gasp from one of the women who gazed at him with shining, compassionate eyes.

Brother Jack gave me a quick look. "Brother, you have heard of Ras? He is the wild man who calls himself a black nationalist."

"I don't recall so," I said.

"You'll hear of him soon enough. Sit down, Brother Clifton; sit down. You must be careful. You are valuable to the organization, you must not take chances."

"This was unavoidable," the young man said.

"Just the same," Brother Jack said, returning to the discussion with a call for ideas.

"Brother, are we still to fight against evictions?" I said.

"It has become a leading issue, thanks to you."

"Then why not step up the fight?"

He studied my face. "What do you suggest?"

"Well, since it has attracted so much attention, why not try to reach the whole community with the issue?"

"And how would you suggest we go about it?"

"I suggest we get the community leaders on record in support of us."

"There are certain difficulties in face of this," Brother Jack said. "Most of the leaders are against us."

"But I think he's got something there," Brother Clifton said. "What if we got them to support the *issue* whether they like us or not? The issue is a *community* issue, it's non-partisan."

"Sure," I said, "that's how it looks to me. With all the excitement over evictions they can't afford to come out against us, not without appearing to be against the best interests of the community . . ."

"So we have them across a barrel," Clifton said.

"That is perceptive enough," Brother Jack said.

The others agreed.

"You see," Brother Jack said with a grin, "we've always avoided these leaders, but the moment we start to advance on a broad front, sectarianism becomes a burden to be cast off. Any other suggestions?" He looked around.

"Brother," I said, remembering now, "when I first came to Harlem one of the first things that impressed me was a man making a speech from a ladder. He spoke very violently and with an accent, but he had an enthusiastic audience . . . Why can't we carry our program to the street in the same way?"

"So you *have* met him," he said, suddenly grinning. "Well, Ras the Exhorter has had a monopoly in Harlem. But now that we are larger we might give it a try. What the committee wants is results!"

So *that* was Ras the Exhorter, I thought.

"We'll have trouble with the Extortor—I mean the Exhorter," a big woman said. "His hoodlums would attack and denounce the white meat of a roasted chicken."

We laughed.

"He goes wild when he sees black people and white people together," she said to me.

"We'll take care of that," Brother Clifton said, touching his cheek.

"Very well, but no violence," Brother Jack said. "The Brotherhood is against violence and terror and provocation of any kind—aggressive, that is. Understand, Brother Clifton?"

"I understand," he said.

"We will not countenance any aggressive violence. Understand? Nor attacks upon officials or others who do not attack us. We are against all forms of violence, do you understand?"

"Yes, Brother," I said.

"Very well, having made this clear I leave you now," he said. "See what you can accomplish. You'll have plenty support from other districts and all the guidance you need. Meanwhile, remember that we are all under discipline."

He left and we divided the labor. I suggested that each work in the area he knew best. Since there was no liaison between the Brotherhood and the community leaders I assigned myself the task of creating one. It was decided that our street meetings begin immediately and that Brother Tod Clifton was to return and go over the details with me.

While the discussion continued I studied their faces. They seemed absorbed with the cause and in complete agreement, blacks and whites. But when I tried to place them as to type I got nowhere. The big woman who looked like a southern "sudsbuster" was in charge of women's work, and spoke in abstract, ideological terms. The shy-looking man with the liver splotches on his neck spoke with a bold directness and eagerness for action. And this Brother Tod Clifton, the young leader, looked somehow like a hipster, a zoot suiter, a sharpie—except his head of Persian lamb's wool had never known a straightener. I could place none of them. They seemed familiar but were just as different as Brother Jack and the other whites were from all the white men I had known. They were all transformed, like familiar people seen in a dream. Well, I thought, I'm different too, and they'll see it when the talk is finished and the action begins. I'll just have to be careful not to antagonize anyone. As it is, someone might resent my being placed in charge.

But when Brother Tod Clifton came into my office to

discuss the street meeting I saw no signs of resentment, but a complete absorption in the strategy of the meeting. With great care he went about instructing me how to deal with hecklers, on what to do if we were attacked, and upon how to recognize our own members from the rest of the crowd. For all his seeming zoot-suiter characteristics his speech was precise and I had no doubt that he knew his business.

"How do you think we'll do?" I said when he had finished.

"It'll go big, man," he said. "It'll be bigger than anything since Garvey."

"I wish I could be so sure," I said. "I never saw Garvey."

"I didn't either," he said, "but I understand that in Harlem he was very big."

"Well, we're not Garvey, and he didn't last."

"No, but he must have had something," he said with sudden passion. "He *must* have had something to move all those people! Our people are *hell* to move. He must have had plenty!"

I looked at him. His eyes were turned inward; then he smiled. "Don't worry," he said. "We have a scientific plan and you set them off. Things are so bad they'll listen, and when they *listen* they'll go along."

"I hope so," I said.

"They will. You haven't been around the movement as I have, for three years now, and I can feel the change. They're ready to move."

"I hope your feelings are right," I said.

"They're right, all right," he said. "All we have to do is gather them in."

THE evening was almost of a winter coldness, the corner well lighted and the all-Negro crowd large and tightly packed. Up on the ladder now I was surrounded by a group of Clifton's youth division, and I could see, beyond their backs with up-turned collars, the faces of the doubtful, the curious and the convinced in the crowd. It was early and I threw my voice hard down against the traffic sounds, feeling the damp coldness of the air upon my cheeks and hands as my voice warmed with my emotion. I had just begun to feel the pulsing set up be-tween myself and the people, hearing them answering in stac-cato applause and agreement when Tod Clifton caught my eye, pointing. And over the heads of the crowd and down past the dark storefronts and blinking neon signs I saw a bristling band of about twenty men quick-stepping forward. I looked down.

"It's trouble, keep talking," Clifton said. "Give the boys the signal."

"My Brothers, the time has come for action," I shouted. And now I saw the youth members and some older men move around to the back of the crowd, and up to meet the advancing group. Then something sailed up out of the dark and landed hard against my forehead, and I felt the crowd surge in close, sending the ladder moving backwards, and I was like a man tottering above a crowd on stilts, then dropping backwards into the street and clear, hearing the ladder clatter down. They were milling in a panic now, and I saw Clifton beside me. "It's Ras the Exhorter," he yelled. "Can you use your hands?"

"I can use my fists!" I was annoyed.

"Well, all right then. Here's your chance. Come on, let's see you duke!"

He moved forward and seemed to dive into the whirling crowd, and I beside him, seeing them scatter into doorways and pound off in the dark.

"There's Ras, over there," Clifton cried. And I heard the sound of breaking glass and the street went dark. Someone had knocked out the light, and through the dimness I saw Clifton heading to where a red neon sign glowed in a dark window as something went past my head. Then a man ran up with a length of pipe and I saw Clifton close with him, ducking down and working in close and grabbing the man's wrist and twisting suddenly like a soldier executing an about-face so that now he faced me, the back of the man's elbow rigid across his shoulder and the man rising on tiptoe and screaming as Clifton straightened smoothly and levered down on the arm.

I heard a dry popping sound and saw the man sag, and the pipe rang upon the walk; then someone caught me hard in the stomach and suddenly I knew that I was fighting too. I went to my knees and rolled and pulled erect, facing him. "Get up, Uncle Tom," he said, and I clipped him. He had his hands and I had mine and the match was even but he was not so lucky. He wasn't down and he wasn't out, but I caught him two good ones and he decided to fight elsewhere. When he turned I tripped him and moved away.

The fight was moving back into the dark where the street lights had been knocked out clear to the corner, and it was quiet except for the grunting and straining and the sound of footfalls and of blows. It was confusing in the dark and I couldn't tell ours from theirs and moved cautiously, trying to see. Someone up the street in the dark yelled, "Break it up! Break it up!" and I thought, Cops, and looked around for Clifton. The neon sign glowed mysteriously and there was a lot of running and cursing, and now I saw him working skillfully in a store lobby before a red CHECKS CASHED HERE sign and I hurried over, hearing objects sailing past my head and the crash of glass. Clifton's arms were moving in short, accurate jabs against the head and stomach of Ras the Exhorter, punching swiftly and scientifically, careful not to knock him into the window or strike the glass with his fists, working Ras between rights and lefts jabbed so fast that he rocked like a drunken bull, from side to side. And as I came up Ras tried to bull his way out and I saw Clifton drive him back and down into a squat, his hands upon the dark floor of the lobby, his heels back against the door like a runner against starting blocks. And now, shooting forward, he caught Clifton coming in, butting him, and I heard the burst of breath and Clifton was on his back and something flashed in Ras's hand and he came forward, a short, heavy figure as wide as the lobby now with the knife, moving deliberately. I spun, looking for the length of pipe, diving for it and crawling on hands and knees and here, here— and coming up to see Ras reach down, getting one hand into Clifton's collar, the knife in the other, looking down at Clifton and panting, bull-angry. I froze, seeing him draw back the knife and stop it in mid-air; draw back and stop, cursing; then draw back and stop again, all very quickly, beginning to cry now and talking rapidly at the same time; and me easing slowly forward.

"Mahn," Ras blurted, "I ought to kill you. Godahm, I ought to kill you and the world be better off. But you *black*, *mahn*. Why you be black, mahn? I swear I ought to kill you. No mahn strike the Exhorter, godahmit, no mahn!"

I saw him raise the knife again and now as he lowered it unused he pushed Clifton into the street and stood over him, sobbing.

"Why you with these white folks? Why? I been watching you a long time. I say to myself, 'Soon he get smart and get tired. He get out of that t'ing.' Why a good boy like you still with them?"

Still moving forward, I saw his face gleam with red angry tears as he stood above Clifton with the still innocent knife and the tears red in the glow of the window sign.

"You *my* brother, mahn. Brothers are the same color; how the hell you call these white men *brother*? Shit, mahn. That's shit! Brothers the same color. We sons of Mama Africa, you done forgot? You black, BLACK! You—*Godahm*, mahn!" he said, swinging the knife for emphasis. "You got bahd *hair!* You got thick *lips!* They say you *stink!* They hate you, mahn. You African. AFRICAN! Why you with them? Leave that shit, mahn. They sell you out. That shit is old-fashioned. They enslave us—you forget that? How can they mean a black mahn any good? How they going to be your *brother?*"

I had reached him now and brought the pipe down hard, seeing the knife fly off into the dark as he grabbed his wrist, and I raised the pipe again, suddenly hot with fear and hate, as he looked at me out of his narrow little eyes, standing his ground.

"And you, mahn," the Exhorter said, "a reg'lar little black devil! A godahm sly mongoose! Where you think *you* from, going with the white folks? I know, godahm; don't I know it! You from down South! You from Trinidad! You from Barbados! Jamaica, South Africa, and the white mahn's foot in your ass all the way to the hip. What you trying to deny by betraying the black people? Why *you* fight against us? You *young* fellows. You young black men with plenty education; I been hearing your rabble rousing. Why you go over to the enslaver? What kind of education is that? What kind of black mahn is that who betray his own mama?"

"Shut up," Clifton said, leaping to his feet. "Shut up!"

"Hell, no," Ras cried, wiping his eyes with his fists. "I talk! Bust me with the pipe but, by God, you listen to the Exhorter! Come in with us, mahn. We build a glorious movement of black people. *Black People!* What they do, give you money? Who wahnt the dahm stuff? Their money bleed black blood, mahn. It's unclean! Taking their money is shit, mahn. Money without dignity— That's *bahd* shit!"

Clifton lunged toward him. I held him, shaking my head. "Come on, the man's crazy," I said, pulling on his arm.

Ras struck his thighs with his fists. "*Me* crazy, mahn?

You call *me* crazy? Look at you two and look at me—is this *sanity*? Standing here in three shades of blackness! Three black men fighting in the street because of the white enslaver? Is that sanity? Is that consciousness, scientific understahnding? Is that the modern black mahn of the twentieth century? Hell, mahn! Is it self-respect—black against black? What they give you to betray—their women? You fall for that?"

"Let's go," I said, listening and remembering and suddenly alive in the dark with the horror of the battle royal, but Clifton looked at Ras with a tight, fascinated expression, pulling away from me.

"Let's go," I repeated. He stood there, looking.

"Sure, you go," Ras said, "but not him. You contahminated but he the real black mahn. In Africa this mahn be a chief, a black king! Here they say he rape them godahm women with no blood in their veins. I bet this mahn can't beat them off with baseball bat—shit! What kind of foolishness is it? Kick him ass from cradle to grave then call him *brother*? Does it make mahthematics? Is it logic? Look at him, mahn; open your eyes," he said to me. "I look like that I rock the blahsted world! They know about me in Japan, India—all the colored countries. Youth! Intelligence! The mahn's natural prince! Where is your eyes? Where your self-respect? Working for them dahm people? Their days is numbered, the time is almost here and you fooling 'round like this was the nineteenth century. I don't understand you. Am I ignorant? Answer me, mahn!"

"Yes," Clifton burst out. "Hell, yes!"

"You t'ink I'm crazy, is it c'ase I speak bahd English? Hell, it ain't my mama tongue, mahn, I'm African! You really t'ink I'm crazy?"

"Yes, yes!"

"You believe that?" said Ras. "What they do to you, black mahn? Give you them stinking women?"

Clifton lunged again, and again I grabbed him; and again Ras held his ground, his head glowing red.

"Women? *Godahm*, mahn! Is that equality? Is that the black mahn's freedom? A pat on the back and a piece of cunt without no passion? Maggots! They buy you that blahsted cheap, mahn? What they *do* to my people! Where is your brains? These women dregs, mahn! They bile water! You know the high-class white mahn hates the black mahn, that's simple. So now he use the dregs and wahnt you black young men to do his dirty work. They betray you and you betray the black people. They tricking you, mahn. Let them fight among themselves. Let 'em kill off one another. We organize—organization is good—but we organize black. BLACK! To hell with that son of a bitch! He take one them strumpets and tell the black mahn his freedom lie between her skinny legs—while that son of a gun, *he* take all the power and the capital and don't leave the black mahn not'ing. The good white women he tell the black mahn is a rapist and keep them locked up and ignorant while he makes the black mahn a race of bahstards.

"When the black mahn going to tire of this childish perfidity? He got you so you don't trust your black intelligence? You young, don't play you'self cheap, mahn. Don't deny you'self! It took a billion gallons of black blood to make you. Recognize you'self inside and you wan the kings among men! A mahn knows he's a mahn when he got not'ing, when he's naked—nobody have to tell him that. You six foot tall, mahn. You young and intelligent. You black and beautiful—don't let 'em tell you different! You wasn't them t'ings you be dead, mahn. Dead! I'd have killed you, mahn. Ras the Exhorter raised up his knife and tried to do it, but he could not do it. Why don't you do it? I ask myself. I will do it now, I say; but somet'ing tell me, 'No, no! You might be killing your black king!' And I say, yas, yas! So I accept your humiliating ahction.

Ras recognized your black possibilities, mahn. Ras would not sahcrifice his black brother to the white enslaver. Instead he *cry*. Ras is a mahn—no white mahn have to tell him that— and Ras *cry*. So why don't you recognize your black duty, mahn, and come jine us?"

His chest was heaving and a note of pleading had come into the harsh voice. He was an exhorter, all right, and I was caught in the crude, insane eloquence of his plea. He stood there, awaiting an answer. And suddenly a big transport plane came low over the buildings and I looked up to see the firing of its engine, and we were all three silent, watching.

Suddenly the Exhorter shook his fist toward the plane and yelled, "Hell with him, some day we have them too! Hell with him!"

He stood there, shaking his fist as the plane rattled the buildings in its powerful flight. Then it was gone and I looked about the unreal street. They were fighting far up the block in the dark now and we were alone. I looked at the Exhorter. I didn't know if I was angry or amazed.

"Look," I said, shaking my head, "let's talk sense. From now on we'll be on the street corners every night and we'll be prepared for trouble. We don't want it, especially with you, but we won't run either . . ."

"Godahm, mahn," he said, leaping forward, "this is *Harlem*. This is *my* territory, the *black* mahn's territory. You think we let white folks come in and spread their poison? Let 'em come in like they come and take over the numbers racket? Like they have all the stores? Talk sense, mahn, if you talking to Ras, talk sense!"

"This is sense," I said, "and you listen as we listened to you. We'll be out here every night, understand. We'll be out here and the next time you go after one of our brothers with a knife—and I mean white or black—well, we won't forget it."

He shook his head, "Nor will I forget you either, mahn."

"Don't. I don't want you to; because if you forget there'll be trouble. You're mistaken, don't you see you're outnumbered? You need allies to win . . ."

"That there is sense. Black allies. Yellow and brown allies!"

"All men who want a brotherly world," I said.

"Don't be stupid, mahn. They *white*, they don't have to be allies with no black people. They get what they wahnt, they turn against you. Where's your black intelligence?"

"Thinking like that will get you lost in the backwash of history," I said. "Start thinking with your mind and not your emotions."

He shook his head vehemently, looking at Clifton.

"This black mahn talking to me about brains and thinking. I ask both of you, are you awake or sleeping? What is your pahst and where are you going? Never mind, take your corrupt ideology and eat out your own guts like a laughing hyena. You are nowhere, mahn. Nowhere! Ras is not ignorant, nor is Ras afraid. No! Ras, he be here black and fighting for the liberty of the black people when the white folks have got what they wahnt and done gone off laughing in your face and you stinking and choked up with white maggots."

He spat angrily into the dark street. It flew pink in the red glow.

"That'll be all right with me," I said. "Only remember what I said. Come on, Brother Clifton. This man's full of pus, black pus."

We started away, a piece of glass crunching under my foot.

"Maybe so," Ras said, "but I ahm no fool! I ahm no black educated fool who t'inks everything between black mahn and white mahn can be settled with some blahsted lies in some bloody books written by the white mahn in the first place. It's three hundred years of black blood to build this white mahn's civilization and wahn't be wiped out in a minute. Blood calls for blood! You remember that. And remember that I am not like you. Ras recognizes the true issues and he is not afraid to be black. Nor is he a traitor for white men. Remember that: I am no black traitor to the black people for the white people."

And before I could answer Clifton spun in the dark and there was a crack and I saw Ras go down and Clifton breathing hard and Ras lying there in the street, a thick, black man with red tears on his face that caught the reflection of the CHECKS CASHED HERE sign.

And again, as Clifton looked gravely down he seemed to ask a silent question.

"Let's go," I said. "Let's go!"

We started away as the screams of sirens sounded, Clifton cursing quietly to himself.

Then we were out of the dark onto a busy street and he turned to me. There were tears in his eyes.

"That poor, misguided son of a bitch," he said.

"He thinks a lot of you too," I said. I was glad to be out of the dark and away from that exhorting voice.

"The man's crazy," Clifton said. "It'll run you crazy if you let it."

"Where'd he get that name?" I said.

"He gave it to himself. I guess he did. *Ras* is a title of respect in the East. It's a wonder he didn't say something about 'Ethiopia stretching forth her wings,' " he said, mimicking Ras. "He makes it sound like the hood of a cobra fluttering . . . I don't know . . . I don't know . . ."

"We'll have to watch him now," I said.

"Yes, we'd better," he said. "He won't stop fighting . . . And thanks for getting rid of his knife."

"You didn't have to worry," I said. "He wouldn't kill his king."

He turned and looked at me as though he thought I might mean it; then he smiled.

"For a while there I thought I was gone," he said.

As we headed for the district office I wondered what Brother Jack would say about the fight.

"We'll have to overpower him with organization," I said.

"We'll do that, all right. But it's on the inside that Ras is strong," Clifton said. "On the inside he's dangerous."

"He won't get on the inside," I said. "He'd consider himself a traitor."

"No," Clifton said, "he won't get on the inside. Did you hear how he was talking? Did you hear what he was saying?"

"I heard him, sure," I said.

"I don't know," he said. "I suppose sometimes a man *bas* to plunge outside history . . ."

"What?"

"Plunge outside, turn his back . . . Otherwise he might kill somebody, go nuts."

I didn't answer. Maybe he's right, I thought, and was suddenly very glad I had found Brotherhood.

THE next morning it rained and I reached the district before the others arrived and stood looking through the window of my office, past the jutting wall of a building, and on beyond the monotonous pattern of its bricks and mortar I saw a row of trees rising tall and graceful in the rain. One tree grew close by and I could see the rain streaking its bark and its sticky buds. Trees were rowed the length of the long block beyond me, rising tall in dripping wetness above a series of cluttered backyards. And it occurred to me that cleared of its ramshackle fences and planted with flowers and grass, it might form a pleasant park. And just then a paper bag sailed from a window to my left and burst like a silent grenade, scattering garbage into the trees and pancaking to earth with a soggy, exhausted plop! I started with disgust, then thought, The sun will shine in those backyards some day. A community clean-up campaign might be worthwhile for a slack season, at that. Everything couldn't possibly be as exciting as last night.

Turning back to my desk I sat facing the map now as Brother Tarp appeared.

"Morning, son, I see you already on the job," he said.

"Good morning. I have so much to do that I thought I'd better get started early," I said.

"You'll do all right," he said. "But I didn't come in here to take up your time. I want to put something on the wall."

"Go right ahead. Can I give you a hand?"

"No, I can make it all right," he said, clambering with his lame leg upon a chair that sat beneath the map and hanging a frame from the ceiling molding, straightening it carefully, and getting down to come over beside my desk.

"Son, you know who that is?"

"Why, yes," I said, "it's Frederick Douglass."

"Yessir, that's just who it is. You know much about him?"

"Not much. My grandfather used to tell me about him though."

"That's enough. He was a great man. You just take a look at him once in a while. You have everything you need—paper and stuff like that?"

"Yes, I have, Brother Tarp. And thanks for the portrait of Douglass."

"Don't thank me, son," he said from the door. "He belongs to all of us."

I sat now facing the portrait of Frederick Douglass, feeling a sudden piety, remembering and refusing to hear the echoes of my grandfather's voice. Then I picked up the telephone and began calling the community leaders.

They fell in line like prisoners: preachers, politicians, various professionals, proving Clifton correct. The eviction fight was such a dramatic issue that most of the leaders feared that their followers would have rallied to us without them. I slighted no one, no matter how unimportant; big shots, doctors, real-estate men and store-front preachers. And it went so fast and smoothly that it seemed not to happen to me but to someone who actually bore my new name. I almost laughed into the phone when I heard the director of Men's House address me with profound respect. My new name was getting around. It's very strange, I thought, but things are so unreal for them normally that they believe that to call a thing by name is to make it so. And yet I am what they think I am . . .

Our work went so well that a few Sundays later we threw a parade that clinched our hold on the community. We worked feverishly. And now the clashing and conflict of my last days at Mary's seemed to have moved out into the struggles of the community, leaving me inwardly calm and controlled. Even the hustle and bustle of picketing and speechmaking seemed to stimulate me for the better; my wildest ideas paid off.

Upon hearing that one of the unemployed brothers was an ex-drill master from Wichita, Kansas, I organized a drill team of six-footers whose duty it was to march through the streets striking up sparks with their hob-nailed shoes. On the day of the parade they drew crowds faster than a dogfight on a country road. The People's Hot Foot Squad, we called them, and when they drilled fancy formations down Seventh Avenue in the springtime dusk they set the streets ablaze. The community laughed and cheered and the police were dumbfounded. But the sheer corn of it got them and the Hot Foot Squad went shuffling along. Then came the flags and banners and the cards bearing slogans; and the squad of drum majorettes, the best-looking girls we could find, who pranced and twirled and just plain girled in the enthusiastic interest of Brotherhood. We pulled fifteen thousand Harlemites into the street behind our slogans and marched down Broadway to City Hall. Indeed, we were the talk of the town.

With the success I was pushed forward at a dizzy pace. My name spread like smoke in an airless room. I was kept moving all over the place. Speeches here, there, everywhere, uptown and down. I wrote newspaper articles, led parades and relief delegations, and so on. And the Brotherhood was going out of its way to make my name prominent. Articles, telegrams and many mailings went out over my signature—some of which I'd written, but most not. I was publicized, identified with the organization both by word and image in the press. On the way to work one late spring morning I counted fifty greetings from people I didn't know, becoming aware that there were two of me: the old self that slept a few hours a night and dreamed sometimes of my grandfather and Bledsoe and Brockway and Mary, the self that flew without wings and plunged from great heights; and the new public self that spoke for the Brotherhood and was becoming so much more important than the other that I seemed to run a foot race against myself.

Still, I liked my work during those days of certainty. I kept my eyes wide and ears alert. The Brotherhood was a world within a world and I was determined to discover all its secrets and to advance as far as I could. I saw no limits, it was the one organization in the whole country in which I could reach the very top and I meant to get there. Even if it meant climbing a mountain of words. For now I had begun to believe, despite all the talk of science around me, that there was a magic in spoken words. Sometimes I sat watching the watery play of light upon Douglass' portrait, thinking how magical it was that he had talked his way from slavery to a government ministry, and so swiftly. Perhaps, I thought, something of the kind is happening to me. Douglass came north to escape and find work in the shipyards; a big fellow in a sailor's suit who, like me, had taken another name. What had his true name been? Whatever it was, it was as *Douglass* that he became himself, defined himself. And not as a boatwright as he'd expected, but as an orator. Perhaps the sense of magic lay in the unexpected transformations. "You start Saul, and end up Paul," my grandfather had often said. "When you're a youngun, you Saul, but let life whup your head a bit and you starts to trying to be Paul—though you still Sauls around on the side."

No, you could never tell where you were going, that was a sure thing. The only sure thing. Nor could you tell how you'd get there—though when you arrived it was somehow right. For hadn't I started out with a speech, and hadn't it been a speech that won my scholarship to college, where I had expected speechmaking to win me a place with Bledsoe and launch me finally as national leader? Well, I had made a speech, and it had made me a leader, only not the kind I had expected. So that was the way it was. And no complaints, I thought, looking at the map; you started looking for red men and you found them—even though of a different tribe and in a bright new world. The world was strange if you stopped to think about it; still it was a world that could be controlled by science, and the Brotherhood had both science and history under control.

Thus for one lone stretch of time I lived with the intensity displayed by those chronic numbers players who see clues to their fortune in the most minute and insignificant phenomena: in clouds, on passing trucks and subway cars, in dreams, comic strips, the shape of dog-luck fouled on the pavements. I was dominated by the all-embracing idea of Brotherhood. The organization had given the world a new shape, and me a vital role. We recognized no loose ends, everything could be controlled by our science. Life was all pattern and discipline; and the beauty of discipline is when it works. And it was working very well.

Chapter eighteen

Only my Bledsoe-
trustee inspired compulsion to read all papers that touched my
hands prevented me from throwing the envelope aside. It was
unstamped and appeared to be the least important item in the
morning's mail:

Brother,
This is advice from a friend who has been watching you closely.
Do not go too fast. Keep working for the people but remember
that you are one of *us* and do not forget if you get too big
they will cut you down. You are from the South and you know
that this is a *white man's world*. So take a friendly advice and
go easy so that you can keep on helping the colored people.
They do not want you to go too fast and will cut you down
if you do. Be smart . . .

I shot to my feet, the paper rattling poisonously in my
hands. What did it mean? Who'd send such a thing?

"Brother Tarp!" I called, reading again the wavery lines of a handwriting that was somehow familiar. "Brother Tarp!"

"What is it, son?"

And looking up, I received another shock. Framed there in the gray, early morning light of the door, my grandfather seemed to look from his eyes. I gave a quick gasp, then there was a silence in which I could hear his wheezing breath as he eyed me unperturbed.

"What's wrong?" he said, limping into the room.

I reached for the envelope. "Where did this come from?" I said.

"What is it?" he said, taking it calmly from my hands.

"It's unstamped."

"Oh, yes—I saw it myself," he said. "I reckon somebody put it in the box late last night. I took it out with the regular mail. Is it something that wasn't for you?"

"No," I said, avoiding his eyes. "But—it isn't dated. I was wondering when it arrived— Why are you staring at me?"

"Because looks to me like you seen a ghost. You feel sick?"

"It's nothing," I said. "Just a slight upset."

There was an awkward silence. He stood there and I forced myself to look at his eyes again, finding my grandfather gone, leaving only the searching calm. I said, "Sit down a second, Brother Tarp. Since you're here I'd like to ask you a question."

"Sure," he said, dropping into a chair. "Go 'head."

"Brother Tarp, you get around and know the members— how do they really feel about me?"

He cocked his head. "Why, sure—they think you're going to make a real leader—"

"But?"

"Ain't no buts, that's what they think and I don't mind telling you."

"But what about the others?"

"What others?"

"The ones who don't think so much of me?"

"Them's the ones I haven't heard about, son."

"But I must have *some* enemies," I said.

"Sure, I guess everybody has 'em, but I never heard of anybody here in the Brotherhood not liking you. As far as folks up here is concerned *they* think you're *it*. You heard any different?"

"No, but I was wondering. I've been going along taking them so much for granted that I thought I'd better check so that I can keep their support."

"Well, you don't have to worry. So far, nearly everything you had anything to do with has turned out to be what the folks like, even things some of 'em resisted. Take that there," he said, pointing to the wall near my desk.

It was a symbolic poster of a group of heroic figures: An American Indian couple, representing the dispossessed past; a blond brother (in overalls) and a leading Irish sister, representing the dispossessed present; and Brother Tod Clifton and a young white couple (it had been felt unwise simply to show Clifton and the girl) surrounded by a group of children of mixed races, representing the future, a color photograph of bright skin texture and smooth contrast.

"So?" I said, staring at the legend:

"After the Struggle: The Rainbow of America's Future"

"Well, when you first suggested it, some of the members was against you."

"That's certainly true."

"Sho, and they raised the devil about the youth members going into the subways and sticking 'em up in place of them

constipation ads and things—but do you know what they doing now?"

"I guess they're holding it against me because some of
the kids were arrested," I said.

"Holding it against you? Hell, they going around brag-
ging about it. But what I was about to say is they taking them
rainbow pictures and tacking 'em to their walls 'long with
'God Bless Our Home' and the Lord's Prayer. They're crazy
about it. And same way with the Hot-Footers and all that. You
don't have to worry, son. They might resist some of your ideas,
but when the deal goes down, they with you right on down
to the ground. The only enemies you likely to have is somebody on the outside who's jealous to see you spring up all of
a sudden and start to doing some of the things what *should* of
been done years ago. And what do you care when some folks
start knocking you? It's a sign you getting some place."

"I'd like to believe so, Brother Tarp," I said. "As long as
I have the people with me I'll believe in what I'm doing."

"That's right," he said. "When things get rough it kind
of helps to know you got support—" His voice broke off and
he seemed to stare down at me, although he faced me at eye
level across the desk.

"What is it, Brother Tarp?"

"You from down South, ain't you, son?"

"Yes," I said.

He turned in his chair, sliding one hand into his pocket
as he rested his chin upon the other. "I don't really have the
words to say what just come into my head, son. You see, I
was down there for a long time before I come up here, and
when I did come up they was after me. What I mean is, I had
to escape, I had to come a-running."

"I guess I did too, in a way," I said.

"You mean they were after you too?"

"Not really, Brother Tarp, I just feel that way."

"Well this ain't exactly the same thing," he said. "You notice this limp I got?"

"Yes."

"Well, I wasn't always lame, and I'm not really now 'cause the doctors can't find anything wrong with that leg. They say it's sound as a piece of steel. What I mean is I got this limp from dragging a chain."

I couldn't see it in his face or hear it in his speech, yet I knew he was neither lying nor trying to shock me. I shook my head.

"Sure," he said. "Nobody knows that about me, they just think I got rheumatism. But it was the chain, and after nineteen years I haven't been able to stop dragging my leg."

"Nineteen years!"

"Nineteen years, six months and two days. And what I did wasn't much; that is, it wasn't much when I did it. But after all that time it changed into something else and it seemed to be as bad as they said it was. All that time *made* it bad. I paid for it with everything I had but my life. I lost my wife and my boys and my piece of land. So what started out as an argument between a couple of men turned out to be a crime worth nineteen years of my life."

"What on earth did you do, Brother Tarp?"

"I said no to a man who wanted to take something from me; that's what it cost me for saying no, and even now the debt ain't fully paid and will *never* be paid in their terms."

A pain throbbed in my throat and I felt a kind of numb despair. Nineteen years! And here he was talking quietly to me and this no doubt the first time he'd tried to tell anyone about it. But why me, I thought, why pick me?

"I said no," he said. "I said *hell*, no! And I kept saying no until I broke the chain and left."

"But how?"

"They let me get close to the dogs once in a while, that's how. I made friends with them dogs and I waited. Down there you really learn how to wait. I waited nineteen years and then one morning when the river was flooding I left. They thought I was one of them who got drowned when the levee broke, but I done broke the chain and gone. I was standing in the mud holding a long-handled shovel and I asked myself, Tarp, can you make it? And inside me I said yes; all that water and mud and rain said yes, and I took off."

Suddenly he gave a laugh so gay it startled me.

"I'm tellin' it better'n I ever thought I could," he said, fishing in his pocket and removing something that looked like an oilskin tobacco pouch, from which he removed an object wrapped in a handkerchief.

"I've been looking for freedom ever since, son. And sometimes I've done all right. Up to these here hard times I did very well, considering that I'm a man whose health is not too good. But even when times were best for me I remembered. Because I didn't want to forget those nineteen years I just kind of held on to this as a keepsake and a reminder."

He was unwrapping the object now and I watched his old man's hands.

"I'd like to pass it on to you, son. There," he said, handing it to me. "Funny thing to give somebody, but I think it's got a heap of signifying wrapped up in it and it might help you remember what we're really fighting against. I don't think of it in terms of but two words, *yes* and *no*; but it signifies a heap more . . ."

I saw him place his hand on the desk. "Brother," he said, calling me "Brother" for the first time, "I want you to take it. I guess it's a kind of luck piece. Anyway, it's the one I filed to get away."

I took it in my hand, a thick dark, oily piece of filed steel that had been twisted open and forced partly back into place, on which I saw marks that might have been made by the blade of a hatchet. It was such a link as I had seen on Bledsoe's desk, only while that one had been smooth, Tarp's bore the marks of haste and violence, looking as though it had been attacked and conquered before it stubbornly yielded.

I looked at him and shook my head as he watched me inscrutably. Finding no words to ask him more about it, I slipped the link over my knuckles and struck it sharply against the desk.

Brother Tarp chuckled. "Now there's a way I never thought of using it," he said. "It's pretty good. It's pretty good."

"But why do you give it to me, Brother Tarp?"

"Because I *have* to, I guess. Now don't go trying to get me to say what I can't. You're the talker, not me," he said, getting up and limping toward the door. "It was lucky to me and I think it might be lucky to you. You just keep it with you and look at it once in a while. Course, if you get tired of it, why, give it back."

"Oh, no," I called after him, "I want it and I think I understand. Thanks for giving it to me."

I looked at the dark band of metal against my fist and dropped it upon the anonymous letter. I neither wanted it nor knew what to do with it; although there was no question of keeping it if for no other reason than that I felt that Brother Tarp's gesture in offering it was of some deeply felt significance which I was compelled to respect. Something, perhaps, like a man passing on to his son his own father's watch, which the son accepted not because he wanted the old-fashioned time-piece for itself, but because of the overtones of unstated seri-ousness and solemnity of the paternal gesture which at once joined him with his ancestors, marked a high point of his present, and promised a concreteness to his nebulous and chaotic future. And now I remembered that if I had returned home instead of coming north my father would have given me my grandfather's old-fashioned Hamilton, with its long, burr-headed winding stem. Well, so my brother would get it and I'd never wanted it anyway. What were they doing now, I brooded, suddenly sick for home.

I could feel the air from the window hot against my neck now as through the smell of morning coffee I heard a throaty voice singing with a mixture of laughter and solemnity:

> *Don't come early in the morning*
> *Neither in the heat of the day*
> *But come in the sweet cool of the*
> *Evening and wash my sins away . . .*

A whole series of memories started to well up, but I threw them off. There was no time for memory, for all its images were of times passed.

There had been only a few minutes from the time that I'd called in Brother Tarp about the letter and his leaving, but it seemed as though I'd plunged down a well of years. I looked calmly now at the writing which, for a moment, had shaken my total structure of certainty, and was glad that Brother Tarp had been there to be called rather than Clifton or some of the others before whom I would have been ashamed of my panic. Instead he'd left me soberly confident. Perhaps from the shock of seeming to see my grandfather looking through Tarp's eyes, perhaps through the calmness of his voice alone, or perhaps through his story and his link of chain, he had restored my perspective.

He's right, I thought; whoever sent the message is trying

to confuse me; some enemy is trying to halt our progress by destroying my faith through touching upon my old southern distrust, our fear of white betrayal. It was as though he had learned of my experience with Bledsoe's letters and was trying to use that knowledge to destroy not only me but the whole Brotherhood. Yet that was impossible; no one knew that story who knew me now. It was simply an obscene coincidence. If only I could get my hands upon his stupid throat. Here in the Brotherhood was the one place in the country where we were free and given the greatest encouragement to use our abilities, and he was trying to destroy it! No, it wasn't me he was worrying about becoming too big, it was the Brotherhood. And becoming big was exactly what the Brotherhood wanted. Hadn't I just received orders to submit ideas for organizing *more* people? And "a white man's world" was just what the Brotherhood was against. We were dedicated to building a world of Brotherhood.

But who had sent it—Ras the Exhorter? No, it wasn't like him. He was more direct and absolutely against any collaboration between blacks and whites. It was someone else, someone more insidious than Ras. But who, I wondered, forcing it below my consciousness as I turned to the tasks at hand.

The morning began with people asking my advice on how to secure relief; members coming in for instructions for small committee meetings being held in corners of the large hall; and I had just dismissed a woman seeking to free her husband, who had been jailed for beating her, when Brother Wrestrum entered the room. I returned his greeting and watched him ease into a chair, his eyes sweeping over my desk—with uneasiness. He seemed to possess some kind of authority in the Brotherhood, but his exact function was unclear. He was, I felt, something of a meddler.

And hardly had he settled himself when he stared at my

desk, saying, "What you got there, Brother?" and pointed toward a pile of my papers. I leaned slowly back in my chair, looking him in the eye. "That's my work," I said coldly, determined to stop any interference from the start.

"But I mean *that*," he said, pointing, his eyes beginning to blaze, "that there."

"It's work," I said, "all my work."

"Is that too?" he said, pointing to Brother Tarp's leg link.

"That's just a personal present, Brother," I said. "What could I do for you?"

"That ain't what I asked you, Brother. What is it?"

I picked up the link and held it toward him, the metal oily and strangely skinlike now with the slanting sun entering the window. "Would you care to examine it, Brother? One of our members wore it nineteen years on the chain gang."

"Hell, no!" He recoiled. "I mean, no, thank you. In fact, Brother, I don't think we ought to have such things around!"

"*You* think so," I said. "And just why?"

"Because I don't think we ought to dramatize our differences."

"I'm not dramatizing anything, it's my personal property that happens to be lying on my desk."

"But people can see it!"

"That's true," I said. "But I think it's a good reminder of what our movement is fighting against."

"No, suh!" he said, shaking his head, "no, suh! That's the worse kind of thing for Brotherhood—because we want to make folks think of the things we have in common. That's what makes for Brotherhood. We have to change this way we have of always talking about how different we are. In the Brotherhood we are all brothers."

I was amused. He was obviously disturbed by something

deeper than a need to forget differences. Fear was in his eyes. "I never thought of it just that way, Brother," I said, dangling the iron between my finger and thumb.

"But you want to think about it," he said. "We have to discipline ourselves. Things that don't make for Brotherhood have to be rooted out. We have enemies, you know. I watch everything I do and say so as to be sure that I don't upset the Brotherhood—'cause this is a wonderful movement, Brother, and we have to keep it that way. We have to *watch* ourselves, Brother. You know what I mean? Too often we're liable to forget that this is something that's a privilege to belong to. We're liable to say things that don't do nothing but make for more misunderstanding."

What's driving him, I thought, what's all this to do with me? Could he have sent me the note? Dropping the iron I fished the anonymous note from beneath the pile and held it by a corner, so that the slanting sun shone through the page and outlined the scrawling letters. I watched him intently. He was leaning upon the desk now, looking at the page but with no recognition in his eyes. I dropped the page upon the chain, more disappointed than relieved.

"Between you and me, Brother," he said, "there are those amongst us who don't really believe in Brotherhood."

"Oh?"

"You damn right they don't! They're just in it to use it for their own ends. Some call you Brother to your face and the minute you turn your back, you're a black son of a bitch! You got to watch 'em."

"I haven't encountered any of that, Brother," I said.

"You will. There's lots of poison around. Some don't want to shake your hand and some don't like the idea of seeing too much of you; but goddam it, in the Brotherhood they gotta!"

I looked at him. It had never occurred to me that the Brotherhood could force anyone to shake my hand, and that he found satisfaction that it could was both shocking and distasteful.

Suddenly he laughed. "Yes, dammit, they gotta! Me, I don't let 'em get away with nothing. If they going to be brothers let 'em be brothers! Oh, but I'm fair," he said, his face suddenly self-righteous. "I'm fair. I ask myself every day, 'What are you doing against Brotherhood?' and when I find it, I root it out, I burn it out like a man cauterizing a mad-dog bite. This business of being a brother is a full-time job. You have to be pure in heart and you have to be disciplined in body and mind. Brother, you understand what I mean?"

"Yes, I think I do," I said. "Some folks feel that way about their religion."

"Religion?" He blinked his eyes. "Folks like me and you is full of distrust," he said. "We been corrupted 'til it's hard for some of us to believe in Brotherhood. And some even want revenge! That's what I'm talking about. We have to root it out! We have to learn to trust our other brothers. After all, didn't *they* start the Brotherhood? Didn't *they* come and stretch out their hand to us black men and say, 'We want y'all for our brothers?' Didn't they do it? Didn't they, now? Didn't they set out to organize us, and help fight our battle and all like that? Sho they did, and we have to remember it twenty-four hours a day. *Brotherhood.* That's the word we got to keep right in front of our eyes every second. Now this brings me to why I come to see you, Brother."

He sat back, his huge hands grasping his knees. "I got a plan I want to talk over with you."

"What is it, Brother?" I said.

"Well, it's like this. I think we ought to have some way of showing what we are. We ought to have some banners and things like that. 'Specially for us black brothers."

"I see," I said, becoming interested. "But why do you think this is important?"

" 'Cause it helps the Brotherhood, that's why. First, if you remember, when you watch our people when there's a parade or a funeral, or a dance or anything like that, they always have some kind of flags and banners even if they don't mean anything. It kind of makes the occasion seem more important like. It makes people stop, look and listen. 'What's coming off here?' But you know and I know that they ain't none of 'em got no true flag—except maybe Ras the Exhorter, and he claims *he's* Ethiopian or African. But none of us got no true flag 'cause that flag don't really belong to us. They want a true flag, one that's as much theirs as anybody else's. You know what I mean?"

"Yes, I think I do," I said, remembering that there was always that sense in me of being apart when the flag went by. It had been a reminder, until I'd found the Brotherhood, that *my* star was not yet there . . .

"Sure, you know," Brother Wrestrum said. "Everybody wants a flag. We need a flag that stands for Brotherhood, and we need a sign we can wear."

"A sign?"

"You know, a pin or a button."

"You mean an emblem?"

"That's it! Something we can wear, a pin or something like that. So that when a Brother meets a Brother they can know it. That way that thing what happened to Brother Tod Clifton wouldn't have happened . . ."

"What wouldn't have happened?"

He sat back. "Don't you know about it?"

"I don't know what you mean."

"It's something that's best forgot about," he said, leaning close, his big hands gripped and stretched before him. "But you see, there was a rally and some hoodlums tried to break up the meeting, and in the fighting Brother Tod Clifton got holt to one of the white brothers by mistake and was beating *him*, thought he was one of the hoodlums, *he* said. Things like that is bad, Brother, *very* bad. But with some of these emblems, things like that wouldn't happen."

"So that actually happened," I said.

"Sure did. That Brother Clifton goes wild when he gits mad . . . But what do you think of my idea?"

"I think it should be brought to the attention of the committee," I said guardedly, as the phone rang. "Excuse me a moment, Brother," I said.

It was the editor of a new picture magazine requesting an interview of "one of our most successful young men."

"That's very flattering," I said, "but I'm afraid I'm too busy for an interview. I suggest, however, that you interview our youth leader, Brother Tod Clifton; you'll find him a much more interesting subject."

"No, no!" Wrestrum said, shaking his head violently as the editor said, "But we want you. You've—"

"And you know," I interrupted, "our work is considered very controversial, certainly by some."

"That's exactly why we want you. You've become identified with that controversy and it's our job to bring such subjects to the eyes of our readers."

"But so has Brother Clifton," I said.

"No, sir; you're the man and you owe it to our youth to allow us to tell them your story," he said, as I watched Brother Wrestrum leaning forward. "We feel that they should be encouraged to keep fighting toward success. After all, you're one of the latest to fight his way to the top. We need all the heroes we can get."

"But, please," I laughed over the phone, "I'm no hero and I'm far from the top; I'm a cog in a machine. We here in the Brotherhood work as a unit," I said, seeing Brother Wrestrum nod his head in agreement.

"But you can't get around the fact that you're the first of our people to attract attention to it, can you now?"

"Brother Clifton was active at least three years before me. Besides, it isn't that simple. Individuals don't count for much; it's what the group wants, what the group does. Everyone here submerges his personal ambitions for the common achievement."

"Good! That's very good. People want to hear that. Our people need to have someone say that to them. Why don't you let me send out an interviewer? I'll have her there in twenty minutes."

"You're very insistent, but I'm very busy," I said.

And if Brother Wrestrum hadn't been wig-wagging, trying to tell me what to say I would have refused. Instead, I consented. Perhaps, I thought, a little friendly publicity wouldn't hurt. Such a magazine would reach many timid souls living far from the sound of our voices. I had only to remember to say little about my past.

"I'm sorry for this interruption, Brother," I said, putting down the phone and looking into his curious eyes. "I'll bring your idea to the attention of the committee as quickly as possible."

I stood to discourage further talk and he got up, fairly bursting to continue.

"Well, I've got to see some other brothers myself," he said. "I'll be seeing you soon."

"Anytime," I said, avoiding his hand by picking up some papers.

Going out, he turned with his hand on the door frame, frowning. "And, Brother, don't forget what I said about that

thing you got on your desk. Things like that don't do nothin'
but cause confusion. They ought to be kept out of sight."

I was glad to see him go. The idea of his trying to tell
me what to say in a conversation only part of which he could
have heard! And it was obvious that he disliked Clifton. Well,
I disliked *him*. And all that foolishness and fear over the leg
chain. Tarp had worn it for nineteen years and could laugh,
but this big—

Then I forgot Brother Wrestrum until about two weeks
later at our downtown headquarters, where a meeting had been
called to discuss strategy.

EVERYONE had arrived before me. Long benches were arranged
at one side of the room, which was hot and filled with smoke.
Usually such meetings sounded like a prizefight or a smoker,
but now everyone was silent. The white brothers looked uncomfortable and some of the Harlem brothers belligerent. Nor
did they leave me time to think about it. No sooner had I
apologized for my lateness than Brother Jack struck the table
with his gavel, addressing his first remarks to me.

"Brother, there seems to be a serious misunderstanding
among some of the brothers concerning your work and recent
conduct," he said.

I stared at him blankly, my mind groping for connec-
tions. "I'm sorry, Brother Jack," I said, "but I don't understand. You mean there's something wrong with my work?"

"So it seems," he said, his face completely neutral.
"Certain charges have just been made . . ."

"Charges? Have I failed to carry out some directive?"

"About that there seems to be some doubt. But we'd
better let Brother Wrestrum speak of this," he said.

"Brother Wrestrum!"

I was shocked. He hadn't been around since our talk, and I looked across the table into his evasive face, seeing him stand with a slouch, a rolled paper protruding from his pocket.

"Yes, Brothers," he said, "I brought charges, much as I hated to have to do it. But I been watching the way things have been going and I've decided that if they don't stop *soon*, this brother is going to make a fool out of the Brotherhood!"

There were some sounds of protest.

"Yes, I said it and I mean it! This here brother constitutes one of the greatest dangers ever confronted by our movement."

I looked at Brother Jack; his eyes were sparkling. I seemed to see traces of a smile as he scribbled something on a pad. I was becoming very hot.

"Be more specific, Brother," Brother Garnett, a white brother, said. "These are serious charges and we all know that the brother's work has been splendid. Be specific."

"Sho, I'll be specific," Wrestrum boomed, suddenly whipping the paper from his pocket, unrolling it and throwing it on the table. "This here's what I mean!"

I took a step forward; it was a portrait of me looking out from a magazine page.

"Where did that come from?" I said.

"That's it," he boomed. "Make out like you never seen it."

"But I haven't," I said. "I really haven't."

"Don't lie to these white brothers. Don't lie!"

"I'm not lying. I never saw it before in my life. But suppose I had, what's wrong with it?"

"You know what's wrong!" Wrestrum said.

"Look, I don't know anything. What's on your mind? You have us all here, so if you have anything to say, please get it over with."

"Brothers, this man is a—a—opportunist! All you got to do is read this article to see. I charge this man with using the Brotherhood movement to advance his own selfish interests."

"Article?" Then I remembered the interview which I had forgotten. I met the eyes of the others as they looked from me to Wrestrum.

"And what does it say about us?" Brother Jack said, pointing to the magazine.

"Say?" Wrestrum said. "It doesn't say anything. It's all about him. What *he* thinks, what *he* does; what *he's* going to do. Not a word about the rest of us who's been building the movement before he was ever heard of. Look at it, if you think I'm lying. Look at it!"

Brother Jack turned to me. "Is this true?"

"I haven't read it," I said. "I had forgotten that I was interviewed."

"But you remember it now?" Brother Jack said.

"Yes, I do now. And he happened to be in the office when the appointment was made."

They were silent.

"Hell, Brother Jack," Wrestrum said, "it's right here in black and white. He's trying to give people the idea that he's the whole Brotherhood movement."

"I'm doing nothing of the sort. I tried to get the editor to interview Brother Tod Clifton, you know that. Since you know so little about what I'm doing, why not tell the brothers what *you're* up to."

"I'm exposing a double-dealer, that's what I'm doing. I'm exposing you. Brothers, this man is a *pure dee* opportunist!"

"All right," I said, "expose me if you can, but stop the slander."

"I'll expose you, all right," he said, sticking out his chin. "I'm going to. He's doing everything I said, Brothers. And I'll tell you something else—he's trying to sew things up so that the members won't move unless *he* tells them to. Look at a few weeks ago when he was off in Philly. We tried to get a rally going and what happens? Only about two hundred people turned out. He's trying to train them so they won't listen to no one but him."

"But, Brother, didn't we decide that the appeal had been improperly phrased?" a brother interrupted.

"Yeah, I know, but that wasn't it . . ."

"But the committee analyzed the appeal and—"

"I know, Brothers, and I don't aim to dispute the committee. But, Brothers, it just seems that way 'cause you don't *know* this man. He works in the dark, he's got some kind of plot . . ."

"What kind of plot?" one of the brothers said, leaning across the table.

"Just a plot," Wrestrum said. "He aims to control the movement uptown. He wants to be a *dictator!*"

The room was silent except for the humming of fans. They looked at him with a new concern.

"These are very serious charges, Brother," two brothers said in unison.

"Serious? I know they're serious. That's how come I brought them. This opportunist thinks that because he's got a little more education he's better than anybody else. He's what Brother Jack calls a petty—petty individualist!"

He struck the conference table with his fists, his eyes showing small and round in his taut face. I wanted to punch that face. It no longer seemed real, but a mask behind which the real face was probably laughing, both at me and at the others. For he couldn't believe what he had said. It just wasn't possible. *He* was the plotter and from the serious looks on the committee's faces he was getting away with it. Now several brothers started to speak at once, and Brother Jack knocked for order.

"Brothers, please," Brother Jack said. "One at a time. What do you know about this article?" he said to me.

"Not very much," I said. "The editor of the magazine called to say he was sending a reporter up for an interview. The reporter asked a few questions and took a few pictures with a little camera. That's all I know."

"Did you give the reporter a prepared handout?"

"I gave her nothing except a few pieces of our official literature. I told her neither what to ask me nor what to write. I naturally tried to co-operate. If an article about me would help make friends for the movement I felt it was my duty."

"Brothers, this thing was *arranged,*" Wrestrum said. "I tell you this opportunist had that reporter *sent* up there. He had her sent up and he told her what to write."

"That's a contemptible lie," I said. "You were present and you know I tried to get them to interview Brother Clifton!"

"Who's a lie?"

"You're a liar and a fat-mouthed scoundrel. You're a liar and no brother of mine."

"Now he's calling me names. Brothers, you heard him."

"Let's not lose our tempers," Brother Jack said calmly. "Brother Wrestrum, you've made serious charges. Can you prove them?"

"I can prove them. All you have to do is read the magazine and prove them for yourself."

"It will be read. And what else?"

"All you have to do is listen to folks in Harlem. All they talk about is him. Never nothing about what the rest of us do. I tell you, Brothers, this man constitutes a danger to the people of Harlem. He ought to be thrown out!"

"That is for the committee to decide," Brother Jack said. Then to me, "And what have you to say in your defense, Brother?"

"In my defense?" I said. "Nothing. I haven't anything to defend. I've tried to do my work and if the brothers don't know that, then it's too late to tell them. I don't know what's behind this, but I haven't gotten around to controlling magazine writers. And I didn't realize that I was coming to stand trial either."

"This was not intended as a trial," Brother Jack said. "If you're ever put on trial, and I hope you'll never be, you'll know it. Meantime, since this is an emergency the committee asks that you leave the room while we read and discuss the questioned interview."

I left the room and went into a vacant office, boiling with anger and disgust. Wrestrum had snatched me back to the South in the midst of one of the top Brotherhood committees and I felt naked. I could have throttled him—forcing me to take part in a childish dispute before the others. Yet I had to fight him as I could, in terms he understood, even though we sounded like characters in a razor-slinging vaudeville skit. Perhaps I should mention the anonymous note, except that someone might take it to mean that I didn't have the full support of my district. If Clifton were here, he'd know how to handle this clown. Were they taking him seriously just because he was black? What was wrong with them anyway, couldn't they see that they were dealing with a clown? But I would have gone to pieces had they laughed or even smiled, I thought, for they couldn't laugh at him without laughing at me as well . . . Yet if they *bad* laughed, it would have been less unreal— Where the hell am I?

"You can come in now," a brother called to me; and I went out to hear their decision.

"Well," Brother Jack said, "we've all read the article, Brother, and we're happy to report that we found it harmless enough. True, it would have been better had more wordage been given to other members of the Harlem district. But we found no evidence that you had anything to do with that. Brother Wrestrum was mistaken."

His bland manner and the knowledge that they had wasted time to see the truth released the anger within me.

"I'd say that he was criminally mistaken," I said.

"Not criminal, over-zealous," he said.

"To me it seems both criminal and over-zealous," I said.

"No, Brother, not criminal."

"But he attacked my reputation . . ."

Brother Jack smiled. "Only because he was sincere, Brother. He was thinking of the good of the Brotherhood."

"But why slander me? I don't follow you, Brother Jack. I'm no enemy, as he well knows. I'm a brother too," I said, seeing his smile.

"The Brotherhood has many enemies, and we must not be too harsh with brotherly mistakes."

Then I saw the foolish, abashed expression on Wrestrum's face and relaxed.

"Very well, Brother Jack," I said. "I suppose I should be glad you found me innocent—"

"Concerning the *magazine article,*" he said, stabbing the air with his finger.

Something tensed in the back of my head; I got to my feet.

"Concerning the article! You mean to say that you believe that other pipe-dream? Is everyone reading Dick Tracy these days?"

"This is no matter of Dick Tracy," he snapped. "The movement has many enemies."

"So now I have become an enemy," I said. "What's happened to everybody? You act as though none of you has any contact with me at all."

Jack looked at the table. "Are you interested in our decision, Brother?"

"Oh, yes," I said. "Yes, I am. I'm interested in all manner of odd behavior. Who wouldn't be, when one wild man can make a roomful of what I'd come to regard as some of the best minds in the country take him seriously. Certainly, I'm interested. Otherwise I'd act like a sensible man and run out of here!"

There were sounds of protest and Brother Jack, his face red, rapped for order.

"Perhaps I should address a few words to the brother," Brother MacAfee said.

"Go ahead," Brother Jack said thickly.

"Brother, we understand how you feel," Brother MacAfee said, "but you must understand that the movement has many enemies. This is very true, and we are forced to think of the organization at the expense of our personal feelings. The Brotherhood is bigger than all of us. None of us as individuals count when its safety is questioned. And be assured that none of us have anything but goodwill toward you personally. Your work has been splendid. This is simply a matter of the safety of the organization, and it is our responsibility to make a thorough investigation of all such charges."

I felt suddenly empty; there was a logic in what he said which I felt compelled to accept. They were wrong, but they had the obligation to discover their mistake. Let them go ahead, they'd find that none of the charges were true and I'd be vindicated. What was all this obsession with enemies anyway? I looked into their smoke-washed faces; not since the beginning had I faced such serious doubts. Up to now I had felt a whole-

Ralph Ellison

ness about my work and direction such as I'd never known; not even in my mistaken college days. Brotherhood was something to which men could give themselves completely; that was its strength and my strength, and it was this sense of wholeness that guaranteed that it would change the course of history. This I had believed with all my being, but now, though still inwardly affirming that belief, I felt a blighting hurt which prevented me from trying further to defend myself. I stood there silently, waiting their decision. Someone drummed his fingers against the table top. I heard the dry-leaf rustle of onionskin papers.

"Be assured that you can depend upon the fairness and wisdom of the committee," Brother Tobitt's voice drifted from the end of the table, but there was smoke between us and I could barely see his face.

"The committee has decided," Brother Jack began crisply, "that until all charges have been cleared, you are to have the choice of becoming inactive in Harlem, or accepting an assignment downtown. In the latter case you are to wind up your present assignment immediately."

I felt weak in my legs. "You mean I am to give up my work?"

"Unless you choose to serve the movement elsewhere."

"But can't you see—" I said, looking from face to face and seeing the blank finality in their eyes.

"Your assignment, should you decide to remain active," Brother Jack said, reaching for his gavel, "is to lecture downtown on the Woman Question."

Suddenly I felt as though I had been spun like a top.

"The what!"

"The Woman Question. My pamphlet, 'On the Woman Question in the United States,' will be your guide. And now, Brothers," he said, his eyes sweeping around the table, "the meeting is adjourned."

I stood there, hearing the rapping of his gavel echoing in my ears, thinking the *woman question* and searching their faces for signs of amusement, listening to their voices as they filed out into the hall for the slightest sound of suppressed laughter, stood there fighting the sense that I had just been made the butt of an outrageous joke and all the more so since their faces revealed no awareness.

My mind fought desperately for acceptance. Nothing would change matters. They would shift me and investigate and I, still believing, still bending to discipline, would have to accept their decision. Now was certainly no time for inactivity; not just when I was beginning to approach some of the aspects of the organization about which I knew nothing (of higher committees and the leaders who never appeared, of the sympathizers and allies in groups that seemed far removed from our concerns), not at a time when all the secrets of power and authority still shrouded from me in mystery appeared on the way toward revelation. No, despite my anger and disgust, my ambitions were too great to surrender so easily. And why should I restrict myself, segregate myself? I was a *spokesman*— why shouldn't I speak about women, or any other subject? Nothing lay outside the scheme of our ideology, there was a policy on everything, and my main concern was to work my way ahead in the movement.

I left the building still feeling as though I had been violently spun but with optimism growing. Being removed from Harlem was a shock but one which would hurt them as much as me, for I had learned that the clue to what Harlem wanted was what *I* wanted; and my value to the Brotherhood was no different from the value to me of my most useful contact: it depended upon my complete frankness and honesty in stating the community's hopes and hates, fears and desires. One spoke to the committee as well as to the community. No doubt it would work much the same downtown. The new assignment

was a challenge and an opportunity for testing how much of
what happened in Harlem was due to my own efforts and how
much to the sheer eagerness of the people themselves. And,
after all, I told myself, the assignment was also proof of the
committee's goodwill. For by selecting me to speak with its
authority on a subject which elsewhere in our society I'd have
found taboo, weren't they reaffirming their belief both in me
and in the principles of Brotherhood, proving that they drew
no lines even when it came to women? They had to investigate
the charges against me, but the assignment was their unsenti-
mental affirmation that their belief in me was unbroken. I shivered in the hot street. I hadn't allowed the idea to take concrete
form in my mind, but for a moment I had almost allowed an
old, southern backwardness which I had thought dead to wreck
my career.

Leaving Harlem was not without its regrets, however,
and I couldn't bring myself to say good-bye to anyone, not
even to Brother Tarp or Clifton—not to mention the others
upon whom I depended for information concerning the lowest
groups in the community. I simply slipped my papers into my
brief case and left as though going downtown for a meeting.

Chapter   nineteen

I went to my first
lecture with a sense of excitement. The theme was a sure-fire
guarantee of audience interest and the rest was up to me. If
only I were a foot taller and a hundred pounds heavier, I could
simply stand before them with a sign across my chest, stating
I KNOW ALL ABOUT THEM, and they'd be as awed as though I
were the original boogey man—somehow reformed and domesticated. I'd no more have to speak than Paul Robeson had
to act; they'd simply thrill at the sight of me.

And it went well enough; they made it a success through
their own enthusiasm, and the barrage of questions afterwards
left no doubts in my mind. It was only after the meeting was
breaking up that there came the developments which even my
volatile suspicions hadn't allowed me to foresee. I was exchang-
ing greetings with the audience when she appeared, the kind
of woman who glows as though consciously acting a symbolic
role of life and feminine fertility. Her problem, she said, had
to do with certain aspects of our ideology.

"It's rather involved, really," she said with concern, "and

while I shouldn't care to take up your time, I have a feeling that you—"

"Oh, not at all," I said, guiding her away from the others to stand near a partly uncoiled firehose hanging beside the entrance, "not at all."

"But, Brother," she said, "it's really so late and you must be tired. My problem could wait until some other time . . ."

"I'm not *that* tired," I said. "And if there's something bothering you, it's my duty to do what I can to clear it up."

"But it's quite late," she said. "Perhaps some evening when you're not busy you'll drop in to see us. Then we could talk at greater length. Unless, of course . . ."

"Unless?"

"Unless," she smiled, "I can induce you to stop by *this* evening. I might add that I serve a fair cup of coffee."

"Then I'm at your service," I said, pushing open the door.

Her apartment was located in one of the better sections of the city, and I must have revealed my surprise upon entering the spacious living room.

"You can see, Brother"—the glow she gave the word was disturbing—"it is really the spiritual values of Brotherhood that interest me. Through no effort of my own, I have economic security and leisure, but what is that, *really*, when so much is wrong with the world? I mean when there is no spiritual or emotional security, and no justice?"

She was slipping out of her coat now, looking earnestly into my face, and I thought, Is she a *salvationist*, a Puritan-with-reverse-English?—remembering Brother Jack's private description of wealthy members who, he said, sought political salvation by contributing financially to the Brotherhood. She was going a little fast for me and I looked at her gravely.

"I can see that you've thought deeply about this thing," I said.

"I've tried," she said, "and it's most perplexing—But make yourself comfortable while I put away my things."

She was a small, delicately plump woman with raven hair in which a thin streak of white had begun almost imperceptibly to show, and when she reappeared in the rich red of a hostess gown she was so striking that I had to avert my somewhat startled eyes.

"What a beautiful room you have here," I said, looking across the rich cherry glow of furniture to see a life-sized painting of a nude, a pink Renoir. Other canvases were hung here and there, and the spacious walls seemed to flash alive with warm, pure color. What does one say to all this? I thought, looking at an abstract fish of polished brass mounted on a piece of ebony.

"I'm glad you find it pleasant, Brother," she said. "We like it ourselves, though I must say that Hubert finds so little time to enjoy it. He's much too busy."

"Hubert?" I said.

"My husband. Unfortunately he had to leave. He would have loved to've met you, but then he's always dashing off. Business, you know."

"I suppose it's unavoidable," I said with sudden discomfort.

"Yes, it is," she said. "But we're going to discuss Brotherhood and ideology, aren't we?"

And there was something about her voice and her smile that gave me a sense of both comfort and excitement. It was not merely the background of wealth and gracious living, to which I was alien, but simply the being there with her and the sensed possibility of a heightened communication; as though the discordantly invisible and the conspicuously enigmatic were reaching a delicately balanced harmony. She's rich but human, I thought, watching the smooth play of her relaxed hands.

"There are so many aspects to the movement," I said.

"Just where shall we start? Perhaps it's something that I'm unable to handle."

"Oh, it's nothing *that* profound," she said. "I'm sure you'll straighten out my little ideological twists and turns. But sit here on the sofa, Brother; it's more comfortable."

I sat, seeing her go toward a door, the train of her gown trailing sensuously over the oriental carpet. Then she turned and smiled.

"Perhaps you'd prefer wine or milk instead of coffee?"

"Wine, thank you," I said, finding the idea of milk strangely repulsive. This isn't at all what I expected, I thought. She returned with a tray holding two glasses and a decanter, placing them before us on a low cocktail table, and I could hear the wine trickle musically into the glasses, one of which she placed in front of me.

"Here's to the movement," she said, raising her glass with smiling eyes.

"To the movement," I said.

"And to Brotherhood."

"And to Brotherhood."

"This is very nice," I said, seeing her nearly closed eyes, her chin tilting upward, toward me, "but just what phase of our ideology should we discuss?"

"All of it," she said. "I wish to embrace the whole of it. Life is so terribly empty and disorganized without it. I sincerely believe that only Brotherhood offers any hope of making life worth living again—Oh, I know that it's too vast a philosophy to grasp immediately, as it were; still, it's so vital and alive that one gets the feeling that one should at least make the try. Don't you agree?"

"Well, yes," I said. "It's the most meaningful thing that *I* know."

"Oh, I'm so pleased to have you agree with me. I suppose that's why I always thrill to hear you speak, somehow you convey the great throbbing vitality of the movement. It's really amazing. You give me such a feeling of security—although," she interrupted herself with a mysterious smile, "I must confess that you also make me afraid."

"Afraid? You can't mean that," I said.

"Really," she repeated, as I laughed. "It's so powerful, so—so *primitive!*"

I felt some of the air escape from the room, leaving it unnaturally quiet. "You don't mean primitive?" I said.

"Yes, *primitive;* no one has told you, Brother, that at times you have tom-toms beating in your voice?"

"My God," I laughed, "I thought that was the beat of profound ideas."

"Of course, you're correct," she said. "I don't mean really primitive. I suppose I mean *forceful,* powerful. It takes hold of one's emotions as well as one's intellect. Call it what you will, it has so much naked power that it goes straight through one. I tremble just to think of such vitality."

I looked at her, so close now that I could see a single jet-black strand of out-of-place hair. "Yes," I said, "the emotion is there; but it's actually our scientific approach that releases it. As Brother Jack says, we're nothing if not organizers. And the emotion isn't merely released, it's guided, channelized—that is the real source of our effectiveness. After all, this very good wine can release emotion, but I doubt seriously that it can organize anything."

She leaned gracefully forward, her arm along the back of the sofa, saying, "Yes, and you do both in your speeches. One just *has* to respond, even when one isn't too clear as to your meaning. Only I do know what you're saying and that's even more inspiring."

"Actually, you know, I'm as much affected by the audience as it is by me. Its response helps me do my best."

"And there's another important aspect," she said; "one

which concerns me greatly. It provides women the full opportunity for self-expression, which is so very important, Brother. It's as though every day were Leap Year—which is as it should be. Women should be absolutely as free as men."

And if I were really free, I thought, lifting my glass, I'd get the hell out of here.

"I thought you were exceptionally good tonight—it's time the woman had a champion in the movement. Until tonight I'd always heard you on minority problems."

"This is a new assignment," I said. "But from now on one of our main concerns is to be the Woman Question."

"That's wonderful and it's about time. Something has to give women an opportunity to come to close grips with life. Please go on, tell me your ideas," she said, pressing forward, her hand light upon my arm.

And I went on talking, relieved to talk, carried away by my own enthusiasm and by the warmth of the wine. And it was only when I turned to ask a question of her that I realized that she was leaning only a nose-tip away, her eyes upon my face.

"Go on, please go on," I heard. "You make it sound so clear—please."

I saw the rapid, moth-wing fluttering of her lids become the softness of her lips as we were drawn together. There was not an idea or concept in it but sheer warmth; then the bell was ringing and I shook it off and got to my feet, hearing it ring again as she arose with me, the red robe falling in heavy folds upon the carpet, and she saying, "You make it all so wonderfully alive," as the bell sounded again. And I was trying to move, to get out of the apartment, looking for my hat and filling with anger, thinking, Is she crazy? Doesn't she hear? as she stood before me in bewilderment, as though I were acting irrationally. And now taking my arm with sudden energy, saying, "This way, in here," almost pulling me along as the bell rang again, through a door down a short hall, a satiny bedroom, in which she stood appraising me with a smile, saying, "This is mine," as I looked at her in outrageous disbelief.

"Yours, *yours?* But what about that bell?"

"Never mind," she cooed, looking into my eyes.

"But be reasonable," I said, pushing her aside. "What about that door?"

"Oh, of course, you mean the telephone, don't you, darling?"

"But your old man—your husband?"

"In Chicago—"

"But he might not—"

"No, no, darling, he won't—"

"But he might!"

"But, Brother, darling, I talked with him, I know."

"You what? What kind of game is this?"

"Oh, you poor darling! It isn't a game, really you have no cause to worry, we're free. He's in Chicago, seeking his lost youth, no doubt," she said, bursting into laughter of self-surprise. "He's not at all interested in uplifting things— freedom and necessity, woman's rights and all that. You know, the sickness of our class—Brother, darling."

I took a step across the room; there was another door to my left through which I saw the gleam of chromium and tile.

"Brotherhood, darling," she said, gripping my biceps with her little hands. "Teach me, talk to me. Teach me the beautiful ideology of Brotherhood." And I wanted both to smash her and to stay with her and knew that I should do neither. Was she trying to ruin me, or was this a trap set by some secret enemy of the movement waiting outside the door with cameras and wrecking bars?

"You should answer the phone," I said with forced calm,

trying to release my hands without touching her, for if I touched her—

"And you'll continue?" she said.

I nodded, seeing her turn without a word and go toward a vanity with a large oval mirror, taking up an ivory telephone. And in the mirrored instant I saw myself standing between her eager form and a huge white bed, myself caught in a guilty stance, my face taut, tie dangling; and behind the bed another mirror which now like a surge of the sea tossed our images back and forth, back and forth, furiously multiplying the time and the place and the circumstance. My vision seemed to pulse alternately clear and vague, driven by a furious bellows, as her lips said soundlessly, *I'm sorry,* and then impatiently into the telephone, "Yes, this is she," and then to me again, smiling as she covered the mouthpiece with her hand, "It's only my sister; it'll only take a second." And my mind whirled with forgotten stories of male servants summoned to wash the mistress's back; chauffeurs sharing the masters' wives; Pullman porters invited into the drawing room of rich wives headed for Reno— thinking, But this is the movement, the *Brotherhood*. And now I saw her smile, saying, "Yes, Gwen, dear. Yes," as one free hand went up as though to smooth her hair and in one swift motion the red robe swept aside like a veil, and I went breath- less at the petite and generously curved nude, framed delicate and firm in the glass. It was like a dream interval and in an instant it swung back and I saw only her mysteriously smiling eyes above the rich red robe.

I was heading for the door, torn between anger and a fierce excitement, hearing the phone click down as I started past and feeling her swirl against me and I was lost, for the conflict between the ideological and the biological, duty and desire, had become too subtly confused. I went to her, think- ing, Let them break down the door, whosoever will, let them come.

I DIDN'T know whether I was awake or dreaming. It was dead quiet, yet I was certain that there had been a noise and that it had come from across the room as she beside me made a soft sighing sound. It was strange. My mind revolved. I was chased out of a chinkapin woods by a bull. I ran up a hill; the whole hill heaved. I heard the sound and looked up to see the man looking straight at me from where he stood in the dim light of the hall, looking in with neither interest nor surprise. His face expressionless, his eyes staring. There was the sound of even breathing. Then I heard her stir beside me.

"Oh, hello, dear," she said, her voice sounding far away. "Back so soon?"

"Yes," he said. "Wake me early, I have a lot to do."

"I'll remember, dear," she said sleepily. "Have a good night's rest . . ."

"Night, and you too," he said with a short dry laugh.

The door closed. I lay there in the dark for a while, breathing rapidly. It was strange. I reached out and touched her. There was no answer. I leaned over her, feeling her breath breezing warm and pure against my face. I wanted to linger there, experiencing the sensation of something precious perilously attained too late and now to be lost forever—a poignancy. But it was as though she'd never been awake and if she should awaken now, she'd scream, shriek. I slid hurriedly from the bed, keeping my eye on that part of the darkness from where the light had come as I tried to find my clothes. I blundered around, finding a chair, an empty chair. Where were my clothes? What a fool! Why had I gotten myself into such a situation? I felt my way naked through darkness, found the chair with my clothes, dressed hurriedly and slipped out, halting only at the door to look back through the dim light from the hall. She slept without sigh or smile, a beautiful dreamer, one ivory arm flung above her jet-black head. My heart pounded as I closed the door and went down the hall, expecting the man, men, crowds—to halt me. Then I was taking the stairs.

The building was quiet. In the lobby the doorman dozed, his starched bib buckling beneath his chin with his breathing, his white head bare. I reached the street limp with perspiration, still unsure whether I had seen the man or had dreamed him. Could I have seen him without his seeing me? Or again, had he seen me and been silent out of sophistication, decadence, over-civilization? I hurried down the street, my anxiety growing with each step. Why hadn't he said something, recognized me, cursed me? Attacked me? Or at least been outraged with her? And what if it were a test to discover how I would react to such pressure? It was, after all, a point upon which our enemies would attack us violently. I walked in a sweat of agony. Why did they have to mix their women into everything? Between us and everything we wanted to change in the world they placed a woman: socially, politically, economically. Why, goddamit, why did they insist upon confusing the class struggle with the ass struggle, debasing both us and them—all human motives?

All the next day I was in a state of exhaustion, waiting tensely for the plan to be revealed. Now I was certain that the man had been in the doorway, a man with a brief case who had looked in and given no definite sign that he had seen me. A man who had spoken like an indifferent husband, but who yet seemed to recall to me some important member of the Brotherhood—someone so familiar that my failure to identify him was driving me almost to distraction. My work lay untouched before me. Each ring of the telephone filled me with dread. I toyed with Tarp's leg chain.

If they don't call by four o'clock, I'm saved, I told myself.

But still no sign, not even a call to a meeting. Finally I rang her number, hearing her voice, delighted, gay and discreet; but no mention of the night or the man. And hearing her so composed and gay I was too embarrassed to bring it up. Perhaps this was the sophisticated and civilized way? Perhaps he was there and they had an understanding, a woman with full rights.

Would I return for further discussion, she wanted to know.

"Yes, of course," I said.

"Oh, Brother," she said.

I hung up with a mixture of relief and anxiety, unable to shrug off the notion that I had been tested and had failed. I went through the next week puzzling over it, and even more confused because I knew nothing definite of where I stood. I tried to detect any changes in my relations with Brother Jack and the others, but they gave no sign. And even if they had, I wouldn't have known its definite meaning, for it might have had to do with the charges. I was caught between guilt and innocence, so that now they seemed one and the same. My nerves were in a state of constant tension, my face took on a stiff, noncommittal expression, beginning to look like Brother Jack's and the other leaders'. Then I relaxed a bit; work had to be done and I would play the waiting game. And despite my guilt and uncertainty I learned to forget that I was a lone guilty black Brother and to go striding confidently into a roomful of whites. It was chin up, a not too wide-stretched smile, the out-thrust hand for the firm warm hand shake. And with it just the proper mixture of arrogance and down-to-earth humility to satisfy all. I threw myself into the lectures, defending, asserting the rights of women; and though the girls continued to buzz around, I was careful to keep the biological and ideological carefully apart—which wasn't always easy, for it was as though many of the sisters were agreed among themselves (and assumed that I accepted it) that the ideological was merely a superfluous veil for the real concerns of life.

I found that most downtown audiences seemed to expect some unnamed something whenever I appeared. I could sense it the moment I stood before them, and it had nothing to do with anything I might *say*. For I had merely to appear before them, and from the moment they turned their eyes upon me they seemed to undergo a strange unburdening—not of laughter, nor of tears, nor of any stable, unmixed emotion. I didn't get it. And my guilt was aroused. Once in the middle of a passage I looked into the sea of faces and thought, Do they know? Is that it?—and almost ruined my lecture. But of one thing I was certain, it was not the same attitude they held for certain other black brothers who entertained them with stories so often that they laughed even before these fellows opened their mouths. No, it was something else. A form of expectancy, a mood of waiting, a hoping for something like justification; as though they expected me to be more than just another speaker, or an entertainer. Something seemed to occur that was hidden from my own consciousness. I acted out a pantomime more eloquent than my most expressive words. I was a partner to it but could no more fathom it than I could the mystery of the man in the doorway. Perhaps, I told myself, it's in your voice, after all. In your voice and in their desire to see in you a living proof of their belief in Brotherhood, and to ease my mind I stopped thinking about it.

Then one night when I had fallen asleep while making notes for a new series of lectures, the phone summoned me to an emergency meeting at headquarters, and I left the house with feelings of dread. This is it, I thought, either the charges or the woman. To be tripped up by a woman! What would I say to them, that she was irresistible and I human? What had that to do with responsibility, with building Brotherhood?

It was all I could do to make myself go, and I arrived late. The room was sweltering; three small fans stirred the heavy air, and the brothers sat in their shirtsleeves around a scarred table upon which a pitcher of iced water glistened with beads of moisture.

"Brothers, I'm sorry I'm late," I apologized. "There were some important last-minute details concerning tomorrow's lecture that kept me."

"Then you might have saved yourself the trouble and the committee this lost time," Brother Jack said.

"I don't understand you," I said, suddenly feverish.

"He means that you are no longer to concern yourself with the Woman Question. That's ended," Brother Tobitt said; and I braced myself for the attack, but before I could respond Brother Jack fired a startling question at me.

"What has become of Brother Tod Clifton?"

"Brother Clifton—why, I haven't seen him in weeks. I've been too busy downtown here. What's happened?"

"He has disappeared," Brother Jack said, *"disappeared!* So don't waste time with superfluous questions. You weren't sent for for that."

"But how long has this been known?"

Brother Jack struck the table. "All we know is that he's gone. Let's get on with our business. You, Brother, are to return to Harlem immediately. We're facing a crisis there, since Brother Tod Clifton has not only disappeared but failed in his assignment. On the other hand, Ras the Exhorter and his gang of racist gangsters are taking advantage of this and are increasing their agitation. You are to get back there and take measures to regain our strength in the community. You'll be given the forces you need and you'll report to us for a strategy meeting about which you'll be notified tomorrow. And please," he emphasized with his gavel, "be on time!"

I was so relieved that none of my own problems were discussed that I didn't linger to ask if the police had been consulted about the disappearance. Something was wrong with the whole deal, for Clifton was too responsible and had too much to gain simply to have disappeared. Did it have any connection with Ras the Exhorter? But that seemed unlikely; Harlem was one of our strongest districts, and just a month ago when I was shifted Ras would have been laughed off the street had he tried to attack us. If only I hadn't been so careful not to offend the committee I would have kept in closer contact with Clifton and the whole Harlem membership. Now it was as though I had been suddenly awakened from a deep sleep.

Chapter twenty

I had been away long enough for the streets to seem strange. The uptown rhythms were slower and yet were somehow faster; a different tension was in the hot night air. I made my way through the summer crowds, not to the district but to Barrelhouse's Jolly Dollar, a dark hole of a bar and grill on upper Eighth Avenue, where one of my best contacts, Brother Maceo, could usually be found about this time, having his evening's beer.

Looking through the window, I could see men in working clothes and a few rummy women leaning at the bar, and down the aisle between the bar and counter were a couple of men in black and blue checked sport shirts eating barbecue. A cluster of men and women hovered near the juke box at the rear. But when I went in Brother Maceo wasn't among them and I pushed to the bar, deciding to wait over a beer.

"Good evening, Brothers," I said, finding myself beside two men whom I had seen around before; only to have them look at me oddly, the eyebrows of the tall one raising at a drunken angle as he looked at the other.

"Shit," the tall man said.

"You said it, man; he a relative of yourn?"

"Shit, he goddam sho ain't no kin of mine!"

I turned and looked at them, the room suddenly cloudy.

"He must be drunk," the second man said. "Maybe he thinks he's kin to you."

"Then his whiskey's telling him a damn lie. I wouldn't be his kin even if I was— Hey, Barrelhouse!"

I moved away, down the bar, looking at them out of a feeling of suspense. They didn't sound drunk and I had said nothing to offend, and I was certain that they knew who I was. What was it? The Brotherhood greeting was as familiar as "Give me some skin" or "Peace, it's wonderful."

I saw Barrelhouse rolling down from the other end of the bar, his white apron indented by the tension of its cord so that he looked like that kind of metal beer barrel which has a groove around its middle; and seeing me now, he began to smile.

"Well, I'll be damned if it ain't the good brother," he said, stretching out his hand. "Brother, where you been keeping yourself?"

"I've been working downtown," I said, feeling a surge of gratitude.

"Fine, fine!" Barrelhouse said.

"Business good?"

"I'd rather not discuss it, Brother. Business is bad. Very bad."

"I'm sorry to hear it. You'd better give me a beer," I said, "after you've served these gentlemen." I watched them in the mirror.

"Sure thing," Barrelhouse said, reaching for a glass and drawing a beer. "What you putting down, ole man?" he said to the tall man.

"Look here, Barrel, we wanted to ask you one question," the tall one said. "We just wanted to know if you could tell us just whose brother this here cat's supposed to be? He come in here just now calling everybody brother."

"He's *my* brother," Barrel said, holding the foaming glass between his long fingers. "Anything wrong with that?"

"Look, fellow," I said down the bar, "that's our way of speaking. I meant no harm in calling you brother. I'm sorry you misunderstood me."

"Brother, here's your beer," Barrelhouse said.

"So he's *your* brother, eh, Barrel?"

Barrel's eyes narrowed as he pressed his huge chest across the bar, looking suddenly sad. "You enjoying yourself, MacAdams?" he said gloomily. "You like your beer?"

"Sho," MacAdams said.

"It cold enough?"

"Sho, but Barrel—"

"You like the groovy music on the juke?" Barrelhouse said.

"Hell, yes, but—"

"And you like our good, clean, sociable atmosphere?"

"Sho, but that ain't what I'm talking about," the man said.

"Yeah, but that's what *I'm* talking about," Barrelhouse said mournfully. "And if you like it, *like* it, and don't start trying to bug my other customers. This here man's done more for the community than you'll ever do."

"What community?" MacAdams said, cutting his eyes around toward me. "I hear he got the white fever and left . . ."

"You liable to *hear* anything," Barrelhouse said. "There's some paper back there in the gents' room. You ought to wipe out your ears."

"Never mind my ears."

"Aw come on, Mac," his friend said. "Forgit it. Ain't the man done apologized?"

"I said never mind my ears," MacAdams said. "You just tell your brother he ought to be careful 'bout who he claims as kinfolks. Some of us don't think so much of his kind of politics."

I looked from one to the other. I considered myself beyond the stage of street-fighting, and one of the worst things I could do upon returning to the community was to engage in a brawl. I looked at MacAdams and was glad when the other man pushed him down the bar.

"That MacAdams thinks he's tight," Barrelhouse said. "He's the kind caint nobody please. Be frank though, there's lots feel like that now."

I shook my head in bafflement. I'd never met that kind of antagonism before. "What's happened to Brother Maceo?" I said.

"I don't know, Brother. He don't come in so regular these days. Things are kinda changing up here. Ain't much money floating around."

"Times are hard everywhere. But what's been going on up here, Barrel?" I said.

"Oh, you know how it is, Brother; things are tight and lots of folks who got jobs through you people have lost them. You know how it goes."

"You mean people in our organization?"

"Quite a few of them are. Fellows like Brother Maceo."

"But why? They were doing all right."

"Sure they was—as long as you people was fighting for 'em. But the minute y'all stopped, they started throwing folks out on the street."

I looked at him, big and sincere before me. It was unbelievable that the Brotherhood had stopped its work, and yet he wasn't lying. "Give me another beer," I said. Then someone called him from the back, and he drew the beer and left.

I drank it slowly, hoping Brother Maceo would appear before I had finished. When he didn't I waved to Barrelhouse and left for the district. Perhaps Brother Tarp could explain; or at least tell me something about Clifton.

I walked through the dark block over to Seventh and started down; things were beginning to look serious. Along the way I saw not a single sign of Brotherhood activity. In a hot side street I came upon a couple striking matches along the curb, kneeling as though looking for a lost coin, the matches flaring dimly in their faces. Then I found myself in a strangely familiar block and broke out in a sweat: I had walked almost to Mary's door, and turned now and hurried away.

Barrelhouse had prepared me for the darkened windows of the district, but not, when I let myself in, to call in vain through the dark to Brother Tarp. I went to the room where he slept, but he was not there; then I went through the dark hall to my old office and threw myself into my desk chair, exhausted. Everything seemed to be slipping away from me and I could find no quick absorbing action that would get it under control. I tried to think of whom among the district committee I might call for information concerning Clifton, but here again I was balked. For if I selected one who believed that I had requested to be transferred because I hated my own people it would only complicate matters. No doubt there would be some who'd resent my return, so it was best to confront them all at once without giving any one of them the opportunity to organize any sentiment against me. It was best that I talk with Brother Tarp, whom I trusted. When he came in he could give me an idea of the state of affairs, and perhaps tell me what had actually happened to Clifton.

But Brother Tarp didn't arrive. I went out and got a

container of coffee and returned to spend the night poring over
the district's records. When he hadn't returned by three A.M.
I went to his room and took a look around. It was empty,
even the bed was gone. I'm all alone, I thought. A lot has
occurred about which I wasn't told; something that had not
only stifled the members' interest but which, according to the
records, had sent them away in droves. Barrelhouse had said
that the organization had quit fighting, and that was the only
explanation I could find for Brother Tarp's leaving. Unless, of
course, he'd had disagreements with Clifton or some of the
other leaders. And now returning to my desk I noticed his gift
of Douglass' portrait was gone. I felt in my pocket for the leg
chain, at least I hadn't forgotten to take that along. I pushed
the records aside; they told me nothing of why things were as
they were. Picking up the telephone I called Clifton's number,
hearing it ring on and on. Finally I gave it up and went to
sleep in my chair. Everything had to wait until the strategy
meeting. Returning to the district was like returning to a city
of the dead.

Somewhat to my surprise there were a good number of
members in the hall when I awoke, and having no directives
from the committee on how to proceed I organized them into
teams to search for Brother Clifton. Not one could give me
any definite information. Brother Clifton had appeared at the
district as usual up to the time of his disappearance. There had
been no quarrels with committee members, and he was as
popular as ever. Nor had there been any clashes with Ras the
Exhorter—although in the past week he had been increasingly
active. As for the loss of membership and influence, it was a
result of a new program which had called for the shelving of
our old techniques of agitation. There had been, to my surprise, a switch in emphasis from local issues to those more
national and international in scope, and it was felt that for the

moment the interests of Harlem were not of first importance. I didn't know what to make of it, since there had been no such change of program downtown. Clifton was forgotten, everything which I was to do now seemed to depend upon getting an explanation from the committee, and I waited with growing agitation to be called to the strategy meeting.

Such meetings were usually held around one o'clock and we were notified well ahead. But by eleven-thirty I had received no word and I became worried. By twelve an uneasy sense of isolation took hold of me. Something was cooking, but what, how, why? Finally I phoned headquarters, but could reach none of the leaders. What is this, I wondered; then I called the leaders of other districts with the same results. And now I was certain that the meeting was being held. But why without me? Had they investigated Wrestrum's charges and decided they were true? It seemed that the membership *had* fallen off after I had gone downtown. Or was it the woman? Whatever it was, now was not the time to leave me out of a meeting; things were too urgent in the district. I hurried down to headquarters.

When I arrived the meeting was in session, just as I expected, and word had been left that it was not to be disturbed by anyone. It was obvious that they hadn't forgotten to notify me. I left the building in a rage. Very well, I thought, when they do decide to call me they'll have to find me. I should never have been shifted in the first place, and now that I was sent back to clean up the mess they should aid me as quickly as possible. I would do no more running downtown, nor would I accept any program that they sent up without consulting the Harlem committee. Then I decided, of all things, to shop for a pair of new shoes, and walked over to Fifth Avenue.

It was hot, the walks still filled with noontime crowds

moving with reluctance back to their jobs. I moved along close to the curb to avoid the bumping and agitated changes of pace, the chattering women in summer dresses, finally entering the leather-smelling, air-cooled interior of the shoe store with a sense of relief.

My feet felt light in the new summer shoes as I went back into the blazing heat, and I recalled the old boyhood pleasure of discarding winter shoes for sneakers and the neighborhood foot races that always followed, that lightfooted, speedy, floating sensation. Well, I thought, you've run your last foot race and you'd better get back to the district in case you're called. I hurried now, my feet feeling trim and light as I moved through the oncoming rush of sunbeaten faces. To avoid the crowd on Forty-second Street I turned off at Forty-third and it was here that things began to boil.

A small fruit wagon with an array of bright peaches and pears stood near the curb, and the vendor, a florid man with bulbous nose and bright black Italian eyes, looked at me knowingly from beneath his huge white-and-orange umbrella then over toward a crowd that had formed alongside the building across the street. What's wrong with him? I thought. Then I was across the street and passing the group standing with their backs to me. A clipped, insinuating voice spieled words whose meaning I couldn't catch and I was about to pass on when I saw the boy. He was a slender brown fellow whom I recognized immediately as a close friend of Clifton's, and who now was looking intently across the tops of cars to where down the block near the post office on the other side a tall policeman was approaching. Perhaps he'll know something, I thought, as he looked around to see me and stopped in confusion.

"Hello, there," I began, and when he turned toward the crowd and whistled I didn't know whether he was telling me to do the same or signaling to someone else. I swung around,

seeing him step to where a large carton sat beside the building
and sling its canvas straps to his shoulder as once more he
looked toward the policeman, ignoring me. Puzzled, I moved
into the crowd and pressed to the front where at my feet I
saw a square piece of cardboard upon which something was
moving with furious action. It was some kind of toy and I
glanced at the crowd's fascinated eyes and down again, seeing
it clearly this time. I'd seen nothing like it before. A grinning
doll of orange-and-black tissue paper with thin flat cardboard
disks forming its head and feet and which some mysterious
mechanism was causing to move up and down in a loose-
jointed, shoulder-shaking, infuriatingly sensuous motion, a
dance that was completely detached from the black, mask-like
face. It's no jumping-jack, but *what*, I thought, seeing the doll
throwing itself about with the fierce defiance of someone per-
forming a degrading act in public, dancing as though it received
a perverse pleasure from its motions. And beneath the chuckles
of the crowd I could hear the swishing of its ruffled paper,
while the same out-of-the-corner-of-the-mouth voice continued
to spiel:

Shake it up! Shake it up!
He's Sambo, the dancing doll, ladies and gentlemen.
Shake him, stretch him by the neck and set him down,
—He'll do the rest. Yes!

He'll make you laugh, he'll make you sigh, si-igh.
He'll make you want to dance, and dance—
Here you are, ladies and gentlemen, Sambo,
The dancing doll.
Buy one for your baby. Take him to your girl friend and she'll
    love you, loove you!
He'll keep you entertained. He'll make you weep sweet—

Tears from laughing.
Shake him, shake him, you cannot break him
For he's Sambo, the dancing, Sambo, the prancing,
Sambo, the entrancing, Sambo Boogie Woogie paper doll.
And all for twenty-five cents, the quarter part of a dollar . . .
Ladies and gentlemen, he'll bring you joy, step up and meet him,
  Sambo the—

I knew I should get back to the district but I was held by the inanimate, boneless bouncing of the grinning doll and struggled between the desire to join in the laughter and to leap upon it with both feet, when it suddenly collapsed and I saw the tip of the spieler's toe press upon the circular cardboard that formed the feet and a broad black hand come down, its fingers deftly lifting the doll's head and stretching it upward, twice its length, then releasing it to dance again. And suddenly the voice didn't go with the hand. It was as though I had waded out into a shallow pool only to have the bottom drop out and the water close over my head. I looked up.

"Not you . . ." I began. But his eyes looked past me deliberately unseeing. I was paralyzed, looking at him, knowing I wasn't dreaming, hearing:

What makes him happy, what makes him dance,
This Sambo, this jambo, this high-stepping joy boy?
He's more than a toy, ladies and gentlemen, he's Sambo, the
  dancing doll, the twentieth-century miracle.
Look at that rumba, that suzy-q, he's Sambo-Boogie,
Sambo-Woogie, you don't have to feed him, he sleeps collapsed,
  he'll kill your depression
And your dispossession, he lives upon the sunshine of your lordly
  smile

*And only twenty-five cents, the brotherly two bits of a dollar be-
cause he wants me to eat.*
It gives him pleasure to see me eat.
You simply take him and shake him . . . and he does the rest.

Thank you, lady . . .

It was Clifton, riding easily back and forth in his knees,
flexing his legs without shifting his feet, his right shoulder raised
at an angle and his arm pointing stiffly at the bouncing doll as
he spieled from the corner of his mouth.

The whistle came again, and I saw him glance quickly
toward his lookout, the boy with the carton.

"Who else wants little Sambo before we take it on
the lambo? Speak up, ladies and gentlemen, who wants
little . . . ?"

And again the whistle. "Who wants Sambo, the dancing,
prancing? Hurry, hurry, ladies and gentlemen. There's no li-
cense for little Sambo, the joy spreader. You can't tax joy, so
speak up, ladies and gentlemen . . ."

For a second our eyes met and he gave me a contemp-
tuous smile, then he spieled again. I felt betrayed. I looked at
the doll and felt my throat constrict. The rage welled behind
the phlegm as I rocked back on my heels and crouched forward. There was a flash of whiteness and a splatter like heavy
rain striking a newspaper and I saw the doll go over backwards,
wilting into a dripping rag of frilled tissue, the hateful head
upturned on its outstretched neck still grinning toward the sky.
The crowd turned on me indignantly. The whistle came again.
I saw a short pot-bellied man look down, then up at me with
amazement and explode with laughter, pointing from me to
the doll, rocking. People backed away from me. I saw Clifton
step close to the building where beside the fellow with the

433

carton I now saw a whole chorus-line of dolls flouncing themselves with a perverse increase of energy and the crowd laughing hysterically.

"You, you!" I began, only to see him pick up two of the
dolls and step forward. But now the lookout came close. "He's
coming," he said, nodding toward the approaching policeman
as he swept up the dolls, dropping them into the carton and
starting away.

"Follow little Sambo around the corner, ladies and gentlemen," Clifton called. "There's a great show coming up . . ."

It happened so fast that in a second only I and an old
lady in a blue polka-dot dress were left. She looked at me then
back to the walk, smiling. I saw one of the dolls. She was still
smiling and I raised my foot to crush it, hearing her cry, "Oh,
no!" The policeman was just opposite and I reached down
instead, picking it up and walking off in the same motion. I
examined it, strangely weightless in my hand, half expecting
to feel it pulse with life. It was a still frill of paper. I dropped
it in the pocket where I carried Brother Tarp's chain link and
started after the vanished crowd. But I couldn't face Clifton
again. I didn't want to see him. I might forget myself and attack
him. I went in the other direction, toward Sixth Avenue, past
the policemen. What a way to find him, I thought. What had
happened to Clifton? It was all so wrong, so unexpected. How
on earth could he drop from Brotherhood to this in so short
a time? And why if he had to fall back did he try to carry the
whole structure with him? What would non-members who
knew him say? It was as though he had chosen—how had he
put it the night he fought with Ras?—to fall outside of *history*.
I stopped in the middle of the walk with the thought. "To
plunge," he had said. But he knew that only in the Brotherhood could we make ourselves known, could we avoid being
empty Sambo dolls. Such an obscene flouncing of everything

human! My God! And I had been worrying about being left out of a meeting! I'd overlook it a thousand times; no matter why I wasn't called. I'd forget it and hold on desperately to Brotherhood with all my strength. For to break away would be to plunge . . . To plunge! And those dolls, where had they found them? Why had he picked that way to earn a quarter? Why not sell apples or song sheets, or shine shoes?

I wandered past the subway and continued around the corner to Forty-second Street, my mind grappling for meaning. And when I came around the corner onto the crowded walk into the sun, they were already lining the curb and shading their faces with their hands. I saw the traffic moving with the lights, and across the street a few pedestrians were looking back toward the center of the block where the trees of Bryant Park rose above two men. I saw a flight of pigeons whirl out of the trees and it all happened in the swift interval of their circling, very abruptly and in the noise of the traffic—yet seeming to unfold in my mind like a slow-motion movie run off with the sound track dead.

At first I thought it was a cop and a shoeshine boy; then there was a break in the traffic and across the sun-glaring bands of trolley rails I recognized Clifton. His partner had disappeared now and Clifton had the box slung to his left shoulder with the cop moving slowly behind and to one side of him. They were coming my way, passing a newsstand, and I saw the rails in the asphalt and a fire plug at the curb and the flying birds, and thought, You'll have to follow and pay his fine . . . just as the cop pushed him, jolting him forward and Clifton trying to keep the box from swinging against his leg and saying something over his shoulder and going forward as one of the pigeons swung down into the street and up again, leaving a feather floating white in the dazzling backlight of the sun, and I could see the cop push Clifton again, stepping solidly forward

in his black shirt, his arm shooting out stiffly, sending him in
a head-snapping forward stumble until he caught himself, saying something over his shoulder again, the two moving in a
kind of march that I'd seen many times, but never with anyone
like Clifton. And I could see the cop bark a command and
lunge forward, thrusting out his arm and missing, thrown off
balance as suddenly Clifton spun on his toes like a dancer and
swung his right arm over and around in a short, jolting arc,
his torso carrying forward and to the left in a motion that sent
the box strap free as his right foot traveled forward and his left
arm followed through in a floating uppercut that sent the cop's
cap sailing into the street and his feet flying, to drop him hard,
rocking from left to right on the walk as Clifton kicked the
box thudding aside and crouched, his left foot forward, his
hands high, waiting. And between the flashing of cars I could
see the cop propping himself on his elbows like a drunk trying
to get his head up, shaking it and thrusting it forward—And
somewhere betweeen the dull roar of traffic and the subway
vibrating underground I heard rapid explosions and saw each
pigeon diving wildly as though blackjacked by the sound, and
the cop sitting up straight now, and rising to his knees looking
steadily at Clifton, and the pigeons plummeting swiftly into
the trees, and Clifton still facing the cop and suddenly crumpling.

He fell forward on his knees, like a man saying his prayers just as a heavy-set man in a hat with a turned-down brim
stepped from around the newsstand and yelled a protest. I
couldn't move. The sun seemed to scream an inch above my
head. Someone shouted. A few men were starting into the
street. The cop was standing now and looking down at Clifton
as though surprised, the gun in his hand. I took a few steps
forward, walking blindly now, unthinking, yet my mind registering it all vividly. Across and starting up on the curb, and

seeing Clifton up closer now, lying in the same position, on his side, a huge wetness growing on his shirt, and I couldn't set my foot down. Cars sailed close behind me, but I couldn't take the step that would raise me up to the walk. I stood there, one leg in the street and the other raised above the curb, hearing whistles screeching and looked toward the library to see two cops coming on in a lunging, big-bellied run. I looked back to Clifton, the cop was waving me away with his gun, sounding like a boy with a changing voice.

"Get back on the other side," he said. He was the cop that I'd passed on Forty-third a few minutes before. My mouth was dry.

"He's a friend of mine, I want to help . . ." I said, finally stepping upon the curb.

"He don't need no help, Junior. Get across that street!"

The cop's hair hung on the sides of his face, his uniform was dirty, and I watched him without emotion, hesitated, hearing the sound of footfalls approaching. Everything seemed slowed down. A pool formed slowly on the walk. My eyes blurred. I raised my head. The cop looked at me curiously. Above in the park I could hear the furious flapping of wings; on my neck, the pressure of eyes. I turned. A round-headed, apple-cheeked boy with thickly freckled nose and Slavic eyes leaned over the fence of the park above, and now as he saw me turn, he shrilled something to someone behind him, his face lighting up with ecstasy . . . What does it mean, I wondered, turning back to that to which I did not wish to turn.

There were three cops now, one watching the crowd and the others looking at Clifton. The first cop had his cap on again.

"Look, Junior," he said very clearly, "I had enough trouble for today—you going to get on across that street?"

I opened my mouth but nothing would come. Kneeling,

one of the cops was examining Clifton and making notes on a pad.

"I'm his friend," I said, and the one making notes looked up.

"He's a cooked pigeon, Mac," he said. "You ain't got any friend anymore."

I looked at him.

"Hey, Mickey," the boy above us called, "the guy's out cold!"

I looked down. "That's right," the kneeling cop said. "What's your name?"

I told him. I answered his questions about Clifton as best I could until the wagon came. For once it came quickly. I watched numbly as they moved him inside, placing the box of dolls in with him. Across the street the crowd still churned. Then the wagon was gone and I started back toward the subway.

"Say, mister," the boy's voice shrilled down. "Your friend sure knows how to use his dukes. Biff, bang! One, two, and the cop's on his ass!"

I bowed my head to this final tribute, and now walking away in the sun I tried to erase the scene from my mind.

I WANDERED down the subway stairs seeing nothing, my mind plunging. The subway was cool and I leaned against a pillar, hearing the roar of trains passing across on the other side, feeling the rushing roar of air. Why should a man deliberately plunge outside of history and peddle an obscenity, my mind went on abstractedly. Why should he choose to disarm himself, give up his voice and leave the only organization offering him a chance to "define" himself? The platform vibrated and I looked down. Bits of paper whirled up in the passage of air, settling quickly as a train moved past. Why *had* he turned away? Why had he chosen to step off the platform and fall beneath the train? Why did he choose to plunge into nothingness, into the void of faceless faces, of soundless voices, lying outside history? I tried to step away and look at it from a distance of words read in books, half-remembered. For history records the patterns of men's lives, they say: Who slept with whom and with what results; who fought and who won and who lived to lie about it afterwards. All things, it is said, are duly recorded—all things of importance, that is. But not quite, for actually it is only the known, the seen, the heard and only those events that the recorder regards as important that are put down, those lies his keepers keep their power by. But the cop would be Clifton's historian, his judge, his witness, and his executioner, and I was the only brother in the watching crowd. And I, the only witness for the defense, knew neither the extent of his guilt nor the nature of his crime. Where were the historians today? And how would they put it down?

I stood there with the trains plunging in and out, throwing blue sparks. What did they ever think of us transitory ones? Ones such as I had been before I found Brotherhood—birds of passage who were too obscure for learned classification, too silent for the most sensitive recorders of sound; of natures too ambiguous for the most ambiguous words, and too distant from the centers of historical decision to sign or even to applaud the signers of historical documents? We who write no novels, histories or other books. What about us, I thought, seeing Clifton again in my mind and going to sit upon a bench as a cool gust of air rolled up the tunnel.

A body of people came down the platform, some of them Negroes. Yes, I thought, what about those of us who shoot up from the South into the busy city like wild jacks-in-the-box broken loose from our springs—so sudden that our gait becomes like that of deep-sea divers suffering from the bends? What about those fellows waiting still and silent there on the platform, so still and silent that they clash with the crowd in their very immobility; standing noisy in their very silence; harsh as a cry of terror in their quietness? What about those three boys, coming now along the platform, tall and slender, walking stiffly with swinging shoulders in their well-pressed, too-hot-for-summer suits, their collars high and tight about their necks, their identical hats of black cheap felt set upon the crowns of their heads with a severe formality above their hard conked hair? It was as though I'd never seen their like before: Walking slowly, their shoulders swaying, their legs swinging from their hips in trousers that ballooned upward from cuffs fitting snug about their ankles; their coats long and hip-tight with shoulders far too broad to be those of natural western men. These fellows whose bodies seemed—what had one of my teachers said of me?—"You're like one of these African sculptures, distorted in the interest of a design." Well, what design and whose?

I stared as they seemed to move like dancers in some kind of funeral ceremony, swaying, going forward, their black faces secret, moving slowly down the subway platform, the heavy heel-plated shoes making a rhythmical tapping as they moved. Everyone must have seen them, or heard their muted laughter, or smelled the heavy pomade on their hair—or perhaps failed to see them at all. For they were men outside of historical time, they were untouched, they didn't believe in Brotherhood, no doubt had never heard of it; or perhaps like Clifton would mysteriously have rejected its mysteries; men of transition whose faces were immobile.

I got up and went behind them. Women shoppers with bundles and impatient men in straw hats and seersucker suits stood along the platform as they passed. And suddenly I found myself thinking, Do they come to bury the others or to be entombed, to give life or to receive it? Do the others see them, think about them, even those standing close enough to speak? And if they spoke back, would the impatient businessmen in conventional suits and tired housewives with their plunder, understand? What would they say? For the boys speak a jived-up transitional language full of country glamour, think transitional thoughts, though perhaps they dream the same old ancient dreams. They were men out of time—unless they found Brotherhood. Men out of time, who would soon be gone and forgotten . . . But who knew (and now I began to tremble so violently I had to lean against a refuse can)—who knew but that they were the saviors, the true leaders, the bearers of something precious? The stewards of something uncomfortable, burdensome, which they hated because, living outside the realm of history, there was no one to applaud their value and they themselves failed to understand it. What if Brother Jack were wrong? What if history was a gambler, instead of a force in a laboratory experiment, and the boys his ace in the hole? What if history was not a reasonable citizen, but a madman full of paranoid guile and these boys his agents, his big surprise! His own revenge? For they were outside, in the dark with Sambo, the dancing paper doll; taking it on the lambo with my fallen brother, Tod Clifton (Tod, Tod) running and dodging the forces of history instead of making a dominating stand.

A train came. I followed them inside. There were many seats and the three sat together. I stood, holding onto the center pole, looking down the length of the car. On one side I saw a white nun in black telling her beads, and standing before the door across the aisle there was another dressed completely in white, the exact duplicate of the other except that she was black and her black feet bare. Neither of the nuns was looking at the other but at their crucifixes, and suddenly I

laughed and a verse I'd heard long ago at the Golden Day
paraphrased itself in my mind:

> *Bread and Wine,*
> *Bread and Wine,*
> > *Your cross ain't nearly so*
> > *Heavy as mine . . .*

And the nuns rode on with lowered heads.

I looked at the boys. They sat as formally as they walked.
From time to time one of them would look at his reflection in
the window and give his hat brim a snap, the others watching
him silently, communicating ironically with their eyes, then
looking straight ahead. I staggered with the lunging of the
train, feeling the overhead fans driving the hot air down upon
me. What was I in relation to the boys, I wondered. Perhaps
an accident, like Douglass. Perhaps each hundred years or so
men like them, like me, appeared in society, drifting through;
and yet by all historical logic we, I, should have disappeared
around the first part of the nineteenth century, rationalized out
of existence. Perhaps, like them, I was a throwback, a small
distant meteorite that died several hundred years ago and now
lived only by virtue of the light that speeds through space at
too great a pace to realize that its source has become a piece
of lead . . . This was silly, such thoughts. I looked at the boys;
one tapped another on the knee, and I saw him remove three
rolled magazines from an inner pocket, passing two around
and keeping one for himself. The others took theirs silently
and began to read in complete absorption. One held his magazine high before his face and for an instant I saw a vivid scene:
The shining rails, the fire hydrant, the fallen policeman, the
diving birds and in the mid-ground, Clifton, crumpling. Then
I saw the cover of a comic book and thought, Clifton would

have known them better than I. He knew them all the time. I studied them closely until they left the train, their shoulders rocking, their heavy heel plates clicking remote, cryptic messages in the brief silence of the train's stop.

I came out of the subway, weak, moving through the heat as though I carried a heavy stone, the weight of a mountain on my shoulders. My new shoes hurt my feet. Now, moving through the crowds along 125th Street, I was painfully aware of other men dressed like the boys, and of girls in dark exotic-colored stockings, their costumes surreal variations of downtown styles. They'd been there all along, but somehow I'd missed them. I'd missed them even when my work had been most successful. They were outside the groove of history, and it was my job to get them in, all of them. I looked into the design of their faces, hardly a one that was unlike someone I'd known down South. Forgotten names sang through my head like forgotten scenes in dreams. I moved with the crowd, the sweat pouring off me, listening to the grinding roar of traffic, the growing sound of a record shop loudspeaker blaring a languid blues. I stopped. Was this all that would be recorded? Was this the only true history of the times, a mood blared by trumpets, trombones, saxophones and drums, a song with turgid, inadequate words? My mind flowed. It was as though in this short block I was forced to walk past everyone I'd ever known and no one would smile or call my name. No one fixed me in his eyes. I walked in feverish isolation. Near the corner now a couple of boys darted out of the Five and Ten with handfuls of candy bars, dropping them along the walks as they ran with a man right behind. They came toward me, pumping past, and I killed an impulse to trip the man and was confused all the more when an old woman standing further along threw out her leg and swung a heavy bag. The man went down, sliding across the walk as she shook her head in triumph. A pressure of guilt came over me. I stood on the edge of the walk watching the crowd threatening to attack the man until a policemen appeared and dispersed them. And although I knew no one man could do much about it, I felt responsible. All our work had been very little, no great change had been made. And it was all my fault. I'd been so fascinated by the motion that I'd forgotten to measure what it was bringing forth. I'd been asleep, dreaming.

Chapter twenty-one

When I got back to the district a small group of youth members stopped their joking to welcome me, but I couldn't break the news. I went through to the office with only a nod, shutting the door upon their voices and sat staring out through the trees. The once fresh green of the trees was dark and drying now and somewhere down below a clothesline peddler clanged his bell and called. Then, as I fought against it, the scene came back—not of the death, but of the dolls. Why had I lost my head and spat upon the doll, I wondered. What had Clifton felt when he saw me? He must have hated me behind his spiel, yet he'd ignored me. Yes, and been amused by my political stupidity. I had blown up and acted personally instead of denouncing the significance of the dolls, him, the obscene idea, and seizing the opportunity to educate the crowd. We lost no opportunity to educate, and I had failed. All I'd done was to make them laugh all the louder ... I had aided and abetted social backwardness ... The scene changed—he lay in the sun and this time I saw a trail of smoke left by a sky-writing plane lingering in the

445

sky, a large woman in a kelly-green dress stood near me saying, "Oh, Oh!" . . .

I turned and faced the map, removing the doll from my pocket and tossing it upon the desk. My stomach surged. To die for such a thing! I picked it up with an unclean feeling, looked at the frilled paper. The joined cardboard feet hung down, pulling the paper legs in elastic folds, a construction of tissue, cardboard and glue. And yet I felt a hatred as for something alive. What had made it seem to dance? Its cardboard hands were doubled into fists, the fingers outlined in orange paint, and I noticed that it had two faces, one on either side of the disk of cardboard, and both grinning. Clifton's voice came to me as he spieled his directions for making it dance, and I held it by the feet and stretched its neck, seeing it crumple and slide forward. I tried again, turning its other face around. It gave a tired flounce, shook itself and fell in a heap.

"Go on, entertain me," I said, giving it a stretch. "You entertained the crowd." I turned it around. One face grinned as broadly as the other. It had grinned back at Clifton as it grinned forward at the crowd, and their entertainment had been his death. It had still grinned when I played the fool and spat upon it, and it was still grinning when Clifton ignored me. Then I saw a fine black thread and pulled it from the frilled paper. There was a loop tied in the end. I slipped it over my finger and stood stretching it taut. And this time it danced. Clifton had been making it dance all the time and the black thread had been invisible.

Why didn't you hit him? I asked myself; try to break his jaw? Why didn't you hurt him and save him? You might have started a fight and both of you would have been arrested with no shooting . . . But why had he resisted the cop anyway? He'd been arrested before; he knew how far to go with a cop. What had the cop said to make him angry enough to lose his head? And suddenly it occurred to me that he might have been angry *before* he resisted, before he'd even seen the cop. My breath became short; I felt myself go weak. What if he believed *I'd* sold out? It was a sickening thought. I sat holding myself as though I might break. For a moment I weighed the idea, but it was too big for me. I could only accept responsibility for the living, not for the dead. My mind backed away from the notion. The incident was political. I looked at the doll, thinking, The political equivalent of such entertainment is death. But that's too broad a definition. Its economic meaning? That the life of a man is worth the sale of a two-bit paper doll . . . But that didn't kill the idea that my anger helped speed him on to death. And still my mind fought against it. For what had I to do with the crisis that had broken his integrity? What had I to do with his selling the dolls in the first place? And finally I had to give that up too. I was no detective, and, politically, individuals were without meaning. The shooting was all that was left of him now, Clifton had chosen to plunge out of history and, except for the picture it made in my mind's eye, only the plunge was recorded, and that was the only important thing.

I sat rigid, as though waiting to hear the explosions again, fighting against the weight that seemed to pull me down. I heard the clothesline peddler's bell . . . What would I tell the committee when the newspaper accounts were out? To hell with them. How would I explain the dolls? But why should I say anything? What could we do to fight back. *That* was my worry. The bell tolled again in the yard below. I looked at the doll. I could think of no justification for Clifton's having sold the dolls, but there was justification enough for giving him a public funeral, and I seized upon the idea now as though it would save my life. Even though I wanted to turn away from it as I'd wanted to turn from Clifton's crumpled body on the walk. But the odds against us were too great for such weakness. We had to use every politically effective weapon against them; Clifton understood that. He had to be buried and I knew of no relatives; someone had to see that he was placed in the ground. Yes, the dolls were obscene and his act a betrayal. But he was only a salesman, not the inventor, and it was necessary that we make it known that the meaning of his death was greater than the incident or the object that caused it. Both as a means of avenging him and of preventing other such deaths . . . yes, and of attracting lost members back into the ranks. It would be ruthless, but a ruthlessness in the interest of Brotherhood, for we had only our minds and bodies, as against the other side's vast power. We had to make the most of what we had. For they had the power to use a paper doll, first to destroy his integrity and then as an excuse for killing him. All right, so we'll use his funeral to put his integrity together again . . . For that's all that he had had or wanted. And now I could see the doll only vaguely and drops of moisture were thudding down upon its absorbent paper . . .

I was bent over, staring, when the knock came at the door and I jumped as at a shot, sweeping the doll into my pocket, and hastily wiping my eyes.

"Come in," I said.

The door opened slowly. A group of youth members crowded forward, their faces a question. The girls were crying.

"Is it true?" they said.

"That he is dead? Yes," I said, looking among them. "Yes."

"But why . . . ?"

"It was a case of provocation and murder!" I said, my emotions beginning to turn to anger.

They stood there, their faces questioning me.

"He's dead," a girl said, her voice without conviction. "Dead."

"But what do they mean about his selling dolls?" a tall youth said.

"I don't know," I said. "I only know that he was shot down. Unarmed. I know how you feel, I saw him fall."

"Take me home," a girl screamed. "Take me home!"

I stepped forward and caught her, a little brown thing in bobby socks, holding her against me. "No, we can't go home," I said, "none of us. We've got to fight. I'd like to get out into the air and forget it, if I ever could. What we want is not tears but anger. We must remember now that we are fighters, and in such incidents we must see the meaning of our struggle. We must strike back. I want each of you to round up all the members you can. We've got to make our reply."

One of the girls was still crying piteously when they went out, but they were moving quickly.

"Come on, Shirley," they said, taking the girl from my shoulder.

I tried to get in touch with headquarters, but again I was unable to reach anyone. I called the Chthonian but there was no answer. So I called a committee of the district's leading members and we moved slowly ahead on our own. I tried to find the youth who was with Clifton, but he had disappeared. Members were set on the streets with cans to solicit funds for his burial. A committee of three old women went to the morgue to claim his body. We distributed black-bordered leaflets, denouncing the police commissioner. Preachers were notified to have their congregations send letters of protest to the mayor. The story spread. A photograph of Clifton was sent to the Negro papers and published. People were stirred and angry. Street meetings were organized. And, released (by the action) from my indecision, I threw everything I had into organizing the funeral, though moving in a kind of numb suspension. I didn't go to bed for two days and nights, but caught catnaps at my desk. I ate very little.

THE funeral was arranged to attract the largest number. Instead of holding it in a church or a chapel, we selected Mount Morris Park, and an appeal went out for all former members to join the funeral march.

It took place on a Saturday, in the heat of the afternoon. There was a thin overcast of clouds, and hundreds of people formed for the procession. I went around giving orders and encouragement in a feverish daze, and yet seeming to observe it all from off to one side. Brothers and sisters turned up whom I hadn't seen since my return. And members from downtown and outlying districts. I watched them with surprise as they gathered and wondered at the depths of their sorrow as the lines began to form.

There were half-draped flags and black banners. There were black-bordered signs that read:

BROTHER TOD CLIFTON
OUR HOPE SHOT DOWN

There was a hired drum corps with crape-draped drums. There was a band of thirty pieces. There were no cars and very few flowers.

It was a slow procession and the band played sad, romantic, military marches. And when the band was silent the drum corps beat the time on drums with muffled heads. It was hot and explosive, and delivery men avoided the district and the police details were increased in number. And up and down the streets people looked out of their apartment windows and men and boys stood on the roofs in the thin-veiled sun. I marched at the head with the old community leaders. It was a slow march and as I looked back from time to time I could see young zoot-suiters, hep cats, and men in overalls and pool-hall gamblers stepping into the procession. Men came out of barber shops with lathered faces, their neckcloths hanging, to watch and comment in hushed voices. And I wondered, Are they all Clifton's friends, or is it just for the spectacle, the slow-paced music? A hot wind blew from behind me, bringing the sick sweetish odor, like the smell of some female dogs in season.

I looked back. The sun shone down on a mass of unbared heads, and above flags and banners and shining horns I could see the cheap gray coffin moving high upon the shoulders of Clifton's tallest companions, who from time to time shifted it smoothly on to others. They bore him high and they bore him proudly and there was an angry sadness in their eyes. The coffin floated like a heavily loaded ship in a channel, winding its way slowly above the bowed and submerged heads. I could hear the steady rolling of the drums with muffled snares, and all other sounds were suspended in silence. Behind, the tramp of feet; ahead, the crowds lining the curbs for blocks. There were tears and muffled sobs and many hard, red eyes. We moved ahead.

We wound through the poorer streets at first, a black image of sorrow, then turned into Seventh Avenue and down and over to Lenox. Then I hurried with the leading brothers to the park in a cab. A brother in the Park Department had opened the lookout tower, and a crude platform of planks and ranked saw horses had been erected beneath the black iron bell, and when the procession started into the park we were standing high above, waiting. At our signal he struck the bell, and I could feel my eardrums throbbing with the old, hollow, gut-vibrant Doom-Dong-Doom.

Looking down, I could see them winding upward in a mass to the muffled sound of the drums. Children stopped their playing on the grass to stare, and nurses at the nearby hospital came out on the roof to watch, their white uniforms glowing in the now unveiled sun like lilies. And crowds approached the park from all directions. The muffled drums now beating, now steadily rolling, spread a dead silence upon the air, a prayer for the unknown soldier. And looking down I felt a lostness. Why were they here? Why had they found us? Because they knew Clifton? Or for the occasion his death gave them to express their protestations, a time and place to come together, to stand touching and sweating and breathing and looking in a common direction? Was either explanation adequate in itself? Did it signify love or politicalized hate? And could politics ever be an expression of love?

Over the park the silence spread from the slow muffled rolling of the drums, the crunching of footsteps on the walks. Then somewhere in the procession an old, plaintive, masculine voice arose in a song, wavering, stumbling in the silence at first alone, until in the band a euphonium horn fumbled for the key and took up the air, one catching and rising above the other and the other pursuing, two black pigeons rising above a skull-white barn to tumble and rise through still, blue air. And for a few bars the pure sweet tone of the horn and the old man's husky baritone sang a duet in the hot heavy silence. "There's Many a Thousand Gone." And standing high up over the park something fought in my throat. It was a song from the past, the past of the campus and the still earlier past of home. And now some of the older ones in the mass were joining in. I hadn't thought of it as a march before, but now they were marching to its slow-paced rhythm, up the hill. I looked for the euphonium player and saw a slender black man with his face turned toward the sun, singing through the up-turned bells of the horn. And several yards behind, marching beside the young men floating the coffin upward, I looked into the face of the old man who had aroused the song and felt a twinge of envy. It was a worn, old, yellow face and his eyes were closed and I could see a knife welt around his upturned neck as his throat threw out the song. He sang with his whole body, phrasing each verse as naturally as he walked, his voice rising above all the others, blending with that of the lucid horn. I watched him now, wet-eyed, the sun hot upon my head, and I felt a wonder at the singing mass. It was as though the song had been there all the time and he knew it and aroused it; and I knew that I had known it too and had failed to release it out of a vague, nameless shame or fear. But he had known and aroused it. Even white brothers and sisters were joining in. I looked into that face, trying to plumb its secret, but it told me nothing. I looked at the coffin and the marchers, listening to them, and yet realizing that I was listening to something within myself, and for a second I heard the shattering stroke of my heart. Something deep had shaken the crowd, and the old man and the man with the horn had done it. They had touched upon something deeper than protest, or religion; though now images of all the church meetings of my life welled up within me with much suppressed and forgotten anger. But that was past, and too many of those now reaching the top of the mountain and spreading massed together had never shared it, and some had been born in other lands. And yet all were touched; the song had aroused us all. It was not the words, for they were all the same old slave-borne words; it was as though he'd changed the emotion beneath the words while yet the old longing, resigned, transcendent emotion still sounded above, now deepened by that something for which the theory of Brotherhood had given me no name. I stood there trying to contain it as they brought Tod Clifton's coffin into the tower and slowly up the spiral stairs. They set it down upon the platform and I looked at the shape of the cheap gray coffin and all I could remember was the sound of his name.

The song had ended. Now the top of the little mountain bristled with banners, horns and uplifted faces. I could look straight down Fifth Avenue to 125th Street, where policemen were lined behind an array of hot-dog wagons and Good Humor carts; and among the carts I saw a peanut vendor standing beneath a street lamp upon which pigeons were gathered, and now I saw him stretch out his arms with his palms turned upward, and suddenly he was covered, head, shoulders and outflung arms, with fluttering, feasting birds.

Someone nudged me and I started. It was time for final words. But I had no words and I'd never been to a Brotherhood funeral and had no idea of a ritual. But they were waiting. I stood there alone; there was no microphone to support me, only the coffin before me upon the backs of its wobbly carpenter's horses.

I looked down into their sun-swept faces, digging for the words, and feeling a futility about it all and an anger. For this they gathered by thousands. What were they waiting to hear? Why had they come? For what reason that was different from that which had made the red-cheeked boy thrill at Clifton's falling to the earth? What did they want and what could they do? Why hadn't they come when they could have stopped it all?

"What are you waiting for me to tell you?" I shouted suddenly, my voice strangely crisp on the windless air. "What good will it do? What if I say that this isn't a funeral, that it's a holiday celebration, that if you stick around the band will end up playing 'Damit-the-Hell the Fun's All Over'? Or do you expect to see some magic, the dead rise up and walk again? Go home, he's as dead as he'll ever die. That's the end in the beginning and there's no encore. There'll be no miracles and there's no one here to preach a sermon. Go home, forget him. He's inside this box, newly dead. Go home and don't think about him. He's dead and you've got all you can do to think about you." I paused. They were whispering and looking upward.

"I've told you to go home," I shouted, "but you keep standing there. Don't you know it's hot out here in the sun? So what if you wait for what little I can tell you? Can I say in twenty minutes what was building twenty-one years and ended in twenty seconds? What are you waiting for, when all I can tell you is his name? And when I tell you, what will you know that you didn't know already, except, perhaps, his name?"

They were listening intently, and as though looking not at me, but at the pattern of my voice upon the air.

"All right, you do the listening in the sun and I'll try to tell you in the sun. Then you go home and forget it. Forget it. His name was Clifton and they shot him down. His name was Clifton and he was tall and some folks thought him handsome. And though he didn't believe it, I think he was. His name was Clifton and his face was black and his hair was thick with tight-rolled curls—or call them naps or kinks. He's dead, uninterested, and, except to a few young girls, it doesn't matter . . . Have you got it? Can you see him? Think of your brother or your cousin John. His lips were thick with an upward curve at the corners. He often smiled. He had good eyes and a pair of fast hands, and he had a heart. He thought about things and he felt deeply. I won't call him noble because what's such a word to do with one of us? His name was Clifton, Tod Clifton, and, like any man, he was born of woman to live awhile and fall and die. So that's his tale to the minute. His name was Clifton and for a while he lived among us and aroused a few hopes in the young manhood of man, and we who knew him loved him and he died. So why are you wait-

ing? You've heard it all. Why wait for more, when all I can do is repeat it?"

They stood; they listened. They gave no sign.

"Very well, so I'll tell you. His name was Clifton and he was young and he was a leader and when he fell there was a hole in the heel of his sock and when he stretched forward he seemed not as tall as when he stood. So he died; and we who loved him are gathered here to mourn him. It's as simple as that and as short as that. His name was Clifton and he was black and they shot him. Isn't that enough to tell? Isn't it all you need to know? Isn't that enough to appease your thirst for drama and send you home to sleep it off? Go take a drink and forget it. Or read it in *The Daily News*. His name was Clifton and they shot him, and I was there to see him fall. So I know it as I know it.

"Here are the facts. He was standing and he fell. He fell and he kneeled. He kneeled and he bled. He bled and he died. He fell in a heap like any man and his blood spilled out like any blood; *red* as any blood, wet as any blood and reflecting the sky and the buildings and birds and trees, or your face if you'd looked into its dulling mirror—and it dried in the sun as blood dries. That's all. They spilled his blood and he bled. They cut him down and he died; the blood flowed on the walk in a pool, gleamed a while, and, after a while, became dull then dusty, then dried. That's the story and that's how it ended. It's an old story and there's been too much blood to excite you. Besides, it's only important when it fills the veins of a living man. Aren't you tired of such stories? Aren't you sick of the blood? Then why listen, why don't you go? It's hot out here. There's the odor of embalming fluid. The beer is cold in the taverns, the saxophones will be mellow at the Savoy; plenty good-laughing-lies will be told in the barber shops and beauty parlors; and there'll be sermons in two hundred churches in the cool of the evening, and plenty of laughs at the movies. Go listen to 'Amos and Andy' and forget it. Here you have only the same old story. There's not even a young wife up here in red to mourn him. There's nothing here to pity, no one to break down and shout. Nothing to give you that good old frightened feeling. The story's too short and too simple. His name was Clifton, Tod Clifton, he was unarmed and his death was as senseless as his life was futile. He had struggled for Brotherhood on a hundred street corners and he thought it would make him more human, but he died like any dog in a road.

"All, all right," I called out, feeling desperate. It wasn't the way I wanted it to go, it wasn't political. Brother Jack probably wouldn't approve of it at all, but I had to keep going as I could go.

"Listen to me standing up on this so-called mountain!" I shouted. "Let me tell it as it truly was! His name was Tod Clifton and he was full of illusions. He thought he was a man when he was only Tod Clifton. He was shot for a simple mistake of judgment and he bled and his blood dried and shortly the crowd trampled out the stains. It was a normal mistake of which many are guilty: He thought he was a man and that men were not meant to be pushed around. But it was hot downtown and he forgot his history, he forgot the time and the place. He lost his hold on reality. There was a cop and a waiting audience but he was Tod Clifton and cops are everywhere. The cop? What about him? He was a cop. A good citizen. But this cop had an itching finger and an eager ear for a word that rhymed with 'trigger,' and when Clifton fell he had found it. The Police Special spoke its lines and the rhyme was completed. Just look around you. Look at what he made, look inside you and feel his awful power. It was perfectly natural. The blood ran like blood in a comic-book killing, on a comic-book street in a comic-book town on a comic-book day in a comic-book world.

"Tod Clifton's one with the ages. But what's that to do with you in this heat under this veiled sun? Now he's part of history, and he has received his true freedom. Didn't they scribble his name on a standardized pad? His Race: colored! Religion: unknown, probably born Baptist. Place of birth: U.S. Some southern town. Next of kin: unknown. Address: unknown. Occupation: unemployed. Cause of death (be specific): resisting reality in the form of a .38 caliber revolver in the hands of the arresting officer, on Forty-second between the library and the subway in the heat of the afternoon, of gunshot wounds received from three bullets, fired at three paces, one bullet entering the right ventricle of the heart, and lodging there, the other severing the spinal ganglia traveling downward to lodge in the pelvis, the other breaking through the back and traveling God knows where.

"Such was the short bitter life of Brother Tod Clifton. Now he's in this box with the bolts tightened down. He's in the box and we're in there with him, and when I've told you this you can go. It's dark in this box and it's crowded. It has a cracked ceiling and a clogged-up toilet in the hall. It has rats and roaches, and it's far, far too expensive a dwelling. The air is bad and it'll be cold this winter. Tod Clifton is crowded and he needs the room. 'Tell them to get out of the box,' that's what he would say if you could hear him. 'Tell them to get out of the box and go teach the cops to forget that rhyme. Tell them to teach them that when they call you *nigger* to make a rhyme with *trigger* it makes the gun backfire.'

"So there you have it. In a few hours Tod Clifton will be cold bones in the ground. And don't be fooled, for these bones shall not rise again. You and I will still be in the box. I don't know if Tod Clifton had a soul. I only know the ache that I feel in my heart, my sense of loss. I don't know if *you* have a soul. I only know that you are men of flesh and blood; and that blood will spill and flesh grow cold. I do not know if all cops are poets, but I know that all cops carry guns with triggers. And I know too how we are labeled. So in the name of Brother Clifton beware of the triggers; go home, keep cool, stay safe away from the sun. Forget him. When he was alive he was our hope, but why worry over a hope that's dead? So there's only one thing left to tell and I've already told it. His name was Tod Clifton, he believed in Brotherhood, he aroused our hopes and he died."

I couldn't go on. Below, they were waiting, hands and handkerchiefs shading their eyes. A preacher stepped up and read something out of his Bible, and I stood looking at the crowd with a sense of failure. I had let it get away from me, had been unable to bring in the political issues. And they stood there sun-beaten and sweat-bathed, listening to me repeat what was known. Now the preacher had finished, and someone signaled the bandmaster and there was solemn music as the pallbearers carried the coffin down the spiraling stairs. The crowd stood still as we walked slowly through. I could feel the bigness of it and the unknownness of it and pent-up tension—whether of tears or anger, I couldn't tell. But as we walked through and down the hill to the hearse, I could feel it. The crowd sweated and throbbed, and though it was silent, there were many things directed toward me through its eyes. At the curb were the hearse and a few cars, and in a few minutes they were loaded and the crowd was still standing, looking on as we carried Tod Clifton away. And as I took one last look I saw not a crowd but the set faces of individual men and women.

We drove away and when the cars stopped moving there was a grave and we placed him in it. The gravediggers sweated heavily and knew their business and their brogue was Irish.

They filled the grave quickly and we left. Tod Clifton was underground.

I returned through the streets as tired as though I'd dug the grave myself alone. I felt confused and listless moving through the crowds that seemed to boil along in a kind of mist, as though the thin humid clouds had thickened and settled directly above our heads. I wanted to go somewhere, to some cool place to rest without thinking, but there was still too much to be done; plans had to be made; the crowd's emotion had to be organized. I crept along, walking a southern walk in southern weather, closing my eyes from time to time against the dazzling reds, yellows and greens of cheap sport shirts and summer dresses. The crowd boiled, sweated, heaved; women with shopping bags, men with highly polished shoes. Even down South they'd always shined their shoes. "Shined shoes, shoed shines," it rang in my head. In Eighth Avenue the market carts were parked hub to hub along the curb, improvised canopies shading the withering fruits and vegetables. I could smell the stench of decaying cabbage. A watermelon huckster stood in the shade beside his truck, holding up a long slice of orange-meated melon, crying his wares with hoarse appeals to nostalgia, memories of childhood, green shade and summer coolness. Oranges, cocoanuts and alligator pears lay in neat piles on little tables. I passed, winding my way through the slowly moving crowd. Stale and wilted flowers, rejected downtown, blazed feverishly on a cart, like glamorous rags festering beneath a futile spray from a punctured fruit juice can. The crowd were boiling figures seen through steaming glass from inside a washing machine; and in the streets the mounted police detail stood looking on, their eyes noncommittal beneath the short polished visors of their caps, their bodies slanting forward, reins slackly alert, men and horses of flesh imitating men and horses of stone. Tod Clifton's *Tod*, I thought. The hucksters cried above the traffic sounds and I seemed to hear them from a distance, unsure of what they said. In a side street children with warped tricycles were parading along the walk carrying one of the signs, BROTHER TOD CLIFTON, OUR HOPE SHOT DOWN.

And through the haze I again felt the tension. There was no denying it; it was there and something had to be done before it simmered away in the heat.

Chapter twenty-two

When I saw them sitting in their shirtsleeves, leaning forward, gripping their crossed knees with their hands, I wasn't surprised. I'm glad it's you, I thought, this will be business without tears. It was as though I had expected to find them there, just as in those dreams in which I encountered my grandfather looking at me from across the dimensionless space of a dream-room. I looked back without surprise or emotion, although I knew even in the dream that surprise was the normal reaction and that the lack of it was to be distrusted, a warning.

I stood just inside the room, watching them as I slipped off my jacket, seeing them grouped around a small table upon which there rested a pitcher of water, a glass and a couple of smoking ash trays. One half of the room was dark and only one light burned, directly above the table. They regarded me silently, Brother Jack with a smile that went no deeper than his lips, his head cocked to one side, studying me with his penetrating eyes; the others blank-faced, looking out of eyes that were meant to reveal nothing and to stir profound uncertainty. The smoke rose in spirals from their cigarettes as they sat perfectly contained, waiting. So you came, after all, I thought, going over and dropping into one of the chairs. I rested my arm on the table, noticing its coolness.

"Well, how did it go?" Brother Jack said, extending his clasped hands across the table and looking at me with his head to one side.

"You saw the crowd," I said. "We finally got them out."

"No, we did not see the crowd. How was it?"

"They were moved," I said, "a great number of them. But beyond that I don't know. They were with us, but how far I don't know . . ." And for a moment I could hear my own voice in the quiet of the high-ceilinged hall.

"Sooo! Is that all the great tactician has to tell us?" Brother Tobitt said. "In what direction were they moved?"

I looked at him, aware of the numbness of my emotions; they had flowed in one channel too long and too deeply.

"That's for the committee to decide. They were aroused, that was all we could do. We tried again and again to reach the committee for guidance but we couldn't."

"So?"

"So we went ahead on my personal responsibility."

Brother Jack's eyes narrowed. "What was that?" he said. "Your what?"

"My personal responsibility," I said.

"His personal responsibility," Brother Jack said. "Did you hear that, Brothers? Did I hear him correctly? Where did you get it, Brother?" he said. "This is astounding, where did you get it?"

"From your ma—" I started and caught myself in time. "From the committee," I said.

There was a pause. I looked at him, his face reddening, as I tried to get my bearings. A nerve trembled in the center of my stomach.

"Everyone came out," I said, trying to fill it in. "We

saw the opportunity and the community agreed with us. It's too bad you missed it . . ."

"You see, he's sorry we missed it," Brother Jack said. He held up his hand. I could see the deeply etched lines in his palm. "The great tactician of *personal* responsibility regrets our absence . . ."

Doesn't he see how I feel, I thought, can't he see why I did it? What's he trying to do? Tobitt's a fool, but why is *he* taking it up?

"You could have taken the next step," I said, forcing the words. "We went as far as we could . . ."

"On your personal re-spon-si-bility," Brother Jack said, bowing his head in time with the words.

I looked at him steadily now. "I was told to win back our following, so I tried. The only way I knew how. What's your criticism? What's wrong?"

"So now," he said, rubbing his eye with a delicate circular movement of his fist, "the great tactician asks what's wrong. Is it possible that something could be wrong? Do you hear him, Brothers?"

There was a cough. Someone poured a glass of water and I could hear it fill up very fast, then the rapid rill-like trickle of the final drops dripping from the pitcher-lip into the glass. I looked at him, my mind trying to bring things into focus.

"You mean he admits the *possibility* of being incorrect?" Tobitt said.

"Sheer modesty, Brother. The sheerest modesty. We have here an extraordinary tactician, a Napoleon of strategy and personal responsibility. 'Strike while the iron is hot' is his motto. 'Seize the instance by its throat,' 'Shoot at the whites of their eyes,' 'Give 'em the ax, the ax, the ax,' and so forth."

I stood up. "I don't know what this is all about, Brother. What are you trying to say?"

"Now there is a good question, Brothers. Sit down, please, it's hot. He wants to know what we're trying to say. We have here not only an extraordinary tactician, but one who has an appreciation for subtleties of expression."

"Yes, and for sarcasm, when it's good," I said.

"And for discipline? Sit down, please, it's hot . . ."

"And for discipline. And for orders and consultation when it's possible to have them," I said.

Brother Jack grinned. "Sit down, sit down— And for patience?"

"When I'm not sleepy and exhausted," I said, "and not overheated as I am just now."

"You'll learn," he said. "You'll learn and you'll surrender yourself to it even under such conditions. *Especially* under such conditions; that's its value. That makes it patience."

"Yes, I guess I'm learning now," I said. "*Right* now."

"Brother," he said drily, "you have no idea how much you're learning— Please sit down."

"All right," I said, sitting down again. "But while ignoring my personal education for a second I'd like you to remember that the people have little patience with us these days. We could use this time more profitably."

"And I could tell you that politicians are not personal persons," Brother Jack said, "but I won't. How could we use it more profitably?"

"By organizing their anger."

"So again our great tactician has relieved himself. Today he's a busy man. First an oration over the body of Brutus, and now a lecture on the patience of the Negro people."

Tobitt was enjoying himself. I could see his cigarette tremble in his lips as he struck a match to light it.

"I move we issue his remarks in a pamphlet," he said,

running his finger over his chin. "They should create a natural phenomenon . . ."

This had better stop right here, I thought. My head was getting lighter and my chest felt tight.

"Look," I said, "an unarmed man was killed. A brother, a leading member shot down by a policeman. We had lost our prestige in the community. I saw the chance to rally the people, so I acted. If that was incorrect, then I did wrong, so say it straight without this crap. It'll take more than sarcasm to deal with that crowd out there."

Brother Jack reddened; the others exchanged glances.

"He hasn't read the newspapers," someone said.

"You forget," Brother Jack said, "it wasn't necessary; he was there."

"Yes, I was there," I said. "If you're referring to the killing."

"There, you see," Brother Jack said. "He was on the scene."

Brother Tobitt pushed the table edge with his palms. "And still you organized that side show of a funeral!"

My nose twitched. I turned toward him deliberately, forcing a grin.

"How could there be a side show without you as the star attraction; who'd draw the two bits admission, Brother Twobits? What was wrong with the funeral?"

"Now we're making progress," Brother Jack said, straddling his chair. "The strategist has raised a very interesting question. What's wrong, he asks. All right, I'll answer. Under your leadership, a traitorous merchant of vile instruments of anti-Negro, anti-minority racist bigotry has received the funeral of a hero. Do you still ask what's wrong?"

"But nothing was done about a traitor," I said.

He half-stood, gripping the back of his chair. "We all heard you admit it."

"We dramatized the shooting down of an unarmed black man."

He threw up his hands. To hell with you, I thought. To hell with you. He was a man!

"That black man, as you call him, was a traitor," Brother Jack said. "A traitor!"

"What is a traitor, Brother?" I asked, feeling an angry amusement as I counted on my fingers. "He was a man and a Negro; a man and brother; a man and a traitor, as you say; then he was a dead man, and alive or dead he was jam-full of contradictions. So full that he attracted half of Harlem to come out and stand in the sun in answer to our call. So what is a traitor?"

"So now he retreats," Brother Jack said. "Observe him, Brothers. After putting the movement in the position of forcing a traitor down the throats of the Negroes he asks what a traitor is."

"Yes," I said. "Yes, and, as you say, it's a fair question, Brother. Some folks call me traitor because I've been working downtown; some would call me a traitor if I was in Civil Service and others if I simply sat in my corner and kept quiet. Sure, I considered what Clifton did—"

"And you defend him!"

"Not for that. I was as disgusted as you. But hell, isn't the shooting of an unarmed man of more importance politically than the fact that he sold obscene dolls?"

"So you exercised your personal responsibility," Jack said.

"That's all I had to go on. I wasn't called to the strategy meeting, remember."

"Didn't you see what you were playing with?" Tobitt said. "Have you no respect for your people?"

"It was a dangerous mistake to give you the opportunity," one of the others said.

I looked across at him. "The committee can take it away,

if it wishes. But meantime, why is everyone so upset? If even one-tenth of the people looked at the dolls as we do, our work would be a lot easier. The dolls are nothing."

"Nothing," Jack said. "That nothing that might explode in our face."

I sighed. "Your faces are safe, Brother," I said. "Can't you see that they don't think in such abstract terms? If they did, perhaps the new program wouldn't have flopped. The Brotherhood isn't the Negro people; no organization is. All you see in Clifton's death is that it might harm the prestige of the Brotherhood. You see him only as a traitor. But Harlem doesn't react that way."

"Now he's lecturing us on the conditioned reflexes of the Negro people," Tobitt said.

I looked at him. I was very tired. "And what is the source of your great contributions to the movement, Brother? A career in burlesque? And of your profound knowledge of Negroes? Are you from an old plantation-owning family? Does your black mammy shuffle nightly through your dreams?"

He opened his mouth and closed it like a fish. "I'll have you know that I'm married to a fine, intelligent Negro girl," he said.

So that's what makes you so cocky, I thought, seeing now how the light struck him at an angle and made a wedge-shaped shadow beneath his nose. So that's it . . . and how did I guess there was a woman in it?

"Brother, I apologize," I said. "I misjudged you. You have our number. In fact, you must be practically a Negro yourself. Was it by immersion or injection?"

"Now see here," he said, pushing back his chair.

Come on, I thought, just make a move. Just another little move.

"Brothers," Jack said, his eyes on me. "Let's stick to the discussion. I'm intrigued. You were saying?"

I watched Tobitt. He glared. I grinned.

"I was saying that up here we know that the policemen didn't care about Clifton's ideas. He was shot because he was black and because he resisted. Mainly because he was black."

Brother Jack frowned. "You're riding 'race' again. But how do they feel about the dolls?"

"I'm riding the race I'm forced to ride," I said. "And as for the dolls, they know that as far as the cops were concerned Clifton could have been selling song sheets, Bibles, matzos. If he'd been white, he'd be alive. Or if he'd accepted being pushed around . . ."

"Black and white, white and black," Tobitt said. "Must we listen to this racist nonsense?"

"You don't, Brother Negro," I said. "You get your own information straight from the source. Is it a mulatto source, Brother? Don't answer—the only thing wrong is that your source is too narrow. You don't really think that crowd turned out today because Clifton was a member of the Brotherhood?"

"And why *did* they turn out?" Jack said, getting set as if to pounce forward.

"Because we gave them the opportunity to express their feelings, to affirm themselves."

Brother Jack rubbed his eye. "Do you know that you have become quite a theoretician?" he said. "You astound me."

"I doubt that, Brother, but there's nothing like isolating a man to make him think," I said.

"Yes, that's true; some of our best ideas have been thought in prison. Only you haven't been in prison, Brother, and you were not hired to think. Had you forgotten that? If so, listen to me: You were not hired to think." He was speaking very deliberately and I thought, So . . . So here it is, naked and old and rotten. So now it's out in the open . . .

"So now I know where I am," I said, "and with whom—"

"Don't twist my meaning. For all of us, the committee does the thinking. For *all* of us. And you were hired to
talk."

"That's right, I was *hired*. Things have been so brotherly
I had forgotten my place. But what if I wish to express an
idea?"

"We furnish all ideas. We have some acute ones. Ideas
are part of our apparatus. Only the correct ideas for the correct
occasion."

"And suppose you misjudge the occasion?"

"Should that ever happen, you keep quiet."

"Even though I am correct?"

"You say nothing unless it is passed by the committee.
Otherwise I suggest you keep saying the last thing you were
told."

"And when my people demand that I speak?"

"The committee will have an answer!"

I looked at him. The room was hot, quiet, smoky. The
others looked at me strangely. I heard the nervous sound of
someone mashing out a cigarette in a glass ash tray. I pushed
back my chair, breathing deeply, controlled. I was on a dangerous road and I thought of Clifton and tried to get off of it.
I said nothing.

Suddenly Jack smiled and slipped back into his fatherly
role.

"Let *us* handle the theory and the business of strategy,"
he said. "We are experienced. We're graduates and while you
are a smart beginner you skipped several grades. But they were
important grades, especially for gaining strategical knowledge.
For such it is necessary to see the overall picture. More is
involved than meets the eye. With the long view and the short
view and the over-all view mastered, perhaps you won't slander
the political consciousness of the people of Harlem."

Can't he see I'm trying to tell them what's real, I thought. Does my membership stop me from feeling Harlem?

"All right," I said. "Have it your way, Brother; only the political consciousness of Harlem is exactly a thing I know something about. That's one class they wouldn't let me skip. I'm describing a part of reality which I know."

"And that is the most questionable statement of all," Tobitt said.

"I know," I said, running my thumb along the edge of the table, "your private source tells you differently. History's made at night, eh, Brother?"

"I've warned you," Tobitt said.

"Brother to brother, Brother," I said, "try getting around more. You might learn that today was the first time that they've listened to our appeals in weeks. And I'll tell you something else: If we don't follow through on what was done today, this might be the last . . ."

"So, he's finally gotten around to predicting the future," Brother Jack said.

"It's possible . . . though I hope not."

"He's in touch with God," Tobitt said. "The black God."

I looked at him and grinned. He had gray eyes and his irises were very wide, the muscles ridged out on his jaws. I had his guard down and he was swinging wild.

"Not with God, nor with your wife, Brother," I told him. "I've never met either. But I've worked among the people up here. Ask your wife to take you around to the gin mills and the barber shops and the juke joints and the churches, Brother. Yes, and the beauty parlors on Saturdays when they're frying hair. A whole unrecorded history is spoken then, Brother. You wouldn't believe it but it's true. Tell her to take you to stand in the areaway of a cheap tenement at night and listen to what is said. Put her out on the corner, let her tell you what's being put down. You'll learn that a lot of people are angry because we failed to lead them in action. I'll stand on that as I stand on what I see and feel and on what I've heard, and what I know."

"No," Brother Jack said, getting to his feet, "you'll stand on the decision of the committee. We've had enough of this. The committee makes your decisions, and it is not its practice to give undue importance to the mistaken notions of the people. What's happened to your discipline?"

"I'm not arguing against discipline. I'm trying to be useful. I'm trying to point out a part of reality which the committee seems to have missed. With just one demonstration we could—"

"The committee has decided against such demonstrations," Brother Jack said. "Such methods are no longer effective."

Something seemed to move out from under me, and out of the corner of my eye I was suddenly aware of objects on the dark side of the hall. "But didn't anyone see what happened today?" I said. "What was that, a dream? What was ineffective about that crowd?"

"Such crowds are only our raw materials, *one* of the raw materials to be shaped to our program."

I looked around the table and shook my head. "No wonder they insult me and accuse us of betraying them . . ."

There was sudden movement.

"Repeat that," Brother Jack shouted, stepping forward.

"It's true, I'll repeat it. Until this afternoon they've been saying that the Brotherhood betrayed them. I'm telling you what's been said to me, and that is why Brother Clifton disappeared."

"That's an indefensible lie," Brother Jack said.

And I looked at him slowly now, thinking, If this is it,

this is it . . . "Don't call me that," I said softly. "Don't ever call me that, none of you. I've told you what I've heard." My hand was in my pocket now, Brother Tarp's leg chain around my knuckles. I looked at each of them individually, trying to hold myself back and yet feeling it getting away from me. My head was whirling as though I were riding a supersonic merry-go-round. Jack looked at me, a new interest behind his eyes, leaned forward.

"So you've heard it," he said. "Very well, so now hear this: We do not shape our policies to the mistaken and infantile notions of the man in the street. Our job is not to *ask* them what they think but to *tell* them!"

"You've said that," I said, "and that's one thing you can tell them yourself. Who are you, anyway, the great white father?"

"Not their father, their leader. And your leader. And don't forget it."

"*My* leader sure, but what's your exact relationship to them?"

His red head bristled. "The leader. As leader of the Brotherhood, I am their leader."

"But are you sure you aren't their great white father?" I said, watching him closely, aware of the hot silence and feeling tension race from my toes to my legs as I drew my feet quickly beneath me. "Wouldn't it be better if they called you Marse Jack?"

"Now see here," he began, leaping to his feet to lean across the table, and I spun my chair half around on its hind legs as he came between me and the light, gripping the edge of the table, spluttering and lapsing into a foreign language, choking and coughing and shaking his head as I balanced on my toes now, set to propel myself forward; seeing him above me and the others behind him as suddenly something seemed

to erupt out of his face. You're seeing things, I thought, hearing
it strike sharply against the table and roll as his arm shot out
and snatched an object the size of a large marble and dropped
it, plop! into his glass, and I could see the water shooting up
in a ragged, light-breaking pattern to spring in swift droplets
across the oiled table top. The room seemed to flatten. I shot
to a high plateau above them and down, feeling the jolt on the
end of my spine as the chair legs struck the floor. The merry-
go-round had speeded up, I heard his voice but no longer
listened. I stared at the glass, seeing how the light shone
through, throwing a transparent, precisely fluted shadow
against the dark grain of the table, and there on the bottom of
the glass lay an eye. A glass eye. A buttermilk white eye distorted by the light rays. An eye staring fixedly at me as from
the dark waters of a well. Then I was looking at him standing
above me, outlined by the light against the darkened half of
the hall.

". . . You must accept discipline. Either you accept decisions or you get out . . ."

I stared into his face, feeling a sense of outrage. His left
eye had collapsed, a line of raw redness showing where the lid
refused to close, and his gaze had lost its command. I looked
from his face to the glass, thinking, he's disemboweled himself
just in order to confound me . . . And the others had known
it all along. They aren't even surprised. I stared at the eye,
aware of Jack pacing up and down, shouting.

"Brother, are you following me?" He stopped, squinting
at me with Cyclopean irritation. "What is the matter?"

I stared up at him, unable to answer.

Then he understood and approached the table, smiling
maliciously. "So that's it. So it makes you uncomfortable, does
it? You're a sentimentalist," he said, sweeping up the glass and
causing the eye to turn over in the water so that now it seemed

to peer down at me from the ringed bottom of the glass. He smiled, holding the tumbler level with his empty socket, swirling the glass. "You didn't know about this?"

"No, and I didn't want to know."

Someone laughed.

"See, that demonstrates how long you've been with us." He lowered the glass. "I lost my eye in the line of duty. What do you think of that?" he said with a pride that made me all the angrier.

"I don't give a damn how you lost it as long as you keep it hidden."

"That is because you don't appreciate the meaning of sacrifice. I was ordered to carry through an objective and I carried it through. Understand? Even though I had to lose my eye to do it . . ."

He was gloating now, holding up the eye in the glass as though it were a medal of merit.

"Not much like that traitor Clifton, is it?" Tobitt said.

The others were amused.

"All right," I said. "All right! It was a heroic act. It saved the world, now hide the bleeding wound!"

"Don't overevaluate it," Jack said, quieter now. "The heroes are those who die. This was nothing—after it happened. A minor lesson in discipline. And do you know what discipline is, Brother Personal Responsibility? It's sacrifice, *sacrifice*, SACRIFICE!"

He slammed the glass upon the table, splashing the water on the back of my hand. I shook like a leaf. So that is the meaning of discipline, I thought, sacrifice . . . yes, and blindness; he doesn't see me. He doesn't even see me. Am I about to strangle him? I do not know. He cannot possibly. I still do not know. See! Discipline is sacrifice. Yes, and blindness. Yes. And me sitting here while he tries to intimidate me. That's it, with his goddam blind glass eye . . . Should you show him you get it? Shouldn't you? Shouldn't he know it? Hurry! Shouldn't you? Look at it there, a good job, an almost perfect imitation that seemed alive . . . Should you, shouldn't you? Maybe he got it where he learned that language he lapsed into. Shouldn't you? Make him speak the unknown tongue, the language of the future. What's mattering with you? Discipline. Is learning, didn't he say? Is it? I stand? You're sitting here, ain't I? You're holding on, ain't I? He said you'd learn so you're learning, so he saw it all the time. He's a riddler, shouldn't we show him? So sit still is the way, and learn, never mind the eye, it's dead . . . All right now, look at him, see him turning now, left, right, coming short-legged toward you. See him, hep! hep! the one-eyed beacon. All right, all right . . . Hep, hep! The short-legged deacon. All right! Nail him! The short-changing dialectical deacon . . . All right. There, so now you're learning . . . Get it under control . . . Patience . . . Yes . . .

I looked at him again as for the first time, seeing a little bantam rooster of a man with a high-domed forehead and a raw eye-socket that wouldn't quite accept its lid. I looked at him carefully now with some of the red spots fading and with the feeling that I was just awakening from a dream. I had boomeranged around.

"I realize how you feel," he said, becoming an actor who'd just finished a part in a play and was speaking again in his natural voice. "I remember the first time I saw myself this way and it wasn't pleasant. And don't think I wouldn't rather have my old one back." He felt in the water for his eye now, and I could see its smooth half-spherical, half-amorphous form slip between his two fingers and spurt around the glass as though looking for a way to break out. Then he had it, shaking off the water and breathing upon it as he walked across to the dark side of the room.

"But who knows, Brothers," he said, with his back turned, "perhaps if we do our work successfully the new society will provide me with a living eye. Such a thing is not at all fantastic, although I've been without mine for quite a while . . . What time is it, by the way?"

But what kind of society will make him see me, I thought, hearing Tobitt answer, "Six-fifteen."

"Then we'd better leave immediately, we've got a long way to travel," he said, coming across the floor. He had his eye in place now and he was smiling. "How's that?" he asked me.

I nodded, I was very tired. I simply nodded.

"Good," he said. "I sincerely hope it never happens to you. Sincerely."

"If it should, maybe you'll recommend me to your oculist," I said, "then I may not-see myself as others see-me-not."

He looked at me oddly then laughed. "See, Brothers, he's joking. He feels brotherly again. But just the same, I hope you'll never need one of these. Meanwhile go and see Hambro. He'll outline the program and give you the instructions. As for today, just let things float. It is a development that is important only if we make it so. Otherwise it will be forgotten," he said, getting into his jacket. "And you'll see that it's best. The Brotherhood must act as a co-ordinated unit."

I looked at him. I was becoming aware of smells again and I needed a bath. The others were standing now and moving toward the door. I stood up, feeling the shirt sticking to my back.

"One last thing," Jack said, placing his hand on my shoulder and speaking quietly. "Watch that temper, that's discipline, too. Learn to demolish your brotherly opponents with ideas, with polemical skill. The other is for our enemies. Save it for them. And go get some rest."

I was beginning to tremble. His face seemed to advance

and recede, recede and advance. He shook his head and smiled grimly.

"I know how you feel," he said. "And it's too bad all that effort was for nothing. But that in itself is a kind of discipline. I speak to you of what I have learned and I'm a great deal older than you. Good night."

I looked at his eye. So he knows how I feel. Which eye is really the blind one? "Good night," I said.

"Good night, Brother," they all except Tobitt said.

It'll be night, but it won't be good, I thought, calling a final "Good night."

They left and I took my jacket and went and sat at my desk. I heard them passing down the stairs and the closing of the door below. I felt as though I'd been watching a bad comedy. Only it was real and I was living it and it was the only historically meaningful life that I could live. If I left it, I'd be nowhere. As dead and as meaningless as Clifton. I felt for the doll in the shadow and dropped it on the desk. He was dead all right, and nothing would come of his death now. He was useless even for a scavenger action. He had waited too long, the directives had changed on him. He'd barely gotten by with a funeral. And that was all. It was only a matter of a few days, but he had missed and there was nothing I could do. But at least he was dead and out of it.

I sat there a while, growing wilder and fighting against it. I couldn't leave and I had to keep contact in order to fight. But I would never be the same. Never. After tonight I wouldn't ever look the same, or feel the same. Just what I'd be, I didn't know; I couldn't go back to what I was—which wasn't much—but I'd lost too much to be what I was. Some of me, too, had died with Tod Clifton. So I would see Hambro, for whatever it was worth. I got up and went out into the hall. The glass was still on the table and I swept it across the room, hearing it rumble and roll in the dark. Then I went downstairs.

Chapter twenty-three

The bar downstairs was hot and crowded and there was a heated argument in progress over Clifton's shooting. I stood near the door and ordered a bourbon. Then someone noticed me, and they tried to draw me in.

"Please, not tonight," I said. "He was one of my best friends."

"Oh, sure," they said, and I had another bourbon and left.

When I reached 125th Street, I was approached by a group of civil-liberties workers circulating a petition demanding the dismissal of the guilty policeman, and a block further on even the familiar woman street preacher was shouting a sermon about the slaughter of the innocents. A much broader group was stirred up over the shooting than I had imagined. Good, I thought, perhaps it won't die down after all. Maybe I'd better see Hambro tonight.

Little groups were all along the street, and I moved with increasing speed until suddenly I had reached Seventh Avenue, and there beneath a street lamp with the largest crowd around

him was Ras the Exhorter—the last man in the world I wanted
to see. And I had just turned back when I saw him lean down
between his flags, shouting, "Look, look, Black ladies and gentlemahn! There goes the representative of the Brotherhood.
Does Ras see correctly? Is that gentlemahn trying to pass us
unnoticed? Ask *him* about it. What are you people waiting for,
sir? What are you doing about our black youth shot down
beca'se of your deceitful organization?"

They turned, looking at me, closing in. Some came up
behind me and tried to push me further into the crowd. The
Exhorter leaned down, pointing at me, beneath the green traffic light.

"Ask him what they are doing about it, ladies and gentlemahn. Are they afraid—or are the white folks and their
black stooges sticking together to betray us?"

"Get your hands off me," I shouted as someone reached
around and seized my arm.

I heard a voice cursing me softly.

"Give the brother a chance to answer!" someone said.

Their faces pressed in upon me. I wanted to laugh, for
suddenly I realized that I didn't know whether I had been
part of a sellout or not. But they were in no mood for
laughter.

"Ladies and gentlemen, brothers and sisters," I said, "I
disdain to answer such an attack. Since you all know me and
my work, I don't think it's necessary. But it seems highly dis-
honorable to use the unfortunate death of one of our most
promising young men as an excuse for attacking an organization that has worked to bring an end to such outrages. Who
was the first organization to act against this killing? The Brotherhood! Who was the first to arouse the people? The Brotherhood! Who will always be the first to advance the cause of
the people? Again the Brotherhood!

"We acted and we shall always act, I assure you. But in our own disciplined way. And we'll act positively. We refuse to waste our energies and yours in premature and ill-considered actions. We are Americans, all of us, whether black or white, regardless of what the man on the ladder there tells you, Americans. And we leave it to the gentleman up there to abuse the name of the dead. The Brotherhood grieves and feels deeply the loss of its brother. And we are determined that his death shall be the beginning of profound and lasting changes. It's easy enough to wait around for the minute a man is safely buried and then stand on a ladder and smear the memory of everything he believed in. But to create something lasting of his death takes time and careful planning—"

"Gentlemahn," Ras shouted, "stick to the issue. You are not answering my question. *What are you doing about the shooting?*"

I moved toward the edge of the crowd. If this went any further, it could be disastrous.

"Stop abusing the dead for your own selfish ends," I said. "Let him rest in peace. Quit mangling his corpse!"

I pushed away as he raged, hearing shouts of, "Tell him about it!" "Grave robber!"

The Exhorter waved his arms and pointed, shouting, "That mahn is a paid stooge of the white enslaver! Wheere has he been for the last few months when our black babies and women have been suffering—"

"Let the dead rest in peace," I shouted, hearing someone call "Aw man, go back to Africa. Everybody knows the brother."

Good, I thought, good. Then there was a scuffle behind me and I whirled to see two men stop short. They were Ras's men.

"Listen, mister," I said up to him, "if you know what's

good for you, you'll call off your goons. Two of them seem to want to follow me."

"And that is a dahm lie!" he shouted.

"There are witnesses if anything should happen to me. A man who'll dig up the dead hardly before he's buried will try anything, but I warn you—"

There were angry shouts from some of the crowd and I saw the men continue past me with hate in their eyes, leaving the crowd to disappear around the corner. Ras was attacking the Brotherhood now and others were answering him from the audience, and I went on, moving back toward Lenox, moving past a movie house when they grabbed me and started punching. But this time they'd picked the wrong spot, and the movie doorman intervened and they ran back toward Ras's street meeting. I thanked the doorman and went on. I had been lucky; they hadn't hurt me, but Ras was becoming bold again. On a less crowded street they might have done some damage.

Reaching the Avenue I stepped to the curb and signaled a cab, seeing it sail by. An ambulance went past, then another cab with its flag down. I looked back. I felt that they were watching me from somewhere up the street but I couldn't see them. Why didn't a taxi come! Then three men in natty cream-colored summer suits came to stand near me at the curb, and something about them struck me like a hammer. They were all wearing dark glasses. I had seen it thousands of times, but suddenly what I had considered an empty imitation of a Hollywood fad was flooded with personal significance. Why not, I thought, why not, and shot across the street and into the air-conditioned chill of a drugstore.

I saw them on a case strewn with sun visors, hair nets, rubber gloves, a card of false eyelashes, and seized the darkest lenses I could find. They were of a green glass so dark that it appeared black, and I put them on immediately, plunging into blackness and moving outside.

I could barely see; it was almost dark now, and the streets swarmed in a green vagueness. I moved slowly across to stand near the subway and wait for my eyes to adjust. A strange wave of excitement boiled within me as I peered out at the sinister light. And now through the hot gusts from the underground people were emerging and I could feel the trains vibrating the walk. A cab rolled up to discharge a passenger and I was about to take it when the woman came up the stairs and stopped before me, smiling. Now what, I thought, seeing her standing there, smiling in her tight-fitting summer dress; a large young woman who reeked with Christmas Night perfume who now came close.

"Rinehart, baby, is that you?" she said.

Rinehart, I thought. So it works. She had her hand on my arm and faster than I thought I heard myself answer, "Is that you, baby?" and waited with tense breath.

"Well, for once you're on time," she said. "But what you doing bareheaded, where's your new hat I bought you?"

I wanted to laugh. The scent of Christmas Night was enfolding me now and I saw her face draw closer, her eyes widening.

"Say, you ain't Rinehart, man. What you trying to do? You don't even talk like Rine. What's your story?"

I laughed, backing away. "I guess we were both mistaken," I said.

She stepped backward clutching her bag, watching me, confused.

"I really meant no harm," I said. "I'm sorry. Who was it you mistook me for?"

"Rinehart, and you'd better not let him catch you pretending to be him."

"No," I said. "But you seemed so pleased to see him that I couldn't resist it. He's really a lucky man."

"And I could have sworn you was—Man, you git away

from here before you get me in trouble," she said, moving aside, and I left.

It was very strange. But that about the hat was a good idea, I thought, hurrying along now and looking out for Ras's men. I was wasting time. At the first hat shop I went in and bought the widest hat in stock and put it on. With this, I thought, I should be seen even in a snowstorm—only they'd think I was someone else.

Then I was back in the street and moving toward the subway. My eyes adjusted quickly; the world took on a dark-green intensity, the lights of cars glowed like stars, faces were a mysterious blur; the garish signs of movie houses muted down to a soft sinister glowing. I headed back for Ras's meeting with a bold swagger. This was the real test, if it worked I would go on to Hambro's without further trouble. In the angry period to come I would be able to move about.

A couple of men approached, eating up the walk with long jaunty strides that caused their heavy silk sports shirts to flounce rhythmically upon their bodies. They too wore dark glasses, their hats were set high upon their heads, the brims turned down. A couple of hipsters, I thought, just as they spoke.

"What you sayin', daddy-o," they said.

"Rinehart, poppa, tell us what you putting down," they said.

Oh, hell, they're probably his friends, I thought, waving and moving on.

"We know what you're doing, Rinehart," one of them called. "Play it cool, ole man, play it cool!"

I waved again as though in on the joke. They laughed behind me. I was nearing the end of the block now, wet with sweat. Who was this Rinehart and what *was* he putting down? I'd have to learn more about him to avoid further misidentifications . . .

A car passed with its radio blaring. Ahead I could hear the Exhorter barking harshly to the crowd. Then I was moving close, and coming to a stop conspicuously in the space left for pedestrians to pass through the crowd. To the rear they were lined up two deep before the store windows. Before me the listeners merged in a green-tinted gloom. The Exhorter gestured violently, blasting the Brotherhood.

"The time for ahction is here. We mahst chase them out of Harlem," he cried. And for a second I thought he had caught me in the sweep of his eyes, and tensed.

"Ras said chase them! It is time Ras the Exhorter become Ras the DESTROYER!"

Shouts of agreement arose and I looked behind me, seeing the men who had followed me and thinking, What did he mean, *destroyer*?

"I repeat, black ladies and gentlemahn, the time has come for ahction! I, Ras the Destroyer, repeat, the *time has come!*"

I trembled with excitement; they hadn't recognized me. It works, I thought. They see the hat, not me. There is a magic in it. It hides me right in front of their eyes . . . But suddenly I wasn't sure. With Ras calling for the destruction of everything white in Harlem, who could notice me? I needed a better test. If I was to carry out my plan . . . What plan? Hell, I don't know, come on . . .

I weaved out of the crowd and left, heading for Hambro's.

A group of zoot-suiters greeted me in passing. "Hey now, daddy-o," they called. "Hey now!"

"Hey now!" I said.

It was as though by dressing and walking in a certain way I had enlisted in a fraternity in which I was recognized at a glance—not by features, but by clothes, by uniform, by gait. But this gave rise to another uncertainty. I was not a zoot-suiter, but a kind of politician. Or was I? What would happen in a real test? What about the fellows who'd been so insulting at the Jolly Dollar? I was halfway across Eighth Avenue at the thought and retraced my steps, running for an uptown bus.

There were many of the regular customers draped around the bar. The room was crowded and Barrelhouse was on duty. I could feel the frame of the glasses cutting into the ridge of my nose as I tilted my hat and squeezed up to the bar. Barrelhouse looked at me roughly, his lips pushed out.

"What brand you drinking tonight, Poppa-stopper?" he said.

"Make it Ballantine's," I said in my natural voice.

I watched his eyes as he set the beer before me and slapped the bar with his enormous hand for his money. Then, my heart beating faster, I made my old gesture of payment, spinning the coin upon the bar and waited. The coin disappeared into his fist.

"Thanks, pops," he said, moving on and leaving me puzzled. For there had been recognition of a kind in his voice but not for me. He never called me "pops" or "poppa-stopper." It's working, I thought, perhaps it's working very well.

Certainly something was working on me, and profoundly. Still I was relieved. It was hot. Perhaps that was it. I drank the cold beer, looking back to the rear of the room to the booths. A crowd of men and women moiled like nightmare figures in the smoke-green haze. The juke box was dinning and it was like looking into the depths of a murky cave. And now someone moved aside and looking down along the curve of the bar past the bobbing heads and shoulders I saw the juke box, lit up like a bad dream of the Fiery Furnace, shouting:

> *Jelly, Jelly*
> *Jelly,*
> *All night long.*

And yet, I thought, watching a numbers runner paying off a bet, this is one place that the Brotherhood definitely penetrated. Let Hambro explain that, too, along with all the rest he'd have to explain.

I drained the glass and turned to leave, when there across at the lunch counter I saw Brother Maceo. I moved impulsively, forgetting my disguise until almost upon him, then checked myself and put my disguise once more to a test. Reaching roughly across his shoulder I picked up a greasy menu that rested between the sugar shaker and the hot-sauce bottle and pretended to read it through my dark lenses.

"How're the ribs, pops?" I said.

"Fine, least these here I'm eatin' is."

"Yeah? How much you know about ribs?"

He raised his head slowly, looking across at the spitted chickens revolving before the low blue rotisserie flames. "I reckon I know as much about 'em as you," he said, "and probably more, since I probably been eatin' 'em a few years longer than you, and in a few more places. What makes you think you kin come in here messing with me anyhow?"

He turned, looking straight into my face now, challenging me. He was very game and I wanted to laugh.

"Oh, take it easy," I growled. "A man can ask a question, can't he?"

"You got your answer," he said, turning completely around on the stool. "So now I guess you ready to pull your knife."

"Knife?" I said, wanting to laugh. "Who said anything about a knife?"

"That's what you thinking about. Somebody say something you don't like and you kinda fellows pull your switch blades. So all right, go ahead and pull it. I'm as ready to die as I'm gon' ever be. Let's see you, go ahead!"

He reached for the sugar shaker now, and I stood there feeling suddenly that the old man before me was not Brother Maceo at all, but someone else disguised to confuse me. The glasses were working too well. He's a game old brother, I thought, but this'll never do.

I pointed toward his plate. "I asked you about the ribs," I said, "not your ribs. Who said anything about a knife?"

"Never mind that, just go on and pull it," he said. "Let's see you. Or is you waiting for me to turn my back. All right, here it is, here's my back," he said, turning swiftly on the stool and around again, his arm set to throw the shaker.

Customers were turning to look, were moving clear.

"What's the matter, Maceo?" someone said.

"Nothing I caint handle; this confidencing sonofabitch come in here bluffing—"

"You take it easy, old man," I said. "Don't let your mouth get your head in trouble," thinking, Why am I talking like this?

"You don't have to worry about that, sonofabitch, pull your switch blade!"

"Give it to him, Maceo, coolcrack the motherfouler!"

I marked the position of the voice by ear now, turning so that I could see Maceo, the agitator, and the customers blocking the door. Even the juke box had stopped and I could feel the danger mounting so swiftly that I moved without thinking, bounding over quickly and sweeping up a beer bottle, my body trembling.

"All right," I said, "if that's the way you want it, all right! The next one who talks out of turn gets this!"

Maceo moved and I feinted with the bottle, seeing him dodge, his arm set to throw and held only because I was crowding him; a dark old man in overalls and a gray long-billed cloth cap, who looked dreamlike through the green glasses.

"Throw it," I said. "Go on," overcome with the madness of the thing. Here I'd set out to test a disguise on a friend and now I was ready to beat him to his knees—not because I wanted to but because of place and circumstance. Okay, okay, it was absurd and yet real and dangerous and if he moved, I'd let him have it as brutally as possible. To protect myself I'd have to, or the drunks would gang me. Maceo was set, looking at me coldly, and suddenly I heard a voice boom out, "Ain't going to be no fighting in my joint!" It was Barrelhouse. "Put them things down y'all, they cost money."

"Hell, Barrelhouse, let 'em fight!"

"They can fight in the streets, not in here— Hey, y'all," he called, "look over here . . ."

I saw him now, leaning forward with a pistol in his huge fist, resting it steady upon the bar.

"Now put 'em down y'all," he said mournfully. "I done ask you to put my property *down*."

Brother Maceo looked from me to Barrelhouse.

"Put it down, old man," I said, thinking, Why am I acting from pride when this is not really me?

"You put yourn down," he said.

"*Both* of y'all put 'em down; and you, Rinehart," Barrelhouse said, gesturing at me with the pistol, "you get out of my joint and stay out. We don't need your money in here."

I started to protest, but he held up his palm.

"Now you all right with me, Rinehart, don't get me wrong. But I just can't stand trouble," Barrelhouse said.

Brother Maceo had replaced the shaker now and I put my bottle down and backed to the door.

"And Rine," Barrelhouse said, "don't go try to pull no pistol neither, 'cause this here one is loaded and I got a permit."

I backed to the door, my scalp prickling, watching them both.

"Next time don't ask no questions you don't want answered," Maceo called. "An' if you ever want to finish this argument I be right here."

I felt the outside air explode around me and I stood just beyond the door laughing with the sudden relief of the joke restored, looking back at the defiant old man in his long-billed cap and the confounded eyes of the crowd. Rinehart, Rinehart, I thought, what kind of man is Rinehart?

I was still chuckling when, in the next block, I waited for the traffic lights near a group of men who stood on the corner passing a bottle of cheap wine between them as they discussed Clifton's murder.

"What we need is some guns," one of them said. "An eye for an eye."

"Hell yes, machine guns. Pass me the sneakypete, Muckleroy."

"Wasn't for that Sullivan Law this here New York wouldn't be nothing but a shooting gallery," another man said.

"Here's the sneakypete, and don't try to find no home in that bottle."

"It's the only home I got, Muckleroy. You want to take that away from me?"

"Man, drink up and pass the damn bottle."

I started around them, hearing one of them say, "What you saying, Mr. Rinehart, how's your hammer hanging?"

Even up here, I thought, beginning to hurry. "Heavy, man," I said, knowing the answer to that one, "very heavy."

They laughed.

"Well, it'll be lighter by morning."

"Say, look ahere, Mr. Rinehart, how about giving me a job?" one of them said, approaching me, and I waved and crossed the street, walking rapidly down Eighth toward the next bus stop.

The shops and groceries were dark now, and children were running and yelling along the walks, dodging in and out among the adults. I walked, struck by the merging fluidity of forms seen through the lenses. Could this be the way the world appeared to Rinehart? All the dark-glass boys? "For now we see as through a glass darkly but then—but then—" I couldn't remember the rest.

She was carrying a shopping bag and moved gingerly on her feet. Until she touched my arm I thought that she was talking to herself.

"I say, pardon me, son, look like you trying to pass on by me tonight. What's the final figger?"

"Figure? What figure?"

"Now you know what I mean," she said, her voice rising as she put her hands on her hips and looked forward. "I mean today's last number. Ain't you Rine the runner?"

"Rine the runner?"

"Yas, Rinehart the number man. Who you trying to fool?"

"But that's not my name, madame," I said, speaking as precisely as I could and stepping away from her. "You've made a mistake."

Her mouth fell wide. "You ain't? Well, why you look so much like him?" she said with hot doubt in her voice. "Now, ain't this here something. Let me get on home; if my dream come out, I'm-a have to go look that rascal up. And here I needs that money too."

"I hope you won," I said, straining to see her clearly, "and I hope he pays off."

"Thanks, son, but he'll pay off all right. I can see you ain't Rinehart now though. I'm sorry for stopping you."

"It's all right," I said.

"If I'd looked at your shoes I woulda known—"

"Why?"

" 'Cause Rine the runner is known for them knobtoed kind."

I watched her limp away, rocking like the Old Ship of Zion. No wonder everyone knows him, I thought, in that racket you have to get around. I was aware of my black-and-white shoes for the first time since the day of Clifton's shooting.

When the squad car veered close to the curb and rolled along slowly beside me I knew what was coming before the cop opened his mouth.

"That you, Rinehart, my man?" the cop who was not driving said. He was white. I could see the shield gleaming on his cap but the number was vague.

"Not this time, officer," I said.

"The hell you say; what're you trying to pull? Is this a holdout?"

"You're making a mistake," I said. "I'm not Rinehart."

The car stopped, a flashlight beamed in my green-lensed eyes. He spat into the street. "Well, you better be by morning," he said, "and you better have our cut in the regular place. Who the hell you think you are?" he called as the car speeded up and away.

And before I could turn a crowd of men ran up from the corner pool hall. One of them carried an automatic in his hand.

"What were those sonsabitches trying to do to you, daddy?" he said.

"It was nothing, they thought I was someone else."

"Who'd they take you for?"

I looked at them—were they criminals or simply men who were worked up over the shooting?

"Some guy named Rinehart," I said.

"*Rinehart—* Hey, y'all hear that?" snorted the fellow

with the gun. "Rinehart! Them paddies must be going stone blind. Anybody can see you ain't Rinehart."

"But he do look like Rine," another man said, staring at me with his hands in his trousers pockets.

"Like hell he does."

"Hell, man, Rinehart would be driving that Cadillac this time of night. What the hell you talking about?"

"Listen, Jack," the fellow with the gun said, "don't let nobody make you act like Rinehart. You got to have a smooth tongue, a heartless heart and be ready to do anything. But if them paddies bother you agin, just let us know. We aim to stop some of this head-whupping they been doing."

"Sure," I said.

"Rinehart," he said again. "Ain't *that* a bitch?"

They turned and went arguing back to the pool hall and I hurried out of the neighborhood. Having forgotten Hambro for the moment I walked east instead of west. I wanted to remove the glasses but decided against it. Ras's men might still be on the prowl.

It was quieter now. No one paid me any special attention, although the street was alive with pedestrians, all moiling along in the mysterious tint of green. Perhaps I'm out of his territory at last, I thought and began trying to place Rinehart in the scheme of things. He's been around all the while, but I have been looking in another direction. He was around and others like him, but I had looked past him until Clifton's death (or was it Ras?) had made me aware. What on earth was hiding behind the face of things? If dark glasses and a white hat could blot out my identity so quickly, who actually was who?

The perfume was exotic and seemed to roll up the walk behind me as I became aware of a woman strolling casually behind me.

"I've been waiting for you to recognize me, daddy," a voice said. "I've been waiting for you a long time."

It was a pleasant voice with a slightly husky edge and plenty of sleep in it.

"Don't you hear me, daddy?" she said. And I started to look around, hearing, "No, daddy, don't look back; my old man might be cold trailing me. Just walk along beside me while I tell you where to meet me. I swear I thought you'd never come. Will you be able to see me tonight?"

She had moved close to me now and suddenly I felt a hand fumbling at my jacket pocket.

"All right, daddy, you don't have to jump evil on me, here it is; now will you see me?"

I stopped dead, grabbing her hand and looking at her, an exotic girl even through the green glasses, looking at me with a smile that suddenly broke. "Rinehart, *daddy*, what's the matter?"

So here it goes again, I thought, holding her tightly.

"I'm not Rinehart, Miss," I said. "And for the first time tonight I'm truly sorry."

"But Bliss, daddy—Rinehart! You're not trying to put your baby down—Daddy, what did I do?"

She seized my arm and we were poised face to face in the middle of the walk. And suddenly she screamed, "Oooooooh! You really aren't! And me trying to give you his money. Get away from me, you dumb John. Get away from me!"

I backed off. Her face was distorted as she stamped her high heels and screamed. Behind me I heard someone say, "Hey, what was that?" followed by the sound of running feet as I shot off and around the corner away from her screams. That lovely girl, I thought, that lovely girl.

Several blocks away I stopped, out of breath. And both pleased and angry. How stupid could people be? Was everyone suddenly nuts? I looked about me. It was a bright street, the walks full of people. I stood at the curb trying to breathe. Up the street a sign with a cross glowed above the walk:

HOLY WAY STATION
BEHOLD THE LIVING GOD

The letters glowed dark green and I wondered if it were from the lenses or the actual color of the neon tubes. A couple of drunks stumbled past. I headed for Hambro's, passing a man sitting on the curb with his head bent over his knees. Cars passed. I went on. Two solemn-faced children came passing out handbills which first I refused, then went back and took. After all, I had to know what was going on in the community. I took the bill and stepped close to the street light, reading.

> Behold the Invisible
> Thy will be done O Lord!
> I See all, Know all, Tell all, Cure all.
> You shall see the unknown wonders.
> —Rev. B. P. Rinehart,
> *Spiritual Technologist.*

The old is ever new
Way Stations in New Orleans, the home of mystery, Birmingham, New York, Chicago, Detroit and L. A.

No Problem too Hard for God.

Come to the Way Station.

BEHOLD THE INVISIBLE!

Attend our services, prayer meetings Thrice weekly
Join us in the NEW REVELATION of the
OLD TIME RELIGION!

BEHOLD THE SEEN UNSEEN
BEHOLD THE INVISIBLE
YE WHO ARE WEARY COME HOME!

I DO WHAT YOU WANT DONE! DON'T WAIT!

I dropped the leaflet into the gutter and moved on. I walked slowly, my breath still coming hard. *Could it be?* Soon I reached the sign. It hung above a store that had been converted into a church, and I stepped into the shallow lobby and wiped my face with a handkerchief. Behind me I heard the rise and fall of an old-fashioned prayer such as I hadn't heard since leaving the campus; and then only when visiting country preachers were asked to pray. The voice rose and fell in a rhythmical, dreamlike recital—part enumeration of earthly trials undergone by the congregation, part rapt display of vocal virtuosity, part appeal to God. I was still wiping my face and squinting at crude Biblical scenes painted on the windows when two old ladies came up to me.

"Even', Rever'n Rinehart," one of them said. "How's our dear pastor this warm evening?"

Oh, no, I thought, but perhaps agreeing will cause less trouble than denying, and I said, "Good evening, sisters," muffling my voice with my handkerchief and catching the odor of the girl's perfume from my hand.

"This here's Sister Harris, Rever'n. She come to join our little band."

"God bless you, Sister Harris," I said, taking her extended hand.

"You know, Rever'n, I once heard you preach years ago. You was just a lil' ole twelve-year-ole boy, back in Virginia. And here I come North and find you, praise God, still preaching the gospel, doing the Lord's work. Still preaching the ole time religion here in this wicked city—"

"Er, Sister Harris," the other sister said, "we better get on in and find our seats. Besides, the pastor's kind of got things to do. Though you are here a little early, aren't you, Rever'n?"

"Yes," I said, dabbing my mouth with my handkerchief. They were motherly old women of the southern type and I suddenly felt a nameless despair. I wanted to tell them that Rinehart was a fraud, but now there came a shout from inside the church and I heard a burst of music.

"Just lissen to it, Sister Harris. That's the new kind of guitar music I told you Rever'n Rinehart got for us. Ain't it heavenly?"

"Praise God," Sister Harris said. "Praise God!"

"Excuse us, Rever'n, I have to see Sister Judkins about the money she collected for the building fund. And, Rever'n, last night I sold ten recordings of your inspiring sermon. Even sold one to the white lady I work for."

"Bless you," I found myself saying in a voice heavy with despair, "bless you, bless you."

Then the door opened and I looked past their heads into a small crowded room of men and women sitting in folding chairs, to the front where a slender woman in a rusty black robe played passionate boogie-woogie on an upright piano along with a young man wearing a skull cap who struck righteous riffs from an electric guitar which was connected to an amplifier that hung from the ceiling above a gleaming white and gold pulpit. A man in an elegant red cardinal's robe and a high lace collar stood resting against an enormous Bible and now began to lead a hard-driving hymn which the congregation shouted in the unknown tongue. And back and high on the wall above him there arched the words in letters of gold:

LET THERE BE LIGHT!

The whole scene quivered vague and mysterious in the green light, then the door closed and the sound muted down.

It was too much for me. I removed my glasses and tucked the white hat carefully beneath my arm and walked away. Can it be, I thought, can it actually be? And I knew that it was. I had heard of it before but I'd never come so close. Still, could he be all of them: Rine the runner and Rine the gambler and Rine the briber and Rine the lover and Rinehart the Reverend? Could he himself be both rind and heart? What is real anyway? But how could I doubt it? He was a broad man, a man of parts who got around. Rinehart the rounder. It was true as I was true. His world was possibility and he knew it. He was years ahead of me and I was a fool. I must have been crazy and blind. The world in which we lived was without boundaries. A vast seething, hot world of fluidity, and Rine the rascal was at home. Perhaps *only* Rine the rascal was at home in it. It was unbelievable, but perhaps only the unbelievable could be believed. Perhaps the truth was always a lie.

Perhaps, I thought, the whole thing should roll off me like drops of water rolling off Jack's glass eye. I should search out the proper political classification, label Rinehart and his situation and quickly forget it. I hurried away from the church so swiftly that I found myself back at the office before I remembered that I was going to Hambro's.

I was both depressed and fascinated. I wanted to know Rinehart and yet, I thought, I'm upset because I know I don't have to know him, that simply becoming aware of his existence, being mistaken for him, is enough to convince me that Rinehart is real. It couldn't be, but it is. And it can be, is, simply because it's unknown. Jack wouldn't dream of such a possibility, nor Tobitt, who thinks he's so close. Too little was known, too much was in the dark. I thought of Clifton and of Jack himself; how much was really known about either of them? How much was known about me? Who from my old life had challenged me? And after all this time I had just discovered Jack's missing eye.

My entire body started to itch, as though I had just been removed from a plaster cast and was unused to the new freedom of movement. In the South everyone knew you, but coming North was a jump into the unknown. How many days could you walk the streets of the big city without encountering anyone who knew you, and how many nights? You could actually make yourself anew. The notion was frightening, for now the world seemed to flow before my eyes. All boundaries down, freedom was not only the recognition of necessity, it was the recognition of possibility. And sitting there trembling I caught a brief glimpse of the possibilities posed by Rinehart's multiple personalities and turned away. It was too vast and confusing to contemplate. Then I looked at the polished lenses of the glasses and laughed. I had been trying simply to turn them into a disguise but they had become a political instrument instead; for if Rinehart could use them in his work, no doubt I could use them in mine. It was too simple, and yet they had already opened up a new section of reality for me. What would the committee say about that? What did their theory tell them of such a world? I recalled a report of a shoe-shine boy who had encountered the best treatment in the South simply by wearing a white turban instead of his usual Dobbs or Stetson, and I fell into a fit of laughing. Jack would be outraged at the very suggestion of such a state of things. And yet there was truth in it; this was the real chaos which he thought he was describing—so long ago it seemed now . . . Outside the Brotherhood we were outside history; but inside of it they didn't see us. It was a hell of a state of affairs, we were nowhere. I wanted to back away from it, but still I wanted to discuss it, to consult someone who'd tell me it was only a brief, emotional illusion. I wanted the props put back beneath the world. So now I had a real need to see Hambro.

Getting up to go, I looked at the wall map and laughed at Columbus. What an India he'd found! I was almost across the hall when I remembered and came back and put on the hat and glasses. I'd need them to carry me through the streets.

I took a cab. Hambro lived in the West Eighties, and once in the vestibule I tucked the hat under my arm and put the glasses in my pocket along with Brother Tarp's leg chain and Clifton's doll. My pocket was getting overloaded.

I was shown into a small, book-lined study by Hambro himself. From another part of the apartment came a child's voice singing *Humpty Dumpty*, awakening humiliating memories of my first Easter program during which I had stood before the church audience and forgotten the words . . .

"My kid," Hambro said, "filibustering against going to bed. A real sea lawyer, that kid."

The child was singing *Hickory Dickory Dock*, very fast, as Hambro shut the door. He was saying something about the child and I looked at him with sudden irritation. With Rinehart on my mind, why had I come here?

Hambro was so tall that when he crossed his legs both feet touched the floor. He had been my teacher during my period of indoctrination and now I realized that I shouldn't have come. Hambro's lawyer's mind was too narrowly logical. He'd see Rinehart simply as a criminal, my obsession as a fall into pure mysticism . . . You'd better hope that is the way he'll see it, I thought. Then I decided to ask him about conditions uptown and leave . . .

"Look, Brother Hambro," I said, "what's to be done about my district?"

He looked at me with a dry smile. "Have I become one of those bores who talk too much about their children?"

"Oh, no, it's not that," I said. "I've had a hard day. I'm nervous. With Clifton's death and things in the district so bad, I guess . . ."

"Of course," he said, still smiling, "but why are you worried about the district?"

"Because things are getting out of hand. Ras's men tried to rough me up tonight and our strength is steadily going to hell."

"That's regrettable," he said, "but there's nothing to be done about it that wouldn't upset the larger plan. It's unfortunate, Brother, but your members will have to be sacrificed."

The distant child had stopped singing now, and it was dead quiet. I looked at the angular composure of his face searching for the sincerity in his words. I could feel some deep change. It was as though my discovery of Rinehart had opened a gulf between us over which, though we sat within touching distance, our voices barely carried and then fell flat, without an echo. I tried to shake it away, but still the distance, so great that neither could grasp the emotional tone of the other, remained.

"Sacrifice?" my voice said. "You say that very easily."

"Just the same, though, all who leave must be considered expendable. The new directives must be followed rigidly."

It sounded unreal, an antiphonal game. "But why?" I said. "Why must the directives be changed in my district when the old methods are needed—especially now?" Somehow I couldn't get the needed urgency into my words, and beneath it all something about Rinehart bothered me, darted just beneath the surface of my mind; something that had to do with me intimately.

"It's simple, Brother," Hambro was saying. "We are

making temporary alliances with other political groups and the interests of one group of brothers must be sacrificed to that of the whole."

"Why wasn't I told of this?" I said.

"You will be, in time, by the committee— Sacrifice is necessary now—"

"But shouldn't sacrifice be made willingly by those who know what they are doing? My people don't understand why they're being sacrificed. They don't even *know* they're being sacrificed—at least not by us . . ." But what, my mind went on, if they're as willing to be duped by the Brotherhood as by Rinehart?

I sat up at the thought and there must have been an odd expression on my face, for Hambro, who was resting his elbows upon the arms of his chair and touching his fingertips together, raised his eyebrows as though expecting me to continue. Then he said, "The disciplined members will understand."

I pulled Tarp's leg chain from my pocket and slipped it over my knuckles. He didn't notice. "Don't you realize that we have only a handful of disciplined members left? Today the funeral brought out hundreds who'll drop away as soon as they see we're not following through. And now we're being attacked on the streets. Can't you understand? Other groups are circulating petitions, Ras is calling for violence. The committee is mistaken if they think this is going to die down."

He shrugged. "It's a risk which we must take. All of us must sacrifice for the good of the whole. Change is achieved through sacrifice. We follow the laws of reality, so we make sacrifices."

"But the community is demanding equality of sacrifice," I said. "We've never asked for special treatment."

"It isn't that simple, Brother," he said. "We have to protect our gains. It's inevitable that some must make greater sacrifices than others . . ."

"That 'some' being my people . . ."

"In this instance, yes."

"So the weak must sacrifice for the strong? Is that it, Brother?"

"No, a part of the whole is sacrificed—and will continue to be until a new society is formed."

"I don't get it," I said. "I just don't get it. We work our hearts out trying to get the people to follow us and just when they do, just when they see their relationship to events, we drop them. I don't see it."

Hambro smiled remotely. "We don't have to worry about the aggressiveness of the Negroes. Not during the new period or any other. In fact, we now have to slow them down for their own good. It's a scientific necessity."

I looked at him, at the long, bony, almost Lincolnesque face. I might have liked him, I thought, he seems to be a really kind and sincere man and yet he can say this to me . . .

"So you really believe that," I said quietly.

"With all my integrity," he said.

For a second I thought I'd laugh. Or let fly with Tarp's link. *Integrity!* He talks to me of *integrity!* I described a circle in the air. I'd tried to build my integrity upon the role of Brotherhood and now it had changed to water, air. What was integrity? What did it have to do with a world in which Rinehart was possible and successful?

"But what's changed?" I said. "Wasn't I brought in to arouse their aggressiveness?" My voice fell sad, hopeless.

"For that particular period," Hambro said, leaning a little forward. "Only for that period."

"And what will happen now?" I said.

He blew a smoke ring, the blue-gray circle rising up boiling within its own jetting form, hovering for an instant then disintegrating into a weaving strand.

"Cheer up!" he said. "We shall progress. Only now they must be brought along more slowly . . ."

How would he look through the green lenses? I thought, saying, "Are you sure you're not saying that they must be held back?"

He chuckled. "Now, listen," he said. "Don't stretch me on a rack of dialectic. I'm a brother."

"You mean the brakes must be put on the old wheel of history," I said. "Or is it the little wheels *within* the wheel?"

His face sobered. "I mean only that they must be brought along more slowly. They can't be allowed to upset the tempo of the master plan. Timing is all important. Besides, you still have a job to do, only now it will be more educational."

"And what about the shooting?"

"Those who are dissatisfied will drop away and those who remain you'll teach . . ."

"I don't think I can," I said.

"Why? It's just as important."

"Because they are against us; besides, I'd feel like Rinehart . . ." It slipped out and he looked at me.

"Like who?"

"Like a charlatan," I said.

Hambro laughed. "I thought you had learned about that, Brother."

I looked at him quickly. "Learned what?"

"That it's impossible *not* to take advantage of the people."

"That's Rinehartism—cynicism . . ."

"What?"

"Cynicism," I said.

"Not cynicism—realism. The trick is to take advantage of them in their own best interest."

I sat forward in my chair, suddenly conscious of the unreality of the conversation. "But who is to judge? Jack? The committee?"

"We judge through cultivating scientific objectivity," he said with a voice that had a smile in it, and suddenly I saw the hospital machine, felt as though locked in again.

"Don't kid yourself," I said. "The only scientific objectivity is a machine."

"Discipline, not machinery," he said. "We're scientists. We must take the risks of our science and our will to achieve. Would you like to resurrect God to take responsibility?" He shook his head. "No, Brother, we have to make such decisions ourselves. Even if we must sometimes appear as charlatans."

"You're in for some surprises," I said.

"Maybe so and maybe not," he said. "At any rate, through our very position in the vanguard we must do and say the things necessary to get the greatest number of the people to move toward what is for their own good."

Suddenly I couldn't stand it.

"Look at me! Look at *me!*" I said. "Everywhere I've turned somebody has wanted to sacrifice me for my good— only *they* were the ones who benefited. And now we start on the old sacrificial merry-go-round. At what point do we stop? Is this the new true definition, is Brotherhood a matter of sacrificing the weak? If so, at what point do we stop?"

Hambro looked as though I were not there. "At the proper moment science will stop us. And of course we as individuals must sympathetically debunk ourselves. Even though it does only a little good. But then," he shrugged, "if you go too far in that direction you can't pretend to lead. You'll lose your confidence. You won't believe enough in your own correctness to lead others. You must therefore have confidence in those who lead you—in the collective wisdom of Brotherhood."

I left in a worse state than that in which I'd come. Several buildings away I heard him call behind me, watched him approach through the dark.

"You left your hat," he said, handing it to me along with the mimeographed sheets of instructions outlining the new program. I looked at the hat and at him, thinking of Rinehart and invisibility, but knew that for him it would have no reality. I told him good night and went through the hot street to Central Park West, starting toward Harlem.

Sacrifice and leadership, I thought. For him it was simple. For *them* it was simple. But hell, I was both. Both sacrificer and victim. I couldn't get away from that, and Hambro didn't have to deal with it. That was reality too, my reality. He didn't have to put the knife blade to his own throat. What would he say if *he* were the victim?

I walked along the park in the dark. Cars passed. From time to time the sound of voices, squealing laughter, arose from beyond the trees and hedges. I could smell the sun-singed grass. The sky against which an airplane beacon played was still overcast. I thought of Jack, the people at the funeral, Rinehart. They'd asked us for bread and the best I could give was a glass eye—not so much as an electric guitar.

I stopped and dropped to a bench. I should leave, I thought. That would be the honest thing to do. Otherwise I could only tell them to have hope and try to hold on to those who'd listen. Was that also what Rinehart was, a principle of hope for which they gladly paid? Otherwise there was nothing but betrayal, and that meant going back to serve Bledsoe, and Emerson, jumping from the pot of absurdity to the fire of the ridiculous. And either was a self-betrayal. But I couldn't leave; I had to settle with Jack and Tobitt. I owed it to Clifton and Tarp and the others. I had to hold on . . . and then I had an idea that shook me profoundly: You don't have to worry about the people. If they tolerate Rinehart, then they will forget it and even with them you are invisible. It lasted only the fraction of a second and I rejected it immediately; still it had flashed across the dark sky of my mind. It was just like that. It didn't matter because they didn't realize just what had happened, neither my hope nor my failure. My ambition and integrity were nothing to them and my failure was as meaningless as Clifton's. It had been that way all along. Only in the Brotherhood had there seemed a chance for such as us, the mere glimmer of a light, but behind the polished and humane façade of Jack's eye I'd found an amorphous form and a harsh red rawness. And even that was without meaning except for me.

Well, I *was* and yet I was invisible, that was the fundamental contradiction. I was and yet I was unseen. It was frightening and as I sat there I sensed another frightening world of possibilities. For now I saw that I could agree with Jack without agreeing. And I could tell Harlem to have hope when there was no hope. Perhaps I could tell them to hope until I found the basis of something real, some firm ground for action that would lead them onto the plane of history. But until then I would have to move them without myself being moved . . . I'd have to do a Rinehart.

I leaned against a stone wall along the park, thinking of Jack and Hambro and of the day's events and shook with rage. It was all a swindle, an obscene swindle! They had set themselves up to describe the world. What did they know of us, except that we numbered so many, worked on certain jobs, offered so many votes, and provided so many marchers for some protest parade of theirs? I leaned there, aching to humiliate them, to refute them. And now all past humiliations became precious parts of my experience, and for the first time, leaning against that stone wall in the sweltering night, I began to accept my past and, as I accepted it, I felt memories welling up within me. It was as though I'd learned suddenly to look around corners; images of past humiliations flickered through my head and I saw that they were more than separate experiences. They were me; they defined me. I was my experiences and my experiences were me, and no blind men, no matter how powerful they became, even if they conquered the world, could take that, or change one single itch, taunt, laugh, cry, scar, ache, rage or pain of it. They were blind, bat blind, moving only by the echoed sounds of their own voices. And because they were blind they would destroy themselves and I'd help them. I laughed. Here I had thought they accepted me because they felt that color made no difference, when in reality it made no difference because they didn't see either color or men . . . For all they were concerned, we were so many names scribbled on fake ballots, to be used at their convenience and when not needed to be filed away. It was a joke, an absurd joke. And now I looked around a corner of my mind and saw Jack and Norton and Emerson merge into one single white figure. They were very much the same, each attempting to force his picture of reality upon me and neither giving a hoot in hell for how things looked to me. I was simply a material, a natural resource to be used. I had switched from the arrogant absurdity of Norton and Emerson to that of Jack and the Brotherhood, and it all came out the same—except I now recognized my invisibility.

So I'd accept it, I'd explore it, rine and heart. I'd plunge into it with both feet and they'd gag. Oh, but wouldn't they gag. I didn't know what my grandfather had meant, but I was ready to test his advice. I'd overcome them with yeses, undermine them with grins, I'd agree them to death and destruction. Yes, and I'd let them swoller me until they vomited or burst wide open. Let them gag on what they refused to see. Let them choke on it. That was one risk they hadn't calculated. That was a risk they had never dreamt of in their philosophy. Nor did they know that they could discipline themselves to destruction, that saying "yes" could destroy them. Oh, I'd yes them, but wouldn't I yes them! I'd yes them till they puked and rolled in it. All they wanted of me was one belch of affirmation and I'd bellow it out loud. Yes! Yes! YES! That was all anyone wanted of us, that we should be heard and not seen, and then heard only in one big optimistic chorus of yassuh, yassuh, yassuh! All right, I'd yea, yea and oui, oui and si, si and see, see them too; and I'd walk around in their guts with hobnailed boots. Even those super-big shots whom I'd never seen at committee meetings. They wanted a machine? Very well, I'd become a supersensitive confirmer of their misconceptions, and just to hold their confidence I'd try to be right part of the time. Oh, I'd serve them well and I'd make invisibility felt if not seen, and they'd learn that it could be as polluting as a decaying body, or a piece of bad meat in a stew. And if I got hurt? Very well again. Besides, didn't they believe in sacrifice? They were the subtle thinkers—would this be treachery? Did the word apply to an invisible man? Could they recognize choice in that which wasn't seen . . . ?

The more I thought of it the more I fell into a kind of morbid fascination with the possibility. Why hadn't I discovered it sooner? How different my life might have been! How terribly different! Why hadn't I seen the possibilities? If a sharecropper could attend college by working during the summers as a waiter and factory hand or as a musician and then graduate to become a doctor, why couldn't all those things be done at one and the same time? And wasn't that old slave a scientist— or at least called one, recognized as one—even when he stood with hat in hand, bowing and scraping in senile and obscene servility? My God, what possibilities existed! And that spiral business, that progress goo! Who knew all the secrets; hadn't

I changed my name and never been challenged even once? And that lie that success was a rising *upward*. What a crummy lie they kept us dominated by. Not only could you travel upward toward success but you could travel downward as well; up *and* down, in retreat as well as in advance, crabways and crossways and around in a circle, meeting your old selves coming and going and perhaps all at the same time. How could I have missed it for so long? Hadn't I grown up around gambler-politicians, bootlegger-judges and sheriffs who were burglars; yes, and Klansmen who were preachers and members of humanitarian societies? Hell, and hadn't Bledsoe tried to tell me what it was all about? I felt more dead than alive. It had been quite a day; one that could not have been more shattering even if I had learned that the man whom I'd always called father was actually of no relation to me.

I went to the apartment and fell across the bed in my clothes. It was hot and the fan did little more than stir the heat in heavy leaden waves, beneath which I lay twirling the dark glasses and watching the hypnotic flickering of the lenses as I tried to make plans. I would hide my anger and lull them to sleep; assure them that the community was in full agreement with their program. And as proof I would falsify the attendance records by filling out membership cards with fictitious names— all unemployed, of course, so as to avoid any question of dues. Yes, and I would move about the community by night and during times of danger by wearing the white hat and the dark glasses. It was a dreary prospect but a means of destroying them, at least in Harlem. I saw no possibility of organizing a splinter movement, for what would be the next step? Where would we go? There were no allies with whom we could join as equals; nor were there time or theorists available to work out an over-all program of our own—although I felt that some-where between Rinehart and invisibility there were great potentialities. But we had no money, no intelligence apparatus, either in government, business or labor unions; and no communications with our own people except through unsympathetic newspapers, a few Pullman porters who brought provincial news from distant cities and a group of domestics who reported the fairly uninteresting private lives of their employers. If only we had some true friends, some who saw us as more than convenient tools for shaping their own desires! But to hell with that, I thought, I would remain and become a well-disciplined optimist, and help them to go merrily to hell. If I couldn't help them to see the reality of our lives I would help them to ignore it until it exploded in their faces.

Only one thing bothered me: Since I now knew that their real objectives were never revealed at committee meetings, I needed some channel of intelligence through which I could learn what actually guided their operations. But how? If only I had resisted being shifted downtown I would now have enough support in the community to *insist* that they reveal themselves. Yes, but if I hadn't been shifted, I would still be living in a world of illusion. But now that I had found the thread of reality, how could I hold on? They seemed to have me blocked at every turn, forcing me to fight them in the dark. Finally I tossed the glasses across the bed and dropped into a fitful nap during which I relived the events of the last few days; except that instead of Clifton being lost it was myself, and I awoke stale, sweaty and aware of perfume.

I lay on my stomach, my head resting upon the back of my hand thinking, where is it coming from? And just as I caught sight of the glasses I remembered grasping Rinehart's girl's hand. I lay there unmoving, and she seemed to perch on the bed, a bright-eyed bird with her glossy head and ripe breasts, and I was in a wood afraid to frighten the bird away. Then I was fully awake and the bird gone and the girl's image in my mind. What would have happened if I had led her on, how far could I have gone? A desirable girl like that mixed up with Rinehart. And now I sat breathless, asking myself how Rinehart would have solved the problem of information and it came instantly clear: It called for a woman. A wife, a girl friend, or secretary of one of the leaders, who would be willing to talk freely to me. My mind swept back to early experiences in the movement. Little incidents sprang to memory, bringing images of the smiles and gestures of certain women met after rallies and at parties: Dancing with Emma at the Chthonian; she close, soft against me and the hot swift focusing of my desire and my embarrassment as I caught sight of Jack holding forth in a corner, and Emma holding me tight, her bound breasts pressing against me, looking with that teasing light in her eyes, saying, "Ah, temptation," and my desperate grab for a sophisticated reply and managing only, "Oh, but there's always temptation," surprising myself nevertheless and hearing her laughing, "Touché! Touché! You should come up and fence with me some afternoon." That had been during the early days when I had felt strong restrictions and resented Emma's boldness and her opinion that I should have been blacker to play my role of Harlem leader. Well, there were no restrictions left, the committee had seen to that. She was fair game and perhaps she'd find me black enough, after all. A committee meeting was set for tomorrow, and since it was Jack's birthday, a party at the Chthonian would follow. Thus I would launch my two-pronged attack under the most favorable circumstance. They were forcing me to Rinehart methods, so bring on the scientists!

Chapter twenty-four

I started yessing them the next day and it began beautifully. The community was still going apart at the seams. Crowds formed at the slightest incidents. Store windows were smashed and several clashes erupted during the morning between bus drivers and their passengers. The papers listed similar incidents that had exploded during the night. The mirrored façade of one store on 125th Street was smashed and I passed to see a group of boys watching their distorted images as they danced before the jagged glass. A group of adults looked on, refusing to move at the policemen's command, and muttering about Clifton. I didn't like the look of things, for all my wish to see the committee confounded.

When I reached the office, members were there with reports of clashes in other parts of the district. I didn't like it at all; the violence was pointless and, helped along by Ras, was actually being directed against the community itself. Yet in spite of my sense of violated responsibility I was pleased by the developments and went ahead with my plan. I sent out members to mingle with crowds and try to discourage any further violence and sent an open letter to all the press denouncing them for "distorting" and inflating minor incidents.

Late that afternoon at headquarters I reported that things were quieting down and that we were getting a large part of the community interested in a clean-up campaign, which would clear all backyards, areaways, and vacant lots of garbage and trash and take Harlem's mind off Clifton. It was such a bare-face maneuver that I almost lost the confidence of my invisibility even as I stood before them. But they loved it, and when I handed in my fake list of new members they responded with enthusiasm. They were vindicated; the program was correct, events were progressing in their predetermined direction, history was on their side, and Harlem loved them. I sat there smiling inwardly as I listened to the remarks that followed. I could see the role which I was to play as plainly as I saw Jack's red hair. Incidents of my past, both recognized and ignored, sprang together in my mind in an ironic leap of consciousness that was like looking around a corner. I was to be a justifier, my task would be to deny the unpredictable human element of all Harlem so that they could ignore it when it in any way interfered with their plans. I was to keep ever before them the picture of a bright, passive, good-humored, receptive mass ever willing to accept their every scheme. When situations arose in which others would respond with righteous anger I would say that we were calm and unruffled (if it suited them to have us angry, then it was simple enough to create anger for us by stating it in their propaganda; the facts were unimportant, unreal); and if other people were confused by their maneuvering I was to reassure them that *we* pierced to the truth with x-ray insight. If other groups were interested in becoming wealthy, I was to assure the Brothers and the doubting members of other districts, that *we* rejected wealth as corrupt and intrinsically degrading; if other minorities loved the country despite their grievances, I would assure the committee that we, immune to such absurdly human and mixed reactions, hated it absolutely; and, greatest contradiction of all, when they denounced the American scene as corrupt and degenerate, I was to say that we, though snarled inextricably within its veins and sinews, were miraculously healthy. Yessuh, yessuh! Though invisible I would be their assuring voice of denial; I'd out-Tobitt Tobitt, and as for that outhouse Wrestrum—well. As I sat there one of them was inflating my faked memberships into meanings of national significance. An illusion was creating a counter-illusion. Where would it end? Did they believe their own propaganda?

Afterwards at the Chthonian it was like old times. Jack's birthday was an occasion for champagne and the hot, dog-day evening was even more volatile than usual. I felt highly confident, but here my plan went slightly wrong. Emma was quite gay and responsive, but something about her hard, handsome face warned me to lay off. I sensed that while she might willingly surrender herself (in order to satisfy herself) she was far too sophisticated and skilled in intrigue to compromise her position as Jack's mistress by revealing anything important to me. So as I danced and sparred with Emma I looked over the party for a second choice.

We were thrown together at the bar. Her name was Sybil and she was one of those who assumed that my lectures on the woman question were based upon a more intimate knowledge than the merely political and had indicated several times a willingness to know me better. I had always pretended not to understand, for not only had my first such experience taught me to avoid such situations, but at the Chthonian she was usually slightly tipsy and wistful—just the type of misunderstood married woman whom, even if I had been interested, I would have avoided like the plague. But now her unhappiness and the fact that she was one of the big shots' wives made her a perfect choice. She was very lonely and it went very smoothly. In the noisy birthday party—which was to be followed by a public celebration the next evening—we weren't noticed, and when she left fairly early in the evening I saw her home. She felt neglected and he was always busy, and when I left her I had arranged a rendezvous at my apartment for the following evening. George, the husband, would be at the birthday celebration and she wouldn't be missed.

It was a hot dry August night. Lightning flashed across the eastern sky and a breathless tension was in the humid air. I had spent the afternoon preparing, leaving the office on a pretense of illness to avoid having to attend the celebration. I had neither itch nor etchings, but there was a vase of Chinese lilies in the living room, and another of American Beauty roses on the table near the bed; and I had put in a supply of wine, whiskey and liqueur, extra ice cubes, and assortments of fruit, cheese, nuts, candy and other delicacies from the Vendome. In short, I tried to manage things as I imagined Rinehart would have done.

But I bungled it from the beginning. I made the drinks too strong—which she liked too well; and I brought up politics—which she all but hated—too early in the evening. For all her exposure to ideology she had no interest in politics and no idea of the schemes that occupied her husband night and day. She was more interested in the drinks, in which I had to join her glass for glass, and in little dramas which she had dreamed up around the figures of Joe Louis and Paul Robeson. And, although I had neither the stature nor the temperament for either role, I was expected either to sing "Old Man River" and just keep rolling along, or to do fancy tricks with my muscles. I was confounded and amused and it became quite a contest, with me trying to keep the two of us in touch with reality and with her casting me in fantasies in which I was Brother Taboo-with-whom-all-things-are-possible.

Now it was late and as I came into the room with another round of drinks she had let down her hair and was beckoning to me with a gold hairpin in her teeth, saying, "Come to mamma, beautiful," from where she sat on the bed.

"Your drink, madame," I said handing her a glass and hoping the fresh drink would discourage any new ideas.

"Come on, dear," she said coyly. "I want to ask you something."

"What is it?" I said.

"I have to whisper it, beautiful."

I sat and her lips came close to my ear. And suddenly she had drained the starch out of me. I pulled away. There was something almost prim about the way she sat there, and yet she had just made a modest proposal that I join her in a very revolting ritual.

"What was that!" I said, and she repeated it. Had life suddenly become a crazy Thurber cartoon?

"Please, you'll do that for me, won't you, beautiful?"

"You really mean it?"

"Yes," she said, "yes!"

There was a pristine incorruptibility about her face now that upset me all the more, for she was neither kidding nor trying to insult me; and I could not tell if it were horror speaking to me out of innocence, or innocence emerging unscathed from the obscene scheme of the evening. I only knew that the whole affair was a mistake. She had no information and I decided to get her out of the apartment before I had to deal definitely with either the horror or the innocence, while

I could still deal with it as a joke. What would Rinehart do about *this*, I thought, and knowing, determined not to let her provoke me to violence.

"But, Sybil, you can see I'm not like that. You make me feel a tender, protective passion— Look, it's like an oven in here, why don't we get dressed and go for a walk in Central Park?"

"But I need it," she said, uncrossing her thighs and sitting up eagerly. "You can do it, it'll be easy for *you*, beautiful. Threaten to kill me if I don't give in. You know, talk rough to me, beautiful. A friend of mine said the fellow said, 'Drop your drawers' . . . and—"

"He said what!" I said.

"He really did," she said.

I looked at her. She was blushing, her cheeks, even her freckled bosom, were bright red.

"Go on," I said, as she lay back again. "Then what happened?"

"Well . . . he called her a filthy name," she said, hesitating coyly. She was a leathery old girl with chestnut hair of fine natural wave which was now fanned out over the pillow. She was blushing quite deeply. Was this meant to excite me, or was it an unconscious expression of revulsion?

"A really filthy name," she said. "Oh, he was a brute, huge, with white teeth, what they call a 'buck.' And he said, 'Bitch, drop your drawers,' and then he did it. She's such a lovely girl, too, really delicate with a complexion like strawberries and cream. You can't imagine *anyone* calling her a name like that."

She sat up now, her elbows denting the pillow as she looked into my face.

"But what happened, did they catch him?" I said.

"Oh, of course not, beautiful, she only told two of us

girls. She couldn't afford to let her husband hear of it. He . . . well, it's too long a story."

"It's terrible," I said. "Don't you think we should go . . . ?"

"Isn't it, though? She was in a state for months . . ." Her expression flickered, became indeterminate.

"What is it?" I said, afraid she might cry.

"Oh, I was just wondering how she *really* felt. I really do." Suddenly she looked at me mysteriously. "Can I trust you with a deep secret?"

I sat up. "Don't tell me that it was you."

She smiled, "Oh, no, that was a dear friend of mine. But do you know what, beautiful," she said leaning forward confidentially, "I think I'm a nymphomaniac."

"You? Noooo!"

"Uh huh. Sometimes I have such thoughts and dreams. I never give into them though, but I really think I am. A woman like me has to develop an iron discipline."

I laughed inwardly. She would soon be a biddy, stout, with a little double chin and a three-ply girdle. A thin gold chain showed around a thickening ankle. And yet I was becoming aware of something warmly, infuriatingly feminine about her. I reached out, stroking her hand. "Why do you have such ideas about yourself?" I said, seeing her raise up and pluck at the corner of the pillow, drawing out a speckled feather and stripping the down from its shaft.

"Repression," she said with great sophistication. "Men have repressed us too much. We're expected to pass up too many human things. But do you know another secret?"

I bowed my head.

"You don't mind my going on, do you, beautiful?"

"No, Sybil."

"Well, ever since I first heard about it, even when I was a very little girl, I've wanted it to happen to me."

"You mean what happened to your friend?"

"Uh huh."

"Good Lord, Sybil, did you ever tell that to anyone else?"

"Of course not, I wouldn't've dared. Are you shocked?"

"Some. But Sybil, why do you tell me?"

"Oh, I know that I can trust you. I just knew you'd understand; you're not like other men. We're kind of alike."

She was smiling now and reached out and pushed me gently, and I thought, here it goes again.

"Lie back and let me look at you against that white sheet. You're beautiful, I've always thought so. Like warm ebony against pure snow—see what you do, you make me talk poetry. 'Warm ebony against pure snow,' isn't that poetic?"

"I'm the sensitive type, you mustn't make fun of me."

"But really you are, and I feel so free with you. You've no idea."

I looked at the red imprint left by the straps of her bra, thinking, Who's taking revenge on whom? But why be surprised, when that's what they hear all their lives? When it's made into a great power and they're taught to worship all types of power? With all the warnings against it, some are bound to want to try it out for themselves. The conquerors conquered. Maybe a great number secretly want it; maybe that's why they scream when it's farthest from possibility—

"That's it," she said tightly. "Look at me like that; just like you want to tear me apart. I love for you to look at me like that!"

I laughed and touched her chin. She had me on the ropes; I felt punch drunk, I couldn't deliver and I couldn't be angry either. I thought of lecturing her on the respect due one's bedmate in our society, but I no longer deluded myself that I either knew the society or where I fitted into it. Besides, I thought, she thinks you're an entertainer. That's something else they're taught.

I raised my glass and she joined me in a drink, moving close.

"You will, won't you, beautiful?" she said, her lips, raw-looking now without makeup, pouting babyishly. So why not entertain her, be a gentleman, or whatever it is she thinks you are— What does she think you are? A domesticated rapist, obviously, an expert on the woman question. Maybe that's what you are, house-broken and with a convenient verbal push-button arrangement for the ladies' pleasure. Well, so I had set this trap for myself.

"Take this," I said, shoving another glass into her hand. "It'll be better after you've had a drink, more realistic."

"Oh, yes, that'll be wonderful." She took a drink and looked up thoughtfully. "I get so tired of living the way I do, beautiful. Soon I'll be old and nothing will've happened to me. Do you know what that means? George talks a lot about women's rights, but what does he know about what a woman needs? Him with his forty minutes of brag and ten of bustle. Oh, you have no idea what you're doing for me."

"Nor you for me, Sybil dear," I said, filling the glass again. At last my drinks were beginning to work.

She shook her long hair out over her shoulders and crossed her knees, watching me. Her head had begun to weave.

"Don't drink too much, beautiful," she said. "It always takes the pep out of George."

"Don't worry," I said. "I rapes real good when I'm drunk."

She looked startled. "Ooooh, then pour me another," she said, giving herself a bounce. She was as delighted as a child, holding out her glass eagerly.

"What's happening here," I said, "a new birth of a nation?"

"What'd you say, beautiful?"

"Nothing, a bad joke. Forget it."

"That's what I like about you, beautiful. You haven't told me a single one of those vulgar jokes. Come on, beautiful," she said, "pour."

I poured her another and another; in fact, I poured us both quite a few. I was far away; it wasn't happening to me or to her and I felt a certain confused pity which I didn't wish to feel. Then she looked at me, her eyes bright behind narrowed lids and raised up and struck me where it hurt.

"Come on, beat me, daddy—you—you big black bruiser. What's taking you so long?" she said. "Hurry up, knock me down! Don't you want me?"

I was annoyed enough to slap her. She lay aggressively receptive, flushed, her navel no goblet but a pit in an earth-quaking land, flexing taut and expansive. Then she said, "Come on, come on!" and I said, "Sure, sure," looking around wildly and starting to pour the drink upon her and was stopped, my emotions locked, as I saw her lipstick lying on the table and grabbed it, saying, "Yes, yes," as I bent to write furiously across her belly in drunken inspiration:

SYBIL, YOU WERE RAPED

BY

SANTA CLAUS

SURPRISE

and paused there; trembling above her, my knees on the bed as she waited with unsteady expectancy. It was a purplish metallic shade of lipstick and as she panted with anticipation the letters stretched and quivered, up hill and down dale, and she was lit up like a luminescent sign. "Hurry, boo'ful, hurry," she said.

I looked at her, thinking, Just wait until George sees that—if George ever gets around to seeing that. He'll read a lecture on an aspect of the woman question he's never thought about. She lay anonymous beneath my eyes until I saw her face, shaped by her emotion which I could not fulfill, and I thought, Poor Sybil, she picked a boy for a man's job and nothing was as it was supposed to be. Even the black bruiser fell down on the job. She'd lost control of her liquor now and suddenly I bent and kissed her upon the lips.

"Shhhh, be quiet," I said, "that's no way to act when you're being—" and she raised her lips for more and I kissed her again and calmed her and she dozed off and I decided again to end the farce. Such games were for Rinehart, not me. I stumbled out and got a damp towel and began rubbing out the evidence of my crime. It was as tenacious as sin and it took some time. Water wouldn't do it, whiskey would have smelled and finally I had to find benzine. Fortunately she didn't arouse until I was almost finished.

"D'you do it, boo'ful?" she said.

"Yes, of course," I said. "Isn't that what you wanted?"

"Yes, but I don't seem t'remember . . ."

I looked at her and wanted to laugh. She was trying to see me but her eyes wouldn't focus and her head kept swinging to one side, yet she was making a real effort, and suddenly I felt lighthearted.

"By the way," I said, trying to do something with her hair, "what's your name, lady?"

"It's Sybil," she said indignantly, almost tearfully. "Boo'-ful, you know I'm Sybil."

"Not when I grabbed you, I didn't."

Her eyes widened and a smile wobbled across her face.

"That's right, you couldn't, could you? You never saw

me before." She was delighted, I could almost see the idea take form in her mind.

"That's right," I said, "I leaped straight out of the wall. I overpowered you in the empty lobby—remember? I smothered your terrified screams."

" 'N' did I put up a good fight?"

"Like a lioness defending her young . . ."

"But you were such a strong big brute you made me give in. I didn't want to, did I now, boo'ful? You forced me 'gainst m' will."

"Sure," I said, picking up some silken piece of clothing. "You brought out the beast in me. I overpowered you. But what could I do?"

She studied that a while and for a second her face worked again as though she would cry. But it was another smile that bloomed there.

"And wasn't I a good nymphomaniac?" she said, watching me closely. "Really and truly?"

"You have no idea," I said. "George had better keep an eye on you."

She twisted herself from side to side with irritation. "Oh, nuts! That ole Georgie porgie wouldn't know a nymphomaniac if she got right into bed with him!"

"You're wonderful," I said. "Tell me about George. Tell me about that great master mind of social change."

She steadied her gaze, frowning, "Who, *Georgie?*" she said, looking at me out of one bleary eye. "Georgie's blind 'sa mole in a hole 'n doesn't know a thing about it. 'D you ever hear of such a thing, fifteen years! Say, what're you laughing at, boo'ful?"

"Me," I said, beginning to roar, "just me . . ."

"I've never seen anyone laugh like you, boo'ful. It's wonderful!"

I was slipping her dress over her head now and her voice came muffled through the shantung cloth. Then I had it down around her hips and her flushed face wavered through the collar, her hair down in disorder again.

"Boo'ful," she said, blowing the word, "will you do it again sometimes?"

I stepped away and looked at her. "What?"

"Please, pretty boo'ful, please," she said with a wobbly smile.

I began to laugh. "Sure," I said, "sure . . ."

"When, boo'ful, when?"

"Any time," I said. "How about every Thursday at nine?"

"Oooooh, boo'ful," she said, giving me an old-fashioned hug. "I've never seen anyone like you."

"Are you sure?" I said.

"Really, I haven't, boo'ful . . . Honor bright . . . believe me?"

"Sure, it's good to be seen, but we've got to go now," I said, seeing her about to sag to the bed.

She pouted. "I need a lil nightcap, boo'ful," she said.

"You've had enough," I said.

"Ah, boo'ful, jus' one . . ."

"Okay, just one."

We had another drink and I looked at her and felt the pity and self-disgust returning and was depressed.

She looked at me gravely, her head to one side.

"Boo'ful," she said, "you know what lil ole Sybil thinks? She thinks you're trying to get rid of her."

I looked at her out of a deep emptiness and refilled her glass and mine. What had I done to her, allowed her to do? Had all of it filtered down to me? My action . . . my—the painful word formed as disconnectedly as her wobbly smile—

my *responsibility*? All of it? I'm invisible. "Here," I said, "drink."

"You too, boo'ful," she said.

"Yes," I said. She moved into my arms.

I MUST have dozed. There came the tinkling of ice in a glass, the shrill of bells. I felt profoundly sad, as though winter had fallen during the hour. She lay, her chestnut hair let down, watching through heavy-lidded, blue, eye-shadowed eyes. From far away a new sound arose.

"Don't answer, boo'ful," she said, her voice coming through suddenly, out of time with the working of her mouth.

"What?" I said.

"Don't answer, let'er ring," she said, reaching her red-nailed fingers forth.

I took it from her hands, understanding now.

"Don't, boo'ful," she said.

It rang again in my hand now and for no reason at all the words of a childhood prayer spilled through my mind like swift water. Then: "Hello," I said.

It was a frantic, unrecognizable voice from the district. "Brother, you better get up here right away—" it said.

"I'm ill," I said. "What's wrong?"

"There's trouble, Brother, and you're the only one who can—"

"What kind of trouble?"

"Bad trouble, Brother; they trying to—"

Then the harsh sound of breaking glass, distant, brittle and fine, followed by a crash, and the line went dead.

"Hello," I said, seeing Sybil wavering before me, her lips saying, "Boo'ful."

I tried to dial now, hearing the busy signal throbbing

back at me: Amen-Amen-Amen-Ah man; and I sat there a while. Was it a trick? Did they know she was with me? I put it down. Her eyes were looking at me from out of their blue shadow. "Boo—"

And now I stood and pulled her arm. "Let's go, Sybil. They need me uptown"—realizing only then that I would go.

"No," she said.

"But yes. Come."

She fell back upon the bed defying me. I released her arms and looked around, my head unclear. What kind of trouble at this hour? Why should I go? She watched me, her eyes brightly awash in blue shadow. My heart felt low and deeply sad.

"Come back, boo'ful," she said.

"No, let's get some air," I said.

And now, avoiding the red, oily nails I gripped her wrists and pulled her up, toward the door. We tottered, her lips brushing mine as we wavered there. She clung to me, and, for an instant, I to her with a feeling immeasurably sad. Then she hiccupped and I looked vacantly back into the room. The light caught in the amber liquid of our glasses.

"Boo'ful," she said, "life could be so diff'rent—"

"But it never is," I said.

She said, "Boo'ful."

The fan whirred. And in a corner, my brief case, covered with specks of dust like memories—the night of the battle royal. I felt her breathing hot against me and pushed her gently away, steadying her against the door frame, then went over as impulsively as the remembered prayer, and got the brief case, brushing the dust against my leg and feeling the unexpected weight as I hugged it beneath my arm. Something clinked inside.

She watched me still, her eyes alight as I took her arm.

"How're you doing, Syb?" I said.

"Don't go, boo'ful," she said. "Let Georgie do it. No speeches tonight."

"Come on," I said taking her arm quite firmly, pulling her along as she sighed, her wistful face turned toward me.

We went down smoothly into the street. My head was still badly fuzzed from the drink, and when I looked down the huge emptiness of the dark I felt like tears ... What was happening uptown? Why should I worry over bureaucrats, blind men? *I am invisible.* I stared down the quiet street, feeling her stumbling beside me, humming a little tune; something fresh, naïve and carefree. Sybil, my too-late-too-early love ... Ah! My throat throbbed. The heat of the street clung close. I looked for a taxi but none was passing. She hummed beside me, her perfume unreal in the night. We moved into the next block and still no taxis. Her high heels unsteadily scrunched the walk. I stopped her.

"Poor boo'ful," she said. "Don't know his name ..."

I turned as though struck. "What?"

"Anonymous brute 'n boo'ful buck," she said, her mouth a bleary smile.

I looked at her, skittering about on high heels, *scrunch, scrunch* on the walk.

"Sybil," I said, more to myself than to her, "where will it end?" Something told me to go.

"Aaaah," she laughed, "in bed. Don't go up, boo'ful, Sybil'll tuck you in."

I shook my head. The stars were there, high, high, revolving. Then I closed my eyes and they sailed red behind my lids; then somewhat steadied I took her arm.

"Look, Sybil," I said, "stand here a minute while I go over to Fifth for a taxi. Stand right here, dear, and hold on."

We tottered before an ancient-looking building, its windows dark. Huge Greek medallions showed in spots of light upon its façade, above a dark labyrinthine pattern in the stone, and I propped her against the stoop with its carved stone monster. She leaned there, her hair wild, looking at me in the street light, smiling. Her face kept swinging to one side, her right eye desperately closed.

"Sure, boo'ful, sure," she said.

"I'll be right back," I said, backing away.

"Boo'ful," she called, *"my* boo'ful."

Hear the true affection, I thought, the adoration of the Boogie Bear, moving away. Was she calling me beautiful or boogieful, beautiful or sublime . . . What'd either mean? I am invisible . . .

I went on through the late street quiet, hoping that a cab would pass before I had gone all the way. Up ahead at Fifth the lights were bright, a few cars shooting across the gaping mouth of the street and above and beyond, the trees—great, dark, tall. What was going on, I wondered. Why call for me so late—and who?

I hurried ahead, my feet unsteady.

"Booo'ful," she called behind me, "boooooo'ful!"

I waved without looking back. Never again, no more, no more. I went on.

At Fifth a cab passed and I tried to hail it, only to hear someone's voice arise, the sound floating gaily by. I looked up the lighted avenue for another, hearing suddenly the screech of brakes and turning to see the cab stop and a white arm beckoning. The cab reversed, rolled close, settling with a bounce. I laughed. It was Sybil. I stumbled forward, came to the door. She smiled out at me, her head, framed in the window, still pulling to one side, her hair waving down.

"Get in, boo'ful, an' take me to Harlem . . ."

I shook my head, feeling it heavy and sad. "No," I said, "I've got work to do, Sybil. You'd better go home . . ."

"No, boo'ful, take me with you."

I turned to the driver, my hand upon the door. He was small, dark-haired and disapproving, a glint of red from the traffic light coloring the tip of his nose.

I gave him the address and my last five-dollar bill. He took it, glumly disapproving.

"No, boo'ful," she said, "I want to go to Harlem, be with you!"

"Good night," I said, stepping back from the curb.

We were in the middle of the block and I saw them pull away.

"Noo," she said, "noo, boo'ful. Don't leave . . ." Her face, wild-eyed and white, showed in the door. I stood there, watching him plunge swiftly and contemptuously out of sight, his tail light as red as his nose.

I walked with eyes closed, seeming to float and trying to clear my head, then opened them and crossed to the park side, along the cobbles. High above, the cars sailed round and round the drive, their headlights stabbing. All the taxis were hired, all going downtown. Center of gravity. I plodded on, my head awhirl.

Then near 110th Street I saw her again. She was waiting beneath a street lamp, waving. I wasn't surprised; I had become fatalistic. I came up slowly, hearing her laugh. She was ahead of me and beginning to run, barefoot, loosely, as in a dream. Running. Unsteadily but swift and me surprised and unable to catch up, lead-legged, seeing her ahead and calling, "Sybil, Sybil!" running lead-legged along the park side.

"Come on boo'ful," she called, looking back and stumbling. "Catch Sybil . . . Sybil," running barefoot and girdleless along the park.

I ran, the brief case heavy beneath my arm. Something told me I had to get to the office . . . "Sybil, wait!" I called.

She ran, the colors of her dress flaring flamelike in the bright places of the dark. A rustling motion, legs working awkwardly beneath her and white heels flashing, her skirts held high. Let her go, I thought. But now she was crossing the street and running wildly only to go down at the curb and standing and going down again, with a bumped backside, completely unsteady, now that her momentum was gone.

"Boo'ful," she said as I came up. "Damn, boo'ful, you push me?"

"Get up," I said without anger. "Get up," taking her soft arm. She stood, her arms flung wide for an embrace.

"No," I said, "this isn't Thursday. I've got to get there . . . What do they plan for me, Sybil?"

"Who, boo'ful?"

"Jack and George . . . Tobitt and all?"

"You ran me down, boo'ful," she said. "Forget them . . . bunch of dead-heads . . . unhipped, y'know. We didn't make this stinking world, boo'ful. Forget—"

I saw the taxi just in time, approaching swiftly from the corner, a double-decker bus looming two blocks behind. The cabbie looked over, his head out of the window, sitting high at the wheel as he made a swift U-turn and came alongside. His face was shocked, disbelieving.

"Come now, Sybil," I said, "and no tricks."

"Pardon me, old man," the driver said, his voice concerned, "but you're not taking her up in Harlem are you?"

"No, the lady's going downtown," I said. "Get in Sybil."

"Boo'ful's 'n ole dictator," she said to the driver, who looked at me silently, as though I were mad.

"A game stud," he muttered, "a most game stud!"

But she got in.

"Just 'n ole dictator, boo'ful."

"Look," I told him, "take her straight home and don't let her get out of the cab. I don't want her running around Harlem. She's precious, a great lady—"

"Sure, man, I don't blame you," he said. "Things is popping up there."

The cab was already rolling as I yelled, "What's going on?"

"They're taking the joint apart," he called above the shifting of the gears. I watched them go and made for the bus stop. This time I'll make sure, I thought, stepping out and flagging the bus and getting on. If she comes back, she'll find me gone. And I knew stronger than ever that I should hurry but was still too foggy in my mind, couldn't get myself together.

I sat gripping my brief case, my eyes closed, feeling the bus sailing swift beneath me. Soon it would turn up Seventh Avenue. Sybil, forgive me, I thought. The bus rolled.

But when I opened my eyes we were turning into Riverside Drive. This too I accepted calmly, the whole night was out of joint. I'd had too many drinks. Time ran fluid, invisible, sad. Looking out I could see a ship moving upstream, its running lights bright points in the night. The cool sea smell came through to me, constant and thick in the swiftly unfolding blur of anchored boats, dark water and lights pouring past. Across the river was Jersey and I remembered my entry into Harlem. Long past, I thought, long past. It was as if drowned in the river.

To my right and ahead the church spire towered high, crowned with a red light of warning. And now we were passing the hero's tomb and I recalled a visit there. You went up the steps and inside and you looked far below to find him, at rest, draped flags . . .

One Hundred and Twenty-fifth Street came quickly. I stumbled off, hearing the bus pull away as I faced the water. There was a light breeze, but now with the motion gone the heat returned, clinging. Far ahead in the dark I saw the monumental bridge, ropes of lights across the dark river; and closer, high above the shoreline, the Palisades, their revolutionary agony lost in the riotous lights of roller coasters. "The Time Is Now . . ." the sign across the river began, but with history stomping upon me with hobnailed boots, I thought with a laugh, why worry about time? I crossed the street to the drinking fountain, feeling the water cooling, going down, then dampened a handkerchief and swabbed my face, eyes. The water flashed, gurgled, sprayed. I pressed forward my face, feeling wet cool, hearing the infant joy of fountains. Then heard the other sound. It was not the river nor the curving cars that flashed through the dark, but pitched like a distant crowd or a swift river at floodtide.

I moved forward, found the steps and started down. Below the bridge lay the hard stone river of the street, and for a second I looked at the waves of cobblestones as though I expected water, as though the fountain above had drawn from them. Still I would enter and go across to Harlem. Below the steps the trolley rails gleamed steely. I hurried, the sound drawing closer, myriad-voiced, humming, enfolding me, numbing the air, as I started beneath the ramp. It came, a twitter, a coo, a subdued roar that seemed trying to tell me something, give me some message. I stopped, looking around me; the girders marched off rhythmically into the dark, over the cobblestones the red lights shone. Then I was beneath the bridge and it was as though they had been waiting for me and no one but me—dedicated and set aside for me—for an eternity. And I looked above toward the sound, my mind forming an image of wings, as something struck my face and streaked, and I could smell the foul air now, and see the encrusted barrage, feeling it streak my jacket and raising my brief case above my head and running, hearing it splattering around, falling like rain. I ran the gantlet, thinking, even the birds; even the pigeons and the sparrows and the goddam gulls! I ran blindly, boiling with outrage and despair and harsh laughter. Running from the birds to what, I didn't know. I ran. Why was I here at all?

I ran through the night, ran within myself. Ran.

Chapter twenty-five

When I reached Morningside the shooting sounded like a distant celebration of the Fourth of July, and I hurried forward. At St. Nicholas the street lights were out. A thunderous sound arose and I saw four men running toward me pushing something that jarred the walk. It was a safe.

"Say," I began.

"Get the hell out the way!"

I leaped aside, into the street, and there was a sudden and brilliant suspension of time, like the interval between the last ax stroke and the felling of a tall tree, in which there had been a loud noise followed by a loud silence. Then I was aware of figures crouching in doorways and along the curb; then time burst and I was down in the street, conscious but unable to rise, struggling against the street and seeing the flashes as the guns went off back at the corner of the avenue, aware to my left of the men still speeding the rumbling safe along the walk as back up the street, behind me, two policemen, almost invisible in black shirts, thrust flaming pistols before them. One

535

of the safe rollers pitched forward, and farther away, past the corner, a bullet struck an auto tire, the released air shrieking like a huge animal in agony. I rolled, flopping around, willing myself to crawl closer to the curb but unable, feeling a sudden wet warmth upon my face and seeing the safe shooting wildly into the intersection and the men rounding the corner into the dark, pounding, gone; gone now, as the skittering safe bounded off at a tangent, shot into the intersection and lodged in the third rail and sent up a curtain of sparks that lit up the block like a blue dream; a dream I was dreaming and through which I could see the cops braced as on a target range, feet forward, free arms akimbo, firing with deliberate aim.

"Get hold of Emergency!" one of them called, and I saw them turn and disappear where the dull glint of trolley rails faded off into the dark.

Suddenly the block leaped alive. Men who seemed to rise up out of the sidewalks were rushing into the store fronts above me, their voices rising excitedly. And now the blood was in my face and I could move, getting to my knees as someone out of the crowd was helping me to stand.

"You hurt, daddy?"

"Some—I don't know—" I couldn't quite see them.

"Damn! He's got a hole in his head!" a voice said.

A light flashed in my face, came close. I felt a hard hand upon my skull and moved away.

"Hell, it's just a nick," a voice said. "One them forty-fives hit your little finger you got to go down!"

"Well, this one over here is gone down for the last time," someone called from the walk. "They got him clean."

I wiped my face, my head ringing. Something was missing.

"Here, buddy, this yours?"

It was my brief case, extended to me by its handles. I

seized it with sudden panic, as though something infinitely precious had almost been lost to me.

"Thanks," I said, peering into their dim, blue-tinted features. I looked at the dead man. He lay face forward, the crowd working around him. I realized suddenly that it might have been me huddled there, feeling too that I had seen him there before, in the bright light of noon, long ago ... how long? Knew his name, I thought, and suddenly my knees flowed forward. I sat there, my fist that gripped the brief case bruising against the street, my head slumped forward. They were going around me.

"Get off my foot, man," I heard. "Quit shoving. There's plenty for everybody."

There was something I had to do and I knew that my forgetfulness wasn't real, as one knows that the forgotten details of certain dreams are not truly forgotten but evaded. I knew, and in my mind I was trying to reach through the gray veil that now seemed to hang behind my eyes as opaquely as the blue curtain that screened the street beyond the safe. The dizziness left and I managed to stand, holding onto my brief case, pressing a handkerchief to my head. Up the street there sounded the crashing of huge sheets of glass and through the blue mysteriousness of the dark the walks shimmered like shattered mirrors. All the street's signs were dead, all the day sounds had lost their stable meaning. Somewhere a burglar alarm went off, a meaningless blangy sound, followed by the joyful shouts of looters.

"Come on," someone called nearby.

"Let's go, buddy," the man who had helped me said. He took my arm, a thin man who carried a large cloth bag slung over his shoulder.

"The shape you in wouldn't do to leave you round here," he said. "You act like you drunk."

"Go where?" I said.

"Where? Hell, man. Everywhere. We git to moving, no telling where we might go—Hey, Dupre!" he called.

"Say, man—Goddam! Don't be calling my name so loud," a voice answered. "Here, I am over here, gitting me some work shirts."

"Git some for me, Du," he said.

"All right, but don't think I'm your papa," the answer came.

I looked at the thin man, feeling a surge of friendship. He didn't know me, his help was disinterested . . .

"Hey, Du," he called, "we go'n do it?"

"Hell yes, soon as I git me these shirts."

The crowd was working in and out of the stores like ants around spilled sugar. From time to time there came the crash of glass, shots; fire trucks in distant streets.

"How you feel?" the man said.

"Still fuzzy," I said, "and weak."

"Le's see if it's stopped bleeding. Yeah, you'll be all right."

I saw him vaguely though his voice came clear.

"Sure," I said.

"Man, you lucky you ain't dead. These sonsabitches is really shooting now," he said. "Over on Lenox they was aiming up in the air. If I could find me a rifle, I'd show 'em! Here, take you a drink of this good Scotch," he said, taking a quart bottle from a hip pocket. "I got me a whole case stashed what I got from a liquor store over there. Over there all you got to do is breathe, and you drunk, man. Drunk! Hundred proof bonded whiskey flowing all in the gutters."

I took a drink, shuddering as the whiskey went down but thankful for the shock it gave me. There was a bursting, tearing movement of people around me, dark figures in a blue glow.

"Look at them take it away," he said, looking into the dark action of the crowd. "Me, I'm tired. Was you over on Lenox?"

"No," I said, seeing a woman moving slowly past with a row of about a dozen dressed chickens suspended by their necks from the handle of a new straw broom . . .

"Hell, you ought to see it, man. Everything is tore up. By now the womens is picking it clean. I saw one ole woman with a whole side of a cow on her back. Man, she was 'bout bent bowlegged trying to make it home—Here come Dupre now," he said, breaking off.

I saw a little hard man come out of the crowd carrying several boxes. He wore three hats upon his head, and several pairs of suspenders flopped about his shoulders, and now as he came toward us I saw that he wore a pair of gleaming new rubber hip boots. His pockets bulged and over his shoulder he carried a cloth sack that swung heavily behind him.

"Damn, Dupre," my friend said, pointing to his head, "you got one of them for me? What kind is they?"

Dupre stopped and looked at him. "With all them hats in there and I'm going to come out with anything but a *Dobbs*? Man, are you *mad*? All them new, pretty-colored *Dobbs*? Come on, let's get going before the cops git back. Damn, look at that thing blaze!"

I looked toward the curtain of blue fire, through which vague figures toiled. Dupre called out and several men left the crowd and joined us in the street. We moved off, my friend (Scofield, the others called him) leading me along. My head throbbed, still bled.

"Look like you got you some loot too," he said, pointing to my brief case.

"Not much," I said, thinking, loot? *Loot*? And suddenly I knew why it was heavy, remembering Mary's broken bank

and the coins; and now I found myself opening the brief case
and dropping all my papers—my Brotherhood identification,
the anonymous letter, along with Clifton's doll—into it.

"Fill it up, man. Don't you be bashful. You wait till we
tackle one of these pawnshops. That Du's got him a cotton-
picking sack fulla stuff. *He* could go into business."

"Well, I'll be damn," a man on the other side of me
said. "I *thought* that was a cotton sack. Where'd he get that
thing?"

"He brought it with him when he come North," Scofield
said. "Du swears that when he goes back he'll have it full of
ten-dollar bills. Hell, after tonight he'll need him a warehouse
for all the stuff he's got. You fill that brief case, buddy. Get
yourself something!"

"No," I said, "I've enough in it already." And now I
remembered very clearly where I'd started out for but could
not leave them.

"Maybe you right," Scofield said. "How I know, you
might have it full of diamonds or something. A man oughtn't
to be greedy. Though it's time something like this happened."

We moved along. Should I leave, get on to the district?
Where were they, at the birthday celebration?

"How did all this get started?" I said.

Scofield seemed surprised. "Damn if I know, man. A cop
shot a woman or something."

Another man moved close to us as somewhere a piece of
heavy steel rang down.

"Hell, that wasn't what started it," he said. "It was that
fellow, what's his name . . . ?"

"Who?" I said. "What's his name?"

"That young guy!"

"You know, everybody's mad about it . . ."

Clifton, I thought. It's for Clifton. A night for Clifton.

"Aw man, don't tell me," Scofield said. "Didn't I see it with my own eyes? About eight o'clock down on Lenox and 123rd this paddy slapped a kid for grabbing a Baby Ruth and the kid's mama took it up and then the paddy slapped her and that's when hell broke loose."

"You were there?" I said.

"Same's I'm here. Some fellow said the kid made the paddy mad by grabbing a candy named after a white woman."

"Damn if that's the way I heard it," another man said. "When I come up they said a white woman set it off by trying to take a black gal's man."

"Damn *who* started it," Dupre said. "All I want is for it to last a while."

"It was a white gal, all right, but that wasn't the way it was. She was drunk—" another voice said.

But it couldn't have been Sybil, I thought; it had already started.

"You wahn know who started it?" a man holding a pair of binoculars called from the window of a pawnshop. "You wahn really to know?"

"Sure," I said.

"Well, you don't need to go no further. It was started by that great leader, Ras the Destroyer!"

"That monkey-chaser?" someone said.

"Listen, bahstard!"

"Don't nobody know how it started," Dupre said.

"Somebody has to know," I said.

Scofield held his whiskey toward me. I refused it.

"Hell, man, it just exploded. These is dog days," he said.

"*Dog* days?"

"Sho, this hot weather."

"I tell you they mad over what happen to that young fellow, what's-his-name . . ."

We were passing a building now and I heard a voice calling frantically, "Colored store! Colored store!"

"Then put up a sign, motherfouler," a voice said. "You probably rotten as the others."

"Listen at the bastard. For one time in his life he's glad to be colored," Scofield said.

"Colored store," the voice went on automatically.

"Hey! You sho you ain't got some white blood?"

"No, *sir!*" the voice said.

"Should I bust him, man?"

"For what? He ain't got a damn thing. Let the mother-fouler alone."

A few doors away we came to a hardware store. "This is the first stop, men," Dupre said.

"What happens now?" I said.

"Who you?" he said, cocking his thrice-hatted head.

"Nobody, just one of the boys—" I began.

"You sho you ain't somebody I know?"

"I'm pretty sure," I said.

"He's all right, Du," said Scofield. "Them cops shot him."

Dupre looked at me and kicked something—a pound of butter, sending it smearing across the hot street. "We fixing to do something what needs to be done," he said. "First we gets a flashlight for everybody . . . And let's have some organization, y'all. Don't everybody be running over everybody else. Come on!"

"Come on in, buddy," Scofield said.

I felt no need to lead or leave them; was glad to follow; was gripped by a need to see where and to what they would lead. And all the time the thought that I should go to the district was with me. We went inside the store, into the dark glinting with metal. They moved carefully, and I could hear them searching, sweeping objects to the floor. The cash register rang.

"Here some flashlights over here," someone called.

"How many?" Dupre said.

"Plenty, man."

"Okay, pass out one to everybody. They got batteries?"

"Naw, but there's plenty them too, 'bout a dozen boxes."

"Okay, give me one with batteries so I can find the buckets. Then every man get him a light."

"Here some buckets over here," Scofield said.

"Then all we got to find is where he keeps the oil."

"Oil?" I said.

"*Coal* oil, man. And hey, y'all," he called, "don't nobody be smoking in here."

I stood beside Scofield listening to the noise as he took a stack of zinc buckets and passed them out. Now the store leaped alive with flashing lights and flickering shadows.

"Keep them lights down on the floor," Dupre called. "No use letting folks see who we are. Now when you get your buckets line up and let me fill 'em."

"Listen to ole Du lay it down—he's a bitch, ain't he, buddy? He always liked to lead things. And always leading me into trouble."

"What are we getting ready to do?" I said.

"You'll see," Dupre said. "Hey, you over there. Come on from behind that counter and take this bucket. Don't you see ain't nothing in that cash register, that if it was I'd have it myself?"

Suddenly the banging of buckets ceased. We moved into the back room. By the light of a flash I could see a row of fuel drums mounted on racks. Dupre stood before them in his new hip boots and filled each bucket with oil. We moved in slow order. Our buckets filled, we filed out into the street. I stood there in the dark feeling a rising excitement as their voices played around me. What was the meaning of it all? What should I think of it, *do* about it?

"With this stuff," Dupre said, "we better walk in the middle of the street. It's just down around the corner."

Then as we moved off a group of boys ran among us and the men started using their lights, revealing darting figures in blonde wigs, the tails of their stolen dress coats flying. Behind them in hot pursuit came a gang armed with dummy rifles taken from an Army & Navy Store. I laughed with the others, thinking: A holy holiday for Clifton.

"Put out them lights!" Dupre commanded.

Behind us came the sound of screams, laughter; ahead the footfalls of the running boys, distant fire trucks, shooting, and in the quiet intervals, the steady filtering of shattered glass. I could smell the kerosene as it sloshed from the buckets and slapped against the street.

Suddenly Scofield grabbed my arm. "Good God, look-a-yonder!"

And I saw a crowd of men running up pulling a Borden's milk wagon, on top of which, surrounded by a row of railroad flares, a huge woman in a gingham pinafore sat drinking beer from a barrel which sat before her. The men would run furiously a few paces and stop, resting between the shafts, run a few paces and rest, shouting and laughing and drinking from a jug, as she on top threw back her head and shouted passionately in a full-throated voice of blues singer's timbre:

> *If it hadn't been for the referee,*
> *Joe Louis woulda killed*
> *Jim Jefferie*
> *Free beer!!*

—sloshing the dipper of beer around.

We stepped aside, amazed, as she bowed graciously from side to side like a tipsy fat lady in a circus parade, the dipper like a gravy spoon in her enormous hand. Then she laughed and drank deeply while reaching over nonchalantly with her free hand to send quart after quart of milk crashing into the street. And all the time the men running with the wagon over the debris. Around me there were shouts of laughter and disapproval.

"Somebody better stop them fools," Scofield said in outrage. "That's what I call taking things too far. Goddam, how the hell they going to get her down from there after she gits fulla beer? Somebody answer me that. How they going to get her down? 'Round here throwing away all that good milk!"

The big woman left me unnerved. Milk and beer—I felt sad, watching the wagon careen dangerously as they went around a corner. We went on, avoiding the broken bottles as now the spilling kerosene splashed into the pale spilt milk. How much has happened? Why was I torn? We moved around a corner. My head still ached.

Scofield touched my arm. "Here we is," he said.

We had come to a huge tenement building.

"Where are we?" I said.

"This the place where most of us live," he said. "Come on."

So that was it, the meaning of the kerosene. I couldn't believe it, couldn't believe they had the nerve. All the windows seemed empty. They'd blacked it out themselves. I saw now only by flash or flame.

"Where will you live?" I said, looking up, up.

"You call *this* living?" Scofield said. "It's the only way to git rid of it, man . . ."

I looked for hesitation in their vague forms. They stood looking at the building rising above us, the liquid dark of the oil simmering dully in the stray flecks of light that struck their pails, bent forward, their shoulders bowed. None said "no," by word or stance. And in the dark windows and on the roofs above I could now discern the forms of women and children.

Dupre moved toward the building.

"Now look ahere, y'all," he said, his triple-hatted head showing grotesquely atop the stoop. "I wants all the women and chillun and the old and the sick folks brought out. And when you takes your buckets up the stairs I wants you to go clean to the top. I mean the *top!* And when you git there I want you to start using your flashlights in every room to make sure nobody gits left behind, then when you git 'em out start splashing coal oil. Then when you git it splashed I'm going to holler, and when I holler three times I want you to light them matches and git. After that it's every tub on its own black bottom!"

It didn't occur to me to interfere, or to question . . . They had a plan. Already I could see the women and children coming down the steps. A child was crying. And suddenly everyone paused, turning, looking off into the dark. Somewhere nearby an incongruous sound shook the dark, an air hammer pounding like a machine gun. They paused with the sensitivity of grazing deer, then returned to their work, the women and children once more moving.

"That's right, y'all. You ladies move on up the street to the folks you going to stay with," Dupre said. "And keep holt them kids!"

Someone pounded my back and I swung around, seeing a woman push past me and climb up to catch Dupre's arm, their two figures seeming to blend as her voice arose, thin, vibrant and desperate.

"Please, Dupre," she said, *"please.* You know my time's almost here . . . you *know* it is. If you do it now, where am I going to go?"

Dupre pulled away and rose to a higher step. He looked down at her, shaking his thrice-hatted head. "Now git on out the way, Lottie," he said patiently. "Why you have to start this now? We done been all over it and you know I ain't go'n change. And lissen here, the resta y'all," he said, reaching into the top of his hip boot and producing a nickel-plated revolver and waving it around, "don't think they's going to be any *mind*-changing either. And I don't aim for no arguments neither."

"You goddam right, Dupre. We wid you!"

"My kid died from the t-bees in that deathtrap, but I bet a man ain't no more go'n be *born* in there," he said. "So now, Lottie, you go on up the street and let us mens git going."

She stood back, crying. I looked at her, in house shoes, her breasts turgid, her belly heavy and high. In the crowd, women's hands took her away, her large liquid eyes turned for a second toward the man in the rubber boots.

What type of man is he, what would Jack say of him? Jack, *Jack!* And where was he in this?

"Let's go, buddy," Scofield said, nudging me. I followed him, filled with a sense of Jack's outrageous unreality. We went in, up the stairs, flashing our lights. Ahead I saw Dupre moving. He was a type of man nothing in my life had taught me to see, to understand, or respect, a man outside the scheme till now. We entered rooms littered with the signs of swift emptying. It was hot, close.

"This here's my own apartment," Scofield said. "And ain't the bedbugs going to get a surprise!"

We slopped the kerosene about, upon an old mattress, along the floor; then moved into the hall, using the flashlights. From all through the building came the sounds of footsteps, of splashing oil, the occasional prayerful protest of some old one being forced to leave. The men worked in silence now, like moles deep in the earth. Time seemed to hold. No one laughed. Then from below came Dupre's voice.

"Okay, mens. We got everybody out. Now starting with the top floor I want you to start striking matches. Be careful and don't set yourself on fire . . ."

There was still some kerosene left in Scofield's bucket and I saw him pick up a rag and drop it in; then came the sputtering of a match and I saw the room leap to flame. The heat flared up and I backed away. He stood there silhouetted against the red flare, looking into the flames, shouting.

"Goddam you rotten sonsabitches. You didn't think I'd do it but there it is. You wouldn't fix it up. Now see how you like it."

"Let's go," I said.

Below us, men shot downstairs five and six steps at a time, moving in the weird light of flash and flame in long, dream-bounds. On each floor as I passed, smoke and flame arose. And now I was seized with a fierce sense of exaltation. They've done it, I thought. They organized it and carried it through alone; the decision their own and their own action. Capable of their own action . . .

There came a thunder of footfalls above me, someone calling, "Keep going man, it's hell upstairs. Somebody done opened the door to the roof and them flames is leaping."

"Come on," Scofield said.

I moved, feeling something slip and was halfway down the next flight before realizing that my brief case was gone. For a second I hesitated, but I'd had it too long to leave it now.

"Come on, buddy," Scofield called, "we caint be fooling around."

"In a second," I said.

Men were shooting past. I bent over, holding on to the handrail, and shouldered my way back up the stairs, using my flash along each step, back slowly, finding it, an oily footstep embedded with crushed pieces of plaster showing upon its leather side; getting it now and turning to bound down again. The oil won't come off easily, I thought with a pang. But this was it, what I had known was coming around the dark corner of my mind, had known and tried to tell the committee and which they had ignored. I plunged down, shaking with fierce excitement.

At the landing I saw a bucket full of kerosene and seized it, flinging it impulsively into a burning room. A huge puff of smoke-fringed flame filled the doorway, licking outward toward me. I ran, choking and coughing as I plunged. They did it themselves, I thought, holding my breath—planned it, organized it, applied the flame.

I burst into the air and the exploding sounds of the night, and I did not know if the voice was that of a man, woman or child, but for a moment I stood on the stoop with the red doorway behind me and heard the voice call me by my Brotherhood name.

It was as though I had been aroused from sleep and for an instant I stood there looking, listening to the voice almost lost in the clamour of shouts, screams, burglar alarms and sirens.

"Brother, ain't it wonderful," it called. "You said you would lead us, you really said it . . ."

I went down into the street, going slowly but filled with a feverish inner need to be away from that voice. Where had Scofield gone?

Most of their eyes, white in the flame-flushed dark, looked toward the building.

But now I heard someone say, "Woman, who you say that is?" And she proudly repeated my name.

"Where he go? Get him, mahn, Ras wahnt him!"

I went into the crowd, walking slowly, smoothly into the dark crowd, the whole surface of my skin alert, my back chilled, looking, listening to those moving with a heaving and sweating and a burr of talk around me and aware that now that I wanted to see them, needed to see them, I could not; feeling them, a dark mass in motion on a dark night, a black river ripping through a black land; and Ras or Tarp could move beside me and I wouldn't know. I was one with the mass, moving down the littered street over the puddles of oil and milk, my personality blasted. Then I was in the next block, dodging in and out, hearing them somewhere in the crowd behind me; moving on through the sound of sirens and burglar alarms to be swept into a swifter crowd and pushed along, half-running, half-walking, trying to see behind me and wondering where the others had gone. There was shooting back there now, and on either side of me they were throwing garbage cans, bricks and pieces of metal into plate-glass windows. I moved, feeling as though a huge force was on the point of bursting. Shouldering my way to the side I stood in a doorway and watched them move, feeling a certain vindication as now I thought of the message that had brought me here. Who had called, one of the district members or someone from Jack's birthday celebration? Who wanted me at the district after it was too late? Very well, I'd go there now. I'd see what the master minds thought now. Where were they anyway, and what profound conclusions were they drawing? What *ex post facto* lessons of history? And that crash over the telephone, had that been the beginning, or had Jack simply dropped his eye? I laughed drunkenly, the eruption paining my head.

Suddenly the shooting ceased and in the silence there was the sound of voices, footfalls, labor.

"Hey, buddy," somebody said beside me, "where you going?" It was Scofield.

"It's either run or get knocked down," I said. "I thought you were still back there."

"I cut out, man. A building two doors away started to burn and they had to git the fire department . . . Damn! wasn't for this noise I'd swear those bullets was mosquitoes."

"Watch out!" I warned, pulling him away from where a man lay propped against a post, tightening a tourniquet around his gashed arm.

Scofield flashed his light and for a second I saw the black man, his face gray with shock, watching the jetting pulsing of his blood spurting into the street. Then, compelled, I reached down and twisted the tourniquet, feeling the blood warm upon my hand, seeing the pulsing cease.

"You done stopped it," a young man said, looking down.

"Here," I said, "you take it, hold it tight. Get him to a doctor."

"Ain't you a doctor?"

"Me?" I said. *"Me?* Are you crazy? If you want him to live, get him away from here."

"Albert done gone for one," the boy said. "But I thought you was one. You—"

"No," I said, looking at my bloody hands, "no, not me. You hold it tight until the doctor comes. I couldn't cure a headache."

I stood wiping my hands against the brief case, looking down at the big man, his back resting against the post with his eyes closed, the boy holding desperately to the tourniquet made of what had been a bright new tie.

"Come on," I said.

"Say," Scofield said when we were past, "wasn't that you that woman was calling *brother* back yonder?"

"Brother? No, it must have been some other guy."

"You know, man, I think I seen you before somewhere.

You ever was in Memphis . . . ? Say, look what's coming," he said, pointing, and I looked through the dark to see a squad of white-helmeted policemen charge forward and break for shelter as a rain of bricks showered down from the building tops. Some of the white helmets, racing for the doorways, turned to fire, and I heard Scofield grunt and go down and I dropped beside him, seeing the red burst of fire and hearing the shrill scream, like an arching dive, curving from above to end in a crunching thud in the street. It was as though it landed in my stomach, sickening me, and I crouched, looking down past Scofield, who lay just ahead of me, to see the dark crushed form from the roof; and farther away, the body of a cop, his helmet making a small white luminous mound in the dark.

I moved now to see whether Scofield was hit, just as he squirmed around and cursed at the cops who were trying to rescue the one who was down, his voice furious, as he stretched full length firing away with a nickel-plated pistol like that Dupre had waved.

"Git the hell down, man," he yelled over his shoulder. "I been wanting to blast 'em a long time."

"No, not with that thing," I said. "Let's get out of here."

"Hell, man, I can *shoot* this thing," he said.

I rolled behind a pile of baskets filled with rotting chickens now, and to my left, upon the littered curb, a woman and man crouched behind an upturned delivery cart.

"Dehart," she said, "let's get up on the hill, Dehart. Up with the respectable people!"

"Hill, hell! We stay right here," the man said. "This thing's just starting. If it become a sho 'nough race riot I want to be here where there'll be some fighting back."

The words struck like bullets fired close range, blasting my satisfaction to earth. It was as though the uttered word had given meaning to the night, almost as though it had created it, brought it into being in the instant his breath vibrated small against the loud, riotous air. And in defining, in giving organization to the fury, it seemed to spin me around, and in my mind I was looking backward over the days since Clifton's death ... Could this be the answer, could this be what the committee had planned, the answer to why they'd surrendered our influence to Ras? Suddenly I heard the hoarse explosion of a shotgun, and looked past Scofield's glinting pistol to the huddled form from the roof. It was suicide, without guns it was suicide, and not even the pawnshops here had guns for sale; and yet I knew with a shattering dread that the uproar which for the moment marked primarily the crash of men against things—against stores, markets—could swiftly become the crash of men against men and with most of the guns and numbers on the other side. I could see it now, see it clearly and in growing magnitude. It was not suicide, but murder. The committee had planned it. And I had helped, had been a tool. A tool just at the very moment I had thought myself free. By pretending to agree I *had* indeed agreed, had made myself responsible for that huddled form lighted by flame and gunfire in the street, and all the others whom now the night was making ripe for death.

The brief case swung heavy against my leg as I ran, going away, leaving Scofield cursing his lack of bullets behind me, running wildly and swinging the brief case hard against the head of a dog that leaped at me out of the crowd, sending him yelping away. To my right lay a quiet residential street with trees, and I entered it, going toward Seventh Avenue, toward the district, filled now with horror and hatred. They'll pay, they'll pay, I thought. They'll pay!

The street lay dead quiet in the light of the lately risen moon, the gunfire thin and for a moment, distant. The rioting seemed in another world. For a moment I paused beneath a low, thickly leaved tree, looking down the well-kept doily-shadowed walks past the silent houses. It was as though the tenants had vanished, leaving the houses silent with all windows shaded, refugees from a rising flood. Then I heard the single footfalls coming doggedly toward me in the night, an eerie slapping sound followed by a precise and hallucinated cry—

> "Time's flying
> Souls dying
> The coming of the Lord
> Draweth niiiiigh!"

—as though he had run for days, for years. He trotted past where I stood beneath the tree, his bare feet slapping the walk in silence, going for a few feet and then the high, hallucinated cry beginning again.

I ran into the avenue where in the light of a flaming liquor store I saw three old women scurrying toward me with raised skirts loaded with canned goods.

"I can't stop it just yet, but have mercy, Lord," one of them said. "Do, Jesus, do, sweet Jesus . . ."

I moved ahead, the fumes of alcohol and burning tar in my nostrils. Down the avenue to my left a single street lamp still glowed where the long block was intersected on my right by a street, and I could see a crowd rushing a store that faced the intersection, moving in, and a fusillade of canned goods, salami, liverwurst, hogs heads and chitterlings belching out to those outside and a bag of flour bursting white upon them; as now out of the dark of the intersecting street two mounted policemen came at a gallop, heaving huge and heavy-hooved, charging straight into the swarming mass. And I could see the great forward lunge of the horses and the crowd breaking and rolling back like a wave, back, and screaming and cursing, and some laughing—back and around and out into the avenue, stumbling and pushing, as the horses, heads high and bits froth-flecked, went over the curb to land stiff-legged and slide over the cleared walk as upon ice skates and past, carried by the force of the charge, sideways now, legs stiff, sparks flying, to where another crowd looted another store. And my heart tightened as the first crowd swung imperturbably back to their looting with derisive cries, like sandpipers swinging around to glean the shore after a furious wave's recession.

Cursing Jack and the Brotherhood I moved around a steel grill torn from the front of a pawnshop, seeing the troopers galloping back and the riders lifting the horses to charge again, grim and skillful in white steel helmets, and the charge begin-ning. This time a man went down and I saw a woman swing-ing a gleaming frying pan hard against the horse's rump and the horse neighing and beginning to plunge. They'll pay, I thought, they'll pay. They came toward me as I ran, a crowd of men and women carrying cases of beer, cheese, chains of linked sausage, watermelons, sacks of sugar, hams, cornmeal, fuel lamps. If only it could stop right here, here; here before the others came with their guns. I ran.

There was no firing now. But *when*, I thought, how long before it starts?

"Git a side of bacon, Joe," a woman called. "Git a side of bacon, Joe, git Wilson's."

"Lord, Lord, Lord," a dark voice called from the dark.

I went on, plunged in a sense of painful isolation as I reached 125th Street and started east. A squad of mounted police galloped past. Men with sub-machine guns were guard-ing a bank and a large jewelry store. I moved out to the center of the street, running down the trolley rails.

The moon was high now and before me the shattered

glass glittered in the street like the water of a flooded river upon the surface of which I ran as in a dream, avoiding by fate alone the distorted objects washed away by the flood. Then suddenly I seemed to sink, sucked under: Ahead of me the body hung, white, naked, and horribly feminine from a lamp-post. I felt myself spin around with horror and it was as though I had turned some nightmarish somersault. I whirled, still moving by reflex, back-tracking and stopped and now there was another and another, seven—all hanging before a gutted store-front. I stumbled, hearing the cracking of bones underfoot and saw a physician's skeleton shattered on the street, the skull rolling away from the backbone, as I steadied long enough to notice the unnatural stiffness of those hanging above me. They were mannequins—"Dummies!" I said aloud. Hairless, bald and sterilely feminine. And I recalled the boys in the blonde wigs, expecting the relief of laughter, but suddenly was more devastated by the humor than by the horror. But are they unreal, I thought; *are* they? What if one, even *one* is real— is . . . Sybil? I hugged my brief case, backing away, and ran . . .

THEY moved in a tight-knit order, carrying sticks and clubs, shotguns and rifles, led by Ras the Exhorter become Ras the Destroyer upon a great black horse. A new Ras of a haughty, vulgar dignity, dressed in the costume of an Abyssinian chieftain; a fur cap upon his head, his arm bearing a shield, a cape made of the skin of some wild animal around his shoulders. A figure more out of a dream than out of Harlem, than out of even this Harlem night, yet real, alive, alarming.

"Come away from that stupid looting," he called to a group before a store. "Come jine with us to burst in the armory and get guns and ammunition!"

And hearing his voice I opened my brief case and searched

for my dark glasses, my Rineharts, drawing them out only to see the crushed lenses fall to the street. Rinehart, I thought, Rinehart! I turned. The police were back there behind me; if shooting started I'd be caught in the crossfire. I felt in my brief case, feeling papers, shattered iron, coins, my fingers closing over Tarp's leg chain, and I slipped it over my knuckles, trying to think, I closed the flap, locking it. A new mood was settling over me as they came on, a larger crowd than Ras had ever drawn. I went calmly forward, holding the heavy case but moving with a certain new sense of self, and with it a feeling almost of relief, almost of a sigh. I knew suddenly what I had to do, knew it even before it shaped itself completely in my mind.

Someone called, "Look!" and Ras bent down from the horse, saw me and flung, of all things, a spear, and I fell forward at the movement of his arm, catching myself upon my hands as a tumbler would, and heard the shock of it piercing one of the hanging dummies. I stood, my brief case coming with me.

"Betrayer!" Ras shouted.

"It's the brother," someone said. They moved up around the horse excited and not quite decided, and I faced him, knowing I was no worse than he, nor any better, and that all the months of illusion and the night of chaos required but a few simple words, a mild, even a meek, muted action to clear the air. To awaken them and me.

"I am no longer their brother," I shouted. "They want a race riot and I am against it. The more of us who are killed, the better they like—"

"Ignore his lying tongue," Ras shouted. "Hang him up to teach the black people a lesson, and theer be no more traitors. No more Uncle Toms. Hang him up theer with them blahsted dummies!"

"But anyone can see it," I shouted. "It's true, I was

betrayed by those who I thought were our friends—but they counted on this man, too. They needed this *destroyer* to do their work. They deserted you so that in your despair you'd follow this man to your destruction. Can't you see it? They want you guilty of your own murder, your own sacrifice!"

"Grab him!" Ras shouted.

Three men stepped forward and I reached up without thinking, actually a desperate oratorical gesture of disagreement and defiance, as I shouted, "No!" But my hand struck the spear and I wrenched it free, gripping it midshaft, point forward. "They want this to happen," I said. "They planned it. They want the mobs to come uptown with machine guns and rifles. They want the streets to flow with blood; your blood, black blood and white blood, so that they can turn your death and sorrow and defeat into propaganda. It's simple, you've known it a long time. It goes, 'Use a nigger to catch a nigger.' Well, they used me to catch you and now they're using Ras to do away with me and to prepare your sacrifice. Don't you see it? Isn't it clear . . . ?"

"Hang the lying traitor," Ras shouted. "What are you waiting for?"

I saw a group of men start forward.

"Wait," I said. "Then kill me for myself, for my own mistake, then leave it there. Don't kill me for those who are downtown laughing at the trick they played—"

But even as I spoke I knew it was no good. I had no words and no eloquence, and when Ras thundered, "Hang him!" I stood there facing them, and it seemed unreal. I faced them knowing that the madman in a foreign costume was real and yet unreal, knowing that he wanted my life, that he held me responsible for all the nights and days and all the suffering and for all that which I was incapable of controlling, and I no hero, but short and dark with only a certain eloquence and a bottomless capacity for being a fool to mark me from the rest; saw them, recognized them at last as those whom I had failed and of whom I was now, just now, a leader, though leading them, running ahead of them, only in the stripping away of my illusionment.

I looked at Ras on his horse and at their handful of guns and recognized the absurdity of the whole night and of the simple yet confoundingly complex arrangement of hope and desire, fear and hate, that had brought me here still running, and knowing now who I was and where I was and knowing too that I had no longer to run for or from the Jacks and the Emersons and the Bledsoes and Nortons, but only from their confusion, impatience, and refusal to recognize the beautiful absurdity of their American identity and mine. I stood there, knowing that by dying, that by being hanged by Ras on this street in this destructive night, I would perhaps move them one fraction of a bloody step closer to a definition of who they were and of what I was and had been. But the definition would have been too narrow; I was invisible, and hanging would not bring me to visibility, even to their eyes, since they wanted my death not for myself alone but for the chase I'd been on all my life; because of the way I'd run, been run, chased, operated, purged—although to a great extent I could have done nothing else, given their blindness (didn't they tolerate both Rinehart and Bledsoe?) and my invisibility. And that I, a little black man with an assumed name should die because a big black man in his hatred and confusion over the nature of a reality that seemed controlled solely by white men whom I knew to be as blind as he, was just too much, too outrageously absurd. And I knew that it was better to live out one's own absurdity than to die for that of others, whether for Ras's or Jack's.

So when Ras yelled, "Hang him!" I let fly the spear and it was as though for a moment I had surrendered my life and begun to live again, watching it catch him as he turned his head to shout, ripping through both cheeks, and saw the surprised pause of the crowd as Ras wrestled with the spear that locked his jaws. Some of the men raised their guns, but they were too close to shoot and I hit the first with Tarp's leg chain and the other in the middle with my brief case, then ran through a looted store, hearing the blanging of the burglar alarm as I scrambled over scattered shoes, upturned showcases, chairs—back to where I saw the moonlight through the rear door ahead. They came behind me like a draft of flames and I led them through and around to the avenue, and if they'd fired they could have had me, but it was important to them that they hang me, lynch me even, since that was the way they ran, had been taught to run. I should die by hanging alone, as though only hanging would settle things, even the score. So I ran expecting death between the shoulder blades or through the back of my head, and as I ran I was trying to get to Mary's. It was not a decision of thought but something I realized suddenly while running over puddles of milk in the black street, stopping to swing the heavy brief case and the leg chain, slipping and sliding out of their hands.

If only I could turn around and drop my arms and say, "Look, men, give me a break, we're all black folks together . . . Nobody cares." Though now I knew *we* cared, they at last cared enough to act—so I thought. If only I could say, "Look, they've played a trick on us, the same old trick with new variations—let's stop running and respect and love one another . . ." If only—I thought, running into another crowd now and thinking I'd gotten away, only to catch a punch on my jaw as one closed in shouting, and feeling the leg chain bounce as I caught his head and spurted forward, turning out of the avenue only to be struck by a spray of water that seemed to descend from above. It was a main that had burst, throwing a fierce curtain of spray into the night. I was going for Mary's but I was moving downtown through the dripping street rather than up, and, as I started through, a mounted policeman charged through the spray, the horse black and dripping, charging through and looming huge and unreal, neighing and clopping across the pavement upon me now as I slipped to my knees and saw the huge pulsing bulk floating down upon and over me, the sound of hooves and screams and a rush of water coming through distantly as though I sat remote in a padded room, then over, almost past, the hair of the tail a fiery lash across my eyes. I stumbled about in circles, blindly swinging the brief case, the image of a fiery comet's tail burning my smarting lids; turning and swinging blindly with brief case and leg chain and hearing the gallop begin as I floundered helplessly; and now moving straight into the full, naked force of the water, feeling its power like a blow, wet and thudding and cold, then through it and able partly to see just as another horse dashed up and through, a hunter taking a barrier, the rider slanting backward, the horse rising, then hit and swallowed by the rising spray. I stumbled down the street, the comet tail in my eyes, seeing a little better now and looking back to see the water spraying like a mad geyser in the moonlight. To Mary, I thought, to Mary.

THERE were rows of iron fences backed by low hedges before the houses and I stumbled behind one and lay panting to rest from the crushing force of the water. But hardly had I settled down, the dry, dog-day smell of the hedge in my nose, when they stopped before the house, leaning upon the fence. They were passing a bottle around and their voices sounded spent of strong emotion.

"This is some night," one of them said. "Ain't this some night?"

"It's 'bout like the rest."

"Why you say that?"

" 'Cause it's fulla fucking and fighting and drinking and lying—gimme that bottle."

"Yeah, but tonight I seen some things I never seen before."

"You think *you* seen something? Hell, you ought to been over on Lenox about two hours ago. You know that stud Ras the Destroyer? Well, man, *he* was spitting blood."

"That crazy guy?"

"Hell, yes, man, he had him a big black hoss and a fur cap and some kind of old lion skin or something over his shoulders and he was raising hell. Goddam if he wasn't a *sight*, riding up and down on this ole hoss, you know, one of the kind that pulls vegetable wagons, and he got him a cowboy saddle and some big spurs."

"Aw naw, man!"

"Hell, yes! Riding up and down the block yelling, 'Destroy 'em! Drive 'em out! Burn 'em out! I, Ras, commands you.' You get that, man," he said. " 'I, *Ras*, commands you—to destroy them to the last piece of rotten fish!' And 'bout that time some joker with a big ole Georgia voice sticks his head out the window and yells, 'Ride 'em, cowboy. Give 'em hell and bananas.' And man, that crazy sonofabitch up there on that hoss looking like death eating a sandwich, he reaches down and comes up with a forty-five and starts blazing up at that window— And man, talk about cutting out! In a second wasn't nobody left but ole Ras up there on that hoss with that lion skin stretched straight out behind him. Crazy, man. Everybody else trying to git some loot and him and his boys out for blood!"

I lay like a man rescued from drowning, listening, still not sure I was alive.

"I was over there," another voice said. "You see him when the mounted police got after his ass?"

"Hell, naw . . . Here, take a li'l taste."

"Well *that's* when you shoulda seen him. When he seen them cops riding up he reached back of his saddle and come up with some kind of old shield."

"A *shield?*"

"Hell, yes! One with a spike in the middle of it. And that ain't all; when he sees the cops he calls to one of his goddam henchmens to hand him up a spear, and a little short guy run out into the street and give him one. You know, one of the kind you see them African guys carrying in the moving pictures . . ."

"Where the hell was you, man?"

"Me? I'm over on the side where some stud done broke in a store and is selling cold beer out the window— Done gone into business, man," the voice laughed. "I was drinking me some Budweiser and digging the doings—when here comes the cops up the street, riding like cowboys, man; and when ole Ras-the-what's-his-name sees 'em he lets out a roar like a lion and rears way back and starts shooting spurs into that hoss's ass fast as nickels falling in the subway at going-home time—and gaawd-dam! that's when you ought to seen him! Say, gimme a taste there, fella.

"Thanks. Here he comes bookety-bookety with that spear stuck out in front of him and that shield on his arm, charging, man. And he's yelling something in African or West Indian or something and he's got his head down low like he knew about that shit too, man; riding like Earle Sande in the fifth at Jamaica. That ole black hoss let out a whinny and got *his* head down—I don't know *where* he got *that* sonofabitch—but, gentlemens, I swear! When he felt that steel in his high behind he came on like Man o' War going to get his ashes hauled! Before the cops knowed what hit 'em Ras is right in the middle of 'em and one cop grabbed for that spear, and ole Ras swung 'round and bust him across the head and the cop goes down

and his hoss rears up, and ole Ras rears his and tries to spear
him another cop, and the other hosses is plunging around and
ole Ras tries to spear him still another cop, only he's too close
and the hoss is pooting and snorting and pissing and shitting,
and they swings around and the cop is swinging his pistol and
every time he swings ole Ras throws up his shield with one
arm and chops at him with the spear with the other, and man,
you could hear that gun striking that ole shield like somebody
dropping tire irons out a twelve-story window. And you know
what, when ole Ras saw he was too close to spear him a cop
he wheeled that hoss around and rode off a bit and did him a
quick round-about-face and charged 'em again—out for blood,
man! Only this time the cops got tired of that bullshit and one
of 'em started shooting. And *that* was the lick! Ole Ras didn't
have time to git his gun so he let fly with that spear and you
could hear him grunt and say something 'bout that cop's kinfolks and then him and that hoss shot up the street leaping
like Heigho, the goddam Silver!"

"Man, where'd *you* come from?"

"It's the truth, man, here's my right hand."

They were laughing outside the hedge and leaving and I
lay in a cramp, wanting to laugh and yet knowing that Ras
was not funny, or not only funny, but dangerous as well, wrong
but justified, crazy yet coldly sane . . . Why did they make
it seem funny, *only* funny? I thought. And yet knowing that it
was. It was funny and dangerous and sad. Jack had seen it, or
had stumbled upon it and used it to prepare a sacrifice. And I
had been used as a tool. My grandfather had been wrong about
yessing them to death and destruction or else things had
changed too much since his day.

There was only one way to destroy them. I got up from
behind the hedge in the waning moon, wet and shaken in the
hot air and started out looking for Jack, still turned around in

my direction. I moved into the street, listening to the distant sounds of the riot and seeing in my mind the image of two eyes in the bottom of a shattered glass.

I kept to the darker side of streets and to the silent areas, thinking that if he wished really to hide his strategy he'd appear in the district, with a sound truck perhaps, playing the friendly adviser with Wrestrum and Tobitt beside him.

They were in civilian clothes, and I thought, Cops—until I saw the baseball bat and started to turn, hearing, "Hey, you!"

I hesitated.

"What's in that brief case?" they said, and if they'd asked me anything else I might have stood still. But at the question a wave of shame and outrage shook me and I ran, still heading for Jack. But I was in strange territory now and someone, for some reason, had removed the manhole cover and I felt myself plunge down, down; a long drop that ended upon a load of coal that sent up a cloud of dust, and I lay in the black dark upon the black coal no longer running, hiding or concerned, hearing the shifting of the coal, as from somewhere above their voices came floating down.

"You see the way he went down, zoom! I was just fixing to slug the bastard."

"You hit him?"

"I don't know."

"Say, Joe, you think the bastard's dead?"

"Maybe. He sure is in the dark though. You can't even see his eyes."

"Nigger in the coal pile, eh, Joe?"

Someone hollered down the hole, "Hey, black boy. Come on out. We want to see what's in that brief case."

"Come down and get me," I said.

"What's in that brief case?"

"You," I said, suddenly laughing. "What do you think of that?"

"Me?"

"All of you," I said.

"You're crazy," he said.

"But I still have you in this brief case!"

"What'd you steal?"

"Can't you see?" I said. "Light a match."

"What the hell's he talking about, Joe?"

"Strike a match, the boogy's nuts."

High above I saw the small flame sputter into light. They stood heads down, as in prayer, unable to see me back in the coal.

"Come on down," I said. "Ha! Ha! I've had you in my brief case all the time and you didn't know me then and can't see me now."

"You sonofabitch!" one of them called, outraged. Then the match went out and I heard something fall softly upon the coal nearby. They were talking above.

"You goddam black nigger sonofabitch," someone called, "see how you like this," and I heard the cover settle over the manhole with a dull clang. Fine bits of dirt showered down as they stamped upon the lid and for a moment I sent coal sliding in wild surprise, looking up, up through black space to where for a second the dim light of a match sank through a circle of holes in the steel. Then I thought, This is the way it's always been, only now I know it—and rested back, calm now, placing the brief case beneath my head. I could open it in the morning, push off the lid. Now I was tired, too tired; my mind retreating, the image of the two glass eyes running together like blobs of melting lead. Here it was as though the riot was gone and I felt the tug of sleep, seemed to move out upon black water.

It's a kind of death without hanging, I thought, a death

alive. In the morning I'll remove the lid . . . Mary, I should have gone to Mary's. I would go now to Mary's in the only way that I could . . . I moved off over the black water, floating, sighing . . . sleeping invisibly.

BUT I was never to reach Mary's, and I was over-optimistic about removing the steel cap in the morning. Great invisible waves of time flowed over me, but that morning never came. There was no morning nor light of any kind to awaken me and I slept on and on until finally I was aroused by hunger. Then I was up in the dark and blundering around, feeling rough walls and the coal giving way beneath each step like treacherous sand. I tried to reach above me but found only space, unbroken and impenetrable. Then I tried to find the usual ladder that leads out of such holes, but there was none. I had to have a light, and now on hands and knees, holding tight to my brief case, I searched the coal until I found the folder of matches the men had dropped—how long ago had that been?—but there were only three and to save them I started searching for paper to make a torch, feeling about slowly over the coal pile. I needed just one piece of paper to light my way out of the hole, but there was nothing. Next I searched my pockets, finding not even a bill, or an advertising folder, or a Brotherhood leaflet. Why had I destroyed Rinehart's throwaway? Well, there was only one thing to do if I was to make a torch. I'd have to open my brief case. In it were the only papers I had.

I started with my high-school diploma, applying one precious match with a feeling of remote irony, even smiling as I saw the swift but feeble light push back the gloom. I was in a deep basement, full of shapeless objects that extended farther than I could see, and I realized that to light my way out I would have to burn every paper in the brief case. I moved slowly off, toward the darker blackness, lighting my way by these feeble torches. The next to go was Clifton's doll, but it burned so stubbornly that I reached inside the case for something else. Then by the light of the smoke-sputtering doll I opened a folded page. It was the anonymous letter, which burned so quickly that as it flamed I hurriedly unfolded another: It was that slip upon which Jack had written my Brotherhood name. I could still smell Emma's perfume even in the dampness of the cellar. And now seeing the handwriting of the two in the consuming flames I burned my hand and slipped to my knees, staring. The handwriting was the same. I knelt there, stunned, watching the flames consume them. That he, or anyone at that late date, could have named me and set me running with one and the same stroke of the pen was too much. Suddenly I began to scream, getting up in the darkness and plunging wildly about, bumping against walls, scattering coal, and in my anger extinguishing my feeble light.

But still whirling on in the blackness, knocking against the rough walls of a narrow passage, banging my head and cursing, I stumbled down and plunged against some kind of partition and sailed headlong, coughing and sneezing, into another dimensionless room, where I continued to roll about the floor in my outrage. How long this kept up, I do not know. It might have been days, weeks; I lost all sense of time. And everytime I paused to rest, the outrage revived and I went off again. Then, finally, when I could barely move, something seemed to say, "That's enough, don't kill yourself. You've run enough, you're through with them at last," and I collapsed, face forward and lay there beyond the point of exhaustion, too tired to close my eyes. It was a state neither of dreaming nor of waking, but somewhere in between, in which I was caught like Trueblood's jaybird that yellow jackets had paralyzed in every part but his eyes.

But somehow the floor had now turned to sand and the darkness to light, and I lay the prisoner of a group consisting of Jack and old Emerson and Bledsoe and Norton and Ras and the school superintendent and a number of others whom I failed to recognize, but all of whom had run me, who now pressed around me as I lay beside a river of black water, near where an armored bridge arched sharply away to where I could not see. And I was protesting their holding me and they were demanding that I return to them and were annoyed with my refusal.

"No," I said. "I'm through with all your illusions and lies, I'm through running."

"Not quite," Jack said above the others' angry demands, "but you soon will be, unless you return. Refuse and we'll free you of your illusions all right."

"No, thank you; I'll free myself," I said, struggling to rise from the cutting sand.

But now they came forward with a knife, holding me; and I felt the bright red pain and they took the two bloody blobs and cast them over the bridge, and out of my anguish I saw them curve up and catch beneath the apex of the curving arch of the bridge, to hang there, dripping down through the sunlight into the dark red water. And while the others laughed, before my pain-sharpened eyes the whole world was slowly turning red.

"Now you're free of illusions," Jack said, pointing to my seed wasting upon the air. "How does it feel to be free of one's illusions?"

And I looked up through a pain so intense now that the air seemed to roar with the clanging of metal, bearing, HOW DOES IT FEEL TO BE FREE OF ILLUSION . . .

And now I answered, "Painful and empty," as I saw a glittering butterfly circle three times around my blood-red parts, up there beneath the bridge's high arch. "But look," I said pointing. And they looked and laughed, and suddenly seeing their sat-

isfied faces and understanding, I gave a Bledsoe laugh, startling them. And Jack came forward, curious.

"Why do you laugh?" he said.

"Because at a price I now see that which I couldn't see," I said.

"What does he think he sees?" they said.

And Jack came closer, threatening, and I laughed. "I'm not afraid now," I said. "But if you'll look, you'll see . . . It's not invisible . . ."

"See what?" they said.

"That there bang not only my generations wasting upon the water—" And now the pain welled up and I could no longer see them.

"But what? Go on," they said.

"But your sun . . ."

"Yes?"

"And your moon . . ."

"He's crazy!"

"Your world . . ."

"I knew he was a mystic idealist!" Tobitt said.

"Still," I said, "there's your universe, and that drip-drop upon the water you hear is all the history you've made, all you're going to make. Now laugh, you scientists. Let's hear you laugh!"

And high above me now the bridge seemed to move off to where I could not see, striding like a robot, an iron man, whose iron legs clanged doomfully as it moved. And then I struggled up, full of sorrow and pain, shouting, "No, no, we must stop him!"

And I awoke in the blackness.

Fully awake now, I simply lay there as though paralyzed. I could think of nothing else to do. Later I would try to find my way out, but now I could only lie on the floor, reliving the dream. All their faces were so vivid that they seemed to stand before me beneath a spotlight. They were all up there somewhere, making a mess of the world. Well, let them. I was through and, in spite of the dream, I was whole.

And now I realized that I couldn't return to Mary's, or to any part of my old life. I could approach it only from the outside, and I had been as invisible to Mary as I had been to the Brotherhood. No, I couldn't return to Mary's, or to the campus, or to the Brotherhood, or home. I could only move ahead or stay here, underground. So I would stay here until I was chased out. Here, at least, I could try to think things out in peace, or, if not in peace, in quiet. I would take up residence underground. The end was in the beginning.

Epilogue

So there you have all of it that's important. Or at least you *almost* have it. I'm an invisible man and it placed me in a hole—or showed me the hole I was in, if you will—and I reluctantly accepted the fact. What else could I have done? Once you get used to it, reality is as irresistible as a club, and I was clubbed into the cellar before I caught the hint. Perhaps that's the way it had to be; I don't know. Nor do I know whether accepting the lesson has placed me in the rear or in the *avant-garde. That*, perhaps, is a lesson for history, and I'll leave such decisions to Jack and his ilk while I try belatedly to study the lesson of my own life.

Let me be honest with you—a feat which, by the way, I find of the utmost difficulty. When one is invisible he finds such problems as good and evil, honesty and dishonesty, of such shifting shapes that he confuses one with the other, depending upon who happens to be looking through him at the time. Well, now I've been trying to look through myself, and there's a risk in it. I was never more hated than when I tried to be honest. Or when, even as just now I've tried to articulate exactly what I felt to be the truth. No one was satisfied—not even I. On the other hand, I've never been more loved and appreciated than when I tried to "justify" and affirm someone's mistaken beliefs; or when I've tried to give my friends the incorrect, absurd answers they wished to hear. In my presence they could talk and agree with themselves, the world was nailed down, and they loved it. They received a feeling of security. But here was the rub: Too often, in order to justify *them*, I had to take myself by the throat and choke myself until my eyes bulged and my tongue hung out and wagged like the door of an empty house in a high wind. Oh, yes, it made them happy and it made me sick. So I became ill of affirmation, of saying "yes" against the nay-saying of my stomach—not to mention my brain.

There is, by the way, an area in which a man's feelings are more rational than his mind, and it is precisely in that area that his will is pulled in several directions at the same time. You might sneer at this, but I know now. I was pulled this way and that for longer than I can remember. And my problem was that I always tried to go in everyone's way but my own. I have also been called one thing and then another while no one really wished to hear what I called myself. So after years of trying to adopt the opinions of others I finally rebelled. I am an *invisible* man. Thus I have come a long way and returned and boomeranged a long way from the point in society toward which I originally aspired.

So I took to the cellar; I hibernated. I got away from it all. But that wasn't enough. I couldn't be still even in hibernation. Because, damn it, there's the mind, the *mind*. It wouldn't let me rest. Gin, jazz and dreams were not enough. Books were not enough. My belated appreciation of the crude joke that had kept me running, was not enough. And my mind revolved again and again back to my grandfather. And, despite the farce that ended my attempt to say "yes" to Brotherhood, I'm still plagued by his deathbed advice . . . Perhaps he hid his meaning deeper than I thought, perhaps his anger threw me off—I can't decide. Could he have meant—hell, he *must* have meant the principle, that we were to affirm the principle on which the country was built and not the men, or at least not the men who did the violence. Did he mean say "yes" because he knew that the principle was greater than the men, greater than the numbers and the vicious power and all the methods used to corrupt its name? Did he mean to affirm the principle, which they themselves had dreamed into being out of the chaos and darkness of the feudal past, and which they had violated and compromised to the point of absurdity even in their own corrupt minds? Or did he mean that we had to take the responsibility for all of it, for the men as well as the principle, because we were the heirs who must use the principle because no other fitted our needs? Not for the power or for vindication, but because we, with the given circumstance of our origin, could only thus find transcendence? Was it that we of all, we, most of all, had to affirm the principle, the plan in whose name we had been brutalized and sacrificed—not because we would always be weak nor because we were afraid or opportunistic, but because we were older than they, in the sense of what it took to live in the world with others and because they had exhausted in us, some—not much, but some—of the human greed and smallness, yes, and the fear and superstition that had kept them running. (Oh, yes, they're running too, running all over themselves.) Or was it, did he mean that we should affirm the principle because we, through no fault of our own, were linked to all the others in the loud, clamoring semi-visible world, that world seen only as a fertile field for exploitation by Jack and his kind, and with condescension by Norton and his, who were tired of being the mere pawns in the futile game of "making history"? Had he seen that for these too we had to say "yes" to the principle, lest they turn upon us to destroy both it and us?

"Agree 'em to death and destruction," grandfather had advised. Hell, weren't they their own death and their own destruction except as the principle lived in them and in us? And here's the cream of the joke: Weren't we *part of them* as well as apart from them and subject to die when they died? I can't figure it out; it escapes me. But what do *I* really want, I've asked myself. Certainly not the freedom of a Rinehart or the power of a Jack, nor simply the freedom not to run. No, but the next step I couldn't make, so I've remained in the hole.

I'm not blaming anyone for this state of affairs, mind you; nor merely crying *mea culpa*. The fact is that you carry part of your sickness within you, at least I do as an invisible man. I carried my sickness and though for a long time I tried to place it in the outside world, the attempt to write it down shows me that at least half of it lay within me. It came upon me slowly, like that strange disease that affects those black men whom you see turning slowly from black to albino, their pigment disappearing as under the radiation of some cruel, invisible ray. You go along for years knowing something is wrong, then suddenly you discover that you're as transparent as air. At first you tell yourself that it's all a dirty joke, or that it's due to the "political situation." But deep down you come to suspect that you're yourself to blame, and you stand naked and shivering before the millions of eyes who look through you unseeingly. *That* is the real soul-sickness, the spear in the side, the drag by the neck through the mob-angry town, the Grand Inquisition, the embrace of the Maiden, the rip in the belly with the guts spilling out, the trip to the chamber with the deadly gas that ends in the oven so hygienically clean—only it's worse because you continue stupidly to live. But live you must, and you can either make passive love to your sickness or burn it out and go on to the next conflicting phase.

Yes, but what *is* the next phase? How often have I tried to find it! Over and over again I've gone up above to seek it out. For, like almost everyone else in our country, I started out with my share of optimism. I believed in hard work and progress and action, but now, after first being "for" society and then "against" it, I assign myself no rank or any limit, and such an attitude is very much against the trend of the times. But my world has become one of infinite possibilities. What a phrase—still it's a good phrase and a good view of life, and a man shouldn't accept any other; that much I've learned underground. Until some gang succeeds in putting the world in a strait jacket, its definition is possibility. Step outside the narrow borders of what men call reality and you step into chaos—ask Rinehart, he's a master of it—or imagination. That too I've learned in the cellar, and not by deadening my sense of perception; I'm invisible, not blind.

No indeed, the world is just as concrete, ornery, vile and sublimely wonderful as before, only now I better understand my relation to it and it to me. I've come a long way from those days when, full of illusion, I lived a public life and attempted to function under the assumption that the world was solid and all the relationships therein. Now I know men are different and that all life is divided and that only in division is there true health. Hence again I have stayed in my hole, because up above there's an increasing passion to make men conform to a pattern. Just as in my nightmare, Jack and the boys are waiting with their knives, looking for the slightest excuse to . . . well, to "ball the jack," and I do not refer to the old dance step, although what they're doing is making the old eagle rock dangerously.

Whence all this passion toward conformity anyway?—diversity is the word. Let man keep his many parts and you'll have no tyrant states. Why, if they follow this conformity business they'll end up by forcing me, an invisible man, to become white, which is not a color but the lack of one. Must I strive toward colorlessness? But seriously, and without snobbery, think of what the world would lose if that should happen. America is woven of many strands; I would recognize them and let it so remain. It's "winner take nothing" that is the great truth of our country or of any country. Life is to be lived, not controlled; and humanity is won by continuing to play in face of certain defeat. Our fate is to become one, and yet many— This is not prophecy, but description. Thus one of the greatest jokes in the world is the spectacle of the whites busy escaping blackness and becoming blacker every day, and the blacks striving toward whiteness, becoming quite dull and gray. None of us seems to know who he is or where he's going.

Which reminds me of something that occurred the other day in the subway. At first I saw only an old gentleman who for the moment was lost. I knew he was lost, for as I looked down the platform I saw him approach several people and turn away without speaking. He's lost, I thought, and he'll keep coming until he sees me, then he'll ask his direction. Maybe there's an embarrassment in it if he admits he's lost to a strange white man. Perhaps to lose a sense of *where* you are implies the danger of losing a sense of *who* you are. That must be it, I thought—to lose your direction is to lose your face. So here he comes to ask his direction from the lost, the invisible. Very well, I've learned to live without direction. Let him ask.

But then he was only a few feet away and I recognized him; it was Mr. Norton. The old gentleman was thinner and wrinkled now but as dapper as ever. And seeing him made all the old life live in me for an instant, and I smiled with tear-stinging eyes. Then it was over, dead, and when he asked me how to get to Centre Street, I regarded him with mixed feelings.

"Don't you know me?" I said.

"Should I?" he said.

"You see me?" I said, watching him tensely.

"Why, of course— Sir, do you know the way to Centre Street?"

"So. Last time it was the Golden Day, now it's Centre Street. You've retrenched, sir. But don't you really know who I am?"

"Young man, I'm in a hurry," he said, cupping a hand to his ear. "Why should I know you?"

"Because I'm your destiny."

"My destiny, did you say?" He gave me a puzzled stare, backing away. "Young man, are you well? Which train did you say I should take?"

"I didn't say," I said, shaking my head. "Now, aren't you ashamed?"

"Ashamed? ASHAMED!" he said indignantly.

I laughed, suddenly taken by the idea. "Because, Mr. Norton, if you don't know *where* you are, you probably don't know *who* you are. So you came to me out of shame. You are ashamed, now aren't you?"

"Young man, I've lived too long in this world to be ashamed of anything. Are you light-headed from hunger? How do you know my name?"

"But I'm your destiny, I made you. Why shouldn't I know you?" I said, walking closer and seeing him back against a pillar. He looked around like a cornered animal. He thought I was mad.

"Don't be afraid, Mr. Norton," I said. "There's a guard down the platform there. You're safe. Take any train; they all go to the Golden D—"

But now an express had rolled up and the old man was disappearing quite spryly inside one of its doors. I stood there laughing hysterically. I laughed all the way back to my hole.

But after I had laughed I was thrown back on my thoughts—how had it all happened? And I asked myself if it were only a joke and I couldn't answer. Since then I've sometimes been overcome with a passion to return into that "heart of darkness" across the Mason-Dixon line, but then I remind myself that the true darkness lies within my own mind, and the idea loses itself in the gloom. Still the passion persists. Sometimes I feel the need to reaffirm all of it, the whole unhappy territory and all the things loved and unlovable in it, for all of it is part of me. Till now, however, this is as far as I've ever gotten, for all life seen from the hole of invisibility is absurd.

So why do I write, torturing myself to put it down? Because in spite of myself I've learned some things. Without the possibility of action, all knowledge comes to one labeled "file and forget," and I can neither file nor forget. Nor will certain ideas forget me; they keep filing away at my lethargy, my complacency. Why should I be the one to dream this nightmare? Why should I be dedicated and set aside—yes, if not to at least *tell* a few people about it? There seems to be no escape. Here I've set out to throw my anger into the world's face, but now that I've tried to put it all down the old fascination with playing a role returns, and I'm drawn upward again. So that even before I finish I've failed (maybe my anger is too heavy; perhaps, being a talker, I've used too many words). But I've failed. The very act of trying to put it all down has confused me and negated some of the anger and some of the bitterness. So it is that now I denounce and defend, or feel prepared to defend. I condemn and affirm, say no and say yes, say yes and say no. I denounce because though implicated and partially responsible, I have been hurt to the point of abysmal pain, hurt to the point of invisibility. And I defend because in spite of all I find that I love. In order to get some of it down I *have* to love. I sell you no phony forgiveness, I'm a desperate man— but too much of your life will be lost, its meaning lost, unless you approach it as much through love as through hate. So I approach it through division. So I denounce and I defend and I hate and I love.

Perhaps that makes me a little bit as human as my grandfather. Once I thought my grandfather incapable of thoughts about humanity, but I was wrong. Why should an old slave use such a phrase as, "This and this or this has made me more human," as I did in my arena speech? Hell, he never had any doubts about his humanity—that was left to his "free" offspring. He accepted his humanity just as he accepted the principle. It was his, and the principle lives on in all its human and absurd diversity. So now having tried to put it down I have disarmed myself in the process. You won't believe in my invisibility and you'll fail to see how any principle that applies to you could apply to me. You'll fail to see it even though death waits for both of us if you don't. Nevertheless, the very disarmament has brought me to a decision. The hibernation is over. I must shake off the old skin and come up for breath. There's a stench in the air, which, from this distance underground, might be the smell either of death or of spring—I hope of spring. But don't let me trick you, there *is* a death in the smell of spring and in the smell of thee as in the smell of me. And if nothing more, invisibility has taught my nose to classify the stenches of death.

In going underground, I whipped it all except the mind, the *mind.* And the mind that has conceived a plan of living must never lose sight of the chaos against which that pattern was conceived. That goes for societies as well as for individuals. Thus, having tried to give pattern to the chaos which lives within the pattern of your certainties, I must come out, I must emerge. And there's still a conflict within me: With Louis Armstrong one half of me says, "Open the window and let the foul air out," while the other says, "It was good green corn before the harvest." Of course Louis was kidding, *he* wouldn't have thrown old Bad Air out, because it would have broken up the music and the dance, when it was the good music that came from the bell of old Bad Air's horn that counted. Old Bad Air is still around with his music and his dancing and his diversity, and I'll be up and around with mine. And, as I said before, a decision has been made. I'm shaking off the old skin and I'll leave it here in the hole. I'm coming out, no less invisible without it, but coming out nevertheless. And I suppose it's damn well time. Even hibernations can be overdone, come to think of it. Perhaps that's my greatest social crime, I've overstayed my hibernation, since there's a possibility that even an invisible man has a socially responsible role to play.

"Ah," I can hear you say, "so it was all a build-up to bore us with his buggy jiving. He only wanted us to listen to him rave!" But only partially true: Being invisible and without substance, a disembodied voice, as it were, what else could I do? What else but try to tell you what was really happening when your eyes were looking through? And it is this which frightens me:

Who knows but that, on the lower frequencies, I speak for you?

PENGUIN ESSENTIALS

THE DAY OF THE TRIFFIDS/JOHN WYNDHAM

'When a day that you happen to know is Wednesday starts off by sounding like Sunday, there is something seriously wrong somewhere.'

When a freak cosmic event renders most of the Earth's population blind, Bill Masen – one of the lucky few to keep his sight – finds himself trapped in a London jammed with sightless mobs who prey on those who can still see. But another menace stalks blind and sighted alike. With nobody to stop them the Triffids – walking carnivorous plants with lethal stingers – rise up as humanity stumbles and falls . . .

'One of those books that haunts you for the rest of your life' *Sunday Times*

THE MAN IN THE HIGH CASTLE/PHILIP K. DICK

'Truth, she thought. As terrible as death. But harder to find.'

America, fifteen years after the end of the Second World War. The winning Axis powers have divided their spoils: the Nazis control New York, while California is ruled by the Japanese. But between these two states – locked in a cold war – lies a neutal buffer zone in which legendary author Hawthorne Abendsen is rumoured to live. Abendsen lives in fear of his life for he has written a book in which World War Two was won by the Allies . . .

'The most brilliant sci-fi mind on any planet' *Rolling Stone*

PENGUIN ESSENTIALS

A MONTH IN THE COUNTRY/J. L. CARR

'That night, for the first time during many months, I slept like the dead and, next morning, awoke very early.'

One summer, just after the Great War, Tom Birkin, a demobbed soldier, arrives in the village of Oxgodby. He has been invited to uncover and restore a medieval wall painting in the local church. At the same time, Charles Moon – a fellow damaged survivor of the war – has been asked to locate the grave of a village ancestor. As these two outsiders go about their work of recovery, they form a bond, but they also stir up long dormant passions within the village. What Berkin discovers here will stay with him for the rest of his life . . .

'Carr has the magic touch to re-enter the imagined past' Penelope Fitzgerald

TENDER IS THE NIGHT/F. SCOTT FITZGERALD

'I don't ask you to love me always like this, but I ask you to remember. Somewhere inside me there'll always be the person I am tonight.'

American psychoanalyst Dick Diver and his wife Nicole live in a villa on the French Riviera, surrounded by a circle of glamorous friends. When beautiful film star Rosemary Hoyt arrives she is drawn to the couple – Dick contemplates an affair, while Nicole believes she's found a new best friend. But a dark secret lies at the centre of the Divers' marriage. A secret which could destroy Dick and Nicole and those close to them . . .

'A beautiful novel about failure' *Independent*